MW01135647

BRIDGET OF ERIN

An Immigrant Finds New Life in America

A Novel

DON AND MILLIE MANG

BRIDGET OF ERIN

An Immigrant Finds New Life in America

A Novel

Book Design by Mike Miller, pubyourbook@gmail.com.

ISBN: 9781085816168

Printed in the United States of America

For Jesus and Mary

and

in Honor of Saint Joseph
Patron Saint of Immigrants

Special Thanks To

Bert Guise-Hyde, Peggy May-Szczygiel, and Joan Graham-Scahill, WATERFRONT MEMORIES & MORE MUSEUM — for their assistance and expertise in matters concerning the history of the First Ward and the Buffalo waterfront.

Father Alfred R. Pehrsson, C.M., whose spirituality and influence was a significant inspiration.

Christine Frappier for cover design.

Lonnie Froman for cover illustration.

Mike Miller for book design.

Christopher A. Mang, our son, for his technical assistance.

Julianna Gauthier, for her never-ending interest and her assistance in formatting.

Josephine Portik for her contribution of great resource material.

Also, Warmest thanks to my grandchildren who prayed for publication of this book: Michael, Patrick, Michael, Shawn, Caitlyn & Christian Anthony

Excerpts on World War I taken from Rev. Francis Duffy's Diary entitled "Father Duffy's Story."

Contents

Preface

The turn of the century was rapidly approaching. America would see many changes in the coming years—electricity, telephone, radios, talking movies, automobiles . . .

Immigrants were flooding her shores by the thousands every month. They came from Ireland. They came from Germany. They came from Italy, Poland, and many other nations. They came to escape rising taxes and tyranny. They came to escape famine and starvation. They came to escape political and religious persecution. They came to the United States because they perceived it as the land of economic opportunity.

And among these multitudes was nineteen-year-old Bridget O'Halloran—alone and afraid. This is her story.

Chapter 1

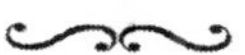

No. 117

It was early that misty morning when young Bridget O'Halloran walked down the gangplank, stepping onto American soil for the first time. This was a new beginning, and the gleam in her eye bespoke her soul's hopeful anticipation of a promising future in this new land. Times had been very hard in the old country. There barely was enough to eat—a struggle just to survive. Ireland's potato famine had gutted the populace and had a grievous effect on the economy of that little nation. So many died of starvation—her parents among them. Leaving Ireland was very difficult for her—breaking the bonds of her enduring friendships was even more traumatic. She felt this loss so deeply that she wondered if she would ever completely recover from it.

She had never felt so alone as she made her way through the crowds to the line forming in front of the immigration inspector. What she expected would take only a few hours turned into days. Completion of the paperwork was difficult and time-consuming, and she would be required to undergo humiliating physical inspections and answer too many questions about her health history, health records being nonexistent in the old country. The nights were cold and damp as she, along with the other newcomers, huddled in drafty rooms, sleeping on rickety old cots covered with scratchy wool army blankets. Acrimonious smells from unwashed bodies permeated the drafty room. Have I gone mad? Did I make a mistake leaving everything and everybody I love? As she looked up at the cracked ceiling—bare spots interspersed with curled up paint chips looking like they were about to fall—she wondered if her life would begin to deteriorate in this strange new land. It was only a short time ago that she closed her little dress shop in the town of Ennis. She reminisced about her customers, so many dear and familiar who she greeted on a first-name basis. And, oh!

that little white church so close to her heart with her beloved Father O'Malley, and the security she felt there! Her musings suddenly ended with the sobering realization of why she gave it all up. One word said it all— SURVIVAL!

This wasn't the first time she had slept in crowded conditions or shared meager fare at a dinner table with other poor souls. As a child, she had never known privacy or decent food—nor could she remember any semblance of family life. The closest thing to family for her was one or two other girls in the orphanage. She never ever referred to that domicile as "home." She did, however, learn something useful there—the one thing she could take with her when she grew up—needlework and sewing. Bridget was a quick learner, becoming extremely adept at creating her own patterns and making clothing from them. Some of her teachers were amazed with what she could do with a needle and thread, eventually searching for a place where the girl could earn her keep through her sewing skills.

Ennis was the perfect place for her talents, and Mrs. Harrigan was fast to hire her to work at "Lady Lovelace." To be sure, life was good for the few short years she was employed there. Although the famine had left so many families impoverished and many of the common folk no longer had resources for these services, there were still some rich landowners' wives who frequented the shop on a regular basis and provided a living wage for both Mrs. Harrigan and Bridget. The apartment above the shop had an extra bedroom in the back, which Mrs. Harrigan granted Bridget for a small rental fee. She had become very fond of the girl, having never had any children of her own. And the warmth of this maternal friend filled Bridget's heart with a pleasurable sweetness which she expected must be like the mother's love she could never remember. The occasional thoughts she had had in the past about the possibility of going to America faded as she began to feel like she actually finally "belonged" to someone.

"My dear, will Mrs. Tillie's dress be finished by four o'clock?"

"Oh, yes, Mrs. Harrigan. I'm sure I can have it ready by then." Those words—"My dear"—how she loved to hear them. It bespoke an endearing message to her heart and made her feel a closeness to another person—a newfound pleasure!

"Good afternoon, Mrs. Tillie. And how are you today?" Bridget smiled at her.

"Oh, my arthritis is bothering me, but I think I'll get through the day, God willing and the creek don't rise! But I might say, you're looking quite chipper today, young lady."

"Thank you. I have your dress all ready for you, Mrs. Tillie."

"What would I do without you, Bridget? I do have this important dinner I must be at this evening, and I *must* look my best."

"Oh, how nice. Where's the dinner going to be?"

"Uh ... well, it doesn't matter really. It's not important. Did I ever tell you that you remind me of the maid-servant I had on our estate in Cork?"

"Really?"

"Yes. Of course, we aren't there at the present time. My husband sold the property to the Duke of Morchester."

"Oh, I had no idea, Mrs. Tillie," as she handed the now-packaged dress to her.

Before leaving, Mrs. Tillie dropped a few important names of people she would be seated with at the dinner. Bridget seemed quite impressed, although she wondered why the woman had neglected to answer her inquiry about where it would take place. Closing the door behind her customer, she turned to Mrs. Harrigan coming from the back room, a broad smile on her face. "I couldn't help but overhear, Bridget. You know, I've been carrying that lady for a while, as we were childhood friends, and I have sympathy for her. But the truth to be known is that she is as poor as a church mouse. She puts on airs to cover up the poverty. I guess she has a little of that Irish pride in her—well ... I mean ... well ... that's not necessarily a bad thing, you know. I mean ..." She realized her words were beginning to sound like gossip.

"Oh, I don't think anything of it at all; it doesn't bother me. But I do feel very sorry to hear it."

"Oh, my dear, she never did have much. She lost her husband at an early age and had to put her children in an orphanage since she couldn't afford to feed them. I really feel quite sorry for her."

"Oh, that's terrible! You know, Mrs. Harrigan, I was brought up in an orphanage myself. Did I ever tell you?"

"No."

Bridget went about the business of closing up, quickly deciding she'd rather not expound about her orphanage days right then. She began to hum her favorite Irish ballad. The conversation ended.

As the days went on, uncomplicated and calm, she reveled in this loving, safe atmosphere of her newfound position—until the day when she was aware Mrs. Harrigan seemed to be coughing quite a bit.

"My dear, I think I will go upstairs and rest a bit. This cold seems to be getting a hold of me. Do you think you can take over?"

"Oh, of course. I'd be glad to. Are you sure you'll be alright?"

"Yes—it's just a little cold."

"Do you think you should go to the doctor? Maybe he could give you a little something for it."

"I'm sure I'll be fine—just need a little rest. Make sure you lock up when you are ready to close, won't you dear? Oh, and might I trouble you to just take a moment and peek in on me when you come up?"

"Yes, I will. Don't worry. Try to sleep."

Bridget did her best to keep the business going by herself, as Mrs. Harrigan's cough continued to get worse, finally turning into pneumonia. Her doctor's remedies seemed to have no effect, and it wasn't long before she passed away. Although Bridget could see her condition deteriorating during the last few months, she had never lost hope that Mrs. Harrigan would recover, and her death had left her with a devastating sense of loss. She kept the shop open and threw herself into the business fully and totally, trying to put it out of her mind.

There was not an empty pew at St. Peter and Paul's that day, and many white handkerchiefs were to be found in the hands of most of the ladies. Bridget was amazed, not being aware of the many in the town who held Mrs. Harrigan in such high esteem. After the service, she was approached at the back of the church by a smartly dressed gentleman. "Are you Miss Bridget O'Halloran?"

"Yes, I am, sir. Are you a friend of Mrs. Harrigan's?"

"Well, yes, I am; and I'm also her attorney. Brian O'Flaherty's the name. Please accept my condolences at the loss of your friend; I understand you were very close."

"Thank you very much, sir."

"I would like to make an appointment to see you, if you might have time one evening after work."

"Oh, yes! I'm so glad to meet you. I have so many questions and didn't know where to turn—you know, about the shop, the business, Mrs. Harrigan's effects ... I don't know what to do about all this."

"We can discuss all of that. Would tomorrow be too soon to meet? After you are done at work? Might I come to see you then?"

"That's fine. Any time after five would be okay."

They sat down at the table in the back room. Mr. O'Flaherty took some papers from his briefcase. "Miss O'Halloran, I will only be reading you the portion of Mrs. Harrigan's will which pertains to you.

'I bequeath my business and the entire store and its contents to Bridget O'Halloran, my dear friend and sweet child, who has brightened my latter years more than she knows.'

Bridget's eyes teared up. The attorney continued, "She didn't have very much besides this store, but the little money she did have she left to the church. I'm sure you knew what a faithful lady she was."

"Oh, yes ... yes." Bridget tried to hold back her tears, as the attorney had her sign some papers. He stood to leave, then turned back to her. "Oh, by the way, I will be sending you the deed, along with some more paperwork that will be needing your signature."

He departed. She broke down and sobbed. His visit had left her with a bittersweet feeling in her heart. The woman she loved like a mother-figure who had taken her in and taught her so much was gone now—yet she was filled with hope for the future for the gift she had been given.

The following few years started out to be exciting. She felt empowered and secure as a business lady—not beholden to anyone. She did thrive for a while in a mainly male dominated business climate. But during this time the potato famine had had a trickle-down effect, and the economy grew worse. Many no longer had enough money to buy clothing, and the business had mainly been reduced to alterations. Food became more and more scarce as the land had grown fallow. What was available was mostly hoarded by the wealthy, and many poor felt the resurgence of famine once again. Many of the populace began to move to the big cities looking for work.

Three years of decline left Bridget no longer able to turn a profit; nor could she manage to pay the taxes on her little shop. Eventually the doors of "Lady Lovelace" had to be permanently closed when the town confiscated the business and the property.

However, despite the adversity, Bridget tried to remain optimistic and hopeful. After she had inherited the store, she felt it might be wise to save up a little money each week whenever she could, due to the uncertainty of the future. Since Mrs. Harrigan's death, thoughts began to return once more of the possibility of life in a new land. Two of her customers had mentioned the accomplishments of their relations who had already emigrated to America. What have I to lose? Mrs. Harrigan's no longer here now. The store is gone ...

"Number 117! Number 117—step forward!" shouted the immigration officer. Bridget sat up, rubbing her eyes, stunned by the loud voice. She was exhausted after a restless night. "Number 117! You are next. Come forward!" Suddenly, she realized that was her number. She felt alarmed—even somewhat terrified! Composing herself as best she could, she raised her arm, waving it a little.

"Here!" she shouted. The officer motioned her to come forward. Thus began another grueling day with more paperwork and much questioning. By afternoon, most of this was finished.

Now began the dreaded eye inspection—she had heard about this from the other girls last night. The doctors were checking everyone's eyes for a contagious disease known as Trachoma which could cause blindness or even death. They did this by turning the eyelid inside out with their fingers or a hairpin. At times they even used a button-hook to check for redness and inflammation on the inner eyelid—an extremely painful experience done by the dreaded "Button-Hook Men." A long sigh of relief escaped her lips when the inspector only used the initial finger manipulation.

"Next!" he shouted, and motioned her along to the next station.

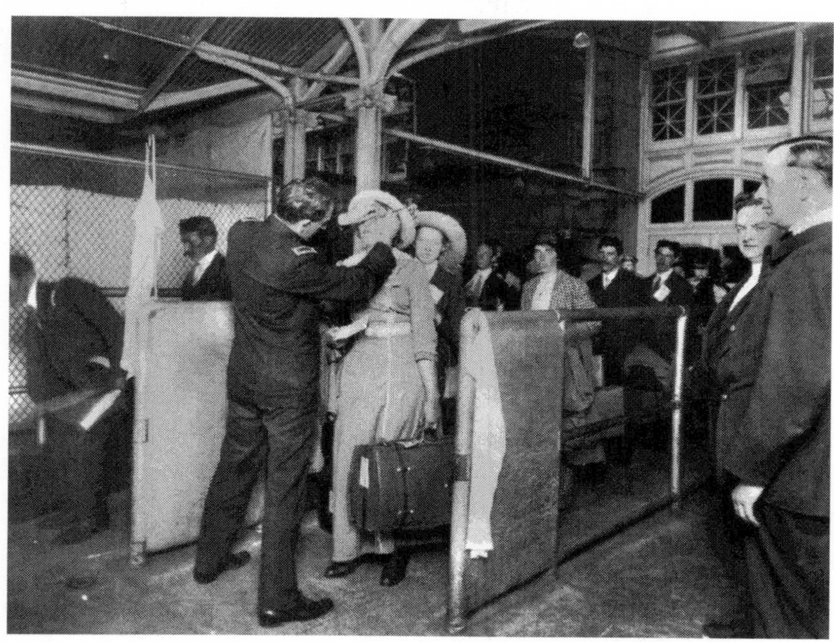

"Please, sit down." Bridget took the seat under the intensely bright light. The woman began to separate the hair with her fingers to see the base of the strands, inspecting for lice. "Oh, oh! What's this?" Bridget's heart froze. Her body stiffened. "Oh, never mind— it's only dandruff." The woman motioned Bridget up from the chair before turning toward the door. "Next!"

Finally, after a complete medical checkup, inspection of her suitcase, and many more questions, it was over! The following day, she received her papers and clutched them tightly to her breast. She was now well on her way to citizenship in a bright new world—a world without food shortages, poverty, desperation, or hopelessness—or so she thought! This was a critical time for her, as she was filled with mixed emotions. The new hope, the endless possibilities, and the excitement of it all was mingled with a tinge of fear as she was herded onto the shore with dozens of other girls. She felt a sudden mistrust in the authorities leading the group—after all, the government authorities in Ireland had allowed thousands to die. She was not about to trust anyone in authority any longer, even here in America, so she purposely walked in the back of the group. As they rounded the corner of a building, she slipped away, unaware she could be placing herself in danger, being totally alone. Unknown to her, newly arrived immigrants were constantly preyed upon by conmen and thieves.

Standing on the shores of her new-found land, she gazed back over that vast ocean. A tear trickled down her cheek.

Surveying her surroundings, she saw a lady—not a person, but a statue—a giant statue! It was the Statue of Liberty. Someone had given her a pamphlet back on Ellis Island explaining what this new statue was all about. It said,

> *This proud lady's right arm holds a great torch raised high in the air. The left arm grasps a tablet bearing the date of the Declaration of Independence. A crown with huge spikes like the rays of the sun rests on the head. At the feet is a broken shackle symbolizing the overthrow of tyranny.*

Her little pamphlet also carried a poem by Emma Lazarus soon to be inscribed on the pedestal of the statue. This read in part,

"Give me your tired, your poor,
Your huddled masses yearning to breathe free,
The wretched refuse of your teeming shore.
Send these, the homeless, tempest-tossed to me.
I lift my lamp beside the golden door."

Bridget suddenly realized she was not alone. Just the sight of that great statue gave her hope. It reminded her of another great Lady—the Mother of Christ. Beginning at an early age, she loved to say the rosary, following the life of Jesus through the mysteries as she prayed the Hail Marys. In a way, she had looked upon the Blessed Mother as her own, for she was too young when her mother died to remember anything much about her. She began to pray silently to her Creator, "Oh, Lord, I give you thanks for the opportunity to live in this free land. With your help, I shall make a new life here."

Chapter 2

Irish Need Not Apply

As Bridget left the Battery and cautiously walked into this huge strange city, she reached in her purse, fingering the small amount of money she had tucked into the side pocket. It wasn't much, but hopefully it would tide her over until she found work. She had converted her earnings into American dollars before leaving Ireland. She had planned well, anticipating she might journey to America in the near future, since her dear old Ireland had started rapidly declining once again and her little dress shop was gradually becoming unprofitable.

She felt like a blind person groping, as it were, through a foreign land, as she made her way into the city. The noise of it all was frightening to her—so unlike her small quiet town of Ennis. At first it was overwhelming—the constant clatter of horse-drawn vehicles, the hucksters selling everything from fruits and vegetables and fresh fish to ladies' hats and gentlemen's watch fobs—it had a hum to it. Bridget thought it sounded like a beehive. "Hey lady! Can you spare a dime?" The young boy tipped his cap upside down, hoping she would drop a coin into it. Caught off guard, she fumbled in her purse and dropped a few pennies into his hat. "Oh, thank you, ma'am. God bless you." Only a few seconds later she was surrounded by more street urchins with dirty faces, raggedy clothes, and grimy outstretched hands.

"We need money for food!" they hollered out at her.

She threw out a few more pennies and quickly slipped away down the next alleyway, hoping to outdistance them. Her heart began beating faster, as she realized she *was* alone and she panicked. She started to run, not really knowing where she was heading. Finally leaving the alley, she breathed a sigh of relief, feeling a little more secure. She had escaped the "invasion," but her heart went out to those poor little ones. So many and so young! Poor little beggars! She had a heart of gold but realized her purse would be empty if she gave to all of them. After all, I *have* to think of my own survival. I don't even know where I will sleep tonight. So many—little beggars. She couldn't get them out of her mind. Maybe things aren't so rosy here after all. Lifting her skirt as she stepped through the muddy intersection, straining to put one foot ahead of the other, she began to sink into the muck, almost falling over. A young policeman standing on the corner quickly approached, stretching out his arm to assist her up onto the wooden sidewalk. "Thank you, sir," she said.

"Well now lass, you seem a bit in distress now; and I might add you don't appear to be accustomed to our New York mud!" His smile was beguiling.

"No ... no, I'm not," she said, catching her breath and straightening her hat.

"And how would things be going in the Emerald Isle now, may I ask?"

"How did you know?" she asked. Hesitating for a moment, she replied, "Oh, it's the brogue now, is it?"

"Yes ma'am. And I might add you look lost—are you?"

"Well, not exactly." She attempted to brush the mud off her skirt.

"Well now, maybe you're not lost—but you sure *look* like you are!"

"Just look at me! My dress and my shoes!" She sat down on her suitcase and began to cry.

"Now don't be cryin', ma'am! Can I help you in some way?"

Patting her tears with her handkerchief, she replied, "I'm hungry and don't know a soul in this strange place." She had always been a strong young woman and prided herself on her independent nature; however, she had never been tested like this before.

"I could tell you're new here. You see, many new people come through here every day. Don't worry— maybe I can help. Do you have a place to stay?"

"No," she said, standing erect as she tried to regain her composure.

"Well now," he said as he reached up and scratched his head, "you wouldn't want to be stayin' around here, I'll tell ya—this neighborhood is filled with hooligans and cutthroats."

"Oh, my goodness! Saints preserve us!"

He thought for a moment—a quizzical look on his face, his right hand stroking the bottom of his chin. "I think maybe Molly might have a back room you could stay in, but it's across town a bit."

"Molly? Who's Molly?"

"Oh, she's a great lady—an old friend of mine."

"Well, I can't really afford to pay very much ... that is... well, I have to find work, you see." She hesitated momentarily. "But, in the meantime, where can I find this Molly? Can you give me directions?"

"I'll do better than that, Miss—oh, I didn't catch your name."

"Bridget—Bridget O'Halloran, Sir."

"Oh, call me Michael." He tipped his cap to her. "Well now, Bridget O'Halloran, if you don't mind waiting for me, I'll be done with me shift in a little while and I can take you to Molly's place myself. Now, there's a little church a few blocks away—St. Michael's. You can wait for me there."

"Oh, Sir—I mean Michael—I can't thank you enough."

"Don't mention it. Get along with ya now— and don't be givin' yer money away. You'll be needin' every penny."

She picked up her suitcase which held everything she owned in the world; and, as she walked through the streets, she observed many passersby, a few hobbling on crutches. One man had only one arm. She wondered why, but not for long.

"Can you help out a veteran who fought for this here United States in the Great Conflict?" She was determined not to give any more to beggars; however, she couldn't refuse this crippled man. Reaching into her purse, she handed him some change and continued to make her way to St. Michael's. She really didn't know much about America's Civil War except that she thought it had something to do with slavery.

It wasn't just the noise and congestion in this enormously big city—there was something else. She couldn't help but overhear people speaking in different languages as she walked through a busy shopping district; in the old country, everyone seemed to look and speak alike. Yet these storefronts told a different story. Wang's Chinese Laundry—Pick Up and Delivery. Schuler's Meat Market. Tony's Fruits and Vegetables. "Fresh apple, Miss?" the vendor asked, holding one out to her.

"Oh, no thank you." She was hungry but didn't want to spend any more of her money and continued walking.

The silence of St. Michael's was an oasis of peace—a holy place to regain her composure. She dipped her fingers in the holy water font and blessed herself. Proceeding up the middle aisle, she took a seat in the front pew. Gazing up at the life-sized Crucifix hanging behind the altar, she prayed, "Oh, Lord, Prince of Peace, guide me and help me find work to support myself. I'm alone and need your help." Holding her rosary beads, she began to recite the Joyful Mysteries. Feeling true peace for the first time since leaving home, she relaxed to the point of falling asleep.

"Miss! Oh, Miss!" Startled for the moment, she looked up to see a grey-haired priest who had nudged her shoulder. "Are you alright? Do you need help with anything?"

"Oh ... oh, no thank you, Father."

"You look tired, my dear. You sure I can't do anything for you?"

"Well ,.. I hate to ask, but would you have a little something that I could eat? I just arrived here and haven't eaten for quite a while."

"You're from the Old Sod, aren't ya?"

"Yes, Father—County Clare."

"I was just gonna have a bite myself come ta think of it. And I'd be mighty pleased ta have ya join me. And, oh! by the way, my name is Father Paddy Norton."

The little wooden frame priest house was small but very clean and tidy. "Have a seat, dear," as Father Paddy pointed to the kitchen table. "Oh, better yet, sit there on the rocker—you'll be more comfortable. I'll put the kettle down. We'll have a nice hot spot of tea with some sandwiches. I'm from County Cork myself—been here ten years now. But ta this day, I can still remember when I first arrived—it's so vivid in my memory! I know just how you're feelin'!" He paused, pulling a chair up to the table. "You'll be fine; just takes a while ta get used to it. What will ya have in your tea, dear?"

"Just a drop of milk and a little sugar, please, Father."

"Here ya are—nothin' like a nice hot spot of tea ta make ya feel better—and help yerself to a sandwich." Smiling, he placed a plate in front of her.

"I appreciate this, Father—but I'd sure feel a lot better knowing if I had a place to stay."

"Oh, my goodness, lass! Ya mean ya don't have any relatives or friends ta put ya up?"

"No. Not a soul. Came over on my own."

"Well, now, I guess you're in a pickle all right!" He scratched his head and looked up at the ceiling, seeming to be deep in thought.

A glimpse of hope came over her, as she remembered Officer Michael's conversation. "Oh, but Father, there *was* a policeman who said he might know of a place."

"Well now," he said as he poured more tea into her cup, "that would be Officer Mike, I'll bet. He's been known ta help many people."

"Yes, that's him—Michael."

The afternoon wore on as they talked about their love for their native land. But, sadly, they could not overlook the terrible tragedy of the potato famine and all the poor souls who died for lack of food. Bridget began to feel a little more comfortable, however, as she now had met two countrymen who reminded her of home.

Father Paddy rose to answer the knock on his kitchen door. "Well now, Michael, come in ... come in, me boy ... and rest those poor brogans! I'll get ya a cup of tea. Must be hard being on yer feet all day, walkin' that beat."

"Thank you, Father. I see you've met Miss O'Halloran." He tipped his cap to her before removing it, and sat down at the table.

"Yes, we've had a nice little chat, mostly about the Old Sod!"

"Oh, yes, it's hard leavin' home like that," Officer Mike responded. "But, ya know, this United States really grows on ya," he said, lighting his clay pipe. "I'm still amazed at the size of it! I learn something new every day. An' I'll tell ya, those boys who went through that great Civil War could tell ya a few things about this country!"

Father Paddy handed Michael his tea. "Yes sir," he added, "many of our own lads from Ireland fought in that war—ta be sure, it was a great cause!" His demeanor became very serious. "Could ya believe some of them joined the Rebel forces and some joined the Yanks—killed one another, they did." He made the Sign of the Cross. "Sad, it was. They came to escape the famine, only to end up on a bloody battlefield. Never had a chance ta enjoy this promised land!"

Bridget became a little unsettled. She never really knew what that war was all about. All she wanted now was to know she had a place to lay her head. Father Paddy noticed that she seemed troubled. "Michael, me boy, Bridget here tells me ya might know of a place for her ta stay."

"Well, Father, I think I know a lady who might put her up. It's not much, but it'll be a roof over her head." He turned to Bridget. "In fact, we'd better get started, young lady. She doesn't like visitors after dark."

"Did ya tell her about the Mission?" Father asked.

"Oh, no! How could I forget? You *could* stay at the Mission for Girls."

"No, thanks," she said, as she reached for another sandwich. "That's not for me; I want to make it on my own."

"Well now," Michael responded, "if you ever have to, the Mission would take you in."

Bridget felt more secure now, looking upon the two men as friends. The warmth of the priest and the supportive assistance of the officer brought peace to her heart.

Michael carried her suitcase, her small strides quickly increasing to keep up with him. Boarding a trolley car, he turned back, reaching down with his right hand to assist her. As she reached into her purse for her fare, he pushed her hand away, winking as he did. "Police ride free, Bridget—and you're with me."

"Thank you, sir." They sat in silence. Michael dozed off. Bridget was enjoying taking in the sights and sounds of this very busy metropolis. Before long, however, that section of Manhattan was behind them and they were entering into what appeared to her to be a very poor section of town. The housing seemed to be quite rundown and some places were boarded up. Untidy looking little children, barefoot, were playing in the streets, many in raggedy clothing.

"End of the line!" The conductor's shout startled Bridget. Michael quickly sat up, rubbing his eyes. He picked up her suitcase and helped her off the trolley. It began to rain as they walked through the darkened streets, void of any lamp posts; however, the dim light of the moon enabled her to see row after row of poorly constructed shanties. A few stray dogs ran across their path.

"Oh, this is terrible!" She shuddered. "How can people live this way?"

"Well, Bridget, you know they're all in the same boat. Some of our people just can't find work. I hope you'll have better luck." She tucked her hands into her sleeves, attempting to keep them warm from the cold night air as they walked on. "Oh, here we are now." He knocked on the door.

"Who is it?" came a husky female voice from inside.

"Michael—Michael Kelly."

Opening the door slowly and cautiously, the woman inspected her visitors to make sure it was Michael. "Come in, come in. Can't be too sure around here, ya know." Looking relieved, she went on, "We've had some robberies in the neighborhood. And who might this be, Michael?"

"Miss Bridget O'Halloran—a newcomer from home."

"Well now, Bridget, what brings ya here? I mean, have ya got people here?"

Bridget, shocked at the gloominess but not wanting to show any disappointment, smiled at her. "Oh ... oh no, ma'am, I don't."

"Well now, sit ya down here and tell me all about yerself," as she pulled a chair out from under the table. "And Michael, you sit yerself down, too," pulling out another.

"Oh, I can't stay, Molly." He glanced at his watch. "The Missus will be waitin' dinner for me." He headed for the door. Turning back, he instructed Molly, "Take good care of this young lass!" He knew well the heart of the old woman. "She's one of us, you know. Lock up behind me now."

Molly shook her head from side to side, looking toward the door. "That Michael! He's got a habit of dropping off stray cats ..." She paused. "Oh, no offense, dear. But that big lug is always givin' people a hand—ya know?"

"Yes, I can see that he's a good man." Bridget looked down at the floor, waiting for Molly to speak.

"Well now, young lady, I'll do what I can for ya. Come with me!" She took her by the hand and led her to a small back room. "Ya can stay here till ya get on yer own two feet. It ain't much, but yer welcome to it—but ya mustn't waste any time getting work. I been havin' a hard time feedin' myself, ya see." She took Bridget's suitcase and laid it on the bed, then lit the small candle on the table. "You look tired, dear. Would ya like to rest? Or have a bite ta eat first?"

"Thank you, ma'am, but I ate a short time ago at Father Paddy's. I *am* a bit tired now." She reached into her purse. "I'd like to pay you something."

"Now, now, Bridget. Don't worry about that. We can talk in the morning. Get yerself some rest now—ya look like ya had a tryin' time of it. Goodnight now."

Before Bridget had a chance to get into bed, Molly was back knocking on the door. "Here's another blanket for ya, my dear, and a little bread and jam just in case ya get hungry. Ya can't go ta bed on an empty stomach now, can ya?" She smiled as she patted her on the hand.

So far, things had not turned out as Bridget imagined they would. The shanties were small and cold, the streets were a muddy mess, and poverty reared its ugly head all around her newfound land. But she was young, strong-willed, and optimistic. For one thing, the few people she had met were generous and kind to her. That's what really matters, she thought. Yes, the people made a big difference! Tomorrow would be the first day of a fine new future. She slept.

A splinter of sunlight peeked through a crack in the ill-constructed wooden wall and awakened her early in the morning. Molly had left a note on the kitchen table.

Bridget — Went to work. Help yerself to the icebox. Be back this afternoon.

Molly

She made a sandwich with some hardboiled eggs and poured herself a glass of milk. Then, after washing up, she quickly dressed, eager to see her new surroundings in the light of day. Stepping outside, she watched as children played tag and jumped rope. A few dogs were fighting over a bone in the middle of the street.

She walked for what seemed hours, soon finding herself near a river. Her senses were accosted by a noisy flurry of activity as peddlers hawked their wares there—each trying to over-shout the others. *"Fish for sale!" "Crab! Crab!" "Oysters!" "Clam Chowder! Come 'n get it! Nice and hot. Clam chowder, Miss?"* She would have liked that warm soup but couldn't bring herself to spend any more of her money at first. Finally, however, that hungry feeling got the best of her and she found herself reaching into her purse.

"That'll be five cents, Miss."

"Thank you, sir." It was warm and wonderful and she felt much better. She continued walking, heading for an area ahead which seemed to have some small shops. There was hope in her heart that she might find a dress shop or even a tailor's where she could find work. That hope, however, suddenly dissipated as she approached "Rags and Riches."

IRISH NEED NOT APPLY

Why? Why would they have a sign like this? What's wrong with the Irish? This was a revelation that she could not understand. She had come to this new country, knowing full well that it claimed liberty and freedom for all. And didn't it actually represent itself proudly at its very doorstep in the form of a Statue of Liberty? Another store! Oh, no! And still another! I can't believe this! She became discouraged and turned to head back to Molly's.

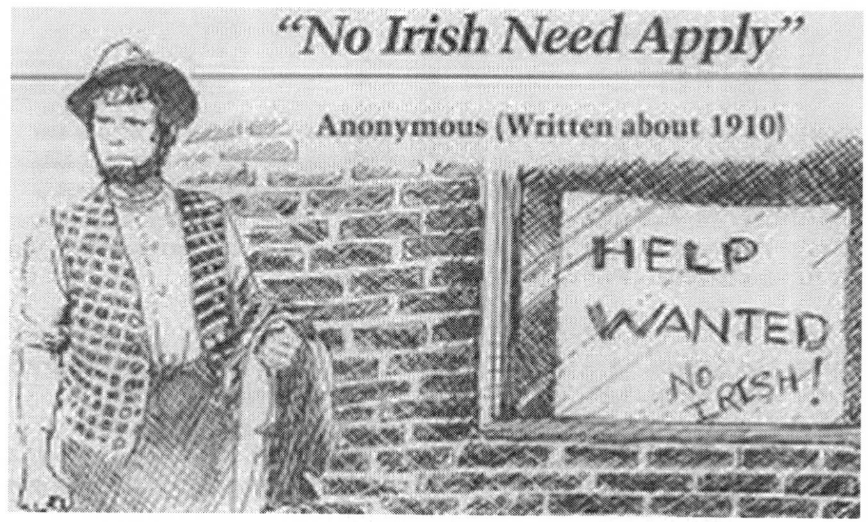

She soon found herself in an area she didn't recognize and realized she was lost. There were people around that she could ask for directions—but what was the name of the street? She couldn't remember—or had she ever been told? "Oh, sir," she asked a barber standing in front of his shop, "I'm lost. Could you tell me where ..." She paused. "I mean ... I came across town from a kind of a poor section ..."

Before she could finish, he broke in. "Oh, you must mean Shanty Town—bad neighborhood down there." Stroking a well-groomed handlebar mustache with his right forefinger, he continued, "You best stay outa there. There's a lot of those wild Irish there— always drinkin' and fightin'."

"I just arrived yesterday and ..." Just then, a customer approached, and the barber hastily gave her directions and went back inside his shop.

Eventually she recognized a small school which she had passed earlier where the children had been playing outside. Things began to look more familiar and she hurried her step so as to be back before dark.

"Well now, and where did ya wander off ta?" Molly asked. Bridget didn't get a chance to answer. "Ya shouldn't be walkin' around by yerself—I mean, a young lady alone! Ya don't know what devils are lurkin' out there."

"I'm sorry," she replied, "but I thought I could find work."

"Well, if its work yer lookin for, why didn't ya say so?"

Bridget looked her squarely in the eye. "I need work badly, Molly. I don't have much money and must find work right away so I can support myself."

Molly smiled. "Ya remind me of myself— when I first came over here. I was anxious, too. But maybe I kin help ya now."

Bridget pulled a chair out from under the kitchen table, sat down, removed her shoes, and rubbed her feet. "I must have walked ten miles today! And *no* one was hiring!" Looking depressed and lowering her head, she muttered, "And to top it all off, I saw these signs in store windows. I don't understand—they said 'Irish Need Not Apply.'"

"Oh, you poor dear! I'll get ya a cup of tea." She filled the teakettle with water and placed it on the old stove in the corner of the room. "Don't ya worry about that! I may have a job for ya," as she glanced back at Bridget.

"A job?" Her face lit up. "Where? What kind of a job?"

"Now don't get yer hopes up—I said I *may* have a job for ya."

"I'll take anything ... I mean, to get started." She looked across the room at Molly. "Later on, though, I would really like to work in a clothing store or a dress shop."

"Why would that be?"

"Well, that's what I did in the Old Country— that's what I did for a living. You know—dress making, ladies' wear, and the like."

Molly began stirring the stew on the stove. "Well, Bridget, that's all well and good. I mean, ya having a skill like that." She turned momentarily to glance over at the girl again. "But I'm afraid you'll have ta take what ya kin get at first."

"Well, what kind of a job were you talking about? Would you mind my asking what it would be?"

"Do you like water?"

"I don't know what you mean," Bridget responded with a quizzical look on her face.

"I mean would ya like workin' on a boat?"

"I don't know—I got pretty seasick on the boat coming over here."

"Well, this would be different. This would only be up and down the river."

"How so?"

"Do you know what a Matron is?"

"No."

"Well, it's a lady who works on those passenger boats that takes people for cruises on the river."

"What do they do?"

"Well, mainly, they're like an aide, ya know—if someone gets sick or needs help of some kind or needs a bandage or feels faint or something. They do what they can to assist them."

"Oh, I think I would like that! I mean, I always liked helping people in need." Bridget's mood began to brighten.

"I got ta tell ya, it doesn't pay much though," Molly said.

Bridget suddenly realized that Molly hadn't said a word as yet about any rent. "Speaking of money, you haven't told me how much rent I owe you."

"I normally charge whatever a person can afford." She looked over at Bridget's purse and old tattered suitcase. "Why don't ya give me three dollars for food and board ta start, and we'll talk about the rest later."

"Yes, that would be fine." Bridget counted out the money and gave it to her.

"So ya don't like the water, huh?"

"Well, I don't know. Maybe the river wouldn't be so bad .... You know, as long as I'd be able to see the land when I'm out there."

Molly laughed. "Well, I've been workin' on boats since I was knee-high to a grasshopper. There's something calming about water, ya know? It's always movin' and helpin' people get from one place to another. She placed the pot of stew on the table. "There's big steamboats, sailboats, barges—yes, my dear, it gets inta yer blood. Wouldn't want ta be anyplace other than on the water."

By now, Bridget was becoming very curious. "Well, what do you do? I mean what is your actual job?"

Molly set a bottle of whiskey on the table after pouring some into her tea. "Care for a little bit of old John Barleycorn?"

"Uh ... no thanks."

"Well now, my dear, it will warm the cockles of yer heart on such a damp day!"

"Oh, no thanks, Molly. The only time I take a little of that is when I'm sick."

Molly sipped her tea and leaned back on her chair. "I'm a tugboat captain."

"You're a *what*?"

"I work on a tugboat. You know—those little boats that move the big ones around and help ta dock 'em."

"Gee, I didn't know a *woman* could do *that*!" She looked surprised. "I mean, I never heard of that back home. I mean ... a *woman*?"

"Yes, my dear. I know it's unusual, but some things in this country are a bit different from back home."

"Boy! I'll say they are! Gosh! I'm amazed that you do that!"

Molly continued sipping her tea. "Mmmm. Nothin' like a good old Irish Whiskey Sling to warm ya up! Would ya like to take a ride on my boat?"

"You mean, *your* tugboat—is it?"

"Yep...an' ya can come along with me tomorrow if ya wish."

"Well, I would like to but ..."

"But what?"

"Well, I think I should spend my time looking for work, don't you?"

"Now, now ... don't worry about that." She smiled at her new friend. "I told ya, I might know someone who might hire ya."

"Oh, yes ... yes, you did."

"Soon as I get a chance, I'll take ya to meet the man who I think will be able to help ya."

"Oh, Molly, I hope it works out." Bridget sounded apprehensive.

"Now, don't ya go worrying yer little head about it."

The following morning, they got an early start and walked briskly for many blocks, Bridget having a hard time keeping up with Molly who was twice her age. They soon came to a wharf where many boats were moored. At the very end was a weather-beaten tugboat with dark green letters— *THE MOLLY-O.*

"Well, Bridget, here she is—my home away from home. I spend a lot of time here. Come on ..."

"Are you sure it's seaworthy?"

Molly laughed. "Well, do ya think I'd spend most of my days on it if it wasn't?"

"I guess not." Looking over at the name on the side of the boat, Bridget asked, "What does the "O" in "Molly-O" stand for?"

"Well, my dear, ya know there's a bad climate among some of our citizen friends over here. As ya already know, some places won't even consider hiring ya if yer Irish."

"That makes me feel terrible!"

"Now, maybe you'll understand about the "O" after my name when I tell ya. My last name is really O'Grady and people know if you have an "O" in front of yer name that yer Irish. Well now, I learned early on when lookin' for a job that if I would leave the "O" off of my name, it would be easier ta get work—me and a couple of my friends as well. In fact, some of them still kid me about it and say I dropped the "O" in the ocean on the way over here! But once I had my tugboat ta work on, I didn't have ta worry about it anymore, so I just went ahead and stuck the "O" back on my name—and there she be, big as life, right on the side of my boat!"

After starting up the old tug, Molly slowly increased her speed until she got into deeper waters. Bridget stood at the front of the boat, her hands clasped tightly on the railing. She glanced nervously back at Molly in the cabin who, upon seeing the look on her face, immediately motioned her to come inside.

"You okay, Bridget?"

"Yes, I'm okay. Just a little wet from the spray." She marveled at Molly's ability in maneuvering the little tug, pushing a large barge. In time a huge steamer passed by, creating a swell which rocked the boat. Bridget rolled her eyes and held her stomach.

Chapter 3

The Matron

For the most part, Bridget enjoyed her day out on the river with Molly—but didn't especially care to do it again. Molly's nautical enjoyments weren't exactly her cup of tea. During the next few weeks, she busied herself around the house—cleaning, cooking, mending, laundry, and anything else she could find to do to show her appreciation for Molly's hospitality.

Soon after, Molly arranged to take her to meet an old friend from the Emerald Isle, James Flynn, who was the person responsible for helping obtain her own job on the tugboat. He now enjoyed his position of attorney for a large shipping magnate, but never ceased to remember his early common and humble beginnings and felt he would always do all he could to assist those who were less fortunate.

Dressed in their "finest," the two ladies rode the horse-drawn trolley all the way to the downtown office of this distinguished lawyer. "Good morning, ladies! Good to see you again, Molly; and this pretty young lady must be Bridget, I take it?"

Bridget smiled and nodded her head but felt a little anxious and inadequate in the presence of this fine looking, immaculately dressed gentleman. His three-piece, navy blue, pinstriped suit, open in the front, revealed a satiny looking vest beneath. The brown wingtip shoes were polished to a high shine.

"Good ta see you again, too, Jim. Bridget here recently arrived from the Old Sod and she's gonna be stayin' with me for a while."

"It's a pleasure. May I call you Bridget?"

"Oh, please do."

"And you call me Jim." He pulled two chairs over in front of his desk. "Here, ladies—please have a seat."

Bridget gazed around at the many books lining the shelves behind the magnificent mahogany desk. She could see out the beautifully red velvet draped windows for what seemed to be miles, as they were on the seventh floor of the building. The two large potted green fern on the sides of each window added a touch of elegance, the likes of which she had never before encountered. The thick, plush, gold-colored carpet made her want to remove her shoes and feel its softness on the bottom of her feet.

"Can you tell me a little bit about yourself, my dear?" Jim smiled broadly at Bridget; and with a twinkle in his eye, he leaned back in his chair, holding his hands behind his head. "First off, what county do you hail from?"

"I'm from County Clare, Sir."

"Call me Jim. Well, what do you know about that? I'm from Cork. And maybe Molly here told you that she's from Limerick? So I guess that makes us all next-door neighbors!"

"Well, no, she never mentioned it." She smiled, nervously waiting for someone else to speak.

Molly sat forward in her chair and shifted her position, straightening her dress. "Jim, we've come here ta see if ya might be able ta help Bridget here find employment and ..."

Before he could answer, Bridget interjected, "I'm a good worker. I can work any hours and I really need work, Sir—I mean, Jim."

"Well, do you have any special kind of work you're looking for, Bridget? Like, do you have any special skills or anything? I mean like secretarial or office work of some kind or anything else?"

Looking somewhat anxious, she responded, "Well, no, Sir, but I am good at dressmaking and ... um ... generally all types of seamstress work. I did manage my own dress shop at home, that is until the economy collapsed. You know, the years after the famine, we couldn't get on our feet—most of us."

"I'm sorry to hear that. I know we've got many of our own countrymen arriving here every day, some poor folks half-starved!"

Molly intervened. "You know, Jim, I heard that one of the matrons on the *River Queen* was leaving. Do ya suppose ya could pull some strings and get that job for Bridget? She's very smart, and I think she would be an asset ta them."

"Yes, Molly, I did hear about that vacancy. I don't really do the hiring ..." He paused, doodling with his pencil, as though he were deciding what to say. "But I do know the Captain of that ship, and I'd be glad to put in a good word for her. Do you think you'd like that kind of work, Bridget?"

"Oh, yes! In fact, Molly took me out on her tugboat, and I just *loved* the cruise down the river!"

The look on Molly's face bespoke her amusement at Bridget's fabrication. "Oh, and Bridget really likes people," she offered. "And I think she would really be good with the public, ya know?"

"I'm sure you would catch on to it, my dear. You seem like a smart young lady. I'll see what I can do."

"Oh, thank you so much. I really do appreciate it," Bridget responded.

Molly chimed in, "Thanks, Jim. I know you'll help if ya can."

Conversation then shifted back into talk of the Old Country and how dear Old Ireland would always be a part of them.

"Excuse me, Mr. Flynn—sorry to interrupt, but your eleven o'clock appointment just arrived—Mr. Simmons."

"Oh, thank you, Marie. Tell him I'll be with him shortly." Molly and Bridget got up to leave. Jim smiled and winked at them, warmly grasping each one by the hand. "Now don't you go worrying, Bridget; I'm sure I can help. I'll be in touch."

Bridget sat outside on the back steps of Molly's little home, fanning herself from the oppressive heat. She gazed at the towering hickory tree standing alone in the field. Funny, she thought. Reminds me of myself—all alone in a strange land. This place had been all open field, Molly had said, before the immigrants swarmed over the land and built their little shanties. Somehow this one hickory survived the invasion. Just the sight of this majestic work of God with its lofty branches and small clusters of nuts brought a sense of peace to her as she pondered her lovely garden back home. When I get a little money, I'll buy some seeds and grow something to eat—and maybe some pretty flowers too. She picked up a few of the hickory nuts that were on the ground and opened the pods. Suddenly a little squirrel pranced up before her. She thought it strange that he got so close but held out her hand with the nut in it. The little animal grasped it with his tiny paws, sitting up on his hind legs to enjoy nibbling the treat. Well, aren't you the friendly one, she thought. Not even afraid. I think I'll call you Nutter.

She was getting bored and becoming impatient waiting to hear from Mr. Flynn. It had been a few weeks since he promised to help her get work. Maybe I'll look again myself—I can't stand just laying around here. Have to get some kind of income—and soon! Dark clouds coming from the west silently drifted across the blazing sky as if a shade were drawn to relieve the sweltering souls below. Bridget lifted her face upward and delighted in the pleasure of the fine mist of rain. Her first impulse was to go indoors, but on second thought she decided to stay right where she was. "Oh, Lord! Thank you for the relief!" she whispered to the heavens, savoring that cool wet blanket enveloping her. If only I *had* planted a garden already, this rain would have been wonderful for it!

She wasn't sure how long she had sat there dreaming of her future; but sometime later, Nutter appeared on the scene once again followed by another little squirrel. She grabbed a nut and held it out. "Here, baby! Here, Nutter!" She noticed a large scar on the back of the other where there was no hair. "Oh, poor thing—what happened to you?" He shied away from taking a nut from her, seeming to be afraid, and ran back to the hickory tree. "I guess I'll call you Scarback!"

She was startled from her enjoyment of the creatures, as she heard Molly shouting. "What are ya doin', Bridget? Don't ya know enough ta come in out of the rain? I've got something here for ya," she said with a lilt in her voice, waving a letter in the air. "Saints preserve us! Ya look like a drowned rat!" Grabbing a towel, she tossed it over Bridget's shoulders. "Dry yerself off, girl—yer floodin' the place!"

Bridget patted her face with the edge of the towel. "Is it about the job?"

"Well, it looks pretty official. Here ..."

Quickly reading it, she grabbed Molly, hugged her, and shouted, "I got the job! I got the job! Mr. Flynn wants me to contact someone who works on the boat. Oh, thank you so much, Molly! Thanks for your help!" She broke down with sobs of relief.

The sun shone brightly and Bridget's hopes were high as she approached the *River Queen* for the first time. She reported to the Captain's quarters on the upper deck. "Come in! Come in! Don't just stand there knockin' away at that door!" He swung around in his swivel chair as Bridget entered, dressed in an all-white uniform with a matching cap. Molly had acquired the apparel from one of her many friends and Bridget altered it perfectly, wanting to appear well dressed for the new position. The old sea captain scratched his bushy grey beard and yawned, sizing up the girl. "Welcome to my ship! Bridget, is it?"

"Yes, Sir."

Coming from behind his desk, he pulled up a chair. "Have a seat, young lady! You're a sight for sore eyes, ya are. We've been without a matron for a few weeks now. You can be a great asset to us."

"Well, thank you, Sir. Yes, Sir—I hope so." She hesitated. "I don't have much experience for this job, but I will do my very best."

"I'm sure you will—I can see your smile will be a good start. Dealing with the public will be hard at times, but it seems you have a pleasant way about you."

She looked down momentarily, feeling a little shy at the compliment. "Well, Captain, I'm sorry, I didn't get *your* name, Sir?"

"Well, blimy! You're right!" He folded his hands behind his back, then continued. "The name is Skully, but you can just call me Captain."

"Yes, Sir ... I mean, Captain."

"What did you say?" as he turned his good ear toward her.

"I said, 'Yes, Sir!'" She spoke a little louder.

"Oh, yes ... yes. I have a little hearing problem at times you see." His mood seemed to become quite serious. "Lost part of my hearing in the damn—oh, I'm sorry ma'am—I mean that *darn* tin can in that War Between the States. Maybe you heard of it?—the Monitor."

"Why, no. I haven't been here for long, you see."

"Well, I won't bore you with the details, but it was a heck of a battle! I mean, I almost bought the deep six. Came close ta meetin' Davey Jones at the bottom of the sea! Guess I was lucky just surviving."

She looked surprised. "Oh, you were in that war?"

"Yes, and a terrible thing it was!" He gazed out the window at the placid waters of the river. "Lost so many ... so many!" A few moments of silence passed. Turning back to her, he quickly changed the tone of the conversation. "Well now, dear Bridget, we won't be botherin' ourselves about the past now, will we. Now that we're friends, I guess you'll want to know your duties."

"Yes, Captain."

Leaning forward with his hands on the desk, he instructed, "Well, your main concern will be for the passengers. You'll be like a representative for the ship. Now, bein' that we're a pleasure boat, we do tours around Manhattan Island every day, up and down the East and the Hudson. So you'll be dealin' with a lot of people. You'll be required to assist anyone in need, like helping someone if they're feelin' sick, providing first aid ... you know—that sort of thing. And you gotta give a little talk about some landmarks, so you'll have to study the information booklet I'll give you. Do you think you can handle all that?"

"I think so. I do like people." She agreed to work the day shift for a nominal wage and felt lucky just to have a job.

"I'm sure you'll do alright. Now off with you. I have work to do." He lit up a big cigar and sat down behind his desk.

As she started to leave, she turned back. "Well, when do I start, Captain?"

"Bright and early! Seven a.m.—tomorrow."

"Thank you, Captain." As she left the ship, she had high hopes for the future, but she couldn't help wondering about the trepidation she had experienced for the water on her voyage to America and again on the tugboat. Well, I'm sure it won't bother me too much. After all, the river is usually calm, it seems. I'll be fine.

The next morning, she stood on the dock, perusing the paddle-wheeler. She was impressed by the long, sleek look of it, as the morning sun cast its light on the gold lettering on the bow, proudly identifying the *River Queen*. She took up her position on the top deck amidships, found a chair, and began to review her landmark pamphlet which she had studied the night before. As she heard the commotion of passengers beginning to board the ship shortly after, she anxiously anticipated her first "customer."

"Oh! My knee!" a young boy was crying. "My knee! My knee!" He was screaming now.

Bridget saw his mother take his hand, as she made her way to the railing where they stood. Kneeling, she tried to hide a slight smile as she observed a small scratch on the child's right knee. "Now there, little soldier, you're a brave lad, you are. We'll just have you all fixed up in a minute. Now I will need your complete assistance—you must hold these bandages for me while I 'paint' on you." The crying ceased immediately as Bridget handed the child the box of bandages and began to apply iodine, followed by some intense blowing on the "wound" right afterward. "Feel better?— now hand me one of those bandages, please."

Bridget's confidence was heightened by this small "urgent" event followed by profuse thanks from the mother, but more especially by a child's smile. She returned to her station and began once again to study her landmark pamphlet.

A young sailor approached, cocking his navy-blue cap back on his head, the initials R.Q. embroidered in gold just above the shiny brim. "Can I be of service to you?" he asked Bridget.

"Why, I'm not sure. Do you work on the ship?"

"Well, sometimes," he responded, leaning back on the railing.

"What do you mean, Sir?"

"Well, I work here part of the year and on the Canal other times."

"What canal is that?"

"You know—Clinton's Ditch—the Erie Canal."

"I haven't been here very long—in America, I mean."

"Yeah, I can tell." He hesitated, then smiled. "I can tell the way you *talk*."

"I really can't talk to you right now," she said, ignoring his remark and holding her pamphlet up to show him. "I have to learn this for my new job here."

"What's to learn?"

"I'm trying to follow this map. I'm supposed to ... Oh, I don't mean to be rude, but I *really* have to study this."

"Could I see it?"

She handed it to him, and he briefly glanced at it. "Oh, I know these landmarks like the back of me hand. Let me show you. I'm not working today—just cruising around. So if you don't mind, I can help."

"Well, I suppose it would be alright." She suddenly realized the ship must have been on its way for a while and wondered if she might have already passed some of the landmarks she was supposed to point out to the passengers. "Oh, my gosh! I think I missed some of the points of interest already!"

"Well now, lass, don't get excited. You'll soon be doin' this in your sleep. Now ..."

"I never caught your name, Sir."

"Well, I never threw it to ya!" he chuckled. "Name's Tom Sexton. And what might yours be, pretty lass?"

She paused momentarily, wanting to smile but deliberately not allowing herself to. "It's Bridget O'Halloran. So tell me, Mr. Tom Sexton—and how do you know so much about *my* job?"

He removed his cap and scratched his head. "If you had spent as much time around these waters as I have, you'd know a thing or two also, Miss Bridget-girl," he responded in a cocky manner. Walking over to a closet, he removed a small megaphone. Smiling, but looking a bit sheepish, he went on to say, "I forgot to tell ya to use this. Ya see, Captain Skully instructed me to show ya the ropes, but I thought I'd get to know ya first."

"Well now!" she retorted, looking him straight in the eye. "And here I thought you were trying to help me out of the goodness of your heart!" She thought her response was quite clever.

"Well now, Bridget-girl ...." He couldn't help smiling at her remark. "I would of helped ya out anyway—orders or no orders from

Skully! So I'm just gonna show ya around and help ya get started, with it bein' yer first day an' all."

The rest of the day seemed to fly by as Tom tried very hard to make amends for his discourteous manner and patiently pointed out the landmarks to her and with her, assisting as needed. "Ladies and gentlemen!" He spoke loudly and clearly into the megaphone. "May I call your attention to the right side of the ship. Very shortly we will be passing the Harlem River Ship Canal which has recently opened, allowing our ships to navigate completely around Manhattan Island. The Army Corp of Engineers dredged the Spuyten Duyvil Creek—also known as the Spitting Devil!—thus enabling the Harlem River to flow freely into the Hudson."

As some of the passengers began to draw around, Bridget moved closer to Tom; and standing on her tiptoes whispered into his ear, "I don't think I can remember all of that."

Feeling the concern in her voice, he replied, "Don't worry. I'll be doing this with ya for the first few days. Before long, it'll be like second nature to ya—you'll see."

Days turned into weeks, and Bridget worked into a routine and gained confidence in herself. Tom seldom visited her, as his own duties in the engine room and assisting the Captain in the pilot house kept him very busy. He also had recently quit his job on the Erie Canal and took another, working part time on the *Mary Powell*, commonly referred to as the "Queen of the Hudson." He found himself thinking about her, however, on a daily basis and decided he was going to make it a point to check in on her and see how she was coming along with the new job. Shortly after, when his duties on the ship allowed, he visited her at lunchtime. Passing the market place the night before, he had purchased six rolls for five cents and brought them, along with some fruit for this occasion.

"Tom! What a surprise!"

"Top o' the mornin' to ya, Bridget-girl!"

"It happens to be afternoon!"

"Well, and don't I know it? I brought some lunch for us. Won't ya join me?"

Thinking he was somewhat rash in expecting her to say yes, yet also not wanting to be rude and refuse his kind offer, she assented. They passed the next hour catching up on her work and his new position on the *Mary Powell*. She thought she smelled whiskey on his breath, as she had on their first meeting. Looking him squarely in the eye, she scolded, "Thomas! Have you been drinking?"

"Well, I only had a wee nip o' the crature today, me girl. You don't think I'm a boozer, do ya?"

"Well, I hope you're not." She paused, looking concerned. "I've seen many good men destroyed by that demon rum back in Ireland— families broken up, children left without enough food, and many bad things caused by the curse of the drink."

He smiled, putting his hands behind his back, and leaned forward so his face was almost touching hers. "Would ya like to smell me breath, Bridget-girl?"

"Oh, get out of here, you rascal!" She tried very hard not to crack a smile.

"How about we go dancin' tonight down at the Shamrock Inn? You do know how to dance now, don't ya?"

"Well, of course I do!" She looked sternly at him. "But I wouldn't get caught dead in a place like that—and you shouldn't even be askin!"

The pleasantries ended only too soon for him, but she was anxious to return to her work, enjoying the food more than the company. She didn't like that smell of whiskey on his breath, nor did she appreciate his crusty demeanor.

And so it went, as summer turned into fall, and Tom had still been unable to get Bridget to actually accept one of his many proposals to date. She was beginning to have some feelings for him; however, she continued to hold back, not wanting to be too involved with a man who definitely seemed so coarse and uncouth. Yet, there was something—something about him—she couldn't quite put her finger on it. But at times she realized there was some kind of attraction there. Maybe it was that cocksure attitude of his. Oh, well, I'm just not going to give it another thought.

The tourist trade was beginning to diminish, and Bridget's hours had to be cut back by Captain Skully. She began to look for other work but was unsuccessful. At times she felt a longing to do something more meaningful with her life. Now that she had more time on her hands, she often sat on Molly's back steps dreaming of better things to come. The old hickory tree was slowly shedding its leaves and the fall air felt invigorating. "What are ya doin' out there?" shouted Molly. "Yer wastin' half yer life sittin' around!"

"I *am* still working, Molly. *You're* the one who got me the job—like—don't you remember?"

"Well, yes, but there's more ta life than workin' and sittin' and workin' and sittin'!" Bridget didn't respond, seeming deep in thought. Something she had seen upon her arrival in America kept reoccurring in her mind from time to time—those images of those little homeless boys begging for money and food. They reminded her of the stories she had heard from her elders who had survived the potato famine—stories of people starving to death. And now this brand-new country of hers showed similar deprivation. Molly shouted again. "Why don't ya make yerself useful and go help out at the Mission or something?"

"What? What did you say, Molly?"

"I said why don't ya go help at the Mission or something?"

"What Mission?"

"Our Lady of the Rosary Mission. Ya know—down on State Street."

"Do they help those homeless boys I saw begging on the streets?"

Molly thought for a moment, a questioning look on her face. "I'm not sure. They help out many of the Irish girls who arrive here and don't have any place ta stay. Well, ya know—like yerself, when ya first came over here."

"Maybe I could have gone there ... but I just don't like being dependent on others if I can help it."

"Well, they only help ya temporarily with food and a place ta stay 'til ya can get on yer feet. But I got ta tell ya—I kinda like ya stayin' with me. I never told ya, Bridget, but I kinda got ta thinkin' of ya as a kinda daughter ta me."

"*Really*?" Bridget moved closer to Molly and placed her hand around her shoulder. She was so moved by this statement and felt a new warmness in her heart for the woman. "Well, I'm beholden to *you*, Molly. I mean, not only letting me stay here but getting me my job, too."

Bridget's next day off was the following Sunday, and she was curious to see the rest of the city. Her job had limited her to working on the *River Queen* and returning to her new home at Molly's every evening. After morning Mass, with the little extra change she had saved, she boarded the trolley heading for uptown Manhattan. As she watched out the window, she was surprised by the stark change in scenery. Behind her were the broken down shanties and the shoeless ragged children playing in the streets. Now she found herself gazing at huge mansions and breathtaking gigantic concrete edifices. The streets were filled with ladies dressed in their elegant Sunday finery, her eye drawn especially to the girl in the lustrous flowing pink dress. The matching wide-brimmed hat was decorated with blue and white flowers and a frilly pink parasol rested on her shoulder. Pink had always been Bridget's favorite color, and she was amazed at the eloquence and grandeur before her eyes. O my gosh! What a gorgeous dress! Maybe ... She tried to imagine how she might look in it, yet it seemed so far removed from her "station" in life. Still, somehow, she might become known and desired for her dressmaking skills, as she was in the Old Country. After all, this is New York City! Big opportunities may be awaiting ....

Most of her day was spent looking in the shop windows decorated with the latest fashions for men and women, expensive watches and jewelry sparkling in the morning sun, as well as the most recent home décor. Continuing her perusal, she found herself seemingly becoming mesmerized with the richness and new technology of the most modern gas-fired stoves and recently developed electrical lighting fixtures. Suddenly, thoughts of Our Lady of the Rosary Mission came to mind, and she found another trolley and headed back to lower Manhattan. The images of those rich clothes remained with her on the ride, but she recalled Molly's speaking of the poorly dressed girls at the Mission. She began pondering about her future. She knew she was skilled in dressmaking and could pursue her own career, but then again ... those girls, those poor girls ...

Chapter 4

No. 7 State Street

A cold rain began to fall, and Bridget ran from the trolley up the stairs of the Mission of Our Lady of the Rosary for Irish Immigrant Girls. Walking into the lobby, she was greeted by a middle-aged, buxom woman with graying hair tucked neatly into a bun at the back of her head.

"Well, young lady, what brings you here on such a rainy day?"

Bridget attempted to shake her shawl and wipe her face with her handkerchief. “Well, a friend of mine told me you help people who can’t help themselves.”

“Well, who would that be?”

“A friend of mine—Molly O’Grady.”

“You don’t mean Molly-O of tugboat fame now, do you?”

“Well, yes, she does work on a tugboat. How do you know her?”

“*Everyone* knows *her*!” Looking a bit concerned at her wet visitor, she continued, “Come over here girl and dry yourself by the radiator.” She led Bridget to the corner of the room. “And, by the way, I don’t even know your name.”

“Bridget. Bridget O’Halloran, Ma’am.”

“Good to meet you, Bridget. I’m Grace O’Brien. Are you looking for a place to stay?”

“Well, no. Molly thought maybe I could help out here. Just part-time—I do have a job. And I stay at Molly’s.”

“Well, you’re lucky to have work. We try to help our girls find work, you know. They’re just comin’ off the boat and don’t know a soul over here.”

“Yes, Ma’am.”

“We’re not always successful, though. Some don’t find work for months.” Grace paused momentarily and folded her arms across her chest, seeming to study Bridget. “Now, how is it you think you can help here? I mean—do you have any special skills? Right now, we actually need cooks, launderers, and maintenance people. Do any of those fit the bill?”

Bridget thought for a moment. “Well, I’m a seamstress and I had my own dress shop in Ennis. And I’m very good at dressmaking and most any kind of needlework.”

“Well, praised be Jesus! You’re just the angel we’ve been hoping for!”

Bridget, taken aback by Grace’s outburst, was at a loss for words.

"You know, young lady—I mean Bridget—you're a sight for sore eyes, you are! These girls who live here are goin' around in rags. Some came here with only the clothes on their backs—nothin' more. We don't have the money to buy any for them; but if we can get some material cheap enough, maybe you could ..."

Bridget interrupted her. "Do you mean, *I* could make the dresses and ..."

"Yes! Yes! What a Godsend you are!—oh! but we couldn't pay you much."

"Oh, don't worry about that! I'd be glad to help out." Bridget looked down at the floor and seemed in a more somber mood. "I know how your girls feel. I'm no different—I mean, we're all cut from the same cloth."

A quizzical look crossed Grace's face. Then laughter erupted, thinking Bridget purposely made the pun. "You've got a great sense of humor, you do. We need more of that around here. Now, let's get down to business!"

As Bridget traveled back to Molly's that evening, she looked forward to the beginning of a new horizon. She felt there would be new meaning to her life. She had had a few previous experiences in helping others in the Old Country which had created a warm glow deep within her soul. Now it seemed like it was beginning to return, as she started formulating plans to make clothing for the girls in the Mission, knowing how poor they were. But who could afford the expense of the material? She had only met a few people since arriving, and they were poor like herself. Molly had no money, and Tom—well, Tom could hardly support himself. Who else ... Who else ...

"I know! I know!" she suddenly cried out, startling the trolley driver, causing him to snap the reins. The horses bolted down the street, missing a mother with two children by only inches. After a short struggle, the driver was able to stop the trolley. He rose from his seat and walked over to Bridget. With his hands on his hips and a glaring look on his face, he reprimanded her sternly.

"We'll have no more of these outbursts on *my* trolley, Miss!"

"Yes, sir. I'm sorry," she responded, glancing down at the floor sheepishly. Though embarrassed, she felt an elation at her thought of a possible donor for the material.

Young Bridget had more skills besides being a seamstress. She had what the Irish refer to as "the gift of gab" or one who "kissed the blarney stone!" She had a way about her that made people feel good. No matter who she met and conversed with, they seemed to walk away feeling good about themselves. Her work as a matron on the *River Queen* was satisfying. She loved meeting new people and aiding them whenever necessary. But now she could begin to use her handiwork to provide for others. Lying in bed that night, she couldn't sleep, as the wheels of her mind created images of dresses, skirts, shirtwaists, and other apparel she could create for the immigrant girls at the Mission.

She wanted to forget the crowds, the teeming masses in steerage on the voyage to America, the confinement, lack of privacy, bad food, and all the foul smells of that ungodly ship. She had struck out on her own to breathe free and soak in the fresh air of freedom and break the bonds of poverty, misery, and domination. She didn't realize at the time that thieves, cutthroats, and worse had been lurking in the shadows anticipating the arrival of unsuspecting new immigrants. Had she realized the dangers of going off on her own, she thought she would have stayed with the crowd and probably gone to the Mission with the rest of the girls. Looking back, she thanked God for who she considered her "two angels"— the policeman and the priest who helped guide her to a safe place.

Before leaving Ireland, she had planned ahead in case any special occasion might arrive in the new land and made herself a new navy blue dress, trimmed in white around the collar and wrists. The everyday clothes she had brought with her were showing wear—but no matter! On her day off, she rose early, fixed her hair so the curls would hang gracefully beneath the pale blue bonnet, borrowed from Molly, which complimented her sky-blue eyes. She wished it were navy or white, so as to pair better with her dress; however, she still felt that she looked pleasing, especially since the length of the dress hid her worn out shoes and the hole in her stocking. Pinching her cheeks for a rosy look, she mustered up her courage and prepared some compliments in hope that Mr. Flynn would respond positively to her appeal.

"Good morning, Miss ... Miss ..."

"Bridget—Bridget O'Halloran. I'm here to see Mr. Flynn."

"Oh yes, I remember you from the last time. Do you have an appointment?"

"No ... no I don't."

"Well, now, Miss O'Halloran, Mr. Flynn is very busy. I don't know if he'll have time to see you today."

"Oh I won't take up much of his time. Oh! Hello, Mr. Flynn."

"Miss O'Halloran stopped in, but she has no appointment, Sir."

"Well, isn't this a pleasant surprise. Nice to see you again, Bridget. It's fine, Marie. I have a little time to spare." He smiled at Bridget. "Please come in, my dear." He ushered her to a brown leather chair in front of his desk. "And to what do I owe the pleasure of your visit?" Before she had a chance to answer, he continued, "And may I say you look quite lovely in that dress."

"Oh, thank you so much, Mr. Flynn. I made it myself."

"Jim—remember?" He circled the desk, seated himself behind it, picked up his pipe and proceeded to light it.

"Oh, yes—Jim."

"Will this bother you?"

"Oh, no. Not at all. I like the smell of tobacco. In fact, you pose a striking figure and look very dashing with it."

"Well, thank you, Bridget. Now ... what can I do for you?"

"Well, first of all, I can't thank you enough for helping me get my job."

"Oh, don't mention it." He drew on his pipe, watching the smoke rise in the air.

"Well, Sir ..."

"Jim."

"Yes—Jim. Well, you see, I have another favor to ask of you ... but I hesitate because ..."

"No, no. Go on. Please."

"Well, it's not exactly for *me*. It's actually for the other girls."

Jim rose from his seat, walked to the front of the desk, then leaned back on it, facing Bridget. "Now, young lady, you've really got my curiosity up."

"Well, there's this Mission down on State Street for Irish immigrant girls."

"Oh, you mean Our Lady of the Rosary?"

"Yes ... yes. Oh, you know about it?"

Smiling, he responded, "Well, Bridget, I don't think there's an Irishman in all of New York who doesn't know about it." Laying his pipe down in the ashtray, he continued, "You see, most all of our people—at least the girls arriving from Ireland—spend their first days there. In fact, I'm surprised you yourself didn't wind up there!"

"I guess I'm lucky that Molly took me in."

Yes, you are. Now what's on your mind, young lady?"

Bridget sat up firmly in her chair and said a silent hurried prayer. "I want to volunteer for the Mission. I mean ... I think I told you before that I was a seamstress." She hesitated, hoping the right words would come.

"Yes, my dear. Go on."

"Well, I was talking to a lady named Grace—at the Mission, I mean. And she said she was hoping I could make some clothing for the poor girls there."

"And how does that involve me?" he asked in a soft voice.

"Well, since I have these skills ..."

"Yes?"

"Oh, I just really need the cloth to work with, you see, but I have no money to buy it!" The words seemed to just tumble out of her mouth.

"Well, why didn't you say so in the first place? I'd be glad to help out. I mean, if you can provide the labor and time, I guess I can be of assistance for such a good cause. How much do you think you'll need?"

"I don't know." She thought for a minute. Raising her eyebrows and looking up at the ceiling, she quietly added, "And then we may even need a sewing machine or two to get started."

"Oh, I see. I'll tell you what, Bridget. Why don't you figure out how much material you'll need and check the prices in some stores. In the meantime, I'll get the word out to some people I know—maybe we can even get some at wholesale prices for you."

"Oh, Mr. Flynn, thank you! I don't know how to thank you enough!"

"Now don't mention it. Let's keep in touch. I will contact you as soon as I have some news." He looked at her apologetically. "Now I really have to go—I have a meeting to attend."

And so, an alliance was formed between the successful lawyer and the poor young seamstress to help the less fortunate at the Mission of Our Lady of the Rosary. Bridget searched many retailers as Jim had asked, only to find ready-to-wear apparel rather than bolts of cloth. She was becoming discouraged, as her day-to-day search expanded into weeks.

Meanwhile, her new friend, Tom Sexton, would call upon Bridget, as he knew he could always find her on the deck of the boat. She had accepted his invitation to share lunch on occasion; however, any further requests to meet outside of work were immediately brushed aside. By now, she had become familiar with the landmarks and no longer needed to look at her little map—nor did she need any more of Tom's assistance.

"May I draw your attention, ladies and gentlemen, to the port side of the boat. That spectacular structure, the Brooklyn Bridge, completed in 1883, is the longest suspension bridge in the world."

Moving from the East River into the Hudson—"Ladies and gentlemen! Riverside Park is to your left where you see the new large granite monument at the top of the hill. This is the burial place of Ulysses S. Grant, the famous Union general of the Civil War and 18th President of the United States."

"Right ahead you will see the Statue of Liberty which was donated to the United States by France in 1884. It had to be shipped over in boxes to be reassembled here. The statue stands 151 feet high and weighs 450,000 pounds The torch rises 305 feet above the base of the pedestal. At the feet is a broken shackle symbolizing the overthrow of tyranny. Listen carefully to this beautiful message which will be inscribed soon on the pedestal." With an almost reverent emotion, she related to the passengers those words she knew so well by now, memorized not only in her mind, but in her heart.

"Give me your tired, your poor
Your huddled masses yearning to be free . . .

This period of time in America was commonly referred to as the "Gilded Age," a term coined by Mark Twain. New technologies were rapidly coming on the scene—electricity, the automobile, factories, railroads, mining. Bridget was now a part of this new and exciting time. However, she had come to discover a seamy side in this new land. Places like The Bowery were filled with cheap saloons, prostitution, tacky lodging houses, tattoo artists, cheap eating "joints", and oh! so many "down and outs." Young children were often seen begging for food in these streets of squalor. Bridget couldn't understand why this new country would have such a great disparity between the rich and the poor, especially after seeing the gigantic Vanderbilt mansions going up on West 57th and West 52nd Streets. Molly was a hardworking woman, yet she still could only afford the little, poorly heated, drafty, and ramshackle shanty.

Although Bridget and Molly had become good friends, she often found herself having lonely nights, still feeling somewhat isolated and alone. These periods seemed to be the times when her thoughts mostly drifted to the hours she had spent with Tom. She hadn't actually detected the smell of liquor on his breath recently—a good sign. She wondered about the times when she hadn't seen him for long periods, however. Does he have a girl? The man does have a really nice sense of humor. He had recently grown a black mustache which, along with his thick head of curly hair and tall, masculine frame seemed to engage her heart somewhat. Well, where has he been? I guess I kind of do miss that man!

It wasn't long before she discovered a secret that he hadn't shared with her. An elderly woman needed Bridget's assistance to push her wheelchair through the door of the ladies' restroom on the *River Queen*. "Well, thank you, dear. You're very kind."

"Oh, you're welcome. It's my job, you know. I'll wait right here until you're ready to come out. Or will you need my assistance inside?"

"No, I can manage myself, thanks."

Exiting a few minutes later, the woman resumed her conversation with Bridget. "Could you wheel me over to the railing so I can get a better view, please?"

"Certainly." She secured the brake on the wheelchair next to the railing.

"Have you been here very long, my dear?"

"You mean here on the boat?"

"No, dear, I mean, have you been here in this country for long."

"Well, no, not really. About a year now."

"My name is Noreen—but my friends call me Reenie. I love to take these boat rides ..." She paused, looking out over the water and the Manhattan skyline, then continued, "I never really liked boats until a friend told me about these tours and talked me into coming along with her one day. Her son had a friend who worked on this boat and he had free passes." She paused again and looked up at Bridget. "And now I come every year. It's so soothing looking out at the water, isn't it?"

"Did you say he worked on the boat?"

"Why, yes... and a handsome young fella he is. Maybe you know him."

"What's his name?" A quizzical look came over Bridget's face.

"Oh, I think it was Thomas—yes, that's it—Thomas. I remember because that was my dear husband's name. We had only been married a year when he was killed at the battle of Gettysburg."

Surprised, Bridget responded, "You don't mean Thomas *Sexton*, do you?" Before Noreen could answer, she added, "Oh, I'm so sorry about your husband; but yes—I *do* know Thomas."

"Yes, I thought you might." She glanced upward at the blue sky adorned with puffy white clouds. "He's a fine lad—does fine work with the little beggars."

"How's that?"

"Oh, he gets them off the streets. Feeds them and always tries to find homes for them."

Bridget spoke under her breath. "So that's where he's been spending his time ..."

"What did you say?"

"Oh, sorry, Ma'am. Just thinking out loud." She couldn't believe this new revelation about Tom. And here all this time I'm thinking he's just a bum, or maybe has another girl! I am definitely going to ask him about this secret thing the next time I see him.

She didn't have to wait long, as he appeared on the deck a couple weeks after just as she finished her duties and was preparing to leave the ship. "Good afternoon, Bridget, and how was your day?" he asked with a broad smile.

"Oh, I'm fine. Just a little tired." She hesitated a moment, then added, "Didn't sleep well last night."

"And why would that be?" he asked with a curious look on his face.

"I don't know—maybe I've got too much on my mind."

"And what would a pretty young lass like yourself have on her mind?"

"Well, I'm hoping to make some garments for the girls at the Mission."

"You're making garments?"

"Well, I *want* to. Mr. Flynn is supplying the material for me, but I have another problem."

"What is it?" He folded his arms across his chest.

"It's the machines. I need sewing machines for myself and a helper."

"Did you say Mr. Flynn?" he asked, unfolding his arms and placing them in his pockets.

"Yes—Mr. Flynn."

"You mean the big attorney?"

"Yes. And a very kind one he is."

"That's a surprise. I mean, how ..."

"How did I get him to help? Well, he is just a very generous man and *wanted* to help." She continued, "And, oh! by the way, not to change the subject, but ..."

"But what?"

"I hear you have another job you never told me about."

"You mean my working on the *Mary Powell*? I did tell you about that, didn't I?"

"Yes, you did. But that's not what I meant."

Leaning back against the deck railing, he looked puzzled. "Well, what *do* ya mean?"

"You know—helping those street orphans."

"Oh, that! Who told ya about that?"

"Oh, just some lady who I met one day. She knew you helped them get off the streets."

"That must be Mrs. Shannon, I presume?"

"Mrs. Shannon?"

"Yes. Noreen Shannon."

"Oh, yes, that's her. She hadn't mentioned her last name."

"Lovely lady ... lovely. She owns a pub down on the waterfront. Everyone knows about Shannon's Pub."

"Well, *I* don't. In fact, I don't like saloons."

"Yes, but I think ya would like Mrs. Shannon's." Observing Bridget's frowning face, he paused a moment before continuing. "She would give ya the shirt off her back if ya needed it. She's always helping people—I mean, those who are down and out. And, by the way, she doesn't like being called Mrs. Shannon—we call her Reenie." Before Bridget could respond, he blurted out, "Hey! it's almost dinner time. How would you like to go there and have a great fish dinner? She has the best seafood in town."

"Well ... I don't know." Bridget hesitated, but was intrigued, after having heard all this new information about Tom's orphan work. His concern for others had certainly improved her impression of him. Maybe he really wasn't the way she had thought—always just thinking of himself. And that Noreen is such a sweet lady! She smiled at Tom. "Well, I guess it would be okay this time. I *am* hungry."

"Great! Let's go! Friday's a busy day over there. Maybe we can beat the crowd. Now don't be surprised if ya see a few characters down there; it ain't the best section of town, ya know."

"Oh! How awful!" Bridget exclaimed, as the ride along the waterfront exposed the squalor and trash of the underbelly of the ever growing metropolis. When she had sailed along on the *River Queen*, it had been at a distance. Tom took her hand. She didn't object, although not understanding if it was out of affection or if he was trying to give her a little security.

Reenie greeted them from her wheelchair as they entered Shannon's Pub. "Thomas! How are you? And who might be this lovely young lady?" She studied her face for a moment. "Oh—the *River Queen,* isn't it*?"*

"Yes, Ma'am."

"Oh, call me Reenie!" She smiled. "Any friend of Tom's is a friend of mine." Reenie took Bridget's hand and squeezed it, then began to wheel herself to a table in the back room, motioning for them to follow. Passing through the bar room, Bridget, unaccustomed to such places, was shocked to see a few "tipsy" men arguing, their language not fit for a lady's ears. Another man had passed out, his head down on the table before him. Now she could understand the sign posted on the wall—"Ladies not allowed in Barroom."

"Here you are. I'm sure you'd like a nice cold beer, Tom! And Bridget, what can I get for you, my dear?"

"A cup of tea would be fine, thank you."

Tom and Bridget seemed to enjoy the private and relaxed atmosphere in the back room, as they had never had much private time with each other in the past. Eventually Tom ordered Shannon's specialty—their fish fry—for the two of them, and they talked and talked long into the evening. She had stories to tell about the devastation in the Emerald Isle caused by the potato famine and reiterated to Tom her years in the orphanage, and he spoke of his abandonment by his parents at a very young age shortly after their arrival in America. "I remember selling newspapers to survive and living in alleyways and abandoned buildings."

They became so enveloped in their conversation, they hadn't realized the room had been filling up with other customers. So much time had been spent talking about their early years, they had barely shared more recent events in their lives.

"You know, Tom, you never answered my question before."

"What was that?"

"You never told me about this work you do now. I mean, with homeless boys."

"Oh, that!" He stared at the candle glowing on the table, then looked directly at Bridget, blurting out, "I'm one of them!"

Saddened at his curt answer, she reached over and took his hand. "Oh, Tom ..."

"You know, I sure would have died if it wasn't for Father Drumgoole."

"Father who?"

"Ya don't know about him?"

"No, I'm afraid I don't."

"It's a long story." Folding his hands behind his head, he leaned back in his chair. "I don't like to think about it—just ... just don't like to think about it."

"Oh, I'm sorry if I'm digging up bad memories."

Tom motioned for the waiter. "Another beer, please." Looking across the table, he asked, "Would ya like another tea, Bridget?"

"No ... no thank you." She smiled at him.

The cold beer left white foam across his black mustache which he immediately wiped away with his sleeve. She didn't seem too happy about his bad manners but couldn't bring herself to say anything about it. He seemed to "mellow out" after this fourth drink. After a moment of silence, Bridget began to feel a little uncomfortable, as she noticed Tom seemed to be staring directly at her. "Did anyone ever tell ya you have beautiful blue eyes, darlin'?"

She looked down, feeling self-conscious. "Now Thomas ..."

"No ... I'm serious! Ya really do!"

Bridget decided she'd better change the subject. "You were saying about Father Drumgoole?"

"Oh, yes. He gave me a roof over my head and fed me. The man was a saint, God rest his soul." He looked very serious now. "Yes, sir, he picked me out of the gutter, half-starved and frozen to the bone. Saved my life, he did."

Bridget was glad to see that Tom seemed more relaxed now and able to speak about some of these hurtful times. "Where was that, Tom?"

"It was an orphanage. Used to be right down here in lower Manhattan. He saved many boys like myself, trying to make enough to eat by hawking papers. Father opened up a home for us and called it "The Newsboys' Home." But later he built a bigger place out on Staten Island."

"Oh! What a wonderful man he must have been!"

"So, anyway, I try to help when I can and be like a father and do things with my boys. Sometimes when the Captain's in a good mood, I'm even able to get them free rides on the *River Queen*—they *love* that!"

"I'm sure they *do*! I can imagine that must be a wonderful treat for them!. Tell me—is the new place on Staten Island still called "The Newsboys' Home?"

"No. He originally named it "The Mission of the Immaculate Virgin for the Protection of Homeless and Destitute Children." But eventually he shortened it to "Mount Loretto." It's a really big orphanage. I don't have much time to spend with the boys since I'm working those two jobs now, but I do help when I can."

"Do they educate them?"

"Of course."

"Well, who runs such a large place now?"

"Eighty angels of mercy."

"Angels?"

"Well not *real* angels, of course. These are Franciscan Sisters from Buffalo. I have a high regard for their selfless work in educating and instilling high morals and character into these poor ragamuffins."

"Oh, that's wonderful! And to think that you devote your time to these boys."

"Just giving a little back. You know, like *I* was helped when I was in that situation." He paused, then added, "And those nuns who taught me were fantastic. Some were like mothers to me, since I never really knew my *own* mother." He leaned his elbows on the table and looked directly at her. "That's enough about *me.* Now tell me more about yourself. What do you do in your spare time?"

She noticed the clock on the wall. "Oh, it's getting late. We should be going."

He raised his eyebrows, surprised at her sudden urge to leave. It seemed to him that she didn't want to talk about her personal life. He grinned. "You have some deep dark secrets to hide, Bridget-girl?"

"Of course not, silly. I'm just tired and must get up for work tomorrow."

He honored her request, made their goodbyes to Noreen, and proceeded to board the next trolley. "Up ya go!" as he turned back and extended his hand to help her up the trolley steps. "I don't even know where ya live, but I'll see ya back to your house."

"You don't have to."

"No, I insist!"

Bridget took her seat, yawned, and laid her head against the window.

"My shoulder's available, Bridget-girl."

She smiled at him and complied. They sat silently, listening to the steady clomp-clomp-clomp of the horses' hoofs. After a while she sat up, as if she had something important to say. Yawning again, she paused for a moment. Finally, she proceeded. "I *do* have a problem, Tom. It's not a deep dark secret, though. It's just ... well, like I said before, I need a couple of sewing machines—for the girls."

"Yes, you did mention that."

"Whoa!" hollered the driver. "End of the line!" The horses came to a sudden halt, lurching Bridget's head forward before snapping it back against the seat. Tom quickly took advantage of her uplifted face and kissed her.

"Thomas!" She immediately rose from her seat, pushed past him, and stepped from the trolley, glancing back at him. "Goodbye!"

"Hey, wait, I'll walk you ..."

"No. I only live a short distance from here. Besides, this is the last trolley tonight."

"She's right, son—better stay on. We're leaving right away."

Chapter 5

The Attic Room

Bridget struggled to find enough money to buy a sewing machine or possibly two. No matter how hard she tried though, she couldn't save enough. After paying Molly her room and board, she just about scraped by with trolley money to and from work. She had almost given up until a day when she was attending Mass at St. Paul's. The priest had made an announcement afterward, asking if anyone knew of someone who could sew.

She entered the Sacristy just as the priest was changing his vestments. "Good morning, Father."

"Good morning, young lady. What can I do for you?"

"Well, Father, I may be able to help you—I'm a seamstress by trade."

"Really? Wonderful! You're an answer to prayer. I have a few robes that really need mending."

"I'd be happy to do that for you, Father."

"Here, I'll show you," as he removed a few of the vestments from the closet and laid them on the table.

She inspected some that were torn at the seams. "Oh, these can be repaired and look like new. Do you have a sewing machine?"

"Well, yes, but I don't think it works very well."

She thought for a bit. "Do you think you could get someone to fix it? You see, I could also use it for the girls at the Mission if you could let me borrow it."

"What Mission is that? There are many missions in New York, you know."

"The Mission of Our Lady of the Rosary—the one for Irish immigrant girls."

"Oh, yes—on State Street. Some of the girls come here for Mass on Sundays." The elderly priest looked up at the ceiling, seemingly deep in thought. Then, after a long pause, he smiled at her. "I'll tell you what. Oh! Excuse me, I'm Father Sullivan."

"Bridget— Bridget O'Halloran, Father."

"Glad to meet you, Bridget."

"My pleasure, Father."

"You know, I think we may be able to help each other out, Bridget. Why don't you come back next Sunday and we'll talk again." He took both her hands into his and gently shook them.

The colder weather soon set in, and Bridget's work on the *River Queen* had been suspended until spring. She felt badly, as Molly was allowing her to stay on temporarily until she could find other work. This wouldn't do, as Bridget was not one to depend on anyone—independence meant too much to her. She finally came to the conclusion that she couldn't possibly stay with Molly much longer. It wouldn't be fair.

She would sometimes walk many miles just to save a few pennies. She could only walk so far, however, on this one particular icy, frigid day, as the cold wind buffeted her face and her hands. Her ears began to freeze, and she pulled her hat down further to cover them. Finally, she was forced to board the next trolley that came along. She watched the horses through the front window, wondering how they could stand the harsh winter wind as they labored to pull that heavy load of humanity, the steam pulsating forcefully from their nostrils. Drawing closer to the Mission, she watched as people walked briskly, bundled up in ear muffs, scarves, and turned-up collars, braving the chilly windy New York winter.

"Our Lady's Mission!" shouted the driver, as he pulled back on the reins, bringing the horses to a halt.

Bridget was greeted by Grace O'Brien as she entered the lobby. "Well, now. Good to see you again, Bridget. How have you been?

I've been wondering when you'd be back," she said with a lilt in her voice and a smile on her face.

"Hello Grace. I've been meaning to come back sooner, but I've been pretty busy."

"Here, let me take your coat. Now what could be keeping a young lady like yourself so busy now?"

"Well, I ..."

Grace interrupted. "Looks like you could use a cup of hot tea." She took Bridget's coat and hat and led her into the kitchen. "Sit down and tell me what you've been up to."

"You know, Grace ..."

"What is it, dear? You look troubled."

"Well, maybe not troubled—just uncertain, I guess."

Before she could go on, Grace interposed, "Oh, I just remembered—a big heavy package was delivered here with your name on it. It just arrived yesterday; and I haven't had a chance to notify you, so I'm glad you stopped in."

"What? Who would ...?"

"Don't know. Come on, it's back in the storage room. Let's see what it is."

After struggling to cut the package open, they found a sewing machine with an envelope attached to it. "Oh, my gosh!" Bridget exclaimed. "It's from the priest—Father Sullivan!" She read it out loud.

Dear Bridget,

Please accept this with my blessing. I hope it will be of great use to you. I know you will be an asset to Our Lady's Mission House and the less fortunate girls who live there.

I took the liberty to send it to the Mission as you mentioned you needed it for your work there. It should be in good working order now, as I found a handy gentleman who was familiar with this type of machine. God bless you.

Father Michael Sullivan

"Oh, that dear priest! He didn't forget! I must go back and thank him in person. Oh, Grace, I can do so much with this machine!" Bridget then muttered something to herself.

"What was that you said?" Grace asked.

"Oh, I just remembered I promised Father I would mend his vestments—can't forget ..."

Hearing the doorbell ring, Grace excused herself and left the room. Alone with her thoughts, Bridget stared at the sewing machine, envisioning all of the many dresses, skirts, and blouses she could now provide for the homeless girls.

Returning, Grace inquired, "Well, my young lady, so tell me! How did you manage this?"

"I prayed a lot, Grace!"

"We did too—the girls and I. We were praying too."

"Oh, I'm so excited! Now I can help out here as well as work on what I love to do best."

"I'm sure you'll do well here, Bridget. Your enthusiasm is contagious!" Grace smiled at her. "You've even got *me* excited about it! What did you mean before when you said you were uncertain about something?"

"Oh! I ... I was ..."

"Out with it, girl! You don't have to be afraid of me! You know, as founder of this fine establishment, having worked with hundreds of girls—I've heard it all!"

Bridget was surprised. "You mean, *you're* the founder here?"

"Well, yes, my dear. I've been working with girls like yourself who have no home—no one to sponsor them or give them a place to stay. Or even worse—could be taken advantage of!"

"Oh dear!"

"It's a long story. But you see, I have seen so much misery among our people who have no one to care for them. I think it all started when I was a child. My father fought for our countrymen back in the Old Country and was arrested and convicted and sentenced to be hanged—just for standing up against the rotten establishment that didn't give a hoot for the starving masses."

"Oh! That's terrible, Grace! I've heard that *my* folks were also part of those poor souls who had to give up their children or see them starve to death."

"You see, dear, maybe you could understand my concern for our people because of the conditions back there. The establishment in Ireland had the food to feed the starving masses; but instead of caring for them, they chose to export the food to other countries for profit. Those damned officials—excuse the language!—will rot in hell for every last person who literally died of starvation. So you see, my father, William O'Brien, was a hero 'cause he fought for those poor souls. Even though his death sentence was commuted, he was exiled to the island of Tazmania. His suffering at the hands of evil men left an indelible mark on me and put this deep conviction inside my heart to do all I could to carry on his fight for righteousness and justice." Grace stood up and walked over to the sewing machine, patting it with her right hand as though it were a baby, then turned back to Bridget. "But that's all behind us now, and I see a bright future for all of us here in our new country. So what do you say? Let's get this machine going and see what you can do with it!"

As they set up the sewing machine, Grace looked deep in thought. "You know, Bridget, I've been thinking—you said you were temporarily unemployed. I mean, now that the *River Queen* has suspended operations for the winter and I know Molly, being such a good soul ... well ... she would never ever evict you. So I was just wondering if you wouldn't be better off living right here—if you'd like to, that is!"

"Oh, I wouldn't want to be a burden—you have enough ..."

"Now, now, young lady, listen to me! You can stay here with us. And seeing that you don't want a handout, you can earn your keep by doing the mending and making the girls' clothing."

"Well, I don't know," Bridget responded, pondering Grace's proposal.

"Think of it this way, Bridget. You have no income right now. You'd have to take the trolley back and forth every day; but if you stayed with us, you wouldn't have that expense. And you'd save on rent besides—*and* the meals here would be free!"

"Oh! You are so kind, but ..."

"But what?"

"Molly might be disappointed if I ..."

"Molly can take care of herself. She's been on her own a long, long time."

"Well, maybe you're right, Grace." Bridget looked down at the sewing machine. "I *do* have many patterns, and I could even teach the girls how to sew—crochet and darning too!"

"Now you're talking! Then it's settled! Come on ..."

Molly was sad to see Bridget leave; but after thinking about it, she realized it was best for the girl. Deep down in her heart, she was glad to see that Bridget would be able to help at the Mission. "I'll miss you, Bridget ..." She reached out and hugged the girl. "...a lot!"

"Oh, Molly, I can never even begin to repay you." Her eyes teared. You've been so good to me."

"Come on. I'll help you get your things together."

Grace had cleaned the attic room and moved a bed upstairs for Bridget, as the space there would allow for the sewing machine as well as a table on which to lay out and cut her patterns. She saw to it that a lacy pink curtain was hung on the window, so as to make it more "homey".

"Come on ..." Grace grabbed Bridget's hand and led her up the stairs. "Here it is! All yours! Not exactly a mansion, but it's clean and you can have some privacy up here."

"Oh, Grace! It's wonderful! And the curtains! How pretty! And do you know—pink is my favorite color!" Bridget walked over to the window, looking out at the alleyway below as her hand gently stroked the material of the curtain.

"Now if it ever gets too hot up here when summer comes, you can always sit right out here on the fire escape."

'Oh, Grace, I don't know how to thank you!"

"You are very welcome, my dear. Now just let me know if you need anything, okay? Oh, and by the way, this is entirely your personal domain—you're in charge of the whole operation. And I know you will be such a blessing for all of us."

Bridget sat alone at her machine, placing her feet carefully on the treadle and her hand on the balance wheel. Suddenly, she was struck with an image of a man plowing a field with a small child on his shoulder. It seemed the man was speaking in a soft but strong voice. "*Put your hand to the plow, Bridget dear.*" Then, as suddenly as it appeared, it was gone! She wondered if she could be the child in that vision—this wasn't the first time she had been impressed with it. She sat quietly, meditating on it. Then, trying to recollect herself, she took in the whole aspect of this new adventure. It was exciting, yet somewhat overwhelming.

The hubbub and clamor coming from the front entrance the following weekend brought many of the girls, bursting with curiosity, to see what was happening. The delivery man was carrying bolt after bolt of material into the Mission as ordered by Mr. Flynn.

"Go get Bridget! Hurry!" Grace was as excited as the girls as she struggled with the commotion of their trying to peek into the brown paper-wrapped bolts. A few had become partially unraveled in the delivery cart, revealing some materials with floral designs and colors.

"Oh, look! How beautiful!"

"Miss O'Brien, can I have the red one?"

"Now, girls, basics first. We will see."

"Gee, this one is all gray!"

"Oh—the flowers! I want the flowers!"

"Here comes Bridget! Bridget, hurry! Look!"

"Oh! How wonderful! Praise God! He answered all my prayers. Oh, that good Mr. Flynn! Now calm down, girls! You'll all have plenty of time to see the material." Bridget picked up the first bolt. "Everyone grab one and help me get these upstairs."

"Yes, girls," Grace chimed in. "Let's get going! Give Bridget a hand here."

"They'll fit nicely right under that big table you gave me, Grace." Bridget could see the girls' happiness at the thought of brand new clothing—something they hadn't had since arriving in the new country. The excitement continued, as the bolts were carried upstairs and piled in neat rows beneath the table. The girls were clamoring to unwrap them and peruse the rest of the materials.

"Not tonight girls! It's getting late—almost time to turn in." Grace made sure the girls obeyed the rules, did their chores, and strictly enforced the nine o'clock curfew every night. The girls did not appreciate the curfew; however, Grace reminded them constantly it was for their own good. They were also under tight restriction during the daytime and could only travel a short distance from the Mission—and then, only with an escort.

Staying warm was a challenge, as the radiator in the corner of the room only worked sporadically; and Bridget needed two sweaters at times. She soon discovered what a tremendous task she had taken on. Hundreds of girls would move through that Mission as time went on. Every girl seemed to need new clothing. Some had come on the voyage from Ireland with her, and she soon felt that she was part of a big family. Some had the same name as hers—Bridget! She had truly "set her hand to the plow" as she labored many hours—measuring, cutting, and sewing—while speaking with each individual girl. Some nights she would go to bed, her fingers hurting and her legs aching from the constant pumping on the treadle. But it was rewarding. She felt a sense of worth. For now, this was her niche in life, as she designed and experimented with patterns, making many shirtwaists, a popular blouse. As she worked fitting each girl individually, time was shared in personal stories and backgrounds, and a closeness developed with many of them. As they were mostly very close in age to her and came from similar circumstances, she looked upon them almost like sisters. Many had very sad stories to tell about their childhood, relating to her personal details which brought tears to both their eyes. She could especially relate her own thoughts and past to those girls who experienced orphanage living in the Old Country.

Occasionally one of the girls would ask Bridget to design something more "modern" than the common but practical clothing she had been providing. The plain gray and black dresses or white shirtwaists with long black skirts had become almost like uniforms to them. And, as young ladies often do, they began to want something "fancier," as they knew they would eventually have to go out in the world and look more attractive to possible future employers, not to mention any young gentlemen who might look their way!

Although Bridget's time was completely utilized in providing the new outfits for the girls, she eventually decided that she somehow had to find time to create clothing to sell outside of the Mission in order to raise extra money to purchase another sewing machine or two. Working diligently with no rest, she was able to accomplish this goal, and began to teach some of the girls her trade, which not only assisted her but would also give them a way to support themselves in the future. She was delighted at their eagerness to work with her; and as they became more proficient, the weight on her shoulders was lightened somewhat which provided her with some sorely needed free time—she needed a rest!

It was a sunny afternoon when Tom came calling. She met him in the lobby and invited him into the parlor. Taking his hand, she led him to the sofa. "Have a seat, Thomas. It's good to see you. What brings you here?"

"I missed you, Bridget." He continued to hold her hand. "I heard you moved when I stopped at Molly's, and she told me you came here."

"Yes, it was much more convenient for me to stay right here where I'm working. And it's been a really busy time. I'm making new clothes for the girls here, as well as teaching them how to sew so they'll learn a trade."

He gazed at her for a moment, a concerned look on his face. "Well, sounds like you made the right decision, and I'm really glad for you, but ... gee, you look so tired!"

She quickly pulled her hand away. "Well, that's a fine thing to say to a young lady! Don't you have something nicer to say ... I mean... since you haven't seen me for quite a while."

Taken back at her remarks, he blurted out, "Oh! Oh, I'm so sorry. I was only concerned about you."

She softened her tone. "Well, I *have* been tired. Sorry—didn't mean to be short with you."

She secretly admired Tom. His unpretentious ways attracted her—something genuine and honest, unlike some refined gentlemen with unscrupulous intentions she had encountered back in Ireland.

"You know, Bridget, you won't believe me, but I *was* going to bring you flowers. But on the way here, I used my last bit of change for a little boy I found shivering and hungry and crying on the roadside. I bought him some food with it."

"Oh, Thomas!" She wiped a tear from her eye, as his comments brought back terrible memories of the starving children in Ireland. "I'm glad you did that—I can't think of a better cause." A warm glow came over Bridget, as she, for the first time, succumbed to his loving and charitable heart. She leaned over and kissed him gently on the cheek.

Tom's response surprised her, as he merely looked down at the floor. "Well, I try to do what I can for the little fellows! But Bridget, I want to hear more about *you.* I guess you're feeling pretty much at home here now?"

"Yes. You know, Thomas, these girls are becoming like sisters to me. I have so much in common with them—all from Ireland, all around the same age, and many were orphaned, as I was. And, of course, they have no one in this country—no relatives or friends to turn to. However, on the bright side, Grace here has been an angel in helping them to find work so they can support themselves. She's the founder—Grace O'Brien."

"Yes, we've met. Molly introduced us once."

"Well enough about all this. I want to hear what you've been up to, Tom."

"Well, since the boats aren't running for the winter, I got a job working at a machine shop until Spring. I'll go back to the *River Queen* then. And probably the *Mary Powell* or the Canal part time, too—wherever I can find the most hours."

"Dinner's ready, Bridget," Grace announced as she entered the parlor. "Oh, excuse me. I didn't realize you had company."

Tom rose to his feet. "Hello, Miss O'Brien. Tom Sexton—Molly's friend."

"Oh, yes. I remember you, young man! Bridget, we're almost ready for dinner. Would you care to join us, Tom?"

"No, I really can't, but thank you anyway. I have to be at work shortly." He turned to Bridget. "So I guess I'd best be on my way, Bridget. It was great seeing you!"

Tom had called upon Bridget a few more times during those long winter months, but she had been too busy to spend much time with him and turned down his requests to go out. They were able to spend short periods chatting together in the parlor, however; and Bridget soon found herself looking forward to these meetings.

Summer came blazing that year, and the city sweltered. Every window was open, and Bridget's little shop in the attic was almost unbearable. Her only relief came at nighttime when she sat out on the fire escape to catch an occasional evening breeze. There were, however, days when she wished for her old job back, sailing around Manhattan Island. She had given notice to Captain Skully that she felt she needed to stay working at the Mission full time, as she hated to leave Grace and the girls, who were in such need of her services. The Captain had hugged her and wished her well, yet saying anytime she ever wanted to return, her job would always be waiting.

Tom showed up late one afternoon, having decided that he would no longer take no for an answer to his requests for a date. "I really think you should take a day off, Bridget. You need it!"

"Well, I guess I *could* use a change of scenery."

Tom reached over and pushed a strand of hair from her forehead. Noticing she was sweating quite profusely, he reached into his pocket for his handkerchief and patted her face with it.

"Thanks, Tom. It's so very hot upstairs." He smiled and stared at her for a moment, as if uncertain what to say next. "What is it, Thomas? You look puzzled."

A broad smile coming over his face, he asked, "How would you like to go to Coney Island?"

"Coney Island? Well ... I suppose."

"Now don't go supposing. You've been working too hard. We can have a great time—maybe even go swimming!"

"I would like that, too, but ..." She remembered she didn't have a bathing suit nor had she even thought about getting one up until now. "I'm not sure about swimming, but it would be nice to be out in the park with some fresh air for a change."

"Great! Then we're goin' and have a swell time of it! How about tomorrow? Would that be okay for you?"

"Tomorrow is Sunday—Mass, you know."

He nodded in agreement. "Of course. We'll do Mass first."

It was a beautiful summer morning when Tom picked Bridget up to attend the early Mass at St. Paul's. Afterwards they had a short chat with Fr. Sullivan, after which Bridget assured him she would definitely come by the following week to pick up his vestments for mending as she had promised and thanked him once again for the sewing machine. Tom shook the priest's hand and started for the door. As Bridget turned to follow him, Father whispered into her ear. "A fine young man, Bridget." She smiled and caught up with Tom.

They decided to walk a few blocks before catching the trolley. "You know, why don't we say a few decades of the rosary while we're walking? Sometimes I'm too tired to say it at night," as she took her crystal blue beads from her pocket. "Do you have one, Tom?"

"I do, but it's home on my dresser."

"Well, I will say the first part of each Our Father and Hail Mary and you say the second part, okay?" She smiled at him.

"Well okay, that's fine. I usually don't say it with anyone—you know?—living alone. I'm used to saying it myself."

"Where two or more are gathered—remember?" She made the Sign of the Cross and began. "I believe in God ..." Tom joined in and they prayed and walked and enjoyed the warm sunlight on their faces. His heartfelt prayer was for their relationship to blossom into a beautiful future together.

As they boarded the newly electrified streetcar, Bridget remarked, "Oh, how strange! It runs without horses?"

"Oh, this is your first time?"

"Why, yes. I haven't been out much lately and ... well, the times I have been, it's mostly close to the Mission so I usually walk."

"It's the newest thing—electric—just like the new light posts going up around the city. Isn't it great?"

"Oh, Tom, it's wonderful! It's so smooth—without the horses, I mean."

"Yes, I guess they're out of a job!" He laughed at his own joke.

"Well, I'm glad. I always felt sorry for them, having to work so hard, even in bad weather and all."

Riding the Coney Island Line, Bridget repeated herself. "What a difference! I can't get over how smooth it is, and so much faster, too! Oh! Listen Tom! Hear that?"

"Sure, it's the Carousel! We'll be there in a couple minutes."

Her eyes beheld a wonderland of excitement as they arrived, and she anticipated a day of fun and joy with Tom. "Come on, let's go!" He grabbed her hand and began walking quickly, pulling her along.

"Oh, my gosh! What's that, Tom?"

"That's the Switchback Railway. Some people call it a roller coaster—first one in the country, they say. Wanna go on?"

"I'm not sure—it's pretty high!"

"Oh, it'll be great! Don't be afraid."

"Well ..."

"I'll get the tickets."

"But ..."

"Come on, Bridget. You'll be fine."

They sat in the front seat. Bridget tried not to look down as the car began its slow ascent toward the high peak. Exiting the car on the platform at the top, they waited until the men turned the car, facing it to go down the track on the opposite side. "Okay, back in, Bridget." Tom seated her first and then climbed in beside her and down they flew. She thought she would scream but the wind took her breath away, and all she could do was bury her head on Tom's shoulder. He quickly took advantage of the situation, putting his arm around her and pulling her close. Back at their starting point, they laughed and joked about their stomachs doing flipflops and understood then why some called it the flip-flop coaster.

Then on to the Shoot-the-Chutes where they stepped from the upper platform into a large, flatbottom boat which rapidly slid down the long waterfilled incline before hitting the large, deep pool at the bottom. Skipping along the water, Bridget laughed as the cooling spray covered her.

"I'm soaked, Tom!"

"Oh, refreshing though, ain't it? You'll dry out in no time, darlin'. Now ... I don't know about you, but I'm hungry. Let's go get a hot dog!"

"A what? What's that?"

"A hot dog. It's a sausage in a bun. You'll like it."

"I never heard of it."

"Brand new over here—some German fellow got the idea. Come on, let's get one."

"How many dogs?" the vendor with the handlebar mustache asked.

"Give us two, please."

"Help yourself to the mustard and pickle to put on them, if you want."

"Thank you. How much do I owe you?"

"Ten cents for the two."

"How do you like it, Bridget?"

"Oh, it's very good! But the name sounds strange— dog?"

"No, no. That's just the name somebody gave it. Something about wanting to name it after their dachshund, but they didn't know how to spell it, so they just said hot *dog*."

"Oh my gosh! That's funny!"

Finding a bench under a tree, they relaxed and finished their lunch, looking out at the water. Tom slid his arm off the back of the bench and onto her shoulder. Her response surprised him, as she reached up and placed her hand over his. "Oh, thank you, Tom. I'm having such a wonderful time!" She breathed in the fresh ocean air, the wind blowing a wisp of her hair gently across her face.`

"I'm so glad, Bridget—you deserve it!" as he gently brushed the hair from her cheek.

"It's so great just to get out of that hot attic! Oh! This summer has been so hot!"

"Maybe you could move your sewing machine into the basement."

"I don't think so. Besides summer's almost over, and I'm not even sure if I'll be there next year."

Tom looked surprised. "Why? Where would you go?"

"I don't know."

"Well, why would you even *want* to leave? You have a place to stay and ..."

"Oh, I appreciate everything they do for me at the Mission, and Grace has been so good to me. And many of the girls are now capable enough to make their own clothing. But I want to get on my own two feet—maybe move out of the city. Maybe even start my own business again. Besides, I miss the country. I mean, back in Ireland, I could breathe free and walk the meadows and enjoy the open spaces and the great expansive blue sky—I really miss all of that, Tom. I really do."

"I know what you mean. I do remember the beauty of the landscape back there, even though I was very young when my folks escaped the famine and came here. I guess they had no choice; there were so many children in our family. They couldn't afford to feed us all. Didn't I tell you that before?"

"Yes, I believe you did mention it." She hesitated a moment. "Didn't you become bitter about that?"

"I never had time back then. I had to beg, borrow, and steal to stay alive." He looked very pensive to Bridget, as he continued staring out at the water. "I hawked newspapers on the street, worked as a bootblack, and even had a job cleaning out horse manure at the police barn. Oh, yeah! *Anything* to survive!" He turned and looked at her. "But you know, Bridget dear, I learned how to depend only on myself and nobody else. As for being bitter, I'd have to think about that. I think if I met my parents today, I wouldn't know whether to hug 'em or slug 'em!"

"Oh, Thomas, I'm sure you would understand their plight." She leaned back, looking at the puffy clouds overhead.

"What are you thinking?"

"Oh, about something you just said."

"What's that?"

"Well, you just called me 'Bridget dear.'"

"Is there something wrong with that?"

"No ... no, there isn't. It's just ..."

"Well, what is it?"

"I ... I guess I can tell you."

"Tell me what?" Tom's curiosity seemed aroused as he waited for her answer.

"I had a ... well ... a sort of a vision the other day. You know—not exactly visual, but in my mind's eye."

"Yes ... go on."

"Well, this image of a man plowing a field with a child on his shoulders—it keeps reoccurring. I feel strongly that it may have been my father and I. Remember, I told you I was very young when my parents died, and I wound up in an orphanage—like yourself?"

"Did you hear anything? I mean, did he say something?"

"Yes. Yes, he did! He said, 'Put your hand to the plow, Bridget dear.'"

"Oh! I see. You think ..."

"I don't know. That's the only time anyone else called me 'Bridget dear.' I just don't know what to make of it. What do you think, Tom?"

"The only thing I can figure out is maybe he wanted to instill in you a good work ethic, or maybe it's just your imagination. But personally, I think it *could* have been your father. You know, you and I have a lot in common. You have that drive to make something of yourself—just like me!" He smiled. "We would make a great team, don't ya think?"

"Thomas! You're jumping the gun! After all, this is only our second date!" She seemed deep in thought for a moment. "I do remember so well one thing I was taught at the orphanage—the old saying, 'Idleness is the devil's workshop.' That's why I keep busy!"

"I'll say you do! But let's not talk about work. I'm having too much fun! So come on!" He jumped to his feet and grabbed her by the hand. "Come on! Let's go!"

They ran up the ramp and both mounted a horse at the Steeplechase Race Track, which took them around on iron rails. Her horse was parallel to Tom's, and she squealed with delight, glancing over at him as her horse began to pull ahead.

"I won!" she exclaimed, laughing, as the ride ended.

"Well, I would have beat you," he said kiddingly. "I whipped my horse, but I just couldn't get the darn thing to go any faster!"

"Oh, you silly!" They both laughed as they walked on to the Sea Lion display.

Their stroll through the park afterward took them past the beer tent. "You know, they don't allow women in there, Bridget, so just sit down here and I'll get us a cold drink. What would you like?"

"Lemonade, if they have it, please."

Loud boisterous voices flowed from the tent which sounded to her like old Civil War veterans reliving their experiences. She wondered what they must have endured to have all this still on their minds and conversing about it after thirty-some years. Those few, however, who were missing limbs, she thought, would no doubt *never* forget!

Her musings were interrupted as Tom handed her an ice-cold glass of fresh-squeezed lemonade and sat down next to her. "Sorry it took so long. They were all out of lemonade and had to squeeze more."

"Oh, it looks wonderful! Thank you, Tom."

"Bottoms up!" He blew the foam off the top of his beer, raised his glass and clanked it against hers. "Here's to you, Bridget. On second thought, here's to *us*!" The cold drinks were refreshing on such a hot day. Tom continued with one of his favorite sayings:

"May the Good Lord take a likin' to ya
But not too soon!"

"Oh, Thomas! That's funny!"

Dusk approached and the lights came on around the park. They watched the old lamplighter as he turned on the gaslights with his long pole. His job only took half as much time now, as the other side of the park was already aglow with the newly installed incandescent lamps. As they strolled along, they could hear a soft melodious waltz coming from the Dreamland Ballroom. Tom paid the fifteen cent admission and they entered the expansive dancehall with its huge revolving mirrored ceiling globe, casting diamond sparkles across the walls, floor, and dancers themselves.

Bridget had never seen anything so lovely. "Oh, Tom! This is like heaven, with its twinkling stars! How pretty!"

"Come on, let's trip the light fantastic, me girl!"

"What?"

"Trip the light fantastic! You know—dancing!"

"Well ... umm ... couldn't we just sit down over here and listen to the music?"

"Why? Don't ya like to dance?"

"Well, you know, Tom, to be honest with you, I never really learned how. I was always busy working. Even in the orphanage, they had all of us working."

"Well, come on now. I'm not all that good a dancer myself anyway, but let's give it a go. I'll try to teach you a little. Come on—it's fun!"

"Well, okay. I'll try." His arm slid around her waist as he began to lead her onto the dance floor. She felt a little awkward; but as the evening wore on, his hand pressed firmly on her back to lead, she began to ease into the rhythmic steps of the music. Soon she was enjoying the sweet feeling of being held close in Tom's arms. Before long, she felt as though she could dance with him all night long.

They both loved Irish ballads and music about Ireland, and as the band began playing "Kathleen Mavourneen," she couldn't help the tears forming in her eyes as the soloist began his moving rendition of the song.

"Mavourneen, mavourneen, my sad tears are falling,
To think that from Erin and thee I must part!
It may be for years, and it may be forever,

Then why art thou silent, thou voice of my heart?
It may be for years, and it may be forever,
Then why art thou silent, Kathleen mavourneen?"

Tom pulled his handkerchief from his pocket and wiped her tears. "I know how you feel. I was small, but I sure remember very clearly how my Mom always seemed so sad after leaving Ireland. I can even remember sitting on her lap while she sang that song to me. But she used to sing it differently—'Kathleen, my darling.'"

"Well, yes. That's what mavourneen means," Bridget explained—"my darling."

"Oh! I didn't know that. Okay, well come on now, Bridget-mavourneen! Listen! It's "In the Good Old Summertime!" He wanted to pull her mind from that melancholy state. He swirled her quickly into a circular motion, and she smiled at this more upbeat music and followed his lead.

More popular tunes followed: "And the Band Played On." "The Man on the Flying Trapeze." And then, as the lights were turned down and it was time to leave, they strolled out into the starlit night, hand in hand, as they quietly made their way back to the streetcar stop, singing along with the background music:

"After the ball is over, after the break of morn,
After the dancers' leaving, after the stars are gone,
Many a heart is aching, if you could read them all—
Many the hopes that have vanished after the ball."

Chapter 6

The Orphans

It wasn't uncommon for the passersby walking down the streets of lower Manhattan to observe young street orphans, waifs, urchins—begging, hawking newspapers, or shining shoes. Tom, having been one of these unfortunate souls long back, had a special place in his heart for them. He had saved many of them after he grew up and got a job. Some of the older boys, however, refused his help as they had become hardened and too proud. When Tom offered to take them to an orphanage, he'd get replies like, "I ain't goin' to no home with nuns tellin' me what to do. That's for sissies!" Many of these homeless boys, some as young as five years of age, got their education in "the school of the streets." They were shrewd and old in vice.

On one occasion, as Tom was walking down State Street, he paused by an alleyway as he thought he heard someone groaning. Investigating, he saw a small boy about five years of age lying semiconscious, soaking wet from rain, with a remnant of bread clutched tightly in his hand. It appeared that he might have fought very hard to hold on to that morsel as he was bruised about his face and neck, his red hair stuck on some blood on his forehead. Tom cradled him in his arms, blotting some of the blood from his face and mouth with his handkerchief. The boy slowly regained consciousness and began to struggle, apparently afraid of this stranger. "It's okay, kid. I won't hurt you. Here—take this." He pulled an apple from his pocket where he constantly stored one in case he saw a starving youngster, remembering well those days when he, himself, was hungry.

Grabbing the apple, the boy responded, "Ya got any money?"

"Well, maybe."

The boy stood up. "Whaddaya mean—maybe?"

Tom answered with his own question. "Do you have a place to stay?"

"Yeah!" the boy defiantly blurted out.

"Where would that be?"

"Over there." He pointed to a spot beneath a stairway which had a grate emanating warm air from a Chinese laundry.

"You have any parents? What's your name?"

"Nah. They got rid a me! No food. Ya got money?"

"That depends," Tom responded.

"Whaddaya mean?"

"Depends if you are willing to work for it."

"What kinda work?"

"Oh, we'll find something. Why don't you come with me? I think I can find a place for you to stay tonight." Tom seemed to detect fear beneath that hard shell. "You got a name?"

Looking at the ground and groaning while holding his head with one hand and chewing on the apple in the other, he looked hesitant and murmured something Tom couldn't understand. "What was that?" Tom asked.

"They call me Small ..." His voice became inaudible.

"Small what?"

"Sm ... sm ..."

"I can't understand you," Tom remarked.

"Small *fry!* Are ya deaf, man?"

"Oh, so ya got a name after all! Now look, kid, I don't have all day! Either ya come to the home for kids like you, or ya don't! You'll get hot food and a warm, dry place to stay."

As the orphan shivered in his wet clothes and devoured the rest of the apple, including the seeds, he looked at Tom. "Ya mean that home for boys?"

"Well, yes."

The youngster took a long hard look at Tom, as though sizing him up. "Well ... okay—but no funny business! If you ain't on the up and up, I got a whistle in my pocket—and I'll warn my buddies if ya try anything."

"Hey, kid, you're talkin' to a guy who came from the streets years ago—and I know just how you feel."

They walked a few blocks, Small Fry following Tom at a safe distance, and arrived at No. 7 State Street. "Hey! What the heck is this?" Small Fry pointed to the sign over the door—*Home for Irish Immigrant Girls.* "Hey Mister, doesn't that say 'girls?'" He did recognize that one word.

"Now listen, Small ..." Tom hesitated. "What's your real name?"

"Dunno."

"Well, we'll fix that later. Come on, let's go in."

"I ain't goin in no girls' school!"

"Look kid, it's late. And it's just for tonight. We'll go to the Newsboys' Home tomorrow."

Small Fry's wet clothing caused him to shiver even more as the cold North wind picked up. "Well, maybe ... Do they have some dry clothes in there? And I want some food, too!"

"I think so. Come on now, it's getting dark!" Tom grabbed Small Fry's hand.

Quickly pulling away, the young boy hollered, "Nah! I still ain't goin in there!"

"Okay," Tom remarked. "Have it your way, but I'm goin in there and havin myself some nice warm food." Tom knocked on the door.

Small Fry began to leave, then suddenly turned on the stairs, murmuring, "Well ... maybe ... Just for tonight."

The door opened a crack and a voice inquired. "Who's there? Who is it? It's very late."

"Hello, Grace. It's Tom. You know—Tom Sexton."

"Oh, Tom! Oh, come right in! I was just about to lock up for the night." Looking at Small Fry, she asked, "And who is this young lad you have in tow?"

"I found him in an alleyway, all beat up. I wonder if he could stay with you just for tonight?"

"Oh, sure. Of course." Looking down at the boy, she introduced herself. "I'm Mrs. O'Brien. And what is your name, young man?"

Small Fry glanced up at Tom, remaining silent. "He doesn't really know his name, Grace," Tom answered for the boy. "You can call him Small Fry for now—that's how he's known. I was going to take him to Father Drumgoole's Newsboys' Home, but it's too far and it's getting late, and with the weather and all, I thought ..."

"Enough said. We have an extra cot in the basement. You take him down there and you'll find some blankets in the closet. Wrap him in these for tonight—his clothes should dry by morning. I'll be down shortly with a sandwich and a hot cocoa. You look like you could use some, too, Tom!"

Small Fry didn't object, seeming to welcome Grace's hospitality. As they descended the stairs, the boy murmured under his breath again.

"Speak up, boy! I couldn't hear you."

"I said I'm gonna get those dirty rats that beat me up! You'll see! I know who they are!"

"I've been in your shoes before; don't waste your time, kid! And, by the way, you *have* to get a new name. I know why they call you that."

"Yeah! 'Cause I'm short!"

Tom smiled. "However, kid, there's an old saying— *Good Things Come in Small Packages.*"

A broad smile came over the boy's face. "I like that!"

"Here we are!" Grace announced. "Hot cocoa and peanut butter sandwiches!"

"*What* kinda butter?" Small Fry asked. "Never heard of it!"

"It's something new—*peanut* butter. You'll love it, kid!" Tom responded.

"Let's just take a minute and get that face and hands wiped off a little, shall we?" Grace carefully wiped his beat-up face with a warm washcloth, gently patting the cut and bruised areas before applying two bandages to the worst cuts, then proceeded to wash his hands.

Small Fry ate ravenously. "Ya got any more?"

Grace smiled. "There'll be a nice breakfast for you in the morning, young man. It's very late now and you really should get some rest. Tom, will you tuck him in? I have to get up early with the girls."

"Sure. And I'll be back tomorrow as early as I can to pick up the boy and take him to Father Drumgoole's if that's okay with you, Grace."

"Oh, I'm sure we can look after the little tyke for one day, Tom. He needs a little scrubbing and some good meals." She lowered her voice to a whisper. "I'm afraid he looks malnourished. But don't worry. He'll be fine. Goodnight now."

"Goodnight ... and thank you, Grace."

After she left, Tom began to tuck the boy in bed. "Hey! Watch it! I'm no sissy kid! I kin do that myself!"

"Sorry." After a long pause, Tom added, "Well, go to sleep now. We'll talk tomorrow about that new name." As he was about to return upstairs, he glanced back at the boy, remembering how he, himself, had had to beg, borrow and steal—and yes! even fight!—just to stay alive. The boy was already fast asleep.

Tom had a satisfied feeling inside as he walked toward the Mission the next morning, knowing Small Fry would be well cared for from now on. Met at the front door by Grace, he knew right away from the look on her face that something was wrong. "Grace—you okay?"

"Oh, Tom! Oh, Tom!" she blurted out. "He's not here!"

"What do you mean?"

"He took off!"

"Oh, no! How? When?"

"Well, we gave him a nice hot breakfast and then I gave him a bar of soap—the good Lord knows he needed a good cleanin'—and then I sent him to the bathroom. I was only gone a few minutes checking on some more bread I was baking, and then—well, then I knocked on the door. I thought he was still washing up, as I heard the water running. He didn't answer. Then I knocked a little louder and called out his name a few times, but there was still no answer. I got so worried, I peeked in and ... Oh, Tom! He was gone! I even had Bridget and some of the girls search the whole building, but there was no trace of him! I'm so sorry! I'm so, so sorry!"

"Why that little scalawag! He purposely left that water running to fool you, Grace. It's okay—don't fault yourself. I think I can find him."

Raising her eyebrows, she asked, "How in the world could you ever find him? You know how these little waifs move around and have no place to call home."

Just then Bridget entered the room. "Oh, Tom! I didn't know you were here!"

"Hello, Bridget."

"Grace already told you?"

"That she did."

Grace looked very serious. "There's something else you should know, Tom."

"What's that, Grace?"

"There were six loaves of bread in the dining room before—now there's only three!"

"Do you think ..." Bridget's words were cut off.

"I don't think—I *know*!" Grace responded.

"Are you *sure*?" Tom asked.

"I'm as sure as the sun comes up in the morning. That little tyke took that bread. That ungrateful little monkey has a funny way of thankin' us for a bed and food."

"Well, I do think I know where to find him."

"Where, Tom?" Bridget looked hopeful.

"Oh, I think he may have gone back to where I first found him."

"Tom, can I go with you? It's okay, isn't it Grace? I can catch up with my work later."

"Better not."

"Oh, Grace! Please let me go with him. I adore these poor little orphans. I only wish I could pick them all up and give them a nice home."

Grace thought for a moment. "Well, okay ... since this is a kind of emergency situation. You stick right close to Tom, Bridget. And Tom, make sure nothing happens to young Bridget here—she's our prize tenant, you know. It's just so darn awful that things like this happen here in this great land of opportunity. And Tom, make sure she's back by dark, you hear?"

The streets were rife with beggars and orphans, as Tom and Bridget began their search for Small Fry. At one point, they observed a few older men with ragged clothing standing around a fire blazing in a large metal barrel, stomping their feet and rubbing their hands over the fire.

"Some of these men lost everything, Bridget. Would you believe?"

"Well ... how?"

"They called it the Panic of 1893. Something to do with railroad financing and bank failures—that's about all I know."

Bridget clutched Tom's arm as they walked by many shadowy alleyways. "Aren't you afraid in this neighborhood?"

"Are you kidding? These streets were once my home. Poverty was my father and starvation was my mother. These streets were my living room, bedroom, and kitchen."

"Oh, I feel so bad for these people. It reminds me too much of the Old Country." She clutched his arm tighter. "Is there any place on God's green earth where people aren't starving?"

"Well, you know, if anything can be said for this lousy poverty, it's this—if you survive, like I did, you will appreciate having a roof over your head and food to eat for the rest of your life."

Arriving at the alleyway where he had first found Small Fry, Tom checked under the stairway—he wasn't there. As he and Bridget turned to go elsewhere on their search, they suddenly heard the cry of a baby. It seemed to be coming from an old abandoned warehouse at the opposite end of the alley.

Wiping the grime from one of the windows, Tom peered inside but saw nothing. Pushing on a nearby door, it slowly creaked open, scraping and scratching against the flooring as it did. Upon entering, they saw a young girl, about nine years of age, huddled in a corner, cradling the crying baby in her arms. She was rocking the infant and singing a soft lullaby. Startled and frightened, she clutched the infant tightly to her chest. "Who are you? What do you want?"

"It's okay, honey. It's okay. We're friends," Bridget responded. "My name is Bridget and this is Tom. And we're friends of Small Fry's. Do you happen to know him? Or where he might be?"

The girl didn't answer and just continued rocking the baby, trying to comfort her and stop her crying. Bridget could see from her gaunt, haggard, emaciated look that she probably hadn't had much to eat lately. Just then, the girl pulled a crumpled-up loaf of bread from behind her, pulling a tiny piece from the soft center, and proceeded to try to feed it to the baby.

"Wait!" Tom commanded. "Can't give that baby bread. She might choke—it's too dry."

Tears ran down the girl's face. "But she has to have *something!* She's so hungry—been crying all morning. Oh, I wish Small Fry would hurry up and ..." Her hand suddenly snapped up to cover her mouth, knowing she had said the wrong thing.

"So you *do* know ..."

Just then the door swung open and Small Fry, short of breath, came running in carrying a bottle of milk. Seeing Tom and Bridget, he stopped dead in his tracks for a split second, then immediately turned and started to "escape."

Tom shouted, "Hey, kid! Wait! We want to help you—all of you!"

With one foot out the door, he suddenly stopped and turned. "You can help my sister and the baby, too?"

"You bet we can!" Tom responded.

Small Fry looked dubious but cautiously approached, taking a seat on an old orange crate. He proceeded to fill the baby's bottle with the milk and handed it to the girl.

"Can I help you?" Bridget asked her.

"I kin do it myself," the girl responded as she wiped the tears from her face with her sleeve and rested her head back against the wall as though she were exhausted.

"Where did ya get the milk, Small Fry?" Tom asked.

"Swiped it off a milk truck." Tom just stared at the boy but said nothing. "Ain't gonna call the cops on me, are ya?"

"No. We just want to help you all get some food and a better place to stay. Remember? The other night?"

Spotting another two loaves of bread behind the girl's back, Tom glanced over at Bridget, whispering, "The other two loaves!"

Bridget nodded, a knowing slight smile on her face. "The poor things!" she whispered back. "What's your name, my dear?"

There was no response. The girl's eyes were closed—a lack of sleep and food had taken a toll on her. Then Small Fry spoke up. "She's scared of strangers—her name's Nellie."

Bridget reached down and gently took the baby and the bottle from Nellie's arms. "What's the baby's name, Small Fry?"

"She don't have a name."

"Oh, she's not your sister?"

"No."

"Where ... Where did the baby ..."

"Found her here cryin'—an' nobody around an' she was all alone."

Bridget gasped. "God have mercy. Who would do such a thing? She could have died."

"This happens all the time in this town, Bridget," Tom said. He turned his attention to Small Fry. "Are you a smart boy?"

"Yeah. I am! Smarter than you, I bet!"

"Maybe you are. But I know a good way you can prove to me just how smart you *are*!"

"I don't have to prove nothin' to *you*, Mister!"

"Tom—call me Tom. I told you my name last night, remember?"

The boy didn't answer.

"Didn't you hear me?"

"Yeah, I remember."

"Okay, then call me Tom."

Small Fry nodded his head.

"Well, now, if you're a smart boy, tell me—don't ya think you would all be better off in a home with food for yourselves and the baby?"

"Well, I guess so."

Tom couldn't get over the adult ways of this street lad; but in a way, he could see himself in him. He was tired looking and skinny, and his red hair looked like it had never seen a comb. He reminded Tom of an old man.

"If we go with ya, ya gotta promise not to tell the cops on me."

"Okay, that's a deal! And that's bein' smart. You're a good lad to help your sister and the baby."

Tom opened the door, only to see the rain coming down in torrents. "We can't take the baby out in this. We'll wait till it lets up." The daylight was growing dim, and Small Fry lit the small candle on top of an orange crate. He pulled over two more crates for Tom and Bridget to sit on, then sat down on the floor himself. "Thank you, Small ... You *really* don't know your real name?" Tom asked, looking at the boy as the flames flickered from the drafts seeping through the old frame walls, causing dancing shadows across the floor.

"Small Fry! That's my name!"

"Well, that's your nickname. What's your *real* name?"

"That's my *only* name—everybody calls me that."

"Didn't your parents call you by any other name?"

"Can't remember," Small Fry answered, staring at the candle's flame.

"Don't you remember your mother or father?"

"Kinda remember my father."

"Can you tell me what you remember?"

"Didn't know any mother. They say she died when I was born."

"I'm sorry."

The baby and Nellie had fallen asleep and the others sat in the darkening warehouse listening to the wind whistle through the walls and the sound of the raindrops on the tin roof.

Bridget then asked, "Well, what do you remember about your Dad?"

"He's a bastard!"

"Hey, kid! Watch your language! There's a lady

present."

"He's a drunk! And he beat me! That's why I left him. I'd rather live on the streets than with him!"

"I'm sorry, but maybe you could start over. You know, son, I think you should have a good name to go through life with. Think about it."

"I'm not your son!"

"Ah, that's just a way of speaking."

Nellie was awakened by a loud clap of thunder. Seeing Tom and Bridget still there made her feel more safe and secure than she could ever remember feeling for a very long time.

"Did you leave home at the same time as your brother, Nellie?" Tom asked.

"Yes," she responded quietly.

"When was that?"

"I ... I don't know exactly. Maybe a few months ago."

"How long have you been living in here?"

"Don't know," Nellie answered, reaching for a piece of bread and devouring it quickly.

Bridget broke into the conversation. "I think the rain stopped. We'd better get the baby to the Mission house where it's warm. The poor thing needs changing and some *warm* milk. We can talk later." Bridget removed her coat and began to wrap it around the infant.

"You're gonna need that on, Bridget. Better to hold the baby close and pull the coat around the two of you together," Tom offered.

Boarding the trolley, they all sat down quietly, listening to the clackety-clack of the streetcar wheels. "I really like this, don't you, Small Fry?" Nellie asked. The boy didn't answer. Nellie smiled, enjoying the ride, as the trolley took them down to No. 7 State Street.

"Come in, my dears!" exclaimed Grace, as she welcomed the children into the Mission. "And what do we have here?" as she looked at the baby.

"Oh, Grace! This is Small Fry's sister, Nellie, and they have been trying to care for this baby since they found her abandoned," Bridget said.

"Oh, Bridget! Not more of these poor little ones!" Grace took the baby from her. "What a little angel! Come on now—let's go down to the kitchen and get you all something to eat." She whispered in Tom's ear, "Keep your eye on the boy, Tom. We don't want him to slip away again." Tom nodded.

After a good warm meal, Grace showed Nellie to a bedroom. "Here you are, my dear. Now don't you worry about anything. You're safe now."

A worried look came over Nellie's face. "But what about the baby? Who will take care of her?"

"Who's baby is she?" Grace asked.

"I don't know."

"Well, how did you come by her?"

"Small Fry and I found her all alone in an old building. She was cryin'."

"Does your brother have a real name?"

"No."

"Well, why not?"

"All I remember was ... well, after Ma died, my Father just always called him Small Fry."

"Oh, that's terrible! He should be christened with a saint's name. But don't worry about the baby. She will be well taken care of at Sister Irene's Foundling Home. There are so many unwanted babies that people drop off there, and the sisters take care of them—Sisters of Charity of Saint Vincent de Paul. And they also find parents to adopt them. In fact, Sister Irene has a cradle in her front hall where a girl can leave her baby if she can't care for him. It is a real blessing for them to know their babies will be cared for. You see, some girls are ashamed and don't want to be known."

Looking relieved, Nellie sighed and crawled into bed.

"I think you will like it here, my dear," as Grace described the education Nellie would get and the new friends she would make. The girl smiled and turned on her side, pulling her blanket up to her ears. Her eyes felt heavy but her heart felt light—and within moments she was asleep.

Grace made arrangements for Small Fry to be placed in Father Drumgoole's home for boys—Mount Loretto on Staten island. The Franciscan Sisters from Buffalo, New York, would give him a good education there.

Chapter 7

The Sailor and the Seamstress

As winter set in, Bridget found herself working long hours. She had been making many shirtwaists, a popular smart-looking, long-sleeved blouse constructed like a shirt with turnover collar and cuffs and a front-button closure. The work was demanding, although she did have some help from the girls, arranging material and cutting patterns. And now, with the new sewing machine acquired through Bridget's extra work, they even took turns with the actual sewing, a great help to Bridget. With so many girls in need, the shirtwaists were their basic "uniform," though Bridget tried to adorn most of them in small ways so as to make each a little different. Buttons of different colors, appliqués, and ribbons at the collars were very much appreciated by the girls.

She found she needed two sweaters at times, as the old radiator in her room still wasn't working well, never quite giving off enough heat. Nevertheless, after a hard day's work and with the comfort of a few extra blankets, she slept like a baby at night. Once, in the very wee hours of the morning, Bridget was suddenly awakened by a loud thwack on the window. Startled, she quickly threw her robe over her shoulders and observed the remains of a snowball splattered on the outside of the window adjoining the fire escape. As she peered out and down into the alley below, there stood Tom motioning to her. "Come on down! It's great out here!" The snowflakes were falling on his upturned face, as he proceeded to pick up more snow for another volley. Shocked by his behavior, Bridget motioned him to go away. Bang! Another snowball hit the window dead on again. She was afraid this would wake up Grace or some of the girls—and that would be big trouble. She tried to open the window, but it was stuck. As she strained to get it open, another figure appeared below. It was a policeman, twirling his billy club at his side as he walked. Unable to hear the conversation, Bridget watched as the policeman shook his finger at Tom and pointed to the alleyway exit with his thumb—Tom got the message.

He came calling a few days later; however, Bridget had mentioned to Grace to explain that she was very busy upstairs if he would come by. During the following month, he continued to call upon her, but she decided she would only allow short visits in the parlor and would no longer accept a date. Not one to give up easily, Tom arranged to escort her to Sunday Mass at St. Paul's, knowing she would need to be accompanied when she left the Mission and would certainly not want to miss the service.

"Here, Missy, let me help you with your coat." She slid her arms into the sleeves, and Tom took hold of the collar area to proceed to "button her up."

"I can do that!" she quipped.

"Oh, okay, and better pull that hat down a little over your ears more. It's really bitter outside."

The snow fell softly but the extreme cold had caused ice to build up and the walking was treacherous. Bridget began to slip, but Tom grabbed her arm instantaneously, keeping her from landing on the ground. "Oh, thank you, Tom. If it wasn't for you, I could really have hurt myself." Taking advantage of the situation, he advised Bridget to hold tightly to his arm. Walking close to him, she had a feeling of wellbeing and security which warmed her heart somewhat toward him once again.

Holy Mass on Sundays became a time when Tom could count on seeing Bridget, being her escort to the church. This seemed to be the one thing they always had in common—their faith. On occasion, Bridget would allow him to stay for a little lunch with her in the parlor afterward which pleased him very much, hoping that perhaps she might be "coming around" again.

And so it went, as the winter winds blew themselves out and the snows began to thaw—as did Bridget's feelings for Tom. And he, knowing Bridget did not work on the Lord's Day, invited her to the park after Mass one Sunday. He had something he wanted to tell her—something that would change the course of their lives—forever! It was springtime, and the lilacs were in bloom. They sat on a bench, enjoying this sweet explosion of nature and the lovely scent of the lavender flowers, feeling the calming warmth of the season after the long winter. Picking one of the lilacs from the bush behind them, he presented this right below her nose so she could take in the beautiful fragrance. She smiled and took the flower from his hand, only to hold it then below *his* nose. “Beautiful, isn’t it, Tom?”

He leaned back on the bench, putting his arm around her shoulder. Looking up at the bright, blue sky, he announced, “I’ll be going away for a while.”

“What?”

“I want to look into working someplace else.”

“Where?” She sat upright, seemingly surprised by this new development.

“Well, I’m working my way up the river—heard they’re lookin’ for men up in Buffalo to work in the grain mills.”

“Buffalo? How far is that?”

“About three hundred and some miles. I have a chance to get work on the Erie Canal again. And since it goes all the way to Buffalo, I thought I could work my way up there. They say the pay is very good.”

“You mean ... we will never see each other again?” In a heartbeat, her feelings were suddenly awakened to the possibility of losing him. She felt regret inside her heart for the times that she thought she hadn’t treated him as well as she should. Even so, she still tried masking her true feelings, casually saying, “Well, Thomas, I guess you must do what you think is best.” She thought for a moment, then continued. “Do you remember I told you a while ago that I wanted to move to the country some day?”

“Yes, I do. We both want the same thing, so why ...” He stopped in midsentence, thinking this would be a perfect time to propose. He took a moment or two to work up some courage before blurting out, “Will you marry me?”

This sudden proposal took Bridget’s breath away, but she calmly said, “Oh, I would definitely need more time to think about such a thing. Don’t get me wrong ... but ... this is quite a surprise, Tom.” She immediately realized that she didn’t want to give him the wrong impression. “I *do* care for you, but ...”

"But what?"

"Oh, I don't know! It would be a big change ..."

"Now, Bridget, dear ..."

Bridget, dear. Those two words always seemed to awaken that deep sensitivity in her soul that quickly got her attention, but she continued on, "I would hate to leave the girls and Grace—they have been so good to me."

"Well, I think you have done so much for them— working your hands to the bone and providing decent clothing and teaching them a trade ..."

"Well, I know. But I've made so many good friends here. And ... and ... what about all those orphan children?"

"I understand. But, you know, I've thought long and hard about this, and I feel we both should have a chance at a new life and, God willing, have our *own* children."

"Oh ... wait a minute, Mister! You're going a little too fast here. I'm flattered by your proposal, Tom; and I am very fond of you, but ..."

"There's that *but* again! Listen, Bridget, I'm sure I can get work; and you just said you want to get out of the city and see the countryside."

"I need more time."

"When we get married, I'm sure you wouldn't want to live in the city. Wouldn't you agree it's no place to raise a family?"

"You're getting way ahead of me, Tom."

"If you need more time, I'll be away for a while. I *am* going to Buffalo and see if they still have job openings. I think it may take three or four weeks before I return ... so how about giving it some thought while I'm gone, okay?"

"I'll miss you, Tom." He leaned over and kissed her.

In the coming weeks, Bridget immersed herself in her job. Although some of the girls would find work and leave the Mission, there always seemed to be new girls arriving off the boats. A few weeks went by and Tom hadn't returned yet. She became concerned but kept herself busy.

Nellie began to visit with Bridget and asked her to give her sewing lessons. Since she was so much younger than the other girls, she eventually became known as "little Nellie Kelly." She was too young when her mother died to remember her last name, and her derelict father was always drunk. So someone at the Mission had begun calling her that nickname, having heard of a famous actress by the same name. And it stuck! The little girl was a quick learner, and Bridget enjoyed teaching her. She had developed a fondness for the girl, causing her to wonder at times what it might be like to have children of her own.

She was becoming concerned for Tom. Day after day, she worried and prayed for his safe return. She had heard there were many dangers on the River and the Canal. Well, he knows his way around. He's a pretty big man—I'm sure he can take care of himself. After all, he *did* grow up on the streets. Oh, God, please take care of him for me.

Bridget was a dreamer and relished the rest she would have after working on her sewing machine all day, especially so when the weather was mild and she could open her window at night and catch the spring breeze. She would often fancy herself a princess who lived in a castle and was courted by a handsome young knight. Sometimes she pictured her third-floor room as the castle prison, from which she would be rescued by this same knight. He would charge up the long staircase, swing open the prison door, and carry her off into the Country Kingdom of beautiful pastures and meadows and flowers of every kind and color, where they would live happily together in beauty and peace and contentment.

But then reality would set in, and her thoughts turned to her flesh-and-blood knight—Thomas. His absence seemed to make her heart long for him, and she found herself growing anxious for his return. Sometimes, she even tried to imagine what it might be like being married to him, but she found she didn't really want to pore over that thought and would soon dismiss it from her mind.

The dining room was the place where many of the new girls had a chance to make friends with those already there, comparing stories and discussing which counties in Ireland they hailed from. Most nights after meals, however, Nellie would go upstairs to visit Bridget in her little shop, which eventually the girls dubbed "Bridget's Boutique."

She had never given up hope to have her own dress shop again and vowed to herself that it would come true, maybe not this year or next. But she was young and promised herself that it would indeed happen one day. Bridget came to look upon Nellie as a sort-of little sister and taught her the art of dressmaking, taking great pains to instruct the little one on every stage of the process. Finishing her work one evening, she sat out on the fire escape to get a breath of fresh air, when Nellie appeared in the doorway. "Can I come out there with you, Bridget?"

"Sure, come on." She motioned to her. "Here, sit down. It's lovely out here tonight."

Nellie sat next to Bridget. "Can I ask you something?"

"Sure, Nellie."

"How come everybody around here talks funny?"

"How do you mean?"

"You know someone said you and the others have an accident."

"Accident?"

"Yes, that's right."

Bridget thought for a moment and then burst out laughing. "Oh, you mean *accent!*"

"I guess that's it." Nellie seemed puzzled at Bridget's laughter.

"Well, honey ... we come from Ireland—it's a land far away across the sea. Oh, Nellie, the grass is greener than you've ever seen and the meadows are lush with colors that come alive with heather on the hills, and the sea laps against the high cliffs and roars like a lion with every wave! And ... well ... along with our memories of that place, we bring the Irish accent, too. You see, my dear? Oh, Nellie! I miss it so!"

Nellie detected a tear rolling down Bridget's cheek and offered a kind word. "I'm sorry, Bridget. Maybe you could go back there someday—and take me with you."

"Oh, my dear, I don't think I'll ever see that land again. You see, I'm here because we didn't have enough food to eat. There was a great famine across the land."

"Yeah, like my brother and I never had enough to eat either ... after my father left us. Small Fry was always out looking for food." Nellie began sobbing. "Oh Bridget, I miss him so, so much! Do you think he's okay?"

Bridget put her arm around the girl. "Oh, look! There's a shooting star up there! Nellie—look!" The girl gazed up. "It's a sign, Nellie! Oh, it's a sign!—Small Fry is okay! I truly believe that!" She wiped Nellie's tears with her handkerchief. "You know, Nellie, we're both orphans and know what it's like to go without—but we're tough! We'll get along just fine. And if we say our prayers every day, God will provide for us. Now, I won't have you worrying any more about your brother. I'm sure we will be able to arrange for you to see him soon."

Nellie continued gazing at the sky, bejeweled with twinkling stars. "Doesn't it look like the stars are winking at us, Bridget?"

"Yes, my dear." Then, with the wry look of an Irish woman, she smiled and continued, "They remind me of a few young men I've known!"

Nellie didn't catch on for a moment. Then, suddenly, she understood and began to laugh. And Bridget joined in, and all seemed well at No. 7 State Street.

The next day found Nellie back at the attic door again, and the day after that ... and again the next! She looked so forward to these times together with Bridget. However, Bridget was becoming concerned that they were growing too close. It almost seemed to her similar to a mother and daughter relationship. She had developed a love for the girl; however, she worried about Nellie's future, as she, on occasion, would find herself contemplating the possibility of marriage, especially since it could mean a move away from the area to Buffalo. How would this affect the girl? Wouldn't it be devastating to Nellie were I to leave? Perhaps I should just "pull back a little bit."

And so Bridget, when finishing her work for the day, began to feign being very tired, so as to go to bed early, since Nellie had also begun to bring afternoon visits into the picture as well as her evening sojourns. Something had to be done—and soon—as Tom arrived back in New York not long afterward.

The following Sunday morning found him at the Mission door, a ring and a postcard of Niagara Falls in his pocket.

"Oh, Thomas, what a surprise! Glad you're back safely," Grace offered. "Have a seat in the parlor. I'll go get Bridget for you."

"Thanks, Grace."

Bridget hurried down the stairway, spotting Tom in the parlor when halfway down. She ran to him, throwing her arms around his neck. "Tom! Oh, Tom! I'm so glad you're home. I was so worried about you! It's been two months!"

He pulled her close to him and just held her momentarily—*too* close, she thought. But who cares? "Love ya, Bridget-girl!"

"Oh, Tom, I missed you *so much*!"

"Bridget ..." He loosened his grip around her waist and kissed her gently on the cheek. "It's Sunday. We can have the whole day together, can't we?"

"Yes ... yes, we can." Her heart was filled with joy.

"Okay. So go powder that little nosey and let's get out of here. We have so much to talk about."

"I have to go to Mass."

"Right. We'll go. Get ready."

The wide brim of her pink hat caught the wind as they walked toward St. Paul's for noon Mass. Her left hand shot up to hold it just in time to keep it from blowing away. It was good to be escorted once again by her Tom, her arm locked within his giving her that feeling of security and protection. His closeness was so comforting and welcome after his long absence.

After Mass, they managed to find a bench that was a little secluded even though the park was very crowded. A few children playing in the grass jumped up when they heard the shrill whistle of the popcorn man pushing his cart down the nearby walkway. "Popcorn, Missy?—I'm kinda hungry, aren't you?"

"Sure. Lots of butter if he has any."

"Here you go. Take *this* one." Tom handed her the bag. "It's got lots of butter, just like you wanted." Tom ate a couple handfuls and set his bag down on the bench. He reached into his pocket, nervously fingering the ring for a few moments, seeming to work up his courage. Waiting until Bridget finished eating, he took her hand and pulled it over to himself. He quickly slid the ring onto her finger, so as to give her no time to possibly refuse him. "Now it's official!"

Bridget began to pull her hand away, but he quickly grabbed it back and squeezed it. "Oh, Thomas! I don't know ..." she stammered.

"But I thought you said you loved me—are you *still* uncertain?"

"Well ... I ..."

"Didn't you say you would know by the time I got back?"

"I guess it's just such a big step and ..."

He pulled the postcard from his pocket. "Look! It's a picture of Niagara Falls! When I was in Buffalo, I visited there. Magnificent! It's a big place for honeymoons! We could go there. Oh, I have so much to tell you! I have a job offer. And there's a little house ..."

She placed her fingers on his mouth. "Wait ... wait, Thomas! It sounds wonderful! But I can't think about these things—I mean ... you're moving too fast."

He looked glum and disappointed, but that steadfast Irish tenacity wouldn't allow him to give up. "Okay, then. Can't we at least be engaged, and ... and ... well, then that'll give you more time to think about it—during our engagement time, I mean."

"Well ... umm ... Well, it just sounds a little backward, doesn't it? I mean, aren't you supposed to think about it first and *then* get engaged?"

"Well, I've done all *my* thinking!"

"I do love you. I've already told you that. Please Tom—be patient. I just have to tie up some loose ends." She looked directly at him with a loving smile. "You know, Tom, I've made a new life here—so many friends ... And moving so far away?"

"Well, now, didn't you come across a whole ocean to get *here*?" He was still gripping her hand tightly. "Alright ... I won't pressure you."

"I promise, by the summer's end ... well, maybe I'll know for sure and we can set the date."

He smiled, relieved by her modified response. He gently pulled her closer to him. "Come here, my little bride-to-be!" His kiss was sweet and tender.

The whistle from the popcorn man had faded off into the distance, and the children had long been gone from the area. The matter had now been settled—in Tom's eyes, at least.

Over time, Bridget had many conversations with Grace O'Brien. They had become good friends, and Bridget had great respect for this fine lady who sacrificed herself to help her fellow countrymen. She was always busy but did take time to talk over tea; and after each occasion, Bridget became more inspired, drawing strength from her. She had provided a home for thousands of young girls who, otherwise, would have found themselves on the street, exposed to the many dangers lurking in the alleyways of lower Manhattan.

But something was bothering Bridget—something she would have to make right —and soon. Sometime after Grace had taken Nellie into the Mission, Bridget thought it might not be the best place for the girl. Little Nellie was only nine years old—several years younger than most of the other girls there. Bridget asked Grace to meet her in the parlor late one evening after the girls were asleep so she could discuss the problem with her. "Now, what was it you wanted to talk to me about, Bridget?"

"It's about little Nellie."

"Yes, go on."

"I'm concerned about her."

"What about her?"

"Well, she and I have become very close, and I think she's beginning to look at me as the mother she hardly ever knew—you know, because of her mother's death when she was so young."

"Yes ... go on."

"I've been thinking a lot about this, Grace. There's more to it." She sighed, then continued. "You see, Thomas and I are talking about getting married—and there's a possibility it could be in the near future, due to certain circumstances. I'm not one hundred per cent certain yet, but ..."

"Well, saints preserve us, Bridget! I didn't know." She looked Bridget straight in the eye. "Are you sure you know him well enough?"

"Well, I think so. I've given it a lot of thought lately."

Grace continued to ask questions about Tom, concerned that Bridget might not be making the right decision. Although Tom had been a fairly frequent visitor to the Mission in the past, conversation generally was between Bridget and himself; and Grace had not really had much opportunity to get to know him personally, although she did admire the fact that he was a church-going man.

"Getting back to Nellie, Grace ..."

"Oh, I'm sorry, my dear. Yes, go right ahead. I didn't mean to 'interrogate' you about Tom. It's just ... well ... I'm concerned about you, my dear."

"Don't give it a second thought, Grace. I know you were only thinking of me. But what I'm concerned about now is that Tom and I would be moving to Buffalo if we get married—Tom already has a job offer there. And if I continue to bond with Nellie, it will only make it harder for her if I have to leave—especially now, since she has been crying to me so often about missing Small Fry. Besides, I've been thinking she might be better off at Sister Irene's Foundling Home since the girls there are closer to her age. And Sister has names of couples who are waiting to adopt—so I'm sure Nellie might in time find a family to love her, especially through Sister's connection with the Orphan Train."

Grace didn't respond, seeming stunned, as she looked at Bridget. After a few moments, she declared, "You're taking my breath away, girl! So much to consider. First off, I'm happy for you. I do know Tom has been helping get little kids off the streets, so ... well ... I guess he must have a good heart. And, second, I'm glad you're concerned for Nellie. Now don't you worry. We'll look into it. I have an idea that might help. Now, I'm tired. It's been a long day. We'll talk again soon."

Bridget would not rest until she found a decent home for Nellie. Although she didn't have any responsibility for the young, plain-looking, and gangly little girl, she felt compassion for her, powerfully identifying with the child.

It wasn't long before Grace asked Bridget to meet her in the parlor once again to discuss Nellie. "I've been doing a lot of thinking, Bridget, and I think I might have a plan."

"Oh, I'm glad! What is it?"

Grace smiled. "I thought that maybe we could 'borrow' a young girl from Sister Irene's to visit here with Nellie. Then, after allowing them some time to get to know one another well, we can think about moving Nellie there, as she would already know and have a good friend. I'm sure she would have a better chance for adoption from there as well."

"Oh, Grace! That's a wonderful idea!"

And so the plan was hatched; and with the agreement of Sister Irene, ten year old Edna Donohue was allowed to come to the Mission on a regular basis to visit with Nellie. Although Edna seemed very shy and introverted, it wasn't long before a strong friendship blossomed between the girls. Nellie began to bring her upstairs, wanting her to get to know Bridget. Soon the girl became very interested in learning about Bridget's art of dressmaking. The two seemed to enjoy their brief visits with Bridget, and she, in turn, loved to teach them a little each time they came.

By now, it had become a routine for Tom and Bridget to attend Mass every Sunday, and it was on one of these days that Bridget explained to Tom the situation with Nellie and her friend. Tom had a suggestion of his own to make. "Wouldn't they love to go to Coney Island for a day?"

"Oh, Tom! What a great idea! I'm sure neither one has ever had an opportunity like that." She paused. "But, wouldn't that be an awful lot of money? The admission and the food and all—for *four*?"

"Now don't you worry about the money. I have a confession to make."

"A confession?"

"Yep. Believe it or not, I've been saving up. Got a little money put aside."

“Really?”

“Yep. Turned over a new leaf. You got me thinking; since we’re getting married, I’ve been trying to save a little toward our trip to Buffalo.”

Bridget threw her arms around Tom’s neck. “Oh, I’m so proud of you, Tom! That’s wonderful! But, getting back to Coney Island ...”

“Well, for the girls’ sake, maybe we could use just a little of it to provide them some happiness. What do you think? I’d like to take them.” Tom smiled. They walked down State Street, making plans for the outing for the girls. “Now Bridget, you’ll be in charge of the girls. You know I’m used to working with boys—used to being a little rough with those little scalawags, you know.”

Bridget looked surprised. “Well, what would you do if we have a girl—*if* we get married, that is!”

“Hey! Hold it! Now *you’re* going a little too fast for *me*, Bridget-girl!” he quipped. They laughed.

It was a bright sunny day, and the girls were so excited. They enjoyed the ride on the new electric trolley, and their anticipation grew the closer they came to the park. Neither of them had ever seen an amusement park before. Tom bought a roll of tickets for the rides, handing them to Nellie and Edna. They stood delighted, not knowing where to begin. Tom pointed to the Switchback Railway. “Why don’t you start there? It’s really fun and ...” Before he could finish, they were running toward the ride. Since money was tight, Tom and Bridget sat on a park bench, just enjoying watching the children laughing and giggling as they boarded their car. They screamed all the way down, approaching Tom at the end of the ride to request another. “Go ahead!” and they were off again! They continued enjoying ride after ride, giving Bridget and Tom time to talk about their future as they watched.

The girls had hotdogs for the first time, and giggled about the name. At first, they recoiled, thinking it was really dog meat. Tom explained to them the origin of the name.

As the day wore on, the sun beat down upon these two young lovers. They were fortunate to find another bench under the shade of a tree. She rested her head on Tom’s shoulder, enjoying the fresh breeze coming off the water. “I can tell you like children,” Tom said, holding her hand.

"Very much," she responded. "They're so innocent and trusting."

"I think it would be nice to have some of each—boys *and* girls. Whacha think, Bridget-girl?"

"Here we go again!" She leaned over and kissed him on the cheek, laughing at her own remark. "Oh, I almost forgot, Tom! Grace wanted the girls back before nightfall."

Walking toward the exit of the park, Nellie exclaimed, "Oh! What's that over there?" as they came upon a little stand—"COTTON CANDY."

"What is it?" Tom asked the attendant behind the counter.

"Some gents in Tennessee invented it. It's really tasty—like a cloud of sweetness!" the man responded.

"Two, please," Tom ordered. He handed them to Nellie and Edna.

The girls looked puzzled for a moment. "Just bite into it!" said the attendant.

"Oh! This is absolutely delicious!" Edna looked over at Nellie who was smiling and shaking her head in agreement.

"Oh, thank you, thank you," the girls remarked in unison, as they rode back to the Mission, thoroughly pleased with their afternoon outing.

"It's so good to see both of you so happy; I know things have been so hard for you two," Bridget remarked.

"Maybe we'll do it again some time," Tom said.

Bridget felt a warm glow as she watched and listened to the girls relive their day of fun to Grace upon their arrival back at the Mission.

"I'm so happy you both had such a good time, girls. Edna, I arranged with Sister Irene for you to spend the night here, as I knew it would be late before you all got back. In fact, it's almost time for evening prayer. Say goodnight to Bridget and Tom now. Nellie hugged Bridget around the neck, as Edna threw her arms around Tom's waist, pressing her head to his chest, thanking him again and again.

Tom's goodness to the girls left a warm spot in Bridget's heart, seeing that he cared more for their happiness than saving his hard-earned money. This, among other things, had brought her to the realization he was the man she wanted to spend her life with.

In the meantime—it took some doing—but after a few more visits, Nellie and Edna had become fast friends and plans were finalized for Nellie to make the permanent move to Sister Irene's. Once this was accomplished, Tom and Bridget went to check on Small Fry. He was settled in, living at Mount Loretto where he was well cared for and educated by the good Franciscan Sisters from Buffalo. Father Drumgoole had financed this new establishment through Saint Joseph's Union and the sales from "*The Homeless Child*" magazine.

"Good afternoon, Sister. I'm Tom Sexton and this is Bridget O'Halloran. We're friends of ..." He suddenly realized Small Fry had no other name. He looked over at Bridget who shrugged her shoulders.

"Yes ... yes? What did you say the name was?"

"Well, Sister, to tell you the truth, I don't know his real name," Tom answered. "The only name he gave us was 'Small Fry' when I picked him up off the streets, half-starved, and took him to Grace O'Brien's place. She was the one who brought him to you afterward."

"Oh, you mean Joseph?"

"Oh, is that what you call him now?"

"The short little boy about six years old?"

"Why, yes."

"Oh, he's a fine lad—eager to learn, he is. I'll get him for you. Now go sit yourselves down," as she pointed to the parlor.

Entering the French doors, they seated themselves on the brown sofa, well-worn around the edges of the cushions. The small table before them held a beautifully bound Bible, a rosary on top of it. A red rose in a small vase had been placed in front of a small statue of the Virgin Mary next to it. Bridget's attention was drawn to a painting of the Holy Family hanging above the sideboard near the door, over which was a golden crucifix.

After a short time, the nun returned. "He'll be down shortly. The children are just finishing their lunch." She noticed Tom and

Bridget looking at the picture of Jesus, Mary and Joseph. "Isn't that a beautiful painting?"

"Yes, it is—just lovely," Bridget answered.

"You know, it was *that* painting that caught the eye of little Joseph when he first arrived here. He said he wanted to know the names of the people in the picture. Later on, the other Sisters and I had to make a decision about a name for the boy. As I informed him that he would no longer be called 'Small Fry' but would have a Christian name, he took me by the hand, telling me he wanted to show me something. I allowed him to lead me here to the parlor where he pointed to Joseph in the painting. 'Can I have *his* name?' he asked."

"'Well, yes, of course, if you would like, I told him. It's a fine name—Joseph. That it will be; and when you are baptized, it will be official. He smiled at me and seemed so happy, it warmed my heart." She paused for a moment, then continued. "And, you know, Joseph said something else ... I mean ... he mentioned a name when he pointed to the Blessed Mother in the picture, and I wasn't sure what it meant."

"What name was that, Sister?" Bridget asked.

Looking at the picture, she smiled. Then, after a moment ... "Nellie! That was the name—Nellie!"

"Yes, of course," Tom said. "You know what he meant?—calling Our Lady by the name Nellie?"

"Well, yes—now I do."

Tom and Bridget both looked at each other, and her eyes began to well up with tears. "Oh, Sister, when we found him, he was taking bread to a young girl and a baby who had no food. We found out later it was his sister, Nellie. The two of them were trying to care for this little abandoned baby in a dirty old warehouse at the end of an alleyway."

"Oh, what a dear boy!" Sister said. "He was trying to be the little man, protecting them, just like Joseph with Jesus and Mary!" The nun glanced over at Bridget, understanding fully her tears within her own heart. "I soon found out why he was always so upset. You see, he came to me crying very often those first few months—crying for his sister. He missed her so much. And I'd ask him her name, yet this just seemed to make him cry harder; so after a while, I just didn't bring it up any more."

A few minutes later, Joseph came bounding into the room, skipping from one foot to the other. "Joseph! You know you must *walk* inside the house!"

"Yes, Sister." The red hair looked freshly cut, parted neatly down the middle of his head, a cowlick sticking up in the back. He was dressed in an ill-fitting but clean white shirt and somewhat worn brown knickers held up by suspenders.

"Well, now," Tom said, "this can't be the young man I brought here just a short time ago now, can it?"

The boy immediately ran over to Tom and grabbed him around his legs, hugging them tightly. Tom reached down, one hand on the boy's shoulder, the other gently lifting up his chin. "Oh, I forgot what a handsome young fella you are, Small Fr ... I mean Joseph. I can see the nuns have been very good to you here."

Bridget immediately stooped down, kissing the boy on the forehead. "Joseph, it's so good to see you again!"

"Oh, I'm sorry," the nun said. "I guess I didn't even introduce myself. I'm Sister Eileen, the principal."

Another nun entered the room. "Oh, excuse me, Sister. I didn't know you had company."

"Oh, Sister, I'd like you to meet Tom and Bridget. This is Sister Teresita. She's our baseball coach."

"Nice to meet you, Sister. Baseball coach, huh?" Tom was impressed.

"Oh, yes! We have a well-rounded program here. A track team also!"

Sister Eileen added, "And our boys compete with other orphanages in the area as well. In fact, we're playing the Children's Aid Society today at three o'clock."

"Yes, that's what I came in to call you for, Sister Eileen—it's almost time." She turned to Bridget and Tom. "Would you care to stay and watch?"

In his excitement, Joseph blurted out, "Oh, yes! Yes! Tom—stay! I want you to stay! I'm gonna be playin!"

"Sounds good to me, Sister! We'd really love to stay," Tom responded. Joseph's face broke out in a big smile.

"The game won't be starting for half an hour. Can we get you something to drink? You can visit with Joseph on the front porch until then if you like," Sister Eileen offered.

"Thank you, Sister. We would like that," Bridget responded.

Sister Teresita brought lemonade and a few cookies. "Joseph will show you where the baseball diamond is when you're through—back behind the building."

"Well now, lad ... I mean Joseph ... you look as if you like it here."

"Yes, Tom ... I mean ... Sir!"

"You don't have to call me sir. Call me Tom. I feel more like a big brother to you."

"Okay, Tom," the boy said, smiling.

"What do you like the best about living here?" Bridget asked.

"The food!"

"What else?" Tom asked.

"The warm bed at night."

"I see. Can you tell us how you spend your days?"

"We go to Mass every morning. But first, we gotta make our beds! And then we get breakfast. And then we go to our classes, and then ..."

"Don't ya have to do any chores or anything?" Tom asked.

"Lots of 'em!"

"Yeah? Which ones?"

"Well, gotta empty the wastebaskets—that's one of 'em. And I'm supposed to sweep up the floor after dinner."

"Wow! That's a big schedule! Sounds like you've got a lot of responsibility there! But don't you get any playtime?"

"Well, sure—after lunch we get to play outside. Is Nellie okay? And the baby?"

"Why, yes, they are both in a good home at Sister Irene's now."

"Where's that?"

"Oh, not far from where we took you, to the Home for Immigrant Girls, remember?" Tom answered.

"Tom, I've been missin' them *real bad*."

"Nellie misses you, too, Joseph," Tom replied.

Just then, Sister Teresita arrived back on the porch. "Time to change your clothes, Joseph. Game starts in fifteen minutes."

The baseball diamond had sandbags for bases and the backstop was an old wooden barn used for storage. The landscape was flat and ideal for baseball. Bridget and Tom took a seat on the few benches that flanked the field for the nuns and a few spectators. These seats were sufficient for the small handful of people; no parents would be there since the boys were all orphans.

Sister Helena, the umpire, a middle aged, rather stout, high-spirited nun, took her place behind the catcher in her long, black habit, rolling up her sleeves and securing each one with a rubber band. She shouted, "Remember the rules now! There will be no stealing bases! You know what the Good Lord said about stealing! We have to *earn* our runs!"

All the boys had nicknames for each other, and the lineup read: "Spike, Small Fry, Swifty, High Top, Freckles, Molasses, Curly, Slick, and Peanuts." As hard as the nuns tried, they couldn't make the boys call themselves by their Christian names—that is, on the ball diamond—especially during the excitement of the game. Classrooms were a different story—only their Christian names could be used, most especially if the nuns were within hearing distance. Otherwise they would be punished with an extra chore such as washing all the blackboards.

Sister Helena flipped a coin and Mount Loretto lost the toss. "Batter up!" she yelled.

The visitors didn't score in their half of the first inning. Then it was Mount Loretto's turn. The first at bat was Freckles who got a single. Then Swifty hit a double, and Freckles advanced to third. Peanuts and Curly followed, but struck out. Things looked dim until Spike hit one over the fence for a home run. Next up was Molasses who popped out to the pitcher, making the score 3 to 0.

The next seven innings were scoreless, as the hot sun bore down and the players became listless and sluggish. Sister Eileen did her best to keep the boys cool, making sure they all took water from the bucket containing a large block of ice. The game seemed to have become a "pitchers' duel." Then the pace suddenly picked up in the top of the ninth when Mount Loretto's pitcher was replaced by Peanuts after a line drive struck High Top in the arm. Peanuts walked three in a row. And then, with the bases loaded, the next batter drove one past third; and by the time Molasses in left field bobbled the ball, the score stood 4 to 3. It wasn't looking good, but Peanuts got lucky as he struck out one player and caught a fly ball from the next one. An excited Sister Helena screamed out in a high pitched voice, "Batter up!" The third batter connected with a drive straight to the first baseman for the third out.

Then, as the bottom of the ninth arrived, Children's Aid Society pitcher, Big Lefty, appeared on the mound—the biggest, fastest pitcher known to mankind! And the Mount Loretto team shuddered just watching him warm up. He had a reputation that brought terror into the hearts of every batter facing him. The boys tried everything to distract him. They tried taunting him with jeers, against the nuns' scolding; but he easily struck out Slick. Then Curly went down with three strikes, and it looked like the end. But Molasses got a single and held on to first. Small Fry was next to the plate. Sister Helena, who was standing behind the plate whispered to him as he came up to bat. "Just get a piece of it, Joseph, and ask your Guardian Angel for a home run!" He wasn't a heavy hitter, but he could run like the wind. With two strikes and two balls against him, he felt doomed. He quickly repeated the prayer, kept his eye on the ball; and as it hurled toward him, he swung as hard as he could and connected with a drive that flew by the second baseman, screamed toward center field, and dropped just short of the back fence.

Sister Teresita, coaching first base, hollered, "Go! Go, Small Fry!" She suddenly caught herself. "Go, Joseph, Go!" The center fielder bobbled the ball, finally throwing it short of the second baseman while Small Fry rounded third. The second baseman grabbed the ball and heaved it toward home plate just as Small Fry slid into home a few feet behind Molasses. The rest of the team hoisted Small Fry up on their shoulders and carried him off the field. He glanced down at Sister Helena who winked at him and raised her finger in the air as if pointing to Heaven. Final score: *VISITORS* 4. *MOUNT LORETTO* 5.

Bridget and Tom shook Joseph's hand, and it took some time for the cheers and excitement to die down. They were invited to stay for the evening meal. Most of the conversation was about the baseball game. Toward the end of the visit, Joseph talked about his new home and school and seemed excited about his classes and the many new things he had learned from the Sisters. After finishing their meal, Sister Eileen rang the bell signifying time for evening prayers. Tom looked across the table at Small Fry. "Well, Joseph, I guess we'd better be going. We really enjoyed visiting you and watching that great baseball game!"

"Thanks, Tom. Will you come back soon?"

"Of course," Tom replied, not wanting to disappoint the lad.

The trolley ride back to the Mission gave Bridget and Tom time to review their afternoon with Small Fry. "Did you notice his good manners, Tom?"

"I *did.* He even called me 'Sir!'"

"I couldn't believe it was the same boy! It was so good to see him in that environment—dressed in clean clothes and having a safe place to live. God bless those sisters! They do such wonderful work with children, living their lives for others. Without them, I don't know where these boys would be."

"You're so right, Bridget. They will have a high place in Heaven!"

"You know, Tom, I hope Joseph is adopted by good parents."

"Yeah, he's a great lad, he is. Given a chance, when he finishes his schooling, I think he'll have great potential!"

Tom leaned his head back, staring at the ceiling. "You know, honey, ever since I first saw Small Fry, I had this image in my mind."

"What kind of image?"

"Have you ever read about martyrs? I mean—of the church? You know, people who were willing to die for their faith?"

"Well, yes—you mean like Peter being crucified upside down? Is that what you mean, Tom?"

"That's right, honey. And one of the first martyrs in the early church was a young lad named Tarcisius— just a little older than Small Fry—I don't think he was even in his teens. Well anyway, you know how the first Christians had to hear Mass in the Catacombs for fear of the Roman soldiers finding them?"

"I remember hearing something about that."

"Well, this boy was carrying the Blessed Sacrament ..."

"It was consecrated?"

"Yes, it was—and he was trying to take it to the Christian prisoners, those who had already been arrested for their faith and had been thrown in jail. Knowing they probably faced death, they had sent a message to the Bishop asking if there was any way they could receive the Lord in Holy Communion to strengthen them. Well, you know, a priest or a bishop would most likely have been stopped on the streets, so Tarcisius begged to be the one to "carry Our Lord" to the prisoners. As a young lad would have been the least suspicious, the Bishop finally gave in and allowed this. However, some ruffians playing in the streets, seeing he was hiding something in his tunic and believing it was something of the Christian faith, beat him to death for trying to conceal it—and all they found was a piece of bread—or so they thought!"

"But, Tom, you mentioned something about an image since you met Small Fry? I'm not understanding ..."

"Well, when I first saw him all beat up in the alleyway, he was grasping tightly a morsel of bread in his hand. It just made me think of that story of Tarcisius, 'cause Small Fry was trying to deliver that bread to Nellie and the baby—and some scoundrels had beat on him trying to get it. He was hurt real bad. Thank God, I heard his moaning."

"Oh, I see your meaning now ..." Bridget smiled. "You know, Thomas, the charity in that little boy's heart is like an extension of God's love."

"Honey, I've taken many lads off the streets and found homes for them—but somehow Joseph is different from the rest. He truly cared more for Nellie and the baby than for himself." Tom became very quiet, unlike his usual outgoing manner.

"What is it, Tom? Cat got your tongue? Is something wrong?" She waited for his response but it didn't come. "It's about saying goodbye to Joseph, isn't it?"

"Well, kind of. But ..." His voice drifted off.

"I know how you feel. I mean, we may never see the boy again."

"It's more than that."

"I don't understand, Tom."

"Well, the problem is ... well ... I just *hate* goodbyes. Never told you—but my whole life has been a series of goodbyes."

"Well, I know you had a rough childhood, but I don't know what you mean exactly."

"I don't like to talk about it."

"Well, sweetheart, I think it would be a good thing if you told me now. If something is bothering you that much—well, it must be terribly important. Shouldn't we discuss it now—I mean, before we get married?"

He looked at her lovingly. "It's about my past. I never told you about my brother and my very early years— before I wound up on the streets ..."

"No ... no you didn't."

He hesitated. "I really don't like to talk about it."

Bridget took his hand. The only sound heard was the humming of the new electric streetcar as it made its way down State Street. "I love you so much, Thomas. You can tell me anything. I mean it. Nothing you say could change my love for you." She squeezed his hand and gently kissed him on the cheek.

"I wouldn't even know where to begin." He looked at her apologetically.

"How about at the beginning? You told me all about your awful time on the streets and about your being saved by Father Drumgoole when he took you to the Newsboys' Home. But now you're saying something about your *earliest* memories and a *brother*?"

"When we just said goodbye to Joseph, it brought back memories of my brother."

"Yes, go on."

"Well, some of it's kinda a blur. I was so young. But other things ... well, I don't think I will ever forget—like... well, like the day they took Michael away." Tom lowered his head and just stared at the floor for a few moments, letting out a deep sigh. Bridget could feel his pain—it was so palpable.

"He's your brother?"

"Yes. All I can remember was our father crying and some people from the home putting us on a train. We watched out the window—our father was waving goodbye to us from the platform. I was calling to him, 'Papa! Papa!' My brother told me it was for the best, but I was devastated. We were with some other children on the train, and somebody had given us some clean clothes and combed our hair. I guess they wanted us to look nice. I didn't know why until we got off the train. They took us to some big building ..."

Bridget observed the pain in Tom's eyes, as he paused for a minute and took a deep breath. "You don't have to tell me anymore."

"Yes ... yes, I do. You *should* know all about me." He stared out the window for a moment, then continued with his story. "I can see it, as though the image is before me even now. They lined us children up on a stage, my brother and I standing next to each other. We were all told to stand still with our hands at our side and smile in front of a lot of adults who were asking questions. Some of them came up and made us open our mouths so they could see our teeth. And I remember one old man feeling my brother's arms and saying, 'I can use a strong farmhand like you.' He took him by the arm, then went over and signed some papers and talked to the people who had brought us there. Then after a few minutes he started to take my brother away. I screamed and hollered to Michael to come back and the last thing I remember, the man was holding him back as he struggled to come over to me. Then the man left with him."

"Didn't those people let you know where your brother was going?"

"No. That was the last I saw of him."

"Oh, that's horrible! Then what happened to you?"

"I was so young—about seven, I think. As I remember, some of the other children were taken away by some other adults; and a few of us remained on the stage. Then the ladies who brought us there—they called them matrons—took us and put us on another train. I cried so hard, I had no more tears left. First my Father. And then my brother. I can remember crying myself to sleep, sitting up on the train. When I woke up in the middle of the night, my sorrow turned to anger—that's when I decided to run away! I snuck into the bathroom and hid there, hoping the train would come to a stop. And after what seemed like hours, it finally did. I pushed the window open and was able to get it up high enough to crawl through and hang from it, then drop to the ground. I quickly ran into some tall grass to hide. The train left after a few minutes, and I looked around in the black darkness. I was cold and afraid and didn't know which way to turn. I didn't know where my brother was, and I only knew that my Father was way back somewhere. So I started out, following the tracks back. I walked a long way, scared that some wild animal might find me. And then, just as the sun was coming up, I spotted a farmhouse with a big red barn behind it. I climbed up into the hayloft. I must have been so exhausted, I fell asleep. When I awoke, I was so, so hungry. A farmer came in and started milking his cows. I stayed very still, so as not to rustle the hay or make a sound. After he finally left, I remained where I was for a while to make sure he wouldn't be returning soon, then came down and started to stuff myself with the cows' feed. And then I saw a basket of apples in the back of the barn. I quickly ate a couple and stuffed my pockets and shirt with as many of them as I could. I hoped I wouldn't get caught. I was scared but determined to get back to my Father. I couldn't understand, being so young, why my Father let me go. I traveled at night and tried to find a hiding place in the daytime—maybe a cave or a deserted building or even a ditch—where I could conceal myself. But the nights were cold, and I wrapped myself in an old burlap bag I had taken from the farmer's barn. My belly ached from too many apples or something—I felt like I would die. There was even a worse and more terrible thing I felt—like I was all alone in the world and no one wanted me. And then, about the third night, while hiking through some woods, I heard a train whistle; and I thought maybe it could be heading back to where my Father was. I couldn't be sure what direction it was going in, but I didn't know what else to do. I ran toward the tracks, but when I got there it was moving so fast, I couldn't hop on. So I just kept walking and walking till I was so exhausted, I just laid down in a ditch for a minute to rest and fell asleep. Next thing I knew, a glint of sunshine flickered in my eyes and suddenly a giant of a man blocked the light, and I tried running away but he caught me by the seat of my pants and picked me right up off the ground, holding me by one hand and laughing really loud. It scared the heck outa me. Then he carried me down and across the tracks where these strange looking people were sitting around a fire and cooking something. 'Look what I found!' said the big man, as he put me down. I was gonna run, but I didn't know which way to go. Besides, something smelled really good—and I was starving! Then, this old scraggly lady with only one tooth and yellow hair asked me if I was hungry. Yes, yes! I said. So she cuts a piece of meat off this animal cooking over the fire and hands it to me. It tasted delicious and I chewed

it up in a hurry. What is it? I asked her. 'Skunk!' she says. Then they all started laughing. I just thought that was so horribly yucky! Then the big fella says, 'What's yer name, kid?' Tom, I said. And then he says, 'Well, Tom, we got to give you a handle—you know, a nickname. Let's see ...' He started scratching his chin. 'How about Tom Thumb? You know, that little guy from the circus?' 'Yeah!' the others replied. 'Tom Thumb it shall be!' Then the big fella says, 'My name's Champ, Mr. Tom! I used to be a champion boxer, believe it or not! Nobody could beat me, see?' Then he pointed over to the old lady with one tooth. 'And this is Sophie, our cook. And over here is Blackie.' He pointed me to a beady-eyed man with a thin black mustache. 'He's a gambler—don't ever play cards with 'im. He'd rob ya blind if he could! And here, we have Bones,' pointing to another guy sitting by the fire. 'He's so skinny, I gotta hold on ta him from blowin' away in a good stiff wind.' Lookin down at me, Champ says, 'Now what in the world are ya doin out here all alone with no one to look after ya?' I ran away, I said in a quiet tone. 'What was that ya said? Speak up, my boy! Some of us don't hear so well, 'specially me. I went half deaf at the battle of Bull Run. A rebel cannonball clipped my ear and I haven't heard outa it since.' I ran away! I shouted. 'Oh, that's better,' Champ says. He wanted to know all about me. After I told him what I had done, he says, 'All the way from New York? Geez, kid, you're a long way from home! But Mr. Tom Thumb, you're in luck,' he says as he gently pretended to box with me. 'We're headin that way and maybe we kin help ya get there. But in the meantime, I'm gonna show ya how ta use your fists. You're a little guy, so ya'd better learn how ta use yer dukes!' Then he says to me, 'Where's yer bindle?' What's that? I said. 'Ya have ta have a bindle, you know—a sack ta carry yer stuff in.' I told him I didn't have anything to carry with me. Just then Bones piped up and said, 'We gotta get ya some clothes and stuff, ya poor lad!' He looked around at the others. 'The poor waif only has the clothes on his back.' Then Champ says, 'Okay, you scoundrels, come on now. Ya must have something ya kin donate to young Tom Thumb here.' Blackie had an extra bindle and he tossed it over to me. And Bones had a comb, and Sophie threw in a bar of soap. Then Champ donated an old jacket of his that hung on me like a big tent. But I didn't care—it was warm. And so, this little group that the world didn't even know about became my family, as rag-tag as it was! They taught me how to jump onto a slow-moving train with boxcars and how to keep from getting caught by the yard dicks."

“Dicks?”

“Yeah. They’re like people hired to police the train yards. So anyway, we begged, borrowed, and stole from trains carrying food, spilled grain that was left in corners of the boxcars, and eating anything on four legs that we could catch. Whenever we got a long ride from city to city, Champ taught me how to box. I think he was really a good boxer, ‘cause he taught me how to jab, weave, and duck and some fancy footwork and timing. He would tie an apple to a string and had me try to punch it as he swung it back and forth before me.” Tom continued. “I’m sorry, I didn’t mean to carry on. But that was a hard time and I’ll never forget those good people. They didn’t even know me, but they were so good to me. I never had that before.”

“I’m so glad they were nice people. But how did you get back here to New York?”

“Well, Champ had been riding the rails for years, and he knew which trains came into New York. So we kept jumping on and off different ones, sleeping in the empty cars and constantly avoiding the train dicks. In a way, I hated to leave them, but I knew I just had to find my Father—and maybe find out where my brother was. It was hard saying goodbye to Champ; so you see, honey, like I said before, my life has been a series of goodbyes.”

“Did you ever find Michael?” Bridget asked.

“No, I’m afraid not. You see, the home that ran the Orphan Trains had strict rules about not giving out any addresses of children who were adopted out. So I guess I just gave up ever finding him a long time ago.”

“And your Father?”

“I tried and tried to find him.” His voice choked up. “Never found him either.”

“I’m so sorry, Tom ... so sorry.” She rested her head on his shoulder and they both sat in silence until the trolley pulled up in front of No. 7 State Street.

Chapter 8

I Now Pronounce You ...

Bridget continued making clothing for the girls at the Mission, as Jim Flynn sent extra bolts of material every month or two for her use. The time spent with Nellie and Mary in her attic room in the past could now be spent in other ways, and she decided to use this time to design and sew a dress for her coming wedding. Molly had mentioned to Jim about her plans, and he decided to surprise her by including some satin and lace in his next shipment of material. She was ecstatic as she opened those bolts. Oh, Jim! Oh, my dear friend! How can I ever thank you?

Meanwhile, Tom had taken on extra hours on the *Mary Powell* which sailed up the Hudson River to Kingston and back every twenty-four hours. He began saving more money, as he would be taking on more responsibility soon and possibly adding some "little responsibilities," as he called them, in the future. He met many sailors from other steamboats, some who worked on the Erie Canal. His plans were coming together, as he made contacts who thought they could get him temporary work on "Clinton's Ditch." A great migration to the West had begun at that time, as employment was abundant in the Great Lakes area, especially in the grain business. Since a job was awaiting him in the Buffalo area, he simply needed to find work on the trip down the Canal.

Those hot sticky summer days and nights in lower Manhattan turned to Fall and the stifled masses breathed a sigh of relief. It seemed to bring a breath of fresh air, diluting the stench of rotting garbage and other repugnant odors that had permeated that pocket of sweltering humanity. Tom, having no snowballs, had to substitute a few small pebbles to announce his arrival at the base of the fire escape. Their previous meetings in the parlor were generally observed on and off by the keen eye of Grace O'Brien, ever vigilant when a male friend would visit one of her girls. It was exciting and romantic when Tom sidestepped the rules by climbing up the fire escape. He was never allowed to enter, but she looked forward to sitting outside the window with him. They spent hours planning their wedding, and she delighted at the times when he would steal a kiss. This seemed to be occurring more often, though they tried to be very quiet, especially when Officer O'Malley was patrolling the alleyway below.

The following month, Bridget went to visit Nellie at Sister Irene's Foundling Home. She hadn't seen her since the day she and Tom took her and Edna to Coney Island.

"Good morning, Sister."

Sister Irene welcomed her into the lobby where the little white cradle stood in the corner. Many infants had been placed in that cradle by unwed mothers or those who couldn't feed their babies. Bridget's admiration for the nun had grown as she learned more about the wonderful way she had saved so many infants.

"Good morning. And how are you today, Bridget?"

"I'm fine, thank you."

"And what can I do for you this fine autumn day, my dear?"

"Oh, I just wanted to see Nellie. I've missed her."

"Oh, Bridget! You didn't know she has been adopted out?"

"Oh, no! I was hoping to have one last visit with her before I leave town." She pulled her handkerchief from her purse and blotted the tears which were rapidly forming in her eyes.

Sister put her arm around Bridget. "I'm sorry, dear. But this very nice couple with good credentials had been looking to adopt, and Nellie seemed to fit all of their qualifications."

"Oh, Sister, could you just tell me where she went?"

"Oh, I'm so sorry. I wish I could tell you, but we are not allowed to give out that information. I'm so, so sorry. I know how fond you are of her."

Bridget sighed. "Oh, Sister, I love her so much. If ever you have any contact at all with those people, please ask them to tell Nellie that I am very happy for her and that I love her and will pray for her always."

"Oh, I will, Bridget. I'm glad you see it that way. And maybe you would also like to know that the little infant you brought us has also been placed in a good home and will be well cared for."

The ride back "home" on the trolley found Bridget deep in thought. Oh, Nellie, I really, really wanted to see you. Now I'm not sure if I'll *ever* see you again! Well, as long as you are safe and happy with your new mom and dad ...

Arriving back at the Mission, Bridget was surprised to see Tom waiting in the parlor. "Oh, Tom! I'm so glad to see you!" She started crying.

"Well, you're not *acting* too glad!" Seeing her break down, he quickly apologized for his quip. "Oh, gosh, I'm sorry, honey. What's wrong?"

"Oh, Tom! I'll never ever see Nellie again!"

"What?"

"I'll never see her again. She's gone. Been adopted."

"Where?"

"They can't say."

He held her close and patted her back, trying to comfort her. "I'm so sorry, honey."

"Nellie's gone. The baby's gone. Well, at least we know they must be in good hands if people wanted them so much to adopt them. But, Small Fry..." Bridget seemed pensive. "Did you ever think of adoption, Tom?"

"Well, yes—sometimes I have. But ya have to be settled to raise a family."

"That's true. Sometimes, in my heart, I feel like I could adopt all those little orphans though!"

"Well, I know how you feel, but that's not too realistic, Bridget!"

"I'll tell you something though, Tom. If we were settled right now, for sure I'd adopt Small Fry right away."

"Yeah, he is special. Maybe we can talk about it later on. Gee, honey, I haven't even started my new job yet! Anyway, he seems happy in his new home—you know, with all his new friends and his eagerness to learn. He'll be fine. And I promise we'll go see him again real soon."

"You're right, Tom. But let's pray that all those poor orphans will find good homes, okay? Besides, you know we may have our own children someday, God willing."

"Now you sit yourself right down here, me girl, 'cause I've got some *good* news for ya!"

Bridget wiped her tears, trying to force a smile. "What is it, Tom?"

"Bridget, me girl, yer lookin' at a man who's got a job all lined up for next spring!"

"Oh, Tom! Wonderful! Where?"

"Well, it'll be temporary—on a Packet Boat on the Canal, but..." A big smile came over his face. "we'll get free passage to Buffalo, 'cause I'm gonna be filling in for the steersman. He's gonna be leavin'. So anyway, the timing will be perfect!"

"But I definitely want to visit Joseph again soon." Her voice was commanding.

"Why sure ... we can do that. Just not right away, honey. Don't ya think we'd better get this wedding business taken care of first?"

She didn't answer, knowing Tom was right but still wishing it could be different.

Bridget had her mind made up to have a big wedding. This was a surprise to Tom, as she had never mentioned it before and he had just assumed they would have a small, quiet ceremony. She got her wish, however, as her friends all offered to help. This was quite a relief for Tom, as he was concerned about the expense. His main priority, however, was for Bridget's happiness. Plans began to fall in place rapidly, as Captain Skully offered the *River Queen* for the reception and Molly rounded up a group of lady friends who agreed to make a buffet.

In time, it was learned that Reenie had offered to provide the drinks from her Pub, and musicians were lined up by Jim Flynn. "Oh, my gosh, Tom! Can you believe all this? Who could ever ask for better friends? Here we're just beginning to talk about getting married, and everybody is getting in the picture already!"

"It's really wonderful, Bridget. Gosh, all I'll have to think about when the time comes is getting myself some suitable clothing." Bridget held her left hand up, pointing to her ring finger. "Ah yes—and one other little item!"

The wedding date was set for the following September. Tom and Bridget felt it was better to wait awhile, so as to put aside a little more money for their needs when they arrived in Buffalo. In addition, Tom had given up his room at the boarding house, as he was allowed to stay in the boatswain's quarters below deck—a great benefit. They couldn't wait to share the news with Father Sullivan and approached him after Mass the following Sunday. He was removing his vestments as they entered the sacristy.

"Oh, hello, my friends. Come in. Come in."

"How have you been, Father?" Bridget asked.

"Oh, I'm fine. And how are you doing—and how is that old sewing machine workin'?"

"Oh, Father, it's been a Godsend. I'll never be able to thank you enough. And I hope those vestments of yours haven't lost their stitches!"

"Ah, ya fixed 'em good as new, my dear! And Thomas, how have you been? Still workin' on the boat?"

"Well, yes, Father, but not too much longer!"

"How's that?"

"Well, that's what we came to talk to you about, Father. We'd like to get married next Fall and then we're moving to Buffalo. I got a job promised me there."

"Well, now! Congratulations! There will have to be some preparation made, of course. But you know, I can't think too well on an empty stomach. Why don't ya come over to the rectory and we'll have a spot of tea and a little bite."

Time spent with Father Sullivan was always most pleasant. His caring demeanor endeared him to his parishioners. "Put the kettle down, Bridget, while I get some muffins. Mrs. Corcoran made 'em for me and brought 'em over yesterday— blueberry—my favorite!"

"Oh, thank you, Father." She filled the kettle and placed it on the stove.

"Now sit down, you two, and tell me all about it!"

They excitedly discussed their plans with Father and he briefly went over the particulars of the church, including the Banns of Marriage. "Now, my dears, since the wedding is some time off, we can go into all this in detail at a later date—maybe about three or four months before the wedding, I want you to make an appointment to see me then and we'll make all the necessary arrangements."

The rest of the afternoon was spent talking about pleasantries—the wedding party and all of the plans their good friends were making on their behalf. Tom showed Father his postcard from Niagara Falls, relating to him the majestic, thunderous beauty of the cataract.

"Ah, yes! I know what you mean, my boy. That was one of the first things I saw when I came into the states from Canada. It is a magnificent sight to behold, it is! A beautiful gift from God! I'm glad you had the opportunity to see it, Tom." The conversation then turned to Joseph, the Newsboys' Home, and the girls at the Mission, as Father liked to be kept up to date on the Catholic organizations that worked with the street children and immigrants in that area.

Time seemed to go slowly, as winter had started quite early that year, the first heavy snowfall arriving in October. Bridget was spending a great deal of time in her little "shop" high up in that attic room which overlooked the Hudson River; and Tom worked on the *Mary Powell* whenever weather permitted, alternating with the machine shop during extreme weather conditions. There were an unusual amount of storms that year, some dumping as much as six to eight feet of snow on the city, making travel impossible. Sometimes weeks went by with no letup, and people found themselves preferring not to venture out but for emergencies such as obtaining food. It was difficult for Tom to make his way to the Mission on many days when he was hoping to visit his new fiance'. Times when he did make it through the high snows culminated in his usual announcement of his arrival, his snowballs hitting Bridget's window. She delighted hearing that "thwack," always anxious to see him.

Finally, the spring thaw arrived and the streets again swarmed with people. Hucksters came shouting their wares, the hum of the electric streetcars resumed, and the chatter of the many languages echoed throughout Manhattan once again. Bridget had decided that, since the time was getting short until she and Tom would be leaving New York, she would try to make one extra outfit for each girl—a big job considering so many lived there; but she wanted to make sure the girls would have what they needed. Nellie was no longer there to help; however, a few of the other girls who had taken previous instruction from Bridget, worked diligently with her to complete this task. In addition, she had designed and sewn the dresses for Grace, her maid of honor, and Molly, her bridesmaid. They had to be pink, of course. No other color would do. The necklines were high, trimmed with lace, and gently rounded with sleeves falling in ruffles to the elbow. The skirt billowed loosely to the ankles, an appliquéd white rose at the bottom right of the hem to match the one at the waist. Her own wedding dress had been completed and was hanging on the back of her door, covered with tissue. At times, she would uncover it and just stand there looking at it, thinking ahead to her wedding day. The lace bodice was joined to the billowing satin skirt which had a pearly white wide tie around the waist. The neck had a high collar which fastened at the back by little round pearl buttons which ran from the neck down to the waist. The upper sleeves were puffy and full, culminating at the wrist with tapered cuffs. On one or two occasions she found herself trying it on, and her imagination carried her back to earlier times when she envisioned herself as a princess being carried off by her white knight. Now, she thought, I really *look* like a princess and Tom will be "carrying me off" to Buffalo where we will live happily ever after. It almost seemed as though it were an actual fairy tale about to come true.

Walking down State Street on the way home from Mass a few months before the wedding, Bridget and Tom discussed the final arrangements they had just made with Father Sullivan. The wedding date had now been set— September 17th. Suddenly Bridget blurted out, "Oh, my gosh! Tom, we forgot about the ring bearer."

"Don't worry—I've got it covered. I've already arranged for Small Fry ... I mean Joseph. He's so excited!"

"Oh, how wonderful! Oh, I'm so glad!"

"Yeah, and also a friend of mine is loaning me his best suit—he only wore it once. So I guess we have all the bases covered, and Father said he will post our Banns of Marriage for the three weeks before the wedding."

"Oh, my gosh! I can't believe it's almost here— everything just seems to be happening so quickly!"

September 17th was a glorious morning. Patches of white fluffy clouds filled the blue skies and the soft winds conveyed just a slight hint of Fall in the air. Bridget was attended by her bridesmaids as they fussed about in the back of St. Paul's Church. A few strands of her hair had been blown about and Molly was pinning them back up into her hairdo and readjusting her veil.

"You look really beautiful, Bridget," Molly said, as she stood back a little to admire her handiwork.

Bridget repeated the compliment to Molly, a smile welling up inside her heart, as she hardly ever saw her dressed in anything but her old navy-blue tugboat pants and shirt. Then she turned to her maid of honor. "You all set, Grace?"

"Yes, my dear. I'm ready."

Joseph appeared a little nervous, although quite proud of the way he looked in a *real* suit donated by Mr. Flynn. He had a fresh haircut, parted neatly in the middle. Tom had given the boy the wedding band, and he kept checking every few minutes to make sure it was still safe there where Tom had placed it in his right pocket. "Now, Joseph, you will be just fine. All you have to do is walk straight down that aisle to where Tom will be standing in the front—and remember, go real slow," Bridget instructed, as she put a white carnation in his lapel and demonstrated to him the proper pace. "Oh, good! Look Joseph! Here comes Captain Skully now." She gave the boy a big hug, then turned to greet the Captain. He had been asked to give the bride away, as he had become like a father to Bridget when she worked on the *River Queen*. He was dressed in his navy-blue jacket, the lower sleeves adorned with gold trim and the two rows of brass buttons running down the front looking as though they had just been polished. His white pants added a look of distinction, matching the white cap resplendent with the shiny black brim boasting of his ship in gold lettering—*RIVER QUEEN.*

"Bridget, you are absolutely lovely!" He leaned over and kissed her on the cheek, taking his cap off and laying it on the table behind them.

She hugged him. "And you, my dear friend, look so distinguished. Thank you so much for being such an important part of my wedding day."

"Are you ready, my dear?"

Nodding, she took the bouquets from the box on the table, handing one to Molly and Grace, took his arm, and motioned Joseph and the girls to their proper places in front of them.

Suddenly, the back door swung open and two sailor-friends of Tom's straggled in at the last minute, unshaven and scruffy looking. "Take yer hat off—yer in church now," one said, as he removed his own cap and slapped the other on the head with it. "Oh, excuse us, ladies," he added, as they entered the inner doors to the church, taking a seat in the back row.

The organist began the wedding march, and Bridget and the entourage began walking slowly down the center aisle. The proud handsome groom stood near the front altar with Jim Flynn, his best man, watching as his bride-to-be made her way toward him with slowly paced strides to the rhythmic flow of "Here Comes the Bride."

On one side of the church, the pews were filled with the good nuns, including Sister Irene from the Foundling Hospital, Sisters Eileen and Teresita from Mount Loretto, and many of the girls from the Mission. Renee from Shannon's Pub had wheeled herself up the side aisle, parking her wheelchair in front of the pews, so as not to block the procession.

The pews on the other side were mostly taken up with Tom's friends—sailors from the *Mary Powell*, the *River Queen*, and the barges on the Erie Canal. Most were unshaven and unkempt looking. Tom couldn't remember ever seeing any of them at St. Paul's before and wondered when they had last stepped foot inside a church.

Captain Skully placed Bridget's hand in Tom's, and the two of them knelt at the foot of the altar as Mass began.

"In the name of the Father and of the Son and of the Holy Ghost. Amen." The intonation of Father Sullivan's prayer seemed to resonate holiness. "Our help is in the name of the Lord, who made Heaven and Earth."

Finishing the beginning prayer, Father then gave instruction to the bride and groom, explaining that they were entering into a union which is sacred and serious and established by God Himself. He explained how the Lord added to the holiness of marriage an even deeper meaning and higher beauty—His own love for His Church. More instruction followed about self-giving and the solemn obligation upon which they were about to embark. Tears of joy fell from many eyes, mostly women's.

Then Father turned to Tom. "Thomas, will you take Bridget, here present, for your lawful wife according to the rite of our holy Mother, the Church?"

"I will."

"Bridget, will you take Thomas, here present, for your lawful husband, according to the rite of our holy Mother, the Church?"

"I will." Her voice was shaky, as her heart seemed fully impressed with the holiness and seriousness of the vow she was making, as she thought of the lifetime ahead she would be sharing with Tom.

The priest then asked Tom and Bridget to join their right hands and repeat after him:

"I, Thomas, take you, Bridget, for my lawful wife, to have and to hold, from this day forward, for better, for worse, for richer, for poorer, in sickness and in health, until death do us part."

"I, Bridget, take you, Thomas, for my lawful husband, to have and to hold, from this day forward, for better, for worse, for richer, for poorer, in sickness and in health, until death do us part."

"I now join you in Holy Matrimony in the name of the Father, and of the Son, and of the Holy Ghost. Amen."

Looking over to Joseph, Father asked if he had the wedding ring. The boy came forward, briefly fumbled in his pocket, and finally with a look of pride on his face, produced the ring and handed it to Father who said a blessing over it, sprinkled it with holy water, and handed it to Tom. Taking Bridget's hand, he placed the ring lovingly on her finger and repeated after the priest, "In the name of the Father, and of the Son, and of the Holy Ghost, take and wear this ring as a pledge of my fidelity." Father Sullivan then blessed the bride and groom and continued with the ceremony.

It was beautiful. There was an air of sanctity that permeated the whole church. It seemed as though an unspoken feeling of wholesomeness and purity was felt by all—these two young people dedicating their lives to one another and God being asked to join their hearts and souls together in His sight, becoming one in the enduring bond of pure love. Father Sullivan read from the First Letter of Paul to the Church of Corinth, Chapter 13, ending with "*In short, there are three things that last: faith, hope and love; and the greatest of these is love.*"

The nuns all rose from their seats, anticipating the coming Gospel reading. Unsure as to what was actually happening, most all of Tom's sailor friends, began to glance over to the pews on the opposite side and a few of them hesitatingly stood up. The rest soon followed as the priest announced from the pulpit, "Please stand for the reading of the Holy Gospel."

> *"...and He said, 'For this cause a man shall leave his father and mother and cleave to his wife and the two shall become one flesh.' Therefore now they are no longer two, but one flesh. What therefore God has joined together, let no man put asunder."*

Following the Offertory and the Priest's Communion, the congregation came forward to receive Holy Communion, as a rich tenor voice softly sang

Ave Maria, gratia plena,
Maria, gratia plena,
Maria, gratia plena,
Ave, Ave, Dominus,
Dominus tecum.
Benedicta tu in mulieribus, et benedictus,
Et benedictus fructus ventris,
Ventris tui, Jesus.
Ave Maria!

After Communion Father Sullivan ended the Mass, giving his final blessing to the congregation. He then placed his hands on Bridget and Tom's shoulders, turning them to face the people. "I present to you, Mr. and Mrs. Thomas Sexton." Resounding applause came forward from those gathered there. "Please know that the newlyweds invite all to a reception on the *River Queen* at Pier #7 at 6 p.m."

The organist then began the Wedding March; and the bride and groom led the wedding party in the procession back down the aisle, taking their places in the vestibule to receive the guests. Afterwards, they were greeted with a shower of rice as they left the church, Bridget being pelted on the side of her face by a handful thrown with some force by Ricky, one of Tom's sailor-friends.

A beautiful surprise awaited the newlyweds, as an all-white open carriage adorned with white ribbons and flowers and pulled by two white horses approached the front of the church, thanks to Jim Flynn's generosity.

"Oh, Tom! Look! How beautiful!"

Tom smiled, having known ahead of time that Jim had arranged for this. Climbing up into the back, he turned to take his bride's hand. "Up ya go, Bridget-girl!"

The coachman turned back to greet them. "Congratulations, Mr. and Mrs. Sexton."

"Oh, thank you so much," Bridget replied, turning that greeting over and over in her mind—Mr. and Mrs. Sexton ... Mr. and Mrs. Sexton ... Mr. and Mrs ...

The coachman snapped the reins, and the sound of the tin cans dragging behind spooked the horses, and off they flew—a quick start to their marriage—as Bridget quickly caught her veil from blowing off. It was a gorgeous day and the coachman reined the horses down to a slow trot to ride around Central Park. Grace O'Brien had packed them a picnic basket, filled with Tom's favorite—fried chicken. She had also included some small delicacies which she had made herself—a lovely assortment of butter cookies. Finding a large willow tree, they sat beneath it and had their lunch, discussing their plans for the future with eager enthusiasm and high hopes.

"Happy, sweetheart?"

"Oh, yes, Tom! Very happy! I love you so much."

"Oh, my girl, can't be even half as much as I love you!" He took her hand and they walked next to the creek behind the willow. A mother duck led a row of seven offspring behind her down the bank into the water. Bridget, having a few cookies remaining in her basket, took them and broke them into small pieces, tossing some of them near the fowl, who immediately converged upon it. She delighted in watching this, as she continued to feed them with the remaining fragments.

"I hope it's okay for ducks to eat cookies!" Bridget quipped.

"Well, I sure don't think they'd rather have that leftover chicken!"

"Oh, Tom, you silly one!" They laughed and continued their stroll.

Tom was suddenly aware the hour was growing late, and they headed back toward the carriage. A park bench nearby was occupied by an unshaven, disheveled-looking older man huddled under an old Army coat. He sat up as they approached. He appeared to be emaciated, his eyes seeming to have a hollow stare. Bridget and Tom exchanged glances, both hearts in the same place. She laid the basket on the bench next to the man. "Oh, thank you, ma'am. God bless you." He immediately reached inside for a piece of the chicken with his right hand. Tom noticed immediately that his left arm was missing.

"Are you a veteran, sir?"

"Yes. Yes, I am." He pointed to the missing limb. "Lost this one at Gettysburg."

Bridget lifted her hand to her face, her fingers covering her mouth. "Oh! Oh! I'm so sorry."

"Don't be sorry, ma'am. It was worth it—whippin' them Rebs like we did!"

"Oh, God!—that it will never happen again!" Bridget sighed.

The man was apparently homeless and just continued devouring the chicken. Glancing up once again at Tom and Bridget, he smiled. "I see you two just tied the knot!"

"Yes," Tom answered.

"I wish you two good people the best all your life. God bless you."

They turned to leave, a tear in Bridget's eyes. "Thank you, sir. God bless you, too."

Riding back in the carriage, neither one spoke for a few minutes. Finally, Tom looked over at Bridget, a serious look on his face. "I hope future generations appreciate what that man and so many others sacrificed for our freedoms."

Back at the Mission, they rested for the remainder of the afternoon before getting ready for the reception on the *River Queen*.

"Ready, Bridget-girl?"

"All ready, husband dear."

"Okay, come on! Our marriage-carriage is awaiting outside!"

They arrived at Pier 7. Bridget was astounded when she saw the boat. "Oh, Tom! Look! Look what they did! Isn't it beautiful?"

Tom smiled, knowing that they had planned to turn the *River Queen* into a wedding extravaganza! Kerosene lanterns hung from the ceiling, ringing the top deck—the white and gold globes casting a soft hue of glistening beauty from stem to stern. Streamers crisscrossed the deck, fastened at each end by white carnations, matching the floral centerpieces in the middle of each table. Flag buntings were draped from the railings on both sides of the ship, the guests lined up along them to watch for the arrival of the newlyweds.

Captain Skully approached them, bowing down from the waist, as they started up the gangplank. In his gravelly voice, he greeted them. "Welcome to our humble ship! We knight you King and Queen for a day, and we lowly river rats and sea urchins give you homage! Your wish is our command." A round of applause broke out from the top deck. Skully kissed Bridget's hand, then turning, tripped over the gangplank, catching himself and making sure he protected the flask of rum in his back pocket. The crew, standing at attention, saluted as the Captain signaled his first mate to blow the shrill boat whistle. Following this, a prearranged symphony of several other boats' whistles, one following the other, echoed throughout the harbor.

Bridget was overwhelmed! She couldn't believe the precious gift before her eyes. "Tom! Can you believe all this! Oh, my gosh! How beautiful! Can anyone have more wonderful friends?" She cried.

"Come on, my baby, dry those eyes! This is *our party*!" He wiped her tears and led her up the gangplank.

Molly had arranged beforehand for her friends to arrive early to begin preparations for the wedding dinner—corned beef and cabbage—as she knew the Irish sailors celebrated St. Patrick's Day *every* day. Fresh fish, caught by Skully's crew the day before, potatoes, vegetables, and salads, along with the ladies' fresh baked bread rounded out the menu. The sailors rolled three large beer kegs up the gangplank, compliments of Renee. Two husky sailors unloaded an upright honkytonk piano from a camion , calling upon another sailor to assist. "Where do you want this?" one of them hollered to the Captain.

"Put it over there next to the cabin wall amidships," Skully yelled back. "And who might be the donor of this fine lookin' instrument?"

"Flynn—Mr. James Flynn the third!"

"And who would be playin' it fer us?"

Just then, Flynn approached. "That would be me, Captain!" Jim was dressed in a rich looking, Navy-blue, pinstriped, three-piece suit. All seemed awestruck to have such a distinguished-looking guest.

The sailors began to pull the plug from one of the barrels, but Renee noticed and quickly wheeled herself over and began to whack them on the knuckles with her cane. "You'll not be gettin' half soused before ya get some food in ya—sit yerselves down till the festivities begin!" she scolded. The sailors knew Renee very well from past occasions at Shannon's Pub, following her orders without a murmur. A short while later, Sister Irene and a few of the nuns from the Foundling Hospital arrived, followed by Grace O'Brien and some of the girls from the Mission. Tom had issued a personal invitation to Sisters Eileen and Teresita, making sure they would see to it that his ring bearer came as well. It was important to him to share their happiness with Joseph.

A tall portly Scotsman, dressed in full plaid kilt, bagpipes over his shoulder, stepped up to the gangplank. "Would this be the wedding of Mr. and Mrs. Sexton, mate?" as he looked at Captain Skully.

"Well, yes, it is ..." Skully removed his cap, and scratching his head, continued, "but what in blazes would a Scotchman like yerself be doin' comin' to an Irish wedding?"

"Well now, whatcha got against the Scotch, laddie?" as he laid down his bagpipes, spit on his hands, and raised his clenched fists.

Flynn noticed the contentious situation which was developing and immediately decided he'd better intervene before things got out of hand. "Now gentlemen, let's not get excited! I'm the one that invited Mr. MacTavish, Captain."

"Well, I don't care! He's got no right comin' aboard my ship and raising a hand ta me!"

The Scotsman's face grew beet-red. "I could take the lot of you Micks on with one hand behind me back!"

"That'll be the day I can't whip someone wearin' a skirt!" the Captain retorted.

"Alright. Alright, gentlemen! This is a wedding, and I'll not have you spoil it for my good friends." Flynn turned to the Scotsman. "Now, Mr. MacTavish, since I have hired you for this party, let's just end all this nonsense! So apologize to the Captain and we can continue on with our evening."

"Are you mad? You want *me* to apologize to this old sea dog?"

"Who you callin' an old sea dog?" The Captain's face was now growing redder than his antagonist's.

Flynn could see this was escalating and getting out of control. As the Scotsman raised his fists once again, he stepped between him and the Captain.

"Git outa my way, you puny little swell!" the Scotsman ordered, as he pushed Flynn to the side.

"If it's a fight you want, it's a fight you'll get!" Flynn challenged as he removed his jacket, loosened his tie, rolled up his shirt sleeves, and handed his eyeglasses to the Captain who stepped back, flabbergasted at this new turn of events.

MacTavish smirked as he watched Flynn getting ready to do battle. "I wouldn't fight a pint-sized runt like you—I'd murder ya!"

"I can handle myself, Mac," Flynn responded, a look of confidence on his face.

The Captain and some others who had gathered nearby to see what all the commotion was about pleaded with Flynn, thinking he'd never last a minute against the big Scotsman. Even so, it was agreed to settle things on the dock so as not to spoil the wedding.

Flynn took a firm boxing stance, putting one foot behind the other, raised his fists, and waited for MacTavish to strike first.

With a fighting spirit in his eyes and a defiant cocky demeanor, Mac threw a punch that Flynn ducked, side-stepping his opponent and throwing a left jab into the soft belly of the Scotsman, who doubled over but quickly came back at Flynn with a vengeance. Swinging wildly, he thrashed again with a jab and a right uppercut, again missing his target. Flynn was light on his feet and fast but never once violated the Queensbury Rules, the new boxing regulations. At one point, Flynn took a jab which grazed his head and knocked him off balance. Quickly recovering, he danced around a lot, while the heavy man's weight seemed to slow him down. The harder he struck at Flynn, the slower he got, which is what Flynn had in mind all the time. He looked for a break, finally finding an opening. With all his might, he struck a strong uppercut to the jaw of his opponent. A crack was heard and the Scotsman went down, momentarily unconscious.

Flynn glanced over at the Captain who was smiling broadly, bent down and shook the Scotty, helping him to his feet after a few minutes. Mac was still dazed, a look of bewilderment on his face, shaking his head from side to side. "No hard feelings, sir," Flynn offered, as he picked up his coat and glasses. "Come on! Let's go to the wedding—I'll buy you a beer!"

"Yeah. Yeah!" the Scotsman replied, wobbling up the gangplank with the assistance of his pugilistic opponent.

The guests had been taken by surprise, seeing the thin Mr. Flynn handle himself so well, winning the fight so easily when they had thought MacTavish would beat him to a pulp.

Just then, Molly arrived and asked Captain Skully what all the commotion was about, having heard the tail-end of the fight when approaching the boat.

"Oh, it's just a little difference of opinion between friends," the Captain offered.

"It sure sounded to me like it was more than a difference of opinion, Skully!"

"Well, actually, Flynn and a Scotchman got into a little trouble."

"A Scotchman?"

"Yeah, Flynn ordered a bagpipe player for the wedding."

"So?"

"So it kinda ended up with a little fisticuffs."

"Flynn fought him?"

"Yeah."

"Well, I can guess who won *that* one!" Molly remarked with a smirk on her face.

"I don't think you'll guess right," Skully replied.

"I bet that fightin' didn't last too long," Molly offered, smiling broadly. "I bet Flynn took 'im in the first few minutes!"

"What? Why in the world would you ever think that skinny gent would beat a big Scotchman?"

Molly looked at the Captain, an all-knowing look on her countenance, yet offering no answer. "Come on—I'm starving! Let's just go and get this party started."

The Captain looked puzzled, wondering what little secret Molly knew that he didn't.

Father Sullivan, seated at the head table with the bride and groom, stood to say grace, taking one of his favorite prayers from the fledgling church.

"Without Thy presence, naught, O Lord, is sweet.
No pleasure to our lips can aught supply.
Whether 'tis wine we drink or food we eat,
Till Grace divine and Faith shall sanctify."

Seeing a puzzled look on some of the sailors' faces, Father then added,

"Thank you for this food, O Lord!"

The meal began, as the band provided soft background music. The sailors and Captain Skully were all seated at the tables on one side of the ship and the nuns and the girls on the other. Suddenly, Small Fry made his way from Sister Eileen's table to the front of the head table, peering over at Tom and Bridget.

"Well, hello, Joseph. Are you enjoying your meal?"

"Well, I kinda wish I could be sitting up here with you and Tom."

Bridget thought he seemed about to cry. "Tom, go get another chair for Joseph. Come right around here, honey. You sit right here next to me."

Joseph's demeanor immediately changed to one of happiness, as he made his way around the table and took the seat Tom had provided. Bridget took his hand in hers and motioned to one of the girls to bring his plate. "There you are, Joseph. Eat up now." She gave him a little hug. His appetite suddenly returned and he began eating again, all the while his eyes examining the three-tiered delightful looking delicacy at the side table, decorated with white flowers made of frosting, the likes of which he had never seen before.

Father Sullivan stood up and spoke. "As I approached your lovely vessel," he began, looking at the Captain, "I wasn't sure if I was coming to a wedding reception or a boxing bout!" Everyone laughed. The priest then made a toast to the newlyweds. "To good health and long life, and may the good Lord keep you both and bless you with many little ones."

Jim Flynn then stood. "I wish you both a blessed and long life together." Raising his glass, the guests joined the gesture as he added, "I have never met a more wonderful couple in my whole life, so may the Good Lord take a likin' to you—but not too soon!" The guests laughed once again, and all toasted Bridget and Tom, including little Joseph who was given a sip of wine from Bridget's glass.

The boy motioned to Bridget to lean down so he could whisper in her ear. "I gotta go—*real* bad!"

"Oh. Okay, honey. Tom, would you please take Joseph to the bathroom?"

Tom took the boy by the hand, leading him to the midships, passing the table with the delicacy on the way. The boy, not being able to resist the temptation, suddenly swiped his index finger across the flowers at the bottom of the cake, hiding it immediately behind his back until he had privacy inside the bathroom to enjoy his ill-gotten prize.

The bride and groom took to the "dance floor" shortly after, following the announcement by the Captain. "Mr. and Mrs. Thomas Sexton!" as he motioned Bridget and Tom to come forward. Tom wasn't the best dancer in the world; however, Bridget enjoyed being held close by her new husband and for a moment, she felt like time had stopped and they were the only two people in the world. A silvery moonbeam cast its glow on the water and a silent joy seemed to invade the two hearts made one. The band continued on with a song known to Tom and Bridget, and they sang along with the music and continued dancing.

Casey would waltz with a strawberry blonde
And the band played on.
He'd glide 'cross the floor with the girl he adored
And the band played on.
He married the girl with the strawberry curls
And the band played on.

"Bridget-girl, we got a *big* problem."

"What? What do you mean, Tom?"

"You don't have any strawberry curls!"

Bridget laughed aloud. "Oh, you silly thing!" They took their seats back at the table, a jovial mood invading the celebration as the piano player, the fiddler, and the harmonica and flute players revved things up with a good old Irish jig. The sailors popped the corks from the barrels and out flowed the "demon rum," as they jokingly called the beer. A couple of the younger sailors, having had a few drinks, eventually made their way over to the table where Grace O'Brien and the girls were sitting and asked them to dance. Grace immediately stood up and asked the rather scruffy-looking lads if they were gentlemen. A tall, blond sailor, his hat cocked back on his head, answered, "Why, yes, Ma'am, we are all gentlemen!" The girls began to giggle until Grace turned and stared them down. Just then, the same young sailor turned to Grace herself, asking, "Would *you* do me the honor of this dance, Ma'am?"

Grace, taken by surprise, seemed at a loss for words, flattered by the invitation proposed to her. After hesitating for a moment, she replied, "You have good taste, lad," and grabbing his hand, they proceeded to twirl around the dance floor, the sailor all the while keeping his eye on one of the younger prettier girls at the table. Afterwards, Grace, then feeling more receptive to the idea, gave permission for the girls to dance with the sailors, though first giving the young men strict instructions to hold them at arm's length.

Some of the more popular songs of the era were then played by the band to the delight of the guests. Grace's favorite, "*While Strolling Through the Park One Day*," was followed by "*On a Bicycle Built for Two*" and "*Sidewalks of New York*." Captain Skully, Jim Flynn, and many of the sailors took turns dancing with the bride. Tom danced with Grace and Molly, while the nuns enjoyed just watching and chatting by themselves. The ladies from the kitchen were the next to enjoy the groom's somewhat less-than-ideal dancing skills.

"Ladies and gentlemen! Please take your seats," Captain Skully announced. "We have here tonight one of our Celtic brothers, Mr. Donald MacTavish"—applause broke out as the big man came forward and bowed from the waist— "who will entertain us with his bagpipes." Again—applause. "And what might be the tune, Mr. MacTavish?"

"'*On the Bonnie Bonnie Banks O' Loch Lomond*', Captain." MacTavish began to play the soft Scottish tune with its haunting melody. The people sat quietly, enjoying the beauty of the bagpipes. About halfway through, the young sailor with the blonde hair stepped up from his table, taking a position next to the Scotsman. In a rich tenor voice, he joined in, singing the lyrics.

"By yon bonnie banks an' by yon bonnie braes...
Where the sun shines bright on Loch Lomond.
Where me an' my true love will never meet again...
On the bonnie, bonnie banks o' Loch Lomond.
O you tak' the high road, and ah'll tak' the low...
And I'll be in Scotland afore ye.
For me an' my true love will never meet again...
On the bonnie, bonnie banks o' Loch Lomond."

It was a song that deeply touched the hearts of all listening. And immediately Flynn stood and asked for an encore. The sailor was only too happy to oblige and continued with the rest of the verses. During this time, Bridget had become concerned as Joseph was not at the table. She searched the deck with her eyes, finally spotting him standing alone at the railing far down from the party area. Having made eye contact with Sister Teresita, she pointed over to the place Joseph was standing. The nun immediately nudged Sister Eileen with her elbow, noticing the boy had just put his head down on the railing, and then got up to go to him. “What is it, Joseph?” Sister Teresita asked. “Aren’t you having a good time?” She bent down and wiped a tear from his eye.

He sobbed, then catching his breath—"I miss Nellie.”

“Oh, Joseph ... oh, you poor boy! I’m so sorry, honey.” Her heart ached for the boy. “But you know, she is in a very good home now.”

“Where is she? Can I see her?”

Just then, Sister Irene walked over to see what was wrong. “Is there a problem with the boy?” she asked.

“He misses his sister and wants to know if he can see her.”

Not wanting to get him more upset, Sister Irene offered, “Joseph, I promise we can look into it tomorrow. Now come along—let’s dance!” She took him by the hand and led him onto the dance floor. He, along with the other guests, were shocked as she began to twirl him around. The onlookers began to clap in time with the music. It seemed strange, as nuns never danced—this was a first! Joseph had temporarily stopped worrying about Nellie, his tears turning into laughter. The band began another Irish jig, and the nun switched to a fast two-step, trying to keep up with the beat of the music. At one point her headgear started slipping off to one side, revealing one ear peeking through her dark brown hair. Joseph found this so funny, he laughed all the louder, bending down and holding his stomach. Sister, almost stealing the show from the bride and groom, tried to adjust her veil inconspicuously but ended up laughing along with the boy as they made their way back to the table.

“Joseph! I had no idea you were such a good dancer!” Sister Eileen quipped. “Sit down here next to me. I’ve hardly had a chance to talk with you all evening.” She glanced up at Sister Irene. “Sister, why don’t you go over there and get Joseph a nice big piece of that wedding cake. They’re just cutting it and I imagine he has a little room left for some dessert.”

“Oh, I *do!* Can you get me a piece with *lots* of frosting, Sister?”

“I’ll see what I can do, Joseph. Would you care for some too, Sister Eileen?”

“The girls will be going up for some in a minute and will bring me a piece, thank you, Sister.”

"Bridget, my dear, little Joseph is requesting a piece with 'lots of frosting!' Do you think you can fill that request?" Sister Irene asked with a wink.

Bridget, glancing over to the table, was relieved to see Joseph looking so happy, She cut a piece from the corner of the cake, so as to have the thickest part of the frosting on two sides of his piece. She then proceeded to take two frosting flowers from another piece and place them on the top of Joseph's.

"Here you are, my dear." Joseph's eyes lit up as he beheld the treat being placed before him.

"Oh, *thank* you, Sister Irene!" he said, as he began to devour his cake.

"You are most welcome, Joseph," she responded as she pulled out a chair next to him.

"Oh! Before you sit down, Sister Irene, please come over to the railing to see how beautifully the moon is shining on the water," Sister Teresita invited with a wink and a nod.

Catching the meaning, Sister Irene followed her. "Now, Sister, can't we at least help the boy write a letter? And you can send it to Nellie's new home? I know it's not allowed to give out the adopted children's new addresses, but..." She paused and looked pleadingly directly into Irene's eyes. "... she is Joseph's only kin, you know."

Sister Irene interrupted. "You know the rule ..." She paused. Then with her wry little smile, she added, "but, we'll see. Maybe a letter wouldn't hurt a bit."

Taking a break from his melodious entertainment of the wedding guests, the Scotsman was standing alone near one of the beer barrels, seeming a little shy for a man of his size and unable to mix with the rest of the folks. But he wouldn't be alone for long. Tugboat Molly approached him. "Well, now, you big bag o' wind, aren't you gonna ask me for a dance?"

"Well ... I ... I ...," he stammered. "I don't dance well."

"Come on, ya big Scotty! Let's dance the light fantastic! I'll show ya!" She pulled him onto the dance floor, Scotty almost tripping over his own feet. Molly led him, and before long he seemed to get the hang of it and began to enjoy himself. After that first dance, they couldn't be separated and became an item for the rest of the night. Renee, watching from her wheelchair, clapped her hands and tapped her feet. Captain Skully came up behind her, grabbed the handles of the wheelchair, and began to twirl her around on the dance floor. Afterward, he spent most of the night telling her war stories, including the violent battles he was in when his ship, the Union Monitor engaged the Confederate Merrimac at Hampton Rhodes during the Civil War.

Every so often, the Captain would go into the Pilot House and blow the ship's whistle, continuing to celebrate the wedding. At one point, the policeman on the beat came aboard the ship. "Skully, you old sea dog, who in blazes keeps tootin' that horn? People are complaining you're keeping them awake!"

"Well, now! If it isn't Officer McGillicuddy! Oh, I'm sorry, but ya see, my friends are celebratin' their wedding." Skully pulled the pint bottle from his back pocket, then offered, "Here—won't ya have yerself a wee nip o' the crature, McGillicuddy? Ya gotta help celebrate a weddin'!"

"Well, I'm not supposed ..."

"Come on—it's good fer what ails ya! Besides, it's a special occasion."

"Well, I guess one little nip won't hurt," the officer replied, as he tipped the bottle to his lips.

The hour grew late and the nuns left with little Joseph, Grace and the girls from the Mission. The big Scotsman made his goodbye, and Father Sullivan left with Renee to help her home. Some of the sailors went to their quarters below deck, leaving those who had passed out right where they were sitting.

One of the last to leave was Jim Flynn. But not before Bridget and Tom thanked him profusely for all he had done. "I just don't think I can ever repay you for all the wonderful kindnesses you brought to our day today, Jim." She reached up and put her arms around his neck, hugging him tightly, before asking Tom to walk him down the gangplank, seeing that he needed a little assistance.

As Tom and Bridget, Molly and Skully watched Flynn depart the ship, the Captain looked over at Molly. "Molly dear, I've been thinkin' about what ya said before when ya said ya weren't surprised that Mr. Flynn beat that big Scotchman in that boxing exhibition."

"Well ... I'm not sure I should tell ya!"

"What's the big secret? You and I go back a long way!"

Molly, who had had quite a few drinks herself, blurted out, "Flynn isn't his real name!"

The Captain, as well as Tom and Bridget, looked very surprised. Skully, taking his cap off and scratching his head, remarked, "What in blazes! Whaddaya mean? Who is he?"

"You wouldn't guess in a million years," Molly responded.

"Come on, Molly—what's the secret?" the Captain asked again.

"Yeah, Molly. Why can't you tell us?" Tom agreed. "The Captain here can keep a secret, and Bridget and I are leaving town anyway."

"Well ... his name is ..." She hesitated.

"Out with it, Molly!" Skully commanded, seeming a little irritated.

"Corby!" she blurted out. "Jim Corby!"

"What? You don't mean the ex-heavyweight champ," the Captain questioned, looking skeptical.

"One and the same!"

"You're kidding!" they all said at once.

"Well, how did he ..." Tom was cut off.

"Well, the way he explained it to me," Molly interrupted, "he wanted to leave the boxing world behind him since he was now a successful attorney. He claimed he was used and, in his words—'they all wanted a piece of me, and they stole much of my earnings.' So after a few years of law school and a bright future, he could do business with gentlemen rather than unseemly characters making backroom deals behind his own back."

"I can't get over it!" Bridget remarked.

Then Tom chimed in. "To think he took the championship from John L.Flanigan—and we never knew his real identity."

"Now I get it, Molly," the Captain quipped. "No wonder ya knew he would have beaten that Scotchman! Scotty never knew what hit 'em!"

"Well, he's a wonderful man, no matter what he was or is. All I know is that he got me a job and provided the material I needed for the girls at the Mission—not to mention all he did in making this day so beautifully happy for Tom and I."

Molly made her goodbyes and was going to sleep on her tugboat for the next few days, leaving the use of her little home to Tom and Bridget before their trip to Buffalo.

Chapter 9

The Honeymoon

The newlyweds had said their goodbyes and were now headed to an unknown future. But they were young and in love and hope filled their hearts, as they looked forward to a bright new beginning.

It was the first day of their journey and the sun shone brightly as they sailed up the Hudson River on the *Mary Powell*, commonly known as the "Queen of the Hudson," heading for the Erie Canal. Bridget hadn't ventured out of the city since her arrival in America. She loved what she saw as they sailed up river. "What a beautiful country!" she remarked, taking in the landscape. "So many trees, greenery, hills, and valleys."

"You're right, Bridget. It is beautiful! I guess I've become used to it. I mean, having traveled this route so many times. You know, sweetheart, you're like a little child. I love your enthusiasm for everything, especially God's nature."

"Oh, Thomas! You know, this lush, green land reminds me of home. I guess I'm a country girl. I miss those open spaces and green meadows."

"Well, dear, maybe after we're settled in Buffalo, we can find a place in the country."

After making landings at Newburgh and Poughkeepsie, they arrived at Kingston early in the evening. "Oh, Thomas, these little towns are so quaint. I would love to live in a small town like these someday. That's what I was used to in Ireland, and we knew all our neighbors. I didn't see that in New York City."

Since the *Mary Powell* only traveled between Manhattan and Kingston, Tom and Bridget transferred to another steamer, also heading north to Albany. The railroad would have been a faster trip for them; however, it would have been more costly, and they wished to save the little money they had. This, in addition to the earnings Tom would make working as a steersman on the packet boat on the Canal, would give them a little "grub stake" for their start in Buffalo.

The packet boat was painted with bright colors, and Captain Finley wore a straw hat and a white shirt, ruffles down the front, bordering the buttons. This jolly old sailor had a pleasant way about him and was seldom seen without a cigar sticking out of the side of his mouth. His wife, Maria, was the boat's cook—a rather stout woman with an Italian accent. After meeting her, Tom and Bridget were ushered into the main cabin where Maria served the passengers hot coffee and muffins at the long rectangular table which ran down the middle of the cabin. Afterwards, the cots which had been folded up against the walls during the day were brought down for sleeping, a curtain separating the men's quarters from the women's. This arrangement wasn't exactly ideal for the newlyweds.

The steersman's job was a big challenge for Tom. His main duty was the operation of the tiller which controlled the rudder and direction of the boat. Since space was so limited, many passengers would sit or lie on the roof. Because of this, he had another responsibility—to warn the people when approaching low bridges. He was very conscientious about *this* duty, as he had heard that a lady passenger had been killed for not heeding the warning in time.

It didn't take long for Tom to adjust to his job at the stern of the boat. He quickly learned the fundamentals in guiding the boat as oncoming "traffic" approached, pulling up to the docks and going through the locks at various stages of the trip. Bridget quickly made friends, as she had a charming and considerate way about her; and she kindly offered to assist Maria with the food preparation. Between making meals, she would visit with Tom in the stern, read an occasional newspaper brought on board by a new passenger, or on occasion, join some of the other passengers on the roof. She made sure, however, to set some time aside for her Bible reading and praying her rosary.

Moving through the Mohawk Valley about sundown one day, as she sat on the roof enjoying the scenery and the fresh air, she overheard a man explaining something to a lady passenger about events that had taken place long ago in the surrounding hills. He was explaining that Iroquois Indians inhabited a village called Ossernenon. Bridget detected that the story concerned her faith, and her curiosity peaked. “Excuse me, Sir, but I couldn’t help overhear what you just said. Do you mind if I listen in?”

The elderly man, a neatly trimmed gray beard covering most of the wrinkles on his timeworn face, broke into a wide smile. “Why no, not at all. It would be my pleasure. May I introduce myself? Claude J. Beaumont at your service, my dear. And this is my wife, Odette.”

“How do you do. It’s so nice to meet you both. I’m Bridget O’Hal ... oh, excuse me, I mean Bridget Sexton. I just got married, you see.”

“Well, congratulations, my dear. I was just telling my wife a little history about this region and what occurred here long ago.” He pointed his finger toward the top of the hill. “It was back in the 1600’s when several Jesuit priests were slaughtered up there by the Iroquois Indians.”

“Oh, that’s horrible!” Bridget gasped.

“Yes, my dear. I believe they were the first missionaries to bring the Christian faith to this tribe—and it cost them their lives. They say those brave priests knew the dangers, but that didn’t stop them. In fact, two of them had such courage while being tortured, that the Indians ripped their hearts out of their bodies afterward, hoping that they themselves would obtain the missionaries’ courage in this way.”

“Oh, no!” Odette gasped.

Her husband continued, “They say the other priests were hacked to death with tomahawks.”

Odette covered her ears momentarily. Then, turning to Bridget, she said, “Please excuse me—I’m going below to get a drink.”

Bridget nodded to Odette, then turned to Claude. “Oh, my good Lord! They suffered a martyr’s death—they must have gone straight to Heaven!”

“I am very impressed with your strong faith, Bridget.”

“Well, it is one of the most important things in my life, Mr. Beaumont. But tell me more about those poor martyrs.”

"Well, one of those missionaries was killed for blessing a child with the Sign of the Cross, and two others were also martyred after being blamed by the Indians for a bad harvest."

"Oh, I couldn't have imagined such atrocities happening in this beautiful country—it looks so peaceful! By the way, may I ask how you know all this history?"

"Well, I travel a lot on business and picked up a lot of information along the way. Yes, ma'am, I've been movin' back and forth on this Canal for many a year." After a long pause, he continued, "Oh, by the way, while we're talking about the Indians, you might be interested to know there was a young Indian girl who lived here—actually, she was around your age, Bridget—who was the first Native American to be converted to the Catholic faith. After her baptism, she was ridiculed and scorned, and her life was threatened by the tribesmen."

"Do you know her name?" Bridget asked. "Do you know what happened to her?"

"Her name was Kateri Tekawitha. It means 'she who bumps into things.' You see, because of smallpox at an early age, she was left not only with a scarred face but also with poor vision. I heard she eventually escaped to a settlement of Christian Indians in Canada and took a vow of virginity, asking the Blessed Mother to accept her as her daughter."

"Wow!" Bridget exclaimed. "She will probably be made a saint one day!"

"Come, my dear, let's go below and join Odette for something to drink."

"Well, thank you, Claude, but I really should join Maria and help her with the evening meal."

The nights were lonely for the newlyweds, having to sleep apart from each other, but there was no other choice. Captain Finley, being aware of the situation, approached Tom in the stern. "Why don't you and Bridget go for a walk along the towpath? I'll take over the tiller for a while, and you two can have a little private time together."

"Oh, that's mighty kind of you, Captain."

"But don't go walkin' too fast, I don't want you to get too far ahead of us," Finley laughed. "This old vessel only goes four miles an hour, ya know. It'll take a few more days to reach Buffalo, considering those mules aren't in any hurry to get to their destination."

Tom smiled. "We'll go *real* slow, Captain!"

"Seriously, though, when you get tired, you can jump back on the boat at our next landing or from the next bridge we come to. Go ahead now, Tom. You youngsters have a nice stroll and enjoy Mother Nature." The Captain then took the tiller and guided the boat close enough to the side of the canal so Bridget and Tom could jump ashore.

For a while, the two young lovers walked the towpath slowly, following the two mules, the young lad walking behind intermittently snapping the reins. Bridget waved to the other lad who was riding one of the animals. Occasionally the boys would switch places. Tom picked up a long blade of grass and chewed on it, as they strolled along talking about their future. After some time, absorbed in their conversation, they noticed they had fallen quite a ways behind the boat when suddenly a cloudburst forced them to look for shelter. Tom threw his jacket over Bridget's head as they ran toward an old weather-beaten barn.

"We'll sit for a while 'til the rain lets up," Tom offered, spreading the jacket over the hay. He put his arm around Bridget's shoulder and kissed her softly. "It's hard being newlyweds when you *can't* be newlyweds!" he remarked, grinning.

"I know, honey. But remember, we have our whole life ahead of us."

"Yes, we do have our whole life ahead of us," Tom repeated, adding, "beginning *now*!" Embracing, they experienced the culmination of pure love which only a new husband and wife could know.

After a while, the sun came back out and they emerged from the barn, only to realize the boat was completely out of sight. After running for quite some time, they finally caught sight of it; and the passengers, sighting *them*, began clapping and cheering. Continuing to run, they paced themselves at a slightly slower jog, laughing as they did, and soon approached a low bridge where they were able to lower themselves onto the roof of the boat.

"I was getting concerned about you two when that rain started. Glad to see you back—thought we lost ya for a while there," the Captain remarked.

"We're okay. We found some shelter but got a little behind ya!" Tom replied. "I'll take over the tiller now, Captain. Thanks so much."

"Oh, no ... no—you two go and get some dinner. You must be starving after that long marathon!" Finley quipped. "I can hold the fort for a little longer."

The next few days they passed by a few small towns and villages, enjoying the outdoors and seeing the new surroundings at every turn of the Canal. Tom was at the helm most of the day and could only take a break when docking for passengers departing or boarding. As they moved on, Bridget took her free moments from helping Maria to be with Tom. "You know, Tom, I can't get over the many kinds of trees around here! There's such a variety—I don't remember so many back in the old country."

"Well, I know a few over here, especially the maples. There's plenty of them ... and pine trees, also."

"I've seen some of my favorite ones in some of the places we've passed."

"What's your favorite?" Tom asked.

"The hickory tree," she promptly answered.

"They say hickory is about the hardest wood there is, honey. They make ax handles and wagon wheels from it."

"Well, I like the hickory because it seems to last such a long time. At least, that's what I heard from Molly. To me, it's like a strong silent sentinel standing over its domain—and it bears nuts besides! You know, Tom, when I was staying at Molly's, she had a hickory tree in the backyard. I loved to watch the squirrels scampering up that tree to get the nuts. Sometimes they would just sit up on the branches where you couldn't always see them. But you could see the shell fragments falling as they chewed the nuts open."

"You were lucky to find a tree like that in the middle of New York City, honey."

Where there were curves in the Canal and two boats approached from opposite directions, one would usually wait for the other to go first. The protocol was that the packet boats containing passengers had the right of way over the cargo boats. There were many times when Tom had to pull hard on the tiller to prevent collision, but so far he had managed very well.

Tom and Bridget enjoyed their passage through the Canal but for the lonely nights when they were separated, and this made them look forward even more to the time when they would finally reach their destination and make their home in Buffalo. "Do you think we will ever *own* our own home?" Bridget asked Tom.

"Oh, yes! In fact, when I was in Buffalo the last time, I met Father Lanigan at St. Bridget's Church; and he told me about a house near the grain mills that may be coming up for rent or maybe even for sale."

"Oh, Thomas! That sounds great! But ... we don't have enough saved for that big an expense!"

"Well, maybe we could rent it at first, and then we'll see what happens. Maybe it might be for sale at a later time. Don't worry—we'll be fine."

"Yes, and I might be able to find work in some clothing shop or dressmakers ... or even do some seamstress work at home."

"Oh, honey, we'll get by. You wait and see!"

As the boat was approaching the last leg of the trip, they rounded a sharp bend in the Canal just as a cargo ship loaded with lumber appeared from the opposite direction. It was a tight squeeze, and Tom threw his full weight against the tiller to steer clear of the barge, just missing it by inches. In doing so, he sprained his wrist. He managed to use his other hand and all his body weight to get to the next stop in a little town called Gasport. The pain grew worse and he thought he might need a doctor. The Captain thought it best for Tom to stay in town and get medical assistance, offering to take over the tiller for the short distance remaining to Lockport. They made their goodbyes, the Captain giving Tom his full payment for his work up to that point. "Can you manage one of these, Bridget?" he asked, holding out one suitcase, as Tom picked up the other with his good arm.

He then steered the boat up to the dock, and a young blonde-haired boy caught the tow line, securing it to the moorings. As Tom and Bridget stepped onto the dock, the boy smiled and greeted them. "Welcome to Gasport. My name is Christian Murphy."

"Well, hello Christian Murphy! I'm Tom Sexton and this is my wife, Bridget."

"Do you work here every day, young man?" Bridget asked.

Tipping his cap, Christian answered, "No, Ma'am. Just on weekends—during the week I go to school. I really like working here and feeding the mules. Sometimes I do odd jobs, too. My dad says I should work and save money."

"Your dad sounds like a wise man, Christian," Tom responded. "He should be very proud of you."

Christian looked down at the ground, seeming a bit shy. "I guess so."

"Well, Christian, I wonder if you know if there's a doctor around here. You see, I sprained my wrist and it seems to be swelling quite a bit."

"Oh, yes, Doc Stephan—he's right up the road here," he said, pointing. "You can't miss it. He's got a sign with his name right in front of his house."

"Thanks, son. You've been a big help."

Dr. Stephan, a tall, brawny, fortyish, congenial-looking man with a thick crop of black hair greeted Tom and Bridget. "Hello, folks. Can I help you?"

"Yes, we just arrived on the packet boat. I'm Tom Sexton and this is my wife, Bridget. We just got married last week in New York City and we were on our way to Buffalo when I hurt my wrist."

"So I see—pretty swollen. Come in! Come in! I'm Doctor Stephan." He ushered Tom and Bridget into a room in the back of his home which was used as his office/treatment room.

"Nasty sprain there, Tom!" He bandaged Tom's wrist tightly and put his arm in a sling around his neck, giving him instructions to keep it there until the swelling went down.

"How much do I owe you, Doctor?" Tom inquired, as he reached into his pocket.

"No, no, my boy! Put your money away! Since you two were just married, please consider my services as a wedding present."

"Oh, thank you!" Tom replied, reaching out with his good hand to shake the Doctor's.

As they turned to leave, Bridget stopped momentarily. "Oh, Doctor, would you know of a boarding house anywhere around here. We need a place to stay tonight."

"Well, yes, but ..." He hesitated, removing his wire-framed spectacles. "Well, actually, there is a place near the Canal, but I wouldn't recommend it, as there are many unseemly characters around there."

"Well, thanks anyway," Bridget said, starting for the door.

"Hold it! I just thought of a place!" the doctor said.

"Oh, good! Is it far from here?" Tom asked.

"No, it's not very far. But, I'm not sure if they still put people up. Anyway, you could give it a try. They're good people."

"Gee, thanks, Doctor."

"The name is Murphy—just up the road about a ten minute walk. You'll see a big red barn—you can't miss it. It says 'Chew Mail Pouch Tobacco' on the side."

"Did you say Murphy was the name, Doc?" Tom asked.

"Why yes—do you know them?"

"Well, no, but we just met a boy named Murphy down by the Canal."

"Oh, young Christian! Yes, he's their son. Wonderful boy! Always helping people."

"Yes, he seemed very polite, too," Bridget added.

"Thanks again, Doc," Tom repeated.

"Now remember, Tom, if there are any other problems with that wrist, be sure to come back. Otherwise, you can probably remove the bandage when the swelling goes down, like I said."

Bridget grasped Tom's good hand as they walked up the dirt road. "Don't you just love the country, Tom?" as she took a deep breath of the fresh air.

"Oh, yes!" Tom replied. "I never really lived in the country. All I ever knew was the crowded city with its congestion, thieves and beggars, and those awful slums permeated with foul smells from the garbage—and those rats!"

"Well, I hope it's better in Buffalo, Tom."

"Yes, it is. And I hear they have areas outside the city with sprawling acres of farmland. Maybe after we get settled down, we could even move out there."

A large golden retriever came tramping down the path leading to the farmhouse. He excitedly began to jump up on Tom, his tail rapidly wagging. "Down, boy—down!" He gently pushed the dog away, protecting his bad arm.

"Gee! What a friendly dog!" Bridget remarked.

"I hope his owners are just as friendly!" Tom said.

After knocking on the door, a middle-aged woman answered. "Hello," she greeted them, wiping her hands on her apron.

"Are you Mrs. Murphy?" Bridget asked.

"Why, yes. Yes, I am."

"Doctor Stephan said you might possibly have a room we could let for the night. You see, Tom here, my husband, sprained his wrist real bad. He's a steersman on the packet boat, and we had to leave to find a doctor."

"Oh, I'm sorry, but we haven't rented out rooms for quite a while now."

"We wouldn't be any trouble. And we could pay you. You see, we were just married in New York City last week and are traveling to Buffalo. We don't know anyone in these parts and ..."

Mrs. Murphy interrupted. "Oh, you're newlyweds?"

"Yes, Ma'am. It would only be for one night."

Just then, the woman's husband came out of the barn and approached the house. "Oh, Christopher!" Mrs. Murphy called. "These people ..." She hesitated. "Oh, excuse me ... I didn't get your name."

"Oh, I'm sorry," Tom replied. "I'm Tom Sexton and this is my wife, Bridget."

"Christopher, these people are newlyweds and they need a room for the night," Mrs. Murphy continued.

Mr. Murphy hesitated and looked as if he was deciding what to say. Then, folding his arms across his chest, he asked, "Do you think we could make room for them, honey?"

"Well, you know," she replied, "we don't have any spare rooms—the four kids and all. Except ..." She didn't want to turn them away. "Christopher, do you think we could fix up the bunk room in the barn for them?"

"Well, yes, I guess they could stay there."

"Oh, that would be wonderful!" Bridget exclaimed.

"We would really appreciate that," Tom added.

"Well, then, it's settled. And you folks are welcome to have dinner with us tonight," Mrs. Murphy invited.

"Oh, you're so kind! We would love to. Thank you so much!" Bridget breathed a sigh of relief, making a mental note to be sure to thank Dr. Stephan before they leave Gasport.

Mr. Murphy glanced over at his wife. "I'll get Michael and Shawn to get some fresh linen and blankets. Mary—could you make sure Kate dusts things off a little." Looking at the newlyweds, he added, "It's been a while since anyone occupied that room."

"Oh, I'm sure it will be just fine, thank you," Bridget remarked.

After getting settled in the bunk room and taking an hour of rest, they made their way back to the house. It was plain inside, the wallpaper was old, and the furniture was well worn. A crucifix was on the wall leading into the dining room, where a statue of the Blessed Virgin stood on the buffet, flanked by two candles. As they all began taking their places at the dining room table, Christian came bounding in the back door. "This is Christian—our youngest—who is about to go in the kitchen and wash up!" Mrs. Murphy quipped, staring at the boy, who apparently got the message, turning quickly from the room.

"Oh, we met him down at the Canal, Mrs. Murphy. He was the one who told us where to find Dr. Stephan," Bridget said.

"Oh, please call me Mary."

"Oh, thank you, Mary. I will."

"And Christopher," Mary added, nodding to her husband. "And these are our other children," pointing across the table—"Shawn, Katy, and Michael." The children smiled.

"It's a real pleasure to meet all of you," Bridget said.

"Same here," Shawn answered, pushing a lock of hair from his eyes and reaching over the table for the mashed potatoes.

"Uh, uh!" scolded his mother. "You will wait, Shawn, until we say grace."

"But I'm real hungry, Mom!"

"Well, here comes Christian now. Father, will you say grace?"

They all bowed their heads, as Mr. Murphy began: "We thank you, Lord, for this good food, for our abundant harvest this year and for our good health, and pray for your continued blessings upon our family and our new friends, Bridget and Tom. Please make this food healthy to our minds and bodies. In Jesus' name. Amen."

"*Now* can I have them mashed potatoes?" Shawn asked impatiently.

"Remember, Shawn—patience is a virtue!" his father advised, smiling. He picked up the platter of roast beef, handed it to Mary, and reached for the potatoes. "The broccoli, squash, and potatoes are all from our garden, Tom."

Katy smiled at Tom. "Ma tells me you're from the big city—New York!" she exclaimed, twisting her braid around her finger as she spoke. "That must be an exciting place!"

"Well, young lady, it may be exciting when you have money, but there are a lot of people there who don't have enough to eat."

"Really?" Katy looked astounded.

"Well, Tom and I are both from Ireland," Bridget added, "but he's right. We've seen starving children right here in New York. And when I see all this food your family grows ... well, I just think it's wonderful!"

"Oh, you're from Ireland?" Mary asked.

"Yes. Tom's been here a bit longer than I, but ... Well, we wanted to make a new life in a better place. New York is no place to raise a family." She turned to Christian, sitting on her left. "Broccoli, Christian?"

"No, thanks."

"Christian, you take a little of that broccoli," his mother commanded. He hesitantly dug his fork into one piece and placed it to the side of his plate, eventually covering it with the mashed potatoes until the coast was clear to slip it under the table to the dog.

Bridget, watching this supposedly hidden deed, had a hard time hiding her laughter, seeing the dog's face appear on Christian's lap once again, waiting for another morsel to be delivered. She was enjoying the meal immensely—especially with the very evident wholesome atmosphere of this family, something that she herself, had never experienced since childhood.

At last the newlyweds had some privacy. It wasn't much—just a small room previously used as a bunk house for migrant workers at harvest time. But Katy had done a great job cleaning and the boys had left the clean sheets and blankets for them—a welcome sight! A kerosene lantern hung on the wall and a soft, late summer breeze floated through the room—and they were oblivious to the world outside for a moment in time.

A rooster crowing at sunup startled them, waking them earlier than planned. Mary Murphy had prepared a large breakfast of bacon, eggs, and muffins with homemade jam topped off with fresh coffee. "Oh, Mary, these muffins are absolutely delicious!" Bridget remarked.

"Oh, thanks. I think they're the best, too, and I make them quite often."

"Do you think I could have the recipe?"

"Why, yes, of course. I'll be glad to write it down for you."

"Yeah, Mary, why don't you share some of your other recipes with Bridget while I show Tom around the farm—" Chris offered, "that is, if the newlyweds don't mind being separated for a little while!" He chuckled.

"Oh, that would be fine," Bridget said, shyly glancing down at the floor. "I could use some advice on cooking. I guess I never had time to learn. I've been too busy with my work as a seamstress."

Christopher jumped into the wagon. "Come on, Tom! Hop in, young man. I'll show you around," as he lit up his pipe and snapped the reins.

"How big is your farm, Chris?"

"Well, we have ten acres on this side of the Canal and eight more on the other side." As they rode along, Chris pointed out the vast corn and wheat fields, two acres of alfalfa and a few acres of soybeans.

"Wow! This is quite a spread, Chris!"

"That's not all—there's more." He snapped the reins once again, and the horse began to trot, crossing the bridge over the Canal. "Now, over here, we have some vineyards— great for making wine!"

"How do you keep all of this up?"

"I'll tell ya, Tom—it takes the whole family to make it work."

"Your harvest must be so plentiful!"

"Oh, yes. We sometimes have to hire some migrant workers, especially if we have an exceptionally good crop."

"Do you sell to people around here?"

"No, actually we sell mostly to the markets in Buffalo and Lockport. This Canal is a blessing—we can ship our crops to points east and west of here for a very nominal fee."

When they returned to the barn, young Christian was brushing down their brown horse, a small colt standing in a corner stall. Michael and Shawn were busy tossing hay up into the loft for winter storage. "Nice looking animals you have here, Chris."

"Thanks. We have a stallion out back, too. And I do occasionally take in horses that some farmers might be going to put down."

"You mean ..."

"Yes, Tom. You see, I can sometimes nurse them back to good health. I kind of like the critters—you know, when you have them for a while, they become like part of the family. Sometimes all it takes is some rest and a good diet. You see, some people just work 'em to death—and then they wonder why they get sick!"

"Really?"

"Yes." Chris suddenly smiled. "In fact, some people in these whereabouts have begun calling me 'the horse doctor!' And I don't mind telling you, I've saved quite a few of them. In fact, I'm headin' up to Niagara Falls on Tuesday to pick up another one."

"Oh! Niagara Falls! About how far is that from here, Chris?"

"Well," Chris responded, as he relit his pipe, "I can make it in under three hours if I can get Betsy here to go at a trot part of the way."

As they pulled up to the farm house, they were greeted with the dog's usual excitement as he ran toward them. "Come on, Moof! Come on, boy!" Chris shouted.

"What did you call him?" Tom asked.

"Moof."

"Oh! That's what I thought you said."

"Yeah. I know. Everyone wonders what kind of a name *that* is!"

"Yeah, I didn't want to say anything, but ... well ... it certainly is kind of an *unusual* name!" Tom stated.

"Well, when he was a puppy, we called him Murph. You know—short for Murphy—" Chris smiled, then added, "because he is part of the family. Then my Dad, who's a little hard of hearing, thought we said 'Moof' and ... well, then all the kids thought it was so funny, they all started calling him that, too. And before you knew it, the name just stuck."

Chris pulled the wagon up to the side of the barn. "Would you like a glass of our homemade wine, Tom? You thirsty? Come on, we'll have a drink together." He took him into a small room which had been built on the side of the barn. "Here's our press. We make the wine for our own personal use mostly. First, we press the grapes in that contraption and let the juice ferment. Then after it reaches a desired stage, we draw it off into these casks until it's suitable for drinking. The secret is in how long you let it ferment. We like making dry wine by allowing most of the sugar to turn into alcohol."

"Excellent!" Tom remarked, after sipping the sample Chris had poured from one of the bottles.

"Let's take the rest of the bottle up to the house, Tom." They took a seat on the front porch overlooking the vast farmland. Just then, Bridget and Mary opened the screen door and came out to join them. "Oh, hi, honey. Why don't you two get some glasses and join us for a drink," Chris invited.

"You have other family around here, Chris?" Tom asked, as the girls returned with their glasses.

"Oh, yes. We have grandparents, cousins, uncles and aunts spread all around the area in nearby towns and villages."

Bridget, concealing her sadness in never knowing any of her relatives, realized for a brief moment the emptiness that only an orphan can feel. She gazed out at the beautiful corn and wheat growing in the warm sunshine. It was like a different world to her. "You know, folks," she said, "you are blessed with all of this. I mean, in Ireland we had a terrible famine, and folks starved to death. I never knew my parents—they were part of those starving masses. I only survived because some good people took me in and raised me in an orphanage. Otherwise, I would probably be under the sod, right next to my parents back in the old country right now."

"Oh, dear!" Mary exclaimed. "I'm so sorry! You poor thing."

"Oh, but," Bridget continued, "I'm so happy now— with Tom." She looked lovingly at him. "*He* is my family now, and, God willing, we will be blessed with little ones." Before anyone could respond, she continued. "I would really like to hear more about your family. I mean, did you always live here or are you from someplace else?"

Chris responded, "We've always lived here in Gasport, as have our folks before us." He paused for a moment, then went on to say, "Except for a few years when I was in the Army."

Tom then asked, "Were you in the Civil War, Chris?"

"Yes ... yes, I was."

"Did you see combat?"

Chris looked out over the corn fields. "You see that field of corn out there?"

Tom responded, "Yes," with a puzzled look. "Yes."

"There isn't a day goes by that I don't look out there at that field that I don't see my fallen comrades lying on cornstalks turned red with blood and the enemy muzzle fire exploding in my direction just yards away."

There was silence on the porch and a slow drizzle of rain began to fall. No one spoke for a brief moment. "Oh, that's horrible! You poor man!" Bridget exclaimed.

"Well, I left many of my buddies there. But we finally drove old Robert E. Lee off that field."

Tom spoke, almost apologetically. "Where was that battle, Chris?"

"It's called Antietam—in Maryland." Chris rolled his pant leg up to expose a large scar on the calf of his right leg. "This here is a souvenir from one of them Rebs in the battle." It was obvious to the others that this was an extremely difficult subject for Chris, who seemed almost as though he was starting to relive that time. "You know, through it all, I could not help but notice a little white church just yards away, and this thought came to me that people would go there on a peaceful Sunday afternoon and pray to Jesus, the Prince of *Peace.*"

"Were you in any other battles, Chris?" Bridget inquired.

"Oh, yes! I was with the 69th at Gettysburg, the Wilderness, Spotsylvania, Chancellorsville, and Cold Harbor. Right up to Lee's surrender at Appomattox. What a glorious day *that* was!"

"It's amazing you survived! Through all that!" Tom exclaimed.

"I did pray a lot—and I *do* thank the good Lord!"

"How old were you when you joined the Army, Chris?" Tom asked.

"Sixteen—I lied about my age! Well, sort of a lie. I mean ... I wrote the number "18" on a piece of paper and put it in my shoe. So when the recruiting sergeant asked me if I was over 18, I really wasn't lying when I said 'yes'!" Everyone laughed and the conversation lightened up, as Chris refilled everyone's glass with his homemade wine.

"Well, I must say, Chris, you were a brave lad to go through that terrible war." Tom raised his glass. "Let's drink a toast to Chris."

"And to all those young men who gave their lives, that others might be free," Chris added.

Mary changed the subject. I've never been to a big city like New York. What's it like living there?"

"Well, there are some sections of the city that have huge mansions where the wealthy live," Bridget responded. "But like I said before, some people are bad off. There are some really poor people living in shanties—most of them are immigrants. In any regard, we just felt we wouldn't want to raise a family there."

Tom spoke up. "Well, I see lots of good things in *our* future—in Buffalo. I know people there who have made a decent living and have bettered themselves."

"I'm glad for you both," Chris said. "I'm sure you'll find Buffalo a thriving city. I've heard there's many jobs to be had there."

"Well, yes. I've got a job all lined up already at the grain mills. And after we get established—I mean in a few years—we may buy a farm! Not as big as yours, but I want to have a place with some land—land we can call our own. You know, the working class, including our people, were never allowed to own land in Ireland. They were at the mercy of the landlords who controlled every inch of that Old Sod—it was a sorry time."

"You know, that's one good thing about this country," Chris said, "Everyone has the same opportunity. If they work hard, they can buy land—and there's plenty for the taking."

As the rain let up, the sun broke through the clouds. They had chatted for a good part of the afternoon. Tom looked over at Bridget. "Well, dear, I think we'd better get moving. We have a ways to go yet." Looking over at Chris, he asked, "I wanted to ask you about the train. I noticed the station back in town and wondered if you knew the schedule? When the next train would leave for Buffalo?"

"Oh, you folks can't start out now! It's getting late, and besides, the last train would have left already," Mary cautioned. "Why don't you stay here another night?"

"Well ..." Bridget began.

"Tomorrow's Sunday and we'll be up early for Mass. Maybe you'd like to join us."

"Oh, thanks, Mary. I almost forgot tomorrow's Sunday. But how did you know we were Catholic?"

"Your Miraculous Medal."

"Oh yes—we both wear Our Lady's medal." Bridget smiled over at Tom.

"You folks are so good to let us stay another night," Tom said. "We would love to attend Mass with you."

"Then that's settled," Mary said, rising from her chair. "Is anybody hungry? How about a little dinner?"

"Well, if you *insist*." Tom quipped. They all laughed.

As they sat around the table, Tom turned to Chris. "I'm beholden to ya, Chris. How much do we owe you?"

"Oh, don't worry about it. We'll talk after supper."

They had just finished saying grace when Katy turned to Bridget. "Can you tell me more about New York City, Bridget? We never get to see other places."

"Katy, why don't you mind your manners—let these folks eat in peace," Shawn reprimanded his sister.

Michael rolled his eyes at Shawn, as if he thought Shawn had spoken out of turn. Christian just sat there enjoying the freshly picked corn on the cob rolled in butter. And Moof sat patiently at the foot of his master, Chris, waiting for some scraps to fall his way.

"Well, young lady," Bridget answered Katy, "I wouldn't discourage anyone from going there. They do have theatres, electric trolleys, the Statue of Liberty, big stores for shopping *and* ... amusement parks!" She paused for a moment. "But two things you'll need if you ever go there."

"What's that—what two things?" Katy asked, eagerly awaiting Bridget's answer.

"Money ... and a chaperone to watch over you. And above all, you must never go into such places as the Bowery."

"What's the Bow ... Bow ...?"

"Bowery, Kate. It's a bad place. If you ever go into it, you may never come out!"

"Oh! Oh, that's terrible!" Katy remarked, still uncertain of what the Bowery actually was. The adults grinned, trying to muffle their laughter, as Bridget's last remarks seemed to take the wind out of Kate's sails.

Mary, waiting to change the subject, looked across the table. "Oh, Tom, I *did* give Bridget some of my best recipes yesterday—so you can look forward to some really good meals when you get settled in Buffalo!"

"Sounds good to me!" Tom said. "Thanks, Mary!" He smiled over at Bridget.

The children began to leave the table. "Hold on a minute!" Chris reprimanded. "I didn't hear anyone ask to be excused."

"Can we be excused, Pa?" Christian asked, trying to please his father.

"Yes, you can all get started on cleanup."

"My turn to dry!" Shawn stated emphatically.

"Hey—you dried yesterday! Remember?" Michael quickly announced.

"I did not!"

"Yes, you did, Shawn. I remember," Katy added. "It's Michael's turn today."

Shawn quickly turned and pulled Katy's pigtail. "Mom! Did you see that? He pulled my hair again!"

"That will be enough out of all of you. I'm ashamed of you, arguing in front of our guests," Mary scolded. "Now I will hear no more of this! Just get started and not another word out of you!"

After the table had been cleared and things quieted down, Tom took the opportunity to talk to Chris and Mary. "I just don't know how I can ever thank you, Chris—putting us up and meals and all. But we don't want to put you out any longer. And I really want to pay you for our stay here."

"I'm glad you brought that up, Tom," Chris answered, remembering that Tom had asked about Niagara Falls. "Were you and Bridget planning to go to the Falls before going to Buffalo?"

"Why, yes, we thought we might, maybe for a couple of days. You know, we won't have a very long honeymoon. I'm anxious to get to Buffalo to secure my job there."

"Well, Tom, Mary and I have been talking, and we thought that, if it's okay with you and Bridget and you could stay 'til Tuesday morning, I could take you to the Falls. I'm going there anyway."

"Oh, that would be wonderful!" Tom exclaimed. "But we still want to pay you."

"We talked about that, too," Chris said, "and if it would be okay with you folks, we could use a couple extra hands to help finish picking the corn crop—not too much left to do. But we have to get it done, hopefully on Monday. It would be a great help to us; and if you two wouldn't mind giving a hand ... well ... we thought we'd just call it even."

"Of *course*," Tom replied, pleased at this turn of events. "We'll be glad to help out any way that we can. You folks have been more than generous."

"Then that's settled," Chris said. "Now we have to be up early for Mass. Let's get some rest."

Tom and Bridget returned to their little room in the barn and retired for the evening. They valued this fleeting privacy on this "traveling honeymoon," as Tom jokingly called it. "You know, honey," Bridget said, "I couldn't be happier if we had a palace to live in.

Just being with you, my husband, makes me happier and more contented than all the riches in the world." They lay on their backs, holding hands and listening to the symphonic rhythm of the crickets interspersed with an occasional hooting of a night owl. Slivers of moonglow penetrated through the small cracks in the old barn wall, lending a tranquil atmosphere to the room.

"I love you, baby." Tom embraced his new wife and they eventually fell asleep. And all was well with these young lovers, as they would face the future together and forge on to their new home with the exuberance reserved only for the young at heart.

The sun burst upon the green fields, as the newlyweds emerged from the barn. Moof was chasing a rodent into the corn fields, barking as he ran. After another hearty breakfast, Chris' family and Tom and Bridget piled into the wagon and Chris snapped the reins, heading for St. John the Baptist Church in nearby Lockport. It was a very hot day and many of the parishioners were fanning themselves, even though the windows of the church were wide open.

After Mass, Chris asked what everyone thought of Fr. Darcy's sermon. "I liked the part about the vines!" Shawn offered.

"Oh, you mean about Jesus saying He was the vine and we are the branches?" Bridget asked.

"Yes—that's a neat way to put it. I know what He means," Shawn answered.

"Well, you know, folks," Tom said, "I don't think I ever saw vines or branches—I mean vineyards. I grew up in the city." He looked out over the golden wheat fields. "This open farmland really grows on you."

Then Mary chimed in. "I think the Bible has many references to plant life. Back in our Lord's day, most people grew their own food and people could relate to Jesus' parables."

Kate seemed in a quandary, as she asked, "But I don't get the part about the dead branches, you know? Did Father say they would be thrown into a fire and burned?"

"Katy," Michael answered, "I think it means that if you don't follow Jesus, you won't be saved—something like that."

Christian was known to be wise beyond his years. Speaking in a soft voice, he said, "Don't worry, Kate, just follow the Ten Commandments and be good and you won't *be* a dead branch. It's that simple!"

Tom and Bridget looked very surprised and seemed impressed at Christian's simplistic explanation. "I think your youngest would make a good priest!" Bridget whispered to Mary, smiling.

There were a few spots on the rutted road that jostled everyone, but they didn't have far to travel back to Murphy's farm. Chris pulled the horses up to the barn, as Moof came running to greet them, quickly jumping up onto Chris, then momentarily to Mary, and then to each of the children, moving excitedly from one to another, not knowing who to greet first!

"Christian, go get General Lee from the barn and bring him out—he needs some exercise!" Chris requested.

"General Lee?" Tom asked.

"Yes," said Chris. "We named him that because of his gray color." Christian did as his father asked, leading General Lee out into a small corral, as he affectionately petted him down the side of his neck.

"He looks a little frail," Tom said.

"He is, Tom," Chris responded. "Got him a short time ago from another farmer down the road. He was movin' and sellin' all his stock; unfortunately, he didn't take care of his animals and there was some kind of trouble over there. Not sure what it was about. But I'll have him good as new in a few weeks. Just needs the right food and exercise." He looked over at Christian and hollered, "Get him runnin' a bit—he's been sittin' around too long."

Tom and Chris took a seat on the porch as the others retired into the house. Chris lit up his pipe and they began to share their views on everything from weather to politics. "I don't suppose you work on the Lord's Day, Chris."

"Oh, no, we rest on the Sabbath, except for necessities, of course, like feeding the animals."

Christian emerged from the barn carrying a baseball and a bat, a long piece of straw sticking out of his mouth. "Mike! Shawn! Come on out! Let's play ball!" he yelled as he approached the house.

His brothers immediately ran out. "Pa, why don't you and Tom play, too?" Michael asked.

"Well, I'm not sure, Mike." Turning to Tom, he asked, "How's the wrist coming along, Tom? Still having pain?"

"Oh, no. It's been much better lately. I forgot to mention it to you."

"Do you feel as though you could handle a ball game then?"

"Sure. I'd really like that—haven't played ball in years!" Tom answered. "But how about the girls?"

Chris hollered through the screen door. "Hey Mary! Bridget! Come on out! Bring Katy—we're gonna have a ballgame."

The boys had a makeshift diamond with bases made of burlap bags filled with dirt.

"I don't know how to play," Bridget said.

"Oh, that's okay," Michael responded. "We'll teach you." To be fair, they put Bridget on Michael's team since he was the best player, then added Tom and Shawn. That left Mary, Chris, Christian, and Katy on the other team. Mary had loaned Bridget a pair of her overalls, as she only had dresses, being a city girl. None of these "athletes" could pitch very well; but if one of them couldn't get the ball over the plate, they simply changed the pitcher.

Bridget was having a problem hitting the ball. Tom finally hollered out to her, "Just hold the bat over the plate!" She did so, and the ball struck the bat and bounced out, landing three feet in front of home plate. "Run! Run!" Tom screamed, and Bridget took off for first base, running like the wind! Mary, fumbling the ball, threw it short of the base. Bridget got a single—and was elated!

Chris, the first baseman, looked at Bridget with a grin. "You didn't have to bring the bat along with you!" he chuckled, taking it from her and tossing it back to home plate.

Later in the game, Christian got a home run, followed by Michael getting two for his team. Heavy-hitters Chris and Tom purposely swung a little easier, so as not to hit the ball "out of the park," thus making it easier for the others—still ending up, however, hitting doubles. Katy and Shawn both scored a few times, but not without a few disagreements, debating close calls as to the runner being out or safe. Both sides hollered and cheered for their team mates, and laughed when they collided at times with the catcher at home plate. At some point in the game, the score was tied, but the final score ended up being 12 to 11—however, which team scored the 12 was still being disputed after the game was over!

Bridget brushed the dirt from the borrowed overalls. "Oh, that was so much fun! What a great game!" She grabbed Tom's hand as they walked back to the barn with Chris. "What a beautiful horse, Chris!"

"Thanks."

"You know, I've never ridden on a horse. Do you think I could try?"

"Why sure! I'll get him saddled up for you."

Tom helped her straddle the horse. "Feels kind of high up here!" Bridget remarked, sounding a little nervous.

"Just sit there for a few minutes," Chris said. "You're doing fine." He handed the reins to Tom. "Wanna walk him around the corral a few times, Tom, 'til she gets used to it?"

After a while, Bridget felt more relaxed, and thought she might be able to manage on her own. Tom handed her the reins. "Okay—go ahead!" He gently tapped the horse on the hind quarters and he began to trot. "I'll be right alongside here—don't worry." A few times around the corral, and Bridget began to get a little more confidence.

"Am I doing this right, Tom? Am I supposed to be bouncing up and down like this?"

"Atta girl, Bridget! You're doing okay!" Tom replied, as she continued "bouncing" around the corral.

"Oh, that was great!" Bridget exclaimed as Tom helped her down from General Lee. "I think I could really get to like this!"

Tom's turn came next, and he galloped down the roadway. The wind in his face was exhilarating. Bridget was amazed how well he could ride, questioning him on his return several minutes later. "I don't know, honey. It just felt so natural sitting on that beauty!"

After dinner that evening, Mary began setting up jars for her canning job the next day. She was anxious to start that yearly process for storing up food for winter. Bridget helped out, offering to assist Katy with the dishes, so the boys could help Chris clean the barn. “Have you ever done canning, Bridget?” Mary asked.

“No.”

“Well, after we get through picking and shucking the corn tomorrow, I’m going to start canning the peaches. Our orchard is small, but it’s more than enough for our family—and peach pie is one of Chris’ favorites, so I try to make it often.”

“Let’s all turn in early,” Chris announced, returning from the barn. “Tomorrow is gonna be a really busy day.”

“But, Pa, I really wanted to play cards with Mike and Christian tonight.” Shawn’s voice had a whining, complaining sound to it.

He was cut off by a stern look from Chris and changed his mind quickly. “Oh, I guess we could do it another night,” he announced, pouting.

“See you all in the morning,” Tom said, as he and Bridget turned to leave for the “bridal suite.”

They all assembled at dawn on the porch, and Chris gave out assignments. “Mike, Shawn, and Katy, you begin over on the north end and start picking. Christian, you see to the animals. Get them fed quickly and then bring the wagon down to the others.” Looking over at Tom, he said, “You and Bridget come with Mary and I, and we’ll get started over by the road.

The sun bore down, and they were extremely uncomfortable, sweating profusely as they worked. Christian brought cold water from the well intermittently to both groups of workers. Around noon, they took a lunch break followed by an hour of rest.

“You folks sure have a lot of work here,” Bridget said, wiping her brow with a handkerchief.

“Yes, we sure do, but you get used to it after a while; and, thank God, this is the end of it for this year’s harvest.”

They returned to the field at midafternoon, when Chris called a halt to the work. “Okay, gang! Let’s haul it all in!”

Christian attached Old Betsy to the wagon filled with corn and led her into the crib barn where the four children took on the task of unloading a small part of the crop which would be used for the family's consumption. The rest would be going to market.

"Now comes the fun part—the shuckin'!" Chris said, beginning to remove the husks from some of the corn, and they all followed, doing the same. As time went by, they were able to increase their speed, hoping to finish early.

Mary stopped momentarily, turning to Bridget and Tom. "You know, folks, some years we invite our relatives and friends to help us—that is, when we have a lean harvest and can get along without the migrant workers. We have a shuckin' party to take away the boredom, and we also get to help one another as we go from farm to farm. Some years, we even have dancing and music—and wine and beer—if we can find a fiddler and harmonica player, that is."

Just then, Katy broke into laughter. "What's so funny?" Mike asked.

"Oh," Katy said with a snicker, "you and Julie and ..." She laughed harder. Michael got up and stormed out of the barn.

"What's wrong with Michael?" Bridget asked.

"Oh," Mary answered, "you see, there's a little custom we have at these shuckin' parties. On occasion we find a few ears of red corn, so we make two big piles—one for our own family and one for a neighboring family helping us. And on the bottom of each pile we hide the red corn, and whoever gets to the bottom first and grabs it—and we always let the young boys do so—gets to kiss the girl of their choice from the other family."

"Oh, that's a cute custom," Bridget said, smiling. "But why did Michael seem so upset?"

"Oh, he was embarrassed because he found the red corn first last year but lost the girl."

The other children began to laugh. "Now don't make fun of your brother," Mary scolded.

Bridget thought she'd better not ask any more questions, so as not to make matters worse. Then Shawn piped up, "When he went to kiss her, she ran away and he got so embarrassed that his face turned beet-red!"

"Oh, the poor boy!" Bridget remarked, watching Michael sulking near the barn door. She raised her voice purposely. "Why, that girl should have considered herself lucky. Michael is such a handsome boy and would be a catch for any girl!" Then she quickly changed the subject. "Did you say you had family in the area?"

"Oh, yes," Mary answered. "Chris' sister and her two sons live down the road apiece."

"Oh, that's nice—having kin so close."

"Oh, yes, we're always helping one another. In fact, our nephews, Patrick and Biggie, are always willing to come over when we need any assistance—and they're ambitious, too. They both work down at the Canal unloading barges."

"I never heard that name before—Biggie," Bridget remarked.

"Well, there's a story behind that," Chris said. "You see, with *our* Michael and my sister's Michael both having the same name, it was confusing at times. So we started referring to *her* Michael as 'Big Michael' since he was taller, and then eventually it was just shortened to 'Biggie' and it stuck." Chris smiled over at Bridget, who seemed a little amused by the explanation.

Just then, Michael returned to help finish the shucking. Mary looked over at Katy and strongly recommended that she apologize to her brother.

"Apologize? For what?"

"You know very well why, young lady."

"Well, gee whiz! Well ... okay, but ..." She stopped mid-sentence, noticing the stern look coming over her father's face.

"Sorry, Michael," she quickly announced.

Mike looked down at the floor. "Well, just don't *never ever* say it again, Katy!" The girl didn't respond.

It began to rain as they were just finishing their shucking. "I think Bridget and I will start some canning," Mary announced. They all made a dash from the barn to the house, getting soaked in the process.

She put the children to work, carrying several bushels of peaches from the front porch into the house and instructing them to begin peeling while she prepared a light meal for all of them.

"I just *hate* peeling peaches," Shawn complained.

"Oh, shush, Shawn! I'm tired of listening to all your grumbling!" Katy remarked.

Mary admonished them once again, "That's enough out of you two!"

"Well, all he ever does is complain, Mom. And I'm getting sick of listening to it!"

"I said that's enough, Katy."

"Oh. Okay." The girl turned to her brother, sticking out her tongue, while her mother's back was turned. Shawn was quick to return the gesture.

After a simple meal of soup and sandwiches, the children returned to their task as Mary began to show the canning process to Bridget. "We have a couple hours before bedtime, so maybe we can at least start the first batch." Bridget watched eagerly, hoping to learn this process so as to use it herself in the future.

She worked right along with Mary. "Gee, there's more to this than I thought."

"Well, it's like anything else—you get used to it after a while. We've been doing it for years."

Chris and Tom had retired to the back porch, Chris lighting his pipe and Tom putting his legs up on a stool. "Boy! You guys really work hard around here!"

"Well, it kinda goes along with having a farm, you know, Tom." They sat quietly, watching Moof just inside the barn door chewing on something.

Sleep came quickly for all that night and after breakfast the following morning, Bridget and Tom said their goodbyes to Mary and the children. They were happy to have made such good friends. They promised to visit whenever possible after getting settled and thanked them for their wonderful hospitality. Tom loaded their two worn suitcases onto Chris' wagon and climbed up, reaching back to grab Bridget's hand. "Up ya go, Bridget-girl."

"Off we go—to Niagara Falls!" Chris announced.

"Oh, how wonderful! I can't wait to see it! Tom showed me a postcard with a picture. It looks beautiful! Have you been there before, Chris?"

" Yes, Mary and I sometimes take the children for a picnic there in the summer. By the way, do you two have a place to stay when you get to Buffalo?"

"No, we don't," Tom responded.

"That could be a problem," Chris remarked. "But I may be able to help you. I know of a priest in the Falls who has helped many in the past."

"Well, that would be wonderful!" Bridget exclaimed.

They marveled at the vast apple orchards on the route. Chris explained they had an abundance of pears, cherries, and peaches as well. "Thomas!" Bridget exclaimed, "Isn't this wonderful? Did you ever see so many fruit trees? And, oh! look over there!" as she pointed to the vast area of vineyards.

"Yes, this is truly God's country."

"Oh, Thomas! Can we buy a farm some day? I'm getting used to this great outdoors and all these farms and fresh air! I just can't believe all this—never see this in the city."

"You're right, Bridget," Chris said. "We are really blessed with rich soil here in the northeast. It's great for growing all kinds of produce."

"Oh! Look over there!" Bridget exclaimed, as they rode by a pumpkin patch.

"Well, you know, folks, you come here in a good year," Chris remarked, pausing to tap the side of the buggy with his pipe to empty the ashes. "Some years aren't as good—maybe too much rain—or maybe not enough. Or could have an early frost which can diminish the harvest. But with the right weather, we thrive. I think the good years outweigh the bad ones." He stopped momentarily to reload his pipe with a new plug of tobacco. "Okay, Betsy, get a move on!" as he snapped the reins once more. "I have to tell you though, the winters can be kinda drab. But all in all, I wouldn't give it up for anything—I like being my own boss."

"Yeah, Chris, that idea sounds really great—being your own boss!" Tom offered.

For much of the ride, Bridget and Tom shared their thoughts of the future with Chris. They turned down a dirt road that ran along the mighty Niagara River. As they traveled along, they could begin to hear the roar of the Falls. "Oh, look at that low cloud up ahead!" Bridget exclaimed.

"Oh, that's not a cloud," Chris explained. "It's the mist rising up from the Falls."

Coming closer, they could see a rainbow forming. "Oh, my! What beautiful colors! And I think that's the largest rainbow I've ever seen!" Bridget squeezed Tom's hand. "I've always loved rainbows—ever since I was a little girl."

Further downriver, just before the rapids, Chris pulled up to a church. "This is St. Mary's of the Cataract. Now you can meet Father Donohue. He's a good friend of mine."

As they approached the front door of the rectory, they heard someone shouting from the surrounding fields. "Can I help you folks?"

"Oh, there he is now," Chris announced.

A tall man in dusty-looking black clothing and a straw hat came walking toward them. "Good afternoon, folks!" the priest greeted them. "Sorry, I didn't recognize you from the fields, Chris. How are you?"

"I'm fine, Father. This is Bridget and Tom Sexton. They're here from New York City."

"Well, welcome ... welcome! I'm Father Donohue."

"Glad to meet you, Father." Tom grasped the priest's hand and shook it, Bridget nodding her head in agreement.

"Why don't we step into the house," Father invited. "I was just coming in to get a cold drink. Please join me."

"Thank you, Father," they all answered.

"Really unusually hot day for the end of September, isn't it?" Father asked. "So what brings you up this way, Chris?"

"Oh, I'm picking up another sick horse that this fella was gonna put down. I believe the poor critter's got more life in him than they think. At least, that has been my experience in the past with a few other animals that I've taken in. And this trip worked out really well, as I was able to bring Tom and Bridget along to see the Falls at the same time."

The priest brought out four glasses and they all sat down at the kitchen table. "Now what might you folks be doing here all the way from New York City?" he asked Tom.

"Well, Father, my wife Bridget and I were just married recently and are on our way to Buffalo. I've got a job lined up there."

"Well, congratulations!" the gray-haired priest said. "This calls for a little more than lemonade!" He stood up and removed a bottle of wine from the cupboard. "Come now," he continued, filling the glasses and lifting his for a toast. "Here's to you, Bridget and Tom, and may you both enjoy a happy and blessed long life together."

"Yes, God bless you both," Chris offered.

Sitting back down, the priest looked over at the newlyweds. "I can tell by your accent you're from Ireland. I've met many of your fellow countrymen here, and they tell me things are pretty bad there—since that famine."

"Yes, Father, we came to America hoping to find better conditions," Tom said.

"Well, I hope you and your lovely bride make a wonderful life for yourselves here. The Lord has really blessed this land of plenty."

"We hope to, Father," Bridget responded.

"Would you be havin' any relatives or friends to stay with?" the priest inquired.

"No, we don't," answered Tom.

Just then, a buxom, middle-aged lady came into the kitchen. "Oh, I'm sorry, I didn't know you had company, Father."

"Mrs. O'Malley, we have company from New York City—Mr. and Mrs. Thomas Sexton," the priest announced. "Tom ... Bridget, this is our housekeeper, Mrs. O'Malley."

"Pleased to meet you," Mrs. O'Malley greeted them, smiling. "I see you've found some refreshments, Father. And where's the food?"

"Well, Mrs. O'Malley," Father blurted out, "our guests have just arrived!"

She quickly responded, "Well, you both look famished. Let me get you all something to eat." Busying herself, she soon had bread, cheese, and sausage on the table.

"So you're on your way to Buffalo, you two ..." Father continued.

Tom sipped the last of the wine in his glass. "Why yes, Father. As I said, I think I will be able to get work there. I've already spoken to someone a while back and it looks promising. He told me there's a great need for grain scoopers on the docks when the boats come in from the Midwest."

"Oh, yes," Father replied. "I met a young man recently who said he was on *his* way there for the same reason you are." The priest seemed very interested in the young couple; and as they talked, Tom mentioned his early years at Father Drumgoole's Newsboys' Home and his admiration of that priest for all his good work.

"Well, Thomas, I know the man well. He and I and Father Baker from Buffalo all went to Our Lady of the Angels Seminary at Niagara University just a few miles from here."

"Wasn't he the founder of the Mount Loretto Home where we took Small ... I mean where we took Joseph, Tom?" Bridget asked. Tom nodded. "I remember we met Sister Teresita and Sister Eileen at that baseball game. They were wonderful—so caring to the boys there! Did you know *them*, Father Donohue?"

"Yes, very well. They both came to Mount Loretto from Buffalo, along with eighty other Franciscan nuns to run that home for boys. So tell me now—how and where did you two meet?"

"It was on a touring boat—the *River Queen*—she goes around Manhattan Island," Bridget explained.

"Really! Well, now doesn't that sound romantic!" the priest stated, smiling.

"Not really, Father! It took some time before I even began to grow fond of Tom."

"Aha! You're a wise young lass, you are! Too many young folks rush into marriage and regret it later." He turned to Chris. "And how is your family doing, Chris? The crops abundant this year?" Father asked.

"Oh, they're fine. And yes, we're having a great crop this year. In fact, Tom and Bridget helped with the harvest."

"Glad to hear it."

"Speaking of the family," Chris said, "I'd better skedaddle. Gotta get that new horse and be home by sundown."

"Yes, you'd better, son. And what would you be naming this one, Chris?" Father asked.

"General Grant."

"Isn't that other horse that you rescued called General Lee, Chris?"

"Yes, it is, Tom."

The priest snickered. "Well, I hope General Lee and General Grant get along, or you might have another Civil War on your hands!" They all burst out in hearty laughter.

"Thank you so much, Father, for the lunch," Chris said, standing up and stretching his arms and smiling. "We'll be back soon—Mary and the young-uns—they love to see the Falls."

"You're always welcome here, Chris," Father responded.

Looking over at Tom and Bridget, Chris said, "It's been so great meeting you, and I wish you both the best up in Buffalo. I hear it's growing by leaps and bounds!"

Tom stood up and shook Chris' hand. "Bridget and I will never be able to thank you enough, Chris, for putting us up—we really appreciate it."

"And please thank Mary for all she did—the cooking tips, too," Bridget added.

"I will. And if you two ever get up our way, please don't hesitate to come see us."

"We'll make a point of it," Tom answered, Bridget nodding in agreement. "Goodbye, my friend."

"Fine man, that Chris!" Father stated. "Now back to you two. You mentioned before, Tom, that you had no special place lined up to stay. You certainly would be more than welcome to stay here tonight. I have an extra room."

Mrs. O'Malley was walking through the kitchen with a basketful of laundry, heading for the back door. "Mrs. O'Malley, just a moment," Father said. "When you are done there, could you kindly make up the guest room for Bridget and Tom here. They'll be staying the night."

"When I'm done hanging these clothes on the line, Father."

As the hour grew late, the newlyweds retired to their room and propped up their pillows, deciding to sit up awhile and just relax and talk a little. "It's kind of warm in here, isn't it, Tom?"

"Yes, Father mentioned it was extremely warm for this time of year, remember?" Tom got up and opened a window. "Listen! Listen, Bridget! Hear that?"

"Yes, what is it?"

"The Falls, honey—the roaring of the Falls! We're really close here."

"Oh my gosh! I can't wait to see it tomorrow, Tom!"

After washing up the next morning, Mrs. O'Malley gave them a huge breakfast of bacon and eggs with toast and coffee. "Gotta give you folks a good send-off meal, so you don't get hungry for a while."

"Oh, thank you so very much. You're very kind." Bridget smiled at her.

"Now, how long did you say you two will be here in the Falls?" the priest asked as he refilled their coffee cups.

"Oh, we'll probably leave later today," Tom answered, sipping the brew. "We're anxious to get to Buffalo to find accommodations there, Father."

"Oh, I see. That's good." The priest paused, then continued. "Well, I can take you around and show you the Falls and other points of interest if you like. Today is my day off, you see."

It was a beautiful sunny day, as a cool breeze swept across the vast Niagara River. They walked on foot, the roar of the cataract growing louder with each step they took. "If you look across the River—" Father said, "that's Canada. There's a lot of history around here. I often think about the slaves who struggled to make their way to this point, trying to find a way to get across to freedom, always fearful of being caught and returned to bondage. There were a number of safe houses near here—you know—people who would help hide them. Unfortunately, some were still caught and sent back to plantations in the South."

The newlyweds listened intently. Coming from Ireland, they hadn't heard much about slavery in America. "Oh, how awful!" Bridget exclaimed.

"It must have been terrible! I've heard some things about your Civil War, Father, but what you're telling us makes it more real. I mean, being right here where the slaves crossed over." Tom glanced down at the floor, shaking his head from side to side.

"Yes, it was a terrible blot on our history—and it took six hundred thousand lives in that War to change things," the priest continued. There was a moment of silence as they all stared across the mighty Niagara to the Canadian shore. "These brave people who tried to hide the slaves in their houses or barns saved many though. They had a name for them—stationmasters. It actually was a very dangerous thing for them to do. They could face six months in prison and be fined one thousand dollars if they were caught. But their Christian beliefs were so primary, they felt they had a duty to help those unfortunate runaways—God bless 'em."

"I wonder if any of those stationmasters ever actually *got* caught," Bridget mused.

"Oh, yes, I think some of them did, my dear."

"You know, Father, *our* people were slaves also. Oh, I mean, they didn't call them that, but what else would you call a man who was beholden to a rich landlord and had to work very hard to produce enough crops to maintain that lord's wealth? And for all his toil and sweat, he was given only a meager few potatoes to feed his family." Bridget had tears in her eyes. "And when the famine hit and the potato crop failed, many souls died of starvation—by the *thousands*, Father!" Tears fell. "And my *parents* were among them! I, myself, was too young to understand. But I do remember my belly always hurt—I was always hungry and cried myself to sleep every night."

Father shook his head in bewilderment. "Oh, I'm so sorry, my dear." There was a long pause in the conversation. Then the priest pointed to the swift turbulent waters thrashing against the jutting rocks as they approached the precipice of the Falls. "These are the rapids."

The vast enormity of it all was breathtaking, and Father had to speak louder than usual, as the noise of the churning waters combined with the loud roar of the Falls grew in intensity.

"What an awesome sight!" Tom remarked, as they came upon the great avalanche of falling water.

Bridget grabbed Tom's arm. "Oh, my gosh! How beautiful! It's absolutely magnificent! *Way* bigger than I ever expected!" She laughed. "But I'm getting kinda wet, Tom!" as the spray from the cataract covered them.

"Aren't we all?" Tom laughed along with her.

"Here, let's walk down this way a little, so we won't get so soaked," Father suggested. "Now these are the American Falls and over there are the Horseshoe Falls," as he pointed to the Canadian side. "They're also known as the Canadian Falls, although one-third is actually in our country. What you see here is what Father Louis Hennepin discovered way back in the 1600's. He, along with Rene de la Salle, another explorer and missionary, were the first Europeans to lay eyes on this magnificent work of God. You see, these two men also went on to discover many parts of this new land together. It was Louis XIV, the king of France, who had given them that mission to not only explore, but hopefully to bring Christianity to any natives who might possibly occupy this new land."

After returning to St. Mary's, they enjoyed a late lunch followed by Mrs. O'Malley's freshly baked sugar cookies. "Don't mean to rush off," Father announced after the pleasant meal, "but I have to get over to the church to hear confessions. You folks make yourself at home." As he started out the door, he turned and said, "Oh, and if you need anything, just ask Mrs. O'Malley."

Bridget and Tom sat a little longer, finishing their tea, after which they decided to take a little walk around the grounds, admiring the beautiful roses and the lilac bushes. "When we get settled in Buffalo, Tom, I want flowers all around our home, especially the lilacs—they smell so sweet."

"I know, honey. I think you mentioned once before how you love lilacs. I'm gonna plant a *million* of 'em for ya, Bridget-girl!"

"Oh, you!"

"Well, tell me now—what is it about lilacs?"

"Oh, Thomas, didn't I ever tell you ..." They walked on for a few more minutes, as though she needed time to think about it. "You see, I often have this vision of a man plowing the fields with me, as a young child, on his shoulders ... and he wears a sprig of lilac in his cap."

Tom looked at her quizzically. "Well, who is he? Does he say anything?"

"Yes. He says, '*Put your hand to the plow, Bridget dear.*" She paused, then suddenly seeming to have an epiphany, she continued. "And then ... And then ..." She seemed lost in another world.

"And then? Go ahead, honey."

"And then ..."

"Bridget, you seem like you're in a dream or something."

"And then he hands me the sprig of lilac from his cap, Tom."

"Can you tell who he is, honey?"

Suddenly tears began trickling down her cheeks. "My Pa—my poor Pa!" She then burst out crying, repeating over and over, "My Pa! It's my Pa! Oh, my poor Pa! I see him now working so hard—sweating—muscles aching—and for what? Only to see his wife and children starving and crying in bed with their empty stomachs. It's all coming back to me now." She cried uncontrollably.

Tom tried to comfort her. "It's okay. It's okay, sweetheart." He led her over to sit in the shade of an apple tree, holding her tight to him until she was able to calm down. He wasn't sure of the whole meaning of the vision, but he vowed to himself never to mention it again.

Returning to the rectory, they found Mrs. O'Malley stirring something on the stove. "Could I trouble you for a cold drink for Bridget, Mrs. O'Malley?"

She handed them two glasses of water. "Well, how's the newlyweds doing? Did you enjoy... Oh, my dear! What happened? You look like you've been crying!"

Tom quickly answered. "Oh, she was just thinking about some hard times when she was younger."

"Oh, thank God! I was concerned you two might have had a fight ... so early in your marriage!"

Bridget lightened up, smiling at Mrs. O'Malley's remark. She wiped a tear from her eye. "He knows better than to fight with me!" They all laughed.

"Now sit ya down, my dears," the sweet, motherly woman requested. "I, too, used to let them old nasty memories eat away at me. But I prayed against them and gradually dismissed them. Now I'm happy in my new-found land here. It's all what ya make of it. No wicked landlord owning your very souls!" She decided to change the subject, realizing this might not be the best time to speak of unpleasant things. "Will you be stayin' for supper?"

"Well, I'm not sure," Tom answered. "We hate to impose ..."

"No imposing stuff now! I'm sure Father will be delighted to have you stay a little longer."

"Thank you so much for your hospitality," Bridget said.

Just then, Father Donohue entered the kitchen. "Oh, hello, Father—all done with the Confessions now?" Mrs. O'Malley asked. "We were just having a nice chat over a cold drink. I'll get you one."

"Thank you. We had some visitors from out of town today—a few who were away from the church for a long time. It's so good when some come back to the fold. Confession refreshes the soul—if only all would take advantage of it. It's an outward sign of repentance, and at the same time renews and strengthens the spirit—end of homily," he laughed.

Mrs. O'Malley had been listening intently and joined in the conversation, wanting to share her knowledge of scripture. "Yes, that is so. John, Chapter 20, verses 22 and 23."

"Oh, really?" Bridget asked. "We never had a Bible back home—never owned one. We were too poor."

"I'm really sorry to hear that," Father said. "Mrs. O'Malley here knows her scripture all right. She's referring to Jesus' appearance to the disciples in the Upper Room after His Resurrection where He breathed on them and said, 'Receive the Holy Spirit. For those whose sins you forgive, they are forgiven; for those whose sins you retain, they are retained.'"

"It's so great that Jesus gave the authority to forgive sins to the apostles." Tom remarked.

"Yes," Father said. And that authority has been handed down from Peter—right down to the present Pope and he, in turn, to the ordained priests."

"Oh, what a wonderful gift!" Bridget remarked.

"Yes, my dear." Father smiled. "Confession *is* truly a gift—it's a sacrament—like Baptism, Holy Communion, Matrimony, Confirmation, Holy Orders, and Extreme Unction."

"Extre ... extre ... How do you say that?" Bridget asked.

"Extreme unction," Father answered. "It's the sacrament we administer to the dying where we anoint that soul and pray for them at their last hour."

"Oh! Oh, yes."

Father smiled. "Well now! We seem to have our own theology class here!" They all chuckled.

By now Tom was getting anxious to get to their destination and start his new job, and he and Bridget decided to set out for Buffalo the next morning. Father Donohue gave them an invitation to stay longer if they wanted; however, the newlyweds graciously declined. They all sat down to Mrs. O'Malley's roast beef dinner and enjoyed her home-baked apple pie for dessert.

"I guess I won't be seeing you before you leave in the morning," Father announced. "After Mass, I have to bring Holy Communion to two of my sick parishioners, but Mrs. O'Malley will accompany you to the train station."

"Well, thank you so much, Father, for everything," Tom said.

"Yes, Father, thank you. We really appreciate it," Bridget added.

"Let me give you a blessing." Father took Bridget's hand and placed it into Tom's. Making the Sign of the Cross over them, he prayed God's blessing for a safe trip and a happy marriage.

They arose early, and after a quick breakfast of coffee and toast, set off for the train station. As they walked, the loud roar of the Falls swept across the open fields. "Oh, my gosh!" Bridget exclaimed. "I just can't get over this! It almost sounds like a hurricane."

"Oh, yes, it's loud all right. But I guess I'm used to it—hearing it every day," Mrs. O'Malley said.

"Thank you so much for everything, Mrs. O'Malley. It was so nice to meet you," Tom said. "And, by the way, your cooking was delicious!"

"God bless you both. Please come back and visit Father and me when you can."

Boarding the train with their two suitcases, containing the only possessions they could call their own, they waved goodbye as it slowly pulled away from the station. Within minutes the great wide, expansive Niagara River came into view as the tracks ran parallel to it. Seagulls were swarming around the banks searching for a meal. Pointing to the opposite shore, Tom said, "Just think, honey. Over there is Canada. Another country! Maybe we could visit there someday."

Bridget nodded her head, as she watched the dark clouds looming in the distance. "Oh, look Tom! Look over there!" she exclaimed as the river emerged up ahead into the broad expanse of Lake Erie. "Wow!"

"Yeah—that's Lake Erie! Isn't it wonderful?"

Chapter 10

The First Ward

"Buffalo! Buffalo! Last Stop! Welcome to the Queen City!" The conductor moved slowly through the aisle shouting his announcement.

After leaving the train, Tom and Bridget began to run to catch a nearby trolley, Bridget reaching up to hold her hat from blowing off as a strong wind came off the lake. Horizontal streaks of lightning flashed across the darkened sky followed by a roaring rumble of thunder.

"Come on—up you go, Bridget-girl!" Tom turned back to assist his wife up the trolley steps just in time to avoid the oncoming deluge. They sat quietly for a few minutes, hands joined together, listening to the hum of the electric trolley and the rain pelting against the windows.

"Gosh! It's really coming down, Tom! I hope we don't have to walk too far when we get off the trolley. We'll get drenched!"

"Don't worry, honey. Maybe it'll stop soon."

"But where will we go? I mean, where will we be staying, Tom?" Her growing apprehension was very apparent to her husband.

"Now you just leave *everything* up to me, little girl— everything is under control. Stop that worrying, honey!"

"But ..."

"I know *exactly* where we're going. I've been here before, remember?" He patted her on the hand. His assuredness seemed to bring a calmness to her heart until, glancing out the window, she noticed there seemed to be a saloon on almost every block they began passing. Before she could speak of this newfound concern, she noticed the rain had stopped. "Oh, good! The rain stopped. Look, Tom!"

"See? All that worry for nothing! Come on, honey. Let's go—we're here." He took her by the hand as they stepped down from the trolley, leading her to a boarding house on the next block.

"Oh, Tom! I'm not sure I like this area too much! Is this whole First Ward thing like this?"

"Oh, honey, this is just temporary. There's a better section not too far from here where we can find better housing eventually." He squeezed her hand.

They were greeted by a short and pudgy lady with a big friendly smile. "And what can I do for ya folks?"

"We'd like a room if you have any available, Ma'am."

"Well young man, you're in luck. I do have two rooms still vacant tonight—very unusual these days. Lotsa folks comin' to Buffalo for work since they put them slingers out."

Tom had saved a grubstake to cover expenses for the short duration between now and the time he could start work and receive his first paycheck. After paying the landlady, he signed the ledger book she placed before him. "Oh, Mr. and Mrs. Sexton!" She studied them momentarily. "Newlyweds, are ya?"

"Yes, we were just married a few weeks ago," Tom answered, "This is my beautiful bride, Bridget," looking over at her with a smile on his face.

"Well, God bless ya both. I hope ya have a long and wonderful life. Ya know, my name's Bridget, too. Bridget O'Leary!" She handed Tom the keys. "Room 201. Second floor—head of the stairs."

"Thank you," Tom said.

"And the toilet is down two doors from your room."

"Thank you," he said once again as he and Bridget walked toward the stairs.

"Oh, and if ya need some extra towels, just let me know. And another thing—don't forget—ya gotta knock on the bathroom door first. It's a common room, ya know."

Tom slept well that night, but Bridget was restless. She laid on her back, just staring up at the ceiling which seemed to be covered with a fine thin layer of brown film. The stale smell of smoke permeated the air, and some anxiety seemed to begin building inside her once again. She decided to open the curtain-less window, hoping it would help; and a chilly breeze, though causing her to shiver, was nonetheless a big relief. She gazed down to the street below where a thin fog was beginning to settle. Beneath the glow of a streetlight, she could see a man leaning against it. Her fears about this area were heightened as the raucous laughter and noise from the saloon on the corner grew. The man below began to walk away from his support, weaving back and forth as he disappeared into the fog. Oh, my dear Lord. I don't want to live around here. Maybe we shouldn't have moved to Buffalo. But I must trust my husband—he must know what he's doing. Surely things will work out. He did say it's only temporary.

She began to pray her rosary, asking God to help them work things out, that Tom's pay would be enough for their expenses, wherever they would settle. Hopefully they wouldn't be here too long. After all, she wanted to have children and live in a decent neighborhood. She thought that, if times became too tough, she could always find another sewing machine and make some extra money.

A ray of sunshine streaming through the grimy window awakened her the next morning. She rolled over, her arm spreading across Tom's pillow—he wasn't there. Alarmed at first, she quickly sat up, noticing a note on top of the blanket.

Honey,

I'll be back by noon. Go down and see Mrs. O'Leary. She will have breakfast for you. I had to go down to the docks 'cause they're supposed to be hiring today and I wanted to be one of the first ones there.

Your loving hubby, Tom

She had to wait to use the toilet room and was uncomfortable when a very sinister looking man with an unkempt long beard dressed in dirty clothes came out. She watched him go down the hall, then quickly entered the room and locked the door behind her. Memories of Queenston and the horrible conditions on the boat in steerage on her trip to America came rushing back. She shuddered, remembering the lack of privacy and men's prying eyes as she and other females slept in those hammock-type contraptions, similar to those on the Canal packet boat.

Coming downstairs afterward, Mrs. O'Leary greeted her. "Good morning, Mrs. Sexton, or may I call you Bridget? Remember I told you yesterday that that's my name as well?"

"Oh, yes, Mrs. O'Leary." Bridget broke out in a big grin. "Or shall I call *you* Bridget, also?"

"Yes, my dear, by all means—please do. Now tell me, how was your stay last night?"

"Oh, pretty good." Bridget didn't want to hurt the woman's feelings with any complaint. "Took me a little while to get to sleep though."

The elderly woman smiled and replied, "Well, maybe this will help you wake up a little," as she motioned her to take a seat at the table. "Fresh coffee and apple muffins—just baked 'em myself."

"Oh, thank you so much. I'm starved!"

"Well, that's not all, love. I've got a few eggs and some bacon just waitin' for someone to eat 'em!"

Bridget felt better now, as the little friendly woman made her feel right at home. They chatted and shared memories of dear old Ireland for a brief time until the bell at the counter rang. "That old bell gets on my nerves sometimes. Half the time it's one of the tenants complaining that they need more soap—and to look at 'em ... well, kinda looks like they hadn't washed in a month of Sundays! Oh, there's that darn bell *again*! Be right back."

"Oh, you're busy. I'll come back later, Mrs. O'Leary. And thank you so much for the breakfast."

"You're welcome, dear. Anything I can do for you—just ask." The bell rang again three times. "Coming ... Coming ... Hold your horses! I'm coming."

As Bridget began to leave, she remembered something she had wanted to ask the landlady, so she decided she'd wait for her return. Within a few minutes, she was back. "Oh, you're still here, dear!"

"Yes, I forgot I wanted to ask you about the housing around here. We hope to find a house to rent if we can afford it."

"Oh, that won't be hard. I can get you some information on that." She smiled, then added, "I have a lot of contacts."

"This is my first time here. Can you tell me how far the grain mills are?"

"Oh, you mean the elevators? Oh, they're not very far from here. Maybe about a twenty minute walk—well, at least in good weather."

"Well, can you find out if there are houses for rent around there?"

"Oh, I believe there might be. However, I think you may want to consider renting a flat instead—it would be a lot cheaper. But don't worry. Maybe after your hubby gets workin' for a while you can look around for something better. And, oh, by the way, speakin' of your hubby—he's a very considerate man! He asked me on his way out this morning if I would keep an eye on you and see that you are well taken care of 'til he gets back."

"Thank you, Mrs. O'Leary. You've been so kind, but I really must get back upstairs. I haven't even unpacked our suitcases yet. And I hope to do a little knitting."

"Oh! You're good with a needle and thread, are ya?"

"Well, I've been sewing for years now. I hope I can find a position where I can do it."

"Well now, young lady, I hope you can."

"Yes. I used to own my own dress shop in Ireland, you see."

"Oh, that's wonderful! But why did you give it up? I mean, wasn't it doing well?"

"Yes, for a time, but eventually the ravages of the famine affected every business—including mine."

"Oh, dear, I'm sorry. I hope you'll be able to find work over here."

"I hope so. At least until Thomas can earn enough at his new job." Departing, she thanked Mrs. O'Leary again.

After unpacking their few belongings, she opened the window and took a seat on the only chair in the room next to it. She first noticed the pungent odor of cereal coming from the new H-O Mill. The early morning fog had evaporated, exposing the gigantic grain elevators in the distance. Now she could see for herself that Tom's workplace *was* only a short walk away.

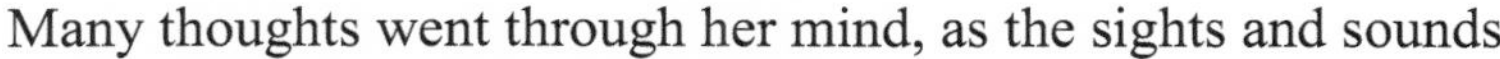

Many thoughts went through her mind, as the sights and sounds

of the neighborhood awakening outside that window became present to her—the buzz of the electric trolley, the clomping of the horses pulling their carriages, the competing cry of the newsboys—"Extra! Extra! Read all about it!" The busy scene before her eyes reminded her somewhat of New York City; however, her thoughts transferred immediately back to the quietude of the Emerald Isle, and a peace seemed to settle into her soul until the shrill whistle of a nearby train jolted her from her thoughts.

She removed her knitting supplies from the suitcase. She had been anxious to begin knitting Tom's Christmas present—a sweater. But it had to be done during his absence, as she wanted so much to surprise him. Suddenly, she felt very lonely. She began to think of the good friends she had left behind in New York—Molly-O, Grace O'Brien, Renee, Jim Flynn, Captain Skully. Tears began to well up in her eyes. Little Small Fry! Oh, little Small Fry! I do miss him so. I hope he is well. Oh, I feel like I left part of my heart back there. I wish Tom would get back soon. She couldn't keep her mind on her knitting and got up to open the window further, searching the streets below for any sign of him. The sun had broken through the clouds and the day seemed to be getting warmer and more humid. Almost like summer, she thought. She picked up the day-old newspaper she had found on the train and fanned herself, unbuttoning the top of her blouse. She decided to leave her reminiscing and think about the future with Tom. I wonder what's taking him so long—maybe he found work for today. I hope he's okay. She took her rosary beads from her pocket and prayed for his safe return. After one decade, there was a knock on the door. "Who's there?"

"It's me—Tom!"

"Oh, Thomas, what took you so long?"

"Bridget-girl, you are now looking at one *employed* husband!"

"Oh, Tom! A job? You got a job? Oh, thank God! How wonderful!" She grabbed him around the waist, giving him a big hug. He grabbed her under her arms and lifted her off the floor, spinning her around twice.

"Give your daddy a big kiss, me girl!" They laughed and kissed and sat on the edge of the bed together.

"Oh, Tom, I'm so relieved! Now we'll have a steady income."

"You had doubts? Where was your confidence that good old Thomas here could land a job?"

"Well, it wasn't exactly that. But, anyway, tell me all about it!"

"Well, ya wouldn't believe the lines down there. Must have been a few hundred guys—well, maybe *one* hundred or so. I don't know. Anyway, that's why I got down there at the crack o' dawn, honey."

"Well, what exactly will you be doing, Tom?"

"Well, I'm not really sure about that yet, but it looks like I'll probably be unloading grain from the boats. I don't have a lot of details yet."

The following Sunday after morning Mass, Tom decided to take Bridget on a little sightseeing into the downtown Buffalo area. "Come on, baby, let's go take a look at the stores down on Main Street. It's a beautiful day for a walk."

"Well, the stores would be closed though, wouldn't they, Tom?"

"Well, sure—but that's okay. We'll just look around and window-shop a little. They probably have furniture stores and clothing stores, and ... well, who knows what else? Come on, let's grab this trolley!"

They laughed and talked, walking along holding hands, peering into the storefront windows. Everything looked so new and wonderful to Bridget. They admired the rich mahogany furniture in the window of Pirson's Appliances and Furniture, the beautiful jewelry in R & L Jewelry sparkling in the afternoon sun, and the high-end men's suits in Kleinhan's.

"Let's sit down for a minute, Tom." Bridget pointed to a small metal bench a few stores away under a lamppost.

"Okay. There's a hot dog cart on the corner over there. How about I get us a couple of dogs? Hungry?"

"Actually, I am. *Really* hungry."

"Wait here! I'll be right back."

Bridget's eye was immediately drawn to a multi-colored mohair coat with a fur collar on a mannequin in the window before her—Adam, Meldrum & Anderson's. She thought she had never seen a coat so lovely—even in New York City.

"Here ya go, me girl! Just like ya like it—mustard and relish!"

She took the hot dog but said nothing. Tom noticed she suddenly seemed quiet. "What's up? Don't ya like the dog?"

"Oh, I'm sorry. Yes, it's good—very good. Thank you."

"Well, you seem quiet all of a sudden."

"Oh, I'm just thinking ..." She decided to mention the coat. "Look at that, Tom—that coat in the window. Isn't it beautiful?"

He felt bad, seeing his new bride admiring—maybe *desiring*—that coat, knowing he could not even begin to think of buying it for her. "Well, yes, it really is pretty, honey, but looks too rich for my blood. Maybe sometime in the future, when we get on our feet ..."

She felt guilty that she had mentioned it, knowing they had no money. I hope I didn't make Tom feel as though he is an inadequate provider. She was determined never to bring the subject up again. Yet, unknown to Bridget, Tom was already starting to formulate ideas about the possibility of purchasing the coat in the future by taking on any extra hours he might be able to obtain at work.

Things began to look up for the newlyweds. Shortly after Tom started his new job, he noticed a sign posted on the bulletin board at the elevators.

FLAT FOR RENT
282 ALABAMA ST.
PARTIALLY FURNISHED

It wasn't much but sufficient for their needs—and Tom could even save the carfare for the trolley, as the docks were walking distance from there.

"Oh, Tom! It's perfect, isn't it?"

"Well, sure honey. I guess it is."

"Well, I mean having two bedrooms. I can use one for my sewing if we are able to save up for a machine. Wouldn't that be great? I could help out and earn a little extra. And besides, that extra room sure would come in handy—just in case, you know—well, you know ... in case we receive a little blessing!"

"Whoa! Slow down, baby! We haven't even moved in yet!"

"And besides, Tom, look how nice and close it is to the church—only a few blocks away."

"Yeah, that's St. Bridget's. They named it after *you*!"

"Oh, you silly!" She nudged him with her elbow.

After settling in, Bridget and Tom joined the parish on Louisiana Street where she began to attend morning Mass on a daily basis. Father Lanigan soon became a good friend, and the church was the main source of their social life. Bridget joined the ladies' Altar and Rosary Society and Tom became an usher and helped out setting up tables and chairs for the weekly Euchre card games. The fall weather had remained beautifully sunny with bright blue skies, and Bridget enjoyed sitting out on the small front porch working on her knitting while Tom was at the docks. Have to get this sweater finished as soon as possible so I can move on to my sewing as soon as we can afford that machine. I hope he likes it.

The First Ward became a way of life, as they settled into a routine. Many of the residents were somehow connected with the grain industry, which was mostly under the control of a dock boss by the name of Fingy Connors. He and a few other men had a monopoly on labor, as they owned saloons and expected the workers to spend part of their pay in these establishments if they wanted work the next day. Tom decided he would stop at Fingy's saloon after work one day and have a beer. Although he had given up drinking, he knew he would fall out of favor with the boss and possibly lose his job had he not gone along with this so-called demand. By the end of the first week on the job, he had already heard so many stories from his co-workers about the extreme difficulties many of the men had suffered who had not complied. He was quite disturbed by these "strongarm tactics," but decided to remain silent so as not to create any problems at this time when he and Bridget needed money.

One day when he returned home from work, Bridget met him with her usual smile. "And how is the love of my life today?" she asked.

"Oh, I'm just fine, my fair lass," he jokingly exclaimed.

"You look cold, Tom ... Are you cold?"

"Well, just a little, honey. That fall wind coming off the lake makes it seem much colder, you know ... Kinda gives ya a chill."

She took his jacket and motioned him to sit down on their only living room chair. "I'll make some hot coffee for you, honey. Here's the newspaper if you want to look at it for a few minutes. Picked it up this morning after church.

"Now I know ya like to have the paper for me every day, dear, but we need every penny we can get, ya know. Besides I can sometimes bring one home from work when the boys are through readin' it, even if it is a day old."

"Well, I have a little surprise for you tonight—I'm going to be earning a little extra money, Tom."

He put the paper down on his lap. "What? How? Where?" he asked with a surprised look on his face.

"Well, you know, I made a new friend—she lives just down the street aways. Her name is Kathleen Masterson. She got a job at the school teaching piano to the children, so she needs a babysitter for her two little ones. So I told her I could help her out. Isn't that wonderful, Tom? Now we can have a little extra—to save."

"That's great, Bridget! We sure can use some extra money." They slept peacefully that night, knowing their financial situation was soon to improve.

Tom's sweater was finally finished and Bridget looked forward to Christmas when she could surprise him with it. In the meantime, it would be hidden in a box behind her hat box on the shelf of the closet. Her next project, in between her babysitting hours, was to start knitting some baby clothing.

One morning before work, as Tom was rummaging through the dresser drawer for his socks, he spotted two little pink baby booties in the back of the drawer. After dressing, he entered the kitchen where Bridget was already making his breakfast. "Good morning, dear." He kissed her on the cheek. "Is Mrs. Masterson having another one?"

"Another what?" Bridget asked.

"Another baby. A little one. You know—an addition to the family."

"Why do you ask?"

"Well, there seems to be some baby booties in the bottom drawer."

"Oh—that!" She looked down at the floor for a moment. Then, without warning, she grabbed him and hugged him. "It's *ours*! It's *ours*! You're going to be a father, Tom!"

"What?" He was at a loss for words. "Oh, my gosh!" He grinned from ear to ear, picking Bridget up off the floor and swinging her around twice before suddenly placing her firmly back down. "Oh, my gosh! Are you all right, honey? I didn't hurt you, did I?"

Bridget laughed. "No, silly. Don't worry. I'm fine." Tom then held her close with her head on his chest, and they simply stood silently for a moment in their embrace, reveling in that indescribable joy of new life evolving from their love.

After the initial shock that he was to be a new father, they had breakfast and sat for a while making plans. Tom seemed to be quite pensive and somewhat anxious and apprehensive to Bridget. "Gosh, we're gonna need a cradle of some kind, and some blankets—oh, and baby food ..."

"Oh, wait a minute, Tom! Hold on! We have a lot of time. I haven't even seen a doctor or anything yet. I mean ... well, I have to make doubly sure, you see? The signs do seem to be all there, but ..."

"What do you mean? What kinda signs?"

"Oh, honey—you know ... Female signs. Stuff that girls know about."

"Oh." He looked perplexed. "Well, okay, whatever you say, dear. But when will we see a doctor?"

"I think I'll just wait a little longer. Then I'll make an appointment. Don't worry. Mrs. Masterson has a good doctor she recommended to me."

Tom took Bridget's hand. He had a curious look on his face. "How do you know it's a girl? I mean ... the booties are pink!"

"I don't know. I can't explain it. I just know in my heart that it's a girl. Oh, Tom! The time! You'll be late for work."

"Oh my gosh! I didn't realize! See you tonight, honey." He quickly kissed her goodbye.

It was a tight-knit community—mostly poor, mostly Irish, and mostly Catholic. Seldom did one venture into another ethnic community and escape harassment or even violence from the locals. A neighbor, Mrs. O'Shea, told Bridget that one day an Italian vendor entered the First Ward selling vegetables. Having parked his horse and wagon in front of a house, he returned to find the horse gone. He did, however, escape without injury. On another occasion, Tom had heard of a young, attractive Irish girl who had an interested young German suitor. Entering the First Ward on his bicycle to call upon her, he found himself involved in a scuffle with a few young men. He narrowly escaped minus his straw hat, his bicycle and the flower he was carrying.

Bridget and Tom enjoyed socializing with their neighbors after Mass on Sunday mornings, on occasion coming together in the parish hall for coffee and pastries. Weddings, baptisms, and funerals were also events that were well attended by those in the area. Many of the housewives also enjoyed one another's company as they met during shopping at the Elk Street market. These casual meetups gave rise to transmission of current events occurring in the neighborhood—quicker than the telegraph! Sometimes the information was not always accurate, possibly being tainted in some ways, as the Irish seemed to have great imaginations and would often add a little color and flavor to the conversation.

Winter arrived early that year, bringing stinging winds that blew off the Lake, whistling by the huge grain elevators and throughout the Ward. Each day Thomas wore extra clothing for his job in the cold belly of the ships, scooping and shoveling tons of grain. Sometimes he thought he could imagine how Jonah felt in the belly of a whale.

After work, he continued to make an appearance at Fingy's saloon, only because it was expected. At first, he thought one beer was a small price to pay to keep his job—but he soon found out there was more to it. After the first few weeks, he noticed most of the men stayed at the saloon somewhat longer than he. Before long, he seemed to feel a little more pressure not to leave as early.

"Another beer, Tom? Sure need some down time and relaxin' after a hard day's work, Fingy always says," the bartender quipped, smiling at him. Somehow that smile seemed more like a smirk to Tom.

"No, thanks. I'd really better get going." He felt a nudge on his arm from Jimmy O'Rourke sitting on the barstool next to him. Understanding that prod, he decided he'd better comply. "Well, on second thought, I guess I'd have time for one more." He quickly drank the second beer, immediately getting up to leave before the bartender could coerce him into another. He walked home with a troubled mind.

"What's wrong, Tom? Are you okay?" Bridget knew the minute she saw his face that something was bothering him. "Tom, what is it?"

"Oh, nothing. What's for dinner? I'm famished," wanting to change the subject. He didn't want her to worry, especially now that she may be pregnant. "Just got the shivers, that's all. Got any hot coffee?"

Turning to take care of his request, she quickly forgot her question and proceeded to make coffee and finish getting dinner ready.

"You're hardly eating anything, Tom! That's not like you."

"Sorry, honey. It was just a really hard day at work today. I'm so tired. I just gotta lay down on the sofa for a little while. Maybe a nap would perk me up." He needed some time to think about the happenings at the saloon and so feigned sleep so as to avoid her questioning. Later in the evening, after Bridget readied herself for bed, she decided not to awaken Tom since he was sleeping so soundly and left him on the sofa, only to find that he had already gone to work in the morning before she was up.

Tom felt the pressure, along with the rest of the men, to continue to spend more of his pay at the saloon. He discussed his feelings with many of the men; however, there didn't seem to be any solution to the problem.

"Hey, man, we don't have much choice. Haven't ya noticed?"

"Better go along with it, Tom, or ya might be out on the streets."

"We all feel the same way, Tom ... but ya really can't do anything about it."

The following week, the scuttlebutt on the boat was that Fingy himself would be at the bar that night. Up until then, Tom had never met him personally, although he had seen him on occasion speaking to the men as a group at times. Tom took his usual seat at the bar and immediately found two glasses of beer being placed before him by the bartender. He said nothing but proceeded to drink, only to find a third glass laid before him before the second glass was even finished.

"Here ya go, man!" the bartender stated.

"Naw—that's enough for me, thanks," Tom answered.

Hearing this, Fingy immediately stepped forward. "Is there a problem here?"

"No," Tom answered, "I was just leaving."

"Why ya just got here! Have another beer!"

"Oh, thanks anyway. But I really have to go; besides, I'm a little short on cash."

"One for the road! I insist! This one's on *me*. And, Jack"—Fingy turned to the bartender—"set up a tab for my friend here. He's a little short on cash he says." Tom was beginning to feel anxious. "Now then, Mr. ... Wait a minute! Aren't you one of the new men? Sexton, isn't it?"

"Yes, sir—Tom Sexton."

"Glad ta have ya, Sexton. Welcome aboard. My name's Connors, but most people around these parts know me as Fingy. Anything ya need—just let me know. And remember, your credit is always good here—always wanna keep my men happy. Let's drink ta that."

Tom found himself lifting his glass to Fingy and trying to fake a smile. Fingy slapped him on the back and turned to leave. Muffled conversation rippled throughout the barroom. Tom stayed a few minutes until it looked like "the coast was clear," then got up to leave at the same time as Jimmy O'Rourke. "Don't believe a word of that, man! He'll turn on ya in a heartbeat. An' he's robbin' us of our hard-earned money. Besides, there's even talk he's gonna be puttin' through a pay cut."

The first few snowfalls of the season were light in that little community down by Lake Erie, This was much appreciated by the residents, as their feet were their main source of transportation. Some trolleys were nearby, but money was tight and they mostly walked whenever they could. It was a time and place when most of the folks had many things in common. They were mostly all poor laborers who lived payday to payday, their faith binding them together even more closely, often sharing joys and sorrows. If a neighbor was sick or injured in some way, it was common—almost a duty—to help out by bringing food or watching others' children. It was also a team effort to help one another with any maintenance of their homes—painting, repairs, etc. In addition, their priests became as guiding lights in a harsh and sometimes dreary environment. However, the coming Christmas holidays brought the beginning of preparations to those small wooden frame homes, inspiring much joy and excitement.

One other commonality that seemed to be pervasive throughout the Ward was the tendency of the Irish to enjoy the spirits in the bottle—"taste o' the crature"—the curse of the drink! One evening, when Tom arrived home late from work, Bridget was taken aback as he seemed a bit "tipsy." "And what have you been up to?" she asked. He threw his hat over toward the coat rack in the corner, and missed—very unusual for him. Bridget was normally a patient, loving individual with a contagious laugh and great sense of humor. However, on rare occasions, if provoked, she could get her "Irish up." And this time, Tom would feel the brunt of it! She looked sternly at him. "What's wrong with you, man? Are you spending the little money we have on liquor? Don't you know I've been doing without to make ends meet and pay the bills?"

"Well, you know, dear, I've told you my job depends on me spending my time at Fingy's saloon."

"Well, don't you think you're overdoing it?" Tom moved toward her, attempting to give her a hug. She pushed him away. "You told me you had to buy a beer at Fingy's—but you never said you had to empty the whole barrel!"

Tom sat down and put his feet up on the stool, trying to relax. Bridget seemed to regret her accusations and stooped down to remove his cold, wet shoes, still covered with a little snow. "You know I love ya, you big lug—but we really need every penny." She leaned over and kissed him on the cheek, mellowing out as fast as she had erupted.

As they lay in bed that night, they gazed out the window watching the clouds drift by the extremely bright moon, as a few remaining leaves fell silently from the large maple tree in the back yard. Tom tried to hide his anxiety from Bridget, as rumors at work began to spread that the scoopers and dock workers were about to have their pay cut in half. Exacerbating the workers' concerns was talk of a reduction in the work force due to the arrival of winter, causing shipments of grain to cease until Spring when the Lakes would thaw. Bridget, however, caught the gist of what was about to "come down" on the workers from the gossip at the Rosary and Altar Society meeting shortly after. She hesitated to bring it up to Tom, as he always seemed so tired after work lately. However, one evening she decided to approach the subject.

"It's nothin', darlin'," he would say. "Just some things at work that are a bit troublesome."

"Can you tell me about them?"

"I didn't want to bother you with it."

"I'm your wife. We should share everything together. Now tell me—what's bothering you?" Before Tom could answer, she added, "Wait a minute. Before you begin, let me make us a hot cup of tea." Tom welcomed the few minutes reprieve to think.

"Okay, now out with it! Tell me, Thomas!"

"Well, there's a lot of things going on at work." He paused to sip his tea, then laid his head back, staring at the ceiling. "I wasn't gonna say anything, but ... well, first of all, it's been hard for me to hang on to my job ..."

"What? Oh, Tom! What do you mean?"

"Well ... Fingy, the boss, prefers single men who not only drink in his saloon but also rent rooms in his boarding house. In other words, they get preference when things slow down. And he wants us to run up a tab so we owe him more on payday. You see, honey, he deducts that from our pay every week, and there's nothin' we can do about it."

"So, *that's* it! Oh, Tom! How awful! Now I'm beginning to understand. And here, I thought ..." Suddenly her countenance began to change rapidly. "Why that no good ... that no good son of a..." She quickly caught herself! "I mean ... well, that man should be tarred and feathered!" There was silence for a moment, and then her voice became strong and severe sounding, almost with a demanding tone. "What you fellows need is a union! Tom, you men *have* to form a union!"

"Fingy owns that, too!"

"Then start your *own*!"

Before Christmas had even arrived, Tom found himself, along with many of the other men, without work. Things looked grim with the holidays fast approaching, their firstborn soon to arrive, and Tom's pay cut off. Tom said that Fingy promised the men he'd hire them back in the spring, but they didn't trust him. By now, Fingy had total control to do anything he wanted, with the large labor force under his thumb.

The next few days, Bridget sat in her rocking chair by the front window, a warm shawl around her shoulders, as the bitter cold winds buffeted their little house. She busied herself with her knitting, always in prayer for help from above. Her concerns deepened, wondering how they were going to survive—literally worrying where their next meal would be coming from. But most of all, she was terribly concerned about the coming baby's welfare. It was obvious to her that she would have to find extra work as the little pay she made babysitting certainly wasn't enough and Tom hadn't been able to find anything as yet. She rocked. She prayed. She rocked. She prayed. Suddenly, that little voice rose up in her consciousness once again. *"Put your hand to the plow, Bridget dear."* As she rocked, the voice seemed to take on a rhythm of its own—

Put your hand
To the plow
Bridget dear
Put your hand
To the plow
Bridget dear
Put your hand ...

Suddenly the sun peeked through the clouds, casting a rainbow of colors across her knitting from the cut glass top of the window. She had always loved rainbows. From the time she was a little girl, she used to picture herself in a beautiful green meadow filled with flowers, the rainbow arching above her, as she sat next to the pot of gold on one end of the multicolored spectrum. This beauty of God's covenant lifted her spirits immediately, and she found herself once again in that meadow. It seemed as though she were a child in her visual gift; however, she looked as an adult. The flowers were so vibrant, she almost felt she could smell them. She took her place at the end of the rainbow; however, the pot of gold melted away, as their little home took its place.

And, as though she could see right through the walls of the house, she and Tom were inside overlooking a baby cradle.

Her heart smiled. She was filled with hope once more, and that hope was in her own hands—all she needed, once again, was a sewing machine. She was a fighter and was determined to have a knockdown, bare-knuckled, dragged-out fight with Old Man Poverty—and *she* would win! She began to look for another sewing machine. She had left the other one in New York at the Irish Immigrant Home for Girls so those who had learned sewing skills from her could continue to assist Grace O'Brien by making the uniforms.

The following Saturday, while shopping for groceries at the Elk Street market, she spotted an old sewing machine for sale. It apparently had seen much use, the wood being scratched quite a bit; however, the condition made the price right. She tested the treadle and the wheel. Good! It works. She turned to the sales person, recognizing him from her church. "Oh, excuse me! You go to St. Bridget's, don't you?"

"Well yes, I do."

"I thought I recognized you." Oh, good! Maybe I can get him to lower the price. "I'm Bridget Sexton."

"Well, how do you do, Miss—or is it Mrs.?"

"Yes, *Mrs.* Sexton. But please call me Bridget."

"I'm Timothy McMahon. It's very nice to meet you, Bridget. I certainly won't have any problem remembering your name—same as the church!"

Her mind whirled. Gotta think how to approach lowering the price. "Well, now, how do you do, Mr. McMahon." She looked down at the ground. "I could really use this machine to help make ends meet. You see, my husband just lost his job at the elevators. And on top of that, well, you see—well, I mean, I'm in a family way."

"Oh, congratulations! I am sorry to hear about your husband though. I know many of the men have been laid off. It's terrible!"

"Yes, it is terrible! Do you suppose there might be any way you could shave a little off the price?"

"Well, I guess maybe I could, being that you're a fellow parishioner and especially now that you're so up against it. I'll tell you what—I'll give it to ya for half price, being that it's Christmas and all."

She wanted to grab him and hug him but thought she'd better not. "Oh, thank you so much, Mr. McMahon. You can't even imagine how much this means to me. It will make all the difference in the world!"

"Do you have a way to get it home?"

"Well, no. I haven't even thought of that."

"Well, where do you live, Bridget?"

"On Alabama Street—282."

"Oh, I go right by there on my way home. I can put it on my wagon and drop it off for ya. Will somebody be home around six?"

"Oh, yes! I will *definitely* be there! And thank you again—so much!" A light snowfall began as she walked home, a warm feeling in her heart replacing the weight that was there previously. She knew now that her rainbow was truly a sign from God. Her newfound half-price gift would enable her once again to use her sewing skills and the days ahead would certainly be better. And if Tom finds work as well, we'll have double the income.

The following day, Bridget awaited Mrs. Masterson's arrival home from the school, wanting to tell her of her good fortune at the market. "Oh, that's wonderful, Bridget! Do you think you could do a few small jobs for me? Those children of mine are so hard on their clothing—well, just a few rips and tears need fixin'. But it's hard to find the time to take care of it with work and all."

"Oh, sure, I'd be happy to—sewing's my trade, you know."

"Well no, I didn't. Did you do that professionally?"

"Well, not recently. But I did have my own dress shop in Ireland. Maybe someday, I'll be able to open one here. It would probably be far in the future though. I can't think of that now—Tom just lost his job."

"Oh, no! Not Tom, too!"

"Too?"

"Yes. My husband, Steve—he's a dock worker—just got laid off, too. But at least, thank God, I have my job at the school. We should be okay. And in the meantime, Steve's going to try to get part-time work tending bar at McCarthy's Tavern."

"Well, I hope that comes through for you two. And Tom is bound to find something soon, I'm sure."

"Next time you come over, Bridget, I'll have those few mending jobs for you. Maybe that will help a little."

"Well, that's kind of you. Thank you." She walked toward the door.

"Wait a minute! I just happened to think—there might be some work your husband could find over at St. Bridget's." She smiled, then continued. "Yes ... yes, I'm sure I heard something about the janitor retiring. You know Stanley, don't you?"

"Yes. Oh, thank you. I'll tell Tom."

Mrs. Masterson took Bridget's hand in hers. "Now don't you worry, dear. I'm sure things will work out." She opened the door for Bridget. "Oh, one last thing—I feel like we're becoming good friends lately and wish you'd call me Kathleen, my dear."

Bridget smiled, gave her a big hug, and left. She pulled up her collar against the chilly winds and tucked her hands in her pockets as she walked the few blocks in the cold, dark night back to 282 Alabama Street. Although Kathleen seemed to lift her spirits somewhat, she couldn't seem to dismiss her worries about Tom's lack of work and the baby on the way.

The next morning, she awoke to find Tom already gone. A snowstorm had begun, and she could only picture him trying to walk through the drifts looking to find a way to earn some money. Great Christmas gift that terrible Fingy gave those men! He sure couldn't care less how any of us will survive the winter ...

The room was chilly and she shivered as she began to dress. Their supply of coal was close to being depleted, and Bridget hadn't found any sewing but for the little work from Kathleen. Her mood grew somber, and she began to have misgivings about leaving New York City. I was single then and had my job at the Mission with no worries. Never had to think where my next meal would be coming from. I *do* love

Tom. Oh, this baby will be coming soon. But oh! How can we ever make it? A feeling of despair seemed to invade her heart, and she threw herself down onto the bed, burying her face in the pillow, and sobbing uncontrollably. She needed that cry. She let it all out, finally looking upward and shouting out loud, "Where *are* You?" She felt exhausted even after her full night's sleep and dozed off once again.

Awakening shortly after, she made it a point to arrive early for Mass to catch Fr. Lanigan. "Father, would you have a few moments to hear my confession?"

"Oh, good morning, Bridget. Certainly," as he motioned her to the confessional.

"Bless me, Father, for I have sinned ..."

"Yes, go on, my dear."

"Well, Father, it's been about a month since I've been to Confession. Father, I'm terribly worried and don't know where to turn. I think my trust in the good Lord is weakening ..."

"Yes?"

"Well, you see, last week I went to see the doctor and he confirmed what I thought ... I'm going to have a baby."

"Well, that's wonderful news, Bridget!"

"Yes, but you see, Tom has no work now that he's been laid off. And Mrs. Masterson said that you might be needing another janitor around here soon. Is that true?"

"That's right—after the New Year. I can't promise you anything exact, but Stanley does expect that he'll be retiring soon. Tell Thomas to contact me in January."

"Oh, thank you so much, Father."

"Is there anything else now, Bridget?"

"No, I just felt awful about not seeming to have enough trust in the Lord. I even screamed at Him last night!"

"Alright, my dear. For your penance, just say one Our Father, for the good Lord knows you have enough penance in your life right now."

"Yes, Father."

"Go ahead now and say your Act of Contrition."

"Oh, my God, I am heartily sorry for having offended Thee, and I detest all my sins because I dread the loss of Heaven and the pains of hell. But most of all, because they have offended Thee, my God, Who art all good and deserving of all my love. I firmly resolve, with the help of Thy grace to confess my sins, to do penance, and to amend my life. Amen."

"God the Father of mercies, through the death and resurrection of His Son has reconciled the world to Himself and sent the Holy Ghost among us for the forgiveness of sins. Through the ministry of the Church may God give you pardon and peace, and I absolve you from your sins"—here the priest raised his right hand, making the Sign of the Cross—"in the name of the Father, and of the Son and of the Holy Ghost."

"Amen."

"Go in peace, my dear."

"Thank you, Father."

Bridget took a seat in the front pew, as Father Lanigan went into the sacristy to robe for Mass. A feeling of calm and contentment had permeated her spirit and she felt totally at peace. She knew Mass was the greatest prayer on Earth, being the prayer of Jesus Christ before the throne of the Father. And she was happy to be there.

The snow was falling lightly as she walked home, though the flakes were so large she could see the design in them as a few landed on her dark-colored coat sleeve. She had heard that every snowflake was different. How could that possibly be, she wondered. There are literally billions and zillions—and all different? Yet, in her heart, she believed. And that heart was singing quite a different song than on her way to church earlier. I'm so happy—Christmas is almost here. And now Tom will possibly have that janitor's job in the near future. She passed two ladies walking in the opposite direction and, although not knowing them, greeted them with a big smile. Shortly after arriving home and taking a light lunch, she found herself humming her favorite Christmas carol, finally breaking into loud song, as though singing to a huge audience.

Silent Night, Holy Night,
All is Calm, All is Bright.

What a wonderful time of the year! I just *love* it! But this house needs something—some decoration or something. Wish we had a little money. Suddenly she thought she had a great idea. Throwing her coat on, she headed to the Elk Street Market once more. I know they sell Christmas trees there, and maybe I can find some of the branches they have trimmed laying around on the ground.

"You don't mind if I take these, do you?"

"Oh, of course not. I would just be picking them up tonight and throwing them out."

"I would love to buy one of your trees, but I can't. You see, my husband lost his job."

"I'm sorry. Go right ahead and take all you want. And have a Merry Christmas."

That's all she needed. She had a red tablecloth and, after trimming the branches a little more, she arranged them in the middle of the table. A candle completed her centerpiece, and she stood back aways just happily admiring it. There! Now it looks a little like Christmas here! She then proceeded to retrieve the box with Tom's sweater from the back of the closet. Wishing to wrap it beautifully but having no paper, she used the leftover yarn from the booties she had made to tie around the box, tucking a little of the greenery under it. At least it looks kind of pretty. Wish I had a tree to put it under. She placed it back on the shelf, making sure Tom would not see it until she was ready to surprise him tomorrow night. After midnight Mass, I think.

Tom's arrival was accompanied by a cold wind blowing through the open front door. He stomped the snow off his boots on the throw rug as he entered and flipped his hat over to the coat rack in the corner, smiling as it made a perfect landing. "Oh, Tom! You look so cold! Sit down here—I'll get you a cup of hot cocoa."

He hugged her and took a seat at the table. "Well, look at this! Where did all this come from? It looks wonderful!"

"I got the branches from the market—they gave them to me—free! Doesn't it look beautiful?"

"Oh, yes, it's nice." She noticed he seemed preoccupied.

"Is anything wrong, honey?"

"Oh, after lookin' all day, I couldn't find a thing. Nobody's hiring!"

"I'm sorry, Tom—but, please, don't feel down—I have something to tell you."

The look on her face seemed to indicate to him it was something good. "Yes? What, hon?"

"Father Lanigan told me to have you contact him next month 'cause Stanley, the janitor, may be retiring and you could possibly replace him."

"No ... really? That's the best news I've heard in a long time. How did you happen to be talking to Father?"

"I made sure I got there early and asked if he could hear my confession before Mass."

They talked about the details of the day over their hot cocoa, and after a meal of beans and toast, they retired early, holding hands between them in bed. Staring at the ceiling, Tom said, "I'm still going out tomorrow, Bridget, and keep looking—just in case that job at church doesn't come through."

"But, Tom! Tomorrow is Christmas Eve!"

"That's all right, honey. I don't mind. I just *gotta* find something soon."

Tom's good intentions to get up early and leave to look for work didn't materialize. Bridget rose at the crack of dawn but decided to let him sleep, knowing the stress that he was enduring during this period of searching for work every day. He really needs rest more than anything. I don't care how long he stays in bed—it's the best thing for him right now.

About eleven o'clock, he sauntered into the kitchen. "Oh, you're finally up, sleepy head!" Tom scratched his head, looking as though he was still half asleep. "Come on, honey. Sit down. I've got a nice hot cup of coffee for you."

"Thanks, honey. What time is it? I feel like my head is thick or something."

"About eleven."

"Eleven? Eleven? Why didn't you wake me? You know I have to look for work."

"I thought you needed the rest, Tom."

"What *I* need is a job and some *money*, Bridget." His voice was stern.

"I'm sorry. I just thought it was best not to wake you. Let me get some breakfast for you." She could see the anxiety and concern on his face as she placed a bowl of cereal on the table. "Please eat something, Tom—you're not eating."

"I'm not hungry. Coffee's enough this morning. Gotta get going."

"No way, mister. You're not going out in that cold with no breakfast in you." Now it was *her* turn to sound a little stern—for his own good.

After a hot bowl of oatmeal, he left the house. Bridget tidied up, wanting things neat and clean for Christmas Day. She had a little flour and sugar, and decided to surprise Tom by baking some sugar cookies, after which she was pleased to find there was enough flour left for a loaf of bread. At least the house will smell good when he comes back. I hope he's not too cold. Maybe he'll be back soon.

It was getting dark. Tom had pounded the pavement for hours, but sure enough, as he suspected, nothing was available anywhere and he finally headed home. As he neared the corner of Elk and Peabody, he passed an elderly, shabbily dressed man, briskly rubbing his hands together. "Here, sonny!" He held out a small, scraggy evergreen tree decorated with a few ornaments. "My last tree—ya can have it cheap. Been out here all day and I wanna get home—I'm freezing!"

"Well ..."

"Ya can have it, ornaments and all, for a quarter."

"Well, thanks, but I'll tell ya, I don't even have a quarter. I just got laid off. Can't afford a tree this year."

"Sorry ta hear that. Well, here! Take it home. Ya can have it, sonny—and have a very Merry Christmas."

"Oh, God bless you, sir. You have a very Merry Christmas, too." He grabbed the old man's hand and shook it profusely. Heading home, his heart lightened from the difficult day by the old man's generosity, he began to whistle his favorite carol, "Angels We Have Heard on High." Light snow began to fall and he lifted his smiling face to embrace the falling flakes.

"Bridget! Bridget!" coming up the steps to the front porch and calling her name. "Bridget! I'm home!"

The door opened. "Oh, Tom! I'm so glad you're back ... Oh my gosh! What ... You got a tree?"

"Uh-huh ... isn't it great?"

"Oh my gosh! How did you ... Bring it in, honey. Come on. You must be cold."

"Nope. Not a bit! Feel just great!" He set the tree aside to take off his coat, flipping his hat over onto the coat rack before grabbing her up in his arms and swinging her around as he always did. They laughed and hugged. "What smells so good, darlin'?"

"I made bread, Tom—and cookies! But sit down first and have a little dinner and tell me about the tree. Well, actually it's only cheese sandwiches, but it will taste wonderful on that fresh bread."

"In a minute. Let's get this tree up first." He set the treasure on the top of a small table next to the sofa as he told her about the "miracle." Bridget rearranged the few ornaments that came with it, then excused herself for a moment and hurried into the bedroom, getting Tom's gift from the closet shelf and placing it under the tree.

"There!" Her happiness was so palpable.

"What's that?"

"Never mind."

"Come on, honey—what's that?"

"Never mind. You'll find out later. Oh, Tom ..."

"What?"

"Well, we don't have a manger." She thought a minute. "I know! We could use that small picture of Baby Jesus from the bedroom. Go get it, Tom, okay?" She smiled as Tom placed it in the center of the table below the tree. Now it was perfect! "There. Oh, I'm so happy!" She hugged him once again, then took his hand, leading him to the table for dinner. She lit the red candle on her homemade centerpiece and, after saying grace, they had their special Christmas Eve meal.

"Oh, listen, Tom—carolers!"

God rest ye merry gentlemen
Let nothing you dismay
Remember, Christ our Savior
Was born on Christmas Day
To save us all from Satan's power
When we were gone astray
O tidings of comfort and joy,
Comfort and joy
O tidings of comfort and joy.

Tom and Bridget peered out the window. There were three young children, well bundled up, now standing in front of the house beneath a halo of light emanating from the streetlamp. The wind was still howling, and Bridget motioned them to the door. "Come inside." Taking the hand of one of the children, she could feel it was freezing right through the glove. "Oh, you children are frozen—come over here and warm your hands," as she ushered them to the warmest spot in the room near the stove. Complying with her instructions, they took off their gloves, some of which had holes in them, and their coats. As they did so, some newspapers fell to the floor.

"What in the world ..." Bridget looked flabbergasted. She suddenly realized the paper was being used inside their jackets as insulation against the cold night air. "Now sit yourselves down here. I'll get you some hot cocoa."

"Thank you, Ma'am," they responded.

"I know you children—aren't you the Sweeney kids from the next block?" Tom asked.

"Yes," they all said in unison.

Bridget placed her plate of freshly baked cookies along with the hot cocoa on the table to the delight of the rosy-cheeked children. They cupped their hands around the warm drinks momentarily, then engaged in devouring the sugar cookies with glee. Bridget began to wonder if any would be left for Tom, but it warmed her heart to see them so happy.

"Mrs. Sexton and I know your parents from church," Tom said, "but we don't know your first names. You have older brothers and sisters, don't you?"

"I'm Michael," the older one said.

"And I'm Steve," said the other boy.

"I'm Mary. And we have five older brothers and sisters."

"Do you all attend St. Bridget's School?" Bridget asked.

"Yes, Ma'am," Steve replied.

Mary set her cocoa down. "I'm in the third grade and Steve's in the sixth grade and Michael's in the eighth grade."

After a short while, Michael said, "We better get going. Got another block to go. Better get your coats on." He motioned his siblings to the coat rack.

"Now wait just a minute," Bridget said. She reached in the kitchen drawer and pulled out a box of chocolates which Mrs. Masterson had sent over for Christmas along with a bottle of wine. "Here! Have a piece of candy, children."

"Oh, thank you, Ma'am."

"Yes, thanks. M-m-m-m."

Mary just nodded.

As they went out the door, Michael turned to wish them a Merry Christmas and thank them for everything.

"Yes, Merry Christmas," the two younger ones added.

"And Merry Christmas to all of you, too, and wish your family a Merry Christmas for us," Tom replied. He and Bridget watched out the door as the carolers proceeded toward the next block, the faint refrains of "God Rest Ye Merry Gentlemen" fading as they soon disappeared from view in the blowing snow.

Bridget quickly closed the door. "Br-r-r! Oh, what wonderful children, aren't they, Tom? To think they would brave that cold just to bring a little cheer to others!"

"And they have so little themselves," Tom answered.

Bridget busied herself clearing the table and began to wash the dishes. Tom came up behind her, grabbing her around the waist. "I love you, Bridget-girl!—and Santa loves you, too! In fact, I think he has something for you up in the attic. I'll go up and get it."

"What?" She hesitated a moment. "Why, you old joker, you! Well, say hello to him for me when you get up there!" They laughed.

Tom returned and placed "Santa's gift," tied with a big red bow, under the tree next to the gift Bridget had placed there earlier.

"Oh, Tom! What is it?"

"Never mind." He laughed as he repeated the words she had said to *him* earlier.

"Tom ... come on! I want to know what's in it."

"Never mind now. You have to wait. Have a little patience—it's a virtue, you know," teasing her a little.

She went over and stood before the tree. "Now, Tom, you know I love surprises. But ... I can't wait! Please let me open it now!"

"Well, let me think about it for a minute!"

"Come on. *Please*?"

"Well, I guess it's okay. But only for an extra kiss!"

She leaned over and quickly kissed him on the cheek, and he handed her the present. She hesitated for a moment, then placed it back down and picked up the one she had for him. "*You* first, Tom!"

"No, honey—*you* first! You can't wait, remember?" He laid his gift aside, sat her down on the sofa, and placed her present on her lap.

"Now what could this be?" as she untied the big red bow and quickly removed the cover of the box. "Oh, my goodness! What ..." She removed the coat and, trying to catch her breath, blurted out, "Tom! Oh, Tom! The coat! How did you ..." Tears welled up in her eyes. She had never had such a beautiful coat in her life.

"Now, now, honey. Don't cry! I thought this would make you *happy*."

"I know. Oh, Tom! It does ... it does," she sobbed, "but of all times, Tom—you don't have a job and we can't ..."

"Don't worry. I'll find something soon."

"Oh, I *do* love it! But ... Oh, Tom ..." He reached into his back pocket and wiped her tears with his handkerchief. She threw her arms around him, squeezing him with all her might.

"I can't have my darlin' going to church and up the avenue dressed in old rags all the time, now can I?"

She collected herself, thought for a moment, and vowed not to spoil their first Christmas together by speaking of the cost any longer.

"Come on, let's try it on ya, honey!" He held the coat as she slipped her arms into the sleeves. She rubbed the soft fox fur collar against her cheek, then putting her chin in the air began a slow strut across the room.

"I feel like a queen or something!" She laughed. "Where are my servants?" She always loved pretending from the time she was a child, and often in her early years would imagine herself to be a princess. And now, here she was—feeling like a real-life *queen*. "Where are my servants?" she repeated, trying to express this in a hoity-toity tone of voice.

Tom, enjoying her little reverie, joined in. "Your servant awaits, my queen!"

Bridget laughed again. "Then kneel, servant!" Tom went down on one knee. Bridget took the newspaper, folded it, and placed one end on Tom's shoulder. "I dub thee Sir Knight of the First Ward."

"My queen, I am your servant forever. But in the meantime, dost thou not have a gift for Sir Knight in honor of his Knighthood?"

Bridget then unfolded the newspaper, holding it up in front of her as though it were a scroll. Pretending to read, she announced: "This day, in the Kingdom of the First Ward, I do bequeath to Sir Knight, here kneeling before me, this gift in honor of his permanent loyalty to Her Majesty, Queen Bridget, and I therefore present him with it with all my love." She took his Christmas present from the table and excitedly gave it to him.

"Oh, my queen! Thouest gift is so wondrous! Humbly dost Sir Knight accept this token of your love." He stood and immediately pulled Bridget's sweater on over his head. "And I shall proudly wear this attire beneath my armor whenst e'er I go into battle for thy kingdom." He sat down on the sofa, pulling her onto his lap. They laughed and embraced and then sat quietly in each other's arms, enjoying the moment. Tom glanced over at the clock on the wall, then exclaimed, "My queen, I do believe thou mayest like to retreat to thy chambers to ready thyself for midnight Mass whilst I instruct your footman to bring your carriage around." He kissed her cheek and gave her a little slap on her derriere.

A warm feeling came over Bridget in church that Christmas Eve, as she and Tom sat in the front row to share in the holy sacrifice of the Mass. They gazed at the Nativity scene on the side altar flanked by evergreens surrounding Jesus, Mary, and Joseph in the stable, the shepherds with their sheep looking on. Father Lanigan came to the podium and all stood for the Holy Gospel. "The Gospel according to Luke."

> *"Now it came to pass in those days, that a decree went forth from Caesar Augustus that a census of the whole world should be taken. This first census took place while Cyrinus was Governor of Syria. And all were going, each to his own town, to register.*
>
> *And Joseph also went from Galilee out of the town of Nazareth into Judea to the town of David, which is called Bethlehem—because he was of the house and family of David— to register, together*
>
> *with Mary his espoused wife, who was with child. And it came to pass while they were there, that the days for her to be delivered were fulfilled. And she brought forth her first-born son, and wrapped him in swaddling clothes, and laid him in a manger, because there was no room for them in the inn.*
>
> *And there were shepherds in the same district living in the fields and keeping watch over their flock by night. And behold, an angel of the Lord stood by them and the*

> *glory of God shone round about them, and they feared exceedingly. And the angel said to them, 'Do not be afraid, for behold, I bring you good news of great joy which shall be to all the people; for today in the town of David a Savior has been born to you, who is Christ the Lord.*
>
> *And this shall be a sign to you: you will find an infant wrapped in swaddling clothes and lying in a manger.' And suddenly there was with the angel a multitude of the heavenly host praising God and saying,*
>
> *'Glory to God in the highest. And on earth peace among men of good will.'"*

Father then motioned for the congregation to be seated and began his homily:

> *"As we see Baby Jesus in the manger, we reflect on God's way being a way of gentleness and tenderness. God's way is not one of violence but gentleness. There is a lack of goodness and love in the world, but God is tender and loving. As we look upon Baby Jesus in the manger, we see that He is the answer to today's problems. Instead of violence, in Baby Jesus in the manger we see gentleness. Instead of hatred, in Baby Jesus in the manger, we see tenderness. Instead of selfishness, in Baby Jesus in the manger, we see God's love for us. Let us ask Baby Jesus to help us to be gentle, tender, and loving with those around us. His coming encourages us to hold out the hand of reconciliation, to help one another, to work for peace—and especially so, today, right here in our own community. Yes, right here—during these trying times in our First Ward."*

Tom certainly understood what Father Lanigan was trying to point out at the end of his homily. Yet, he was determined to try to keep his mind on the Mass itself now and to pray for better times to come to the working poor of the First Ward, especially those now unemployed. He reached over and squeezed Bridget's hand, as though attempting to communicate his hope through this touch.

After Mass ended, most all the parishioners gathered briefly in the back of the church, wishing one another a Merry Christmas.

"Oh, my dear! What a lovely coat! I haven't seen that on you before," Mrs. Masterson said.

"I know. Isn't it beautiful? Tom surprised me. I love it, too!" She felt like a *real* queen—not just a pretend one! "And, I just want to thank you once again for the candy and the wine. That was so good of you, my dear friend." Another woman approached and complimented her on the coat as well, asking where she had bought it. Bridget smiled, thanked her, and explained it was her Christmas gift from her husband.

Upon arriving home that night, Tom poured two glasses of wine; and as they stood before their little tree, admiring it, as sparse as it was, he clicked his glass on hers and held it up high. "Merry Christmas, honey!—Merry *first* Christmas! Here's to my wonderful wife and to our beautiful baby-to-be! I'm a lucky man!"

They sipped their wine and snuggled on the sofa. He put his hand on Bridget's belly. "Honey! I just felt something. I just felt him!"

"*Him*? Tom! It's a *her*!"

"Oh, yeah. I forgot!" They sat there in a total embrace, just listening to the cold winter winds blowing outside. But their young love was stronger than that wind buffeting the little white house on the shores of Lake Erie beneath those towering grain elevators in that little community called the First Ward.

But there was more than young love in that Ward. There were whispers and dark clouds of animosity fermenting. The unrest rippled through the ranks of the laborers, the grain scoopers, and the dock workers. It only seemed to escalate and would have to be resolved one way or the other. And the genesis of that trouble could be found in the greed of a handful of dock bosses—the biggest being a man by the name of Fingy Connors.

The holidays came and went without much fanfare that New Year's, but for a quiet toast together with the wine they had saved from Christmas. 1899 burst on the scene with a blizzard. Tom began his relentless quest for finding work, talking to merchants and knocking on doors. He finally found a temporary job shoveling the snow off the railroad tracks. Every night he would come home cold and exhausted from the backbreaking work. His fingers and toes often were numb, and Bridget worried he would get frostbite. She would wrap his feet in a blanket and place a towel which she had warmed near the oven over his hands. He tried to "play it down" so as not to have her worry, always concerned about the baby.

"Tom! Hold up a minute!" Father Lanigan called out to him after Mass one Sunday. "I need to talk to you."

Tom waited while Father shook hands with his parishioners as they exited the church, then turned to him, taking him by the hand and leading him back inside where they sat in a pew. "Thomas, Stanley has decided to stay on for another year or two."

Tom looked down, a hopeless feeling coming over his heart.

"Tom, you didn't give me a chance to finish. I have *good* news for you! I just got wind they are shorthanded doing the finishing work inside Our Lady of Perpetual Help—you know ... the new church being built over on O'Connell Street."

"Yes, I know of it, Father."

"Now, Thomas, they do need another man over there, and I thought of you—with the little one on the way and all. I know you're handy and probably wouldn't have a problem with that kind of work. Now, mind you, I don't know what the pay is, but it might tide you over for a while—at least until spring, I suspect."

Tom had a broad smile on his face. "Oh, Father! *No doubt* I can handle that job. When can I start?"

"Not sure, Thomas. I'll give you the name of the foreman—tell him I sent you. And I'll be askin' the good Lord to get you the job."

Tom grabbed Father's hand and shook it. "Oh, thank you. Thank you so much, Father!"

"Now off with ya, lad—and good luck to ya!" He turned to leave, then turned back. "Oh, and Tom! I'd suggest you get over there at the crack o' dawn before anyone else gets wind of it."

Bridget was just finishing collecting all the Mass books from the pews and placing them back in the rack at the rear of the church, as she did every Sunday. “Come on, honey,” Tom said. “Let’s get home. Father can lock up—and I’m anxious to talk to you.”

She could sense the excitement in his voice. “What ... what is it, Tom?”

“Come on, honey. I’ve got something to tell ya!” He grabbed her by the arm and rushed her out of church. Bending down, he scooped up a small pile of snow in his hands, making a snowball. Pretending as though he were a baseball pitcher, he “wound up” and hurled it toward a big oak tree. As it splattered against the trunk, he picked Bridget up and whirled her around, laughing.

“What’s wrong with you, Tom? Why are you acting so nutty?” she said curiously, smiling at his antics.

“Bridget-girl! You won’t believe this, but ...” He purposely stopped midsentence, thinking he’d keep her in suspense for a moment.

“Thomas! If you don’t tell me right now what in the world is going on here ...” She had to turn on her “stern voice.”

“Oh, baby! I’ve got a job! I mean, I *think* I have a job. And it’s *inside*!—over at the new church on O’Connell.”

“What? Oh, Tom!” Her heart had always been heavy as he trudged off every morning for the railroad, knowing he’d be out in freezing cold weather all day doing such hard labor. This was almost too good to be true—*inside* work! “Oh, Tom, I’m so, so happy. I can hardly believe it! How ... I mean, when will you start?”

“I hope right away. Father said to talk to the foreman early tomorrow.” As he talked, he bent down and packed another snowball. Bridget hurriedly made one of her own while his back was turned, throwing it at his posterior before he straightened up. A few more snowballs went through the air, as they laughed and played like two children. They finally headed home, strolling slowly down Alabama Street, holding hands and talking excitedly about the good news, not minding the cold or the snow.

Chapter 11

The Strike

The frigid March winds coming off the lake had blown themselves out, just as the winds of change in the Ward were beginning to intensify. The men had become accustomed to quiet conversations in shadowy corners of saloons, as Fingy had spies infiltrating the ranks throughout the neighborhood. These whispers spilled over behind the closed doors of neighbors' homes and onto street corners and eventually began to solidify and to speak as one unstoppable voice. This voice grew louder and louder, as these fragmented groups of men joined forces—and the whispers escalated into a roar culminating in the First Ward's groaning with shouts of STRIKE! STRIKE!

Tom had made a close friend at work shortly after he and Bridget had arrived in Buffalo. Being from France, he soon was dubbed by the men with the nickname, “Frenchy.” Just as Tom, he, too, had been abandoned by his parents in childhood; the two men seemed to have much in common to discuss. They worked in the same crew on the boats, and Tom made it a point to try to assist him to become more fluent with his very limited English during their lunch hours. Though Frenchy spoke little because of the speech hindrance, he was well liked by the men for his sincere personality. A man of great stature, he stood about six feet, seven inches, yet was a very mild-mannered person—Tom began to refer to him as the “Gentle Giant.”

Frenchy had asked Tom to meet him one evening after work at the Shamrock Saloon, feeling the need to talk. He always felt comfortable speaking with Tom, more so than with the others, Tom being the first to befriend and mentor him.

“Hey! Bon’Jour Mon’Ami!”

Tom raised his right hand in a mock salute and took the stool beside his friend. Frenchy motioned to the bartender for a beer for Tom. After a short while, the conversation turned to the “subject of the day.”

“We strike, Mon’Ami?”

Tom motioned to Frenchy to lower his voice, concerned that some of Fingy’s undercover men might be there. “Maybe so,” he whispered.

“Is bad we strike, no?” Frenchy asked.

“It’s bad *and* good.”

“What you mean—bad *and* good?”

“I mean it’s bad we have to strike—but good if it means we get our fair pay for an honest day’s work.”

“Honest? What honest mean?”

“You know—like you tell the truth,” Tom replied.

“Oh, yeah! Truth. I know now. You mean do good work, right? Not cheat boss. Frenchy do very good work.” Pounding his chest, he went on. “Frenchy don’t cheat boss. Frenchy sweat ass off in them ships.”

"You're right, big guy. And you and the rest of us deserve better than getting our pay *cut*."

"You bet, Mick!"

Tom smiled at his friend's use of the word "Mick." They ordered another beer and then Frenchy continued his questioning. "How we strike?"

"Sh-h-h. We *gotta* keep it down here."

"Don't strike mean hit somebody? Like this ..." He slapped Tom on the back, almost pushing him off his bar stool.

"Whoa, big fella! Not quite! You're right in a *way*— it does mean to hit someone, but it also means to refuse to work. And that's what we all must do—refuse to work to fight for our fair pay!"

"Me ready to fight!"

"No ... no! We shouldn't fight. We must all just refuse to work—and then maybe we will win."

"Okay, Mick! I do what *you* do—you smart egg!"

Tom's smile quickly turned to dismay, as he noticed three men with baseball bats enter the room. He recognized them as part of a local gang of street thugs. One of them hollered out, "This is a warning! We know there is a walkout being planned—don't even think about it!" All three began slapping their bats against their hands in a threatening manner. Frenchy didn't like this intimidation and bolted from his bar stool, grabbing the leader's bat with his massive hand, as he pushed him against the wall, throttling him by the neck with his other hand. The other two thugs looked on in utter disbelief, then dropping their bats, made a hasty retreat out the door. Tom quickly ran over to Frenchy. "Frenchy, let him go!" he shouted. "You're gonna kill him!"

"He bad man, Mon'Ami," Frenchy answered as he loosened his grip on the thug, who immediately bolted from the room, choking and coughing.

The unrest grew and grew, continuing into Spring, when some dock bosses recruited more thugs and ruffians from *other* cities to come to Buffalo to escalate the intimidation against the men. Tempers flew as these hired thugs entered the saloons with clubs and blackjacks—and a powder keg of violence began to smolder.

And so it began. There was no turning back now. The will of these hard-working laborers, hands all calloused from scooping grain all day and going home with aching backs night after night, would be heard loud and clear, as the men refused to show up for work and unload the grain in the holds of the ships. They were blindsided when Fingy's hirelings began to intensify their threats, however. It became unsafe to walk the streets alone at night. Unable to intimidate all the men at once, these ruffians would roam around in gangs of four or five men, looking for one or two scoopers after dark— then "hit and run," after roughing them up piecemeal, often attacking with baseball bats. On occasion, however, these attacks backfired, as the workers would overpower the thugs and give them a severe beating.

The lakes had thawed out, but the heat of tempers continued to build in what used to be that little peaceful First Ward community. And along with this unrest and work stoppage, came boatloads of grain beginning to stack up along the shore—an armada of forty-three!

Reports of attacks and beatings began to surface from around the area, some ending in injuries to both sides; but up 'til now this had been limited to black eyes, bruises, and a few broken bones—UNTIL a body was found floating in the Canal one damp, foggy morning. It was Frenchy! Tom was horrified! A local newspaper portrayed the death as an accident, and a certain someone who had control of that newspaper was suspected of suppressing the truth. That same someone was Fingy Connors who had previously purchased that newspaper to use as a conduit to influence the community—especially the politicians. The news of the fatality sent shock waves through the Ward and ultimately reached other papers in surrounding areas. As Frenchy's death had been reported as an accident, the authorities closed the case—many seeming apathetic. Tom and most of the other scoopers, however, were convinced it was due to reprisals for Frenchy's actions in the saloon, and Tom became terribly upset and angry—and took the anger home with him.

Returning home after picketing one afternoon, Tom sat down to his hot cocoa, as was Bridget's custom to have ready, hoping it might relieve a little of the stress she saw in his eyes. "I can't believe Frenchy's gone!" Tom's voice was so angry. He shook his head from side to side. "Those SOB's did it!—I know it!"

"Now Thomas, don't be getting yourself all riled up! Leave it alone and just pray for his soul."

"I'll pray ..." He stared out the window. "...but I won't forget! I'll *never* forget!"

Bridget's heart ached for her husband. She knew he had felt a great loss from Frenchy's death. But worse, she was terribly concerned about the anger that had built up in him, worried that he might say or do something to provoke more violence, especially toward *him.* She decided to speak to him further about this after dinner. Always feed a man first. Better wait 'til he calms down a bit—then talk. "Tom, why don't you go lie down for a little while and I'll make some dinner."

"Not hungry."

"You have to eat *some*thing!"

"Bridget, I said I'm not hungry—didn't you hear me?"

"Please don't take your anger out on me, Tom!" Now *she* was getting a little perturbed.

"Just leave me alone, Bridget. I just don't want to discuss it any more—*period*!"

Bridget felt extremely frustrated at this point and decided to leave the room. She could see that she'd get nowhere trying to warn him, yet feeling that she *must.* She threw herself on the bed and cried into her pillow so he wouldn't hear and get upset. As morning broke, she was still lying there fully clothed, having cried herself to sleep. She rolled over, her arm reaching out to embrace Tom—he wasn't there! She rose quickly to check the living room. No Tom!

In the days to come, more arguments followed. Tom finally decided to keep his thoughts to himself, so as not to upset Bridget any longer and create more discord in the home.

And then the rains came. Those April showers were more like a deluge that year, raining steadily for days with no letup. So, too, there was no letup in Tom's anger. It continued to grow, just as tempers flared on both sides, but mostly with the workers.

"Who the hell do they think they are?"

"Yeah! I'm sick of all this!"

"Yeah! Sick and tired of those greedy bastards takin' advantage of us!"

That angry mob with the loud voices only needed a spark to set their cause in motion. And that spark was ignited when some of Fingy's men burned down McMahon's Tavern at 161 Elk Street, where the rank and file had been meeting to discuss forming their *own* union—and Tom made sure he was present, having completed his temporary job at Our Lady of Perpetual Help and rejoining the scoopers' workforce, for he certainly knew full well the hardships they had all been forced to endure in the past in order to feed their families.

A meeting was called by Father Patrick Cronin, an Irish Catholic priest and advocate for the workers' cause, to be held at St. Bridget's parish hall. During Father's speech, the men were delighted to see another familiar man of the cloth in the hierarchy of the church make his way through the crowd—James Edward Quiqley, Bishop of Buffalo. He addressed the men in his usual calm, collected manner, issuing a mandate to the strikers that specifically forbade them from working until conditions improved. A loud cheer arose from the men, standing to acknowledge their champion. The influence of the good Bishop, along with other priests and Protestant ministers, grew, in addition to the growing public sentiment and pressure from the grain shippers whose cargoes were still unloaded. All this soon brought the pressure to a boiling point, forcing Fingy and other dock bosses to cave in to the workers' demands.

"I am now a proud member of ...." Tom hesitated, grinning.

Bridget waited expectantly for whatever this news was. "What, Tom? What? Now don't you go leave me hanging again! I hate it when you do that!"

"109, Bridget! 109!"

"109? What's 109?"

"*Local* 109, Bridget-girl! Our brand new Union!" He grabbed her around the waist, lifting her into the air and swinging her around, as he loved to do.

"Tom! Honey, put me down!—the baby!"

"Oops! Sorry honey." He patted her belly. "Well?"

"Well, oh, my gosh! I don't know what to say! How wonderful! You guys did it! I'm so proud of you, Tom!"

"Give your daddy a great big kiss, me darlin'!"

She kissed him and he gently hugged her. It finally came through. Now their problems would be over, she thought. Or would they? I hope this is the end of all the trouble. Not wanting to spoil the joy of the moment, she decided to let it be—for now.

Most of the men were satisfied and relieved that the old ways of intimidation and fear of being fired were now a thing of the past. But there was *one* man who was far from being satisfied—Tom Sexton! There was still some unfinished business that the rank and file had all but forgotten—Frenchy. No one had claimed the body which was still in the morgue. Tom, having been the closest friend of the deceased, was determined that Frenchy would not be buried in a pauper's grave, but would have a Christian burial. He made arrangements with Father Lanigan for a funeral Mass at St. Bridget's and took up a collection from his fellow workers for a gravesite for the man.

The official settlement of the strike on May 23 brought a new life of relief and calm to the scoopers of that old First Ward. And on that very day, another new life was soon to come into being.

"It's okay, honey. Hang on! Doctor Niles is on his way."

"Oh, Tom! Oh! Oh!"

Tom was nervously pacing back and forth, wanting to help Bridget but not knowing what to do. "He's coming, hon. He'll be here in a minute!"

"Oh ... Tom ... O-o-o-o!"

"Do you want some tea, honey? I can make you some tea."

"Oh ... no ... no ..." It was apparent that she was experiencing quite a bit of pain, and he felt utterly helpless.

"He's on his way—I'm sure he'll be here in a minute."

"Tom! Oh my gosh! Oh, Tom—the baby's coming! She's coming!"

"Oh, thank God, Bridget. He's here! The Doctor's here!"

"So, my dear, we're going to have a baby, are we?" Dr. Niles calmly asked, smiling.

"Oh, Doctor, hurry!—Oh my gosh!"

After a brief examination, Dr. Niles instructed Tom to place several extra clean sheets over the bed. "There's no time to waste, Tom. Why don't you go out to the kitchen and start some water boiling." The doctor turned back to Bridget. "Another minute and I'd have been too late, my dear!" he announced. "This baby is in quite a hurry to make its entrance into the world," he laughed. "Hold on ... Here he comes!" Bridget was in exceptionally hard labor by this time and had no concern that the doctor had used the wrong pronoun. She tried to muffle her moaning as her body seemed to be pushing on its own, without her cooperation. "Almost here," the doctor announced. "One more push!"

Bridget let out a slight scream, and the doctor placed the newborn on her mother's chest. "She's a beauty!"

Tom was speechless. He felt as though his heart was so filled that it was hard to contain himself. "Oh, my gosh! Baby, she is absolutely beautiful!" as he leaned over to kiss Bridget on the cheek.

"I told you she would be a girl!"

"You told me *she* would be a *girl*?" He laughed at the way she phrased her statement.

Teresa Sexton, weighing 7 pounds and 1 oz, would carry the name of her mother's favorite saint, Therese' of Lisieux, commonly known as the "Little Flower of Jesus." The new parents were filled with joy over their firstborn, talking and laughing for days about the birth. It was a time of adjustment—and great joy with their new little one. Bridget felt that she had the whole world in her grasp, and things seemed to be looking up as the warm Spring breezes filtered through the Ward and nature blossomed once again as flowers and trees came into bloom.

After dinner one evening, Tom was relaxing on the sofa, smoking his pipe and reading the newspaper. Laying it aside, he smiled up at Bridget. "You know, honey, I really haven't told you lately that I love you, but I *do*, even though I don't tell you very often."

"Oh, you're so sweet! I love you, too." Bridget walked over to the cradle, picked up Teresa, and brought her over to Tom, laying her in his arms. "And, you know, Tom, Teresa told me this morning how much *she* loves you, too!"

Smiling, Tom bent down and kissed the baby. "Well, thank you, Teresa!"

"I'm so happy, Tom!" Bridget leaned over to kiss the child, too.

"Come on, honey—sit down here next to me—I mean to *us*," as he patted the cushion of the sofa. He put his arm around her back, pulling her close to him, and they sat quietly, relishing this time of peace and their love for one another and their newborn.

It was wonderful to be back at work full time, especially now with the scoopers having Local 109 behind them and being able to bring their *full* paycheck home each week. But deep within, Tom could not shake off thoughts of Frenchy's death, and it began to surface in conversation with Bridget. Lying in bed one night, restless and unable to sleep, he got up and opened the window. Immediately the aroma from the H-O mill invaded the room.

"What is it, Tom? Something wrong?"

"Oh, sorry, honey. Didn't mean to wake you."

"Well, is something wrong?"

"Oh, no." He hesitated, then added, "Well, maybe."

Bridget sat up in bed and rubbed her eyes. "What do you mean—maybe?"

"Oh, it's nothing," he remarked matter-of-factly.

"Now tell me! I'm your wife!" she quickly retorted. "Oh! I know—it's about Frenchy, isn't it?"

Tom hesitated, as though he didn't want to answer, then blurted out, "Yes! ... Yes, it is! I *have* to find out who killed him!"

"You'll be doin' no such thing, Thomas! Just forget it and just keep lookin' after your wife and baby girl now!" Her voice had taken on a commanding tone.

Continuing to stare out the window as though in a trance, Tom raised his voice in anger. "I'll get to the bottom of this if it's the last thing I do—so help me, God!"

The baby awoke and began crying. "Now see what you've done, Thomas! You woke the baby!" Bridget scolded.

Tom became very quiet, Bridget fed Teresa and put her back in her crib, and everyone finally got back to sleep.

At least something was much better now with Tom bringing home more money. Bridget continued babysitting the Masterson children which helped pay the expenses they had fallen behind on. She had a strong will and fortitude about her, something which Tom had always admired. He was grateful to have such a good wife, her attitude toward her family being soft and generous, as she always placed his and the child's needs ahead of her own.

Shortly after, Bridget was elated with the wonderful news that Tom was promoted to a position in the cupola, located at the top of the grain elevators where the grain was cleaned and weighed. He found this to be a more challenging job as well as being less strenuous—the pay was better, too!

The last half of that year was uneventful, however, the Ward basically remaining calm. Local 109 had planned a New Year's Eve party to welcome in the new century. And what a party it was! The O'Tooles, O'Reillys, O'Learys and Murphys. O'Connors, O'Flannigans—even the Hennigans!

"You know, Bridget-girl, I think I'm gonna have to change our name."

"What? What do you mean?"

"Well, like maybe we should change it to *O'Sexton!"*

"Oh! You silly!" Bridget laughed. "Well, *I am* an O'Halloran!"

"True ... true."

"And since you are with me, you're all set!"

"Well, thanks, me girl!"

The kegs of beer seemed to be emptied as fast as they were brought in. The music was right from the Old Sod. They had brought Old Ireland with them, as they danced the Irish jig to many upbeat Irish tunes, clapping and singing and stomping their feet.

"Courtin' in the Kitchen!" the fiddler shouted.

Come single belle and beau, unto me pay attention
Don't ever fall in love, it's the devil's own invention
Once I fell in love with a lady so bewitching
Miss Henrietta Bell down in Captain Kelly's kitchen
Sing too-ra-loo-ra-lie, singing too-ra-loo-ra-laddie
Sing too-ra-loo-ra-lie, singing too-ra-loo-ra-laddie

Tom grabbed Bridget around the waist and started swinging her around the dance floor, at the same time singing his heart out.

At the age of seventeen I was apprenticed to a grocer
Not far from Stephen's Green where Miss Henri used to go, sir
Her manners were so fine, she set my heart a-twitchin'
When she invited me to a hooley in the kitchen.
Sing too-ra-loo-ra-lie, singing too-ra-loo-ra-laddie
Sing too-ra-loo-ra-lie, singing too-ra-loo-ra-laddie

"Tom! I'm getting out of breath—let's sit down a minute."

"Okay, honey. I'll go over and get us a drink ... Be right back"

As the night wore on, they enjoyed listening to patriotic and marching cadence tunes of long ago, one of when their forefathers fought and died for their liberty— "O'Donnell Abu:"

On with O'Donnell then, fight the old fight again
Sons of Tir Connail are valiant and true
Make the proud Saxon feel Erin's avenging steel
Strike for your country O'Donnell Abu.

Hearts were stirred and a few tears shed by the women as the band proceeded to play "The Wearing of the Green" and "The Rising of the Moon." But when Jimmy O'Rourke took the stage to sing "God Save Ireland" in his beautiful Irish tenor voice, it really touched the crowd.

High upon the gallows tree
Swung the noble hearted three
By the vengeful tyrant stricken in their bloom
But they met him face to face
With the courage of their race
And they went with souls undaunted to their doom.
God save Ireland, said the heroes

God save Ireland, said they all
Whether on the scaffold high
Or the battlefield we die
Oh what matter when for Erin dear we fall?

"Tom, this makes me feel so homesick for Ireland."

"I know what you mean, honey. I'm feeling the same way. It would have been a great place to bring up a family if the famine hadn't hit and the damn British didn't care if we starved to death!" He stopped momentarily, then offered, "Ah! But look at it *this* way, me girl—we might never have met had we not come to America!" He squeezed her hand and kissed her cheek.

She smiled. "Oh! You're right, Tom! Thank God then that we did!"

Jimmy O'Rourke took the stage once again. He began a countdown at sixty seconds to midnight. "ten... nine... eight... seven... six... five... four... three... two... one... HAPPY NEW YEAR!" The band struck up *Auld Lang Syne* as merriment went through the crowd, horns blowing, confetti flying, and men hugging and kissing their wives—along with some of the other girls! The men were shaking hands and slapping each other on the back. "HAPPY NEW YEAR!" "HAPPY NEW YEAR!"

"Oh, Tom! Can you believe? 1900! Imagine— 1900! A whole new century!"

The dancing and drinking continued on into the wee hours of the morning. Bridget was getting tired and anxious to leave, as the baby was being watched by Mrs. Masterson. "In just a minute, babe—there's me buddy over at the bar— Shawn O'Shaunessey. Gotta have just one more beer with him and wish him a Happy New Year."

"Make it only one now, Tom! Promise? I told Mrs. Masterson we'd be back early."

"Happy New Year, buddy!" Tom greeted his friend, motioning the bartender over. "Two beers for O'Shaunessey and me!"

"Yeah, let's *hope* it is, Tom!"

Tom looked puzzled, until O'Shaunessey leaned over a bit and whispered something in his ear.

"Who told you?" Tom asked in a loud excited voice.

"Sh-h-h!" Shawn warned. He immediately glanced around to see if anyone had overheard.

Tom lowered his voice. "Do you have names? I need the names of those bastards!"

Just then, Bridget came over and pulled at Tom's sleeve. "Let's go, honey. It's late," she whined.

Shawn got off his stool, nodded to Bridget, and leaned toward Tom once again. "I'll let you know as soon as I find out," he whispered.

"What was that all about, Tom?" Bridget inquired. "Why was he whispering?"

"Oh, nothing. Just talkin' about the new work rules for Local 109, hon."

"Well, come on, let's go."

"In a minute. Just wanna finish my beer."

"Oh, come on, Tom! You've had more than enough! Let's go. I want to get home to Teresa."

Walking home in the early morning hours of that first day of the year, Bridget asked once again, "What did you say that was all about—that talk you were having with Shawn?"

"Oh, nothing! Just a little joke between men!"

"You can't fool *me*, Thomas Sexton! I didn't see you laughing about anything."

"Nothin' important," he said, lighting up his pipe as they walked down the dimly lit street. "Button up, honey." He tried to change the conversation as he reached over to fasten the top button of her coat.

"I hope not," she replied. "You know, we can't be having any secrets now. If it's something serious, I should know," she said with a worried look on her face.

He grabbed her hand and squeezed it. "Did anyone tell you they love you today?"

"Oh, Thomas! You *know* you asked me that this morning!"

"And do you remember what you answered?"

"Now Thomas! Stop all that blarney! I think you had a little too much to drink."

"Well ... *I* love you baby! And *God* loves you even *more*!"

"Well, okay, thank you." She smiled at him. "Here we are."

New Year's Day began with a blinding snowstorm, and Tom considered himself lucky to have the day off. The harbor had frozen over and there were no ships to unload. The day started with a nice hot breakfast and a leisurely morning reading the newspaper, while Bridget bathed and fed and cared for Teresa. Tom laid the paper in his lap and stared out the window, as the wind off the lake continued to howl and dump snow in its wake.

"A penny for your thoughts."

"Oh, I wish I knew what happened ..." He abruptly stopped in midsentence.

"You wish what? What happened?"

"Oh, nothing." Tom tried to think of something to say quickly to change the subject, not wanting Bridget to see his concern. "I was just thinking about last night, honey, and wondering how long the party went on after we left."

"You can't fool me, Thomas," Bridget said, walking over to him while drying a dish. "It's about your old friend, Frenchy, again, isn't it?"

Tom looked at her with an apologetic look, realizing Bridget was too astute and was able to see right through his façade.

"It is, isn't it? I *know* it is! Can't you forget about that?" she shouted. "It's history now, Tom. Just let the poor man rest in peace."

Tom felt that he was the only one who cared about Frenchy. Even Bridget didn't seem to care. Nor did his fellow workers. Not even the police, as they had ruled his death an accidental drowning. Tom knew this wasn't true, as a police officer who had sided with the scoopers had indicated to him that the body had been badly beaten—but swore him to secrecy. It was hushed up, as the officials thought that information would cause reprisals by the rank and file and greatly affect the outcome of the negotiations of Local 109.

Tom's intentions to get more information about Frenchy's death from Shawn O'Shaunessey were stymied, since he had become quite elusive since their conversation at the New Year's Eve party. After some time, Tom finally decided he would have to approach him at his jobsite—it wouldn't look suspicious, he thought, as there was often talk between employees and he would make it brief.

"O'Shaunessey? Shawn O'Shaunessey?" The boss took a big drag on his cigar.

"Yes—Shawn. You know him."

"Uh ... yeah ... Sure, I know him."

"I'd like to speak with him for just a moment. Where can I find him?"

"Your guess is as good as mine. He hasn't reported for work for three days now!"

"Oh, my gosh! I didn't know that!" Tom's heart sank, suspecting the worst.

The boss flipped the stub of his cigar into the Canal. "If ya see that slacker, tell 'im ta get back here or he'll be out of a job."

The following day, a letter arrived in the mail, addressed to Tom. It was marked "personal," and there was no return address. He quickly opened it.

Red Rafferty and Sammy Jablonski.

I'm goin' back to Ireland. You should too if you

care about livin'. Destroy this letter after reading.

Your friend,

S.

Chapter 12

Put Your Hand to the Plow

This was the tipping point. Tom grappled with his feelings and knew he should drop it, but something inside said "search for the truth." And that truth was to bring Frenchy's murderers to justice. He made up his mind. But unfortunately, in his passionate quest, he used poor judgment—asking questions in neighboring saloons. A few beers seemed to bolster his courage, and he became *too* vocal in some of his inquiries. Some of the men he knew from the boats seemed to shy away from conversation with him, knowing full well he was interested in obtaining information about certain people—and they wanted no part of it.

At times Tom dropped his guard after a few drinks, unaware there were still some anti-union men frequenting the neighborhood pubs. Several had continued their loyalty to the man who still held much power in the area, having obtained excellent jobs at some of Fingy's other enterprises after the 109th came into existence. In any case, "don't rock the boat" seemed to be the widespread philosophy of the men in the First Ward.

Tom's quest continued. He was not going to let this pursuit be set aside. He began to resent the workers, previous friends included, for their indifference in the matter; and his questioning sometimes came across in an angry tone.

"Ya think it's not important?" There was silence. "Well ... do ya? It coulda been *you*, ya know!"

Silence.

"I'll get to the bottom of this if it's the last thing I do!"

Silence.

"So help me, God, I will!" He stormed out of Clancy's Bar that night, fuming.

On to McCarthy's ... on to the Shamrock's ... on to O'Grady's ... on to Dinny's Pub ...

No one was talking. No one knew anything ... or if they did, they were not about to reveal it. Tom was becoming discouraged. Arriving home that night much later than usual, an argument ensued. This scenario was occurring more and more often in the past month or two, and Bridget felt she could no longer endure the worry. Not only was Tom drinking again, but was *his* own life now in jeopardy? And the money... Their finances were becoming problematic once again. Too much was going out the window in the pubs during Tom's pursuit for information—money that was needed at home, especially now with the baby. Tom *was* able to get himself to work every day; at least Bridget was grateful for that. But these evenings alone were filled with worry.

"Tom, you *must* stop this. You *must*!" Tom walked over to her, put his arms around her, and tried to kiss her. "You smell like a brewery," as she pushed him away. "I'm going to bed. Maybe you'd better, too—sleep it off!" she said angrily.

Nothing changed. The next evening, he was gone again—out on his search. Bridget was getting desperate. She even began to think she would take Teresa and leave—the stress was so great. She just wanted all this to end. Maybe if I leave, he will stop. We could stay at Grace O'Brien's—she would put us up. Then maybe Tom will come around and stop all this and we can live in peace again. She hated thinking such thoughts, but in her mind the end justified the means.

More time passed—still no change. But Bridget had not been able to pull herself away from her husband. It was not unusual for her to sit up night after night after putting Teresa to bed. She couldn't sleep anyway. One evening, she found herself pacing back and forth as the hour grew later and later. 1 a.m ... 2 a.m ... 3 a.m ... She felt exhausted, both physically and emotionally. She sat on the couch and began to pray. The pubs must be closed by now. He should be coming... Where could he be? 4 a.m... Now she was growing frantic. She kept going to the front door to look down the street. No sign of him. Oh, God, where is he? Please get him home.

The baby's cries awakened her. It was sunup. She jumped up from the couch and ran to the bedroom to see if Tom had come home. He wasn't there. She grabbed the baby from her crib and began to warm a bottle. Her heart began to pound. Where is he? Oh, God! Is he all right? Fear began to build up inside her. She quickly changed and fed Teresa, then fashioned a pouch-like carrier out of a blanket, hoisting it over her shoulders to carry Teresa, then headed out to search for her husband, her heart filled with dread.

Starting at the docks, she checked to see if he had come in to work that morning but was told by his boss that he hadn't seen him since the day before at quitting time. It was obvious to Bridget that he most likely must have decided to continue his pursuit for Frenchy's killers right after he had left work.

Quinn's Tavern was her next stop. "Sorry, Ma'am. I know Tom—but I haven't seen him in a couple days."

Dinny's Pub came after that. "Oh, hello, Bridget," the bartender said.

"Dinny, by any chance, have you seen Tom lately?" she asked anxiously.

"He's been around a lot lately, Bridget, but I haven't seen him for maybe a couple days now." Dinny noticed she looked terribly concerned. "Is anything wrong?"

"He didn't come home last night ... I'm worried sick."

Dinny knew Tom had been asking a lot of questions at his place lately, but didn't want to concern Bridget any further. "I'm sure he'll be alright. Probably just sleeping it off somewhere. I'll keep my eyes open for him. Maybe you and the baby should go back home."

She didn't answer—just turned and went out the door. And so it went—on and on from one place to the next, her baby in tow, asking questions. It was always the same answer. No one had seen him since a couple nights ago. She began to comb the neighborhood, stopping at all their friends' homes. Same responses.

"Sorry, Bridget, haven't seen him."

"Saw him at church last Sunday—not since."

“Did ya check with Father Lanigan? He might know something.”

There was no sleeping that night. Early the next morning Bridget was back on her rounds, continuing her search. Later that afternoon, she spoke with a man named Timothy O’Shea at Mulligan’s.

“You say the last time you talked with Thomas was a week ago?”

“Yes, Ma’am. He came here after work and said something about ...” He stopped in midsentence.

“Yes ... yes ... go on!” Bridget said excitedly.

“Well ... he made me promise not to say anything.”

“My God, man! My husband is missing!” Bridget shouted. Teresa started crying. Bridget cradled her in her arms to try to calm her down.

“Sorry, Ma’am. All he said was ‘I’ll get those two devils no matter what!’”

“Did he give you any names?” she asked, now beginning to cry herself.

Timothy handed her his handkerchief, patting her on the shoulder. “I’m sure he’ll turn up soon. I’ll let you know if I hear anything.”

“But did he give you any *names*?” she asked again, raising her voice.

“Well, no Ma’am. That’s all he said—about the two devils, I mean. And then he stormed out of here like a man on a mission!”

Bridget tramped the streets, sometimes almost ‘til dawn when she was able to leave Teresa with Mrs. Masterson. Day after day, she continued to search every saloon in the First Ward. She had questioned every neighbor and merchant, as well as all her church friends. She had reported Tom’s disappearance to the police after the first twenty-four hours.

One week later, there was a knock on the door. She opened it to find Sgt. Sweeney. Removing his cap, he greeted her, “Good morning,

Mrs. Sexton." Her heart grew fearful, as she could tell by his demeanor that it was not good news.

"What is it, Officer?" She had no time for niceties.

"Mrs. Sexton, have you, by any chance, heard anything from your husband yet?"

"No. No, Officer. What is it? What is it?"

"Well, we found a body in the Canal last night, and we need you to come down to the morgue to see if it could be your husband."

"Oh, dear God! Oh my God!" She started to shake and felt lightheaded. "Oh ..."

"Come and sit down for a moment." He led her to the sofa, just as the baby began to cry.

"Oh, dear God. I have to get the baby."

"You sit. I'll get her for you, Mrs. Sexton."

After bundling up Teresa, Bridget climbed into the police wagon with the help of the officer. She shook as she was taken to the morgue and led to a table where a body was covered with a white sheet. Trying desperately to keep some sort of composure as she was still holding the baby in her arms, she breathed a sigh of relief as the sheet was lowered from the face of the body.

Her meager savings were running out, and she had to force herself to stay at home part of the time to do sewing jobs just to keep herself and Teresa in food and pay the rent. She had no relatives and only a few friends who often brought food. Father Lanigan also helped as much as he could, giving her part of his small allowance as pastor of the parish. She was often seen walking the railroad tracks at the end of Alabama Street, collecting coal that had fallen from the cars for cooking and storing up for future use. She stood in line at local markets that sometimes gave away day-old bread. She considered herself lucky to obtain a loaf with no mold on it. At one point, her landlord was about to evict her from her house when she had no money for the rent; however, she happened to come across an ad in the newspaper for a seamstress at Kobacker's in downtown Buffalo.

As she entered the big double doors on Main Street, she was met by a well-dressed man in a three-piece suit. "May I help you, Madam?" he inquired in a business-like tone.

"Yes. I'm answering your ad for a seamstress."

"Oh, yes. That would be Mrs. Flannery you would want to see. Just go to the back of the store and you will find her in the ladies' dress department over to the right."

"Thank you."

A portly woman was holding a tape measure up to another lady's shoulders with one hand while removing pins from her mouth with the other, then attaching them to a paper pattern. Bridget, not wanting to disturb her, waited patiently until Mrs. Flannery finished with her client. Removing the remaining pins from her mouth, she turned toward Bridget.

"Can I help you, dear?"

"Are you Mrs. Flannery?"

"Yes. Yes, I am. Can I help you with something?" She leaned over a table, writing some figures down as she spoke.

"Well, I'm here about your ad for a seamstress," Bridget answered.

"Oh, yes. Well, you kind of caught me at a bad time though, my dear. Do you suppose you could come back about three?"

"Well ..." Bridget thought for a moment, as she was expected back at Mrs. Masterson's at four o'clock to pick up Teresa. "Well ... yes, I can," she finally offered, uneasy at the time limitation but not wanting to miss this opportunity.

Biding her time, she walked by the stores on Main Street looking at the window displays. She was getting hungry and decided to sit on the bench in front of Adam, Meldrum, & Anderson's to eat the sandwich and apple that she had packed. Looking up, she noticed the beautiful display of spring clothing in the window of the store. Yet, suddenly, in her mind's eye, the window seemed to change, becoming as it was so long back when she sat on that very same bench admiring the beautiful mohair multi-colored coat with the fur collar. Her eyes began to well up with tears. She dabbed them with her handkerchief and tried to compose herself so she could finish her lunch in time to return to Kobacker's. Two women walked by; and, noticing their coats also having fur collars was enough to cause tears to flow once again as she thought of Tom's sweetness in making sure she had that coat for Christmas. Anguish built up within her heart, but she tried her best to dismiss the feeling, as she attempted to pull herself together and calm down. She tossed the rest of her lunch into a nearby trash basket, unable to eat, and began the walk back to see Mrs. Flannery. She wondered if possibly it might be better just to sell her coat—it might bring enough money for a few weeks of food for Teresa and herself. But the bittersweet image of Tom's Christmas gift would not allow her to contemplate the thought any longer—it was the only thing she had from him. Besides, she was holding onto that hope of his return. She noticed the big round clock high on a pedestal at the intersection—2:55 p.m. Better hurry. Don't want to be late. Too important.

"Come in. Come in, my dear." Mrs. Flannery pointed to a chair across from her desk in the back room, as she peered over the top of her eyeglasses to check the clock on the wall. "You are right on time. Very good. Now, as to this job ..."

"Yes, I would like to apply, please."

"Now tell me—well, first of all, your name please?"

"Bridget Sexton."

"How do you do, Bridget. May I ask if you have any experience with fashion or design—or even sewing in general?"

Bridget sat erect in her chair, straightened her dress, and responded, "Yes, Ma'am. I owned my own dress shop in Ireland."

"Well, well, young lady ... I'm impressed. However, we generally always need references before we hire."

"I see ... and I do understand. However, I learned my trade from a friend of my mother's in the Old Country. But you see, she has since passed away."

"Oh?"

"I might possibly be able to get you some references from some of my customers back in Ennis, however. Some of them frequented my shop quite often and were very satisfied." She knew Mrs. Tillie would be happy to write her a reference. "It might take a little time though, being that I would have to write and then wait for a response. And I would be happy to do that for you if it is absolutely necessary. But I was really hoping that I could line up the job right away though. You see ..." Her eyes began welling up again. "Oh, I'm sorry."

"What is it, my dear?"

Bridget wiped her tears and shifted her position on the chair. "I'm so sorry, Mrs. Flannery. Well ... well, it's just... well, you see, my husband has been missing for some time now."

"What?"

"He's been gone for quite some time. We don't know where he is. I don't know if he's safe. I have no money. And my baby needs food ..."

"Oh, my dear!" Mrs. Flannery's heart was touched. She put her arm around Bridget's shoulder, handing her a handkerchief from her pocket as she did so. As she watched Bridget trying to compose herself, she thought perhaps she could do without the references after all. "Now Bridget, I suppose we might be able to make an exception about the references in this case. Perhaps we might just be able to hire you like on a trial basis, in which case you could begin right away. What do you think of that?"

"Oh, Mrs. Flannery! Oh, I promise I will do my very best work for you. I don't know how to thank you."

"Now don't you worry about anything, dear. But, just one question—by any chance do you have any experience on the new electric machines?"

"Well, no, not really." Bridget's heart grew concerned at the question. "But I'm really a very fast learner. I'm sure I could pick it up right away."

"Oh, I'm sure you could, my dear. Actually, it's so much easier than that old foot pedal."

Bridget nodded, smiling, relieved that experience with the electric machine could be so easily dismissed.

"Now write your name and address down here," Mrs. Flannery directed, handing Bridget a pad and pencil. "I will contact you as soon as I can. And, just so you know, it would be three days a week to start. Then maybe we could look into adding more hours down the road a bit."

"Oh, that would be fine, Mrs. Flannery. Thank you so much."

She was able to relax on the trolley ride back home, comforted with the thought that she could earn enough to feed herself and Teresa. There had been so many times when she didn't know if she could go on living with the gnawing feeling in her heart that never seemed to leave since Tom had gone missing. There wasn't a night gone by that she hadn't cried herself to sleep; and her burden had become even heavier, not knowing if she would have enough food for the baby to stay alive for even another day. But strange as it may seem, she would find herself getting angry at the situation. And that anger would somehow strengthen her to go on and bolster her resolve to overcome it all.

Her salvation came in the form of a letter from Mrs. Flannery. She was informed she could start her new job the following Monday morning. With a lilt in her voice, she sang out, "Teresa ... Teresa ... look baby!" as she waved the letter in front of the child. "Mommy's got a job!" Grabbing Teresa from her crib, she began to swing her around.

Suddenly the joy changed to sorrow. She stopped abruptly, practically in tears, and laid the baby back down. *Tom ... Tom ...* She would have given anything in the world to have that joy she had always experienced when he would grab her up and swing *her* around. Those strong arms! Tom, I miss you so! She flopped backward onto the couch, her head in her hands, and sobbed her heart out. What seemed like hours of agony over her lost love suddenly ended. It was back. Back again. As if someone was whispering into her heart—"*Put your hand to the plow, Bridget dear.*"

Bridget informed Mrs. Masterson that she wouldn't be able to babysit for her anymore because of the new job. But now, *she* had a problem—finding someone to watch little Teresa. She tried all weekend to find someone, asking around the neighborhood as well as at the church; no one was available. Monday morning came and she felt she had no choice but to go in to the store and explain the situation to Mrs. Flannery, hoping she could obtain more time from her to find the help she needed in order to keep the job.

She arrived at work, Teresa in tow, and explained her situation to the good lady. "I'm so sorry, Ma'am, but I couldn't find anyone to watch my baby. Could I ..."

Mrs. Flannery, seeing that Bridget seemed upset, broke in. "Now, now, my dear. It's alright that you brought her. Don't worry—we can handle this. She won't get in the way." She paused momentarily, reaching over to pat the baby on the shoulder. "What a pretty little thing!"

"Mrs. Flannery, I know I'm supposed to be starting my job today—but could you possibly give me a couple more days to try again to find a babysitter for Teresa. I hate to even ask—but I need the job so badly."

"But, my dear—you have already been hired!"

"Well ... but ... I know, Mrs. Flannery. But you see, I thought I wouldn't have a problem finding someone to watch her."

Mrs. Flannery broke out in a big smile. "Come over here, Bridget—over here to the storeroom." She led her to a side room filled with floor-to-ceiling shelving, mostly holding bolts of every kind of material and every color in the rainbow. "There!" the kind lady announced as she pointed to a small cradle at the back of the storeroom.

"A cradle? I don't understand."

"Well, let me explain something to you, my dear. The city fathers, along with some of the merchants, including us, have agreed to collect donations for the Fresh Air Mission."

"What is that?"

"It's a camp for underprivileged children. You know—those whose families can't afford to take them on vacation to the beach. It's located down on the lake shore where the children can go swimming in the hot summer months."

"Oh, that's wonderful!"

"Yes, dear—that's where the cradle comes in. You see, each store will have a cradle just like this one," as she pointed to it, "hanging from the ceiling and customers can donate, putting money into it. With many stores participating, we hope there will be enough money collected for many children to enjoy the camp. Actually, they call it Cradle Beach now."

"Oh, I see the connection. What a beautiful idea!" Bridget looked over at the cradle before her.

"So seeing as we have a cradle here, my dear, and our program won't be starting for a few weeks, you are welcome to use it for little Teresa until you can find a babysitter. So let's get you started right now. Today! How does that sound?"

Bridget wanted to hug her, but thought it might not be appropriate. "Oh, how will I ever be able to thank you, Mrs. Flannery?"

Before the woman could answer, a few of the female employees came over to see the baby and began fussing over her. They were so demonstrative, Bridget wondered if they had never seen a baby before. "Her name's Teresa," she announced, enjoying their attention to her child.

"Oh, how cute!" one said.

"She's beautiful!" another added.

A few minutes later, Mrs. Flannery spoke up. "Girls, this is our new girl—Bridget." They all welcomed her, then returned to work. "Bridget, bring the baby over here," Mrs. Flannery said, as she moved the cradle from the storage room and placed it next to her desk. "Now, my dear, if you have to feed little Teresa before you start work, I will leave you for a few minutes. Just let me know when you are ready, and I'll give you some instructions." She left, closing the door behind her.

"Did you hear all that, baby? What good fortune! I can hardly believe it! Thanks be to God—we're in!" She proceeded to unbutton her blouse, surprised that Teresa hadn't cried even though it was quite a while past her feeding time. "Come on baby ... but don't take too long. Mommy's got to work, you see," she announced to Teresa, caressing her cheek. Afterward, she opened the door and motioned to Mrs. Flannery that she was ready to begin work.

Bridget was fascinated with the new electric sewing machine and adapted to it well. Mrs. F., as Bridget came to call her employer, was amazed at the girl's skills as she demonstrated some techniques that she used in Ireland and showed the lady some of the patterns she had worked with and thought to bring along with her. This "mass production" was not exactly to her liking, however, as she had been used to the old, much slower, way of doing things. But she was a quick learner and so thankful to be working. She could have used a few more hours; however, three days a week was all that the job required.

Although it provided food for the table, she was still having a hard time making ends meet.

She decided she would only take the streetcar to lower Main Street and walk the rest of the way to save the fare of the second car. Another warning letter from the landlord threatening eviction if her rent was late one more month, prompted her to begin a search for a cheaper place to live. It wasn't long before she found a place at 149 Fulton Street, just around the corner. It was only a one bedroom flat with a small kitchenette attached, but it would do for now. Father Lanigan made sure Stanley was available to assist her with moving, letting him know that the church would survive without his good janitorial services for a day.

The struggle continued. Tom was still missing. Many nights were spent crying into her pillow. Bridget had vowed to herself that she would never give up her search—*never.* She had to find him ... had to find him. Every week she would stop back at the police station, hoping there would be some news ... *any*thing. But to no avail. She continued to stop at the pubs from time to time—someone might possibly have caught a glimpse of him. Nothing ... Nothing ...

One day she sent an ad to be placed in the Buffalo News.

A MISSING MAN

> *Being a constant reader of your valuable paper for years, knowing that you are ready to help those in trouble, I would like to know if any of your kind readers would have any information of the whereabouts of Thomas Sexton, 149 Fulton Street. I think he must have met with an accident or some trouble. He has been from home four weeks.*
>
> HIS WIFE

Every day after work, she immediately checked the mail to see if there was any response. Since no replies were forthcoming, she thought she would submit a similar ad to all newspapers in the major cities around the country; however, this turned out to be too expensive for her meager income.

Meanwhile, she continued to take her daughter to work with her every day, thanks to the goodness of Mrs. Flannery. The baby seemed to like the trolley as it hummed along, often having a drowsy effect on her and lulling her to sleep.

One of the ladies who frequented the store was extremely satisfied with Bridget's work, asking specifically for her dresses to be done by the girl rather than the other employees. Mrs. Kennedy was a very dignified lady who had exceptional taste in female fashion. She often wore wide-brimmed hats and fox furs over her shoulders. A new dress or two was definitely on her agenda every month or so, due to the fact that her husband was a politician and they were frequently at social gatherings. Mrs. Flannery felt this request for Bridget's skills was quite a "feather in her cap," and was extremely pleased with herself for hiring the girl.

Over time and many conversations, Mrs. Kennedy discovered that she and Bridget were both from County Clare. This led to reminiscing about Ireland, both agreeing that land would always have a special place in their hearts. She soon found herself becoming quite fond of the girl, treating her like the daughter she had lost years before. But their background seemed to be the only thing the middle-aged lady and Bridget had in common.

One day, as Bridget was fitting the woman for a special dress for a convention, she began to share more about her life with the woman and soon found herself discussing her lost husband.

"Oh, Bridget! Oh, that's terrible! You poor thing!"

"It really has been so difficult," she answered, tears welling up in her eyes.

Mrs. Kennedy's mood changed drastically, as she thought of the many times she had bragged about her husband and his success when she had first met Bridget. She felt remorseful and saddened by this boasting, knowing full well now how much it must have hurt the girl. She took a lace-edged handkerchief from her purse and handed it to Bridget. "Is there anything at all I can do, my dear?"

"Well, I suppose there is one thing, Mrs. Kennedy." Bridget wiped the tears from her eyes. "I really must find a second job, as I can't get enough hours here to support my little Teresa and myself. So if you ever hear of anything ..."

"Oh, dear, why didn't you tell me sooner?" Looking in the mirror while primping her hair, she added, "I'm sure my husband could find you work at the Pan-Am Exposition. He has people under him who are in charge of hiring, and a word from him, I am sure, will bring something for you there."

"The Pan-Am Exposition?"

"Yes ... you know of it, don't you?"

"Well, kind of. I mean ... I have heard that it's coming here, but I'm not exactly sure what it's all about. Oh, excuse me, but would you please lift your arm so I can pin this."

"Oh, of course. Yes, actually it's like a World's Fair, Bridget. Among other things, it has information on machinery, manufacturing, the arts, music, new technology, medicine, and many, many other exhibits."

"That sounds exciting! Oh, I would be so very appreciative! But I do have to be here during the day—three days a week, that is."

"No problem, my dear. I know that arrangements can be made for you to work the evening hours there. Don't you worry—consider it done!"

"Now the other arm, please."

"Oh, of course."

"I'm sorry, didn't mean to interrupt you, Mrs. Kennedy."

"Not at all. Anyway, it's so exciting that we should be hosting this world renowned event right here in our own backyard!"

It wasn't long before the rich politician's wife returned for another fitting, and she had good news for Bridget. The construction was nearly completed for the Exposition to begin, and Mr. Kennedy had already arranged for Bridget to work in the maintenance department, cleaning the Temple of Music at night. In the meantime, Bridget had found a teenage girl in the neighborhood to watch the baby during the hours she was at Kobacker's, but it was only temporary. She knew she would have to find another sitter—one who was able to babysit for longer hours into the evening once she started at the Expo.

Some time passed and Bridget was surviving—but barely. She made a little extra money doing alterations at home. She looked forward to her new evening job, as it would afford her and the baby a little more than the bare basics of life. Every evening as she rode home on the trolley, she would take her rosary from her purse and say the prayers slowly as she fingered the beads.

Mrs. Kennedy, on one of her visits, had given a little poem to Bridget that her husband's nephew had sent them from England. This young aspiring poet, G.A. Studdert Kennedy, was gaining notoriety there. Bridget always had had a love of poetry, but this particular work touched her very deeply. She read it over and over until she knew it by heart, often meditating on it.

WHEN JESUS CAME TO BIRMINGHAM

When Jesus came to Golgotha,
they hanged Him on a tree.

They drove great nails through hands and feet
and made a Calvary.

They crowned Him with a Crown of Thorns,
red were His wounds and deep

For those were crude and cruel days,
and human flesh was cheap.

When Jesus came to Birmingham,
they simply passed Him by.

They would not hurt a hair of Him;
they only let Him die.

For men had grown more tender,
and they would not give Him pain.

They only just passed down the street
and left Him in the rain.

Still Jesus cried, "Forgive them, for they know not what they do.

And still it rained the winter rain
that drenched Him through and through.

The crowds went home and left the streets
without a soul to see

And Jesus crouched against a wall
and cried for Calvary.

Bridget's wounds were also deep, as the hole in her heart and her longing for Tom had not lessened. She took some comfort in uniting her sorrows to those of Christ and continued to focus on the fact that she and her husband would meet again ... if not in this world—in the next. Yet she would *never* give up her search for him. She asked Mrs. Kennedy if her husband could help her in any way, and he did try by having some of his friends in government begin some inquiries ... but to no avail.

Loneliness continued to creep in more and more in the evenings, as she would lie on the bed in the darkness—her heart holding tightly to her memories.

Chapter 13

He Didn't Know, Poor Fellow

1901 was looking a little better. Mr. Kennedy pulled a few more strings, allowing Bridget to be the *head* of maintenance in the evenings at the Temple of Music building in the center of the Pan-American Exposition—a square, ornate, red and gold trimmed building with bluish-green dome panels. Angels surrounded St. Cecilia with her harp on the southeast corner of the structure.

It would take some stamina for Bridget to hold down her day job at Kobacker's and work the evening shift at the Expo. But she was strong, energetic, and determined. After worrying about a babysitter who could watch Teresa for her expanded working hours, a solution in the form of a new arrival on Fulton Street was a blessing.

Mrs. Ryan was hanging clothes in her yard at the same time Bridget was doing the same. "Good morning, young lady! I'm Megan Ryan, your new neighbor," she said, leaning over the fence.

"Oh, good morning! Welcome! It's a pleasure to meet you, Mrs. Ryan—and I'm Bridget Sexton."

Mrs. Ryan mentioned she had eight children, which was no surprise to Bridget, noticing her many lines of clothing. Three of the children were playing beneath the clean laundry, running in and out between the shirts and pants, hiding and laughing as they did. "Children, come over here!" Mrs. Ryan instructed. "You can't be running around through my wash with those dirty hands. Come here—I want you to meet someone."

The children came out from under the laundry lines, grabbed a few dandelions and blew the parachute balls into each other's faces.

They slowly made their way over to the fence where Bridget stood smiling at their antics.

"This is Adam, Brian, and Connor," Mrs. Ryan announced, pointing to each as she did.

"Well! Hello there, children. I'm so happy to meet you." Bridget smiled down at them, reaching through the fence to take each one's hand. Adam would have no part of it, shying away. But the other two seemed to take delight in Bridget's attention. "You must be very proud of your beautiful children, Mrs. Ryan."

"Oh, please ... I hope you will call me Megan—now that we are such good friends!" She broke into a big smile. "And *your* little Teresa is beautiful."

"You know Teresa?"

"Oh, yes, your babysitter sometimes brings her out on the front porch during the afternoons. In fact, my Kathleen has taken quite a liking to her."

Bridget soon discovered the Ryans were also from the Emerald Isle. Megan was a strong and hearty, middle-aged woman. Her husband was an executive at the new H-O cereal mill. Wanting to be close to his work, but having to move his family quickly, they rented the house next door to Bridget's until they could find time to search for a larger place. Mr. Ryan's family were upper-class Irish who were horse breeders in the old country; however, the blight had even affected *their* financial status, and they decided to sell everything and come to America while most of their fortune was still intact.

Mrs. Ryan obviously took great delight in her "little angels," as she was prone to speak of them. A few days after meeting over the fence, she and Bridget sat on the porch steps enjoying a cup of coffee, watching their children at play. Bridget couldn't help wondering, as they chatted, if Megan could possibly babysit Teresa, being that she lived right next door; however, she didn't dare think of asking, as the woman already had eight of her own.

"Adam! Don't let me see you go near that street again! Kathleen—keep your eye on your brother!" The girl stepped over to take Adam's hand, only to have him pull away from her, tripping as he did and skinning his knee right through his pants. "Oh, no! Not another hole! I can't keep up with these kids. They go through their clothes so fast, and I just can't seem to find time for mending. I was thinking of buying a sewing machine, but it's more a matter of time than anything else."

"Well, Megan, maybe I could be of help. I'm a seamstress—and I do have a sewing machine. I'd be glad to help with the mending. In fact, I also do alterations."

"Really? Oh my gosh! That's great! Just what I need! But are you sure *you* would have the time? I mean ... didn't you tell me the other day that you were going to begin a second job?"

"Well, yes. But don't worry, I can find time on Tuesday or Thursday afternoon before I go to the Expo."

"I'll pay you, of course."

Bridget knew she could always use more money; however, she felt this might be a good time to bring up the sitting problem. "Oh, I wouldn't think of it, Megan!"

"Well, how *can* I thank you?"

"Well, actually I've been thinking maybe one of your older children could watch Teresa for me. I really do need someone, as I'll be working long hours during the summer."

"Well, that would work out fine. We can take your little angel whenever you want. In fact, I'm sure the children would welcome having her—they are quite fond of her, especially Kathleen. She always wanted a sister!" She laughed.

"I just want you to know I'll be working two jobs, as I mentioned; so I'll be gone from early morning 'til midnight— except for Tuesdays and Thursdays when I'm off from Kobacker's."

"Now don't you worry about a thing," Megan offered. "We'll take good care of Teresa, and you can be sure there's enough love to go around. We may even spoil her a bit!" she said with a broad smile. Megan had wondered in the short time she had known Bridget why she had not seen a man around her home. She wanted to inquire, yet felt too uncomfortable with that idea.

Gazing at the snow-white puffs of clouds against the azure blue sky, Bridget breathed in the fresh spring air and felt a weight taken from her shoulders. She wondered if Tom might be somewhere looking up at this same beautiful sky ... or could he be ...? She quickly dismissed the next thought that was beginning to form in her mind. Megan noticed a sudden change in Bridget's demeanor. "Is something wrong, my dear?"

Bridget didn't feel comfortable going into Tom's disappearance right then with all the children around, but she couldn't hold back the tears. "Oh, Megan ..."

"What's wrong, dear?"

"Oh, Megan ..."

The woman reached over, taking Bridget's hand in hers and placing her other arm around Bridget's shoulder, saying nothing and giving the girl time to compose herself. "It's alright, Bridget. You don't have to say anything."

"Oh, no ... it's not that." Bridget leaned over a little to whisper in Megan's ear, not wanting the children to hear. "It's my husband—he went missing some time back, and I still don't know what happened to him." More sobs came, but she tried to stifle them, taking her handkerchief from her pocket and blotting her eyes.

"What? Oh my gosh, how horrible! I'm so sorry. Oh, we will be praying for him, Bridget." They sat in silence for a few moments, Bridget taking some comfort from the woman's touch.

"Thank you, Megan. I'd appreciate that so much. But I think I'd best be going in now—I've got a lot of catching up to do."

"Of course. Just let me know when you will be needing us, Bridget."

The First Ward began like that—the educated and uneducated—rich and poor—were close neighbors. At that time, each nationality settled in its own area of the city—the Irish, of course, *being* the First Ward. There could be a janitor living next door to the mayor, mostly because these different nationalities settled in their own enclaves.

Bang! Boom! Clang! The construction site was a beehive of activity as the workers wrestled with the time limit to meet the May 1st deadline for the opening of the Expo. Every loud noise one could imagine was the first thing Bridget heard as she stepped from the trolley on Elmwood Avenue. A small wooden building just inside the entrance gates was surrounded by tables covered with blueprints for the many buildings on the grounds. Bridget approached one of the men at the site. "Do you know where I can find Mr. Jacobs?"

"Who?" asked the man with the handlebar mustache and grimy hands, brushing off the sawdust from his overalls.

"Mr. Jacobs—he's from the maintenance department I was told," she hollered, hoping to be heard above the shrill sound of a buzz saw.

"Oh, *that* Jacobs! He's over at the Temple of Music."

"Where's that?" she asked, looking around.

"Over there—that red and gold building," he shouted back, pointing to it.

"Oh, yes ... now I see it. Thank you, sir."

The man nodded, tipped his cap, and returned to his work. Bridget entered the round building and was in awe as she looked up at the high dome and four large balconies, then down at the shiny granite floors. Men on ladders of all sizes were scattered about, working on fixtures, painting, polishing, and positioning seats on the main floor—a great hubbub of motion and action. She found Mr. Jacobs giving instructions to a few of the workers. "Can I help you, Ma'am?" he asked, wiping his brow.

"My name is Bridget Sexton, and I was told ..."

"Oh, yes. You're a friend of Mr. Kennedy—he said you would be coming."

"Well, yes. I am a good friend of his wife."

"Well, I only have a few minutes, but I'll tell you a little about the job. Then you can decide if you want it."

"Oh! But I *do* want the job!" she said emphatically.

"Oh!" he said, lighting up a big cigar. "Alright then, your hours will be four to twelve, Monday through Friday. And your pay will be seventeen dollars a week."

"Oh! Mondays through Fridays?"

"Yes. Mr. Kennedy made the arrangements for you to have all weekends off. Beats me!—weekends bein' the busiest, you know. But he mentioned something about a family situation?"

Bridget was so pleased but thought it best to say nothing more about the "family situation." "Oh, I see. Very well. Thank you so much."

"You will be in charge of all the maintenance in this building. And, by the way, this is only temporary, as the Expo ends in November, you know."

"Yes, sir, I'm aware of that."

"After hours, you will clean up any litter, sweep the floors, clean the toilets, water the plants, and generally have the place clean for the next day. Oh, and make sure there's no litter left under the seats. People sometimes get careless, you know? And don't worry about scrubbing the floors— there will be a team coming in at 10 p.m. to do that. They will report to you before beginning, and you can give them any other instructions as you see fit. Make sure they scrub good between the rows of chairs. In other words, it will be *your* responsibility to see that the place is spotless for the next day. You will also be given maps of the grounds to hand out if anyone has need of them."

"Yes, sir. When do I start?"

"Well ... two days before opening—just to make sure everything is ready," he answered, puffing on his cigar and blowing smoke in the air. "You sure you're up to all this?"

"Oh, yes, Mr. Jacobs. I've been doing hard work most all my life. Don't worry. I'll see that the job is done right. You can be sure of that."

"Good. I'll see you at the end of April then—better make it *three* days before we open—probably have last minute cleaning up to do after the workers are finished. Do you have a white shirtwaist and a dark colored skirt?"

Bridget thought for a moment, then remembered she still had one of the uniforms she had sewn at the Mission— exactly what she needed. "Oh, yes, I do."

"Fine. There will be a name tag waiting for you at the Main Gate when you report for duty."

"Yes, sir." She reached over to shake his hand, as he began once again shouting out orders to his workers.

Soon the beehive of workers was replaced by swarms of visitors to the Expo. It didn't take long for Bridget to settle into her new routine. She was able to travel from Kobacker's to the Expo in time by transferring just once on the trolley. She was a quick learner and took pride in her new job, actually enjoying most of her duties, but for one—cleaning the water closets. But always being ready for a challenge, she adapted very well.

It was a hot summer, and she would take her lunch break outside on a park bench in the cool shade of her favorite tree—a shagbark hickory. She always made sure she had maps and directories with her to accommodate any visitors, offering any other assistance they might need. People from foreign countries sometimes had problems making their needs understood; however, Bridget would do her best to be of service. Her name tag read:

B. Sexton, Attendant
Pan-American Expo

Her one regret now was the fact that her time with the baby was so limited. She valued her weekends with Teresa, trying to make up for her absence during the week. She had some comfort knowing this would be temporary, with the Expo ending in November. She tried to get any sewing or mending jobs done on Tuesdays and Thursdays during the day, both for Mrs. Ryan and a few other neighbors who had heard of her skill. Saturdays were spent going to the Elk Street Market with Teresa, a routine she enjoyed sharing with the girl, showing her the many vendors selling their wares and allowing Teresa to pick out a special treat for herself, which usually ended up being a cookie. There were times when the girl pointed out other things she wanted, pulling on her mother's skirts and begging. But Bridget often had to dismiss her pleadings, saying "Mommy doesn't have enough pennies for that, Teresa." At times, however, a rolled-up piece of boloney would be given the girl by Mr. Fred, a kindly butcher known in the area for his love of children.

The market thrived with activity on Saturdays, the area being filled with horse-drawn wagons and approximately fifty or more stalls and stands, and Teresa delighted in being led from one to another, at times being the one pulling her mother along. The sights and sounds delighted the child, as she spent most of the time in her own home during the week while her mother had to work. Kathleen had been the primary sitter during the summer, at times bringing Teresa next door to play with her brothers.

Sunday was the day for worship and a time to rest, which Bridget sorely needed. Her schedule had seemed to become quite grueling for her, especially on days when the temperature soared. She often felt exhausted, literally flopping down on her bed at night. Sleep came almost immediately. In a way this was good, as there was no repetition of the long sleepless nights spent wondering about Tom.

Bridget observed many dignitaries coming through the Temple of Music. She would have liked very much to meet some of them personally; however, she felt it better to remain “on the sidelines.” As the summer months were drawing to a close, excitement was growing as talk of President William McKinley’s coming visit spread throughout the city. Bridget had heard that he would actually be receiving visitors at *her* building, and her mind began whirling, wondering if there could possibly be any way she could meet him herself. Before any answer came to mind, she was called aside one afternoon by Mr. Jacobs.

“Now, Bridget, you probably have heard by now that the President will be coming on September 6th.”

“Yes.”

“I’m going to need your help. I want you here early that day; is there any way you can arrange that?”

“How early, Mr. Jacobs?”

“Well, the President is scheduled to be here at 4 p.m. I’d like you here by noon if there is any way possible. This place must be clean as a whistle!”

“I’m sure it can be arranged, Mr. Jacobs.”

From noon until three p.m., Bridget checked the whole building to make sure every single thing was spotless and in order. Shortly before the President’s time of arrival, she purposely went to wait in the storage room, out of sight, but having a clear view of the spot where the President would be greeting the public. Many well-dressed ladies and gentlemen were beginning to line up to shake the President's hand. The organist began to play some popular music of the day as they waited. One of the tunes was "After the Ball was Over"— that same tune that Tom and Bridget had danced to back on the pier at Coney Island just a few years before. Bridget was raw with emotion—all of the excitement of the President of the United States arriving mixed with the hole in her heart for Tom. She quietly wept in silence away from the crowd.

"The Star Spangled Banner" followed as the President entered the room precisely as scheduled at 4 p.m. and began shaking hands with the crowd, a swell of applause breaking out. He was led up to a spot circled by green plants in the middle of the auditorium. A large American flag had been hung on the wall behind.

It was such a hot afternoon that many people could be seen wiping their brow with handkerchiefs. After a short while, a young girl, about twelve years of age, greeted the President and asked if she could have the red carnation from his lapel. He politely obliged her. Bridget, peering out from the storage room on the side, viewed the whole proceedings. She thought it so nice of the President to give the flower to the girl. She began to hope that, maybe if she spruced herself up and fixed her hair a bit, she might come in at the tail end of the greeting line and shake his hand herself. She knew that he had only limited time before leaving for another engagement. Looking at the large clock on the wall, she was wishing the long line would quickly dwindle so she could carry out her little plan.

She continued watching, when, a few minutes later, a man reached over to shake hands with the President. A handkerchief covered his hand, concealing a small revolver. Shots rang out and the President began to fall over, his personal guards grabbing him and lowering him to the floor.

Bridget shuddered in horror, first closing her eyes, then peering out the door once more to see the guards grappling with the assassin and pulling him down as the visitors panicked, screaming and pushing as they ran toward the exits. She quickly pulled her rosary from her pocket and tried to pray. The President was immediately removed to the Exposition Hospital and the Temple of Music was put on lockdown until further notice. All remaining visitors and employees were evacuated but for Bridget who received instruction from Mr. Jacobs to remain.

Bridget was a strong person, but cleaning up the President's blood proved to be traumatic and, coupled with the extreme heat that day, she found herself growing faint. She took a few moments, returned to the storeroom, and sat on a chair, placing her head downward toward the floor, afterward wiping her face with a cold cloth and taking a cold drink of water. She then returned to finish the gruesome task assigned her. Tears fell. Kneeling there, a sudden chill came over her sweating body as her tears co-mingled with the President's blood. This horror gave rise to a new thought—could this possibly be what might have happened to Tom? She felt sick. Will Mrs. McKinley be left alone—like I am? Oh, dear God! Let him live!

Riding home on the trolley, she couldn't shake that image of the President's face in writhing pain as he fell to the floor. She hoped no one would notice the stains of blood on her clothing from her grueling task.

The evening had cooled off, and she opened the windows to a welcomed evening breeze. Her first duty was to herself—she needed a good long bath, almost as though she felt she had to wash away all the evil that had seemed to rule the day and brought the Commander-in-Chief low—but not dead.

The next day, things looked somewhat brighter, as the Expo had returned to its normal state. However, even though the crowds were dense before, they came in even greater numbers to see the spot where "the dirty deed" had taken place. Bridget approached Mr. Jacobs upon her arrival to inquire as to the President's condition.

"It appears he's doing pretty well, Bridget. He was on the operating table yesterday, as you probably know."

"Well, no, I didn't, Mr. Jacobs."

"Yes, there's quite a story about that. As he lay there, he said of his assassin, 'He didn't know, poor fellow, what he was doing. He couldn't have known.'"

"Really?"

"Yes. Amazing, isn't it? Well, anyway, he's over at the Milburn House right now with his wife at his side. Well, here—here's last night's paper." He handed her a copy of The Buffalo Evening News. "I'm through with it anyway and you might want to read the rest."

"Thank you." Bridget glanced at the headline as she made her way to the Temple of Music.

BUFFALO EVENING NEWS

Buffalo, N.Y. Friday, September 6, 1901

EXTRA! *EXTRA!* *EXTRA!* *EXTRA!*

PRESIDENT M'KINLEY SHOT

Two Bullets Sent Into His Body By a Stranger at the Pan-American

He Sank Down and Was at Once Taken to the Exposition Hospital

She breathed a sigh of relief—as did the nation— knowing the President appeared to be out of danger and the assassin, Leon Czolgosz, had been arrested. People once again could enjoy the beauty and the excitement of the Expo.

Eight days later, however, the nation would be plunged into sadness, suffering another shock when the President succumbed to gangrene and infection from the wound in his abdomen.

EXTRA! BUFFALO EVENING NEWS EXTRA!

Buffalo, N.Y. Saturday, September 14, 1901

M'KINLEY'S DEATH WAS CALM AND PEACEFUL

Resigned to the Will of God, the President of the United States Died at 2:15 o'Clock This Morning

Through the grapevine at the Expo, Bridget heard of McKinley's deathbed conversation with his wife, Ida. She had said to her husband, "I want to go, too. I want to go, too." The President had replied, "We are all going—we are all going. God's will be done, not ours." Then he had put his arm around her, it was reported, and passed from this world to the next.

Although with each passing day, Bridget found her hopes dwindling, she fought her inner demons that suggested she may never have closure for Tom. Her sorrow at the President's death seemed to give way to the thought that "at least Mrs. McKinley had *that*."

The last two months of work at the Temple of Music weren't the same. A pall seemed to hang over the building, as people continued to stream into it just to see where the President had been shot. It wasn't unusual to see ladies now and then wiping tears from their eyes, blessing themselves, or saying a quiet prayer.

The heat of summer turned to the cooler days of Fall and the Expo came to a close. As Bridget was leaving the grounds on the last night, the music ceased and the bright lights were being turned off building by building. She had said her goodbyes to Mr. Jacobs and her fellow workers and began her walk to the trolley. It was November 2nd, All Souls Day on the Catholic calendar, and she prayed for the President and all her deceased relatives and friends, hoping against hope that Tom was not among them.

It was good for her to have a breather from working two jobs. Now she could spend more time with little Teresa, soon turning three years of age. Things would be tighter now, however, without that extra income. Her last thought before falling asleep that night was to approach Mrs. Flannery about some extra hours at Kobacker's. She collapsed on her bed exhausted, hoping Teresa wouldn't wake up too early in the morning.

Chapter 14

The Man With the Monocle

It wasn't long before the excitement of the Expo had worn off and the death of the President had faded in the minds of many, for he now belonged to the ages.

Good fortune had come to Bridget with the increase in her working hours from three days to five per week. This worked out well for her, as she could finally enjoy spending evening hours at home with Teresa. Within a year, her talents became more evident at the store, especially since she had now begun designing many of the garments herself. Word had spread throughout the neighborhood as women began noticing her handiwork. This had brought new customers to Kobacker's, and she soon found herself accepting the position of Mrs. Flannery's main assistant. This gave her more responsibility as well as an increase in pay, as she was now being placed above the other three seamstresses who would work under her direction. Many of the regular customers who frequented the business, however, still requested Bridget by name.

One day when business was slow, a very distinguished- looking couple came into the store. "Good morning! May I help you?" Bridget asked, trying not to stare. Something so familiar with that man.

The middle-aged woman's brown hair was swept up under a wide-brimmed blue and lavender hat which matched the blue dress trimmed in purple ribbon. She held a folded-down parasol in her right hand and a very small clutch bag in her left. A short fur jacket was over her shoulders and Bridget, thinking she looked quite stunning, wondered if it might be mink. The gentleman accompanying her was wearing a three-piece suit, a gold watch fob hanging from the vest.

"Yes, my dear, you *may* help me," the woman answered. I would like to look at a few dress designs."

"Of course. We have many, and also have custom designs in addition. Would you care to step in the back room and I can show you some of them?" Now who *is* that man—I know I've seen him somewhere.

"Thank you." The couple followed Bridget, who placed some of her patterns along with pictures of the final garments before the woman. After perusing several, she pointed to three of her favorites, asking Bridget if they were from a New York City designer.

"Well, actually, *I'm* the main designer for the store. Were you interested in one of these?"

"In *all* of them!"

"All *three*?"

"Yes, all three. I must say you are certainly young to be a designer—and such a talented one at that!" She smiled at Bridget.

"Well, thank you so much. Would you care to be measured today while you're here?"

"Yes, I would, thank you."

The gentleman, sitting toward the side of the table, stood to take a better look at the pictures and nodded his approval of his wife's selections. After fifteen minutes, glancing at his watch fob a few times, he finally spoke. "We really must get back soon, dear. How much longer will this take, young lady?"

"I'll be done measuring in just a few more minutes, sir," Bridget responded, as she drew the tape from under the bosom almost to the floor, "but we also need to pick out the material your wife would like."

"I see." Looking over to his wife, he suggested, "Edith, it would be better for you to return another time. We really should be on our way now. The dinner, you know ..."

"Oh, of course." The woman looked over at Bridget. "Well, my dear, you have my measurements now and you can see from the pictures what I like. We'll be back in town next month and you can show me what you've come up with. I will leave the whole matter in your hands. You will most likely know the best materials for the patterns I've picked. From the looks of these pictures, I feel I can trust your professional judgment."

The gentleman nodded to Bridget. "Thank you, young lady. It's been a pleasure." His wife slipped her hand through his arm and they started for the door. She turned back, handing Bridget a small piece of paper and asking, "Oh, by the way, what is your name?"

"I'm Bridget Sexton."

"Thank you, Bridget."

As Bridget watched them exit, she noticed two well-dressed men standing at each side of the door leaving just behind them. She glanced down at the paper from the lady. It read:

Mrs. Theodore Roosevelt
1600 Pennsylvania Avenue
Washington, D.C.

A slight gasp exited her lips. As she turned, she realized that some in the store had already surmised who these people were, as a low "buzzing" seemed to pervade the atmosphere. Whispers behind cupped hands, smiles, and heads nodding each to the other continued for a few moments.

"Wow! Bridget's designing a dress for the First Lady! Can you believe it?"

"Oh, my gosh! The old Rough Rider himself!" a male clerk murmured.

"Rough rider?" another clerk questioned.

"Well, yes ... that's his nickname—from the Spanish American War!"

Mrs. Flannery finally brought the scuttlebutt to a close by indicating to all to return to work.

Soon after, Bridget heard that President and Mrs. Roosevelt had been to Buffalo at that time on a brief unofficial visit to the Wilcox House at 641 Delaware Avenue where the President had taken his oath of office after McKinley's assassination the year before. She worked hard making the befitting garments for the First Lady—they had to be rich and elegant looking, yet still give a stately impression to any onlookers.

There had been great anticipation in the store for the return visit of the distinguished couple; however, it wasn't meant to be. Bridget received a note the following month:

Dear Bridget,

I am sorry to say that our return visit to Buffalo has been cancelled due to a change in the President's itinerary.

I am looking forward to wearing your dresses for state dinners at the White House. May I ask that you send them to me at the address I gave you last month, along with the bill. It was a pleasure meeting you, and I hope this is not too much of an inconvenience.

My best regards,

Edith Roosevelt

The normal routine had resumed at Kobacker's until a month later, when a photograph of the President and the First Lady appeared on the front page of the newspaper ... and there it was!—Bridget's personally designed dress on display for all the world to see! Bridget soon found herself a local celebrity, as the news spread rapidly throughout Buffalo, especially so in fashion circles. Kobacker's was now in the spotlight, and the paper ran a followup article about the designer herself, once again bringing much new business to the store.

Other than a little recognition for her dressmaking skills in her hometown in Ennis, Ireland, she had never had such accolades afforded her as she was now experiencing. Having the work of her own hands become a garment worthy of the First Lady was a great joy to her humble spirit, and she gave all honor and glory to God—after all, she thought, who else could possibly have arranged all this? A healthy raise was soon in Bridget's paycheck, and she found her financial difficulties starting to diminish as she began catching up on past bills. This, in itself, soon brought much happiness to her heart, as she was now able to provide little niceties for Teresa, a pleasure which was denied her for so long—a new dress, a stuffed bear, and a new baby doll.

The following Sunday, Mrs. Ryan came to call. "Good morning, dear," said the mother of eight. "How are you today?"

"Good morning, Megan. It's so good to see you again. Come in. Can I get you a cup of tea?"

"Well, yes, that would be nice—but I can't stay long."

Bridget was glad Teresa was still asleep, so she and Megan could enjoy a cup of tea and chat for a while. "I just had to hear all the details about your meeting the President," Megan offered, as she pulled the picture from the newspaper from her apron pocket. "Oh my gosh! How awesome!"

"Oh, I know! It really was! Awesome, I mean!" Bridget laughed, still hardly believing it herself. "I didn't even know who it was at first, Megan. Well ... I mean ... I thought I had seen the face somewhere, but it didn't connect right away. Just knew he looked familiar, you know?"

"Well, yeah, but, who else wears a monocle? Wasn't that kinda a clue?"

"Well, no. He didn't have that on when he came in."

"Oh."

Megan wanted to hear all the details, especially about *Mrs.* Roosevelt and what she was wearing that day, how her hair was done, and did Bridget think she was pretty. Bridget shared the whole experience with her, and Megan just kept shaking her head, saying, "Imagine, *you* meeting the President and his wife—I can't believe it!" She stood up. "Oh, I'd better get back before ..." She stopped at the door, then added, "Oh, I almost forgot what I came for!"

"What's that?" Bridget asked.

"To tell you the news."

"Well, I hope it's *good* news!"

"Oh, kinda both good *and* bad!"

Bridget looked concerned. "Oh?"

"Well, you see, it's good for us, but not too good for you, I guess. Bridget, we're going to be moving. We bought a house over on Delaware Avenue—really needed more room, as you know, with all the kids! I just wanted you to know we will all miss you and little Teresa a lot." She seemed to be holding back tears. "Although it's really not that far from here. I just hope you will be able to come and see us occasionally."

"Oh, Megan! I'm going to miss you, too. You've been such a good friend, and your children have been wonderful to little Teresa. I will hate to see you go ... but I'm so happy for you—having a new home." She gave Megan a hug.

"I'm sorry, but I really have to run, Bridget. Mr. Ryan's probably looking for me. We'll talk later."

"But you didn't tell me when you'll be leaving..." Bridget's concern was growing as she wondered who could watch Teresa when Megan moved away.

"Well, I'm not sure yet, exactly. Mr. Ryan has all the red tape to go through. It might be some time before we actually go." Megan suddenly realized Bridget's plight. "Oh, Bridget, I'm so sorry—of course you're concerned about Teresa. How stupid of me! I should have told you first. I was at the card party at church Friday night and Mrs. Masterson mentioned that her husband was on good footing now at work ... with the union and all ... you know? So anyway, thanks be to God, she mentioned that she is going to give notice at the school and is so happy about it, 'cause all she ever really wanted was to be able to be at home with her children."

"She's giving up her piano lessons?"

"Well, not exactly. You see, she feels she might take in a few students right at home. It wouldn't be difficult and she'd always be there for her children."

"Oh ... oh, yes."

"Now let me tell you the rest quickly, 'cause I really gotta run. I mentioned to her about our moving to Delaware, and she asked about Teresa."

"She did?"

"Yes, she did. And I really think you might want to contact her—sounds like it might be a definite possibility for you. A little switch here—after all, you watched *her* children. Maybe now she can watch *yours*. Bye, love."

Bridget felt a great loss when her neighbors left. Even little Teresa missed them, often crying for her babysitter—"Kaf-ween—Kaf-ween!" But she was happy for her friends finally having more room for their beautiful family at 472 Delaware Avenue. Megan had mentioned that a very famous author had lived there at one time about 30 years prior. His name was Samuel Clemens, but most people knew him by the name Mark Twain.

Bridget was quite contented with her full-time hours at work and her raise in pay. Her greatest joy, however, was the time she could now spend with Teresa in the evenings. She had developed much confidence in her ability now to be the breadwinner and was grateful to God that she no longer had to worry about paying the rent from month to month.

She had lost contact with most of Tom's old friends, even the ones who had helped her when he first went missing. Even the few who had come by to support or assist her in small ways eventually dwindled. She had made new friends at work, but most of them were married with families of their own. She didn't seem to care about being active in any social activities, being contented with her job and her evenings with Teresa.

When the child began school at St. Bridget's, it was difficult for Bridget to keep from hurting—Tom was not there to see this important step in Teresa's life. She felt empty inside. As she would lie awake during the nights, she couldn't help thinking there had to be more to life than working, eating, and sleeping. Her hope had continued to dwindle the last few years, but she fought to keep even the smallest spark alive within her heart. She had her memories, but memories couldn't hold her close in bed or swing her around in moments of joy—*or* carry a child piggyback. Oh, my poor little girl!—no daddy.

Every day at work, she wondered where the time had gone as she glanced up at the cradle hanging from the ceiling. One minute, Teresa was an infant; the next—school!

"Have you ever been there?" a voice came from behind. Bridget turned to the customer, an older, gray-haired woman smiling at her. "Cradle Beach, I mean. Have you ever been there?"

"No, I haven't," Bridget answered.

"It's a great place! I volunteer there."

"Oh, you do? What do you do there?"

"Oh, just about anything and everything. You know, helping watch those poor young children at the beach, dressing the little ones, playing games and sports events—whatever is needed. Some folks donate their time and more-or-less supervise the youngsters by spending a week or even just a day watching them."

"That's wonderful!"

"It's a beautiful beach. Do you have any children?"

"Yes, I have a daughter, Teresa."

"Oh, bring her down next summer, why don't you."

Bridget hesitated, her eyes glancing downward. "Well, thank you. But, I don't think I could afford it."

"Well, my dear! *That's* what it's for!" She squeezed Bridget's hand. "The next time I come in, I'll bring some literature for you. How would that be?"

"Oh, thank you so much." Summer was some time away, yet Bridget needed this happy thought just at that time. Her little girl—playing at the beach! She could just picture it in her heart—and that heart smiled at the thought.

Teresa seemed to thrive at school. Bridget had arranged for her daughter to walk back and forth with Mrs. Masterson's children which gave her much comfort, after school remaining at their home until their mother returned from work. The arrangement was perfect. After their dinner every evening, the child would happily show her mother all her "goodies," as she called them, that she had worked on at school that day. She was a quick learner and found school stimulating.

Tears welled up in Teresa's eyes one evening, as she related how Jimmy had pushed her in the hall and made her "fall down and bump her chin." An examination of the injured area didn't seem to show any redness or swelling, but Bridget accepted her hurt feelings, embracing her and holding her tightly to her breast. "It's okay, baby—you're okay. That naughty Jimmy!" This calming caress seemed to stop the tears almost immediately. These were the moments Bridget cherished—those moments that had been denied her for so long due to her work schedule. Bridget called them her "precious moments."

The autumn chill had set in, and Bridget made sure Teresa would be dressed warmly, having knitted her a purple "snuggle hat", as Teresa called it, with matching mittens. A pair of little black boots were on a small rug near the front door, just in case snow came early. She wanted to make sure Teresa was well prepared to trudge through the snow drifts that formed when the winds came sweeping off the lake and down Fulton Street, as they had the previous winter.

It wasn't long before temperatures plummeted, bringing thoughts of Christmas to her mind. She was determined to have everything ready for the holy day early, so she could enjoy a calm and serene Christmas with her little one. She would try to get some of her close friends for a little Christmas party for the child's sake—maybe Mastersons and Ryans. The day was upon her before she knew it. She now was living only for Teresa. Although her faith remained unshaken, her loneliness became magnified at this time of the year. She was determined that the girl would have an afternoon nap on the 24th, wanting to take her along to midnight Mass. That evening, as in previous years, she couldn't help but remember when she and Tom sat in the front pew, together feeling Teresa's little kick in her tummy. Now here she was, sitting in the front row, holding a little hand in her own.

St. Bridget's had become a comfort for her. She would never forget Father Lanigan and how he had helped her through those dark days when she had little food and Tom was nowhere to be found.

Megan Ryan had become her closest friend, but she hadn't seen her since they moved away. Shortly after Christmas, though, an invitation came in the mail, and she and Teresa happily boarded the trolley, heading for 472 Delaware Avenue. In a bag were eight pair of mittens which Bridget had knitted over the past month or so—seven of different colors and one of pink—for the only girl, Kathleen. She had wrapped them in tissue and each had a name attached on a little card—Adam, Brian, Connor, Daniel, Kathleen, Kevin, Kyle, and Shane.

The snow was falling gently as they arrived, being greeted at the door by the oldest child. Little Teresa grabbed her immediately around her legs, squeezing her, delighted to see her once again. "Kaf-ween! Kaf-ween!"

"Mom, Mom!—it's Bridget and Teresa!" Kathleen immediately picked up the child in her arms, hugging her tightly. "Oh! It's so good to see you both! Come in. Come in."

Before they finished removing their coats and hats, a stampede was seen coming down the red carpeted stairway. Hugs and kisses were the order of the day, amongst the confusion of it all. Megan arrived on the busy scene, wiping her hands on the white apron which covered her deep green skirt and white blouse. A small sprig of fake holly berries was attached at the neckline. "Now, now, children," Megan loudly announced, "give them some breathing room!" She came over and hugged her two guests, as Kathleen tried to help bring some order to the chaos. Megan instructed the twins to take their guests' coats and led them into the parlor.

A large red brick fireplace was on the far wall, a cozy warmth emanating throughout the room from the flames within. The floor-to-ceiling mahogany bookcases on either side were filled with many books—some on grain and milling, others on economics, transportation, and railroads. Bridget noticed copies of "Huckleberry Finn" and "Tom Sawyer" as well, among the many green plants and pictures of the grain elevators that also graced the shelves. She picked up "Tom" and began to page through it. "Oh, that's my *favorite* story!" said Shane, one of the twins, the freckles on his nose seeming to fade outward across his cheeks.

"Mine too," offered the other twin. "The best part is when Tom and Huck were pirates and ..."

"Yeah, remember?" Shane broke in excitedly. "The Black Avenger and the Red-Handed! An' how Huck put that weed in the old corn cob pipe and smoked it!"

"I wish I could go down a river on a raft like they did," Daniel added. "Did ya ever read it, Bridget?"

"*Mrs. Sexton*, Daniel!" Megan strongly corrected.

"No, but I've heard it's a very good story," Bridget replied, smiling at the two boys as she returned the book to the shelf. "And to think the man that wrote it lived right here, in this very house! But I suppose you already know that, don't you?"

"Mmm—Hmm." Both twins nodded their heads.

"Please, have a seat." Megan pointed to the red velvet couch, as the youngsters took a spot on the floor in front of the fireplace.

"Sit here, Teresa! Come on, sit down here with us!" Kevin called over to the child, standing close to her mother.

"Go ahead, Teresa—sit with them. Your home is absolutely lovely, Megan," Bridget offered, as she glanced at the shiny hardwood oak flooring and the tapestries on the wall. "And someone did a really beautiful job decorating that Christmas tree!"

"I helped!" Shane declared.

"I did too!" his twin remarked.

"And Kyle and Kathleen put the garlands around," Megan said.

"Did the little ones help, too?" Bridget asked.

"Yes, they hung some of the ornaments on the lower branches," Megan replied, smiling at Adam, Brian, and Connor, who were so obviously proud of themselves.

Megan took a seat next to Bridget. "It's so good to see you again, Bridget. It seems so long."

"Oh, Megan, I've been so busy."

"Oh, I know, you poor dear. It must be so hard." She looked sympathetically at Bridget before turning to Kathleen. "Warm some milk up, dear—for hot cocoa."

"Yes, Mother."

"We'll have a little something to warm you up; you look so cold," Megan said to Bridget.

After a short while, the children's chatter made conversation a little difficult. "Okay, children—go in the other room and show Teresa some of your toys," Megan instructed. "Now—that's better," she said, smiling. "They tend to get a little rambunctious at times."

Kathleen entered the room with a tray full of muffins and two cups of hot cocoa. "This should warm you up," Megan offered, passing one of the cups over to Bridget. "It's such a bitterly cold day today!"

The pleasantries of renewing old acquaintances over the delicious drink in front of the beautiful fire made for a lovely time—at least for a little while!

"What smells so good in here?" Daniel asked, rushing into the room with the others.

"It's muffins!" squealed little Brian with delight.

"Hold It!" shouted Megan. "One at a time!" Just then a little hand reached over the side of the tray and Megan gently slapped it away. "Guests come first! Wait your turn!" After passing the tray to Bridget, then to little Teresa, she set it back down on the table. "Okay, you ruffians—*now* you can have one." In the blink of an eye, the tray was empty!

Bridget had always looked on Megan as a mother-figure, and one in whom she was comfortable confiding in when she used to live next door. It felt good to be in her presence once again, and they spoke quietly together on the sofa as the children finished their treats and returned once again to the "toy room."

"You know, Megan, I've been thinking lately about moving back to New York City. I mean ... I have many friends back there and ... well, since Tom is no longer with me any..." Bridget teared up, stopping in midsentence. She quickly held her handkerchief up to her face to conceal her emotions.

"Oh, dear, I'm so sorry. Is there anything I can do?" Megan took Bridget's hand in hers.

Bridget just shook her head. "No, not really, I guess. Except maybe—would you pray with me?"

"Yes, of course." After praying the "Our Father" together, Megan continued, "Oh, Lord, have mercy. Help Bridget and give her your strength to get through this terrible ordeal. Bless her, Lord, with wisdom and guide her steps as she enters this new phase of her life. In Jesus' name, we pray. Oh, and Lord, keep her and Teresa safe in their travels."

It was a short prayer, but very comforting to Bridget. "Drink your hot chocolate before it gets cold, dear. It'll make you feel better." Megan handed Bridget her cup. They sat in silence for a few moments as Bridget composed herself, Megan's hand still in hers.

"Now tell me, Bridget," Megan inquired, breaking the silence and trying to change the subject. "How is your job going? You're still at Kobacker's, I presume?"

"Yes, I am," Bridget responded, beginning to feel better. "I received a promotion. I think I told you, didn't I, that I'm designing some new fashions for the store?"

"How wonderful! I always knew you were talented along those lines."

"Thanks, Megan."

"What I'm wondering, though, Bridget, is why you're thinking of moving when things are going so well for you at the store?"

"Well, you know ... I've been thinking ... well, this place has so many hurtful memories now. Everywhere I go, I'm reminded of Tom and ..." She hesitated, looking down at the floor. "Well, I just want to get away. I want to make a new start. And I'm thinking of Teresa also, you see. Like, there's trade schools in New York for young ladies. So I'm thinking of her, too. And, everything considered, I'm thinking ... well ... maybe it would be better for both of us. A change of scenery, I guess. You know what I'm trying to say, don't you, Megan?"

"Of course. And I'm sure you'll make the right decision, dear." Megan hugged her.

"Thank you, dear friend," Bridget said, hugging her back. "Now tell me about *yourself.* Well, I know you sure do have your hands full with the kids and all. And, oh! That Kathleen—I can't get over how she is blossoming into such a beautiful young lady!"

"I know—isn't she though? Well, I thank God every day that they are all healthy. They do keep me runnin' though—that's for sure!"

"And, by the way, how is Mr. Ryan?"

"Oh, he's doing well—working hard, as usual. He wasn't even able to get more than two days off for Christmas. Said to tell you he was sorry he couldn't be here."

"Oh, that's okay. I understand." Bridget reached over to the side of the sofa where she had laid a large shopping bag on arrival. "I have a few gifts for you and the children here, Megan."

"Oh, Bridget, you didn't have to ..."

"But I *wanted* to." She handed Megan her gift. "Merry Christmas, Megan. It's not much, but I hope it keeps you warm."

Upon opening the gift, Megan pulled out a pink scarf. "Oh! How beautiful! Did you make this *yourself*, Bridget?"

"Yes, I did."

"Well, thank you so much, but you shouldn't have. I know how terribly busy you've been. But I do appreciate it—it's just lovely!"

"I'm glad you like it, Megan."

Megan wrapped the scarf around her neck. "How does it look? It will keep me nice and warm." She rose from the sofa. "Oh, wait, I'll be right back. I have a little some- thing for you, too."

A few minutes later, she returned with an envelope. "Merry Christmas, Bridget. I didn't have time to go shopping, but I hope you'll like this."

"Oh! Oh, my gosh!" She took the two new five-dollar bills from the envelope. "Oh, Megan, this is *way* too much!"

"Now, now, my dear, I want you to get what you need for Teresa and yourself!"

Bridget was overwhelmed and hugged Megan, thanking her profusely. "You don't know how much this means to me!"

Unbeknownst to the two women, some little eyes had been peeking from the sides of the parlor door, watching them opening their presents.

"Can we come in now, Momma?" little Adam asked.

Before "Momma" could answer, the children came running into the room shouting, "Do we get some presents, too?"

Megan rolled her eyes. "Where's your manners, children? You shouldn't even be asking now."

"Oh, that's all right," Bridget said, as she removed the other gifts from her shopping bag. "It's okay—they're so anxious!"

"Well," Megan responded as she looked over at the children, "if you know how to ask."

"Please ... please ..." they all shouted.

"Oh, all right. All of you sit down," as she pointed to the floor in front of the sofa.

Bridget handed the children their gifts and they proceeded to rip them open. Mittens! Some had red and some had green. Some were happy and some were not. But surprisingly enough, they negotiated for their favorite color; and eventually, after a few squabbles, they all ended up happy.

Megan spoke up. "Now what do you say to Mrs. Sexton?"

"Thank you, Mrs. Sexton," came the choir of voices, ranging from toddler to teen.

Adam jumped to his feet and threw his arms around Bridget's legs. Bridget hugged him and kissed him on the forehead. "Me got a present for you, too," he proclaimed with a big smile on his face. He quickly rushed from the room, soon to return with a somewhat faded, threadbare teddy bear which appeared to have survived many, many a hug. He thrust it forward to Bridget, grinning from ear to ear.

"For me?" Bridget asked.

"Uh, huh."

"Oh, thank you, Adam."

"But that's your *favorite* bear, Adam!" Connor advised, a look of surprise on his face.

The other children just sat there, watching to see what would happen next. Bridget wished to acknowledge Adam's sweet generosity in granting her his favorite bear but didn't want to take it from the child. "Adam, this is such a wonderful gift. I just don't know how to thank you. I love your little bear, but I'm wondering, darling, if he might get lonesome for his other toy-friends if I take him home with me. But mostly, I'm just afraid he would miss *you* an *awful* lot."

Adam looked pensive. "Yeah ..."

"Well now, I'll tell you what. How would it be if we shared him? He could stay here for now with you so he wouldn't get homesick ... and every time I come over I could play with him." She laughed inside herself, thinking her solution would most likely be accepted by the child.

"Uh, huh." Adam smiled and took his bear back, hugging it close as though it were a long-lost friend once again found.

"Now that all our gifts have been opened, let's not forget whose birthday is today," Megan announced.

"I know!" Kevin hollered.

"Me too! I know. too!" chimed in Adam.

"All right then," let's all go over to our manger and speak to ..."

"*Jesus!*" shouted Connor.

"Yes, so let's offer a little prayer. Kathleen, would you like to lead us?"

"Yes, Momma," Kathleen replied, taking little Teresa by the hand over to the Christmas tree where the children all sat on the floor in a semicircle before the manger.

"I think the third Joyful Mystery of the Rosary would be appropriate, Kathleen."

"Yes, Momma." The girl took her rosary from her pocket and began:

"*The Third Joyful Mystery—The Birth of Jesus*"

Kathleen began the Our Father, followed by ten Hail Marys in remembrance of the Lord's birth, and the children all joined in.

Afterward, Brian announced that he wanted to sing a song for Jesus' birthday. "Very well, go right ahead," said Megan.

"*Oh, Come all the faceful*
Joyful on my trumpet
Oh, come me and come me
to best of the hem."

Holding in her laughter, Megan told the four-year-old how very nice and pleasing his gift was to Jesus. Not to be outdone, Connor decided he, too, had a present for the Lord and quickly laid his new mittens at the manger. But the tenderhearted little Adam once again stole the show by presenting Jesus with his bear.

Suddenly Teresa broke into tears. "What's wrong, Teresa?" She continued sobbing with no answer. "What is it, baby?" her mother asked.

"I don't have no present for Baby Jesus," she stated through her sobs.

"Oh, honey!" Bridget said. "I know the best present you could give Him, and you have it right now."

The girl looked up at her mother. "What? What present, Momma? I didn't bring no present for Him."

"Teresa, do you know what the Baby Jesus wants more than anything else?"

"Huh?"

"Love. That's the most important thing of all to Him—for us to love Him." Bridget smiled.

"*I* love Him!" Teresa said. "Here—I'll show Him." She took the statue of the Baby Jesus from the crib and kissed it, happy to be able to give Him her gift, afterward holding it close to her chest for a "big, big hug!"

They closed their "birthday celebration" with a few more Christmas carols before being called to the table by Megan for ham sandwiches and cranberry juice followed by an assortment of Christmas cookies. Glancing out the window, Bridget noticed the dark clouds coming off the Lake, announcing a coming barrage of snow.

"Oh, oh Megan! Look!" as she pointed to the window.

"Looks like we're in for a storm," Megan warned.

"Yes, maybe I'd better be on my way, I'd like to be home before dark."

Bridget and Teresa boarded the trolley just as the snow began to fall. " Oh, look Mommy! Snow!" Teresa announced excitedly. "Can you make me a snowman?"

"We'll see tomorrow, honey. By the time we get home, we'll need a bath and a little more to eat—then it'll be time for bed."

"Oh ... all right."

As the trolley made its way to the First Ward, Teresa was a nonstop talker, excitedly re-living the fun events of the afternoon with their friends. "When can we go back there, Mommy? I like to play there. They have lots and lots and lots of toys."

"We'll try to visit again soon, Teresa. I'm glad you had such a nice day."

Arriving back in the First Ward, a bitter wind had picked up, and they hurried along, walking against the snow blowing in from the Lake. Bridget pulled Teresa's collar up and her hat down a little more to cover her ears, as they trudged the few blocks through the snow, hand-in-hand, to their humble home at 149 Fulton Street.

After a warm cup of cocoa and some toast, Bridget got the child ready for bed and sat down with her on the sofa for a bedtime story. It seemed impossible, however, to read more than a line or two without interruption, as Teresa continued her remarks about the afternoon. "Let's get a house like theirs, okay, Mommy? I like that house really a whole lot. It's so nice and big and you can play hide and go seek in it."

"Is *that* what you children did, Teresa?"

"Mmm—Hmm."

"Oh, my goodness! I hope you weren't running all over the place there."

"No, just hidin'. It was lots of fun." She smiled for a minute, then continued. "I found Collin—Adam too!"

"Really? Where were they?"

"Collin was behind the chair."

"And Adam?"

"Well, I couldn't find him for a while, but then I looked behind the door and he was there."

Bridget tucked the child in bed and heard her prayers.

"God, I like your snow and I hope I
could get a snowman tomorrow and ..."

"Teresa, we start like this: In the name of the Father, and of the Son, and of the Holy Ghost, Amen," her Mother interrupted, taking the child's hand to remind her to bless herself.

"And please tell Bobby to stop
pulling my hair in school. And bless
Mommy and me. And I don't like spinach,
but it's not your fault ... well ... kinda it is

but you make good stuff too ... like cookies.
So goodnight God."

Bridget smiled and kissed Teresa on the forehead. "Goodnight, baby. Love you."

Loneliness. Loneliness. It always seemed worse at this time of the year, especially in the evenings. The quietude. The stillness. It never did seem to create a stillness in her heart though. More like a shattered feeling. Like something was broken long back and had never been repaired. Bed was empty. No one to hold her. No one to whisper in her ear. No one to snuggle up to. No one to smile at when awakening and rolling over in the morning. She needed her rest but wanted to stay up until she couldn't keep her eyes open, so as to doze off to sleep right away when finally going to bed. It didn't work that way that night, however. She lay in bed listening to the howling winds outside for what seemed to be hours—alone with her thoughts. Tom ...

The bitterly cold winter was followed by a very wet Spring that year. It was a relief when Summer finally arrived, and Bridget's two-week vacation enabled her to volunteer to supervise the children at Cradle Beach on the shores of Lake Erie. It did her heart good to see Teresa enjoying the many activities and interaction with the other children. The girl loved the sing-alongs around the campfire in the evenings, her voice the loudest to be heard. Within two days, she had a "best friend,"—Susie. They always sat together, sang together, swam together and ate their meals together. Their cots were side by side, and they spent time whispering "secrets" to each other at bedtime.

The sunshine and the fun at the Lake were like a breath of Heaven, considering this was the first time in Bridget's life spent without worry of survival. There was something about this brief respite that felt like a healing of all her cares and worries. Here she could lie awake at night, more relaxed and calm after the beauty of the fresh air and the constant lapping of the waves on the shoreline of Lake Erie. More so, the joy of seeing her child having such a wonderful time made her heart rejoice. This two-week period seemed to be the closest she had come to being able to put Tom out of her mind for a while. But she knew she could never really give up the search. Sometimes she would still think about leaving Buffalo, as she heard of opportunities in the fashion industry in New York City. But how could she leave? There could still be a chance that Tom would be found, she continued to tell herself. Sometimes she wondered if she would ever marry again if she found out the worst. But surely, she could never love another man. There was only room for one man in her heart—that's all there was to it.

Teresa was sad at the end of the vacation, knowing her friendship with Susie might not be able to continue. Susie had told her she lived "far, far away," and Teresa could not comprehend exactly where that would be. They hugged each other as they departed, and Bridget and Teresa came back to the First Ward refreshed. That evening after prayers, the girl had a question for her Mother. "How come people are different colors, Mommy?"

Bridget had never mentioned Susie's "color." She didn't think it at all strange that the child would ask such a question, however. And it certainly wasn't a difficult one at that. "Well, darling, we are all a part of the beautiful and wonderful creation of God."

"Well, but how come Susie looks different from me?"

"Teresa, remember all the times when we were at the Elk Street Market?"

"Yes."

"Well, do you remember the florist there? The man who sold the flowers to people?"

"Mmm—Hmm.

"Which were your favorites?"

"Oh! The little ones that were shaped like hearts." She thought for a minute. "And ... the yellow ones where the middle part stood up."

"Those are daffodils, honey. And the ones that look like hearts—the pink ones—those are called bleeding hearts." Like mine, she suddenly thought, pushing it immediately to the back of her mind.

"I really liked the blue ones, too, Mommy."

"Teresa, is it hard to decide?"

"Mmm—Hmm."

"It is for me, too. They are all beautiful. All different sizes and shapes—and *colors*."

"Mmm—*Hmm.*"

"So you see, all God's children are beautiful and wonderful too—even if *they* come in different sizes, and shapes—and *colors*."

Teresa smiled. "And nice, too. Isn't Susie nice, Mommy?"

"Very nice, darling. Now go to sleep. I love you."

"Night, Mommy."

And so it went. Bridget resumed her daily work at Kobacker's and Teresa continued attending school at St. Bridget's. The months flew by and turned into years, and each year Bridget's hope for Tom's return had continued to dwindle. Now was the time that she had to make a change. Teresa was entering her early teens, and Bridget wanted more for her daughter. After much thought, she just about decided to return to New York. She could renew some of her old acquaintances and locate a trade school for Teresa. She had saved a small grubstake that she hoped could tide the two of them over until she might find employment there.

The great grain elevators—the ships—the scoopers— and the saloons—they had no significance in her life anymore. All of these things were *once* part of life—with *Tom.* She had just about accepted that terrible and hurtful conviction in her heart that it certainly was a very strong possibility that Tom was gone—*forever.*

Chapter 15

The Tragic Years

"Oh, my! How fast these new trains go!" Bridget remarked, as they rolled out of the city and moved into the countryside.

"Yes, Mom, isn't it exciting?" Teresa responded.

"Well, it sure beats the horse and buggy, and even those new electric streetcars!" Mother and daughter were certainly enjoying the experience of riding the new improved steam engine. In a short while, however, Teresa fell asleep. Bridget continued watching out the window as the scenery flashed by, catching glimpses of farmlands displaying their abundant fruit orchards and rows of vineyards and some small towns. Along the way, a few brief stops were made to pick up several passengers, as others would disembark. At one stop, she noticed a farmer tending his crops in the fields, bringing her a brief remembrance in her heart of her own people laboring in the fields back in Ireland. The memories were dim and veiled as if looking through a misty haze, but her sense was that it was a dark, unforgiving time for her whole family. But the one vision that remained completely clear was that of her father plowing the field—that field that never seemed to yield enough potatoes to keep them alive.

"ALBANY! NEXT STOP! ALBANY!"

The conductor's loud voice woke up Teresa.

"Well, sleepyhead! You've been missing the scenery," her mother said, as the train jerked to a stop.

"I'm hungry, Mom."

"Go down to the washroom, why don't you, and splash a little water on your face and wake up a little."

"I'm hungry ..."

"Yes, I know dear. We'll go down to the dining car afterward."

"Oh, a *dining* car?"

"Yes. Run along now. I'll wait for you and then we'd better get some lunch before they are done serving."

Bridget opened the menu: "Hmm. Broiled mutton chops, breaded veal cutlets, freshly hunted buffalo." The prices caused her to close it immediately, only to see a budget menu on the back cover. "Oh, here, Teresa—we can order from this. They have sliced tomatoes with baked beans for fifty-five cents or smoked haddock for ninety cents."

"Good afternoon, ladies," the waiter greeted them. "Would you care to order?"

"Yes, I think we will have the beans and tomatoes," Bridget replied.

"Mom, I want that veal thing," Teresa whined.

"We will have the beans, please," Bridget repeated.

"Yes, Ma'am."

"Don't do that, Teresa," Bridget scolded as the waiter walked away. "That's not very nice. You *know* we can't afford more. As it is, the beans are quite expensive."

"Are we poor, Mom?"

"Well, not exactly—but we certainly aren't wealthy!"

"Sorry."

"Excuse me, ladies." Bridget looked up to see a tall, handsome young man, smartly dressed in a white shirt with a striped navy and white tie. A lock of his coarse black hair was hanging down upon his forehead, and his friendly smile emitted a warm feeling. "I hate to impose upon you, but seeing this is the last table with any room, I was wondering if I might join you?"

Teresa, having taken notice of his fine demeanor, nodded her head to her mother.

"Why, of course, young man. Please have a seat." She pointed to the chair next to Teresa, which seemed to delight the girl.

"Thank you so much. Billy Darly's the name."

"How do you do," Bridget responded. "I'm Bridget Sexton and this is my daughter, Teresa."

"Very pleased to meet you both."

"Traveling to New York City, Mr. Darly?" Bridget inquired.

"Yes, I am. Actually, I'll be attending school there."

"Oh, me too!" Teresa smiled at him.

"And where would that be—your school, I mean?" Bridget asked Billy.

"Cooper Union. I'll be studying telegraphy."

"That sounds really interesting. We'll be looking for a school for Teresa when we get there. Possibly a trade school of some sort."

"Really? Western Union is hiring a lot of young ladies, I hear. They are even offering free courses."

"Oh! Where?" Bridget asked.

"Right there, at Cooper Union, where I'm going."

"Oh, Mom! That sounds so exciting! Maybe I could do *that*!"

"I'm sure you could learn that easily, Teresa," Billy said. "I have a buddy who is already working there. He says it's easy. All you have to do is learn to operate the key and tap out some dots and dashes."

"Oh, Mom! That sounds so simple. I can do that, I bet!"

"Did you wish to order anything, sir?" the waiter asked as he served the beans and tomatoes.

"Oh, I'll just have the same, please," Billy replied.

During their meal, Bridget explained a little of her background—coming from Ireland, working at the Mission, and moving to Buffalo and about her job at Kobacker's.

"And why did you decide to leave Buffalo?" Billy asked.

Not wishing to go into any details, Bridget simply replied that she felt the wages in New York would be higher and that Teresa might obtain better schooling there. "And where are *you* from, Mr. Darly?"

"Well, my family was originally from Syracuse, but we moved to Albany several years ago because of my Dad's work."

"Oh, yes. I saw you board at the Albany stop," Bridget offered.

"Mom, I think I'd really like to do that teleg ... teleg ..."

"Te—leg—ra—phy, Teresa." Billy pronounced it slowly for her.

"Would it be possible for us to contact you once we get settled in New York, Mr. Darly? Maybe we could use a little of your assistance in this schooling thing."

"Why don't you call me Billy? I feel like we're friends already. And yes, I'd be happy to help you in any way I can. Here, let me write the address where I'll be staying. At my friend's—you know—the one I was telling you about."

"Oh, the one who works at Western Union?" Bridget inquired.

"Yes, my good friend, Fergus—Fergus O'Sullivan."

"That's an unusual name—Fergus." Bridget mused.

"Well, there's a little story behind that, but I'll tell you another time." Billy jotted his friend's address on a piece of paper and handed it to Bridget. "I'll be looking forward to seeing you both in New York soon." He excused himself.

"Oh, Mom, I'm really excited. Doesn't that sound so exciting to you?"

"The telegraphy school, you mean?"

"Well, yeah. Everything. The school and his friend and ... well, Billy's real nice, isn't he? And kinda cute."

"Teresa! You are much too young ..."

Bridget's first arrival in New York City years before was traumatic and filled with apprehension and uncertainty. But now she was returning to a place where many wonderful friendships had developed long back. Approaching State Street, Bridget noticed the great increase in the number of motor cars and new electric streetlamps. They crossed the street cautiously, as the motorists seemed to be oblivious to the pedestrians.

They finally arrived at Our Lady of the Rosary Mission for Irish Immigrant Girls, Bridget's "home" for those few years long back. The young girl at the desk smiled as they entered. "Can I help you?"

"Yes," Bridget answered. "Would Grace O'Brien be here?"

"I think she's in the office. I'll get her for you."

"Thank you."

"Who shall I say is calling?"

"Oh, just say an old friend."

"Yes, Ma'am."

Teresa looked around, surveying the lobby. "Who lives here, Mom?"

"Oh, honey, there's many young homeless girls here. "*I* used to live here myself—before you were born."

"Really?" Teresa looked surprised. "You lived *here*, Mom?"

Before Bridget could answer, Grace O'Brien entered the room—a little grayer and a little stouter. She lowered her glasses, peering over the top at the two standing before her. "Well, as I live and breathe, is that *you,* Bridget?" They hugged one another, Grace stepping back to look her up and down. "Well, you turned out to be a handsome young lady, you have." She looked over at Teresa. "And who might this young one be?"

"She's my daughter—Teresa."

"Oh, she's beautiful! How old are you Teresa?"

Teresa, seeming a little shy, responded, "I'm thirteen ... going on fourteen."

"I can't believe you have daughter, Bridget. It seems like such a short time since you and Tom ..." She hesitated. "Oh, I'm so sorry—I heard about Tom."

Bridget glanced down at the floor. "Thank you, Grace. It's been quite difficult—but I'm moving forward now. My sewing, you know."

"Oh, of course. You do have a wonderful skill there. Always did. I'll never forget how much you helped our girls here."

"I'm glad about that, Grace. Actually, I'm even better qualified now, as I was able to add fashion design to my sewing skills when I was employed at Kobacker's in Buffalo. So I'm hopeful there might be something for me in the fashion industry here in New York."

"Sounds like a good possibility. I hope it will all work out for you, Bridget. You deserve it."

Grace brought them into the parlor to talk over tea and cheese sandwiches. "Have a little bite now. You must be very hungry. I assume you just arrived in New York," glancing over at their suitcases.

"Yes—actually this is the first place we've stopped."

"Do you have anywhere to stay, my dear?"

"Well, no, not yet, Grace. I was going over to Molly's after this, hoping she might put us up, at least temporarily. She never did like being alone, you know."

"Well, obviously you don't know, Bridget ..."

"Know? Know what, Grace?"

"Well, Tugboat Molly is now *Mrs.* Tugboat Molly!"

"What?"

"Yep! She and MacTavish tied the knot—not too long after your wedding."

"No! The Scotsman?"

"Mmm—Hmm. She is now Mrs. MacTavish! Don't you remember how chummy they got during your reception on the boat?"

"Oh my gosh! I can't believe it! Tugboat Molly— now an old married lady!" Bridget snickered. "Well, she sure deserves much happiness. She was so good and kind to me when I was with her."

"Yes—but guess what happened to her."

Bridget had a quizzical look on her face. "What? What happened?"

"You won't find her at her old address any more. She lost her house to the government."

"The government?"

"Yes, they condemned all those shanties and built a new housing project. Molly was forced to move and she and MacTavish have been living on the tugboat."

"No kidding! Gee, I'm sorry to hear that. But, well, she always did love the water, you know!"

"Yeah!" Grace smiled. "So, tell me, dear, why don't you both stay right here with us—at least, until you get settled and find work, or whatever. You are certainly welcome, and I'd love to have you back."

"Oh, thank you, Grace. You are so kind." Bridget had much to share—Buffalo, the First Ward, the Strike of '99, the Pan Am Expo, the assassination of McKinley ...

Grace was shocked to hear that Bridget actually witnessed the shooting. "Oh, how horrible—to see something like that!"

"Oh, it *was*, Grace, and, you know, what made it worse was my thought of Mrs. McKinley actually having closure of *her* husband's passing and I having nothing ... nothing but wondering and waiting and hoping and praying ... Oh, I'm sorry. I'm sorry, Grace."

"It's okay, honey. I understand." She put her arm around Bridget and tried to change the subject. "And what school did you go to, Teresa?"

"I just graduated from St. Bridget's," the child answered proudly.

"Good for you! Do you have any idea what you want to do? For work, I mean?"

"Umm ... I kinda thought I'd do what Mom does— make dresses and things. But then, we met this man on the train and he's goin' to school here and gonna be a—what do you call that thing, Mom?"

"Well, he's going to telegraphy school, Grace. We might look into that for Teresa," Bridget replied.

"Sounds like it might be a good idea. You'd probably be good at it, Teresa," Grace offered, hoping to be encouraging to the girl.

"If I can make a lot of money, me and Mom can have an easier life."

They whiled away the afternoon, Grace trying to bring Bridget up to date about her old friends and acquaintances, as well as the news about the Mission.

"Tell me, Grace, have you had occasion to see Jim Flynn at all lately?"

"Oh, I guess you didn't know, Bridget. Actually, he was transferred to Michigan some time back."

"Oh, gee, I really wanted to see him. What a great man, wasn't he? He did so much for all of us."

"Yes, he was. I've often thought about him."

"You know, Grace, I think I'd better get going for now. I promised Teresa I'd take her to see Molly's tugboat. And I'm really anxious to see her myself."

"That's fine. I will have a room fixed for you both by the time you get back."

"Thank you so much. You always do everything for your friends—just like you do for the girls here."

"Well, I feel it's my duty, since they all come over here with only the shirts on their backs, so to speak."

The trolley approached the area where Molly used to live. The new housing project had been completed, but there was one thing still standing. "We're getting off here, Teresa. I want to show you something." She took her daughter by the hand and walked to a small green space in the center of the project, where a few children were playing in a sandbox near the swings.

"What is it, Mother? Why did we stop here?"

"Look, honey—it's my tree!" It was still there. They didn't cut it down. There it stood, tall and strong, just as she remembered it in Molly's back yard.

"What's so special about a tree? Did you say *your* tree, Mom?"

"Yes, my dear. It's *my* hickory tree!" Bridget sat down on the grass, and Teresa followed.

"Did *you plant* it, Mom?"

Bridget laughed. "Oh, no, honey. No, but you see, I always admired it when I lived here with Molly. So tall and majestic—God's beautiful creation! When you think of it, it's kind of a home."

"A home, Mom?"

"Sure. The birds live there, you know."

"Oh, well, yeah ..."

"I just thought it was a really pretty thought. The way they build nests in the branches. I'd sit out on Molly's back steps and just look at it. And there were two squirrels, you see—Nutter and Scarback—and ..."

Teresa laughed. *"Nutter* and *Scarback*?"

"Yep. My little friends. I'd get the nuts that dropped from the tree and open them, and Nutter would come over and sit up on his hind legs and take the nut with his little hands right from mine."

"Squirrels don't have *hands*, Mom!"

"Now you know what I mean, silly. He'd take the nuts with his *paws!"*

"A-w-w-w."

"He was so cute, honey."

"What about that other one? What'd you call *him*, Mom?"

"Scarback—that little guy had an area about the size of a half-dollar on his back where no hair grew. He must have been hurt somehow and it left a scar there. Maybe that's why he stayed close to the tree. I never could get him to come over to me for a nut the way Nutter did."

"Oh! Look!" Teresa exclaimed. "Mom—look!" A squirrel suddenly ran down the trunk of the tree, chased by another closely behind. She laughed at their antics, wondering if one was a male chasing a female. "Can you see a scar?"

"Oh, darling, I really don't know if those two little friends would still be around. Anyway, I don't see any scar—these are probably two different squirrels."

"Oh, yeah, I guess so. Wonder how long squirrels live. Do you know, Mom?"

"Well, not exactly. But Molly told me once she thought about five years or so."

"Oh. Well, anyway, do you think I could go on that swing for a few minutes?"

"Oh, sure, go ahead. I'll just sit here—but don't be too long, okay?"

Bridget's tree had always reminded her of her home in Ireland—maybe that's why it was so ingrained in her heart. Her early years in the orphanage there began to flood into her mind. Those difficult years in that harsh environment were overshadowed in her thoughts, however, by the fond memories of those hikes in the woods and the instructors who taught the girls about the various plant life and trees. She had loved these excursions into nature. These memories, although dim, were like precious jewels that never lost their value—a thread to the past—that past that she was too young to understand at the time. But still they belonged to her and would forever be in a place that no one else could ever find—not even Teresa.

The old tugboat, moored at the dock, was just the way Bridget had remembered it. A slight wind was blowing small ripples of waves which lapped at the bow. A puff of smoke came from the window; and as they came closer, Molly could be seen smoking her clay pipe. Bridget knocked on the side of the little tugboat. "Ahoy, mate! Anybody here?" She squeezed Teresa's hand.

Molly poked her head out the window. "Who is it? Oh, my gosh! Is that *you*, Bridget? Oh, my gosh! Come aboard! Come aboard!"

Molly embraced the girl she had come to look upon as a daughter, after which she turned to Teresa. "Now who might this little lass be, Bridget?"

"She's my daughter, Molly. Teresa—my daughter."

"What a pleasant surprise! I'm so glad to meet you, Teresa! You're a spittin' image of your Mom." Molly smiled. "Now come and sit down here at the table. I'll put the kettle down. We've got a lot of talkin' to do—a lot of catchin' up. My, you just look absolutely wonderful, Bridget! I can't tell you how happy I am to see you. Now I want to hear all about everything. Well, gee, how many years is it anyway?"

"Too many. I've missed you, Molly—thought about you so often. Would you believe we just came from that new project—my favorite tree was still there!"

"Yep. They didn't take *that* one down. Okay, now—you first! How was Buffalo?"

Bridget glanced down. "Well, we managed—but we had a rough time for a while." She paused. "Grace—Tom went missing."

"What? What do you mean—went missing? What happened?" Molly's face took on an extremely serious look.

"Well, it's a long story," Bridget answered, glancing over at Teresa and thinking she shouldn't have brought up the subject. "We'll have plenty of time to talk about all that later. Right now, I want to hear about *you.*"

Molly got up to pour the tea and put out some cookies. "Now don't ya eat too many of them, Teresa! It'll ruin your appetite for dinner. Ya *are* gonna stay for dinner, aren't ya?" she asked Bridget.

"Well, I ..."

"Now, I'm not about to take no for an answer. Besides, we got the freshest fish in town—right there outside that window!"

"That's for sure!" Bridget remarked.

"But, hold it! Before we talk any further, I really wanna tell you something, Bridget."

"Yes?"

"You don't know it, but, I am *Mrs. Molly MacTavish* now." She stood with a broad, proud smile on her face, awaiting a surprised response from Bridget.

"Oh, Molly! I know. Grace told me just this afternoon. How wonderful! I'm so happy for you!" She gave her a big squeeze, then held her at arm's length. "Well now, *Mrs. Molly MacTavish,* tell me how that all happened."

"Well, that Scotty ... he kinda just swept me off my feet. Or shall I say, 'I swept *him* offa *his*!"

Bridget laughed. "I do remember you two dancing around at the reception. Kinda looked like *some*thing was going on."

"Well, he just latched onto me and something clicked. We seemed to get along so well and, after all, I wasn't a ravin' beauty, ya know, and was gettin' on in years. So thought I'd better grab him—or let him think he was grabbin' *me!"*

"Well, I wish you both all the happiness in the world, Molly. You deserve it."

"Oh, here comes my Scotty now! He'll be so surprised to see you."

"I don't know if he'd even remember me. It's been so long."

"Ah, hello, and how's me sweet wife today?" Scotty planted a big kiss on Molly's cheek and hugged her against his broad chest, almost taking her breath away. Noticing Bridget and Teresa, he added, "And who might these pretty lassies be?"

Before Bridget could answer, he realized her face looked familiar. "The bride, right?"

"Yep, it's Bridget O'Halloran!" Molly interrupted. "I mean Bridget *Sexton*. You remember her from the wedding reception, don't you?"

"Of course. How could I forget a wedding with all them Micks?" he laughed. "And where's the mister?"

Before Bridget could answer, Molly nudged Scotty in the ribs with her elbow and quickly changed the subject. "And this is Bridget's daughter, Teresa." She cupped her mouth with her hand and whispered in Scotty's ear, "I'll tell ya later."

Scotty grabbed the girl's two hands in his and shook them voraciously. "And a bonnie fair lass she is—takes after her mother." He smiled over at Bridget, then turned to Molly. "Have ya got a tattie or somethin' fer yer guests, Mrs. MacTavish?"

"I *do*, Mr. MacTavish, *and* some nice fresh fish to go along with it."

"Well, me darlin' wife, how's about takin yer little bahoochie inta the galley and cookin' it up?"

"Oh, we'd really love to stay, but I did promise Grace I'd be back early to help her set up our room—we'll be staying there temporarily. But we'll see each other again soon and catch up on old times—I'll make that a point!" At that she hugged Molly once again and shook Scotty's hand.

Stepping onto the dock, she and Teresa turned to wave goodbye once more. "I really like them a lot, Mom! And I like that tugboat, too. Let's come back soon, okay? I really want to go out for a ride on it."

"We will, Teresa. I'm sorry we didn't have enough time for that today—next time, honey."

In the days to come, Bridget, after answering newspaper ads and following many leads, finally found a job in a small dress shop in uptown Manhattan—"Molly-Maureen's Boutique." And after a temporary stay with Grace, they finally settled into a small, three-room apartment on Canal Street—living room, walk-in kitchen, and one bedroom to be shared.

Teresa, although extensively excited about living in the "big city," had some misgivings about this new humble abode. "Gee, Mom! It sure is small! I wish we had a nice big huge place like Kathleen's Mom and Dad bought in Buffalo. I remember all the rooms—so many. We had so much fun playing there."

Bridget felt bad. She knew Teresa wasn't realizing the difficulties since her father had disappeared. She wanted to show the girl a comparison between the Ryans who had a father with a high-paying job and a mother who was the only breadwinner for the two of them. She couldn't get those thoughts into words, however, not wanting Teresa to feel so much less fortunate than others. "I know, honey. This will be fine for now. And once we both are working, we will be able to afford something a little nicer."

"Oh. And Mom, when I get my job at Western Union, I'm gonna give you all my money." Bridget smiled at the girl's sweet offer, wondering if it would be so easy for her to do when the time came. She kissed her.

Billy Darly took Teresa "under his wing" at Cooper Union. Bridget considered it a blessing that her daughter was able to obtain this education at no cost. Having Billy at the same place was a double blessing. Thank God things are looking up. The girl took very quickly to Morse Code and soon became very adept at the key. She continually tried to obtain better marks than Billy but was unable to do so. Nevertheless, he would tease her, calling her a "little smarty pants" as he continued to mentor her after classroom hours, his hand upon hers tapping out messages. This gave her a warm feeling in her heart, yet made her a little uncomfortable at the same time. He was becoming quite fond of her, although aware of the difference in their ages. "Going on fourteen" was a little too young for an eighteen year old man; however, he could see that she was quite mature for her age and felt there could be something for the two of them in a few years or more. For now, he would "bide his time" and try to look at her like a little sister. She seemed to sense his interest, however, and couldn't help but enjoy the fact that she might be growing into an attractive young lady. His attention to her was appealing, but only in a way as a girl might look upon a big brother. It gave her a feeling of security though—a feeling that was very different from the way she had felt under the roof of her mother. It was new—it was a feeling somewhat of safety—maybe even protection. He seemed like a "tower of strength" to her, something she never knew before, having no father. She liked it—that "male thing."

"Mom, guess what? Billy likes me."

"Well, of course he does, dear."

"No, Mom. I mean I think he *really likes* me."

"Teresa, you are not even quite fourteen and Billy is much older than you. You are probably imagining things."

"I'm *not* !"

"Well, sit down. Dinner's ready. You can tell me all about school today."

"It was good. I'm learning a lot and Billy's helping me. But Mom, I really wanted to talk about something else."

"Oh? What's that, Teresa?"

"I want to start earning some money."

"Well, yes, you will—when you are done with school."

"But Mom, a lot of the girls at the school have part-time jobs and I thought maybe I could ..."

"Now you just keep your mind on school. I'm sure you'll get a good job after you graduate. Remember what Billy said?"

"What?"

"About his friend who is already working at Western Union."

"Oh, yeah, that's right. They are going to be hiring, right?"

"Yes. So just look forward to that time. It'll be here before you know it. Besides, you still have more to learn before you can obtain a good job like *that*. Billy said they pick from the top of the class."

"But Mom, I saw an ad in the newspaper and it was about girls wanted to work in a place called the Triangle Shirtwaist Factory—right *now*. They want people right *now*, Mom. I think I could do that with all the stuff you taught me about sewing. And I could still stay in school at the same time. Come on, Mom!"

"No. Absolutely not, Teresa! And that's final!" Teresa began to pout. "Now stop that!"

"Well ..."

"Now listen—you concentrate on school and I think we will take a couple days off at Thanksgiving time. How does that sound?"

"Why?"

"Well, there are some wonderful people here in New York that I really want to see—and to meet *you*, too."

Teresa still didn't look too happy. "So, who are these people, Mom?"

"My friends. The ones I met when I first came to America."

"Well, okay. But I really wanna go back to Molly's and ride on that tugboat." Her demeanor seemed to perk up at the thought.

"We will. Next summer when school's over. It's nice on a hot day. And I know Molly will be glad to take us."

Winter came early that year and by Thanksgiving, the ground was covered with a foot of snow. Bridget revisited her old friends on Staten Island.

Not much had changed at Mount Loretto since she and Tom took "Small Fry" there many years ago. As they entered the foyer, a nun approached who Bridget immediately recognized. "Sister Eileen! How are you?"

Sister looked puzzled for a moment. "Oh! Bridget! How wonderful to see you again!"

"It's so good to see you, too, Sister." Bridget put her arms around her old friend and hugged her tightly for a moment, then turned to Teresa. "Sister, this is my daughter, Teresa."

"Oh, my goodness! It's wonderful to meet you, my dear!" Sister reached over and grasped the girl's two hands within hers. "Come ... come in to the parlor. I want to hear all about everything. Here, sit down. I'll get us some tea. Be right back."

In a short while, Sister returned with a tray followed by Sister Teresita. Bridget began to stand up.

"Now, now, stay right where you are", Sister Teresita directed. "You don't have to get up for me." She bent over and kissed Bridget on the forehead. "Bridget, I can't tell you how happy I am to see you. It's been so long!" She glanced over at Teresa. "And you must be Teresa. I'm so pleased to meet you, dear. Sister Eileen was telling me all about you in the kitchen."

"Hello, Sister. I'm glad to meet you, too. My Mom has told me a lot about *you* both also."

"Tell me now, Bridget—about your time in Buffalo," Sister Eileen said as she poured the tea.

"Well, let me just say it's been very difficult. I had to work two jobs since Tom went ..." She stopped herself.

"It's okay, Mom," Teresa advised, putting her arm around her mother's shoulder. "I'm over it now."

Bridget's eyes began to tear up. "Oh, honey."

Sister Teresita had a sad look on her face. "You don't have to talk about it right now, Bridget."

"No ... no, that's alright. I *do* want you both to know." She blotted her eyes with her handkerchief. "Well, actually it was a terrible time! You see, there was a strike and the men walked out. And then this led into some awful violence. And anyway, sometime during all this, Tom's best friend was found floating in the canal and Tom wanted justice for him, and I think he got too close to finding out who his killers were and one day he just didn't come home after work and ... well ... well, that was the last I saw of him ... and we never could find any trace of him after that. I searched everywhere, put ads in the newspapers, and spent weeks and weeks inquiring of everyone all over the Ward who had had any connection with him at all. Even ... oh Sisters! I even had to check the morgue a few times—it was horrible!"

"Oh, my good Lord, no!" Sister Teresita exclaimed. She clutched the rosary beads hanging at her side and held them to her chest, her mouth beginning to form the words of prayer silently.

Teresa quickly interrupted, not wanting her mother to relive those difficult moments. "Well, Mom and I are doing okay *now* though. I'm going to school here and Mom's got a job at "Molly-Maureen's" uptown."

"School? Well, that's wonderful! Where is that, my dear?" Sister Eileen asked.

"It's at Cooper Union. I'm gonna be a telegraph operator!" The girl's words rang with self-esteem.

"Good for you!" Sister Eileen remarked. "And I'm sure you will be a wonderful telegrapher!" Teresa smiled proudly. The nun got up and asked to be excused for a moment. "I have a surprise for you. I'll only be a minute."

The "surprise" was tall and handsome! His thick red hair had a coarse but wavy look to it, and one strand of it had fallen over his forehead. He ran his fingers through it, trying to place it back where it had previously been. "Now tell me, Joseph," Sister Eileen stated, "do you know this lady?" as she pointed to Bridget.

Before he could answer, Bridget exclaimed, "Joseph? This is *Joseph?"*

Her voice cemented in his heart who he thought was sitting before him. "Oh, Bridget! My dear Bridget!" Those old beautiful tender thoughts from years back welled up inside him. He bent down to hug her and kiss her cheek. "I'm so happy to see you! Is Tom here?"

Bridget patted the seat next to her, motioning for Teresa to move over. "Sit down here next to me, Joseph." He knew immediately there was something grievously wrong and reached over to take her hand, grasping it tightly.

"What is it? What is it, Bridget?"

She was brief. She retold the story but with few details. Joseph looked down at the floor. He shook his head from side to side. "I loved that man. I loved that man!" He looked up at Bridget. "I'm so, so sorry, Bridget. I'll never forget him—he saved my life—and Nellie's—and the baby's!"

For a moment, nobody spoke. Then Bridget smiled at Joseph. "I can't believe you, Joseph! You're so tall! And to think they used to call you 'Small Fry!'" They all laughed.

Teresa cleared her throat, as if to say "remember me?" "*This* is '*Small Fry*?'"

"Oh, I'm sorry, Teresa. Yes, this is 'Small Fry!' At least he used to be Small Fry when we brought him here years ago. Now he is Joseph." She turned to him. "Joseph, this is my daughter, Teresa."

"So nice to meet you, Teresa." He reached over and shook her hand lightly.

"You, too, Joseph." She liked his touch. "Do you go to school here?"

"No, not anymore." Joseph laughed. "I graduated a few years ago but I stayed on to work as the Athletic Director. I loved sports so much, and the good nuns offered me the job."

Teresita added, "Yes, I was getting a little overextended at that time with my other duties, so it was a blessing to have Joseph take over."

"Now tell me, what ever happened to Nellie?" Bridget asked Sister Teresita. "The last I heard she had been adopted."

"Yes, that's right. She was adopted out; but after a year or so, the father of the family died, and the mother wasn't able to raise her on her own."

"Oh, no!" Bridget exclaimed. "So what happened?"

"She was sent back to Sister Irene, but that home is mostly for infants and toddlers now, so they took her in at the convent of the Sisters of Mercy over on Willoughby Avenue and she was raised there. In fact, she joined their order and is presently a novice."

"Oh my goodness!" Bridget remarked. "I was just about to say 'how sad' but I guess now I'll have to say 'how wonderful!'"

"Isn't it though? And they do such wonderful work over there," Sister Eileen said, "teaching those girls a trade."

"Oh that's good! What kind of trade?" Bridget asked.

"Well, many learn sewing on the new machines—some learn to make artificial flowers, and some make shirt collars for the Manhattan haberdasheries."

"Well, I really want to see her. Maybe we can stop there when we leave, if it's not too late. Gosh, she was only nine years old when I last saw her—just before Tom and I left for Buffalo."

Teresa had been listening quite attentively. "I wonder how it feels to be a nun ..."

The two sisters looked at each other and grinned.

"Can you tell me?—how it feels? Must be different, I guess, from just being an ordinary person, isn't it?"

"Well," Sister Teresita laughed, "we certainly *are* ordinary people, too, Teresa!"

"Oh!" Teresa looked puzzled. "But you *must* be special!"

"Don't you know, my dear, that we are *all* special in God's eyes*?"*

"I can't wait to meet Nellie. She's gonna be a new nun so maybe I can ask *her* how it feels."

"Excuse me, Teresa. I don't mean to interrupt my dear, but Sister Eileen and I have a meeting with our priest-director in twenty minutes. Bridget, I'm so sorry, but we must excuse ourselves."

"Oh, we really must be on our way anyway, Sister. I'm not sure how the trolleys run around here and I do want to get over to Willoughby Avenue to see Nellie before we go back home."

"You won't have any problem; the next one doesn't leave for another forty-five minutes and you can catch it right outside the door. So you and Teresa can stay right here where it's warm until it comes," Sister Teresita advised.

"That sounds good to me," Teresa said. "We can stay here and talk with Joseph." She smiled at him.

"Oh, I'm so sorry," Joseph replied, "but I have to be at the meeting as well. But it was wonderful meeting you," as he hugged the girl. "And Bridget, I will never forget what you and Tom did for me. Please come back soon."

The snow had intensified and the East River was hardly visible below as the trolley crossed the Brooklyn Bridge back to lower Manhattan and the Mercy Home for Children. A figure dressed in a long black habit formed a sharp contrast against the drifting white snow. The sister slowly made her way up the front steps, slipping at one point and grabbing the iron railing to keep from falling. Teresa ran up from behind. "Oh, Sister, are you okay?"

"Yes. Thank you, dear."

"We're coming to see Nellie—my Mom and me."

Entering the foyer, the nun introduced herself and removed her shawl. "How do you do, Sister? I'm Bridget Sexton and this is Teresa."

"How do you do, Teresa. Now then, you said you were coming to see Nellie, did you, my dear?" the nun asked with a broad smile.

"Mmm—Hmm."

"I'm an old friend of hers, Sister," Bridget said. "I heard that she is now a novice here?"

"Oh, yes—that would be Sister Mary Jane. Excuse me for a minute and I will let her know you are here, Bridget, and see if she can have visitors right now."

"I hope she will remember who I am." Bridget hesitated for a moment, then added, "Oh, Sister, just mention 'Bridget and Tom.' I'm sure she'll know then."

A young nun came down the main staircase. Teresa nudged her mother's arm. "Mom, how come she's got a *white* veil on her head?"

"Bridget! Oh, Bridget! Is it really *you*?" Sister Mary Jane stretched out her hand and grabbed Bridget's and they hugged each other affectionately. A few tears trickled down the nun's cheek; and she pulled a handkerchief from inside her sleeve to dab them, then turned to Teresa.

"Are you Nellie?" the girl immediately inquired.

"Yes, and who might *you* be, my dear?"

"I'm Teresa!"

"She's my daughter, Nellie."

"Oh, my goodness! How wonderful to meet you, Teresa!" Nellie led them to a small room containing a desk, a long wooden bench, and a large picture of the Sacred and Immaculate Hearts directly under a Crucifix on the wall behind it. "I can't begin to tell you how happy I am to see you, Bridget. Please, sit down."

"I'm so pleased to see you survived your ordeals, Nellie. Sister Teresita told me what happened with your adoption and the unfortunate incident that brought you back to New York."

"Oh, I know, Bridget. It was terribly hard for me at the time, but ... oh, I'm so much happier now! This was the life I was always meant for. I realized that this was God's will for me shortly after I returned. I was somewhat dejected at first and so ... well ... I began to pray more. And the more I prayed, the more I realized that I had a calling to the religious life. So here I am! Thank God!"

"I'm so happy for you, Nellie. I know you had such a hard beginning," Bridget said.

"Yes, I'm taking the name of a friend, an older nun who helped me and guided me when I first arrived here. Sister Mary Jane was her name—the sweetest person I've ever met." She quickly added, "Besides *you*, of course!"

"Oh, *I* had a favorite nun at St. Bridget's, too!" Teresa volunteered. "That was my school in Buffalo."

"What grade are you in, Teresa?"

"I already graduated from there, Nellie. Oh, I mean, Sister."

"That's okay, you can call me Nellie. I haven't taken my final vows yet."

"My Mom and Dad took vows."

"Yes, that's right, my dear. They took vows in the sacrament of Matrimony."

"That means getting married, right?" Teresa seemed quite interested in the nun.

"Yes, you're right."

"So when you take your vows, that's kinda like that?"

"Yes. I'll be married to Jesus."

"What?"

"It's a spiritual marriage—my religious vocation."

"Oh." Teresa thought for a minute, not quite understanding. "I was wondering—how does it feel to be a nun?"

Nellie smiled. "Oh, it's very exciting, Teresa. To be able to live your life loving and serving God and His people."

"That sounds so nice," Teresa mused, pondering the words she had just heard.

"Have *you* thought about a religious life, Teresa?" Nellie asked.

"No, not really. Actually, I just started school at Cooper Union. I'm studying to be a telegraph operator."

"Well, good for you! There seems to be more and more young women going into the work force these days. I hope you do well, dear."

"Thanks, Nellie. Me too."

"Now tell me—how's Tom?" Nellie asked, turning to Bridget.

Bridget expected the subject would be coming up and really hesitated to go into it again. But she couldn't just ignore Nellie's question so briefly tried to explain to her what had happened.

"But didn't the police ..." Nellie was cut off.

"They worked hard trying to find him ... Well, anyway, we just never were able to and never could find closure."

Teresa quickly changed the subject, as usual. "Mom and I are doing okay now though, Nellie. Mom's got a job here already, and I'll have one when I finish school. Then we'll have more money and get a better place to live—like my friend, Kathleen's got."

"I see. Now tell me, where are you working, Bridget?"

"Uptown in a women's apparel store—at "Molly- Maureen's." I'm a dress designer now."

"Well, that doesn't surprise me. I remember how good you were, teaching me how to work that sewing machine in that attic room at the Mission. I just loved visiting you up there. You were like a big sister to me, and I kinda felt like it was our little hideaway where we could tell secrets. And remember that night when we were sitting out on the fire escape and that shooting star went overhead?"

"Yes, I sure do. My recollection was that you were missing Small Fry—wasn't that it?"

"Yes. That *was* it. I was so worried about him and couldn't help wondering if he was okay. And then you said the shooting star was my sign from God that he was— remember?"

"Yes. And wasn't it true? He turned out to be such a fine young man. And who would believe he'd become the Athletic Director at Mount Loretto. I'm so proud of him."

"Me too." Nellie reached up to straighten her veil. "And remember that night you were reminiscing about Ireland, Bridget, and talking about wanting to go back there? I wanted you to take me with you when you went. But ... well, that never did happen."

"No. No, it didn't. But you know, Nellie, I still carry that land in my heart. I always have. I always will."

Nellie excused herself and returned to the room with tea and cookies for her guests. They shared about old times at the Mission and the outing at Coney Island. "I often remember how exciting that day was, Bridget. I had never seen an amusement park before. We had so much fun, remember?" Her musings were suddenly interrupted by a little tinkling bell. "Oh, I'm sorry. I must go now. That bell signals all of us to meet in the Chapel for evening vespers."

"Oh, Nellie, I hope we haven't held you up too much."

"Not at all. In fact, you are both welcome to join us if you like."

"I would absolutely love that, but ..."

"Me too," Teresa chimed in. "Oh, let's do that Mom, okay?"

"I'd like to, Teresa, but you know how bad the weather is outside. So I really think we'd best be on our way, Nellie. But thank you. Hopefully we can join you another time."

Bridget and Teresa settled down to a routine of work and school that winter. It was a long time coming, but now the window of hope seemed to be opened wider. Bridget had made new friends at work and became an asset to the little boutique uptown. Billy Darly continued his tutoring sessions with Teresa, always using the opportunity this provided to see her more often. His fondness for the girl had been growing; however, he still tried to conceal his feelings toward her, knowing her mother felt the difference in their ages to be too much. She did, however, allow him to spend Christmas Eve with them, as the young man was unable to get home to Albany due to the severe weather conditions. He was good company and they enjoyed sharing a dinner of ham with potatoes and peas and carrots. Teresa was quite excited to have a friend over and made it a point to bake her own Christmas cookies. Billy was determined to make Teresa feel as though she were the best baker in town, and so consumed more than his share. The girl was delighted, as she had never baked before and was relieved to see that her cookies certainly must be good since Billy ate so many.

"Let's show your Mom how good you're getting, Teresa," Billy offered.

"Oh, you first."

Billy moved the dishes from in front of him and began tapping out a message in Morse code on the table.

A slight blush came over Teresa's face. "Oh! Billy!"

"What did he say?" Bridget asked.

"Oh, he's just being silly, Mom. He just said 'you are so sweet, Smarty Pants!'"

"Smarty Pants?"

"Yeah, he calls me that sometimes, Mom. Isn't that silly?" Teresa's face suddenly lit up and she tried to muffle a laugh as she turned to her friend. "Hey, Silly Billy!" She grinned at him and waited to see how he would reply, feeling that she had "topped" him.

"Well, you got *me* now!" Billy laughed.

"Okay, you two funny ones," Bridget joined in, "come on—let's relax in the living room for a while."

Billy took two small packages from his pocket—one wrapped in red paper and one in green. "Merry Christmas to you both!"

"Oh, Billy! You shouldn't have!" Bridget exclaimed.

Teresa had her gift unwrapped in a second and opened the small box within. "Oh, thank you, Billy! A medal! Oh, it's beautiful!" She leaned over and kissed him on the cheek. "Here, do this for me, okay?" she asked as she turned around and held the ends of the chain to the back of her neck. "What did you get, Mom?"

"I have a medal, too, honey. Thank you so much, Billy."

"You're very welcome. I had them blessed already." He turned to Teresa. "This is a very special medal, Teresa."

"Oh?"

"It's the Miraculous Medal of Our Lady," he offered. "Do you know of it?"

"I guess I do now. Will I get a miracle?" She smiled.

"I hope you will." He smiled back at her. "You see, it was originally called the Medal of the Immaculate Conception; however, many people did, in fact, have miraculous things happening in their lives when they wore it—and it soon became known as the Miraculous Medal."

"Here, let me help you, Mom." Teresa closed the clasp on her Mother's medal.

"Billy, I don't know how to thank you. These are lovely."

"Oh, I'm the one who should be thanking *you*, Mrs. Sexton. I'd have been all alone for Christmas Eve if it wasn't for your kind invitation."

"Oh? I thought you mentioned on the train that you have a roommate?"

"Yes, that's right. But, you see, Fergy's parents don't live too far away, so he was able to make it home for the holidays."

"Oh, yes," Bridget said, "now I remember. He's the one with that unusual name. In fact, didn't you mention that there was some kind of a story behind that name?"

"Yes, you remember correctly. Actually, Fergus is an old Irish name. I don't think it's used much anymore. He told me he was named after his grandfather, a Civil War sergeant in the 69th Irish Brigade. Apparently, he was awarded the Medal of Honor for bravery."

"Oh, I wonder what he actually did," Bridget remarked.

"Well, it was at the Battle of Antietam. He crawled out onto the battlefield to rescue another soldier who had been wounded and was able to drag him back behind their lines—all this while under heavy enemy fire. And if that wasn't enough, he crawled *back* out to retrieve the colors which had gone down with the wounded boy. Then, while crawling back with the flag, he himself was pinned down by the heavy enfilade sweeping across the field and was hit in the leg."

"Oh, my! Whatever happened to him?"

"He eventually was rescued and went on to fight in seven more major battles. He did live through the war and I guess Fergy's parents wanted to honor him by naming their son after him. In fact, they gave him his grandfather's medal."

"Wow!" Teresa remarked. "That's some story!"

"Oh, my! Look at the time! I didn't realize it was getting so late," Bridget said. "Maybe we'd better think about cleaning up the table, Teresa. We don't want to be late for Midnight Mass."

"Okay, Mom."

"Billy, would you like to come along?"

"Yes, I'd like that very much. Where are you going?"

"To Transfiguration—that's our church—over on Mott Street. We just registered there when we arrived in New York. It's only a couple blocks from here—we can walk."

"Oh, yes, I know where that is."

On the way, Billy supported each of them with his arm through theirs. "Don't want you two slippin' on this ice."

"Thanks, Billy. You're such a gentleman!" Teresa remarked, enjoying that male protective presence.

They arrived at Transfiguration a little early to hear the choir singing carols before the service. The church lights had not been turned on, and the candles gave a soft glow which seemed to exude holiness, shining around the manger and in front of the statuary.

O Holy Night
The stars are brightly shining
It is the night of our dear Savior's birth.
Long lay the world in sin and e'er pining
'Til He appeared and the soul felt its worth.
A thrill of hope, the weary world rejoices
For yonder breaks a new and glorious morn.
Fall on your knees - O hear the angels' voices
O night divine, O night when Christ was born
O night divine, O night, O night divine.

Bridget's eyes beheld the beauty of the Manger scene, then glanced over at Teresa, as she placed her hand on her belly, instinctively recalling the midnight Mass long back when her daughter announced her presence to her mother and father with a strong kick.

Bridget had heard the Gospel message of Christ's birth many times in past years but never tired of listening to it. It was a time of rejoicing—a time of happiness—a time of gift-giving—as the Father had given His Divine Son to the Earth.

After Mass, Billy walked Bridget and Teresa home. The weather had turned worse and the snow was coming down in large flakes. They quickened their steps and pulled up their collars as they made their way back to Canal Street. "Would you care to come in for a cup of hot cocoa before you leave, Billy?" Bridget asked.

"Oh, thank you so much, but I really better be going. It's late. But I just want to thank you again for such a beautiful evening."

"You're welcome, Billy," Bridget responded. "We enjoyed having you with us."

"Yes, we liked having you here, Billy—I mean, Silly Billy." Teresa laughed at her own remark.

"Thanks, Smarty Pants," Billy joked back. "I liked *being* here." He tipped his hat. "Goodnight now."

Bridget and Teresa sat near the small tree they had put up a week ago and warmed up with the hot cocoa. "Mom, would you like one of those cookies I made? I didn't have any money to get you anything for Christmas, so my cookies are kinda my present—what's left of them! Billy ate so many, didn't he?"

"Yes, he really enjoyed them."

"Well, anyway, by next year, Mom, maybe I'll be working—I'll have money to get you something for sure then."

"Oh, honey. That's okay. I have everything if I have *you*."

Teresa leaned over and kissed her mother. "I love you too, Mom. I know things have been hard on you all these years with Dad gone."

"It's alright, honey. We're fine. And you're doing well at school—with Billy's help. You'll be a good telegraph operator, I know. We'll just keep on doing the best we can and look forward to a good future. And with God's help, we will have one!" Bridget hugged her daughter. "Now I think you'd better get some rest. It's late. Go ahead now—I'll be in in a minute."

"Okay. Nite Mom."

Bridget laid her head back on the sofa. The evening had given her warm though bittersweet feelings. Thoughts of Tom ran through her mind—that first Christmas ... the coat ...

"I can't have me darlin' going to church and up the avenue dressed in old rags all the time, now can I?"

"My queen, I am your servant forever. But in the meantime, dost thou not have a gift for Sir Knight in honor of this great event?"

Oh, Tom ... I'll always love you! Always ... always... Sleep—the Morpheus of the dreamer.

As 1911 arrived on the scene, Western Union found itself with a shortage of telegraph operators. This created a more immediate need for employees; consequently, they hired some of the students from Teresa's class for further training on-the-job. This took place for three months under the watchful eye and close scrutiny of their supervisor. Billy, Teresa, and a dozen others had been selected due to the progress and skills they had already acquired at Cooper Union. Teresa loved the excitement of being a telegrapher, as it put her into the mainstream of news—sending and receiving messages ranging from mundane, personal information to big news events taking place around the world.

March of that year burst on the scene like a lion, but the end of the month went out like a lamb. The warm spring breezes caressed Teresa's face as she was riding home from work one day on the trolley, which was stopped by police at one point. "Can't go on! Fire up ahead." Sirens were screaming, and she could see horse-drawn fire engines converging on a building at Washington Place and Greene Street. The passengers stepped off the trolley to observe dark black smoke and flames billowing from the top three floors.

"It's the Asch Building!" the driver exclaimed.

"Oh, no!" A woman screamed out. "That's the Triangle Shirtwaist Factory! My niece works in there!"

They stood in horror, the crowd screaming and weeping as girl after girl jumped out the windows to their deaths. It appeared that the firefighters didn't have ladders tall enough to reach those poor unfortunate souls.

"They're jumping! Oh, dear God! Oh, no! They're jumping!"

"Can't they get out? Why can't they get out?"

"Oh, look—the fire escape—some are getting out."

About twenty terrified employees crowded out onto the fire escape. Within minutes, however, the heat began to twist the iron structure and it pulled away from the building

"Oh, no! Look! It's collapsing!"

"O-o-o-o! Oh, my God! Oh, my God!"

The victims were hurled one hundred feet to their deaths. Bodies fell upon bodies and workers began covering them with white sheets.

Teresa stood watching with the ever-growing crowd. It could have been me ... it could have been me! She trembled at the thought. Thank God Mom said no.

A man in the crowd became angry and shouted out, "Someone will pay for this!"

Another cried out, “Oh, my God, have mercy!” The groaning and the screaming made people shudder. Some wept as they watched the horror of flames licking at the poor girls who were hesitating at the windows momentarily before jumping.

“It’s like Dante’s Inferno!”

It was all over in about eighteen minutes. Teresa and the others shuffled along like zombies and boarded the trolley on the next street to get home. Not a word was spoken.

The following day, all the newspapers carried the complete coverage of the disaster. Most of the victims were eighteen and nineteen-year-old girls—Jewish and Italian immigrants. Some had been trapped because the doors had been locked from the outside. Some leaped into the elevator shaft, attempting to grab the cable and climb down.. A few survived by climbing a stairway to the roof. Statistics were listed.

49 workers burned to death or suffocated by smoke

36 found dead in elevator shaft

58 died from jumping

2 more died later from their injuries

145 total people killed

The disaster was the main topic of conversation in a shocked community for many weeks. The backlash from the public was so great—people were infuriated and demanded change and more regulation of safety standards. This became a catalyst for new safety rules to be introduced, new equipment to facilitate fighting fires in high rise buildings, and the requirement of more frequent inspections at workplaces. Because of these changes being made, the hubbub decreased in time, but for those who were actual witnesses to the horror and found it difficult to erase completely those images in their minds.

Teresa was one of these and, although not *wishing* to discuss it, found herself *needing* to have an outlet to speak of it. Billy became this outlet. She had always felt completely comfortable with him—able to talk and discuss most anything that came up. And right now, that fire was what she needed to release from her memories, having had numerous nightmares since it had occurred. She couldn’t get the picture of those girls falling to their deaths out of her mind. Billy was a good listener and Bridget felt that he was good company for her daughter, not realizing he was using this need of Teresa's to be with her more often. He had always been attracted to her and had grown fond of her over the past year. She no longer appeared as an awkward teen but was rapidly developing the attributes of a very attractive young woman with a pretty face and obvious curves who could turn the heads of many a young man. Her long red hair would "bounce" as she walked and her wide-set blue eyes were embellished by long, thick lashes. From time to time, Teresa still felt that Billy's interest in her was more than a friend. However, she continued to look upon *him* as a kind of father-figure—a replacement perhaps for the man she had never known.

"Too bad Billy's not a little bit older, Mom. He'd be a good boyfriend for you."

"Oh, honey. You're cute. But I'm not sure I could ever be interested in *any* man again. Your Dad will always be alive in my heart. I only wish you could have known his dear, sweet ways. Our love was so beautiful, Teresa."

Teresa hung her head, sorry she had brought up the subject. "I didn't mean to make you feel bad, Mom."

"Oh, no, you didn't, hon. I'm fine." Bridget patted the cushion on the sofa next to her. "Sit down here a minute, Teresa."

"Yes, Mom?" She sat.

"Teresa, I think maybe now might be a good time for us to look for another place. You know, one with *two* bedrooms, and in a little better neighborhood."

"Oh, you think so?"

"Well, with *both* our incomes now, I think we can do it."

Teresa reached over and hugged her mother. "Oh, I'm so excited! Yes, let's do it, Mom." The news lifted the girl's spirit and she jumped from the sofa, threw her arms up in the air, and began to spin herself around. "Whe-e-e-e!"

"Well, I'm certainly glad you seem to approve of the idea!" Bridget laughed.

"Oh, Mom! Do you think we could find a place closer to the water? I love the water! Oh! and that reminds me— we never did get back to Molly's for my ride on the tugboat."

"Well, maybe next Saturday when we're both off. I'll see."

"Thanks, Mom!" Teresa hugged her.

"I know just the place for you two!" Molly announced. The day was warm and sunny, and Teresa enjoyed the ride down the river, especially the few minutes that Molly allowed her to steer the tug.

"Really?" Bridget asked. "Where, Molly? Where is it?"

"Not too far from here—a nice neighborhood. I've seen it myself."

"Oh? Were you and Scotty looking for a place?"

"Well, actually we were tossing the idea around a bit, but we decided to stay right here on the tugboat."

"Oh ..."

"Just one thing, though—" Molly added, "it's on the third floor so you do have to go up a few flights of stairs."

"I don't care!" Teresa exclaimed. "Does it have two bedrooms?"

"Yes, it does," Molly answered. "Sound good?"

"Oh, yeah! That'll be great! I'd love having a bedroom of my own, Molly."

"And the best part, my dear," Molly continued, "is that you can see the river from there!" as she docked the boat.

"Wow! Let's go see it, Mom! Can we go see it, Mom?"

"Hold on a minute, Teresa! You're going too fast for me. Can I ask you how much this apartment is, Molly?"

Just then, Scotty arrived home from work and was delighted to see the company. "Well, hello. Good to see ya both again. What's fer dinner, me darlin'? I'm famished."

"Everything is ready. Just set yourself down," Molly said, as she planted a big kiss on her husband's cheek. "Sit here, Bridget. And

Teresa, you can sit *here*." She proceeded to bring a large bowl of boiled potatoes to the table, along with fried fish. Molly described the apartment in detail to Bridget over dinner, answering all her questions.

"Gosh, I don't know, Molly. It seems a little high. I might have to think about it."

"Why don't we take you two over to see it tomorrow? What time will you be going to Mass in the morning?"

"Noon," Bridget answered.

"Okay, that's good. How's about you meeting us here at the boat at about one-thirty? The landlord lives on the first floor and he's generally always home on Sundays. It's only about a mile or so from here, so we can walk."

"Good afternoon. Can I help you?" The landlord smiled. "Oh, Mrs. MacTavish, how nice to see you again. Did you decide to rent the apartment?"

"Well, no. Actually, my husband and I decided to stay where we are for the time being, but my good friend, Bridget here, is looking for a place."

"Could we see it? Could we see the apartment, sir?" Teresa piped up.

"Why certainly. Follow me. Right up these stairs."

"Oh, Mom! Look! I can see the river!" Bridget nodded as she walked over to the window. "See, Mom?"

"I'll wave at ya as I pass by in my tug," Molly snickered. "I've pushed many a barge up that river in my day!"

"And you know, honey," Bridget said, turning to Teresa, "I used to be a tour guide on a boat called the *River Queen*. That's where I met your Dad. He was a sailor then." Bridget stood momentarily staring out the window.

"Would you like to see the bedrooms?"

"Oh! *I* would!" Teresa announced.

He led them to the rear of the apartment where there was a fairly large room with another smaller one separated by a bathroom. Teresa wanted to announce her request to have the largest room for herself, but decided it would be incorrect for her to do so. "Well, when can we move in here, Mister .., Mister ..."

"Stein."

"Oh—Mr. Stein. Can we move in tomorrow?" Teresa asked excitedly.

"Not so fast, Teresa," her mother said. "Perhaps we could go into the kitchen for a moment, Mr. Stein ..."

"Yes, of course. Come with me, Bridget."

They discussed the cost and moving arrangements. Bridget offered to clean the hallways and the stairs for a slight reduction in the rent, and Mr. Stein was happy to oblige, releasing him from one small duty as a landlord. Molly offered Scotty's services to help them move the following weekend, and Bridget asked Billy Darly to lend a hand as well.

"You can put that chair right over there by the window, Billy," as she pointed to the spot. "Yes, that's good. Right there."

"Can you give me a hand now, Billy, with the sofa?" Scotty asked.

"Sure."

"And my sewing machine will go in the bigger bedroom, Scotty."

"Oh, I love it! I just love it, Mom! Gosh, it's so much nicer than the other place. We're gonna be so happy here. I just know it." Teresa reached over and hugged her mother.

"Alright now. We have a lot of work to do. Gotta get everything in order this weekend, Teresa. Let's start unpacking right now, okay?"

"Okay. Gee, I can't wait to tell everybody at work all about our new place!" Teresa thought for a moment. "Maybe we could even have a party here for my birthday, Mom!"

"Oh, honey, we'll talk about that later. That's still a couple months away. Too much to do right now."

Time seemed to fly with the busyness of settling into the new apartment and working full time jobs as well. It was a cold and rainy

April and it seemed the rain and wind would never let up. But the following month brought warm and beautifully sunny days, and Teresa's thoughts returned to making plans for her birthday. "It's almost here, Mom! What do you think?"

"Now you just leave everything in my hands, little girl! I've got a surprise in the works."

"What? You do?" Teresa seemed delighted. "What, Mom? Tell me."

"Not yet. I have a little more to do."

"Oh, gee! Come on, Mom—I can't wait. *Please* tell me."

"Nope." They both laughed.

The evening before the birthday, after Teresa had gone to bed, Bridget packed a large picnic lunch for four. She rose early the next day and took a large piece of paper, writing the words "Happy Birthday Teresa" and hanging it on the cupboard door.

"Well, good morning, birthday-girl! I thought you'd never get up. It's a beautiful day—just for you!" She kissed her daughter and gave her a big hug. Teresa noticed the sign and smiled. "Sit down, honey. Let's have breakfast."

"Okay, Mom, but ..."

"Yes?"

"But, where's my surprise?"

"Oh, yes, the surprise! I almost forgot!"

"You did? You forgot? Gee, Mom, I've been dying of curiosity!"

"Oh, I'm just kidding. But you will have to be a little patient. It's coming. Eat up and then we'll go."

"Go? Where we goin'?"

"Well, that's the surprise!"

They finished breakfast and dressed. Bridget took two of the blankets from their beds and began to fold them. "Whatcha doing?" Teresa asked.

"You'll see. Here, give me a hand folding these blankets."

"Mom, what the heck is going on?"

Bridget just smiled. "Now grab yourself a sweater, just in case the weather gets cooler later."

It was a short trolley ride to the park. They walked for a short distance when Teresa stopped in her tracks. "Look! Mom, look!"

"What?"

"Up there." Teresa pointed ahead to a massive maple tree. "Look at that! There's balloons on that tree!"

As they got closer, they could see the big "Happy Birthday" sign nailed to the front of the huge trunk, the multi-colored balloons hanging from many of the branches above. "A-w-w-w Mom! How cute! Oh, gee—thanks! I *am* surprised!"

Suddenly, Billy jumped from behind the tree trunk, startling Teresa, and began to toot Happy Birthday on a kazoo.

"Oh, my gosh!" Teresa laughed, filled with joy. "Oh, my gosh! What the heck is *that* thing, Billy?"

"Let me hug the birthday girl! Happy birthday honey!"

"Oh, thank you! So *this* is my surprise! How nice ... this is so nice, Mom!" She turned back to Billy. "But what is *that* thing?"

"This is my wonderful new instrument—it's called a kazoo."

"I never heard of such a thing, Billy," Teresa remarked.

"That's because it's brand new. Just came into New York State from Georgia."

"Oh, what a funny thing. But how do you get the tune into it?"

Billy smiled at her. "*I'm* the tune!"

"What do you mean?"

"You just blow the tune into it. Here—wanna try it, honey?"

"Mmm—Hmm." She thought for a moment, then proceeded to play "In the Good Old Summertime." Bridget and Billy listened attentively, as Teresa swayed back and forth to her own "music." "Oh, I love it! I want one! Where did you get this, Billy?"

"At the Happy Birthday store."

For a moment, Teresa looked puzzled, then realized what he was saying. "Oh, Billy! You mean it's for *me*? My *present*?"

"That's exactly what I mean," he replied, kissing her on the cheek. "Play us another tune, sweetie, while your Mom and I spread the blankets."

"I know just the one," Teresa laughed, as she began to play "Strolling Through the Park."

"Hey, you're getting really good at that thing!" Billy remarked, noticing Fergy a couple blocks away on his bike. "How about "A Bicycle Built for Two," Teresa?" He winked at Bridget.

"Okay, I know it." She began to play, when suddenly Fergy rode directly up to the tree on his bike. Surprised at the stranger's approach, she stopped her tune, wondering who he was.

"Well, well, if it isn't my good old friend, Billy Darly. And what might you be doing here this fine day?" Fergy remarked, grinning, as he removed his straw hat and wiped his brow.

"Well, I might ask you the same question," Billy answered, looking up from the blanket.

"Well, actually, it seems I was just sitting home this morning when I happened to look out the window at this nice sunny day. And I thought it would be a good time to take a ride to the park to see if by any chance there might be a birthday party going on there for some pretty young lass!"

"Oh, you two jokers!" Teresa laughed, still unsure who the stranger was.

"I'm so glad you could join us, Fergy. It's nice to finally meet you," Bridget said.

"Fergy? You mean *you're Fergy*?" Teresa asked, impressed with the handsome features of his face.

"Fergus O'Sullivan at your service, my dear," he replied, placing his hat against his chest and bowing from the waist.

"Well, I can't begin to tell you how very nice it is to make your acquaintance, Mr. O'Sullivan," Teresa laughed.

Fergy removed a very small gift from the basket of his bicycle. "Happy birthday, Teresa." He sat down on the blanket next to her.

"Oh my gosh! Another surprise!" as she tore open the small box. "Wow! Look at this, Mom!"

"What is it, honey?"

"Tickets—tickets to a concert! It says 'Featuring the famous Gaslight Orchestra.' Oh, thank you, Fergy! I've never been to a concert."

"How nice of you, Fergy," Bridget remarked.

"I wonder if they will allow me to play my kazoo at the concert," Teresa joked.

"Well, I wouldn't doubt it for a minute—you're so good at it!" Billy remarked, laughing. "They'll probably give you a solo!"

"Yes, it did sound quite good," Fergy added. "I only had the pleasure, of course, of hearing a small part, however, when I rode up. Was that 'A Bicycle Built for Two' you were playing?"

"Mmm—Hmm. Wanna hear the rest?" Teresa asked.

"Well, I'd like that, but *my* bike is only built for *one*."

"That's okay. I'll play it anyway!"

Teresa began once more to play the kazoo, as Bridget began to unpack the lunch of sandwiches, cheese and crackers, and fresh fruit. "Billy, would you run over to that stand and get four glasses of lemonade, please." Bridget reached into her purse for some money, but Billy refused, insisting on buying them himself.

After lunch, Bridget brought out a pound cake and lit a small candle on the top. Teresa was "in her glory" as they all sang to her.

"Billy tells me you both graduated from telegraphy school, Teresa," Fergy said.

"Yeah, she's a natural on the key—quicker than most! She's already got Morse Code down pat!" Billy remarked. "Hard keeping up with her—that little Smarty Pants!"

Teresa laughed, poking Billy with her elbow. "None of that now, Mr. Silly Billy!"

"Funny we've never met, Teresa." Fergy remarked. "I'm up on the fifth floor in accounting, you know. But actually I seldom get down to the message center where you two are." He paused. "Maybe we could meet in the lunchroom some afternoon. Do you and Billy generally have the same lunch hours?"

Billy answered the question. "Well, yes, we do. But all that will be changing soon. I hear they're going to put all us newer people on the night shift when our on-the-job training is over. They said we have to start there when we are done with our mentoring since there's fewer communications on the night shift and it will give us more time to get our feet wet."

Bridget seemed surprised. "You didn't tell me about that, Teresa!"

"Oh, sorry Mom. I meant to let you know but we've been so busy lately with all the moving and everything."

"Well, I'm just not very comfortable with that, honey."

"What do you mean, Mom?"

"Well, being alone and waiting for the trolley after dark, and ..."

"Oh, don't worry about that, Mrs. Sexton," Billy interrupted. "I'm only a few blocks away and I'd be glad to walk over and escort her to work since we'll be on the same shift."

"What would we do without you, Billy? Thanks." Bridget smiled at him.

"Let's not talk about work on my birthday, okay Mom?"

Fergy reached into his pocket, taking out a deck of cards. "Anybody for a good game of Euchre?"

"Me!" Teresa shouted.

"We used to play that at the card parties on Saturday nights at church," Bridget remarked. "Tom used to love that game ..." She hesitated, suddenly realizing she might have to explain Tom's disappearance again.

Billy, noticing Bridget's unsettled demeanor, quickly stated, "Oh, it must be so hard for you. I know about Teresa's father, Mrs. Sexton. She mentioned it to me some time ago. I'm sorry."

After a moment of silence, Fergy announced, "Okay now, who's gonna deal?" He began shuffling the deck.

Two hours of play seemed enough for Teresa. She decided she'd like to take a little walk down to the lake. "Wanna come along?" she asked, glancing over at Fergy.

"Sure! Come on, Billy."

"Oh, yes, of course. You come, too, Billy," Teresa added.

"Good idea," Bridget said. "And I'll start packing things up here while you three take your walk. Don't be long though. Looks like some pretty dark clouds over there."

"Okay, Mom." Teresa looked up at her balloons. "What about those?"

"I'll cut them down for you, honey," Billy said.

"Just two, Billy. Leave the rest on the tree in case any kids come along. They'd enjoy seeing them."

"Okay."

"Oh, but I *do* want my sign—my Happy Birthday sign."

Billy removed the sign from the tree trunk and laid it on the blanket. "Be right back, Mrs. Sexton."

It wasn't long before a light rain began to fall, and the three came running back, helped Bridget finish packing up, and headed for the trolley, the girls holding the blanket over their heads.

By the end of the year, Teresa and Billy had become full-fledged telegraphers, able to work with confidence and proficiency in their skills. They had settled nicely into the routine of the night shift and had begun to make many new friends at work. That Christmas was the first time Teresa would attend a Christmas party being held for the employees of Western Union, but for a skeleton crew of those who volunteered to man the keys for an extra remuneration. It was an exciting time for her and she had asked Bridget to make "something real pretty" for her to wear. The material they chose together had a lovely sheen to it, pale coral in color. It was fashioned by the "designer-mom," as Teresa had begun to call her mother, into "the prettiest dress I ever saw in my whole life." The square neckline was outlined by a deep pink satin band, as was the midcalf hem. A matching band, somewhat wider, circled Teresa's waistline. Tiny flowers were then appliquéd above the hem's band and below that on the waistline. "I feel like a princess or something."

"You look like one, honey."

"Oh, Mom, thanks. Thanks."

"You're welcome. Have fun, darling." Can this possibly be that little girl I've been living with? She looks like a beautiful young lady. "Oh, answer the door, honey. Is that Billy?"

"Wow!" Billy remarked as he entered the room. "Who is this beauty?"

Teresa blushed. "Oh, you know it's me, Billy. Silly Billy."

"Teresa, you look absolutely gorgeous, hon."

"Doesn't she?" Bridget agreed.

"Thanks, Billy. It's all due to Mom making me this beautiful dress."

"Yes, and the beautiful girl who's wearing it! We won't be too late, Mrs. Sexton," Billy assured her.

"Take good care of her now."

"Don't worry, I will."

The conference room on the third floor of Western Union had been decorated with red and green streamers hanging diagonally across the ceiling culminating in a huge silver Christmas bell in the center. In the corner of the room was a seven-foot, green Douglas fir decorated with lights, strings of beads and popcorn, tinsel, paper flowers, pine cones and bows made from ribbons. Teresa's eye was taken by the attractive ornaments—the little gold trumpet, the sparkling snowflake, the brown teddy bear, the tiny stocking, the little teapot, the miniature Christmas tree, and the beautiful red cardinal. "Isn't this just beautiful, Billy?" as the two stood together admiring the tree. "My favorite is the cardinal; what's yours?"

"*You're* my favorite!"

"Oh, Billy!"

"So what are you two gonna do—stand here all day?"Fergy asked, poking Billy on the shoulder from behind.

"Hi Fergy."

"Yes, hi Fergy!" Teresa announced, purposely swirling her dress as she turned to greet him. Oh, that face!—that handsome face! "We were just admiring the tree. Isn't it beautiful?"

"Yeah, they did a nice job on this alright. Kinda puts you in the Christmas spirit. But let's grab a table. There aren't many left," Fergy said.

"Well, you two go get that one." Billy pointed to an empty table near the door. "I'll get some drinks for us."

Fergy pulled out a chair for Teresa. The red tablecloth was the perfect background for the centerpiece of small evergreen branches and pine cones tied with a sparkling gold ribbon. "I just love this party, don't you, Fergy? Everything is just so pretty," Teresa remarked, leaning over to smell the fresh greenery.

"It *is* nice. And, by the way, *you* look very pretty yourself tonight, Teresa."

"Oh ... thank you, Fergy." She blushed, having wondered if he would ever notice.

"Oh good! Coca-cola—I love that!" Teresa remarked, as Billy set the drinks on the table.

"Oh, I wasn't sure if you had ever had it, Teresa."

"Yes, I had it a couple times."

"They also have punch there, in case you'd rather have that."

"No, this is fine, Billy. Thanks." Teresa patted the chair next to her for Billy to sit down.

"The waiter said the band will be starting in five or ten minutes, honey."

"Oh, they have a band? How great!" Teresa remarked.

"Yes, and I insist on having the first dance, my dear," Billy responded.

"Who is *that*?" Teresa asked Fergy, noticing a young lady waving at him from another table.

"Oh, that's Alice. She works with me in accounting."

"Kinda nervy, isn't she? I mean, waving over to a man who is sitting with another girl."

"Oh, she's just a real friendly gal. Everybody likes her," Fergy remarked, waving back to Alice.

"Well, it just seems *very* forward to *me*," Teresa added.

Billy noticed her voice sounded a little testy. "Come on, kiddo—let's dance. The band's starting," he said, hoping to get her mind off Alice as he led her onto the dance floor. "It's 'Meet Me Tonight in Dreamland.' Nice, huh?"

"Oh, sorry ... what was that?" Teresa asked, her eye on Fergy who was making his way to Alice's table.

"I said that's a nice tune."

"Oh! Yes ... yes, it is."

"Aren't you having a nice time, Teresa?"

"Sure."

"A penny for your thoughts, hon."

Teresa didn't respond, continuing to watch Fergy, now leading Alice onto the dance floor.

"Teresa?"

"What? Did you say something?"

"Yes, I said a penny for your thoughts."

"Oh. Oh, I'm sorry, Billy. I guess I just have a little headache."

"Do you want to sit down?"

"Mmm—Hmm."

"Just relax, Teresa, and listen to the music, okay? Can I get you another cold drink?"

"Maybe I'll try that punch, if you don't mind, Billy," Teresa answered, never taking her eyes off Fergy and Alice. If this keeps up, I really *will* get a headache!

Billy returned with her drink just as the music ended and Fergy returned to the table with Alice. "Alice, I'd like you to meet two very dear friends of mine—Teresa Sexton and Billy Darly. They're on the first floor."

Alice nodded to Teresa. "A pleasure." She turned and nodded to Billy.

Some pleasure, Teresa thought. Maybe for *you*—not for *me*. She tried to be polite and responded to the girl. "Yes—a pleasure."

"I understand you both are working the night shift," Alice said, trying to make conversation in what she felt was a slightly icy atmosphere.

"Yes." Teresa didn't intend to carry on much of a conversation with her.

"They're putting out the food," Billy said, feeling things were getting out of sorts. "I don't know about all of you, but I'm famished. Come on, let's eat." He reached for Teresa's hand and she grasped his, feeling she needed his strength once again.

"Well, it was nice meeting all of you," Alice remarked. "I'd better get back to my friends."

Good idea, Teresa thought, as Billy led her away from the table. She turned back. "Come on, Fergy. Aren't you going to have something to eat?"

"Be right with you."

"Are they going to play again, Billy?" Teresa asked as they returned to their table with their food.

"Oh, I imagine so. Eat, honey! Maybe it'll make your headache go away."

"Where's Fergy? Don't you think we should wait for him?"

"I think he just got at the end of the line. We can start without him. He won't mind."

"Well, I think I'll wait. I'm not too hungry anyway."

"Okay. Do you mind if I start? I'm really starved."

"Go ahead, Billy."

"Teresa ..." Billy hesitated for a moment.

"Yes?"

"What's the matter?"

"What do you mean?"

"Well, something's wrong. I can tell."

Teresa was silent. Billy reached over, putting his hand below her chin and turning her head to him. "Teresa ... now I know something is bothering you. Why don't you tell your good friend Billy all about it before Fergy gets back, hmm?"

"It's nothing."

"Come on, baby. What's going on?"

"Billy, I already told you—I have a headache."

"Okay, okay." He decided not to push the point. Besides, Fergy was headed back to the table.

As soon as Fergy started eating, Teresa's headache suddenly disappeared and she decided she was hungry. "I can't wait till the band comes back. We're gonna dance, aren't we, Fergy?"

"Sure. But I want to eat first."

"Oh, I'm sure you'll have time. Don't you love dancing, Fergy?"

"It's nice."

"Well, you sure look like you enjoyed it when you were out there with that Alice."

"Oh, come on, Teresa!"

"Ladies and gentlemen!" came a voice from the stage. "For your dining pleasure, may I introduce our Barber Shop Quartet—The Singing Santas." Suddenly, four men dressed as Santa Claus ran out onto the stage, each one carrying a large black sack on his back which was placed on the floor before them.

"Oh, look at that! Isn't that cute? Santa Claus! Four of them!" Teresa laughed. A round of applause broke out.

"It's supposed to be a surprise," Billy said.

"Well, it is! I'm surprised! Aren't you, Fergy?"

"Well, actually, a rumor was kinda going around up on the fifth floor, Teresa. In fact, I think that one on the left is my friend, John, from Security."

The blending of the four voices as they harmonized "Sidewalks of New York" and "Sweet Rosie O'Grady" was a delight to the listeners. Afterwards, the Santas made their way around the tables, treating all the employees to little green cloth sacks filled with hard candies and tied with red ribbons. "Ho! Ho! Ho!" said one Santa as he approached the table. "And have you all been good little children this year?"

"Oh, yes, Santa!" Teresa responded. "Very good! We've all been very good!"

"Well, Merry Christmas to you all!" He laid a favor before each of them.

"Is that you, John?" Fergy asked.

"Ho! Ho! Ho!" was John's answer, as he winked at Teresa.

A couple more songs were done by the quartet, after which the band resumed its dance music. Would you like to dance again, Teresa?" Billy asked.

"Oh, thank you, Billy, but I believe I promised Fergy."

A questioning look was momentarily on Fergy's face, but he immediately rose and took Teresa's hand. "Oh, yes, of course. Excuse us, Billy."

The music was slow and sweet, and it seemed to Teresa that she could sway in Fergy's arms all night. She wanted him to hold her tighter, but Fergy just held her at arm's length and made small talk. "Are you enjoying yourself, Teresa?"

"Oh, yes! It's just lovely, isn't it?" Am I dreaming? I feel like my feet are not even on the floor. I think I'm in love. I *must* be in love. I'm *sure* I'm in love.

"And how's it going down there on the first floor? Like the work?"

"What?"

"I said how do you like working at Western Union?"

"Oh ... oh, yes. It's fine."

"It's a good job for a girl," Fergy added.

"Yes, and now that all our mentoring is over with— Billy's and mine—I've got my own telegraph key now."

"Billy says you're really good at it."

"Not as good as him, but at least I feel comfortable with it—secure—you know?"

The tap on Fergy's shoulder allowed Billy to cut in on their dance. "Hi honey. I was missing you at the table."

"Gee, Billy, that wasn't very nice."

"It's a guy thing—we all do it. Nothing wrong with it."

"Well, it seems to me like it's kinda barging in."

Billy felt bad, as though he was being disciplined or something.

"How would you like it if Fergy cut in on us when *we* were dancing?"

"Oh, Teresa! It's no big deal." Billy started feeling a little irritated. "Let's just sit down."

"After the Ball Was Over" was the last song of the evening. Neither Billy nor Fergy asked Teresa to dance, so she decided to take matters into her own hands. "Billy, why don't we dance this together?" she asked, wanting to make amends for her harshness with him, but also hoping it might make Fergy jealous.

As the song came to the end, the lights were turned up and everyone applauded. "Come on Fergy," Billy said, "we'll see Teresa home."

Old Man Winter bombarded the city with his howling winds and deep snow for the next three months. Somehow the trolleys kept running through it all with the extras hired by the city to keep the tracks cleared so people could get to their jobs. When spring finally arrived on the scene, it was greeted with joyful hearts by the weather-weary inhabitants of New York.

Arriving at work one April night, Bridget noticed there seemed to be a "buzz" throughout the room. She immediately realized that everyone was totally absorbed in an unusual amount of activity. Walking toward her desk, she could see the other operators seemed to be receiving incessant emergency distress calls.

MGY—MGY—the Titanic!

Hurriedly she sat at her key; messages apparently had been coming in for some time. They continued on—one after another—one after another. And on and on they came. Her heart froze ...

MGY CQD SOS SOS CQD CQD DE MGY

We are sinking fast ...

She quickly turned to Billy at the desk next to hers. He could see the fear in her eyes. She was shaking.

Passengers are being put ...

Suddenly the signal faded. A sickening feeling came over her, and it appeared that the others were experiencing the same. Sometime after the initial reports were received, statistics began coming in from another ship, the *Carpathia.* She was the first vessel on the scene, and began to pick up the survivors from the lifeboats. Early reports coming in were indicating that approximately seven hundred passengers had already been rescued.

Teresa, seeing reports that approximately twenty-two hundred passengers were originally aboard, broke down and cried. Billy tried to be of comfort to her; however, being unable to leave his desk, could only reach over to take her hand. She was still shaking. His touch seemed to have somewhat of a calming effect on her, however—that strength that always seemed to flow through from him. She noticed some of the other female telegraphers wiping away tears. A dark cloud of gloom seemed to hang over the entire office.

"Oh, God! How could this be?" the supervisor said.

"They hit an iceberg!"

"Maybe they'll still find more people ... in the water ..." one woman said, her voice sounding hopeful.

A man at the desk behind her said, "I'm sorry ma'am. People couldn't survive very long in those ice cold waters. They would die of hypothermia."

"How horrible!" another cried.

"Didn't they say that ship was unsinkable?" a man suggested.

"O-o-o-o. Oh, yes. Yes, that's right. I heard that the ship's captain said, "Not even God Himself could sink this ship!"

As the reports continued to come in, the horror of the tragedy continued to grow. The employees fulfilled their duties, although under the strain of the constant bombardment of messages. Some could be heard mumbling prayers under their breath as they worked.

Teresa was deeply affected and seemed to be in a daze as she rode home from work on the trolley with Billy. Images of the disaster floated through her young mind, and she could not seem to dismiss them as hard as she tried. She reached over and took Billy's hand in hers. He grasped it, pulled the other one over, and enclosed them both between his, wishing he could just enfold her completely in his arms and protect her from anything that could harm her. She leaned over and placed her head on his shoulder, closing her eyes.

Bridget, having a day off work, immediately noticed Teresa's downcast demeanor as she came through the front door. "And what would be so terrible that makes my lovely daughter so sad looking? Isn't Billy coming in?"

Teresa disregarded the question. "Mom ... you haven't heard? Haven't you heard?"

"What?"

"The Titanic—the Titanic sank!"

Bridget looked confused. "What? Sank?"

"Mom, that big ocean liner! All those people! Oh, Mom! It just kept coming in all night!—the reports. I couldn't stand it! I couldn't stand it, Mom!" She broke down and started crying again.

Bridget got up and held her daughter. "Oh, honey! Oh, how terrible! Saints preserve us! Those poor souls!" They stood quietly, Bridget holding her close and patting her back, trying to calm her. "I'm sorry, honey. I'm so sorry. What a horrible thing for you to go through." Bridget wanted to inquire as to the cause of the disaster, but decided not to ask any questions, as she could see that Teresa was traumatized by the incident. She sat the girl down on the sofa, removed her shoes and lifted her legs, swinging them up onto the cushion. "I'm going to put the kettle down, honey. Be right back. You rest."

She returned with a pillow and placed it behind Teresa's back before handing her a hot cup of tea. Teresa just stared straight ahead, holding the cup. "They say it hit an iceberg, Mom ..." Nothing more was said.

The tragic stories of that doomed ship covered newspapers for weeks and months to come. It seemed that each new report of the number of deaths was constantly changing, keeping the nightmare alive. In time, however, the number of fatalities on that ill-fated ship was settled at fifteen hundred and seventeen. Teresa continued to suffer visions in her mind's eye of the ship tipping over, spilling those poor souls to their deaths in that deep, cold Atlantic Ocean. She drew heavily on Billy's support during these months, to the point where Fergy was almost erased from her mind.

Eventually stories of the disaster faded onto back pages of the newspapers and, by 1913, whispers of unrest in Europe began to trickle along the telegraph lines, hinting of war.

Chapter 16

War

"Fifteen is the pits, isn't it, Mom? Do you remember?"

"What do you mean, Teresa?"

"Well, you know, it's kinda like you're not a woman yet, but you're not a kid anymore, either. Just kinda stuck somewhere in the middle, you know?"

"Oh, honey! You're so funny. Just relax and enjoy each year ... well, each day actually, for what it brings."

"Good advice, Mom!" Teresa seemed satisfied with that.

"Besides, in my eyes, honey, you truly are grown up. After all, you've been working your job for almost three years now and helping with all the expenses. Thanks to you, we have this nice place to live and ... well, anyway ..." She smiled at her daughter. "Did I tell you how much I love you today, Teresa?"

"Nope."

"Well, I love you today, and God loves you even more!"

"Oh, Mom! That's so nice!"

"You know, honey, your father used to say that to me all the time!"

"A-w-w-w. I love him so much—even though I never had him with me."

Although Bridget had long back recovered from the initial shock of Tom's disappearance, that little ache in her heart still lingered below the surface. On a few occasions, that heart fluttered upon seeing someone at a distance who resembled Tom, only to find out at closer range, it wasn't him, quickly dissolving that fleeting hope once again. But life went on. She was a strong woman of faith all through her struggles and never faltered in her belief in Jesus Christ. Her undying faith was a bulwark against the rare occasions of hopelessness.

On Sundays Bridget and Teresa would attend Mass at Saint Patrick's on 5th Avenue and 50th Street, eventually registering at that parish. Bridget made friends easily and soon decided to involve herself in the church activity of helping the poor, knowing first-hand the many difficulties these people were experiencing. Bridget's work at "Molly-Maureen's" had evolved mostly into designing, although she liked the "hands on" work of stitching and cutting that she had done in the past. She decided to use these old skills, taking one or two evenings a week to work at home to sew for those less fortunate, the material being donated by the parish. Teresa, wishing to assist others through her mother's good example, joined in by knitting mittens and hats, as Bridget had taught her long back.

Bridget felt that she had now gained much more security through her trade and the second income from Teresa, who seemed to be well on her way to a promising future at Western Union. Through all their suffering after the disappearance of Tom, it seemed as though Teresa had matured much faster than would have been expected in someone her age. Bridget was very proud of her daughter, remarking to her quite often how she was a blessing from God. The two had grown even closer through their trials than most mothers and daughters. Billy had also noticed the growth in Teresa; she seemed to him to be closer to an eighteen or nineteen-year-old instead of just "going on 16," her way of speaking of her age—as of the coming birthday. He had become more and more infatuated with her sweet and perky ways the past couple years, though mostly trying to hide his feelings. By now, however, he felt more comfortable with inviting her out, hoping Bridget might approve.

"Mom, do you remember a long time ago when I told you that I thought that Billy really liked me a lot?"

"I *do* remember that, Teresa. Why do you ask?"

"Well, I was *right*."

"Oh?"

"Mmm—Hmm."

"Yes? So what are you trying to say, Teresa?"

"Umm ..."

"Teresa? What is it?" Bridget was beginning to get the idea of where her daughter was going with all this.

"He asked me for a date, Mom," the girl blurted out.

"Oh, Teresa! Honey, you know how I feel about that."

"But M—o—m—m ..."

Bridget's thoughts flew through her mind. She had always tried to be both mother *and* father to her daughter. "Now don't go rushing things right now—there'll be plenty of time for that. You're young yet."

"I'm almost *sixteen*!"

"Exactly. You're young yet."

"But M—o—m—m, he only asked me to go for a walk with him down in the park and ..."

"Oh! Well ... well I guess that would be alright. Yes, that's a good idea. We'll all go for a walk together—maybe on Sunday?"

"Umm ... well ... I kinda think he meant *me*—I mean, *just* me."

"Now, Teresa, if he really likes you and wants to spend some time with you, he should be glad to go even if I go along."

"M—o—m—m ..." the girl's voice whined out once again.

"That's it, Teresa. Yes or no. It will be my way or not at all."

"Gee! Don't you *trust* me with *Billy*?"

"Well, that's not the point. You are only fifteen, my dear."

"Almost *sixteen*!"

"I know, but still ..."

Teresa interrupted, "It's not like we're madly in love or something, you know, Mom!"

"Well, I certainly hope not!"

"We're just good friends. It's just that Billy makes me feel so good. I mean, I just like being around him. He's... well, he's comforting. Yeah, he just makes me feel so comfortable."

"Well, don't you see enough of him on the trolley and at work?"

"Yeah, but we don't have that much time to talk on the trolley and we're too busy at work."

"Oh."

"Well, you know, Mom, don't you feel real nice about him? Like ... I mean, like when he's around?"

"Well, honey, I kind of know what you mean."

Teresa pushed her point. "He's good and kind and strong and ... well ... and sweet." She thought a moment. "Remember a few times when you were talking about Daddy and you kept telling me how sweet he was?"

"Yes." This reminiscing brought her Tom so fully back into her heart, it felt as though it were about to break. She quickly tried to diminish the feeling. "Yes, I do, honey."

"So maybe Billy is kinda like Daddy was, you think?"

"Well, maybe you're right on that point, Teresa."

"So maybe he just makes me feel how I would have felt if I had Daddy around all those years—do you think so, Mom?"

Bridget's heart was beginning to open. She realized that perhaps Teresa had substituted Billy for the father she never knew and thought that maybe it *would* be good for the girl to have him around more.

"Mom, he's just my best friend. That's all. So don't you think I could go?"

"Yes. But like I said before—we'll all go."

Teresa could see that her mother was not about to give in and allow her to go alone on a date.

Clang! Clang! Clang! The trolley was crowded, but Billy finally found a seat toward the back for Teresa and him. "Guess what,

Teresa? There's a rumor going around that we're gonna be put on days soon—I'm gonna check it out when we get to work."

"Oh, that's good news! Guess this is "good news day," Billy!"

"What do you mean?"

"I can go on our date."

"Oh, that's great, hon!"

"Well, yeah ... kinda ..."

"Kinda?"

"Mmm—Hmm. It's umm ... like, I can go with you on Sunday, Billy, but how about if another person comes along?"

"Oh, you mean you want me to invite Fergy?" Billy asked in a disheartened tone.

"No, that's not it."

"So, what's the story?"

"Well, would you believe my Mom wants to come along with us?"

"Oh, really? Gee, I was hoping ..." He thought a minute. "Well, I guess if she insists."

"Yeah, she does!" Teresa said with a half-smile on her face. She hesitated, then quickly added, "But feel free to invite Fergy, too."

"He might be busy this Sunday, Teresa," Billy offered.

"Well, it certainly won't hurt to ask him, Billy. Maybe he won't."

"Well, why don't we just bring the whole office!" Billy mumbled under his breath, shaking his head, as they got off the trolley.

"What was that?"

"Nothing. Come on, here we are!"

The following Sunday after Mass the four met, as planned, under Teresa's "birthday tree." After a light lunch, they set out for their walk along the lake, Billy having pre-warned Fergy not to join them. A gaggle of longnecked geese flew low over their heads, honking loudly, and Teresa tripped as she looked upward to see them. "Watch your step!" Billy cautioned, taking advantage of the situation and reaching out to grab her in his arms, as the fowl began their slow glide to a gentle landing on the still water.

"Oh, thanks, Billy." She walked closer to the edge of the lake and sat on the grass, watching another landing by a second group. "Come on, sit down!" They spent some time relaxing there, mostly talking about work, Teresa a little annoyed that Fergy had decided to stay at the picnic spot with Bridget. Well, at least I might have the opportunity to see more of him now that we'll be going on the day shift.

"Come on, you two, let's have a game of Euchre!" Fergy remarked on their return, taking a deck of cards from his pocket. "So how's it going down there on the first floor? You two keeping things running smoothly?" Fergy smiled at Teresa and Billy, as he began to deal.

"Well, I'll tell ya, Fergy—I hear we're the Number 1 team in the building!"

"Is that so?" Fergy laughed. "Funny, I was under the impression that the Accounting Department was rated Number 1."

"Hah!" Billy was trying to think of a good response to that one.

Fergy reached over and plucked a handful of grass, tossing it into the air. "And Billy, I've been meanin' to ask you, how come you work with us common folk when your Pa has so much dough?"

Billy took the question seriously. "Well, to begin with, I love working as a telegrapher. Besides, I intend to work my way up the ladder—right up to the top!"

"Is that so?" Fergy remarked. "Well, you might bump into me on the way up!"

"Yeah? Well, maybe—or maybe I'll just have to pull you up behind me!" Billy smirked, glancing over at Teresa. "But mostly, I've got to keep my eye on this cute girl who sits at the desk next to mine." Teresa smiled, as Bridget just sat there, enjoying the bantering going on between the boys.

"And anyway, Fergy, I just like the excitement of working there. You know, being right on top of the news coming in every day. Kinda like firsthand knowledge of big stuff going on around the country and hearing about big events right away—you know?"

"Yeah—like the Titanic sinking, you mean?"

"Yeah, exactly," He paused, then added, "As terrible as it was." Billy was sorry the subject had come up, knowing how difficult it had been for Teresa to erase it from her mind after the occurrence.

She quickly jumped into the conversation. "I heard something interesting the other day over the wire. I don't understand it, but all these messages were going to some diplomat—something about the Balkan War in Europe. And then something about an Ottoman Empire—whatever *that* is! Then they called it 'Powder Keg of Europe'. I don't know what all that means, but I don't like the sound of it!"

"Yeah, I heard all that, too, Teresa. And I know one thing—" Billy remarked, "there's gonna be a war over there."

"Well, I hope *we* don't get into it," Fergy added.

"This is *supposed* to be a pleasant afternoon," Bridget interrupted. "I hate to think about such serious stuff on such a beautiful day. Anyway, it's getting kinda late. Maybe we should head for home."

In time, Bridget and Teresa became even closer friends to both Fergy and Billy. Mother and daughter had already shared much about their past in Buffalo and had also come to know much about the boys. Their families were from opposite ends of the social ladder. Billy's family was from well-to-do English landowners, while Fergy's came from poor Irish immigrants. Bridget had come to notice that Teresa's instinct about Billy's interest in her being more than friendship certainly seemed to be correct. Having known poverty herself for so many years made her wonder if perhaps it would be to her daughter's benefit one day to have a husband who would have no problem whatsoever supporting her and any possible children. For the time being, however, she kept these thoughts to herself, deciding to allow Billy more leeway to visit on occasion.

The days turned into weeks and the weeks into months—everyday work, Mass at St. Patrick's, sewing for the poor, card games, picnics, ice skating in Central Park, and get-togethers at Bridget's. Life was good for the four friends; however, talk of unrest overseas surfaced more and more in newspapers and on telegraph, war becoming a major topic of conversation across the country, although the four of them could not even begin to imagine how all this would affect their future.

"More potatoes, Billy?" Bridget passed the dish without waiting for an answer.

"Oh, thanks. I'd really like some, but ..." He placed the dish back on the table.

"No?" Bridget looked surprised, as potatoes were his favorite.

"I'm not too hungry, actually," Billy explained.

"Oh?"

"Well, it's just that some of this stuff we're getting in at work is starting to bother me a lot."

"Oh, I'm sorry. I didn't know. Teresa hasn't said anything about work lately," as she looked over at her daughter. "What's going on?"

"Well, I didn't mention it, Mom, but the news yesterday didn't sound very good. It was all about some guy called an Archduke."

Billy interrupted. "That's right. It was Archduke Franz Ferdinand from Austria. They assassinated him."

"And his wife, too!" Teresa added.

"Oh, how terrible!" Bridget remarked.

"And worse—there's every possibility this could lead to a war in Europe!" Billy said.

"I just hate hearing all this," Bridget said. "Why don't you two just go out for a little walk or something while I clean up the dishes. Then we can have some coffee when you come back."

"Oh, I'll help, Mom!"

"No, no, Teresa. You two have been working all day. I can do these few dishes. Go get a little air."

"Okay. We won't be long, Mom."

Bridget busied herself, trying to forget the foreboding news and thinking it would be good for the two young people to do so as well. Billy is so good. I can understand why Teresa feels so much comfort when he's around. Maybe she... Her thoughts continued as she cleared the table.

"Gee, Billy!" Teresa remarked as they started down the street. "How Mom's changed. Have you noticed?"

"What do you mean, Teresa?"

"Well, it didn't seem that long ago that I couldn't go for a walk with you at the park without her tagging along. But just now ... well didn't it seem to you that she was kinda encouraging us?"

"Yeah, that's right—kinda," Billy answered.

"Probably 'cause I told her we were just good friends."

Billy stopped walking, took Teresa's arm and turned her toward him. "Is *that* what I am to you, Teresa—just a good friend?" he asked in a very serious tone of voice.

"Ummm ... well, a very, very *dear* friend, Billy."

"Teresa ..."

"Oh, look at this Billy!" the girl interrupted quickly. "Hopscotch!" She started jumping ahead from square to square following the markings on the sidewalk.

"Come on, Teresa," Billy said, "let's head back."

"No, let's not. You come on and try this, Billy," she retorted, laughing, as she turned on square eight.

"We're heading back, Teresa!" She didn't like the curt tone of his voice but could see that he was not about to walk any further.

"So how was the walk?" Bridget inquired. Neither answered.

"How was your walk?" she asked again.

"Oh, umm ... it was nice," Teresa answered.

"Well, coffee's ready."

"Oh, thanks. I really appreciate it, but I think I'd better be going," Billy said.

"Oh, come on, Billy! Have some coffee. Come on!" Teresa insisted.

"No, really, I think I'd best be going. Thank you so much for the wonderful dinner, Bridget."

"You're very welcome, Billy—anytime. Goodnight now," she answered, holding the door while wondering if anything was wrong. She turned back to her daughter, a quizzical look on her face. "Well?"

"Well what, Mom?"

"Now honey, something's wrong. I can tell."

"Billy didn't like me playing Hopscotch!"

"*What*?"

"Yeah, that's all. He didn't wanna do Hopscotch."

"Don't you think you are getting a little too old for Hopscotch? And where were you playing that anyway?"

"Oh, just a couple blocks from here. It was on the sidewalk."

"Obviously. So?"

"That's all, Mom. That's all."

"Come on, this sounds like nonsense, Teresa."

"Well, it's just that ... ummm ... I don't think he liked it when I said we were just good friends. I think he got mad. At least he *sounded* mad. And then I jumped on the Hopscotch—and that was the end of it."

"Well, Teresa, I think maybe Billy must be quite fond of you."

"Yeah, don't I know, Mom? Didn't I tell you that a long time ago?"

"Yes, but you were too young to even begin to be thinking of those things at that time."

"Well, I'm not *now*."

"Sometimes, Teresa, young men who are good and kind and strong and sweet—like you always call Billy—can grow on you in time. I ought to know."

"Yeah, I know—Dad!"

"Yes."

"Well, anyway, I don't feel like talkin' about it anymore, Mom, okay?" Teresa didn't think she should bring up her feelings about Fergy right at that time.

The conversation came to an abrupt end; there was a moment of silence. Then Bridget began working on her sewing machine for her church project. A few minutes later, she looked back at Teresa who seemed totally absorbed in a book she had brought home from the library the day before.

"What's the book about, honey?"

"It's about the Civil War," Teresa responded, never taking her eyes from her reading.

"You know, honey, I've been doing a lot of thinking lately."

"Oh."

"About maybe moving back to Buffalo."

"Oh, sure, that's good, Mom," Teresa responded, half listening.

Bridget raised her voice. "We're moving back to Buffalo!"

Teresa dropped the book. "*What?*"

"Yes. I've been thinking. What if your father ever returned to Buffalo—he wouldn't know where to find us."

"You really think he could return? I mean ... after all this time? Besides, Mom, even if by a miracle that could happen, somebody there would know where we are—the Ryans maybe."

"He never knew the Ryans, and we never told anyone else we were coming here, honey."

"Oh, Mom!" Teresa felt so much sadness to see that her mother was still pining away from her father's disappearance, thinking she had overcome that long back. "I'm so sorry, Mom." She got up from the sofa, went over to the sewing machine, and bent down, putting her arms around Bridget, just holding her close for a few minutes. "I love you, Mom."

"I love you, too, honey."

"Don't sew now. Come on ... sit down over here with me." Bridget sat next to her daughter, holding her hand. "Mom, I understand how you must be feeling right now, but don't you think it's a little unrealistic? I mean, I'm just doing so good on my new career and I'm up for a raise soon. Besides we just got this nice apartment and ... well, your job is good. And another thing—we have our two best friends here. I just think ... well, what would we be going back to? We'd have to start all over."

Bridget didn't respond.

But there was another unsaid reason Teresa didn't even want to *think* of moving away—that "Fergy with the handsome face!" She watched for him every day at lunch in the cafeteria. On one occasion, Alice stopped by their table to say hello to Billy and her.

"Nice to see you both again," she said, smiling.

"You too," Billy responded.

Teresa simply nodded her head, determined not to say *anything*. Then, on second thought, "Is Fergy working today, Alice?"

The girl simply nodded back and mentioned that he had taken an earlier lunch.

"Well, say hello to him for me," Teresa said. Alice nodded again, saying nothing, and left.

"Well," Teresa said to Billy, "the least she could have done is say 'okay.'"

"Maybe if you tried to be a little friendlier, Teresa, she might have. Your tone of voice was kinda testy."

"Well, I don't wish to speak about it anymore," Teresa snapped at Billy. "I have to get back to work." She got up to leave, Billy immediately following her.

"What's with you anyway, Teresa?"

"I said I don't want to talk about it."

That evening after dinner, Teresa tried to keep her mind on her reading once more. That sudden interest in the Civil War seemed to baffle Bridget, but Teresa had a definite plan in mind. Maybe Fergy would take more interest in her, being knowledgeable about the Civil

War in which his grandfather had fought, especially since he carried his name. Bridget decided to invite the boys for dinner one evening shortly after, continuing to wonder if Teresa and Billy's friendship might develop into something more serious. Fergy's presence, however, gave the girl occasion to share much of what she had learned; and the conversation mostly gravitated around the War. Teresa expected this might give Fergy occasion to ask her out; however, that was not to be the case.

Billy continued his quest of pursuing Teresa, though mostly keeping it in a quiet mode, giving her support whenever she needed it and seeing her safely back and forth to work. She, in turn, not wanting to raise his ire, decided to keep her feelings about Fergy under wraps. She wasn't going to take any chances of losing the comfort of her best friend. The age-old eternal triangle was in place, and what was soon to come would change the innocence of it all.

The following May, war escalated on the European continent when a German U-Boat sunk the British ship, *RMS Lusitania*, killing 128 Americans. The United States continued to remain neutral through the following year; however, in March of 1917, three US cargo ships were sunk by another German U-Boat. Shortly thereafter, America made the discovery that Germany wanted to ally themselves with Mexico and start hostilities against the United States. In exchange for the conflict, Germany would support any action undertaken by Mexico to reclaim the territory which they had lost to the United States previously, including Texas and Arizona. This was the tipping point which culminated shortly after with President Woodrow Wilson asking Congress to declare war against Germany, stating "The world must be made safe for democracy."

"Look at this, Teresa! Look at this!" Bridget called out to her. "Oh, God! We're going to war!" She held the New York Times before her, pointing to the headline and reading as she did.

The New York Times

PRESIDENT CALLS FOR WAR DECLARATION,

STRONGER NAVY, NEW ARMY OF 500,000 MEN,

FULL CO-OPERATION WITH GERMANY'S FOES

Washington, April 2 -- At 8:35 o'clock tonight, the United States virtually made its entrance into the War. At that hour, President Wilson appeared before a joint session of the Senate and House and invited it to consider the fact that Germany had been making war upon us and to take action and recognition of that fact in accordance with his recommendations, which included universal military service, the raising of an army of 500,000 men, and cooperation with the Allies in all ways that will help most effectively to defeat Germany.

"I know, Mom. Everybody in the office figured it would come to this, seeing the messages that were coming through."

"Oh, of course." Bridget continued reading to herself, shaking her head from side to side. "This is terrible! Just terrible!" she murmured.

So now the "Gilded Age," as Mark Twain had called it, faded into the past; and America was now on a war footing, ill-equipped as it was. The new recruits had to train with wooden rifles in the beginning. The Germans, referred to as the Huns, were now America's new enemy. "Hell is too good for the Hun" became a common slogan throughout the land, and our Army Infantry soldiers were now known as "Doughboys." Patriotic music echoed in cities and towns across the nation, flags waved in the breeze from poles attached to storefronts and homes, and prayers for our nation became commonplace in churches of all denominations. And in New York City, a foursome would soon be reduced to a twosome, as Billy and Fergy were among the thousands and thousands of young doughboys who had volunteered for the work of war awaiting across the seas.

Camp Mills, Long Island. Barracks, infantry drill, bayonet drill, marching, inspections, calisthenics, rifle range, physical hygiene, guard duty, combat training—in rain, mud, or dust! By October, the boys were exceedingly anxious for the pass which would bring them back to Manhattan for five days. Each one spent the first few days with their parents, after which they decided to spend one more afternoon at their usual favorite picnic spot with Bridget and Teresa.

It was the last Sunday in September when they all met at the park. A definite chill could already be felt in the soft breezes, and Teresa's "birthday tree" was adorned in majestic golds, oranges, and reds. The meeting was bittersweet; the boys would soon be shipped overseas, and Bridget and Teresa tried to hide their concern. So happy to be back together, they all hugged one another, Teresa kissing both boys on the cheek. She had sorely missed the two and those few months they were away made her realize how very important they had become in her life—almost like family. Billy, of course, was her "best friend," but her feelings for Fergy had blossomed into what her young heart believed was true love, even though he had never responded in any way that had given her any hope that he felt the same. This, in itself, caused her no feeling of dejection, as she always believed her "Fergy with the handsome face" would come around in time. But *now*, time had run out—at least for the moment.

The boys had brought their baseball gloves and played catch for a while after lunch. They tried to get Teresa to join in, but she refused and sat on the blanket with her mother, trying to hold back her tears.

"Oh, Mom! I'm so worried! What if something would happen? Oh, we'll have to pray every day for their safety."

"We will, honey. Don't worry. I'm sure the Good Lord will watch over them for us."

"But, Mom, what if something *would* happen?"

"Teresa, you mustn't think like that. Try not to think that way, honey."

Teresa rose from the blanket and walked quickly toward the lake, so as to hide her sobbing from the rest. Billy spotted her after a few moments. "Teresa, wait up!" She heard but didn't stop and continued walking straight ahead. "Teresa!" he called again. Finally, he ran and caught up with her. Tears were streaming down her cheeks. "Oh, baby!" He grabbed her up in his arms, her feet dangling, and held her tightly. "Honey, what is it?" She just continued sobbing. "Come on. What's wrong?"

"It's this war thing—this terrible war! I don't want you two to go away."

"Now, now, honey," setting her back on her feet. "We'll be back before you know it. We'll beat those Huns in no time at all."

"I don't know what I'll do without you, Billy. You're my best friend."

"There's that 'best friend' stuff again!"

"Oh, I'm sorry. You know you mean the world to me."

"And you *are my* world, Teresa." He wanted to tell her how much he loved her again and again, but she seemed so fragile at the moment, he didn't want to cause her any more concern. "Come on, honey. Let's head back. They'll be looking for us." He lifted her chin and kissed her softly on the lips. He took her by the hand and they started back. A voice in the distance was calling out, "Come on, you two! We need you for a Euchre game."

Billy hollered back. "Comin' Fergy!"

Teresa couldn't keep her mind on any card game but played anyway, trying to push her worry from her mind. "Won't be able to play too long," Fergy said. "Have to be back tonight, you know."

"You have to go back to the *Camp* tonight?" Teresa asked.

"Oh, yes. Then we leave from the train station right here in Manhattan tomorrow—both of us."

"Well, perhaps we should pack up; you two have a lot to take care of, I'm sure, to get ready to leave," Bridget offered, beginning to pick up the cards.

"We'll see you home," Billy said, offering his hand to Teresa. "Oh, one last thing," He took his pocket knife from his jacket and began to carve on the side of the tree.

Billy

Teresa

Fergy

Bridget

"There! Now that makes it official! It's *our* tree!" he announced.

Standing at the door of Bridget's apartment, the four of them held hands, not speaking for a moment. Bridget lowered her head and started a short prayer, asking God to keep them both safe.

"We'll be praying every single day," Teresa remarked, tears welling up in her eyes.

"Yes. And we'll write," Bridget added, reaching over to hug Billy and then Fergy.

Billy, wishing to lighten things up, turned to Teresa. "Now you make sure you keep the telegraph lines going. Maybe by the time we get back, you'll be a supervisor!" he chuckled. "My little Smarty Pants!"

"Oh, Billy!" Teresa reached over and hugged him around his waist. "My Silly Billy!" He leaned down and kissed her on the forehead. She then reached up and pulled his face down, returning the kiss to his.

Fergy reached over and took Bridget's hands in his, warmly shaking them and thanking her for everything. Turning to Teresa, he did the same. Pulling her hands from his grasp, she hugged him tightly. "Sorry, honey," he said. "We just really have to get going," shifting from Teresa's hug, leaving her feeling somewhat slighted. "Come on, Billy. We *really* gotta go. Not much time left. Gotta be back to camp by nine tonight, remember?" Billy nodded. Bridget and Teresa waved them off as they headed toward the trolley.

Bridget was awakened at seven the next morning to the sound of sobbing. She quickly entered Teresa's room, finding her sitting on the edge of the bed. “What is it, dear? Are you alright?” Teresa didn’t answer but covered her tear-stained face with her hands. Bridget sat down next to her and put her arms around her. “They’ll be alright, honey. They’ll be okay.”

“Well, that’s not it, Mom. Not exactly.” she sobbed.

“Well, what?”

“Oh, Mom, I just can’t let them go without a final goodbye.”

“Now dear, don’t you worry. They can take care of themselves. We did our goodbyes last night, remember?”

“No, Mom, you don’t understand.” Bridget looked puzzled. Teresa repeated herself. “You don’t understand.” The girl had a pained look on her face. “Mom ... it’s ... it’s *Fergy*!”

Bridget was afraid she knew what was coming. She had surmised from Teresa’s actions the night before that there was something more than friendship here. “What about Fergy, Teresa?”

“Well, I never told you, but ...” She hesitated.

“What about him, honey?” Teresa started crying harder. “That’s alright. I’ve seen you around him.” She put her hand under her daughter’s chin, raising it slightly and looking into her eyes with a look that only a mother can give. “You really love him, don’t you?”

“Oh, yes, Mama. I do. I do. But I never told him.” Bridget mumbled something Teresa couldn’t make out. “What did you say, Mother?”

“Oh, nothing.”

Teresa persisted, “I know you said *some*thing.”

“Well, I just said that *I* never had a chance to say goodbye.”

“You mean my father?”

“Yes, dear. I never had a chance to say goodbye.” Bridget suddenly straightened up and said, “If you truly love him, tell him so. It’s only right.”

“But how?”

“Honey, their train doesn’t leave ‘til nine. *We’re* gonna be there! Hurry! Get dressed!”

The brisk cold wind that morning seemed to be a precursor of the cold winds of war the boys would soon be entering. The 42nd Rainbow Division stood shivering on the platform awaiting the arrival of the train which would deliver them to the shores of the Atlantic Ocean, from there to be shipped overseas. "Oh my gosh! I hope we can find them, Mom—there's hundreds and hundreds and hundreds!" They pushed their way through the crowd of khaki-clad uniforms, Teresa searching frantically. Bridget began to call out. "Billy! Fergy! Billy!"

A band suddenly struck up the popular tune, "Over There." Immediately, a patriotic fervor was aroused in the crowd and a crescendo of voices filled the air.

Over there, over there
Send the word, send the word over there
That the Yanks are coming
The Yanks are coming
The drums rum-tumming
Everywhere
So prepare, say a prayer
Send the word, send the word to beware
We'll be over, we're coming over
And we won't come back till it's over
Over there

Teresa started crying. "They'll never hear us, Mom. Not with all this noise," she shouted to her mother.

Bridget removed her hat and told Teresa to do the same, holding them as high up over their heads as they could and frantically waving them back and forth. Suddenly, a voice was heard yelling from behind. "Teresa! Bridget!" And again—"Teresa! Bridget!" Billy was struggling to push his way through the crowd, yelling as he did so, Fergy following shortly behind.

The clackety-clack of the heavy metal wheels rolling over the steel tracks announced the arrival of the train which would transport Fergy and Billy off to war.

Teresa grabbed Fergy around the neck and whispered into his ear. "I love you!" Unable to hear over the din of the crowd, Fergy cupped his ear with his hand. Teresa raised her voice, shouting, "I said I love you, Fergy!"

The captain, having taken a position on the top step of the train, yelled through a megaphone. “Okay you men, time to board. Let’s get some kind of order here. On the double!”

“I’ll write you Teresa,” Fergy quickly responded to the girl’s dismay, hoping to hear something more from his lips.

Billy reached over, a disturbed look on his face, and hugged Teresa but said nothing, afterward kissing her on her cheek. Bridget had only a moment to grab both their hands and shake them, as they were pushed forward by the mob of soldiers boarding the train. On the steps, Fergy turned back, yelling, “Don’t forget to save us a spot at the park! We’ll be back for another picnic!” He laughed and disappeared into the train.

“What did he say, Mom?”

“I couldn’t hear him either, Teresa.” The two stood silently in the midst of the confusion until all the men had boarded. The shrill whistle, followed by the loud hissing sound of the train’s steam engines laboring to gain momentum, seemed to bring about the stark reality in Teresa’s heart that Fergy could possibly be gone from her forever. Tears ran down her cheeks. “What if he never comes back, Mom?” she asked amid her sobs.

“Oh, honey, the Good Lord will watch over him. You mustn’t think that way. We’ll pray every day.” Bridget took a handkerchief out of her pocket and wiped her daughter’s tears. They stood there, watching as car after car slowly began passing them by. The great spurts of steam spit out from the engine began to cloud their view, as Teresa frantically searched window after window hoping to catch one last glimpse of the one she loved. Men were hanging out from the windows, waving and shouting their goodbyes. The train began moving faster, and Teresa started pushing her way through the crowds along the platform, finally running, trying to keep up with the speed of the train, only stopping when the caboose rolled out beyond the platform. She stood there watching as the train pulled out of sight carrying the precious cargo of young warriors to an unknown destination to do mortal combat with a strange enemy called “The Hun.”

“I hope he heard what I told him, Mom. I mean, he really didn’t say anything much—just that he’d write. Do you think he heard me?”

Bridget thought perhaps the boy could have heard what her daughter had said but wasn't about to admit that. "I don't know that anybody could hear *anything* with all that racket, honey. Come on, let's head home, hmm?" They turned to leave, the last two on the platform. Teresa broke down again.

The War Between the States had been over for fifty-two years, and only a few veterans were still alive. Some were missing limbs and needed crutches or wheelchairs—they were the remnants of war. Some were poverty stricken and needed relatives or friends to care for them. Behind each one was a story—a story that most likely began in their youth—in a tragic kind of war. Brother against brother. And when it began, these brave young men were filled with patriotism and willing to face the jaws of death. It was either a bullet, an exploding shell, or disease that crippled these young men for the rest of their lives—or suddenly ended that life. It was as if a pattern had been set—men fighting and dying in most every generation. The causes would be different, but the devil would have his "pound of flesh."

Now it was beginning all over again—some countries would be victorious and some defeated. New technologies brought even more destruction—airplanes, the rapid-firing machine guns, tanks ...

The world would go on, but the results would leave another generation trying to bury the horror in their hearts—*or* being buried beneath crosses dotting the landscape in every little town across this great nation and on foreign shores.

And now, this new conflict they called "The Great War" was just beginning for 125,000 American boys. It seemed to many just a token, but that was all the President and Congress would allow.

Bridget and Teresa returned to their respective jobs and prayed daily for the boys to be safely returned to their homeland, often stopping by St. Patrick's to pray a rosary, not only for Billy and Fergy, but for all the boys in harm's way. Teresa's prayer life had become more fervent, as her heart feared the loss of her Fergy, bringing a greater understanding of her own Mother's heart at the loss of her father.

Just before Christmas, Teresa received a letter from Billy saying his outfit arrived in Brest, France and was in training. He sounded homesick and wished she and Bridget a Merry Christmas. Teresa wondered why he hadn't mentioned Fergy. She answered his letter, inquiring about him at the end.

New Year's came—still no letter from Fergy. Then, finally, in February, one did come. He was in Baccarat, France. Teresa was so excited, she quickly tore open the envelope, almost ripping the letter.

Dear Bridget and Teresa,

I hope all is well with you both. I am fine. Shortly after arriving here in France, I was called into the Captain's office who introduced me to the Regimental Chaplain, Father Duffy. I couldn't imagine why I had been called to his office at first and was a little concerned. The priest asked me if I was any relation to a Fergus O'Sullivan. I told him he was my grandfather who fought In the Civil War. In the ensuing conversation, the priest mentioned that he saw my Grandpa's name listed on the roster of the 69th Irish Brigade, including a citation for bravery—above and beyond the call of duty. I felt very proud and told him how my grandfather used to show me his scars from being wounded in the Battles of Fredericksburg and Gettysburg. The priest smiled at that and said, "Well, son, you look like a chip off the old block, carrying on the grand old Irish tradition of fighting for freedom. I'm sure you'll be as brave as your Grandpa."

Then, to my surprise, he offered me the Chaplain's Assistant job! What an honor!

By the way, Billy and I are in different outfits now— they transferred him a few weeks ago, so I don't get to see much of him anymore. My new job will be to guard Father Duffy, as well as assisting him at Mass and in his rounds caring for the spiritual needs of the men.

We'll most likely be going into action soon, so am asking for your good prayers. God bless you both.

Your friend,

Fergy

Teresa sat back in her chair, staring down at the letter still in her hand and began to sob. Just then, Bridget, hearing her cry, rushed from the kitchen. "What is it, honey?"

"Mom!" Teresa blurted out between her sobs. "Oh, Mom! It's a letter from Fergy!"

"Oh, my gosh! What's wrong—is he hurt?"

"No, but ..." She handed the letter to her mother. "Look! It's addressed to *both* of us!" Bridget read the letter, but before she could speak, Teresa sobbed, "Mom! He doesn't love me!"

"Now, now. Why do you think that?"

"Can't you tell? The letter wasn't to me alone, but to the *both* of us!" Her crying became more profuse. "I should have known back at the train station when I told him how I loved him and he never said it back!"

Bridget sat down next to her and put her arm around her daughter's shoulder. "Now don't get all excited, honey. You know, he probably has a lot on his mind right now—give him time to settle in. You don't know how he may feel about going into harm's way."

"You think so? Maybe he's a little worried?"

"It very well could be. We can't even imagine—being over here and safe. He's probably keeping a lot inside."

Teresa laid her head on Bridget's shoulder and the two just sat in silence for some time, each buried in their own thoughts.

Billy's response to Teresa's letter came a short time after Fergy's. As usual, his words had a calming effect on her, as he had a gift of relating the news from the front in a way that seemed to make her believe they were in no danger. Her "best friend" related nothing of his feelings for her in his correspondence, having noted well her words to Fergy at the train station. She enjoyed reading his mail, as those same nice soothing feelings enveloped her, even though his mail came from across the sea.

As time went on, Teresa wrote less and less to Fergy, as she couldn't quite find the words to say to him, still having some hope for his affections but not wishing to push her *own* on him. His letters seemed to her somewhat cool and distant, and it gave her great cause for concern. What she did write were simply of current events from home—daily affairs and news from Western Union. Her continued correspondence with Billy, however, was lighter and more upbeat, as she had always found it so easy to relate to him her thoughts and feelings.

The 42nd Rainbow Division, comprised of the 69th Irish Brigade from Manhattan, the 14th Regiment from Brooklyn, and the 4th Alabama, was fast approaching the front. This volatile combination of units, having been on opposite sides during the Civil War, were now united, about to fight a common enemy—The Hun!

"Mom! Mom!" Teresa sounded excited. "Another letter!" It had been a while since they had heard anything from overseas and opened it quickly. "It's from Billy, Mom!"

My dears,

I apologize that I have not written in so long, but circumstances have made it quite difficult to find the time. As I have a few brief moments right now, I thought I'd try to bring you up-to-date a little. I've been transferred into Division Headquarters and assigned to the Communications Unit, working with high-ranking officers, sending and receiving messages—Guess I learned something useful at Western Union! I must have "lucked out," as my duties here with "the Brass" bring me some fringe benefits, the best being the great food! We also are lucky to find a building that still has a roof to grab some z-z-z's on occasion.

Have to go—getting the high sign that we're moving out again. Miss you both.

Love, Billy

p.s. Haven't seen or heard anything from Fergy. In different outfit now. Hope you like my picture.

"Mom, do you think that "moving out" means Billy will be in danger?" Teresa looked terribly concerned.

"Oh, honey, I think he'll be alright since he's in the Communications Department. He'd most likely be behind the lines." Bridget's words seemed to erase the worry from her daughter's mind.

As the winter months dragged on, Teresa was growing weary from all work and no play. She had rapidly matured into a very attractive young woman of eighteen years and had been approached for dates on occasion by some of the young men at Western Union, Tony being the most persistent. None had been able to secure a positive response, however, as her infatuation with her "Fergy with the handsome face" had always been foremost in her heart; although, of late, the initial spark which had been ignited in that heart when she first laid eyes on him was beginning to fade into embers somewhat.

The Christmas and New Year's holidays were uneventful that year but for Mass. Hearts were deep in prayer for the safety of the men overseas and the end of the war. Bridget and Teresa had made no plans, as things were simply not the same without "their boys." Western Union had their big holiday party once again; however, Teresa had no inclination to attend.

Feeling that her daughter needed a little diversion in her life, Bridget was more than happy to make a little announcement after dinner one evening. "How would you like to go to a Broadway show Saturday night?"

"Oh, Mom!" Teresa straightened up in her chair. "How could we afford that?"

Bridget smiled. "We don't have to! A friend at work gave me two tickets. Seems something came up and he and his wife won't be able to make it. Isn't that great?"

"Oh, how wonderful! What's the name of the play, Mom?"

"It's called "Going Up," honey—a musical comedy—something about an aviator and his high-society girlfriend. And it's even supposed to have a full-size bi-plane in the production."

"You mean there'll be a plane on the *stage*? A *real* plane?"

"Yes, exactly."

"Oh, my gosh! That's amazing!"

The Liberty Theatre was filled to overflowing that night. Bridget and Teresa, dressed in their finest, were thrilled to see their seats were in the second row behind the orchestra. "I can't believe this, Mom!"

"S-h-h. The curtains going up, honey." She snickered. "Oh—no pun intended!"

The chorus burst onto the stage, their costumes glittering as they danced to the music of the catchy song by the same name as the play. As the show progressed, the audience broke into loud laughter during the comedic episodes, especially as Edith Day did her routine of song and dance to the famed tune of "Tickle Toe." Her number was applauded with such unabated exuberance, it was repeated twice over for the audience. Bridget and Teresa sat spellbound, enjoying immensely the extravaganza before them.

"Wasn't it fun, Mom?" The trolley moved slowly over the snow-covered tracks, the two still bubbling over with enthusiasm as they reviewed the evening's entertainment, Teresa humming and tapping her toe.

"I'm so glad you enjoyed it, honey." She laughed at her daughter. "Looks like you've got *tappy* toe instead of "Tickle Toe!"

They laughed together. "It's so good to see you having such a good time, Teresa. "It's been such a big relief tonight, after all this talk about the war and everything."

"Yeah, Mom! Let's do it again! That Edith Day was really great, wasn't she? Wish *I* could sing like that."

"I'm freezing. Let's make some cocoa," Bridget said as they approached the steps of their apartment.

"Good idea, Mom."

Bridget hung up her coat and hat, turning to go to the kitchen. "Where'd you go, Teresa?"

"I'm in my bedroom. Be right out."

The dancing entrance from her bedroom to the kitchen, heels clicking against the linoleum, was accompanied by a melodic imitation of "Tickle Toe" on Teresa's kazoo.

Bridget broke up laughing; then began humming along with it, putting one arm through her daughter's and spinning her around. They spent the rest of the evening chatting about the play and making plans to see another as soon as they could save the money.

The following week brought letters from both Billy and Fergy. "Here, honey—open Fergy's and I'll open Billy's."

Teresa reached over and took Billy's letter from her mother's hand. "Let's read Billy's first, Mom."

"Oh ... well, sure. Okay, honey." Bridget seemed surprised.

My dearest girls,

Sorry I was cut off the last time I wrote. Everything had to be packed up in a hurry, as we had to advance immediately to keep up with the main body of the Army which was moving to the front. Being in Communications, we are like the "nerve center" where all orders originate. So it's important for us to be close behind, yet far enough from the fighting so as not to endanger "the Brass."

I received your last letter some time ago and sorry it took so long to answer, but I know you understand. I am issuing strict orders to you both that you are not allowed to worry! I am fine and, I'm sure, in no immediate danger. I thank you both for your prayers—please continue to pray for our men and for an end to this terrible war.

I often think of all the good times we had and cherish the memories. I hope you are doing okay there. Look forward so often to the time when I can beat you both at Euchre again!

Can't tell you too much about Fergy. All I know is his outfit is ahead of us, moving west.

Stay well, my dear friends. You are sorely missed and much loved.

Billy

"Oh, it's so good to hear from him, isn't it, Mom? Even in his letters, he's concerned about *us*—not wanting us to worry."

"Well, that's Billy!"

"I know. I just miss him being around, don't you?"

"Sure I do." Bridget held out the other letter to her daughter. "Here—wanna read Fergy's mail now, honey?"

"Oh ... oh, sure. Of course. Sorry, I almost forgot there was another letter."

Bridget looked puzzled. "Go ahead—read it!" as she tore open the envelope and handed it to her daughter.

Dear Bridget and Teresa,

Sorry I haven't had a moment to write you two, but our outfit has been constantly on the move. I have been very busy assisting Father Duffy. Honestly, I have a hard time keeping up with the man. If he isn't saying Mass or administering the sacraments, he is aiding the wounded returning from the front. I have developed a great admiration for him—he is truly a saint on the Earth!

I think of you both very often and hope everything is going well for you. Never seems to be much time to write these days. Now here it is already time for lights out (a few small candles). We are in a bombed-out church. At least there is a small section of the roof remaining which gives us a little protection from the elements. Will be moving out tomorrow. God bless you both and please pray for this war to end soon.

Your friend,

Fergy

"Sounds like they are both okay, Mom."

"Thank God, honey." Teresa nodded her head. "Let's send a letter back right now. Do you want to?" Bridget grabbed a paper to respond to the mail. "What do you want to say, Teresa?"

"Oh, you know what to say, Mom—why don't you just drop a line to Fergy? I'm awfully tired—have to be up so early for work tomorrow. I think I'll just hit the sack and I'll drop a line to Billy on my lunch hour tomorrow."

"Oh, well, alright, dear. I'll write a few lines to Fergy before turning in. Maybe you could add to it tomorrow when you write Billy."

"Well ... sure, I guess. Goodnight, Mom." Teresa left the room—Billy's letter clutched tightly in her hand.

The next few months, Bridget seemed to notice Teresa's slump back into a melancholy state. One Saturday afternoon she grabbed the evening paper from the front porch, proceeding to show the headline to Teresa.

"Congress Calls 'Over There' American Victory Hymn."

"You remember that song, don't you, Teresa?—from the train station?"

"Sure. It was wonderful!"

"They did that song at that Red Cross Benefit—they did it for the troops."

"I know. I've heard about it, Mom." She hesitated a minute. "Wanna go see another play? I'd really like to."

"I think that might be a good idea, honey. I've heard this 'Cohan Revue' is absolutely delightful—the music is supposed to be great!"

"Sounds good, Mom. Let's get some tickets." She thought a moment. "Oh! Is it very expensive?"

To Bridget, the cost would be secondary, as they really needed a little pleasure in their lives right now. "Oh, not too, I don't think."

George M. Cohan's great musical extravaganza afforded the two girls some much needed diversion and enjoyment. The tune, "Over There," lifted the country's spirit, and the patriotic blood of the land flowed through its veins from coast to coast.

Other plays afforded much needed mirth, especially the "Ziegfield Follies." Bridget really enjoyed watching W.C. Fields, one of her favorites, as well as Eddie Cantor and Will Rogers. But the dancing was Teresa's greatest enjoyment, especially the ballroom duo, Fred Astaire and his sister, Adele.

Spring had passed with no further communications from either Billy or Fergy, and the girls couldn't help but be concerned. Teresa had responded to Billy's last letter but had never taken the time to answer Fergy's, feeling that her mother's response was adequate.

Early in June, a letter finally arrived from Billy stating the 69th would be advancing toward the front with the rest of the 42nd Rainbow Division. A month later they found themselves traveling by train to Champagne-Marne where they became attached to the French Army, the 69th earning a reputation as a great fighting force.

Shortly after, another message came—this one from Fergy. He explained that Father Duffy was dictating events to him, as they happened, for the Company's records. He had also given Fergy his permission to send any to the home front; and Fergy felt this was a good way to keep both his parents and his friends up-to-date. He mentioned it might be considered somewhat as Father Duffy's diary, so to speak, as it would be in the priest's own words.

> *On Easter Sunday, when arriving at Magnieres, we selected a bombed-out church to hold Mass. Both sides had used it to fight from, and both sides had helped to wreck it. The roof was gone and most of the side walls. The central tower over the entrance still stood, though the wooden beams above had burned, and the two big bells had dropped clean through onto the floor. The cure' used a meeting room in the town hall for his services, but that would not do for my congregation. The church faced a long paved square, so I decided to set up my altar in the entrance and have the men hear Mass in the square. The church steps served excellently for Communion. It is one of the things I wish I had a picture of—my first Easter service in France; the old ruined church for a background, the simple altar in the doorway, and in front that sea of devout young faces paying their homage to the Risen Savior. My text lay around me—the desecrated temple, the soldier-priest by my side, the uniforms we wore, the hope of triumph over evil that the Feast inspired, the motive that brought us here to put an end to this terrible business of destruction, and make peace prevail in the world. Here more than a thousand soldiers were present, and the great majority crowded forward at Communion time to receive the Bread of Life.*

Before the month was out, another communication arrived; Fergy was sending more excerpts from the good priest's diary.

> *There is no doubt anyway about the opinion of the good priests who are carrying on the work of the dead and gone saints. They are full of enthusiasm about our fellows. What attracts them most is their absolute indifference to what people are thinking of them as they follow their religious practices. These men of yours, they tell me, are not making a show of religion; they are not offending others; they touch their hats to a church, make the Sign of the Cross, or go to Mass just because they want to, with the same coolness that a man might show in taking coffee without milk or expressing a preference for a job in life. They run bases with scapulars flying, and it doesn't occur to them that they have scapulars on, any more than they would be conscious of having a button of their best girl or President Wilson pinned to their shirts—they may have all three.*
>
> *Come to think of it, it is a tribute not only to our religious spirit, but to the American spirit as a whole. The other fellows don't think of it either—no more than I do and one of our Chaplains who is closest to me in every thought and plan wears a Masonic ring. We never advert to it except when some French people comment on our traveling together—and then it is a source of fun.*

"I can just picture that, can't you, Mom?"

"Picture what, dear?"

"Those boys running around playing baseball with their scapulars flying in the wind!"

"Well, what would you expect now from a bunch of good old Irish Catholic lads?" Bridget snickered.

Teresa started giggling. "Oh, Mom, you're so funny!"

"Seriously though, I'm glad those boys wear our Lady's garment for protection."

"I hope Billy has one—why didn't we think to give him one, Mom?"

"Don't worry about that, Teresa. I'm sure Father Duffy has looked after all the men—Fergy, too!"

"Oh, of course—Fergy too, Mom." Teresa looked pensive. How could she have neglected thinking of Fergy.

"Teresa? What is it dear?"

"Oh, nothing. Do you think we should drop a line back right now, Mom?" Before her mother could answer, she added, "I mean ... actually, you really don't know what could happen from one day to the next, you know—when there's war."

"Alright, let's do that. I'll get some paper, dear."

Dear Fergy,

Received your letter just today along with your notes from *Father Duffy's "diary." We were so impressed with our boys over there—practicing their faith in the middle of all that turmoil. Father Duffy sounds like a wonderful man—how fortunate to be his assistant. I mean, how fortunate for him to have you as his assistant—well, you know what I mean.*

We think of you and pray for you every day—Billy, too.

Not too much to report from around here. Mostly people talk about the things over there. We pray a safety prayer for our troops every week after Mass at St. Patrick's, and many of the neighbors get together in each other's homes for an evening rosary a few times a week, praying for each and every one of our loved ones by name.

I'm still working at the dress shop every day, and Teresa says most all her communications at work are constantly coming across the wire with the ongoing war news.

Last Sunday we took a walk around Central Park, chatting about the wonderful times we had on our little picnics with you and Billy. We stood reminiscing in front of "our tree."

We did get a little treat when a friend gave me some tickets for a Broadway show called "Going Up." I can't tell you how much we enjoyed the music and the dancing—it was great! We loved it so much, we decided to splurge and get tickets for another show—the "Cohan Revue." They played that song, "Over There" in the show—do you remember the troops singing that at the train station?

Teresa is asking if you ever do run into Billy, to give him her love.

Will close for now. Stay safe, my friend.

Love, Bridget and Teresa

Bridget had long suspected that Teresa's true affections seemed to be leaning more toward Billy recently. It appeared that possibly her daughter's heart had begun to mature into the realization that there was more to love than physical attraction. All this seemed to bring back thoughts of her first meetings with Tom, and she decided to spend an afternoon with Teresa on the "*River Queen*".

The gangplank crashed down onto the dock. "I can't believe this old boat is still running, honey."

"And you *worked* on this boat, Mom?"

"Honey, this is where your Dad and I met." Bridget quickly dabbed a tear from her eye, hoping Teresa wouldn't notice.

"Need my hanky?" The girl reached into her purse.

"I'm okay—really. It's just ... well ... so many beautiful memories."

"Tell me all about it, Mom. I'd really like to hear."

Bridget took her hand, leading her to a railing on the upper deck. "This is it, Teresa—this is where it all started."

"Oh?"

"When I first came to work here. I was standing here—right here, in this spot—trying to study my map of the points of interest. You see, I was supposed to announce these places to the passengers as we approached each one."

"That sounds like a nice job."

"Yes, but it was a little confusing at first. I was kinda left on my own."

"Nobody showed you how to do it?"

"Well, yes." A smile came across Bridget's face. "This is where your Father came in."

"Oh? Dad?"

"Teresa, he was so cute. He had this navy-blue cap on—the brim was shiny black and above it were gold initials—R.Q."

"*River Queen*!"

"Yes, that's right."

"Did you fall in love with him right away?"

"No, not at all. He was too smart-alecky—too cocky. Actually, to me, he almost seemed a little on the wild side."

"Really?"

"Yes, and I smelled booze on his breath a number of times."

"Oh gosh, Mom!" A concerned look came over Teresa's face. "Umm, so how did you come to ..."

"Well, even though he was impertinent at times, he began to help me to learn the job the first few weeks and I got to know him a little better. And, you know, there was always *something* about that man—maybe it was the way he always called me 'Bridget-girl', or 'pretty lass', or maybe it was just that cocksure attitude he had. I don't know. Anyway, he sure did grow on me." She looked out over the water. "How I loved him!"

Teresa put her arm around her mother, holding her close for a moment. "Oh, Mom! How I wish I could have known him. He sounds like such a *character*! But such a *wonderful* character!" They stood in silence for a few moments, each with their own thoughts of their loved one.

Suddenly, Bridget broke into laughter.

"What the heck?"

"Oh, I'm just thinking about our reception and how it started with a boxing match—right down there on the dock—at our wedding reception!"

Teresa looked puzzled. "What are you talking about, Mom? A *boxing* match!"

"Oh, a couple of gentlemen had a little misunderstanding but ... well, it was soon smoothed over and the rest of our reception was wonderful—a little unusual though—sailors dancing with nuns ..."

"*What*?"

"... and Captain Skully twirling an old friend around the dance floor in her wheelchair. Oh! and, believe it or not, Molly grabbing MacTavish and pulling him onto the dance floor."

"You mean Scotty, Mom?"

"Yes, that's where they actually met, honey. And Molly made all the advances. They just seemed to "click" right away. Anyway, it was quite a night. And Captain Skully kept blowing the boat whistle, and all the other boats in the harbor joined in. I guess there were some complaints from some of the neighbors living around here, but the Captain was a good friend of the local gendarme!"

"Hah! Sounds like a blast! But get back to the boxing match, Mom. I'm curious."

Bridget continued sharing with her daughter, often bringing tears which seemed to flow from the two hearts as one, but they were tears of healing—long overdue.

Further news of the war came once again from Fergy, quoting from Father Duffy.

> *I never hear confessions in a church, but always in the public square of a village, with the bustle of army life and traffic going on around us. There is always a line of fifty or sixty soldiers, continuously renewed throughout the afternoon, until I have heard perhaps as many as five hundred confessions in the battalion. The operation always arouses the curiosity of the French people. They see the line of soldiers with man after man stepping forward, doffing his cap with his left hand,*

and making a rapid Sign of the Cross with his right, and standing for a brief period within the compass of my right arm, and then stepping forward and standing in the square in meditative posture while he says his penance. "What are those soldiers doing?" I can see them whispering. "They are making the Sign of the Cross. Mon Dieu! They are confessing themselves." Non-Catholics also frequently fall into line, not of course to make their confessions, but to get a private word of religious comfort and to share in the happiness they see in the faces of the others.

Officers who are not Catholics are always anxious to provide opportunities for their men to go to confession; not only through anxiety to help them practice their religion, but also for its distinct military value. Captain Merle Smith told me that when I was hearing confessions before we took over our first trenches, he heard different of his men saying to his first sergeant, Eugene Gannon, "You can put my name down for any kind of a job out there. I'm all cleaned up and I don't give a damn what happens now."

Fergy ended the correspondence with an indication that he was unsure when he'd get another chance to write, as they "are in the thick of it." However, a short time later, another letter did arrive from him.

Dear Bridget and Teresa,

We are up front now and occupy the trenches. Our losses here have been heavy, but we are holding our own. Already we have repulsed one attack by the Hun. I couldn't believe how Fr. Duffy was so cool-headed under fire! I am awed at the bravery of the man who goes out into no-man's land under enemy fire—from mortars and machine guns—to help retrieve the wounded. I sometimes wonder if he has a special angel who protects him. I have offered to assist him on these occasions, but he says, "You stay back, son. Someone has to record what happens here. Your job is just as important as any soldier's in this man's army." I am doing my best to document all of this terrible war—including the carnage, I hate to say, that goes with it. But, on the other hand, I am so lucky and proud to be associated with this brave, holy priest.

The food is pretty bad—we live mostly on trench rations, otherwise known as bully beef (combination of beef and salmon). We generally have to eat it cold, as cooking facilities are nil. We're living in deplorable conditions, the trenches sometimes being wet and muddy—very little drainage. We place boards across from side to side and sleep on them when the Huns aren't lobbing shells at us. Earlier today their shells were falling far behind our lines—hope Billy's unit was far enough behind that they weren't affected. Haven't got any news from back there as of yet. Pray for me. Gotta go.

Affectionately, Fergy

"Why don't *you* write him back this time?" Bridget asked Teresa.

"Oh, Mom, I'm really tired. It was tough at work today. Messages just never stopped coming all day long—one after another after another—mostly all war stuff, you know? I hate seeing all this stuff. Wish it would just be over! Honestly, sometimes it just gets me so down! Wears me out. And besides, I worry about Billy. We haven't heard from him for a while."

"Come on, honey. What's going on with this Billy stuff lately?"

"Nothin'."

"Never mind nothin'. Something's going on. I'm not dumb, you know!" Bridget thought it best to get her daughter talking about what was beginning to be so obvious.

"I'd just rather not talk about it right now, Mom. Really. I'm really tired."

"I'm sorry, honey. Guess I wasn't thinking. Why don't you lie down for a while 'til I get dinner ready. I can take care of this letter later."

"Not hungry, Mom."

"Teresa, do you suppose maybe you should look for another type of work? Like maybe something similar to mine? I could probably get you into "Molly-Maureen's." It wouldn't be as stressful working in a place like that."

Oh—boredom for sure! "Thanks, Mom, but you know I have a trade now." How can she stand sewing all day? "And, don't forget—I think I told this to you before—they mentioned there might be a chance for advancement down the road. Besides, if this God-forsaken war ever ends, it'll be back to normal stuff the way it used to be. And, by the way, rumors are even going around that they might be needing people in the Washington office—wouldn't *that* be something!"

"This is all getting to be too much for me, honey. Come on, let's just sit down and have a bite to eat, okay? Settle for a sandwich?"

"Sure, okay, Mom." Teresa felt badly for her mother. The day shared on the *River Queen* was another reminder that Bridget never really had any closure from her father's disappearance. "I'm just wondering, Mom, if maybe there might be some gentleman at work—you know, you're really very pretty."

"Now none of that blarney, Teresa!"

"No, *really* Mom! You *are*!"

"What are you trying to say, my dear?" Bridget asked with a little smirk on her face, knowing well what her daughter was implying.

"Umm ... I just think it might be a good idea for you to get a nice big handsome gentleman friend! Might be the best thing for you, Mom, you know?"

"Well, my dear, it just so happens that 'gentleman-friends' generally do not work in ladies' boutiques. Nor are they usually the type of clientele we get."

"Well, then maybe *you're* the one who should be looking for another type of employment!"

Bridget laughed. "Touche'!"

Weeks passed before they heard from Billy again. His letter had been dated a month earlier. He stated that his unit had been moving so fast, there had been no time to write. In addition, they had received orders from headquarters to cease and desist all communication with the "outside world" until further notice due to the close proximity of the enemy and fear of intercepts.

Teresa grabbed her mother's arm. "Oh, no! Oh, they're in danger! Oh, Mom!"

"Teresa, he's alright, honey—he's alright. Look, you just got a letter from him."

"I know, but ..."

"Now honey, please don't worry. I'm sure he'll be safe—you know—with all the prayers going up for our troops."

"I'd just die if anything happened to Billy!"

"Oh, honey, you *are* in love with him, aren't you?" Teresa didn't answer. "I was beginning to wonder what was going on in that little heart ... I mean, with Fergy seeming to take a back seat lately."

Teresa broke into tears. "I just ... I just miss *Billy* so much. I don't know ... I just miss him *terribly*, Mom."

Bridget started to fill the teapot with water. "Want to talk about it, honey? I'll make us some hot tea."

"I'd really just rather lie down a bit. Do you mind? I've got a little headache."

A month passed before any more mail arrived. Upon opening the letter, Bridget noticed it was longer than usual. "Oh, here's more about the good priest from Fergy, Teresa."

"Read it, Mom."

Dear Bridget and Teresa,

It's been awhile—hope you two are doing well. Just a note to give you the latest from the front. I made copies of some of the excerpts from Father Duffy's latest report which he just compiled yesterday—one for you two and one for my parents. Fortunately, we had a lull in the action last evening, and I took advantage of the time. Father Duffy's diary speaks for itself. As I have said before, I am always at his side.

No time for more.

Pray for us
Fergy

"It's kinda long. Wanna have dinner first, honey?"

"No ... no, go ahead," Teresa answered apprehensively.

July 15, 1918

It was 12:04 midnight by my watch when it began. No crescendo business about it. Just one sudden crash like an avalanche; but an avalanche that was to keep crashing for five hours. The whole sky seemed to be torn apart with sound—the roaring B-o-o-o-m-p of the discharge and the gradual menacing W-h-e-e-e-e-z of traveling projectiles and the nerve-racking W-h-a-n-g-g of bursts. Not that we could tell them apart. They were all mingled in one deafening combination of screech and roar, and they all seemed to be bursting just outside. Some one of us shouted, "They're off"; and then nobody said a word. I stood it about twenty minutes and then curiosity got the better of me and I went out. I crawled around the corner of the shack and looked toward the enemy. Little comfort there. I have been far enough North to see the Aurora Borealis dancing white and red from horizon to zenith; but never so bright, so lively, so awe-inspiring, as the lights from the German Artillery.

I stepped inside and made my report to Lieutenant Young, who was busy writing. He called for a liaison man. Harry McLean—just a boy—stepped out of the gloom into the candlelight. He looked pale and uneasy—no one of us was comfortable— but he saluted, took the message, made a rapid Sign of the Cross, and slipped out into the roaring night. A liaison man has always a mean job, and generally a thankless one. He has neither the comparative protection of a dugout or fox-hole under shelling, nor the glory of actual fight. Our lads—they are usually smart youngsters—were out in all this devilment the whole night and I am glad to say with few casualties. Every last man of them deserves a Croix de Guerre.

Corporal Jelly of H—a fine soldier—and Private Hunt of E—he had a cablegram in his pocket announcing the birth of his first born—had been killed by the shell that struck in front of our dugout, and my friend Vin Coryell wounded. We found later that some men of Company H who had been sent to the French for engineering detail, had also been killed. The enemy were appearing around the corners of the approach trenches. Rifle and machine gun fire crackled all along the front. The Germans, finding that this was the real line of resistance, went at their job of breaking it in their usual thorough fashion. Their light machine guns sprayed the top of every trench. Minenwerfer shells and rifle grenades dropped everywhere, many of them being directed with devilish accuracy on our machine gun positions. Many of ours were wounded. Sergeant Tom O'Rourke of F Company was the first man killed and then one of the Wisconsins.

That day the Badgers showed the fighting qualities of their totem. Several of their guns were put out of action at the outset of the fight, and practically all of them, one by one, before the battle was over. In each case, Captain Graef, Lieutenant Arens, and the other officers, together with the surviving gunners, set themselves calmly to work repairing the machines. Corporal Elmer J. Reider fought his gun alone when the rest of the crew was put out of action, and when his gun met the same fate he went back through a heavy barrage and brought up a fresh one. Privates William Brockman and Walter Melchoir also distinguished themselves amongst the brave, the former with the cost of his life. There were many others like Melchoir, who, when their gun was made useless, snatched rifles and grenades of the fallen Infantrymen and jumped into the fight. As specialists, they were too valuable to be used up this way and an order had to be issued to restrain them. Sergeant Ned Boone, who knows a good soldier when he sees one, said to me, "Father, after this I will stand at attention and salute whenever I hear the word Wisconsin."

Our own stokes mortar men fought with equal energy and enthusiasm under Lieutenant Frank McNamara and Sergeants Jaeger and Fitzsimmons with Corporals John Moore, Gerald Harvey, and Herbert Clark. They did not take time to set the gun up on its base plates. Fitzsimmons and Fred Young supported the barrel in their hands, while the others shoved in the vicious projectiles. The gun soon became hot and before the stress of action was over, these heroic non-coms were very badly burned.

Again and again the Germans attacked, five times in all, but each time to be met with dauntless resistance. By three o'clock in the afternoon the forces of the attacking division was spent and they had to desist until fresh infantry could be brought up. In spite of these events, the issue of the day's battle was not in doubt after ten o'clock that morning. There had been anxious moments before, especially when many machine guns were put out of action and the call for further fire from our artillery met with a feeble response. I dropped in on Anderson, true to his motto, "Fight it out where you are." He was putting the last touches to his preparations for having his clerks, runners, and cooks make the last defense, if necessary. "Do you want some grenades, Padre?" was his question.

The fighting at The Marne continued until the 18th of July when the United States Rainbow Division was relieved by French troops. Father Duffy and Fergy stayed on temporarily to help carry the wounded off the battlefield to the Aid Station. Any dying or seriously wounded had the comfort of the sacraments given them by the priest. This quiet composed serenity brought to the hearts of the men had a similar effect in Fergy's own heart. He seemed able to share in the warmth and tranquility he, too, needed after witnessing the hostilities and carnage of war.

The end of the month found their Division attacking strongly held German positions in the battle of Croix Rouge Farm. The Americans, in an unusual advance across open fields and in the crossing of the Oureq River, suffered heavy losses from the German machine guns in nearby woods—184 officers and 5,469 men.

After returning to full strength, the Division went on the offensive at Saint Mihiel on September 11. After the German defeat there, they traveled to the Argonne Forest the following month, relieving the physically and mentally exhausted First Division—that storied unit which had lost 1,750 men killed during the previous week's battle. By the 14th of October, the battle had gone back and forth as the Rainbow, suffering the violent intenseness of the fighting there, had been attempting to penetrate the Hindenburg lines. Two days afterward, at a hill called Co'te de Chatillion, they successfully assaulted the most formidable part of an in-depth network of barbed wire and carefully prepared German defenses.

The Rainbow's continued participation in the final Allied offensive which stretched along the entire Western front culminated in the final victory against the Hun, the armistice being signed on November 11th.

Marching two hundred miles to Germany, they remained as part of the occupation troops there until April 15, 1919. A brief note had come from Fergy letting the girls know where they could send mail for the next few months.

My dear friends,

Here I am in the northern section of the Koblenz Bridgehead in Germany, Thanks be to God this horrible war is ended—all the men are already making plans for their arrival home with joy-filled hearts, looking so forward to being with their wives and families once again.

For me, the story will be a little different. You see, I intend to stay here on the Continent for some time, as I need to discern something that I've been thinking about for some time now. As I've mentioned before in my letters, my life has been so greatly impacted by the work I've been privileged to do with Father Duffy. I've had many discussions with the good priest—and have seen many men badly wounded or killed—and my whole outlook on life has changed after looking into the eyes of the wounded and dying, seeing the peace Father was able to impart to them at that crucial time. Watching him in the performance of his duties has given me a greater insight into the beauty of a man who gives of himself for others. His noble altruism has caused me to think deeply on the way I wish to spend the rest of my life. Therefore, I am thinking of entering a seminary to take some time for deep prayer, asking the good Lord to show me the way.

Pray for me, Fergy

P.S. Please write me and send any mail to the address on the front of my envelope.

"Oh, my gosh! Can you imagine, Mom? Fergy—a priest!"

"Well, I'm just as amazed as you are, Teresa. But, well, it's kind of wonderful, isn't it?"

Teresa just stared straight ahead. "He never mentioned anything about Billy, Mom. Did you notice?"

"I'm sure he's fine. After all, we haven't heard anything otherwise. Fergy most likely hasn't seen him or heard anything or he would have let us know."

"Mmm—Hmm."

April 25th found three battleships delivering American doughboys back to New York City—minus Fergy *and* Billy. The Rainbow Division had seen more days of combat than any of the other American divisions during the Great War and suffered 14,683 casualties. Red Cross nurses were waiting as they disembarked on Pier 54, the Marine Band playing "There'll Be a Hot Time In the Old Town Tonight," "How Dry I Am," "Pack Up Your Troubles in Your Old Kit Bag," and other old songs—and the boys yelled themselves hoarse.

The soldiers proudly marched down Fifth Avenue, people in tall buildings throwing ticker tape and waving American flags out the windows.

"Hold onto my arm, Teresa—we could get separated in this mob."

"Oh, Mom, isn't this exciting? There must be a million people here—maybe more!"

"Here they come! Look Teresa. Here they come!"

"Oh, my gosh! How are we ever going to spot him, Mom? There's so many! Oh, how grand! How grand! Look at them! Aren't they gorgeous?"

The military spectacle of 25,000 doughboys in trench helmets and full combat gear marched steadily before them—line after line after line—being greeted with clapping and loud cheering from the crowd as they waved flags, the girls throwing kisses and roses to the troops. Bridget and Teresa were trying to push forward so as to see better, but to no avail. They found a staircase to one of the buildings and pushed their way up to the top stair, so at least they could see the whole spectacle. Teresa was highly disappointed, knowing there could be no way she could possibly make out the soldiers' faces from that distance. "What are we going to do, Mom? How will we ever find him?"

"I guess it seems like that might be impossible, Teresa. But don't worry. Knowing Billy, he will make it a point to come over to the house as soon as possible."

"I suppose so," Teresa remarked dejectedly.

"Let's just enjoy this wonderful day and thank God the war is finally over."

They didn't have long to wait before hearing from Billy. But it was a letter—not a visit. Teresa excitedly ripped the envelope open as she yelled to Bridget to come from the kitchen. Grabbing her mother's arm, she pulled her down onto the couch next to her to enjoy his mail together.

Dear Teresa (and Bridget),

"He's addressing it to me!" She squeezed Bridget's hand, a big smile on her face.

I know it's been ages since I've written and I apologize. It was almost an impossible situation to try to write home, especially after I was injured.

"Oh, no! He's been injured, Mom!"

Things got so heavy in the fighting that I was literally on that telegraph key, well, it seemed like twenty-four hours a day. You are probably wondering how I could have been hurt, mostly being behind the lines. You see, at the battle of the Argonne Forest, our headquarters got hit with a shell, as the Huns were overshooting our lines. We lost one of our men and two others were badly wounded. I guess I was the lucky one. Only my legs got it.

"Oh no! His legs! Oh my gosh! I hope he's not crippled!"

Anyway, the bones in my right leg were shattered pretty badly and I was evacuated to the nearest field hospital. I was there through Christmas—got great care from the doctors and nurses. But it took quite a bit of time and lots of energy to get back on my feet. I'm doing pretty good now, but am still on crutches and have been told I will always have a limp. Considering the alternative, I guess I'm good with that!

Now the good news. I was fortunate to have a wonderful nurse—Annette. She took such good care of me that I truly believe I would have needed a much longer recovery time had she not been there. Needless-to-say, I was quite dejected at first, wondering if I would even ever walk again.

She not only cared for my wounds—she helped so much with my mental anguish, sometimes even praying at my bedside when she thought I was asleep at night. I never let on actually, as it was such a comfort to just lie there with my eyes closed and listen to her dear prayers for my recovery.

As the months passed, we grew closer and began to share some of our personal lives with one another. I had occasion to speak of you so often, as you were such an important part of my life, Teresa. It did me good to have someone to confide my deepest feelings to. You see, when I overheard you confess your deep love to Fergy at the train station—well, I guess I wasn't too surprised, but it hurt me so deeply since you had really done a job on my heart! I always hoped that in time the feeling would become mutual. Anyway, time heals all; and, although it took a while, I tried to move on and make a new life for myself.

Annette and I are now engaged to be married.

Teresa gasped and dropped the letter on the floor. "No! No! No!" She began to sob and threw her head in Bridget's lap. "Oh, Billy ... Billy ..."

"Oh, honey, I'm so sorry."

Through her sobbing, she blurted out, "He never even knew, Mom. He never even knew how much I loved him! Oh, dear God! Oh, God!"

Bridget reached down and picked up the letter.

It will be awhile before we can tie the knot, as I want to be able to walk without crutches by then. I suppose Fergy might be coming home soon, if he is not there already. I lost track of him way back, before my injury. I'm not sure if he even knew I was wounded. Anyway, I know how you cared for him, and I hope you will realize your dream of spending your life with him.

Know that there will always be a place for you in my heart. Sending love to you both. God bless, Billy

Western Union received a note the following Monday morning. It seems one of their telegraphers was suddenly taken quite ill and would not be available to work for at least a week.

"I really think it would do you *more* good to be at work, Teresa. It might get your mind off things."

The girl didn't respond.

Bridget put her arms around her daughter. "I know how badly you must be feeling, honey. Believe me, I understand totally how painful it is to lose the person you love more than anything in the world. But you have to pull yourself together! Come on, sit down. I'll make some tea."

"Don't want any, thanks."

"They might be needing you at work, honey." Bridget was trying her best to console her daughter, at the same time wanting to encourage her to return to work.

Another few months passed, and although Teresa had returned to her job, she never seemed to come out of her slump, seemingly always in a state of depression. Bridget continued to try cheering her up, taking her to a few more Broadway shows, hoping to take her mind off Billy.

And so it went week after week—until Bridget made up her mind to change things. It was late in the evening and she was working on her sewing machine, pumping the pedal with her feet, while Teresa was laying out her clothing for another day's work ahead. "I'm *never* going to get married!" she suddenly blurted out.

"It's Billy again, isn't it?"

Teresa didn't reply.

"I think we both need a change of scenery, honey. You know, I hear that they might be closing our boutique. The bookkeeper told me in confidence, although he wasn't supposed to say anything as yet, that the sales are falling due to the competition of the larger department stores uptown. I don't know how much longer I'll have a job."

"Oh, Mom! Why didn't you tell me? How long have you been worrying about this?"

"Oh, not too long, but ... well, anyway, I've been doing a lot of thinking about it lately. And, with circumstances being what they are, maybe this is a good time for us to discuss what you brought up a while back."

"What?"

"You know—what you were telling me about the possibility of a transfer to Washington, D.C.—*and* at a higher rate of pay. Isn't that what you said? Do you know if it is still an option, Teresa? Have they talked any more about it at work?"

Teresa perked up. "Yes! Yes, they have! I think I might have a good chance of being considered for it—last I heard they hadn't specified anyone as yet. Oh, my gosh! Wouldn't it be exciting, Mom? Washington, D.C! I mean, wow! The Italian Embassy there is right across the street from the White House!"

"Italian Embassy?"

"Yes, that's where it would be—in that Embassy—we have an office there!"

"But you can't speak Italian! So how could ..."

Teresa laughed. "Oh, no, Mom. I wouldn't have to learn Italian. I'd actually be sending *out* messages after they had been interpreted by others on the staff."

"Oh." It did Bridget's heart good seeing her daughter "coming alive" once again. "And I'm not the least bit concerned about work. You know I could get a job anywhere in Washington with my sewing. After all, I *did* make a dress for the First Lady, you know."

"What? What are you talking about, Mom?"

"Didn't I ever tell you, hon?"

"Hmm—Mmm."

"Well, you see ..."

After relating the story about Mrs. Roosevelt's dress, Bridget poured a glass of wine for the two of them. "I think this night calls for a celebration, my dear! This is the beginning of our new chapter!" She held her glass up to Teresa's, tapping hers against it. "Here's to us!"

Teresa chimed in. "And here's to Washington! Watch out, Washington! Here we come!"

"Yep—here we come!" They laughed heartily, chatting about all the things they imagined they would do in the Capital."

"Perhaps I shall have you design me a new dress, Mother dearest, for my visit to the White House. After all, I'm sure the President will want me for lunch when I arrive!" Teresa had a hard time speaking without laughing.

Bridget picked right up on her mirth. "But of course, Miss Sexton. You absolutely *must* have a new garment."

"I'm so excited that I don't know if I'm even gonna be able to sleep tonight, Mom."

"It is getting a little late. Maybe we should think about turning in, as much as I hate to end this wonderful evening, honey."

Lying in bed later, Bridget prayed in thanksgiving that her daughter once more seemed to have new hope. She was tired and wanted to sleep, but couldn't, as the darkness and quiet of night once again brought back memories of Tom. She often wondered if his hair was becoming gray, or if he had put on weight—*or* if he was still walking the Earth. Sometimes when the light of the moon would glide across her window and brighten up her bedroom, she wondered if he could be gazing up at its beauty as she was. A tune seemed to dance in her head—"*After the Ball is Over*—" again and again, as though it were a recording of their favorite song. The tune was suddenly joined by a vision of Tom leading her across the dance floor at Coney Island.

"Come on—let's trip the light fantastic, me girl!"

She turned over on her side, pulled the blanket up to her chin, wanting never to let go of these visions filling her heart. Finally ... finally ... sleep ...

Chapter 17

The Capital

The heat of summer was rapidly approaching an end, as Bridget and Teresa boarded the train for Washington. They had said their goodbyes to New York and all their friends at work and church. They found an upper apartment owned by an elderly gentleman and his wife in an old section of town which had been used many, many years before as a carriage house. The ground level had stored horses and a carriage, and the upper level had been slaves' quarters. However, with the coming of the age of the automobile, there was no more need for either horses or carriages; and the slaves had been emancipated half a century earlier.

Convenience was an important factor for Teresa, as her new job at the Italian Embassy was only thirty minutes from the apartment by trolley. Arriving home from work one evening, she flopped on the sofa and kicked off her shoes. "Oh, boy! That really smells good, Mom! I'm starved!"

Bridget, stirring a pot of stew, turned her head slightly, and replied, "Well, sit down, honey. It's all ready."

"You'll never guess who I saw today, Mom."

"The President?"

"How did you know?" Teresa asked, looking surprised.

"Oh, just a good guess. I remembered that you told me about the Embassy being across the street from the White House."

"How did you do on your job hunting today, Mom?"

"Oh, honey, I couldn't wait 'til you got home to tell you. I actually found one, believe it or not, right around the corner!"

"Really?"

"Yes, there was a sign right in the window—'Alteration Lady Wanted.' So I went right in and they hired me on the spot when they heard about all my experience. I start tomorrow." She hesitated a moment. "The only thing is ... it's only part-time."

Teresa was glad to hear this, as she had noticed her mother had been starting to look weary and fatigued for the past several months, but hadn't wanted to say anything about it to her. She always hoped there could be a time when Bridget wouldn't have to work so much. It had been almost twenty years since her father's disappearance, and Bridget had shouldered the burden, both physically and mentally, for too long. "Oh, that's okay, Mom! Actually. you don't even have to work at all any more. I'll be making enough on this job to support the two of us."

"Now you know I'm not the type to just sit around, honey. Not while I have two good hands to work with. How about some more stew?"

"Mmm—Hmm. It's really good!"

The five weeks since their arrival in Washington had flown by, but they were pretty much settled by now. Bridget had a problem getting to sleep most nights in this new environment. She hoped against hope for that miracle—I guess it would really take a miracle—that Tom might still return, but worried that he would never be able to find her. How would he know she was in Washington?

President Woodrow Wilson had a regular routine of a morning ride in his horse-drawn carriage. Although he had an automobile, he still preferred his customary transportation in his open buggy. He felt it important that the people could see their president, often waving to passing motorists or pedestrians. Teresa could observe him getting into his carriage most mornings, as it was just about the same time that she would be arriving at work. On more than one occasion, she herself was the recipient of a smile and a wave in her direction.

She missed seeing him when he left the city to tour the country, as he was trying to promote the formation of the League of Nations. A few weeks later, she had heard of his return but there was no sign of him. Eventually news was leaked that the president had suffered a severe stroke, forcing an end to the tour. Word had gone around the Embassy, however, that he was still able to continue his work from the White House.

About that same time, Congress passed legislation known as the Volstead Act which resulted in prohibition becoming the law of the land the following January—the Eighteenth Amendment to the Constitution. This was followed shortly after by the addition of a Nineteenth Amendment in August 1920, which guaranteed women the right to vote. This became an exciting thing for Bridget and Teresa, as they took very seriously what they felt was their "sacred duty" and studied carefully the following months before the presidential election so as to be well informed as to what each candidate stood for and what they espoused to do for the country. That November saw Warren G. Harding's landslide victory over James Cox—404 to 127 in the Electoral College voting.

The country was recovering from the Great War, and it was an exhilarating time to be living and working in the nation's Capital. In the weeks and months to come, Bridget found herself taking advantage of her days off work. She had three days a week to do as she pleased—a well-deserved rest from all the years she had labored to survive without a husband. She decided to take one day to attend a Mass that was being held at the laying of the cornerstone for the foundation of the Shrine of the Immaculate Conception. More than ten thousand people attended, including many dignitaries, foreign ambassadors, United States officials, military officers, and many priests. Cardinal James Fitzgibbons, Archbishop of Baltimore, blessed the foundation which was placed on land being donated by the Board of Trustees of the campus of the Catholic University of America.

The following weeks, she found herself continuing her touring of her new locale, including the Capital Building, the Smithsonian Institute, the Washington Monument, Arlington Cemetery, and the half-constructed Lincoln Memorial.

Each day Bridget returned home from her jaunts, she would share new information of her exploits with Teresa. "Hi, honey," she greeted her daughter, arriving later than usual one afternoon, shaking the snow from her headscarf.

"Hi, Mom! And just where were you gallivanting around today?" Teresa asked as she was setting the table for dinner.

"Oh Teresa! You should see this new monument they're building to honor Lincoln! It's only half-completed, but it's *huge*!"

"Oh, you saw that? Yeah, some of the people at work were talking about it the other day."

"It's mammoth! But only the bottom of his chair and his legs have been assembled so far, and his hands are laying on the ground! They're so big you could probably lie down in one of the them!"

"No thanks! I prefer my bed." They laughed. "Where's the head, Mom?"

"I don't know, but I imagine it's in one of the crates laying at the base of the statue."

"Gee, Mom! You could get a job as a tour guide. You're always coming home at night with the latest news and the most interesting stories."

"Well ... just trying to keep up with my telegrapher daughter!"

"Hah! Very good, Mom! Now that the table is set, what do you say we think about some dinner? What are we having anyway?"

"Oh, I'm sorry, honey. I guess I was just so absorbed in relating all this to you—well, I kinda just wasn't even thinking about dinner."

"What? Well, here I am starving to death and my own mother hasn't even thought about my stomach with all her travels going on! I guess I'll just have to hire a cook!"

"Are you *really starv*ing to death? I mean, we could just settle for some soup and a sandwich or something that won't take any time."

"Well, actually, I was kinda thinking about steak and a baked potato and a big salad!" The girl snickered.

"Oh, you!" Bridget came over and tapped her daughter on her rear. "Silly one! Come on, we can have the salad and the potato if you don't mind a hamburger patty with it instead of the steak!" Bridget grinned back.

"So where's your next jaunt, Mom?" Teresa asked over dinner.

"I was thinking of maybe going to Ford's Theatre."

"Oh, that sounds interesting. What's playing?"

"Nothing. Don't you know it was closed after Lincoln was shot?"

"Oh, what a stupe!" Teresa tapped the base of her right hand against her forehead, laughing at herself. "I should have known that."

"But I still want to see it, even if it's just from the outside. And then, I was also thinking about how interesting it would be to see the Supreme Court."

"Wow! Yeah!"

"But I found out they're actually not even in session right now—so that's out."

"You know, I'm kinda feeling left out of all this great stuff you're doin', Mom. I'd like to see some of this, too. But with working every day ... well, I guess you'll just have to keep briefing me on all of it 'til I get some time off or something. Or maybe on a weekend."

"Oh, speaking of weekends, I heard at work that the Catholic University of America ..."

"Where you were a couple weeks ago?"

"Yes."

"Don't tell me you're gonna go to college, Mom?" Teresa grinned.

"Honey, will you be quiet for a minute and let me talk?"

"Just kiddin'."

"Oh, I know. Well, you'll be surprised to hear who's going to be speaking there."

"Who?"

"None other than Father Duffy!"

"What? No kidding. Father Duffy? You mean *the* Father Duffy?"

"None other. He's coming on a Sunday afternoon at three and doing a talk on the campus—about the War."

"Oh, my gosh! Do you think we'd be able to talk to him? I feel like I know him from all Fergy's mail."

Two weeks later, the girls arrived at Divinity Hall on the University Campus two hours before Father Duffy's program was to begin. "I want to make sure we can get a seat near the front, Teresa." Entering, they were amazed to see they would indeed be fortunate to find a place to sit at all. "Oh my gosh! He must be an awfully popular priest! Oh, there's two over there, honey—grab them before anyone else spots them!" An usher at the door handed them a brochure with the priest's picture on the front.

Taking their seats, they perused the information therein as they waited for the program to begin. "Look at this, Mom," Teresa said as she turned to the inside back cover. "He got all these awards!"

Distinguished Service Cross
Distinguished Service Medal
New York State Conspicuous Service Cross
Legion of Honor (France)
Croix de Guerre (War Medal)

Father Duffy is the most highly decorated cleric in the history of the United State Army. He was involved in combat and accompanied litter-bearers into the thick of battle to recover wounded soldiers.

Teresa laid the program in her lap and turned to her mother but said nothing.

"What? What is it, dear?"

"Well, don't you think they should have mentioned Fergy? I don't see anything in here about him at all!"

"Umm ... well, maybe Father will say something in his talk ..."

"Sh-h-h!" someone murmured from behind.

"Good afternoon, ladies and gentlemen," Reverend Thomas Shahan greeted the audience, "and welcome to the Catholic University of America. It is my great honor and privilege to introduce to you today Father Francis Duffy, Chaplain of the famous 165th Regiment of the United States Army."

A loud applause went up from the congregation as the priest took the stage and approached the podium. Father Shahan grasped both his hands within his own, shaking them profusely. "Welcome, Father Duffy—welcome!"

"Thank you so much. It's *my* privilege to be here," the priest responded to the rector. Father Shahan gestured to him with his right hand that the podium was all his and took a seat in the center of the stage.

"Thank you so much, Father." Rev. Duffy turned and nodded to the rector. "And good afternoon, my dear friends. It's a real honor to be here in our nation's Capital. I can't tell you how proud I am to have had the privilege to serve with our young men overseas during the War. I thank God for our victory and will never forget the sacrifices of so many which enabled us to obtain that victory. Having been their chaplain, I have been witness to valiant courage, dauntless heroism, and selfless camaraderie."

The stillness of the audience was constantly maintained as the good priest spoke of his experiences during hostilities, often including personal ordeals and trials which his men had shared with him during times of extreme turbulence on the battlefield—from machinegun fire, exploding bombs, and on some occasions, mustard gas—not knowing from one minute to the next if they would still be alive at the end of the day. An occasional gasp could be heard during his speech, and some of the women kept their handkerchiefs handy, as the good priest continued to share what he referred to as some of his last reflections:

"My duties, like my feelings, still lay in the past. With men from all the companies, I went round the battlefields to pay, as far as I could, my last duties to the dead—to record and, in a rough way, to beatify their lonely graves, for I knew that soon we would leave that place that their presence hallows, and never look upon it again."

Bridget seemed to sense the heaviness in Father's heart as he spoke these final comments. She squeezed Teresa's hand, as though it would pass the same sensitivity into *her* heart.

Father Shahan returned to the podium, as the audience gave Father Duffy a standing ovation. "We should all be very proud of Father Duffy and all the men who made these sacrifices to preserve freedom in this world. We, as a nation, must always stand as a guiding beacon for all freedom loving people and stand against tyranny wherever it rears its ugly head." He once again shook Father Duffy's hand and thanked him for coming. Loud applause erupted once again.

Teresa, determined to meet Father Duffy, rushed to one of the ushers at the side door. "Please, would you go backstage and give a message to Father Duffy for me. It's *really* important."

"What is it, Miss?"

"Tell him a friend of Fergy's is here. He'll understand."

After a few minutes, the usher returned, smiling. "He said to come backstage, Miss."

"Oh, thank you so much." She felt like giving him a big hug, but instead motioned to Bridget who was still seated.

"So, this is the friend of Fergy's?" the good priest asked with a warm smile, taking Teresa's hands in his own.

"Yes, I'm Teresa Sexton and this is my Mom—Mrs. Sexton. I mean, *Bridget* Sexton."

"Oh, yes, Bridget and Teresa! Yes, Fergy spoke of you often."

"He *did*?" Teresa asked, wondering for but a moment if she had possibly actually made an impression on him prior to his leaving for the service.

"Yes, and I'm so very pleased to meet you," the priest continued.

"Oh, me too!" Teresa responded. "I feel like we've met already."

"How's that?" the priest interrupted.

"Oh, we read your *whole* diary."

"You did?"

"Yes, Fergy sent it to us little by little. So, you see, we know all about you and that's why I wanted to meet you in person."

"I see." The priest smiled warmly at her.

Bridget stood by, not being able to get a word in as Teresa continued the conversation. "We were best friends, you know." She smiled broadly, wondering if she should have made that statement a little "stronger," but decided against it.

"Well, my dear, your "best friend" made a strong impression on me, I'll have you know.'

"Oh?"

"Yes, from the moment I met him in the Company Commander's office. You see, from that time, I felt a strong sensitivity that the Lord had His hand on him."

"Really?" Bridget questioned, finally able to join the conversation.

"Yes, my dear. And then, working so closely with him on the battlefield, it was reinforced within me."

Mother and daughter looked at each other, amazed at the priest's perception.

"He'll make a great priest!" He hesitated. "You *did* know he was in a seminary in France, didn't you?" suddenly wondering if Teresa had something different in mind.

"Yes, we knew, Father; he did write us about it," Bridget responded.

"Well, have you heard from him lately, Father?" Teresa inquired.

"No, but I intend to write him soon. I'll mention to him that I met you, my dear." The priest hugged her. "Now I *must* go. I only have an hour until my train leaves for New York."

Teresa was grateful for her good job and Bridget as well, even though she only worked part-time, since tensions had begun mounting among the war's veterans who were having problems finding work, not only due to scarcity, but also because of new immigrants being infused into the population. In addition to this, many rural inhabitants began migrating into urban centers, compounding the problem. Racial tensions also added to the unrest as the rebirth of the Ku Klux Klan began to grow by leaps and bounds.

Teresa's work at the Italian Embassy seemed to help her recovery from the news of Billy's engagement. There were a number of young male interpreters, some of whom began flirtatious encounters with her. At first, she ignored their advances, not wishing to give them any encouragement; however, she secretly enjoyed the attention. After several weeks, while eating lunch in the cafeteria, she was approached by a young man with jet black hair and an immaculately trimmed mustache. "Excuse me, Miss, would you mind if I share your table? There's no other place to sit; it's all filled up, you see?" as he pointed around the room.

Noticing that all the tables were indeed occupied, she answered, "Well, yes, you may. I'm almost finished."

"Well, thank you, Miss. You're most kind." Placing his lunch on the table, he unfolded a newspaper, burying his head behind it. He began eating but said nothing.

Teresa had been prepared to rebuff any advances as she saw him approach; however, none had come. Trying to be sociable, she asked, "Have you been here long?"

"No," he responded, only lowering the paper long enough to answer.

"What department do you work in?"

He lowered the paper once again. "Way up top—accounting."

Finally, she stood up, slightly shaking her head from side to side. "Well, back to work. Be seein' ya." What a strange person he is, she thought—he never even introduced himself. Kinda rude!

She was getting used to a few of the men pursuing her with compliments and flattery, unlike her luncheon visitor. She finally determined that his indifference and aloofness must have been due to the fact that he was a married man; why else would anyone act so distant?

The environment at the Embassy was very strict. The employees were forbidden to fraternize on the job; and Teresa's boss, Mr. Slattery, constantly had his eye on his subordinates. Because of this, notes would circulate around the office unbeknownst to him, which became a joke amongst the workers, some comparing it to grade school shenanigans. It seemed that this unfriendly atmosphere was a catalyst which created a need for a more friendly environment for the workers. That need, though not being met in the workplace, was soon to have an unlikely outlet in the ambience of the new speakeasies which had arisen since the passage of the recently created Prohibition Amendment. What could be better than music, dancing, and "booze"—and the illegality of it all made it even more exciting! Jazz was born, the Flapper arrived— THE ROARING TWENTIES!

By the following year, Prohibition being the law of the land, the speakeasies had spread to most every big city in the country. It took some time, but sooner or later, those looking for an alcoholic drink or music and fun found their way to a secret location where they could enjoy themselves.

One day Teresa found a note on her desk.

I would like to get to know you better. Would you like to go out with me on a date?

Tony

p.s. Please leave a note on the corner of your desk and write yes or no and I will pick it up.

She wondered who this was from, as she knew of at least three men in the Embassy with that name. Whoever it was obviously waited until she was away from her desk to drop his invitation. He could have seen her after work or in the lunch room and asked her then, she mused. After some thought, she responded with her own note which read,

"Yes and no. Meet me in the lobby next to the mailbox after work tomorrow and I will give you a definite answer."

Arriving at work the following day, she noticed her note had apparently been picked up. Her curiosity grew, as she wondered if her "secret admirer" was handsome—or might he be homely! Nice—or maybe not so nice! Tall—or short? Fat?—Gosh, I hope not!

The afternoon dragged on—Fridays always seemed to—and the telegraph traffic slowed way down. Then, as she watched the big clock on the wall, the hands finally showed five o'clock. She finished the report she was working on, closed up her desk, and hurried to the ladies' room to check her hair and powder her nose before hurrying to the rendezvous at the mailbox. Descending the stairway to the front lobby, she observed a man standing next to it. Getting closer, she noticed he was the "man behind the newspaper."

"Tony?"

"Yes—that's me. So glad we could meet up again." He smiled at her.

"So! The man from the cafeteria!"

"Yes, I do apologize for my behavior that day, too."

"Well, why so secretive? I mean with the mysterious note on my desk."

"My apologies again! You see, I almost got fired one time—just for talking to someone. Nothing to do with work either. Since then, I've been ultra-careful that those old taskmasters don't catch me committing such a terrible transgression!"

"Gee! I had no idea it was *that* bad!"

"Crazy, huh?" They laughed. "So, anyway, you gave me a "yes and no" on your note. I hope you've decided it's a yes." He looked at her with a questioning countenance. For a moment she didn't answer. "Teresa? That *is* your name, isn't it?"

"Yes."

"Well, may I take you to dinner one evening?"

Glancing out the front entrance, she noticed it had begun to snow. It seemed the wind was picking up and blowing it forcefully sideways against the front of the building. Turning up the collar of her coat, she casually answered him. "Well—maybe. I'll let you know," as she turned to exit the building, leaving him standing there with a befuddled look on his face.

His first indication to Teresa that they might enjoy an evening at a speakeasy with some friends from the Embassy was strongly rebuffed by the girl. However, after listening to much of the scuttlebutt and hearing a few of the girls relating to her how much fun these clandestine places were—the new sounds of jazz—the dancing—not to mention the drinks!— finally brought her to relent. After all, how could it hurt anything? Everybody needs a little fun and excitement in their life. Anyway, nobody ever got caught, as far as I know.

"Who is this Tony-fellow you're going out with?" Bridget asked.

"Oh, he's just a fella I work with. I gotta get ready, Mom," Teresa responded as she walked toward her bedroom.

"Well, do you know anything about him?" Bridget continued, raising her voice so as to be heard from the kitchen.

"Well, I know him from work. He's been there awhile—since before *I* came."

Bridget wanted more information. "I mean, do you know anything *about* him? You know—like where he's from, his family, if he has any religion ..."

"Not really, Mom. Gee, we're just going out for the first time. I can't give you his whole past history yet!" Teresa remarked with a perturbed sound in her voice.

"I'm concerned about you."

"Oh, I'm sorry. I know. Anyway, I should have mentioned right away—we'll be with Betty and her boyfriend. So don't worry, Mom. We're actually going out to dinner— the four of us!" I best not tell her *where* we're going to dinner!

"Well, just be careful, and come home at a decent hour."

Suddenly, they heard a loud horn beeping outside. Teresa ran from her bedroom and peeked out the living room window. "It's my date, Mom," she related, as she observed a shiny new automobile out front.

"You'll not be runnin' out there now. No girl of mine will be runnin' out to the beep of a horn. You wait for him to come to the door and introduce himself properly like any gentleman would."

"Oh, Mom, I ..."

"No 'Oh, Moms' now. If the young man wants to date my daughter, he'll come in and escort you to the car."

After a few more beeps, Tony, getting no response, finally came and knocked on the door. "I'll get it, Mom." Teresa motioned the young man inside. He wore a full length raccoon coat and a flat, straw boater hat which concealed his hair but for the short sideburns. "Tony, this is my mother." He immediately removed his hat, revealing his jet-black, shiny, slicked back hair, parted down the middle.

"Nice to meet you, Ma'am." He smiled at her.

“I hear you work with Teresa at the Embassy,” Bridget said, sizing him up.

“Oh, yes, I do, Ma’am,” he responded, intending to introduce her to the fact that he had a good job in the accounting department. However, Bridget immediately continued with her instruction.

“Now, I am entrusting my daughter to you and I expect you to have her home at a decent hour.”

“Oh, yes, of course.”

“I understand, Tony, that you will be with another couple?” she inquired, wanting to make sure Teresa had that story right.

“Mother, didn’t I already mention that?” That perturbed sounding voice again.

“Yes, Ma’am. They’re waiting in the car.”

“Have a nice evening,” Bridget offered, still unsure that she liked the idea of Teresa dating someone she knew so little about.

Tony held the door as Teresa got in the passenger side, then went around to get behind the wheel. Betty introduced her date to Teresa. “This is Gerald, Teresa—we’re practically engaged!”

Teresa looked back and nodded her head at the man, unsure whether or not being “practically engaged” required a “congratulations.” “Oh, how nice!” Betty smiled and snuggled her head on Gerald’s chest.

“Where are we going?” Teresa asked, glancing over at Tony. “To an Italian restaurant?” She was hoping, Tony being Italian, that perhaps he had changed his mind about the speakeasy but was still concerned that they might possibly have decided to go to one of those “dens of iniquity.”

“Well ... not exactly,” Tony replied. Betty laughed.

“What’s so funny?” Teresa asked, adjusting her skirt over her knees as she turned around to face the girl.

“Before Betty could answer, Tony quipped, “We’re going to Charlie’s.”

“Charlie’s?” Teresa asked.

“Yes, Charlie’s. We’ve been there before; it’s a lot of fun.”

"It's not a speakeasy, is it?" Teresa seemed worried.

"Well, where else do you think we could get a little hooch?" Betty remarked.

"Well, gee, I'm not sure I want to ..."

"Oh, come on, dear," Betty retorted, "let your hair down for one night."

Tony and Gerald joined the conversation, reassuring Teresa that everything would be fine. She felt trapped. What could she do? Three against one!

The foursome made their way through a back alley and up a long flight of stairs. Tony knocked on a door. An eye appeared through a small round hole. "Who is it?" someone shouted in a gruff sounding voice.

"Charlie sent me," Tony responded. The door swung open and they entered a long hallway which led to another flight of stairs and another door. The six foot tall muscular bouncer seemed to recognize Tony and allowed the four of them to enter.

Teresa was in awe, glancing around the heavily smoke-filled room, not knowing where to look first. The shrill sound of a trumpet reverberated across the room, accompanied by a saxophone, bass fiddle, piano, and drums. Couples were dancing together to the fast and jumpy beat.

"Oh, I love that Charleston!" Betty announced.

Teresa couldn't care less just then, her eyes burning from the smoke. She blinked several times, trying to relieve it.

"You okay, Teresa?" Tony asked.

"It's just ... well ... pretty smoky in here."

"Sorry. You'll probably be okay in a few minutes. Your eyes will adjust to it." She doubted that, but just shook her head to be agreeable.

"Take your coat, Betty?" Gerald asked.

Betty turned, opening the elongated fur collar, as her date helped her off with her coat. Teresa's mouth almost dropped open as she observed that beautiful rose-colored dress. The floating fabric of the handkerchief bottom brushed the lower calves of her legs, partly hiding the shining, honey beige colored rayon stockings. Teresa quickly glanced around, trying to see, as best she could through that smoky fog, what the other girls were wearing. An insecurity suddenly came over her as she felt quite out of place in her plain, everyday dress.

"Teresa?" Tony interrupted her thoughts. She hadn't realized he was waiting to take her coat.

"Oh, I'm really still chilly, Tony. I think I'll just leave my coat on for a while."

"Follow me, please." The waiter led them past the long bar that filled the whole side of the room opposite the band to a small table in the corner.

"Pitcher of beer okay?" Tony queried the others. They all nodded in agreement. "You try to grab the waiter and order awhile, Gerald. Come on, honey, let's dance," as he took Teresa's arm and whisked her off to the dance floor.

More embarrassment. I wish I wasn't here. "I guess I'll have to take my coat off, Tony."

"Oh, sure, Teresa. Come on," as he led her back to the table, throwing her wrap on the back of her chair just as the waiter hurriedly set four glasses on the table, followed by a large pitcher of beer, spilling some over the edge.

"Looks like we got here just in time!" They laughed at Tony's remark as he pulled Teresa's chair out for her before pouring her drink.

Oh my gosh!—this is *awful*! she thought. How can anybody drink this stuff? Not wanting to appear prudish, she put on a fake smile and acted like she was enjoying the beer. The waiter placed a small bowl of pretzels on the table; Teresa grabbed a few right away, hoping to relieve that awful taste in her mouth. By the second round, however, it seemed as though the brew was starting to go down a little more smoothly. She began to wonder if she should bring up the idea of dinner. Let's see. He *did* invite me out to dinner. I *think*. I'm getting awfully hungry.

"Have another drink, Teresa," Tony invited, pouring the third round before she could respond.

"When the heck are we gonna get something to eat?" Betty whined.

"Waiter!" Gerald called. "Could we get a menu?"

"Well, we actually don't have any menus. We only serve finger foods here. Oh! And egg sandwiches."

"Oh, I really like those!" Teresa quipped, her stomach growling.

"Well, bring some hors d'oeuvres, please—and an egg sandwich for Teresa here," Tony ordered.

"Me, too!" Betty added. "I'll have one of those sandwiches, too," as she nodded to the waiter.

Gerald, finishing off the few remaining pretzels, remarked, "I'm fine with a few horses doovers—leaves more room for the liquid refreshment!"

Betty knocked him with her elbow. "You silly!" she remarked, laughing.

Teresa, beginning to feel the effects of the three rounds, stood up and grabbed Tony's hand. "Come on! Let's go dance!" She pushed through the crowd, pulling Tony by the hand, to the dance floor, only to realize she was a little unsteady on her feet. Tony could see her plight and immediately put his left arm around her waist, drawing her tightly to him. She wanted to push him away from this close embrace, but he was already leading her—and she was following! Relaxing a little, she began to enjoy this bodily contact, even as her conscience seemed to be saying "too close—too close."

They danced for the next few songs, all the while Teresa keeping a close eye on the table, watching for the waiter to deliver the food. "Here it comes! Let's go eat!" Tony didn't release her from his grasp, continuing to dance. Normally she probably wouldn't have said anything; however, that growling stomach came first. "Come *on,* Tony!" she insisted, and immediately disengaged herself from his close embrace and pushed through the crowd back to the table.

"I'm famished!" she announced to Betty and Gerald.

"Helpy-selfie!" Betty remarked. "Try these yummy hors d'oeuvres!"

"Hold it!" Gerald grabbed her arm as she began to pass the plate to Teresa, grabbing a few of the delicacies for himself.

They sat out the next few songs, just enjoying eating and listening to the mellow trumpet of the black musician. "Wow! That guy's so good! Who is he?" Teresa asked.

Gerald, wiping some foam from his lips, said, "He plays the meanest trumpet in town! His name's Armstrong— Louie Armstrong—otherwise known as "Satchmo."

"Isn't that the cat's meow? His sound, I mean," quipped Betty.

Teresa sat back, mesmerized, just soaking up the sweet sound of jazz, not realizing she was also soaking up too much beer. A fat lady trying to squeeze through the crowd accidentally bumped Teresa's chair just as she was taking a sip of the brew, spilling it down the front of her dress. "Oh, sorry dearie."

"Look what you did! My dress—it's ruined!"

The woman paid no attention and simply continued on her quest to find the bathroom. This upset Teresa even more. "That stupid woman!"

"Yeah!" Betty agreed.

Tony handed Teresa a few napkins from the table. As she started dabbing the wet dress, she suddenly started to cry.

For a minute, Tony didn't know what to do. "It's okay, Teresa. It's okay."

This made her cry even harder. She was thinking it was a good thing there was so much noise in the place so nobody could hear her. Maybe her tears would make her burning eyes feel better anyway. Suddenly the good time didn't feel so good anymore. "I want to go home, Tony. Take me home, okay?"

"Oh, come on, Teresa!—just because a little beer spilled on your dress?" Tony responded.

"Well, I don't feel good anyway."

"You'll ruin the party for all of us!" Betty insisted.

"I don't care!"

"Oh, great! Just great!" Betty frowned at Teresa. "Come on, Gerald. Guess we have to go. She's not gonna stop that bawling."

The ride home was quiet. Nobody said a word. Tony had a disgruntled look on his face. Teresa felt terrible. Her eyes were still burning and she thought she might have to throw up. Worse, what would her mother say to see her in this state. She'll smell that beer all over me—my dress and all.

Tony reached over and pushed the door open for her. She didn't care if he was rude, not walking her to the door. Maybe it's better. Mom won't light into him. Besides, he never even stood up for me to that snotty Betty. She quickly removed her shoes and tiptoed inside. Oh, thank you, God! She's asleep. Tucking herself immediately under the covers after removing her wet dress, she passed out.

Teresa kept her distance from Tony after that. A few other suitors came along, but Teresa felt most of the men left much to be desired, however—far cry from my Billy. Well, he *used* to be my Billy. I wish I could go back and re-live those days over again. I'd sure do things differently. And he can't be the *only* man in the world who I could fall in love with—can't be. She was thinking about the saying her mother always told her—"Men are like streetcars. There'll be another one along every five minutes!" Sure enough, though not exactly every *five* minutes, others did come along, but no one she was interested in. Besides, she didn't like the fact that they always wanted to spend the evenings in speakeasies.

Betty had apologized to Teresa and had mentioned that Gerald had a best friend—Norman. She thought that he would be a good one to line up with Teresa, since Norman loved the "good times."

"You know, Teresa," Betty advised, "he might be just the thing you need right now. You're still in that shell of yours."

"Oh, I don't know. I guess I'm just not with it or something. Anyway, this guy at church keeps asking me out. I might just say yes one of these days."

"Well, that's nice, but let's line up a night with Gerald and Norman. What do you say?"

"Well, I still don't feel comfortable in those speakeasies, though, Betty. I really just kinda feel out of place."

"Honey, all you need is a new dress—and maybe a new hairdo!"

"You think that'll help?"

"I *know* so. In fact, I'll go with you and bring you 'up to date!'"

The following Saturday morning, Teresa met Betty at Madison's Department Store. The front windows were a delight to their eyes, offering the latest in flapper fashions. "There's yours!" Betty announced. "The yellow one!"

"Oh, I don't know, Betty. It looks awfully expensive."

"Who cares! Come on. Let's go in, honey. We'll check it out."

Teresa hesitantly followed her into the store, wondering if she could afford the beautiful dress. "Oh, my gosh! I'm not sure I can afford this, Betty," Teresa said, coming out of the dressing room. "I really do love it, but ..."

"That's it! You're getting it!"

"But ..."

"No buts. It's gorgeous, and it fits like a dream."

"I just can't ..."

"Look! Turn around and look in the mirror."

"Well ..."

"Shake your bottom, girl!" Teresa did. "Cute eh?— the way those fringes wiggle. I can just see you on the dance floor in *that*! Every guy In the place will be wanting to dance with you. Come on! Hurry up and change! You're gettin' it!"

Bridget checked out the dress, and Betty grabbed her hand and led her out of the store. Hurrying her steps down the street, she announced, "Let's get moving. Can't be late for our appointment, girl."

"We have an appointment?"

"Yup, we sure do! We'll be absolutely magnificently gorgeous in a little while."

"Betty, what are you planning?"

"You'll see."

Teresa was getting a little nervous. "It better not cost much. I don't have too much left. Where's our appointment?"

"It's a surprise! But don't worry. It's the best of the best!"

Oh, oh. I'm not sure about all this. Teresa was *really* beginning to think twice about everything, when she was almost pushed through the Red Door of the salon by Betty. "Oh, no! Elizabeth Arden!" She turned abruptly. "Betty, let's get out of here!"

"Good afternoon, ladies. Come right in." The gentleman at the small desk to the right of the entrance was dressed in a black suit. The jacket was unbuttoned, revealing a gray satin-looking vest topped by a black bow tie. His gray beard was meticulously trimmed and his thick head of hair gave him a distinguished look. "And you have an appointment, do you, ladies?"

"Yes," Betty answered. "For Miss Sexton here."

"Oh, yes—that will be with Miss Angela. Please have a seat and she will be right with you," as he pointed to the red velvet chairs on the opposite wall.

"Oh my gosh, Betty!" Teresa was nervous. She glanced around the elegant salon at the pink and white flocked wallpaper decorated with an assortment of lovely framed art. The back wall had five large oval shaped mirrors within the mahogany woodwork. Each had a turquoise chair facing it, two presently occupied with customers, gold smocks covering their dresses. One woman was connected to some kind of paraphernalia which had a number of wires coming down and clasped to strands of her hair through three-inch long black rods. Good grief! What the heck is that? I'm getting out of here. Oh, oh—too late.

"Miss Sexton?" Miss Angela invited, motioning her to the nearest turquoise chair.

Teresa didn't move. "Go on, hon, that's you!" Betty said, giving her a push on her arm.

Miss Angela placed a gold smock over Teresa. "So, we're ready for a more modern look, are we?"

"Well, I ..."

"You'll look terrific with the new bob," Miss Angela stated as she began to cut Teresa's hair. Oh, no! Teresa watched in the mirror as her beautiful hair began to fall to the floor. Oh, my gosh! What am I doing? All my curls are gone. Oh, no! No, that's too short! She wanted to cry but didn't dare—not here. Too late now.

It was over in no time. "Pretty, hmm?" the beautician remarked, making a last-minute half curl on each side just slightly over the ears.

Teresa wished she could say what she really felt, but for what purpose. "Umm ... oh yes," she lied, thinking she would buy a cloche hat which would cover it all up.

Since there wasn't enough money left to even think about buying anything more, Teresa arrived at her front door with nothing on her head but for the little hair that was remaining. Oh, I hope Mom's not home.

"Saints preserve us! What have you done to your hair, girl?" Bridget exclaimed in a loud voice.

"Oh, Mom! It's the latest style—the flapper haircut," Teresa answered, trying to convince her mother it looked good, though feeling very uncomfortable herself with most of her crowning glory gone.

"Well, you just sit down here, young lady—we have to talk. I've been meaning to have a talk with you for some time now anyway. I don't like what I see—and I don't mean just that hair! Or lack of it! You've been coming home smelling like a brewery, and your clothes reek of smoke! And I don't know half of the gentlemen you've been seein'. As a matter of fact, I don't even know if they *are* gentlemen!"

"Oh, Mom, I'm sorry. But I just wanted to have a little fun. Besides, I usually only have one drink—just to be sociable," Teresa offered, crossing her fingers behind her back.

"Well, you better slow down, girl. You're partying too much."

Teresa sat still, just looking at the floor. A loud sigh escaped her lips. After a short period of silence, she said in a quiet voice, "You know, Mom, you're right. I have been overdoing it."

Bridget breathed a sigh of relief. Her daughter was still intact, admitting what her mother thought she would never admit.

At work the following day, Teresa was joined by Betty in the lunchroom. "Okay, all set!" Betty announced, smiling.

"What's that?"

"Our foursome. You, me, Gerald, and Norman. It's all set for this Saturday."

"Oh, I'm not going," Teresa said

"What? Just what the heck are you talking about, Teresa?"

"I'm just not going."

"And why not, may I presume to ask," Betty questioned in a not-too-friendly voice. Before Teresa could answer, she continued, "After everything I did for you—I spent my whole day just trying to make you more presentable!"

Teresa was taken aback by her nasty remark. "Oh, really! I wasn't aware that I was so *un*-presentable, Betty." The conversation confirmed in Teresa's heart what she had been burying for some time. That initial glamour and glorification of the "Roaring Twenties" had been wearing off, and she felt there was a decadence about it. After all, it's all about self-gratification, she had thought, and only could lead to a degradation of society.

Although she wasn't yet finished with her lunch, she got up from the table, leaned over to Betty, and assertively announced, "Besides, I *hate* this haircut!" at the same time giving a hard yank to a strand of the girl's hair.

The next few weeks became troubling for Teresa. She had noticed there was a lot of snickering and whispering going on in the office, especially as she walked by certain girls' desks. There was finally an explanation of the cause of her uncomfortable feeling, as a co-worker, Margaret, approached her in the ladies' room after work one day.

"Uh, as long as we're alone here, Teresa, I thought maybe you should know ..." The girl hesitated, seemingly unsure if she should continue.

Teresa knew very little about Margaret—only that she was quiet and seemed introverted, mostly keeping to herself, her desk in the far corner of the office. "Hello, Margaret."

"Teresa, I'm so sorry. I just kinda wondered if maybe I should tell you something ..."

"Oh?"

"Yes. Well, you see, it seems ... well, there's some nasty rumors going around the office—unfounded, I'm sure."

"About *me*?"

"Yes. I'm really sorry."

"I don't understand."

Margaret didn't want to reveal any names, but offered, "Well, it seems someone has it in for you."

"Oh, I get it." Teresa understood completely now. "Thanks, Margaret, for being my friend."

At least I know now, Teresa thought, as she rode the trolley home that evening. Bridget was preparing dinner as she entered the kitchen. "Mom, sit down—I want to talk to you." After relating the whole incident to her mother, she listened to what she felt was good advice.

"You know, Teresa, I'm glad you did pull that snot's hair. I never did like that nervy thing. But for now, honey, I think the best thing is just to ignore those ignoramuses. Sounds to me like they're all lowbrows, like that Betty."

After a while, the undertones seemed to diminish somewhat, Teresa hearing that Mr. Slattery had a talk with some of the girls about keeping their minds on their work. This relieved much of the stress on Teresa; however, the following month, she noticed that Betty hadn't shown up for work for several days. At first, she thought nothing of it, thinking the girl was on vacation. However, when three weeks had gone by, she began to wonder. Eventually she learned that the girl had been let go.

"Why? What happened?" she inquired of Margaret.

"You didn't hear?"

"Hear what?"

"Well, at first I thought it was because she was disrupting things, but actually—well, it was because of her beginning to show ..."

"You mean ..."

"Yep, that's it. Four months."

"Oh my gosh!" Teresa gasped, covering her mouth with her hand.

"I can't believe you didn't even notice, Teresa."

"Umm ... well, I noticed she had gotten a little heavier, but I just thought it was because she had been doing a lot of weekend partying at the speakeasies." Teresa hesitated, not knowing if she should ask. "Who ..."

"Gerald."

"Oh, gee. I feel kinda sorry for her, Margaret. But, you know, my Mom always used to say, 'What goes around, comes around.'"

"Yeah, I guess."

Teresa thought for a moment. "I hope all that drinking she's been doing won't hurt the baby." Oh, my gosh! Wait 'til Mom hears about this!

The Roaring Twenties continued to roar—but Teresa was no longer a part of it. She threw herself back into church work and began to make new friends. Washington had another side besides the big government with all of its trappings and the young, better-off partygoers. There were more poor people living in the shadows who could barely feed their families and countless numbers of orphans, just like in New York City.

The wind picked up as Bridget and Teresa were walking back home from Mass one Sunday. "I can't believe this cold," Bridget said, pulling her coat collar up around her neck and slipping her hands in her pockets. "Only the middle of October—too soon."

They discussed the priest's sermon. "You know, Mom, Father was right. I mean, about helping the poor. Wish I had more money to do that." Teresa pulled her scarf up to cover her nose and mouth as she added in a muffled tone, "I see little ones begging over by my work—and right across from the White House! It doesn't seem fair."

"I know, dear. I've seen plenty in my time. Whole families dying in the Old Country for lack of food. Even when I arrived here, the little beggars came at me from all sides. Seems like it never ends. But the priest was right—we can at least make a difference by helping a few if we can."

A freezing rain began, pelting them in their faces. They quickened their pace, finally arriving back home, slamming the door behind them. After removing their coats and hats, Bridget filled the kettle to make tea.

"Mom ..."

"What is it, dear?" She thought her daughter's voice sounded pensive. Looking over her shoulder, she continued, "Is something wrong?"

"No—but I *really* want to do something to help those poor beggars," as she looked over at her mother pouring the tea.

"Well, that's a noble thing you want to do. But how do you propose to do it?"

"I don't know," Teresa replied, staring down at the floor. "I really don't know where I'd even begin."

Bridget handed a cup of the hot brew to her daughter. "Well, maybe I can help," she said, smiling warmly. "There are many ways to help the less fortunate."

There was a long silence. Bridget placed a plate of cookies on the table. "You know, honey, I don't know that I ever told you very much about how your father and I helped those orphans in New York City."

"Oh, Mother! I wish I had known him."

"He had a big heart, Teresa."

A look of sadness came over the girl's face. "I know it's been awfully hard for you since Daddy went away."

"Yes, but we're not talking about me right now. I just wanted to remind you that your father was an orphan himself—same as me. So you can easily understand why he had such a soft spot in his heart for those little ones."

Teresa began to cry. "Where is he? Why did he leave us?"

Bridget hugged her daughter, surprised at her outbreak. "I've asked myself that question for years, darlin', and I've tried every way to find him. Oh, Lord! If only I knew ..." Her voice trailed off and she just stared out the window—wondering ... wondering...

Some time went by, and Bridget still hadn't found full time work. This left much time for her to sit and think, although she continued to do a little more sightseeing around the Capital. The following November, on Armistice Day, she and Teresa decided to attend the internment ceremonies for the Tomb of the Unknown Soldier in Arlington Cemetery, officiated by President Warren Harding. Shortly afterward, the Lincoln Memorial was finally completed, and they were fortunate to be able to attend the dedication at the National Mall.

"Glad he's got his head on!" Teresa quipped.

"Hands, too, hon," her mother added.

"Mmm—Hmm." Teresa was gazing at the inscription over the statue's head.

IN THIS TEMPLE
AS IN THE HEARTS OF THE PEOPLE
FOR WHOM HE SAVED THE UNION
THE MEMORY OF ABRAHAM LINCOLN
IS ENSHRINED FOREVER

"Very impressive, isn't it?"

"Mmm—Hmm, it really *is*, Mom."

It was a hot summer the following year. The telegraph keys were all clicking in the office at the same time, revealing the death of President Harding after his trip to Alaska. The White House was soon draped in black—and the nation mourned. Calvin Coolidge, the Vice President, was sworn into office within hours after Harding's death.

The employees at the Embassy usually had all windows opened wide, and multiple fans were scattered throughout the office. Half of Teresa's paper work landed on the floor one afternoon. As she struggled to pick it all up before it blew further, a handsome lad was suddenly on his knees beside her, assisting. How nice of him to help me. Dino was the new employee. He was straight from Italy but could speak English well. His good looks had caught Teresa's eye when he arrived, as well as every other girl's in the office. Something about him seemed to remind her of Fergy. "Now hold these down while I get you an anchor," he advised, taking her hand in his and placing it on the pile of papers they had returned to the desktop.

He returned with the "anchor"—his glass ashtray. She thought he would be needing it and was about to hand it back when he said, "I have another. You keep this one. I think it will do the trick, Teresa. It *is* Teresa, isn't it?"

"Yes. I didn't realize you knew my name." I wonder if he thinks I'm pretty.

"Oh, yes. I've heard it around the office."

"Really?"

"Yes. Quite often."

She thought she could say something funny—maybe like "I didn't know I was so famous," but a sudden concern came into her heart, wondering why people would mention her "quite often." She thanked him for his assistance and went back to her work, deciding she was just being silly to worry—it was probably nothing.

She noticed he would glance her way from time to time, smiling and winking at her when Mr. Slattery wasn't around. In the cafeteria, he would tap her on the shoulder as he passed by, often taking a seat next to Tony. I can't imagine why he sits with that jerky Tony.

Wiping the sweat from her brow, she began to exit the building after work, only to have a hand offered to assist her down the front stairs. "Oh, thanks, Dino."

"Want a lift home, Teresa?"

"You have a car?"

"Tony's driving."

"Oh. No thanks. I feel like walking."

"Come on. You don't want to walk in this heat."

"It doesn't bother me, but thanks anyway." She turned away and started down the street to catch the trolley.

He quickly caught up with her and took her by the arm. "I'd really like to see you sometime, Teresa."

"I have to go or I'll miss the trolley." The ride seemed to last but a second—her thoughts were so preoccupied with this new romantic interest.

"Hello, honey. How was your day?" Bridget inquired as her daughter entered with a big smile on her face.

"Busy, Mom. *Real* busy! And, oh, Mom! There's this gorgeous new guy at work! And he seems interested in *me.* You should see him, Mom—he's *so* handsome—well, all the girls have their eye on him."

"Oh, so that's the reason for the big smile, hmm?"

Teresa just laughed.

"Well, you can tell me all about him in a minute, honey. Not to change the subject, but I'm sure you heard the news about the President?"

Teresa shook her head. "Oh, sure. The wires were hot all day. Some of the employees stayed on overtime, there was so much information coming in—and going out. I probably should have stayed. We could use the extra money. But it was so, so hot in there, I couldn't wait to get out; and he *gave* us a choice."

"Here," Bridget said, handing her a cold lemonade. "It's okay, honey—that you came home, I mean."

"Well, did you hear anything about the *new* President, Mom—Coolidge?"

"Not much yet."

"Well, listen to this—I wrote it down. He says he wants to preserve the old moral and economic precepts of frugality amid the material prosperity which many Americans were enjoying."

"Material prosperity? Gosh! *I* don't feel too prosperous! Seems like we never have a penny left over, honey."

"Sorry, Mom."

"Oh, no. That's okay, honey." Bridget had given much thought about moving back to Buffalo, but decided not to bring it up to Teresa on a day that she was feeling so "up" about her new male friend.

The next few months were a time of confusion for Teresa. She was strongly attracted to Dino but couldn't help being a little disturbed about him. He seemed so full of himself, purposely flirting with the other girls in the office when she was around. Is he trying to make me jealous? Or maybe he's one of those men who thinks he's just a gift to women—a gigolo or something. The more she watched these comings and goings, the more she decided to hold off dating him, even though he had continued to tell her he wanted to take her out. Margaret had mentioned to her that none of the girls in the office would ever have thought twice about accepting an invitation for a date from him. She, herself, would have "given the world" if he'd ask *her* out. "Do you know how lucky you are, Teresa? Gosh! He's always wanting to date you. How can you refuse? He's gorgeous!"

"I know, Margaret. But he flirts with *every*body!"

"Well, *almost* everybody. He doesn't flirt with *me*! Wish he did."

Teresa felt sorry for Margaret. Besides being so introverted, mostly keeping to herself, she was taller than most of the male employees and walked in a "stooped down" way, trying to make herself look shorter. Her black-rimmed glasses were much too heavy looking for her face, and her hair was naturally frizzy.

"Oh, I don't know, Margaret. Maybe I'm making too much of it. But don't you think it's strange that he acts that way in front of me? It just leaves a bad taste in my mouth, so to speak."

"I wouldn't even care about a taste in *my* mouth. I'd grab an invite from him right up! Gosh Teresa! Why don't you just give him a chance? You're stupid not to,,." Margaret surprised herself with her own words. "Oh my gosh! I'm so sorry. I really didn't mean that, Teresa."

"No, it's okay. I know you didn't."

"Well, did you ever stop to think that maybe he really *is* trying to make you jealous—that maybe that will make you want to date him?"

"I never thought of it that way." Teresa glanced over at Dino, working diligently at his desk across the room. "I guess maybe I should."

Margaret smiled. "Lucky girl."

"Thanks, Margaret. You're such a good friend. I guess I never told you how much I appreciate your sincerity and friendship."

"Miss Henderson!" a voice boomed. "Get back to work!"

"Sorry, Mr. Slattery," Margaret apologized, quickly whispering into Teresa's ear. "Gotta go."

The following week, Dino surprised Teresa from behind as they exited the building, placing his hands over her eyes. "Guess who?" he asked, disguising his voice.

"I give up. Who is it?"

He leaned over her shoulder and whispered in her ear—"Me!"

"Oh, Dino!" she laughed as she turned around. His funny little gesture seemed to take her off guard, revving up within her a desire to spend some time with him.

"Saturday night—let's do the town. What do you say?"

"Well, I guess we could."

"Great! Pick you up at six?"

"Where would we go? Not to a speakeasy, I hope."

"Why not?"

"It's just not my thing anymore, Dino."

"Hmm." Dino thought for a moment. "Well, how about we grab a bite to eat and see a movie?"

"Sounds good to me," Teresa responded. She seemed delighted that the man was instantly responsive to her wishes.

"The 'Hunchback of Notre Dame' is playing at the Avalon. Lon Chaney's supposed to do a great job as the hunchback!"

"That sounds wonderful, Dino; I'd love to see it."

"Settled then. Saturday it is."

A cool breeze made the walk to the trolley enjoyable. Teresa was glad Dino didn't show up in Tony's car; she wanted nothing to do with the man—or his belongings. After helping her up the trolley steps, he stood to the side, allowing her to take the window seat. She liked that. He makes me feel secure—kind of like he's safeguarding me from any shuffling going on in the aisle. Halfway to the theatre, he slid his arm along the top of the seat behind her, at the same time reaching over with his other arm and taking her left hand in his. That secure feeling suddenly started to change into a little insecurity. How forward of him. It's only our first date—actually, only the *beginning* of our first date. Well, there's not too much I can do about it, I guess. Besides, we're almost there.

Standing in line for tickets, she noticed two of the other men from the office in the lobby. Are they looking at me? Or *him*? Oh, for heaven's sake, I must be getting paranoid.

"Teresa?"

"Oh, sorry. Just thinking of something."

"Come on, let's get our seats, honey."

Honey? He's already calling me honey? And those two men are still staring at us. Suddenly, she was wishing she was home. Her Mom was right all along; she always said she shouldn't go out with people she hardly knew. There was nothing she could really put her finger on—it was just that uncomfortable feeling within. "Do you know those two men over there, Dino?"

"Sure. They work in the office. Don't you recognize them, Teresa?"

"Well, yes. It's just that ... well, they seem to be staring."

"Nah, hon. They're just friendly." He nodded over to them, as he ushered Teresa into a seat in the back row.

"Maybe we should sit a little closer, do you think? Might be able to see better," she offered.

"Oh, I would, of course. It's just that I'm a little farsighted. Do you mind?"

"I'm sorry. No, of course not." She took her seat, at the same time noticing the two men sat down at the end of the row in front of them.

As the lights dimmed and the movie began, Dino's arm once again slid behind Teresa's back, his hand brushing up against the side of her neck. That feeling again! She reached up and moved his hand to the back of the seat, which only led to his grasping her shoulder. In the meantime, she noticed the two men were glancing back at them and snickering. "Dino," she whispered, "what is going on here? Those men are looking at us again."

"Oh, they probably just think you're very pretty. Don't pay any attention to them," as he took her hand in his and squeezed it, at the same time squeezing her shoulder with the other.

She felt hemmed in by his grasp, until her attention was suddenly drawn to the screen where a grotesque looking hunchback was being chained to a large wheel fastened to the top of a platform. The look of helplessness on the face of the creature drove a feeling of compassion deep into her heart. The organ player in the front of the theatre leaned heavily on the keys, the music dramatizing the whole scenario unfolding before their eyes, the caption on the screen reading, "Again was a slave to suffer for his master's crime." This compassion was soon replaced, however, by a feeling of revulsion as a black-cloaked person began to lash the poor soul's back.

Her attention stayed riveted on the screen for the next hour until a sudden advance was made by Dino pressing his lips firmly on the side of her neck as he tightly grabbed her hand. "Dino!" she exclaimed in a whisper, quickly pulling her head away. Oh, no! They're watching *again.* I don't know what the heck is going on—but whatever it is, I don't like it. "Excuse me," she whispered to her date, "I'm going to the restroom for a moment." She released herself from his grasp and walked to the back of the theatre, passing the ladies' room and exiting the lobby just in time to catch the trolley pulling up outside. She felt like crying—like she'd been made a fool of. What was he trying to prove? I don't understand. And those men?

Monday morning came quickly—much too quickly for her. She had spent most of the weekend thinking how upset this whole situation had made her—the date, those men, the whispers amongst some of the other employees in the office—it just all seemed to be catching up with her. Later, at lunch, Margaret, almost hesitantly, asked about her movie date. The final straw came as Teresa began to relate the incident to her, and Margaret admitted she had already heard Dino whispering with the other two men about it. She apologized to Teresa, feeling sorry that she had encouraged her to date the man. "Who does he think he is anyway? Just cause he's so good looking, I guess he thinks all the girls are drooling over him! I'm so sorry, Teresa."

"It's not your fault, Margaret. But, my gosh! It's worse than I thought. That Betty—she really did a job on my reputation, didn't she?"

"Yeah, I know. I didn't know how to tell you—that whole thing, you know? The devil was in that girl, I swear!"

Teresa toughed out the rest of the workday, arriving home that night only to pour out her heart to her mother.

Bridget took her daughter in her arms, as she began sobbing and relating how she wished she didn't ever have to step foot in that office again. "It's become so embarrassing, Mom—unreal!"

"Oh, darling! Oh, how terrible! That dirty skunk! How awful! I can't believe it! How can people be so cruel?" She wanted to cry herself but tried to stay strong for her daughter. She took Teresa's hand and led her over to the sofa. "Sit down, honey. I want to talk to you." She pulled a chair over to the sofa, sat down and took Teresa's hands in hers. "Maybe this is the right time to tell you what's been on my mind lately. I've been thinking a lot about moving back to Buffalo. I do have a few contacts back there, you know; and I think they would take me back at Kobacker's. And living's a lot cheaper there, too."

"Oh, Mom!"

"And now that you say things are so difficult at work— well, what do you think about this idea? And do you think you could get a transfer?"

The pain in Teresa's heart began to diminish, being replaced by a feeling of hope. She sat upright on the edge of the sofa, squeezed her mother's hands, and smiled. "Oh, Mom! Yes! Yes—let's go back! I'd love to go back! I'm sure there's a Western Union office in Buffalo, and I could transfer. Well, I'm pretty sure I could anyway—Mr. Slattery told me one time that my work was so good, I could probably transfer anywhere in the country and they would take me!"

Bridget brought sandwiches from the kitchen, and the discussion went on. "And you know what else?" she offered. "Maybe we'd have two incomes again—if I could find full-time work! That would make a really big difference, honey!"

“Sounds great to me, Mom!” She added, “And just think, we’d be able to see all our old friends again—Mrs. Ryan and all the kids. Gee, they wouldn’t be kids anymore! Maybe we could spend Christmas with them, like we did before. It was such a beautiful day, remember?”

“Sure I remember. But I think we might have to wait until after the holidays, honey. It would be too much to make all the arrangements and everything—besides, you really would have to give notice at work.”

“I don’t even care if I do!”

“But you must. I mean, if you are aiming at being given a transfer, you really have to do things the right way.”

“Yeah, true.”

The following week, Teresa approached Mr. Slattery to inquire of him the possibility of being transferred to Buffalo. He indicated to her that he would be sorry to see her leave as her work had been exceptional but would contact the Buffalo office for her. Two weeks later, a reply came from them stating that one of their telegraphers would be leaving and they would be glad to have her transfer without an interview, based on the performance record sent them by her supervisor. However, the position would not be open until January 1st.

Teresa made up her mind to face that formidable intimidation in the office for the last month of the year, her spirit lifted at the thought of a new beginning in Buffalo.

December arrived on the scene, the area gifted with a blanket of white. “B-r-r, it’s freezin’ out there, Mom! Beautiful though, isn’t it?” Teresa asked, stomping the snow from her boots. She removed her coat and shook the snow from her hat. “What’s cookin’, Mom? Chicken soup? Smells good.”

“How was work today, honey—did everything go okay?”

“Well, I managed to get through it. Actually, there was a little bit of excitement today. Everybody was at the front windows watching workers putting a huge Christmas tree up on the ellipse.”

“Really?”

“Mmm—Hmm. The President is gonna be lighting it on Christmas Eve, I guess. It’s a big one! Forty-eight feet high!—a little bit higher than ours, Mom!”

Bridget laughed. "Oh, I'd really like to see *that*," she remarked.

"Me, too! I guess they'll have a big crowd there, don't you think?"

"Probably. But let's go anyway, and we'll still have plenty of time to get to Christmas Eve mass afterward."

They stood in the winter chill among thousands as snow fell lightly listening to the 3,000 city school children singing Christmas carols and the United States Marine Band with their Christmas-themed music delighting the crowd. At exactly 5 p.m., President Coolidge, standing at the foot of the huge balsam fir, flipped a switch, and 2,500 red, white, and green electric bulbs illuminated the first National Christmas Tree.

"O-o-o-o!"

"Ah-h-h!"

"Look at all the lights, Mommy! Wow!" The child was jumping up and down with excitement.

"Oh, how beautiful!"

The awesome spectacle brought cheers from the thousands and children clapped their hands, beaming with joyous excitement.

"Oh, I'm so glad we came, Mom," Teresa exclaimed as they stepped off the trolley afterward. They began the six-block walk home, the snow falling lightly. "Wasn't it wonderful?—the President himself lighting up that huge tree!"

"It was beautiful!" Bridget replied, brushing some snow off her eyelashes. I just love this time of year! The only thing that could make it any better would be if we ..."

"If we what?"

"Well, what I was going to say, honey, was ... well, if we only had your father here to share it with."

"Oh, Mother, I'm so sorry. I thought ..."

"I know, I know. You were going to say you thought by now, after all these years, I'd be over it. I know. It's just that I couldn't help thinking back to our first Christmas while we were standing there. Your Dad was so excited when he was able to bring this scrawny little Christmas tree home that Christmas Eve. A kind old man at the Elk Street Market gave it to him late that night. Otherwise, we'd never even have had one—couldn't afford it."

"A-w-w-w." Teresa squeezed her mother around the waist.

It was truly a silent night. Neither one spoke for a while. The only sound that was heard was the snow crunching beneath their feet. A cold wind had sprung up suddenly, belting the snow into their faces. Bridget pulled her hat further down over her ears and slipped her hands into her pockets, her thin gloves unable to keep out the cold.

"Let's get some hot cocoa on, okay?" Bridget asked.

"I'll bring it in the living room, Mom. Why don't you sit down by the tree."

"Thanks, honey. Not too much sugar!"

"We have a lot to be thankful for, my dear," Bridget said, looking up at the star on the top of their tree as Teresa handed her mother a cup.

"I know, Mom," Teresa replied.. "I *am* thankful. for you, my warm house to come home to, and my job—I mean, being able to get the transfer and all." Her eyes fell upon their manger scene. "Oh, and for our faith, of course!" The two sat silently admiring their decorated tree. "Pretty good job, hmm?"

Bridget, disregarding the question, seemed deep in thought. She placed her cup on the end table and took Teresa's hand. "There's just one other thing, Teresa—and then I won't bring it up again. You see, it's not only hanging onto a hope which, of course, seems inconceivable—well, it's kinda like just wanting to be near my memories—it just makes me feel like I'm near him." She had secretly coveted her hope in silence, trying not to mention it. Many times she tried to dismiss the emptiness from inside, but it held her hostage and time never was able to release her beloved from the recesses of her heart.

"I understand, Mom. Really I do."

Bridget, gazing out the window at the light snow still falling, continued, "You know, honey, your father and I used to talk about some day moving to the outskirts of the city. His dream was to buy a small piece of land where we could have a little farm and raise chickens—a place of our own. You know, my Mom and Dad and I lived on a farm—but it wasn't ours." Her face showed the sadness in her heart as she added, "We probably could have been happy there if those mean old landlords didn't treat us like slaves!"

"Slaves?"

"Well that's kinda how we lived—with just the clothes on our backs and the meager food they allowed us from our labors." She hesitated a minute, then looking over at Teresa, she smiled and, taking the girl's hands in hers, continued, "But that's all behind us now. Let's get back to our plans. What I wanted to tell you was about this new little village just north of Buffalo. It's a little rural and sparsely populated. Wouldn't it be nice to get a little piece of land there away from the city and live in our own house—something no one could take away from us. We could even grow our own food!"

Before Teresa could answer, Bridget took a beautifully-wrapped gift from under the tree.

"I've been wondering what's in there, Mom!" Teresa quipped, smiling as her mother handed it to her.

"Merry Christmas, honey!" She leaned over and kissed her daughter on the cheek.

"I hate to open it—it's so pretty!" Teresa quickly untied the red ribbon and ripped the paper off.

The pink sweater and matching gloves delighted the girl and she proceeded to put them on and strutted across the living room, as though she were a model on a runway. "Very pretty, honey. Very pretty!"

"And a perfect fit! Thanks, Mom. I love it!" She returned her mother's kiss. "Now it's *your* turn." She smiled as she bent down, pulling a small package from under the couch.

"What?" Bridget grinned at her daughter.

"Merry Christmas, Mom."

"You stinker! I can't believe that hiding place!"

"Hah! Bet you thought I didn't get you anything!"

"You funny one!"

"It's kinda small ..."

"Well now, my dear, you know the old saying ..."

Teresa interrupted. "Mmm-Hmm. Good things come in small packages!"

"Oh! Oh my gosh! Teresa, you shouldn't have!" Gold gilded over black surrounded the square face of the watch, Roman numerals showing the hours. In tiny lettering in the center was the word "Elgin." The links in the stretch band expanded easily as she pulled the gift over her left hand. "Oh! It's beautiful, honey! And it fits perfectly!" She stared down at the lovely timepiece. "I don't think I've ever seen anything so beautiful! Oh, thank you honey! Thank you so much, but gee!—it must have cost you a month's salary!"

"Well, Mom, you're worth every penny! And *more*!"

"Oh my gosh, Teresa!" Bridget looked down at her gift. "Would you believe it's time to get ready for Mass?"

"Already?"

"Yes. It's 11 o'clock!"

Chapter 18

Home Is Where the Heart Is

Bridget's heart was back with her memories—back by the giant grain elevators, the Buffalo waterfront with its grain-filled boats, and the First Ward where her love was robbed from her in the flower of his youth.

The move back to Western New York was not difficult for her, as their rented apartment in D.C. was furnished, and their clothing and a few mementoes were all they needed to pack. They had given prior notice to their landlord and boarded the train to Buffalo.

Clackity-clack. Clackity-clack. Bridget's forehead was tightly pressed against the train window as the scenery sped by, the morning sunlight creating diamond sparkles on the blue rushing stream the train seemed to be following. Where had all those years gone? It couldn't have been that long back that she left that "Isle of Green" behind her—that land of her ancestors. It was almost as if each turn of the wheels brought a new image to her mind. Her Mom. Her Dad. The mud cabin. The hunger that had slowly crept into that humble earthen home like a thief in the night. Memories flashed through her mind—some she had blocked out for years. Images of her mother crying in bed at night, her little sustenance being mostly given to her child. Her father coming in from the fields, exhausted and dirty from laboring since sunup. The few potatoes he was able to salvage for his family once the Great Famine had spread throughout the land. His anger at "those damn English!" The death of both parents within a short period of time. She became so deep in thought she didn't even hear her daughter addressing her. Finally, the girl nudged her with her elbow.

"Mom?"

"Oh, I thought you were sleeping, honey."

"I *was*." Teresa yawned as she stretched over her mother's lap so as to get a better look at the mountains. "Can we switch seats, Mom?"

"Sure."

"Are we in Pennsylvania already?"

"Yes." The mountain range before their eyes seemed to dwindle in height as the train made its way toward New York State. "You missed some breathtaking scenery! You can see the hand of God in this land."

"Were there mountains in Ireland, Mom?"

"I heard there were some, Dear, but I never saw them. We were never able to travel at all; and then, of course, I had to be taken to that orphanage when my folks passed, you know."

"Yeah. Sorry, Mom."

"But I do remember some meadows and streams and high cliffs by the sea when they would take us on an outing once a year for a picnic near the water."

"Well, where did you go after you left there?—the orphanage, I mean."

"Well, the officials there took me to a little town called Ennis. There was a lovely woman who was looking for help in her dress shop—Mrs. Harrigan. I could sew pretty well, and she hired me and let me live in the small apartment above her store." Bridget had tears in her eyes. "I grew to love the woman very much—treated me like I was her own child. Probably would have stayed in Ireland if she hadn't passed." She looked over at her daughter. "Well now, haven't I already told you about all this?"

"Well, Mom, I like hearing about your youth and about your family in Ireland, even though I know so much of it was sad."

Bridget didn't respond right away. She just sat staring out the window. Then she said, "Well, honey, some things were really bad; and I don't want you to think any more about it. I'm already sorry I shared some of that with you."

Teresa grabbed her mother's hand. "I'm so sorry for all you went through, Mom."

"Oh, that's all behind me now. We'll just look to the future and make the best of things. We're doin' fine."

They sat quietly for some time, Bridget seemingly deep in thought, before Teresa, reminiscing about another train trip, interrupted her musings. "Remember when we met Billy, Mom? On that train to New York?"

"Oh, hon!" Bridget was taken by surprise at her daughter's question. "Well, sure—of course I do." She waited to see what Teresa would have to say next, but nothing came. Oh, I hope she isn't still suffering from Billy's loss.

Teresa took a book from her tote.

"Still working on that "Able McLaughlin" story, honey?" Bridget wanted to change the subject from Billy, being uncomfortable with the possibility that her daughter might be enduring similar heartaches as she herself had been all these years.

"Yeah, it's a good story, Mom—historical fiction. This guy returns home from the Civil War and finds his girl ... well ... uh ... in a compromised situation—you know what I mean?"

"Well, sure. Sure I do, honey!"

"So anyway, he takes over the whole situation and chases that bad guy right out of town and ... well, he kinda saves the girl's honor, even though some people don't think too much of him when the baby is born early."

"I see."

"But then, that other guy comes back and ..."

"Yes?"

"Well, that's where I'm at right now. I'll let you know what happens." She picked up the book, but within a few moments laid her head back and closed her eyes. Bridget thought she detected a small tear in the corner of the girl's right eye and reached for her handkerchief but decided to ignore it.

"ALBANY! NEXT STOP! ALBANY!"

Teresa opened her eyes, another tear suddenly falling. Bridget now understood what was going on in her daughter's heart. "Oh, no, honey! Still? Still Billy? I didn't know."

The girl denied her own feelings, wiping her eyes with the back of her hand. "I'm fine. Fine. Really I am, Mom." Bridget suddenly realized that Albany was the stop where Billy had boarded that train so long back. She put her arm around the girl and just held her.

After some time, Bridget reached into her tote and took out some ham sandwiches she had packed. "Come on, honey, let's have a little bite."

"Not hungry, Mom. Thanks anyway."

"Okay, then, I guess I won't eat anything either." Bridget returned the sandwiches to the bag.

"Well, I guess I could eat a little," her daughter said, not wanting her mother to go without lunch. After eating, the sun beginning to set behind darkening clouds, they rested for a short time before falling asleep.

The conductor's loud announcement rang in their ears.

"BUFFALO! BUFFALO! NEXT STOP! BUFFALO!

As the train station wasn't far from the old First Ward and the grain elevators, the first thing Teresa noticed as they stepped off the train was the strong smell of cereal emanating from the H-O Company. "Smell *that*, Mom?"

"Yep! When you smell that, you know you're in the old First Ward!"

"It's good to be here, Mom. Really, I just feel it's so good to be here."

"Bridget! Oh, Bridget! Over here!" Mrs. Ryan was rushing down the dimly lit platform toward them, waving her arms above her head.

They almost collided into one big hug—the three of them together. Bridget cried. "Oh, Megan! Oh, it's so good to be back! Thank you for coming."

"This *can't* be little Teresa!" She held the girl at arm's length, so as to get a better look. "My goodness! You're a young lady!"

"She's a *telegrapher*, Megan—with Western Union."

"Really? That's wonderful, Teresa," smiling at the girl. "You must be very proud of her, Bridget."

"Oh, I am! She's done very well. That's how she was able to get the transfer to the Buffalo office. Her supervisor said her work was exceptional!"

Teresa blushed, feeling a little self-conscious though enjoying the accolades. "Oh, oh! Did you feel that?" Teresa asked, holding her hand palm up.

Within moments, a flash of lightning at the edge of the platform was followed by a deafening crack of thunder. "Oh, dear!" Megan exclaimed. "Come along now, before it pours. I have my car waiting." They scrambled quickly from the station and stepped up onto the running board to climb into the Maxwell Touring Car. The red body was highlighted by a black roof and red wheels with whitewall tires. Leaning forward and tapping on her chauffeur's shoulder, she said, "Take us home, Steven."

"Yes, Ma'am."

"I'm so glad you got my letter to meet us, Megan."

"Oh, I was so delighted to hear you were coming back, Bridget."

"I hope you didn't have to wait too long—the conductor said that we were running late."

"Oh, I just got here a little while ago myself."

Bridget and Teresa couldn't help but notice the shiny chrome door handles and the ash trays in the backside of the front seats, the black leather upholstery matching the roof of the car.

"Oh, I never rode in an automobile before. I always took the trolley, you know," Bridget said, turning to Megan and smiling.

"But I have!" Teresa exclaimed. "At least a few times on some dates in Washington."

"Well, this is our first one," Megan answered. "Mr. Ryan bought it for us a few years back."

"How wonderful! It's just lovely, Megan," Bridget remarked.

"Mmm—Hmm! I *love* it!" Teresa added.

"Could you drop us at the boarding house on Louisiana Street? We can stay there until we find an apartment."

"Oh, no way! I'll not have my dear friends staying at any boarding house, especially since I have so much room!"

"Oh now, Megan, we couldn't impose on ..."

"Now you'll be stayin' at *our* place. Mr. Ryan and I have already discussed it and that's all there is to it! Besides, the children are all looking forward to seeing you again. They missed you all these years."

"Well, I don't know." Bridget looked over to Teresa, looking to get her input.

"Yes! Yes!" her daughter exclaimed. "I want to see the kids again!"

Megan laughed. "Well, you won't find *the kids* hiding behind the bedroom doors this time!"

"Oh, how kind of you, Megan," Bridget said, laughing. "Well, maybe for a few days, until we can find an apartment."

A big smile came over Megan's face. "Oh, splendid! Then it's all settled."

The rain was coming down in torrents now, making visibility difficult, and Steven slowed the speed to a crawl. Passing Alabama and Fulton Streets, memories flooded Bridget's mind like a re-run of a movie. A few tears trickled down her cheeks. Megan handed her a handkerchief. "Oh, honey, it's okay. I understand." She put her arm around Bridget's shoulder.

Teresa, who had been gazing up at the tall grain elevators, reached over and took her mother's hand. "Mom, it's okay. We'll be fine."

The conversation seemed disconnected and distant, as the memories of Tom continued to swirl through her heart. This isn't like I thought it would be. It just isn't the same. How could it be?—without him.

It was heartwarming for Bridget and Teresa to visit with the Ryans at 472 Delaware, the warm reception giving them much comfort. The thirteen years since they had left Buffalo had brought many changes at the Ryan home. Most of the children had moved away—gone off to college or got married and had places of their own. Kathleen had become a lay missionary of the Vincentian order working in Panama, as Megan had written to Bridget some years back. Only one was left at home—Adam—a proud new uncle to Daniel's one-year-old twins. The pitter-patter of little feet was often heard once again in that residence on many weekends.

Mr. Ryan invited the guests into the library after dinner that evening. Seating himself in his favorite large, black leather wingback chair with the polished silver nailhead trim and lighting up his pipe, he proudly pointed out that his home had once been occupied by the famous author, Mark Twain. He always enjoyed telling people about the celebrated previous owner as though it were a "feather in *his* cap," so to speak.

"Oh, we remember!" Bridget quipped, looking over at the glowing embers in the fireplace.

"Did you know his real name was Samuel Clemens?" Before Bridget could answer, he continued, "His father-in-law gave him this house in 1870. Can you imagine him writing some of those famous stories right here in this room?" Mr. Ryan continued, as the smoke rose upward from his pipe.

"Yeah, I felt the urge to get a pencil and paper and start writing the minute I walked through that door!" Teresa quipped, smiling at her own humor.

"He was also a writer for the Buffalo Morning Express," Mr. Ryan continued, oblivious to Teresa's little input. "He had quite a sense of humor, often referring to himself as 'the laziest man in the newspaper business.' But..." His demeanor suddenly changed, as he looked down at the floor. "But, you know, the man also had much sadness roaming these halls. His father-in-law died shortly after they moved in. And then another close friend of his wife's fell ill while visiting and died right here as well. And then they even lost their first child in infancy."

"Enough of that Mark Twain business now, dear," Megan said, smiling over at her husband. "Let's hear all about our guests' news!" She turned to Bridget and Teresa, sitting together on the sofa. "Now tell me all about yourselves. You both look well and you don't look any the worse for the wear—I mean, living in those big cities!"

"Well, we tired of New York after a while; and, like I told you in my letters, we moved to Washington," Bridget offered. "Now *that's* an interesting place!"

"Oh, is it now?" Megan asked with a grin on her face. "And did you meet the President?"

Teresa chimed in, "We never actually met him, Megan, but I did see him almost every day when he went out on his carriage. Our Western Union office was right across the street from the White House."

"And, you know, we did just watch last month when President Coolidge lit up the first national Christmas tree on the Ellipse!" Bridget added.

Megan smiled. "Well, I'll be! Hobnobbin around with the elite of the Capital, were ya?"

"Well, of course!" Bridget decided to return Megan's jest. "The First Lady and I got together often for tea!"

"Speaking of tea, can I get some for you?" Megan offered, smiling at Bridget's remark.

"Oh, thank you, Megan," Bridget replied. "I'd love some."

"No tea for me!" Mr. Ryan spoke up. "A beer, please, my dear," as he nodded to his wife.

The conversation continued as the evening wore on, Bridget relating her many sightseeing trips in the Capital and Teresa telling of some of the highlights of her work, especially about the Titanic.

Megan then inquired as to any suitors Teresa may have had. Not being the girl's most favorite subject, she decided to dismiss the topic quickly, simply mentioning that two young men, Tony and Dino, were just not her 'cup of tea,' laughing at her own pun, as she sipped the brew. Deciding to change the subject right away, she mentioned, "I can't wait to hear about Kathleen's mission work, Megan."

"Oh, I'd love to share that with you, but maybe tomorrow? It's getting late and you both have had a long trip today. Let me take you upstairs and show you your room."

It was just two weeks later that an apartment became available right on Delaware, though much further north from the Ryan's, across the street from Forest Lawn Cemetery. Teresa started her job at Western Union on Main Street in downtown Buffalo, easily accessible by trolley. Bridget's arthritis had steadily grown worse over the winter, and her hands had stiffened, thus making her sewing quite difficult. She knew she would be unable to use her skills, as she had in the past, to make a living and decided to look in a different direction. She had time, however, to set up housekeeping in their new home. During the next few months, her search for work continued with no results, until spring when she spotted an ad in the Buffalo paper. This sounded perfect, she felt, as a matron was needed for the popular passenger ferry, *The S.S. Canadiana*, which transported people from Buffalo to Crystal Beach, Canada. Her experience from years earlier on the *River Queen* impressed the management and was helpful in obtaining the job, although it would only be seasonal, from May through September.

In the meantime, she took an afternoon to tour Forest Lawn, learning a great deal. "Listen to this, Teresa."

"Can it wait just a minute, Mom? I just want to change my clothes and get into something comfy. We were so busy today!"

"Okay, I'll set the table a while." During dinner, Bridget was eager to share her acquired history of the cemetery. "So there's this man buried there, Teresa—Ely Parker his name is. He was an Indian, a tribal diplomat in the Seneca Nation. He was an attorney, too—*and* an engineer! Imagine that! And *then* he became a lieutenant colonel during our Civil War under Gen. Ulysses Grant."

"Wow!" Teresa exclaimed.

"Oh, there's more! Believe it or not, he actually wrote the terms of the Confederate surrender at Appomattox!"

"Pass the mashed potatoes, Mom—I'm awfully hungry tonight."

"Teresa, aren't you even interested in this? *I* think it's fantastic!"

"Oh, I'm sorry, Mom. Yeah, sure, really I am. I just couldn't get a word in. Go ahead. Tell me more."

Bridget smiled. "Then there's this little girl. She stands in the middle of Mirror Lake there."

"*What?*"

"Well, I mean a statue, silly."

"Oh."

"She represents all children. You know, Teresa, I couldn't help thinking of all the orphan children back in New York—you know, when I first came here."

"Like Small Fry?"

"Yes, honey. He was one of many." There was a moment of quiet. "Well, anyway, let me finish ..."

"Go ahead, Mom, and pass me another wiener please."

"Then there's another Indian there by the name of Red Jacket."

"Oh. Did he have one?"

"What? What do you mean, dear?"

"Did he have a red jacket?" Teresa thought her question was so funny, she burst out laughing.

"Well, yes, as a matter of fact, he *did*, Missy," Bridget answered thoughtfully. "He just happened to be a very prominent Seneca chief who negotiated neutrality on the part of his powerful Indian Nation in the War of 1812. His statue actually does show that jacket and the famous medal given him by President George Washington. Now *I* think that is quite the thing!"

"Oh, yeah—me too, Mom."

As May arrived, Bridget boarded the *Canadiana*, anxious to begin the few weeks of briefing and orientation. The vessel was similar to the *River Queen*, though somewhat smaller. Bridget's position was mainly to provide assistance to anyone in need. She was to help with first aid and also make sure supplies were available for the women's rest rooms, handing white hand towels to those who used the facilities. Pausing at the railing one afternoon, overlooking the waters of Lake Erie, her thoughts went back to the orphanage in Ireland when the girls were taken for their annual outing to a nearby lake, a cherished time for her. And that long voyage across the vast ocean that brought her to her new land. Then there was Molly's tugboat and the *River Queen*. Funny how water always seems to be a part of my life. Her eyes teared up as she envisioned herself and Tom traveling on that packet boat down the Erie Canal on their honeymoon. She wiped her eyes, collecting herself. And now, here I am *again*—on the *Canadiana*.

This boat would have a constant stream of passengers, many of them youngsters, sailing to a "land of dreams," anticipating a day of frivolity on amusement park rides. Bridget was anxious for her maiden voyage, never having seen Crystal Beach, although Captain Foley had described much of it to her.

"I've been makin' these trips over there for many years, Bridget. It warms me heart ta see the happy faces and the broad smiles on these youngsters' faces when I pick 'em up. Sometime—not right now 'cause ya still got a lot ta learn—but sometime I'll let ya roam the park while the boat is docked. I might even go with ya! Ya might want to ride the Carousel or the Backety-Back Railway or the ..."

"Oh, I've been on that Railway, Captain Foley. They have one at Coney Island."

"Did ya live in New York, Bridget?"

"For a short time. I worked at the Mission of Our Lady of the Rosary for Irish Immigrant Girls. That was before I got married."

"I thought ya said ya worked on the *River ... River ...*"

"*River Queen*. Yes, I did. In fact, that's where I met my husband."

"So you're married to another sailor, eh?"

"*Was* married, Captain. He's been gone many years."

"So sorry to hear that, Bridget," the Captain offered in a sympathetic tone, reaching over and patting her hand.

The big day was suddenly upon them. It was sunny but windy, the swell of waves licking the side of the *Canadiana* as she was being prepared to leave the Buffalo harbor. Bridget was just as excited as the people coming up the gangplank, handing their tickets to Captain Foley, and rushing to find a good seat alongside the railing. The older children were quick to make their way to the top deck, many rushing to the bow, expecting to be the first to spot that paradise as they approached. Squeals of joy and anticipation were heard over all three levels as the clang of the hoisted gangplank and the chug of the engines were heard.

As the ship got underway, the Captain could be heard on his loudspeaker inviting the crowds to gather on the second floor. "Ladies and gentlemen ... and all you youngsters! Welcome to the *S.S. Canadiana*, the largest, finest, safest, and most up-to-date steel excursion steamer in the world! She was built right here in Buffalo, New York in 1910. I'm your Captain—Captain Foley." He reached up and tipped his cap to the crowd. "As we begin our little voyage, you may be interested to observe the rich mahogany décor and the beautiful brass railings and lighting fixtures. The grand stairways with the sweeping bannisters are another fine feature of the ship," as he pointed with a sweeping motion of his arm to the staircase. "And one of our most popular features is our large dance floor—if you glance downward, you will see you are standing on it!" He smiled. "Your voyage to Crystal Beach will be approximately one hour. Enjoy your trip—and the cooling breezes!"

Bridget's duties made the time fly by. Before she knew it, the Canadian shore could be detected in the distance, the giant roller coaster and the Ferris Wheel being the first to come into view. Suddenly, there was a mad dash to the bow. The crowd pointed excitedly toward the land ahead, the cool spray licking their faces. Coming closer, the cacophonous sounds of the carousel, the calliope, the Backety-back clatter, and the screams from the Ferris Wheel grew louder and louder as they approached, intensifying the excitement of those onboard. Bump! Bump! Bump! and the boat docked at the pier, releasing the gangplank with an ear-splitting crash. A sea of happy children quickly rushed down and stormed the immigration turnstile.

"Where were you born?"

"Buffalo."

And again and again, "Where were you born?"

And again and again, "Buffalo"—but for an occasional "Batavia" and "Rochester."

And off they flew! Scrambling over one another to be the first to get through the entrance gate.

Bridget had the whole afternoon to do her few small jobs while the people were at the park—sweeping the decks and cleaning the rest rooms. Afterward the Captain asked her to assist him in his office with some paper work. Finishing this, he took her for a tour of the Engine

Room below, where he introduced her to those “unseen workers” who were responsible for keeping the ship running smoothly.

The afternoon seemed to fly by, and before she knew it, the passengers were once again coming aboard. Bridget stood at the top of the gangplank as they approached. “That’s a mighty big sucker you have there!” she remarked to a youngster, laughing. He smiled at her but continued licking. “What flavor is that, little man?”

“Sim-a-mim.”

“Oh, yes! Cinnamon. I love that flavor!”

“Wanna lick it?” the child asked, holding his sucker up to Bridget.

“Oh, thank you, dear, but I’m so full from lunch—maybe later.”

“That should keep him occupied all the way back to Buffalo!” his mother stated. “Anyway, if by any chance he finishes it before we get back, I still have a butterscotch and a lemon in my bag here—but I doubt he will!” Bridget laughed.

The moonlight cruises were mostly quiet, couples dancing to the soft sounds of a four piece band as they sailed around Lake Erie. “Rhapsody in Blue” was a favorite on the boat, as was “It Had to be You”. On occasion, however, a request would be made from the younger people for the more lively “Charleston.”

Bridget couldn’t help but think of Tom holding her close as they danced at the ballroom that night on Coney Island. A feeling of melancholy came over her, as she turned and glanced out at the dark waters. The moonlight made a glimmering path of light which seemed to travel across those deep blue fathomless waters ending just at the spot where she stood.

Come on, let’s trip the light fantastic, me girl!

“Excuse me, Miss. Miss?”

Bridget was jolted from her memory. “Oh, I’m sorry. Yes, can I help you with something?”

“Yes. Could you direct me to the ladies’ room?”

“Of course. Actually, I was just on my way there myself.”

Things began to look up for Bridget and Teresa, as they worked into a routine after settling into their new apartment. They were quite content with the location which was halfway between downtown Buffalo where Teresa worked and the rapidly developing farm country north of the city where they hoped to settle one day. Bridget hopped the trolley in front of their apartment one afternoon to survey the area. She and Teresa had decided they would definitely try to save some of their earnings whenever possible, now that they *both* had jobs once again, with the hope of one day being able to purchase a plot of land and a home of their own.

Entering the Village of Kenmore, she was surprised to see so many homes already built or under construction. She decided to ride to the end of the line into Tonawanda with its open spaces and a few farms dotting the landscape. After dinner that evening, she was anxious to share her thoughts with her daughter. "I took the trolley up north this afternoon. Teresa, it's so nice there—just beautiful! Lots of houses already built ... churches ... farms. Anyway, I just had this feeling inside of me—like that's where we're gonna go one day. When we can, I think this will be the place. It's called Kenmore. Can't wait to show you."

"Sounds nice, Mom."

"I guess I've told you, honey, how your father and I used to talk about having our own house someday."

"Yup, you sure did, more than once!" Teresa smiled, then continued. "Well, I guess this is a good time then to tell you the good news."

"Good news? What? Tell me."

"I'm gonna get a raise very soon!"

"You're kidding!" Bridget looked puzzled. "How can that be? I mean ... well, you just started here a few months ago."

"But my seniority was transferred from the D.C. office to Buffalo. Great, huh?"

Bridget hugged her. "Wow! That's wonderful! This calls for a celebration!" She poured two glasses of white wine which she had put away for a special occasion. They immediately clinked their glasses together, laughing as they did. "Here's to our *own place*!"

"Yes, our very own place! Oh, Mom, I'm so happy!"

"Then it's agreed! I'm not getting any younger, you know!"

Chapter 19

Country Boy and City Girl

The apartment had a front veranda overlooking the cemetery across the road which Teresa took advantage of, especially on evenings when the temperature never seemed to fall below eighty degrees. She picked up the copy of "Ladies' Home Journal" from the table between the rocking chairs and began to fan herself. Oh! This heat! Wish it would cool down. "Hey, Mom! Bring me a cold drink, will ya?" she hollered, glancing toward the screen door.

"Lemonade or iced tea?" a voice hollered back.

"Oh, I don't care!" Her mind focused on the graves across the street. She had been pondering her mother's words about "not getting any younger" for some time and couldn't seem to get them out of her mind. It was one thing not to ever have had her father, but what if something happened to her *mother*. She dabbed the sweat from her forehead.

"Here you go, honey," Bridget said, handing her a glass of lemonade.

"Thanks."

Usually when Bridget took one of the rockers, Teresa would purposely make sure she would rock in unison with her mother, mostly because she thought it was funny. It was different this evening. She sat very still, not moving the rocker at all.

"Something bothering you, hon? You seem kinda sullen—not like yourself lately."

Teresa just shook her head from side to side. "No ... no, nothin', Mom."

"Now who do you think you're foolin', young lady? Come on. What's up?"

"Really, nothing." Teresa stared down at the worn wooden porch floor. "Well, actually ... well, it's just kinda that I worry sometimes."

"About what, honey?"

"Well, what if anything ever happens to you?" Teresa looked up at her mother, her eyes beginning to tear.

"Oh, honey! Oh, my gosh!" Bridget got up from her chair and leaned over to hold her daughter. "What in the world are you thinking?"

Teresa grabbed her around the waist, burying her head in her mother's apron. "Well, you know, with Dad never being with us ... well, it's just that if anything ever happens to you, I don't think I could stand being alone!"

Bridget stooped down and took Teresa's hands in hers. Looking up into her eyes, she emphatically stated, "*Nothing* is going to happen to me."

They held each other quietly for a few moments, Teresa finally breaking the silence. "Besides, what if I end up being an old maid?" The tears suddenly let loose, falling down her cheeks.

"Oh, so *that's* it!"

"Well, kinda *part* of it."

"Oh, honey! You're young and beautiful. You'll find someone—you'll see."

"Oh, I don't know if there'll ever be *anybody* who could compare with my Billy!"

Bridget's heart ached for the girl, knowing full well the pain of losing one you love.

Three weeks later, Teresa dropped her change purse as she was giving her carfare to the trolley conductor. A tall, handsome young man picked it up and handed it to her, tipping his hat and smiling. He didn't say a word, but she liked his face and good manners. "Oh, thank you, sir," she said as she sat down in a front seat facing the aisle. He took a seat directly opposite, looking over at her, still smiling. She glanced downward, a little self-conscious.

At the next stop, a man who had obviously had too much to drink, stepped onto the trolley. After paying his fare, he lost his balance and knocked off the young man's hat, causing it to fall right in front of Teresa. She bent over and picked it up, reaching across the aisle to hand it back to its owner. "Now it's *my* turn to say thank you," he stated. They both laughed, and her self-awareness seemed to disappear.

During the ride, she noticed that he kept glancing over at her from time to time. When her eyes met his, however, he then quickly looked away, and she wondered if he might be somewhat shy. She secretly hoped he would talk to her, but he never said a word. Maybe *I* should start a conversation— no, maybe not. It wouldn't be very ladylike. Besides, she remembered how her mother always said never to talk to strange men. She turned sideways on her seat, so as to be able to better look out the front window of the trolley and avoid any uncomfortable feelings.

Arriving at her stop on Delaware at Delavan, they both rose to exit the trolley simultaneously. He motioned to her to step ahead of him but immediately changed his mind and stepped down first, turning to offer his hand to assist her. Surprised, she hesitantly took his hand and thanked him once again, as she departed the trolley and stepped out into the rain, holding her purse over her head, hoping to protect her hair. They both ran to a nearby storefront with an awning. The rain continued to pour, drumming on the covering overhead, as they stood in their dry oasis next to baskets of fresh fruits and vegetables.

"Can I help you?" the old man asked with a strong Italian accent, smiling and wiping his hands on his long, dirty apron. His handlebar mustache made Teresa smirk, thinking it looked so silly.

The young man responded, "Well, no, we just ..."

"Here! You take one-a my nice apples for you and your lady. You look like such a nice couple—here, you two take an apple from Tony." His eyebrows rose up and down. "It's so nice to see young people like you—reminds me when my wife and I were young."

The young man was taken by surprise. "Oh, we're not together!"

"Wadda you mean?"

"Well," the young man said, "we just got off the trolley at the same time, but we actually don't know each other."

"Whatsa your name?"

"Joe—Joe Mang."

"Whatsa your name, young lady?"

"Teresa Sexton."

"Okay then," said Tony. "Joe, I want you to meet Teresa." Then looking over at Teresa—"This is Joe." He smiled. "Now there, look at that! The rain stopped! A good sign! Now you two just run along and make a good life for yerselves—ya look like ya belong together."

"Nice to meet you, Teresa," Joe remarked, shaking her hand.

"Well, you, too," she responded with a slight laugh.

"Are you going my way?" he asked her, pointing down the street.

"Why, yes. Yes, I am."

"You live around here?" He tossed his apple in the air as they began to walk, catching it on the way down.

"Yes, just a few minutes from here. How about you?"

"Well, I live in Kenmore," he said, taking a big bite from the fruit.

"So why did you get off here?" she inquired. "Aren't you a few miles from your home?"

"Well, because *you* did!" he responded with a wry smile. Before she could think of the next thing to say, he continued, "Well, to be honest, I wanted to talk with you on the trolley, but I didn't want to seem too forward or rude."

Teresa felt at ease with him. It was flattering getting a compliment from such a handsome young man; but, remembering her mother's warning, she was cautious as she knew nothing about him. Before long, she stopped. "This is where I live." She waited to see what he would say next, but he seemed at a loss for words. "Well, thank you for walking me home, Joseph."

He reached over and took her hand and shook it profusely. “It was very nice to meet you, Teresa.”

“I think you might have missed the last trolley, Joseph.”

“Oh, that doesn’t bother me. I like to walk—real good exercise. Besides, it’s not that far. Only about three or four miles!”

“Well, goodnight.” She turned and walked up the front steps. Looking back, she added, “Nice meeting you, too, Joe.”

He tipped his hat. “Maybe we’ll meet again.”

“Well ... maybe,” as she fumbled through her purse for her keys.

That evening, Bridget noticed a slight change in Teresa’s mood. After dinner she was humming a tune as she washed the dishes, occasionally breaking into song.

“After the ball is over, after the h-m-m-m-m
After the dancers’ leaving, h-m-m-m the stars are gone,
Many a heart is aching, if you could read them all—
H-m-m-m h-m-m-m h-m after the ball.”

“I love that tune, Teresa.”

“You do?”

“Yes. Actually, it reminds me of a beautiful evening long, long ago.” Bridget grabbed a towel and began drying. “You seem pretty happy tonight, honey.”

Teresa just smiled, continuing to wash the dishes. Bridget peered over her glasses and with a slight grin said, “Now listen Missy, something’s going on with you. Did you win a million dollars or something? You can’t fool your old mom, you know.”

“Oh, it’s nothing, Mom. Just a fella I met on the trolley and ...”

“I *knew* it. I knew something was going on in that little head of yours! How did you happen to meet? He’d better be a good, upright young man. Nothin’s too good for my daughter, you know!”

“Oh, Mom, I *just* met him. Maybe he won’t even call on me.”

“Well, he’ll be missin’ out if he don’t.”

Bridget felt that her own life was slipping by, as she was entering her fifties. Now she lived for her only child, doing what she could to make things better in her life.

A few weeks later, as summer was at its peak, Teresa came out on the porch, fanning herself with a magazine while holding a lemonade in the other hand. She never *could* stand the heat, especially on muggy days. It made her hair "droop," she always told her mother. And after all the time she spent with her curling iron, it was quite aggravating. Maybe there *was* something to that awful short haircut Betty made me get, after all. Oh, I don't even want to think about that nervy thing. Taking a seat on her favorite rocker and looking out over the porch railing, she noticed a crop of black wavy hair heading toward the house. She stood back up to see who was approaching, happy to see who the visitor was.

"Hi there," Joseph greeted her, as if he had come to visit an old friend.

"Oh, hello. I didn't recognize you at first."

"Well, I guess I was pretty wet when we met last," he said.

"You're right. We *both* were!" They laughed. "We probably looked like drowned rats!"

Standing at the foot of the porch steps, he reached into his pocket, taking out a handkerchief and wiping the sweat from his brow. "Hot one today, huh?" He seemed a little ill at ease until Teresa motioned for him to come up on the porch.

"Did you walk all the way from Kenmore again?"

"Yes, I did! It's good exercise, you know!"

"Yes, I *do* know. You told me that the *last* time, remember?"

"Uh, yeah. Yeah, that's right! I did, didn't I?" Caught in his pretext, he tried to think quickly. "Besides, I save a lot on carfare!" He was quite pleased with himself for his fast, clever response.

"How about a nice cold glass of lemonade?" she asked.

"Oh, yes! That would be great!."

"Please, sit down. I'll be right back." The screen door slammed behind her.

A few minutes later she returned with his drink. "Here you are—Joe, isn't it?" Teresa knew full well his name but felt it better he didn't understand how much she had been thinking of him.

"Oh, thanks—looks good." He took a quick sip of the cool refreshing beverage. "And yes ... yes, it *is* Joe!"

Teresa soon detected that Joe was a man of few words, as she seemed to be the one to keep the conversation going. "You work around here?" she asked.

"Yes, I work at the Pierce-Arrow Plant over on Elmwood Avenue."

"Oh. What do you do there?"

"I work in Timekeeping, but I don't think I'll be there much longer."

"Oh, really? How come?" She thought maybe she shouldn't have asked, wondering if he would feel she was prying.

"Well, I recently took this test ..."

"Oh? What kind of test?"

"For a policeman."

"Gee, that sounds great! A cop, huh? In Kenmore? Where you live?"

"Yep."

Teresa wished that Joe was more forthcoming. I don't like having to "pull" everything out of him with questions. Oh, well ... "So tell me, Joseph, how long have you lived there—in Kenmore?"

"All my life. My folks own a farm there. Been in the family for a couple generations."

"You know, my Mom always talks about buying a piece of land there and maybe growing our own food." She leaned her head on the back of the rocker, but suddenly noticed a spider building a web in the corner of the ceiling above her. She cringed, leaped off her chair, and quickly jumped away.

"Oh, it's only a little spider, Teresa," Joe offered as he reached up and squashed the spider between his fingers.

"O-o-o-o!" she exclaimed with a squeamish look on her face, turning away. "How could you *do* that?"

"Well, when you live on a farm, you get used to that stuff," he said, wiping his fingers on his overalls. "Come on, Teresa, sit down. He can't hurt you now!" He snickered.

"Are you spoofin' me, Joseph?"

"Naw—I wouldn't do that."

"You *are*!"

Joseph was unaware that Teresa was simply spoofin' him back and decided to return to the pre-spider subject. "So you were saying—about your Mom and her interest in Kenmore. You know, I just overheard my folks talking about selling off some of their land the other night."

"Oh, really? Gee, I'd love to see your farm sometime and ..." She hesitated. "Oh, but I'm not sure if we could afford anything quite yet."

Joe, not wishing to miss another opportunity to spend time with Teresa, responded quickly. "Well, I could *still* show it to you—anytime at all, Teresa."

"Gosh, I'm not sure, Joseph, if that's a good idea. I wouldn't want Mom to get all interested right now. After all, we did just move in here from D.C."

"Oh, sure. I understand. Anyway, keep it in mind," he said, disappointed at the missed opportunity. "I didn't realize you just moved in."

The storm clouds had grown darker and darker, and soon a cool breeze swept across the porch bringing with it a fine spray of rain. "Oh, doesn't that feel good, Joe?" Teresa asked, glad the mugginess in the air would soon dissipate.

"Yeah, sure does. Now, tell me, Teresa, you said you just came from Washington?"

"Yes, but we used to live in Buffalo years back—in the First Ward—when I was younger." Before he could respond, she continued, "Then Mom and I moved to New York City."

"New York? No kidding."

"Yes. You see, I had an opportunity to go to school at the Cooper Union there. And then, my training was continued at the Western Union Office."

"Western Union? You mean you do telegraph work?"

"Oh, yes. That's my job now. That's my trade. I just recently was transferred here to the Buffalo office."

"But, I thought you said you came from Washington."

"Yes, I did. We moved to D.C. because I was offered a better position there at the Italian Embassy. Better pay." Teresa decided not to bring up any further details about the move back to Buffalo.

Joseph noticed there was no mention of Teresa's father as she spoke of life in three cities. Hoping he was not being too forward, he asked, "Teresa, you never mention your father. Is your father still living?"

"We don't know." Joseph looked puzzled. "Well, you see, he went missing right after I was born." She glanced down at the floor. "And ... well, anyway, we don't like to talk about it—Mom and I. She gets really depressed."

Joseph felt very uncomfortable. He felt he had spoken out of turn and decided not to pursue the subject. "Well, sounds like your job must be really interesting!"

"Oh, it is—*very* interesting." She hesitated. "It can be very difficult at times though, as well. Like, for instance, when the first reports came in about the Titanic."

"Gosh, I can't even imagine."

"Well, at first there was hope. They were putting people into the lifeboats. But as the night wore on, messages were fewer and fewer and sounded more distressing, and it went on and on. And then there was nothing at all coming through. It was horrible!"

Joseph could see that her eyes were tearing up and knew she would probably never forget it. "I'm so sorry you had to go through that, Teresa. I know just a little of the horror of it. Our neighbor, Henry Sutehall, was on that ship."

"Really? Your neighbor?"

"Yes, he was lost. He and another man from this area—Edward Austin Kent, an architect." Joseph stood up. "I hope I haven't upset you."

"It's okay. I'm okay."

"Well, I guess I'd best be going. Looks like the rain is letting up. Thanks for the lemonade," as he set his glass on the railing.

"Oh," she said, surprised at his short visit, "thanks for stopping by." She watched him walking down the street, turning once to wave goodbye. I hope he comes again. He's nice.

Since most people had no cars or telephones at that time, Joseph's communication with Teresa occurred when he walked to her house or took a trolley. A few weeks later, however, their paths crossed—this time at the Buffalo Zoo. Teresa, with her friend, Harriet, from Western Union, were enjoying the capers of the monkeys in the warm, summer sunshine when she felt a tap on the back of her right shoulder. "Hello again," Joe said. "Fancy meeting you here!"

"Oh, my gosh! Hi Joseph. Where did *you* come from?"

"I was just taking a bill to the office here," he remarked, nodding over to Harriet so as not to ignore her presence.

"A bill?" Teresa asked inquisitively.

"Yes. We supply the zoo with feed for the animals. I mean, my Dad grows it on the farm and we sell it to them."

"Gee, you must have an awfully big farm to feed all these animals!"

Joe laughed. "Oh, no. We only supply *some* of their needs—wheat, oats, and barley. They buy from other farmers as well."

Harriet cleared her throat. "Oh, I'm sorry, Harriet," Teresa apologized. "I want you to meet Joseph Mang. Joe, this is my friend, Harriet Bender—we work together."

"Nice to meet you, Harriet," Joe offered.

Harriet nodded and smiled. "Same here."

"I'm glad I ran into you, Teresa. Actually, I was going to stop by your house to see if you'd like to come to our church social next Sunday."

"Well," Teresa replied, stalling as though considering what was on her social calendar. "Well, yes, I think I'm free on Sunday."

"Great! I'll pick you up at one o'clock." He turned to leave, tipping his cap as he did so.

Walking back to Teresa's home through Delaware Park, Harriet reached over, grabbing Teresa's arm. "Wow, Teresa! Where did you ever find *him*? He's so handsome!"

"Isn't he? I think so, too. Actually, we met by chance on the trolley."

"Really? How's that?"

"Well, I dropped my change purse when I was trying to pay the conductor."

"And?"

"That's all. He picked it up for me."

"What a lucky break, Teresa!"

"I don't know him very well yet, but he does seem nice. Maybe a little on the shy side though."

One other mode of transportation was available on rare occasions to young Joseph—his father's horse and buggy. These occasions usually came to be after much persuasion by the lad.

Joseph pulled up in front of Teresa's home promptly at one o'clock the following Sunday. "Whoa, Annabelle!" he hollered, pulling tightly on the reins. Teresa had been watching for him through the living room window, not wanting to appear too anxious to see him by waiting on the porch. He jumped down from the buggy, bounding up the front steps two at a time, and knocked three times loudly on the door.

Teresa quickly glanced in the mirror, pinching her cheeks to give them color and checking to see if her hair looked alright, primping it with her fingers. She wondered if Joseph would think she looked pretty. Well, he'd better, after spending all this time with my curling iron. "Oh, Joseph! How nice to see you again," she offered as though she hadn't even expected him, although she had taken two hours to ready herself for this meeting. Her favorite pink dress with the pleated skirt had been taken from the closet and hung on the bedroom door two days prior, the matching hat adorning the dresser top next to it.

"Up you go!" as Joe assisted Teresa onto the buggy. She opened her parasol, shielding herself from the glaring sun. "Okay, Annabelle! Off we go!" He pulled the reins to the left, and the horse turned around, heading back toward Kenmore. Crossing the city line and entering into the Village, Teresa noticed new home construction in the first few blocks. Soon after they passed a large farmhouse on the corner of Mang Avenue. "This is where I live, Teresa."

"Oh, what a big house!" Looking around, she asked, "And is this all your land?"

"Well, most of it. We did own those three blocks under construction back there, but my father sold them off to a builder." Joe pulled up behind the church, tying the horse to the wooden fencepost there.

"Is this a *new* church, Joseph?"

"It's *fairly* new. My father donated three acres of his land, and he and a few other farmers built it."

"That's wonderful! I'm impressed!"

"Well, he's a generous man; but most of all, his faith was extremely important to him. Besides, a church was badly needed around here so everybody wouldn't have to take that long ride up to St. Joe's on Main Street, especially during the cold winters—we all had open buggies. I remember when I was a kid, having to hold a blanket over my head during blizzards. Didn't keep me from freezing, though!"

Joe helped Teresa from the buggy, and they began to stroll around, looking over the tables laden with all kinds of homemade pies, cakes, cookies, and other delights.

"Oh, look, Joe! Fudge!"

"Like that?"

"Mmm—*Hmm*!"

"Two pieces, please," as he took some change from his pocket. "Here you go!" handing one to Teresa, who began to nibble little bites so as to make it last longer.

Some children ran by, chasing each other, and some boys were playing baseball out in the field. A group of men were playing horseshoes; however, many more could be seen under the tent which housed a few barrels of beer. Some women had peaches and pears and tomatoes in Mason jars on a nearby table, the sign in front reading: "*Donation only— Assist the Poor of our Parish.*" And the Holy Name Society was cooking hotdogs next to the church.

"Come on over here, Teresa," Joe said, taking her by the arm and leading her to a nearby table. "I want you to meet some of my family." He introduced her to the many Mang relatives—brothers, sisters, cousins, nieces, aunts and uncles. "Where's Mom and Dad, Louie?" he asked his younger brother.

"Haven't seen 'em yet, Joe. Com'on, have a seat."

"Gonna go get something to drink right now, Lou. Catch ya later."

Teresa, waving her hand slightly toward the group, remarked, "Nice to meet all of you." She turned to Joseph. "Oh, my gosh, Joseph! This is all your *family*?"

"That's only part of 'em, Teresa," he chuckled. "Come on, let's go get a Coke—I'm thirsty, aren't you?" He wiped his forehead with his handkerchief.

"Sounds good to me. It's awfully warm today!"

"Here you go, ladies," Joe said with a smile, handing one of the buxom women two nickels in exchange for two green glass bottles of the cold beverage. Handing one to Teresa, he took her by the hand and led her to a small bench beneath a tree, preferring to spend a few moments alone with her before the rest of the clan showed up.

"Oh, my gosh!" Teresa exclaimed. "Do you know how lucky you are to have such a wonderful family around?"

"Well, I guess. I mean, everybody has families."

"Well, no. Everybody *doesn't*." Teresa noticed by the look on his face that her comment puzzled him. "You know, I really never knew *any* of my relatives, Joseph. It's just been my mom and me since I was born."

"You mean, you don't even have *any* other relatives?"

"No. I was just a baby when my father disappeared, and my mom came from an orphanage in the old country 'cause her people were all wiped out in the potato famine."

"I'm sorry, Teresa. Sorry."

"It's okay, Joseph."

"Oh, here they come now!"

"Who?"

"My mother and father. Here they come!" He pointed to them, walking across the fields from the farmhouse. "Come on!" He took her hand, pulling her to her feet, and they headed over to greet them.

"Joseph! Did you give Annabelle any water since you left?" his father immediately inquired.

"Uh, actually, I was just about to do that, Pa ..." He hesitated momentarily. "But I just want to introduce you first to my friend, Teresa."

"How do you do?" Frank offered, reaching his hand outward to shake hers.

"Yes, how do you do, Teresa?" Joseph's mother added.

"Joseph, you really *must* water the horse!" Frank looked over at Teresa, apologetically. "Sorry, but these horses ... well, they just gotta have water on these hot days."

"Come on, Teresa. Come with me. I really have to take care of Annabelle."

"I understand, Joseph."

"The water trough is right back here, Teresa," as he untied the horse from the post.

"Oh, my gosh! He sure *was* thirsty, poor thing!"

"It's a *she*—I wouldn't name a male horse Annabelle, silly!" Joe laughed.

"Oh, of course!" Teresa smiled. "Gee, I hope nobody took our bench. It was the only one that was in the shade."

"Sorry, Teresa. Looks like somebody stole it right out from under us!" Joseph looked around for another spot, but to no avail. Noticing a few moments later that the couple on the bench seemed to be getting ready to leave, he instructed Teresa, "Hurry over there and stand next to the bench while I get us some hot dogs. Then grab it the minute they get up—before anybody else gets a chance." His plan worked well, and they once again had a shady spot to sit for their lunch. He thought he might put his arm around her, but decided against it. "I'm still hungry—are you?" She didn't have a chance to answer. "Wait here and I'll grab us some cherry pie." Teresa enjoyed simply sitting there and staring out at the open fields of corn and wheat between the church and Joseph's farm.

"Did you forget the pie, Joseph?" as she watched him returning empty-handed.

"Would you believe they were all out of cherry? My favorite, too!" He looked disappointed.

"How ironic! No cherry pie when right over there are a million cherry trees!" She laughed.

"Yeah! Come on! We'll go take a walk," he said with a grin, leading her the short distance to the orchard. "There you go! Cherry pie galore, minus the crust! All you can eat!" as he pulled a branch down.

A gentle cooling breeze drifted through the orchard, playing with a few locks of her hair, blowing some onto the side of her pretty face. He wanted to brush it away but thought this might seem too forward. Suddenly, however, without thinking, he found himself leaning over and kissing her quickly on the cheek.

She lifted her hand to her face, taken by surprise yet pleasantly pleased. "Oh, Joseph!" she remarked, not knowing what else to say or do. She felt a warmth come over her face but wasn't sure if she was blushing or if it was just the heat of the day.

"You're really pretty, Teresa." She glanced downward, thinking he apparently wasn't so shy as she had previously thought.

She couldn't wait for her mother to get home that evening, wanting to share with her the lovely afternoon she'd had at St. Paul's social, but this was Bridget's Sunday evening dinner cruise and she'd be working late. Falling asleep on the sofa, Teresa was suddenly awakened about midnight when her mother finally arrived home. "Teresa, what are you doing up so late? Don't you have to work tomorrow?"

"Yeah, sure I do, Mom. But I just wanted to tell you about my day—it was so nice."

"You mean that church social you told me about?"

"Yes. I had such a nice time. And Mom, you should see all the relatives that Joseph has! Such a big family!"

"Did you meet his folks? Were they there?"

"Yes."

"And?"

"Well, I really didn't get much of a chance to talk with them. Joseph had to go right away to water Annabelle."

"Annabelle?"

"Oh, that's their horse. He picked me up with his Dad's horse and buggy."

"Oh."

"So anyway, when his parents showed up, his Dad was more concerned with the horse getting water, so Joseph and I had to go do that right away. Then, by the time we finished, his dad had joined some of the men playing cards and his Mom was helping sell the pies. So we really didn't spend any more time with them. We kinda sat in the shade and then walked through their orchard eating crustless cherry pie!" Teresa grinned, thinking her mother wouldn't understand what she was talking about.

"Crustless cherry pie?" Bridget asked, then immediately added, "Oh, I get it! Think you can fool your old mom, eh?" she laughed. "Come on, now, you funny one! Better get to bed. It's awfully late—morning comes fast." She hugged Teresa and turned off the lights.

The work week passed quickly. "Again? Again, Teresa? Gosh, you just saw him last week!"

"Well, we made plans to go to Niagara Falls today with Harriet and Ted, Mom. He's Harriet's fiance'—he's got a Tin Lizzie! That's what he calls his car! Funny, huh?"

"I really think I'd better meet this Joseph. It's only proper, Teresa," Bridget answered, as though she hadn't heard a word her daughter said.

"Well, gosh, Mom! You're always working when he comes around."

Bridget simply continued, "I don't even know him. So I think you'd better have him come in here before you go anywhere."

"Okay, I will. But you know, Mom, maybe sometime you could just come out with us for a day—that would give you a chance to *really* get to know him. Besides, it might do you good. All work and no play, you know..." Teresa had always felt some sadness as she left to go anywhere, leaving her mother alone at home. She wanted so much to see her have a little social life and some fun.

"Oh, but honey, you know I have to work."

"See what I mean?" Teresa seemed frustrated. "Gee! You'd think Captain Foley could do without you for one day!" A horn beeped and footsteps were heard bounding up the stairs. "Here he is, Mom!"

"How do you do, young man," Bridget said.

"Oh, fine, Ma'am. Very nice to meet you." Joseph wasn't sure if he should reach over to shake her hand but decided to anyway. Bridget noticed his hand felt callused as he took hers in a firm grip. He must be a hard worker, she thought. She could see her daughter seemed quite pleased to have her mother finally meet him.

"I hear you're going to be a policeman, Joseph."

"Yes, Ma'am. Still waiting to get called."

"Well, I guess I won't have to worry about Teresa when she's with a policeman-to-be!"

"Oh, yes, Ma'am. I'll take good care of her. Don't you worry." Teresa was trying to hold back a smile, seeing how seriously Joseph took her mother's words.

"I guess we really should get going, Mom. Harriet and Ted are waiting."

"Go along then. Not too late though."

"We'll just be up at Niagara Falls, Ma'am. It's not too far and I'll have her back at a decent hour."

Teresa kissed her mother goodbye. "I'm really excited about seeing it!"

Bridget sat down on the sofa, thoughts of Fr. Donohue taking Tom and her to view the Falls that day so long back as they made their way to Buffalo. Such happy times ... such happy times. It seemed like flashbacks were jumping through her mind, one after another. Tom. The Falls. Fr. Donohue. Tom. The gorge. That rainbow. The rapids. Tom. Tom. Those ever-present memories brought forward once again from the deep recesses of her heart. Tears fell.

Arriving at the Falls, Teresa was stunned by the beauty before her. "Oh, my gosh! How awesome!—absolutely awesome! Isn't this *beautiful*, Harriet?" She was so engrossed with the view, she hadn't even noticed the spray from the Falls had taken the curl from her hair.

"Wait 'til you see it from the *Canadian* side!" Harriet answered.

"Right! But now, we're going down into the Cave of the Winds," Ted said.

"Come on, Teresa," Joseph said, taking her by the hand. They entered a room where their valuables were checked, after which they were issued flannel garments covered with oilskins and felt slippers for their feet. Joseph pulled Teresa's hood up over her now-straight hair and tied the strings tightly under her chin before they began the descent down the wooden staircase, walking into a fine mist from the gigantic cascade before them. As they grew closer, the deluge and roar of that magnificent wonder grew louder and louder. Teresa clutched the railing tightly with one hand and Joseph's arm with the other. She was getting extremely anxious about the whole thing, feeling it was very dangerous. She turned to Harriet but saw no indication that *she* felt any uneasiness, although this did nothing to reduce her stress.

"Oh, Joe! Let's go back!" she exclaimed, frightened.

"Oh, just a little further," he insisted, raising his voice so she could hear above the thunder of the cascading water. "You can do it. We're almost there."

She stopped. "*I'm* going back," she yelled.

"Okay," he shouted back to her, turning once more to behold the beauty of the majestic sight before him.

Their wet garments were deposited at the drying room, and Joseph picked up his wallet and watch from the office. Ted and Harriet soon returned and did likewise.

"Wow! That was really, really amazing! You guys should have stayed," Ted announced. "Well, anyway, I don't know about you, but *I'm* starved!" The foursome found a quiet spot in the park away from the crowd and sat down beneath a large maple tree. "You three stay here and keep our good spot—I'll get the lunch from the car."

Teresa spread the tablecloth out on the grassy knoll. "Thanks for packing this, Harriet," as she took a large, crusty loaf of Italian bread and a large brick of cheddar cheese from the basket.

"Oh, you're welcome. There's apples and sugar cookies too, Teresa. I don't know about the lemonade—the ice is probably melted by now. Hope it's not too watery."

Enjoying the lunch, Joe suddenly burst into laughter. "What the heck you laughing at, Joe?" Ted asked.

"Just thinkin' how you two looked like a couple of drowned rats when you came up!"

"Well, yeah," Ted snickered. "Kinda felt that way, too! Pass the cookies and a little more of that hot lemonade!"

"Sorry, all the ice melted," Harriet said apologetically.

"Oh, honey, I'm only joshin ya!" Ted replied, leaning back on his elbow, tossing a few blades of grass in the air. "You know, they call this the 'Honeymoon Capital of the World.'"

Joseph squeezed Teresa's hand. "Yeah, great place for a honeymoon!" he nodded, staring at her.

"Speaking of honeymoons, won't we be going over the Honeymoon Bridge to Canada?" Harriet asked

"Absolutely. We'll go as soon as we're done eating," Ted answered.

The bridge was crowded, being a weekend. "Now, Teresa," Joe said, "they will be asking you where you were born."

"Really? Why would they care where I was born?"

"Oh, it's just security stuff," Joe answered.

"Yeah," Ted interrupted. "Once I said I was born in 'Boof-a-lo,' thinking it was funny. But I was sorry afterward 'cause they detained me for an hour, thinking I was a foreigner or something. You can't fool around with this stuff."

After passing through Customs, they followed the signs leading them to the Whirlpool Aero Car. Oh my gosh! What in the world? Teresa's mind began racing, as they approached the attraction before them. "Joseph, I'm not sure ..."

"How many?" the operator asked.

"Four," Joseph answered, as Teresa was tugging at his sleeve, hoping to get her comment in before he answered the man.

Waiting for the aerial tramway to return to its landing spot, the operator gave a short introduction to the ride.

> *"Sometimes called the Spanish Aerocar, it was developed in Bilboa, Spain by engineer Leonardo de Torres Quevedo and has been in operation since 1916. Suspended by six steel cables, it travels 250 feet above the whirlpool—a thrilling trip over the vortex of water."*

"O-o-o-o, it looks like a big red basket hanging out there, Joseph," Teresa remarked, a foreboding feeling coming over her as she watched it make its way back to the landing.

"Step aboard, ladies and gentlemen!" the operator announced after the passengers had disembarked.

"I don't think I'll go, Joseph," Teresa stated, leaving go of his hand, as she turned and started back to the road.

"Teresa, *come on*." Harriet encouraged. "It's perfectly safe. And beautiful to see. I've been on it before. Come *on*." She caught up with Teresa and took her by the hand, almost dragging her onto the car.

"Don't worry," Joseph reassured her. "You're safe. There's a policeman on board."

"Where?" Teresa asked, looking around at the others.

"Right here," Joe announced, pointing his thumb to his chest and placing his left arm tightly around Teresa's waist, hoping to comfort her.

"Oh, Joseph!" Teresa couldn't help smiling. Just then the car lurched from the landing and she found herself hanging high above the swirling waters below. Something happened inside her stomach—something that didn't feel too pleasant. She tried closing her eyes, but her mind still told her it was a very, very long way down. She found herself burying her face tightly into Joseph's chest, turning her head only to catch a breath of air but never opening her eyes. She could hear his heart beating. It seemed so steady, just like Joseph seemed to be. He held her tightly.

"It's only a ten-minute ride," he mentioned, not indicating that was the one-way time. She didn't answer. "Did you hear me, Teresa?"

"Mmm—Hmm," she responded, nodding her head up and down against his chest.

"You're missing it, Teresa!" Harriet said. Again no response. "Teresa, listen—try just putting your hand over one eye."

"Can't," came a muffled voice.

"It's okay, Harriet," Joseph said, shaking his head back and forth, indicating to the girl not to pressure Teresa.

Suddenly, Teresa seemed to lose that fear, feeling some relief at his remark. It was a feeling of protection—of someone who stood up for her—of someone she could rely on—of someone who would care for her. It was that same feeling she always had when she was with Billy years ago. That strong solid steady presence—comforting—sweet. This reassurance in her heart showed her that she *could* open her eyes and look at the beauty in the gorge. Still, not wanting to leave her "spot of comfort," she hesitated a few minutes longer.

"Here we are! The halfway point!" Ted announced.

"Maybe I could take just a little peek," Teresa said softly, lifting her head upwards from Joe's chest but not opening her eyes.

"Sure, go ahead, honey," Joe answered. "Your 'parking spot' will still be here if you need it!" He kept one arm around her while turning her slightly to face the side of the car. "Okay, open up!"

She opened her eyes, trying to relax, but grasped his hand tightly in her own. She decided she wouldn't look down however, keeping her gaze straight ahead. "It *is* pretty!"

"There you go! I knew you could do it!" Joe kissed her lightly on her cheek. It felt nice. She wanted to hold her hand on that spot as though to "cement" it in place but decided against it. She noticed Harriet watching her and grinning, as if she understood what she was thinking. "I'm really proud of you, Missy Brave One!" Joe remarked as they once again stepped on solid ground.

It was only a short distance to the Horseshoe Falls. The close view of the roaring cataract was thrilling, as a beautiful rainbow drew its colors across the mist. "Oh! Look, Joe! A rainbow! I *love* rainbows! Don't *you*?"

They were soaked by the spray but didn't seem to mind. So many couples holding hands seemed almost in romantic ecstasy, and it was obvious a great number were newlyweds. She knew Harriet and Ted would be planning their marriage soon and wondered if they would come back on their honeymoon. "I need a towel. My hair is dripping." Teresa was a little uncomfortable, wondering if she looked less than pretty but knowing there was nothing she could do about it.

"Me, too," Harriet announced. They laughed as they pushed their wet hair back behind their ears.

"*Natural* beauties!" Ted quipped, always having some remark for any occasion. "Come on, my beauty—into the Tin Lizzie!" he instructed Harriet. The ride home was filled with joy, the four starting a round of "Little Brown Jug," one of Joe's favorite songs.

"Quite good, I would say," Ted remarked. "We could easily land a radio job, I'm sure! I can drop you off first, Joe. It's on the way."

"Oh, that's okay, Ted. Maybe it would be better to take Teresa first. I like to walk from her house—the exercise, you know. It's good for you."

"Oh, yeah, sure, Joe. The exercise! I understand," Ted remarked, hoping Teresa couldn't see him grinning.

It was dark now, but Teresa could see Bridget was still up with the lights on in the living room. "We could sit on the porch a little while," Joe offered.

"Oh, I don't know, Joe. Mom's still up."

"She can come out and sit with us."

"I don't think so—she's probably ready for bed. Gotta work tomorrow, you know."

"Oh."

"As a matter of fact, I do, too. I really think I'd better get in."

Joseph was disappointed and didn't want to leave. Taking her hand in his, he bent over and kissed her on the cheek.

"I'm sorry you have to walk all the way home now, Joseph." It wasn't too difficult to understand why he had asked Ted to drop her off first.

"Oh, I don't mind. It's good ..."

"Exercise—I know!" she interrupted. What a sweetheart he is! She quickly returned his kiss, surprising him. He bounced down the stairs, whistling "Little Brown Jug" as he did.

Bridget was contented with her job on the *Canadiana* and enjoyed meeting new people every day, especially the little ones. Their excitement was so palpable as the boat would approach the landing at Crystal Beach, parents having to hold their children's hands tightly as the gangplank crashed down and the crowd pushed forward to disembark. Thinking ahead at times, she wondered about her future when Fall would come and the boat would stop running until the following year. They could always rely upon Teresa's job, of course; however, Bridget didn't want to be dependent upon her daughter. Well, I'm not going to worry about that right now.

One evening that summer, shortly after Joe and Teresa went to Niagara Falls, mother and daughter sat outside, using magazines to fan themselves from the extreme heat and oppressive humidity. "How was your day, honey?" Bridget asked.

"Hot. Hot, Mom. All our windows were wide open at work, and all the fans did was blow that hot air around." She wiped the sweat on her forehead with the back of her hand. "And how was *your* day, Mom? I bet you caught a nice cool breeze sailing around out there on the water."

Watching the sun setting in the distance and continuing to fan herself, Bridget replied, "Oh, yes, I do enjoy standing on the upper deck near the bow when I get a break. It's so refreshing! Some days, when the wind is just right, a fine mist sweeps right across."

"Sounds great. I kinda envy you."

Neither one spoke for a moment. The only sound to be heard was the rhythmic squeak of Bridget's rocker on the wooden floor of the porch. Teresa thought her mom had a pensive look on her face. "What's up, Mom? Whacha thinkin' about?"

"Oh, I was just wondering how your date with Joseph went the other day. Did you have a good time?"

"Oh, Mom!" Teresa exclaimed, smiling. "Yes, it was wonderful! The Falls were gigantic! I never realized the enormity of it all!"

"I know. It's beautiful! Dad and I were there on our honeymoon."

"You spent your honeymoon there? I didn't know that."

"Well, not exactly. We came through there on our way here from New York City and a good priest-friend took us around a little."

"Oh. Well, I'm glad you had a chance to see it anyway." She reached over and squeezed her mother's hand. "I love you, Mom." She wanted to continue sharing her pleasant time with her mother but felt she should take a break from it momentarily. "Let me get you a drink, Mom. Want some ice water or iced tea?"

"Oh, no thanks, honey. I'm fine. But go ahead—tell me about the rest of your trip."

"Well, we started out and went down into this place called the "Cave of the Winds" but I got scared and didn't make it. So I ended up getting soaked for no reason." She laughed.

"Oh, no!"

"Yeah, and I guess I wasn't a very good date for Joseph. I'm afraid I put a little damper on everybody's day actually."

"Really? How's that? I mean, was the day really spoiled?"

"Well, sorta. When we got to the Aero Car, I just didn't want to be on that thing at all. It looked so awfully scary and ... well, I just tried to get out of it. But then Harriett grabbed my hand and actually pulled me."

"What? *Pulled* you?"

"Mmm—Hmm. But it all worked out okay after all. I just hid my face and wouldn't look. My stomach did flip-flops. It's a wonder I didn't throw up, I felt so awful!"

"Oh, my gosh! So what did you do? You couldn't get off, could you?"

"No. It started right out across the gorge, so when Harriett tried to get me to look, I just kept my face hidden. And then, Joe indicated to Harriett to leave me be. He was great—kinda stickin' up for me. I felt a little better and ... well, it seemed like I lost some of that fear. And ... well, after a while I did look out—but I didn't look *down*! And he held me tight and it kinda gave me this protected feeling. And it ended up that I really did have a good time after all."

"Well! That's quite a story!"

"He's real nice, Mom."

"Oh? Do I detect this is getting a little serious? Kinda soon, Teresa."

Teresa ignored the question. "He's like ... well, he's kind and understanding. And I just feel good when I'm with him. You really have to get to know him, Mom—he's a real gentleman—really he is."

"Well, he'd better be! Nothin's too good for my daughter, you know."

"Yes, I *know*, Mom!"

"Well, the little I've seen of him—he seems like a decent fellow."

"Oh, he *is*!"

Bridget smiled. "I've been thinking about how I could get to know him better."

"What's that, Mom?"

"Well, just yesterday, I talked to Captain Foley and he gave me next Saturday off. Maggie's gonna stand in for me, and the three of *us* are invited to cruise over to the Beach and have a day of fun—you and me and Joseph!"

"Really? No kidding! That would be wonderful! I do so want you to get to know him better."

Saturday morning was perfect—bright sun, wispy white clouds, and a cool breeze. "Answer the door, Teresa! I have to finish packing the lunch."

"Oh, no, I can't, Mom! I haven't even combed my hair yet! Can't you get it?"

"Joseph, how nice to see you again. Teresa will be out in a moment." He tipped his cap and sat down on the porch steps.

Bridget went back inside, the screen door slamming behind her, only to be re-opened in a few moments. Teresa sat next to Joe on the top step. He immediately pulled his cap from his head. She thought he looked exceptionally handsome, his curly hair almost having a fuzzy look to it. It made her want to run her fingers through it. Before they could say anything, however, a taxi cab pulled up in front and a well-dressed man in a three-piece suit stepped out and walked up to the house.

"Does Bridget Sexton live here?" he asked.

Teresa was immediately impressed with his appearance. "Why yes, that's my mother. I'll get her for you."

"Tell her an old friend is inquiring. Flynn's the name—Jim Flynn."

Teresa went inside. "Mom! Mom! There's this *gorgeous* gentleman outside, and he's inquiring for *you*!"

"How do you do, young man?" Flynn held out his right hand toward Joseph who came down the steps to greet him.

"How do you do, sir. I'm Joseph—Joseph Mang—but most people call me Joe." He took Flynn's hand and shook it profusely.

The screen door slammed. "Jim! Is it really *you*?" Bridget scurried down the steps, throwing her arms around his neck and hugging him as Teresa and Joe looked on in amazement. "I can't believe it! Oh my gosh! I'm so happy to see you!"

"You, too, Bridget," Jim responded, removing his straw hat and returning the hug. "It's been a long time." He stood back, still holding her hands, and smiled broadly. "You haven't changed a bit!"

"And neither have *you*," she quipped, hugging him again. "What brings you to Buffalo? How did you find me?"

"Business—company business. Much of our shipping covers the Great Lakes, remember?"

"But, how did you find *me*?"

"Well, it wasn't all that difficult since we have a register of all the boats on Lake Erie, you know. And I happened across the name of the *Canadiana* and saw that it sailed from Buffalo to Canada. Anyway, Bridget, I remembered you worked on the *River Queen* and wondered if possibly you might be working on another vessel around here. So I checked into the roster of employees."

"I can't believe it! I just can't believe it!"

Teresa cleared her throat. "Oh, sorry Teresa," her mother apologized. "Jim, I want you to meet my daughter. And this is her friend, Joseph."

"Yes, we met—Joe and I. I'm very pleased to meet *you*, Teresa." He reached over and took her hand in his, shaking it lightly. "And you're just as pretty as your mom!"

Bridget smiled, inviting all to come up on the porch. "I'll get some cold drinks. Please sit down," she invited Jim.

"Thank you," Jim responded, seating himself on Bridget's squeaky rocker and placing his hat on the porch rail. Teresa kept her eye on the fine gentleman, her head spinning with thoughts.

Handsome! Single? Looks about Mom's age. Wonder why he *really* came.

"Here we go!" Bridget announced, handing out the refreshing looking lemonade, the ice clinking in the glasses.

Jim lifted his glass toward her. "And here's to the renewal of old acquaintances!" They all followed his lead and did likewise.

"So, anyway," Teresa stated, placing her half-empty glass on the railing, "I hope you two wouldn't mind if Joe and I left for a short while. You see, he had just mentioned how nice it would be to take a walk on such a beautiful day!" Noticing by the look on his face that Joe was about to question her statement, she quickly took his glass, depositing it next to hers, and grabbed his hand. "Come *on*, Joe!" as she headed down the steps.

"Not too long now, Teresa," her mother cautioned. We have to leave in about forty-five minutes, you know," understanding full well what her daughter was up to.

"Oh, I'm so sorry, Bridget," Jim stated. "I guess I came at an inopportune time."

"No. No, not at all. We're just going over to Canada for the day." She hesitated for a slight moment. "Oh, won't you come with us? That would be great! Come with us!"

"Oh, I wouldn't want to intrude."

"You wouldn't be intruding, Jim. I'd love it if you'd come. Besides, wouldn't you like to see the *Canadiana*?"

Jim glanced down at his suit, pulling the vest outward from his chest. "I'm a little overdressed, I think. Maybe I could take my suitcoat and vest off?"

"Then you'll come?"

"I'd be delighted. Is Tom coming? Is he home?"

Bridget was taken aback momentarily. "Oh, I'm sorry, Jim—I guess you didn't know. Well ... you see, he's been gone a long time."

"You mean ..."

"I know what you're going to say." She looked down. "We don't know if he's dead or alive. He disappeared when Teresa was a baby." She held her tears back.

"Disappeared?"

"Yes, disappeared. It's a long story." Before Bridget could say another word, she saw Joseph and Teresa returning. "We'll talk again, Jim."

"Oh, of course, Bridget." He squeezed her hand. "Where should I put my suitcoat?"

"I'll take it," she answered.

"Do you have a telephone, Bridget? I'd better call for a cab."

"We don't have one, Jim, but Mrs. Block next door says we can use hers any time."

"Are we all ready to go, Mom?" Teresa asked, coming up the steps.

"There's a little change of plans, honey. Jim's coming along and is getting us a cab."

"Oh! Oh, that's nice!"

"Now I want you to go over to Mrs. Block's and call for a Checker Cab. She can give you the number—she's taken them before. Tell them to come in a half hour—I still have to finish packing the lunch."

"My home away from home!" Bridget remarked as the foursome headed up the gangplank in the midst of the shoving crowd.

"Stay together," Jim announced, taking Bridget by the hand.

"We're goin' up top to the bow," Teresa announced, grabbing Joe's hand. "See ya later."

As the boat pulled away from the dock, Jim found two deck chairs near the railing. "Here we go! Perfect!" he announced, gesturing to Bridget with his right hand to take a seat. "Well now, Bridget, tell me all about yourself. It's been a long, long time! You and ..." He halted in midsentence.

"It's okay, Jim. You were going to say 'Tom,' weren't you?"

"I'm sorry."

"No, not at all. Nothing to be sorry about. I can talk about it, Jim." She peered out over the water, the sparkling brightness causing her to squint. She hesitated, trying to get her thoughts together. "Well, you see, to make a long story short, Tom was able to get a job as a scooper on the docks when we came to Buffalo, and we were doing okay for a while. But then he went to work one day ..." She paused for a moment, trying to collect herself, "and never came home. I was frantic! I went to his workplace and talked with everybody there but nobody seemed to know anything at all. After that, I searched everywhere and questioned everyone I could—neighbors, church friends, Tom's work friends, saloon keepers ..."

"Well, did you report it to the police?"

"Oh, sure, right away. Especially since Tom was hellbent on finding the killers of his good friend, Frenchy."

"His friend was killed?"

"Well, he was found floating in the canal—yes. And I'm afraid Tom might have found out who did it."

"Oh, no! Oh, I'm so sorry, Bridget. How terrible!"

"Anyway, nothing seemed to help. I even ran an ad in the Buffalo News and wrote to the Old Country. At one point, I was even called down to the Morgue—it wasn't Tom, though. And the worst part was that people seemed afraid to talk to me. They just all clammed up and I couldn't get anywhere."

"Oh, Bridget! Oh, I wish I had known. I'm sure I could have helped somehow. Is it possible that I might still be able to do something?"

"Thanks, Jim. Your company gives me a lot of comfort." She smiled at her old friend.

"Come on, Bridget," Jim stated, thinking she needed a break from her story, "let's take a walk around the deck for a little while."

"Yes, let's do that. We'll go up to the wheelhouse. I want you to meet Captain Foley—he's my boss, you know!"

The Captain, after being introduced to Jim, was most gracious, inviting them to have a seat and sharing a few Maritime stories with them.

The boat whistle blew, announcing the coming arrival at Crystal Beach, and the railings were suddenly filled with those wanting the first glance at the Park. After the boat was secured to its mooring, the gangplank was lowered; and the surge of humanity converged on the lone customs agent.

The picnic grove, situated under a green roof of giant elm trees, had a number of tables which were unoccupied. Bridget spread her tablecloth across one and unpacked their lunch. “So tell me, Joe,” Jim inquired, helping himself to a piece of fried chicken, “what kind of work do you do?”

“Well, I’m presently working at Pierce-Arrow but I’m on the list for a policeman’s job in Kenmore.”

“Well, that’s an honorable profession—good luck with that. I actually have a couple friends who are in ‘New York’s Finest!’”

“Thanks. I’m looking forward to it. My brother, Louie, just started as an officer in Tonawanda. He likes the job a lot.” Joe went on to tell Jim a little about his family, the farm, and St. Paul’s Church.

Teresa, feeling that Joe was getting a little lengthy and being anxious to go on the rides, interrupted. “Now Joseph, let’s not monopolize the conversation, shall we?” Before he could answer, she continued, “Are you done eating? ‘Cause I’m anxious to get on that giant roller coaster!”

“Oh! Oh, sure, Teresa! Yeah, I’m done. Come on. We can go now.”

“Teresa! How rude!” her mother admonished. “Let the boy eat!”

“No, really, Mrs. Sexton, I’m done. Would you excuse us?” as he took Teresa’s hand and headed toward the amusements, first grabbing a couple sandwiches to take with him.

“Now we can take our time and finish eating, Jim.”

“Yes. And you can finish your story if you’d like, Bridget, but you don’t have to—only if you want.”

"Well, actually, Jim, after Tom disappeared, I was left with nothing. As I said before, Teresa was an infant. It was a pretty hard time, Jim." She stopped for a moment, biting her bottom lip and staring at the ground. Jim reached over and put his hand on hers. "Some times were really bad, like when we couldn't afford to heat the house—I actually had to find wood or pieces of coal that fell off the coal cars onto the railroad tracks. So it kinda was hand-to-mouth for us for a while." She hesitated once more, thinking it was futile to re-live all this. Straightening up and trying to smile, she continued, "But that's all behind me now. Teresa got some schooling in telegraphy and got a job at Western Union."

"No kidding. That's great! I'm so glad things turned out okay. You have a lovely daughter. You can be proud of that girl!"

"A little outspoken at times though!" Bridget laughed. "Maybe Joseph better get used to it—things seem to be getting a little on the serious side. But enough about that—let's hear about *you*."

"Well, there's not too much about *me*, Bridget. Actually, my work seems to be my whole life these days."

"Oh?"

"Well, since my wife died."

"Oh, I'm so sorry, Jim."

"No, no, that's alright, Bridget. It's been some time now—seven years to be exact."

"Do you have any children?"

"No, we never had any. Wish we did, but ..."

"Oh, sorry. I didn't mean to pry."

"Not at all."

"We have cookies for dessert," Bridget offered, hoping to lighten the conversation.

"Wonderful. Pass 'em over," Jim responded with the same thought.

Conversation continued, Jim relating his transfer to Michigan shortly after Bridget and Tom left New York. It was as though twenty-some years had not even passed and their friendship had flowered throughout all that time. At one point, Jim suddenly burst out laughing. "What? What's so funny, Jim?"

"I don't know. I just happened to have a kinda flashback or something."

"What kind of flashback?"

"Oh, of that wild wedding reception on the *River Queen*!"

Bridget smiled. "Well, let's say wild and *wonderful*! Thanks to you, Jim. You made it wonderful for Tom and I. I'll never forget what you did—all our beautiful friends. Renee, Captain Skully, Molly, Sister Irene, Small Fry, Sister Eileen, Grace O'Brien, Sister Teresita, Father Sullivan ..."

"Don't forget my antagonist!" Jim stated, laughing harder.

"Oh, you mean the old Scotsman? Scotty?"

"Yes—MacTavish. Good old MacTavish. I have to say I really didn't want to fight him, but I was afraid he'd *kill* Skully!"

"Well, you know about him and Molly, don't you?— tying the knot!"

"Yes. Actually, I was out of town at the time, but I did have a message on my desk when I returned and sent them a little gift."

"Oh, how good of you, Jim."

One memory brought to mind another, and then another; and they enjoyed reminiscing for the rest of the afternoon.

"Brought you some loganberry!" Teresa announced as she and Joe returned from the amusement park.

"Thanks," Jim responded, taking a sip. "*Very* good! Never heard of a loganberry drink."

"Oh, its kinda new, Jim," Bridget said. "Thanks, Teresa."

"Come on, you two! Don't you want to go on some of the rides? We walked all the way back to get you, " Teresa announced.

Bridget just looked over at Jim with a look on her face that said "not really."

"Whatever *you* want to do, Bridget," Jim said. "It's up to you." Bridget was not too happy that he passed the decision back to her.

"Well, why don't you both go on ahead for now, Teresa. Maybe we'll catch up in a little while," Bridget offered.

"No way, Mom! You're just trying to get out of it!" Jim couldn't help chuckling.

Bridget finally gave in and agreed to join her daughter and Joe on some of the rides. She was surprised at the fun time she began to have, but for the first dip of the roller coaster which had the same effect on her stomach as her first ride on Molly's tugboat. "Isn't it great, Mom?"

"Oh, yeah, sure! *Really* great!" Bridget responded with a slightly sarcastic tone in her voice.

"Well, the Ferris Wheel's next! Come on everybody!" the girl announced.

"O-o-o-o, I don't know about that," her mother responded.

"Oh, don't worry, Mom. It's nothing like the roller coaster. It's real smooth—and the view across the lake from up there is so pretty. You'll love it!"

"Come on, Bridget." Jim encouraged her. "It is a nice ride. And we'll be sitting together."

Joseph and Teresa climbed into a seat, and the handler moved the wheel slightly until another empty seat was ready for Bridget and Jim. And up and up they went. "See the *Canadiana*?" Bridget asked, pointing down to the dock. The seat rocked a little, frightening her. She grabbed Jim's arm.

"It's okay, Bridget. I'll try to hold the seat steadier for you." He put his arm around her shoulder, giving her some comfort. Arriving at the top, the wheel stopped completely.

"Oh, no! We're stuck!" She tightened her grip on Jim's arm.

"They're just stopping for a minute to let some people off, Bridget," he said. "It'll only be a minute."

"Get me off this thing, Jim—*please*. I don't like it—scares me."

The wheel suddenly started up again and after three more rounds, their seat was stopped at the base so they could get off. Joseph and Teresa were waiting for them, having finished their ride moments before.

"Ready for the next one?" Teresa asked.

"No more for me!" Bridget stated emphatically.

"Maybe you should try the Merry-Go-Round, Mom!" Teresa giggled.

"Good idea. I think I will do just that," her mother replied, making Teresa laugh even more. Jim helped Bridget up on a silver horse with a blue saddle, the reins sparkling with rhinestones. Placing his left foot in a stirrup on the green dragon with the flaring nostrils next to the silver horse, he swung his other leg over the top just as the ride began. He reached over and took Bridget's hand, her horse rising up as the dragon went down. The calliope music added to the delight of the moment, "Gee, I feel like a kid again!" Bridget smiled over at Jim.

"Yeah, me too! I haven't had this much fun since I can remember!" He squeezed her hand. "Come on—I'll race ya!"

Up and down. Up and down. He was down when she was up. She was down when *he* was up. They laughed and stayed for two more rides, then decided to walk back to the park.

"I certainly didn't expect I'd be riding Merry-Go- Rounds when they sent me to settle these Buffalo accounts, Bridget. What an enjoyable day this has been! Thanks so much for asking me to join you." He bent down and kissed her lightly on the cheek.

"Oh, look, Jim! The sun isn't even set yet and the moon is out," she announced, trying to avoid acknowledging what had just occurred. "It's lovely, isn't it?"

"It is," Jim agreed, wanting to respond by saying that *she* was lovely, too, but thinking it best not to since she seemed to ignore his kiss. "Let's grab a hot dog," he offered. "Would you believe I'm hungry *again*?"

"Okay. Sounds good to me." They strolled around the grounds—two old friends getting re-acquainted. As they walked along, Jim chatted about the time Molly brought Bridget to see him.

"Funny how the years can change things, isn't it, Bridget?"

"How do you mean, Jim?"

"Well, considering you were just a kid when I got you the job on the *River Queen*. At least, at that time, you seemed like a kid to me."

"Well, yes, I suppose."

"But now, you see, after all these years ... well, it's like you don't seem that much younger than I am—you know what I mean?"

"Oh, yes, I think so. I guess I never thought of it that way. You mean, like now we are both *adults*? Is that it? Your meaning, I mean."

"Right—exactly!" Jim thought it best not to use the words "middle age."

"Wait up!" Teresa's voice yelled from behind.

"So there you two are!" Bridget said. "You finally done riding all those dangerous things?"

"Oh, we had lots of fun, didn't we, Joe?" Teresa quipped.

"Sure." Joe looked a little tired. "She's a tough one to keep up with!" Teresa nudged him in the ribs with her elbow.

"Hear that?" Teresa asked, as music began drifting across the park from the new ballroom.

"Yes. It's beautiful!" Bridget answered.

"Come on, let's go. Let's go dance! Come on, Jim! Come on, Mom!"

Teresa grabbed Joe by the arm and turned to lead everyone to the Ballroom.

"Hold on a minute, Teresa," her Mother cautioned. "What time is it, Jim?"

"Just about seven."

"Well, let's not forget the last boat leaves at nine. So... well, I guess we'd have a little time to go there. What do *you* think, Jim?"

"Fine with me," Jim answered. "Let's go!"

A large crystal globe hanging from the center of the ceiling projected tiny shards of light from ceiling to floor as it rotated, creating a dream-like atmosphere for the dancers. Teresa had Joseph on the dance floor almost immediately. "Isn't that a wonderful song, Joseph? I just love this music!"

Jim took Bridget's hand. "How about it, Bridget? Should we show those two that us old timers can still trip the light fantastic? Nice song, that 'Rhapsody in Blue.'"

Bridget hesitated. "Oh, I don't know."

"Oh, come on, Bridget. I've seen you dance before. You know you can."

A little more coaxing, and Jim managed to get Bridget to her feet. After the first few dances, the band played 'After the Ball Was Over.' It all came back—flooding into her... that favorite tune. She had to sit down. "Are you alright, Bridget?" Jim asked, leading her to one of the benches.

"I'm sorry, Jim. I'm sorry. After all this time. It's just ... Well, it's just ... That song—was our favorite. Mine and Tom's."

"Hey, you two!" Teresa exclaimed as she and Joseph approached. "Boy! You really looked good out there!—not as good as *us* though!"

Bridget pulled herself together, not wanting to put a damper on the evening. "Oh, of course not, my dear. You two should win the gold cup!"

"Oh, Mom! Listen! The Charleston! You know how to do that, right?"

"Just sat down, Teresa. You and Joe go ahead. We'll watch for a minute—gotta catch my breath."

"You okay now, Bridget?" Jim inquired as the two young people made their way back to the dance floor.

"I'll be fine, Jim."

"We can just sit here and relax awhile if you'd like. Or maybe you'd like to go outside and take a short stroll on the Promenade? Maybe a little fresh air would do you good."

"Yes, let's do that. Just wait a minute—I'll tell the kids."

The bench behind the Ballroom afforded a lovely view of the sunset over the water as the waves licked the Lake Erie shore. They continued reminiscing and sharing stories about their pasts. "You know, Jim—I never knew you had been a boxer at one time until that little fisticuffs on the dock at my wedding! Actually, Molly was the one who explained to us afterwards about your boxing career.'.

"Oh, she did?"

"Yes."

"Well, it was great for a while. I took the Championship from John L Flanigan. Not bragging—just mentioning. Terrific feeling being at the top, and I kinda reveled in it until..."

"Until what?"

"Well, you see, I made great money and loved all the attention—but it got dirty."

"Dirty?"

"Well, yes. The fight game was highjacked by a criminal element, and they tried to force me into their corruption."

"How could they do that, Jim? I don't think Molly went into an actual explanation."

"They offer you big money to take a dive."

"A dive? I don't understand."

"Well, that's when they pay you to pretend you're knocked out. Anyway, that's long past." Jim glanced at his watch. "It's getting a little late."

"What time *is* it?"

"Well, actually, we have to be back at the boat in about 40 minutes."

Bridget hadn't realized it was so close to the time they had to leave. Since they had arrived, it seemed like only a couple hours had passed. "I guess time flies when you're having a nice time," she remarked to Jim, smiling. "I'm so glad you could come along."

"Couldn't let a pretty lady be all by herself on those dangerous rides now, could I?"

"Oh, you!"

Jim continued, "Come on. We'd better go get those two."

Walking back toward the dock, the four approached a small stand with some very large suckers in huge round glass containers. "Oh, look, Jim!" Bridget remarked.

"You want a sucker?" Jim laughed.

"Not just *a* sucker—these are *special* suckers—*Crystal Beach* suckers!" Bridget responded.

"Really? Well, they are kinda *big* suckers. Haven't seen any *that* big anywhere—not even in the Big Apple!"

"Let's get one, Jim."

"Okay. Hmm, let's see now. There's cinnamon, lemon, coconut ..."

"I guess I'll take cinnamon." She hesitated. "Oh, I love lemon, too ..."

"We'll take two of each flavor, young man," Jim said. "How much do I owe you?"

"That'll be forty-two cents, sir."

"Wait 'til we get on the boat—they'll last us all the way home," Bridget said.

"And then some, looks like," Jim added.

The moonlight skipped across the water as the *Canadiana* pulled away from the Ontario dock. Bridget and Jim took a seat next to the railing across from the dance floor, watching Teresa and Joe once again who looked like they could dance all night to the mellow tunes of the four-piece band. Intermission brought a request from the girl for one of the cinnamon treats. "What are you picking, Mom? Which one do you want, Joe?"

Both chose lemon and Jim decided on the coconut. They looked like four little children, sitting there licking their suckers. "That lemon looks pretty good, too, Mom. Can I have a lick?"

Bridget held her sucker over to Teresa whose tongue had turned bright red from the cinnamon. The girl wondered why the three burst out laughing as she licked Bridget's lemon treat.

The next hour passed quickly, Jim asking Bridget if she'd like to dance on one occasion. She claimed she was too tired and just wanted to sit.

Two cabs were at the Buffalo dock when they arrived and Jim quickly hailed one. "1574 Delaware, please."

"Yes, sir!"

"You'll come in for pie and coffee, I hope," Bridget inquired. " I made it myself—apple!"

"Yeah! And my Mom makes the best apple pies you *ever* had in your life, Jim! There isn't a bakery in Buffalo that could touch them!"

"Oh, I can *always* make time for homemade pie!" Jim smiled at Bridget.

"Can you come back in an hour?" Jim asked the cab driver as he paid the fare. "Keep the change, Cabbie."

"Yes, sir!" the cabbie replied, quite pleased.

"Would anyone prefer tea?" Bridget inquired. "Don't want to lose any sleep tonight."

"Coffee for me!" Joe responded.

"Yes, that will be fine, Bridget," Jim agreed.

"Don't we have any milk, Mom? I'd rather have milk. Gotta get up early for work tomorrow, remember?"

"I do, too, Teresa," Jim mentioned. "But omehow I can drink coffee all night—never keeps me awake."

Joseph finished his pie quickly and decided on a second piece. "Really great, Mrs. Sexton!"

"Yes, I see what you mean about Mom's pie, Teresa!" Jim said.

The hour quickly flew, and Joe noticed the taxi pull up in front of the house. "Your ride's here, Jim."

"Oh, guess I'd better get going. I can't tell you how much I enjoyed this reunion, Bridget."

"I feel the same way, Jim."

"When can we get together again?"

"Well, how long do you expect to be in Buffalo?"

"Depends how long it takes to finish this assignment. Might be three or four days yet."

"Oh, that's wonderful! Where are you staying?"

"I have a room at the Statler. You know, they have a nice dining room right at the hotel. Why don't you join me for dinner some evening—I hate eating alone."

"That would be nice."

"Okay, pick you up on Wednesday—about six, okay?" He took her hand in his and squeezed it.

Bridget hesitated for a moment, thinking she might have to leave Teresa alone for dinner. But before she could speak, her daughter immediately let it be known that she was going out with Joseph that night, much to the boy's surprise.

"So it's all set then," Jim declared, looking around the room. "Where did you put my jacket and vest, Bridget?"

"It's in the other room," Teresa offered. "I'll get it."

"Do you need a lift home, Joseph?" Jim asked.

"No thanks, Jim. I like to walk. It's good exercise."

"Oh, yes! Very good exercise. We know *all* about it, Joseph!" Teresa quipped, laughing as she returned from the bedroom and handed Jim his jacket.

Jim gave her a little hug. "Thank you, my dear. It was so nice to meet you. And you, Joseph."

"You, too, Jim. Thanks for coming with us. Glad Mom had someone to keep her from falling off that big silver horse!"

"Oh, you!" Bridget laughed.

"Goodnight now. Thanks again, Bridget. It was a wonderful day!" Jim hugged Bridget at the door, kissing her cheek. She heard him whistling as he walked down the porch steps.

"You know, something about that Jim looks sorta familiar. I don't know what it is," Joe remarked.

"Well, he did some acting for a while after his boxing career ended."

"He was an actor, Mrs. Sexton? *And* a *boxer*?"

"Yes. Actually, he was the heavyweight champion. You probably have heard the name Jim Corby.'"

"That's it! I've seen him in sports magazines. Oh, my gosh! I can't believe I was with a champion boxer all day and didn't know it!" Joe scratched his head, looking befuddled.

Teresa yawned. "I really apologize, Joe, but I'd better call it a night. That old job, you know!"

"Oh, gosh, I'm sorry, Teresa. I guess I'd better be going. Thanks a lot for the pie, Mrs. Sexton."

"I'll walk you out, Joe," Teresa offered.

Fifteen minutes later, Bridget couldn't help but comment, "Hmm, what happened to the tired girl who had to excuse herself and get some sleep?" She reached over and brushed Teresa's hair back with her hand. "Just a little messy there, Missy."

Ignoring her mother's remark, Teresa grabbed her hand. "Sit down here a minute, Mom," she said, pointing to the sofa. "Mom, guess what?"

"Okay. What now?"

"I think I'm in love!"

For a moment there was silence, as the girl waited for a response from her mother.

"Well, honey, I was kinda getting the impression lately that you two were getting a little serious. But, take your time. Don't rush into anything. Remember, once you're married, it's forever, you know? If it's meant to be, it will be."

"I know, Mom, but you know the first time I even laid eyes on Joe ... well, it was kinda like I felt the first time I saw Fergy."

"Yes, my dear. But, remember what happened with that situation. That attraction you felt for Fergy ended up with the realization that it was Billy you *really* loved. So go slow. You need more time."

Her response was less than pleasing to Teresa. "But Mom, Joe's so nice. He's so sweet. I mean, gee! Don't you just love him? I mean, you just can't help but love the guy!"

"Yes, he's nice, Teresa, but I really think we had better get to bed now. It's terribly late and we have to get up for work tomorrow. We can talk again about it, okay honey?" She kissed her daughter goodnight. "Just say a little prayer before you go to sleep."

"Two roast beef dinners, please," Jim nodded to the waiter.

"Yes, sir. Would you care for a side salad with dinner?"

"That will be fine." Jim smiled across the table at Bridget. "I'm so glad you could make it, Bridget."

Bridget enjoyed the dinner and the lovely surroundings. The elegance of the dining room, as well as the delicious meal were so enjoyable for her, not being used to such grandiosity.

Riding back in the cab that night, Jim told Bridget that he had to leave early the next morning for an appointment in New York. "Oh, that's too bad, Jim. I was hoping you could stay a little longer."

"I expect I'll have to return here in the fall, though. I'll have a report due from the summer shipping season. Anyway, we'll see each other then?"

"Why, sure. I'd love that. I can't thank you enough for such a beautiful evening."

"It was my pleasure, my dear." He walked her up to the door, suddenly tipping her chin up with his hand and kissed her.

"Thank you again, Jim," she said, a little flustered at the unexpected kiss.

"I'll call you when I get back, Bridget."

Entering the living room, she caught her daughter quickly backing away from the front window. “Teresa! What? Were you spying on me, Missy?”

“Oh, no, Mom. I was just glancing outside ‘cause I thought I heard a noise or something.”

“Oh?”

“So how was it, Mom?”

“How was what, Teresa?” knowing full well her daughter’s meaning.

“Come on, Mom! You know—do you like him? I mean, a lot?”

“He *is* a lovely man, honey. Just old friends, you know, he and I.”

“That’s it? Gee, Mom!”

The rest of the summer seemed to fly by. Teresa was busy working her job at Western Union and Bridget on the *Canadiana*. She was trying to put a little of her earnings aside, knowing the ship would stop sailing at the end of the season, and money would be a little tighter again.

The trees in Forest Lawn were picturesque, embellished in their red, orange, and gold splendor. The October days brought bright blue skies adorned with billowy white clouds and soft, gentle cool breezes. The squeak of Bridget’s porch rocker could be heard on an occasional afternoon as she enjoyed her favorite season of the year. She had received a telegram from Jim stating he was soon to arrive once again in Buffalo,

“So happy to see you again, Bridget. How was the rest of your summer?” he asked, giving her a hug.

“Hot! Very hot!” she laughed. “Come on in, Jim. I’ll make a pot of coffee.” She continued, “But it’s always great on the *Canadiana*—always a cool breeze off the Lake.”

The two caught up on the past few months and were soon joined by Teresa when she arrived home from work. “Oh, my gosh! Jim!” She walked right over and hugged the man. “I’m so, so, so glad to see you!”

"Wow! What a nice greeting!" Jim hugged her back. "And how are you, Teresa?"

"Oh, just great! Just great, thanks."

"And how's that young man of yours?"

"Oh, he's just great, too! We both are!"

Jim smiled at her exuberance. "Well, mighty glad to hear it, my dear."

"Coffee, Teresa?" her mother asked.

"No thanks, Mom. Joe should be here any minute. We're going out for a little while." She looked over at Jim. "Sorry, Jim. Don't mean to be rude or anything. It's just that we already had this planned. Didn't know you were coming."

"Not at all, my dear. Not at all."

"Oh, here he comes now!" Joe came bounding up the porch steps, as usual. "Hey honey! How's my girl? Got a surprise for you!" He reached in his pocket and pulled out a folded-up paper. "Here it is! Here's the official notice! I'm now an official member of the Kenmore Police Department!"

"Oh, Joe!" Teresa exclaimed. "Oh, Joe! How great!"

Jim stood and walked over to Joe, extending his hand.

"Hi, Jim! When did you arrive? I didn't know you were coming," Joe said. Now aware of Jim's background, he looked at the man with new eyes. This wasn't Jim *Flynn* before him—it was Jim *Corby*, the heavyweight boxing champion! He took his hand and shook it, knowing full well those hands were once filled with great power. He seemed in awe of the man, temporarily forgetting his excitement about his new job.

"Just got here, Joe. Looks like I picked a good time. Congratulations, son!"

"What are you staring at, Joe?" Teresa asked.

"Oh ... oh, nothing."

"So, well, when do you start being a full-fledged copper?" Teresa joked.

"Well, soon," Joseph replied seriously. "Couple more things to take care of. Gotta get my drivers' license and my uniform."

Teresa hugged him tightly and he responded by lifting her up in the air and hugging *her*. "I hate to say this," he said, placing her feet back on the floor, "but gosh, we have to leave. My Mom and Dad are having a dinner for me. You know, to kinda celebrate. They're so happy about it."

"Oh, I didn't know we were going to *your* house, Joe."

"Well, neither did I. I mean ... umm ... the invite just came a couple hours ago. So it's kinda spontaneous. But I couldn't very well refuse."

"Certainly not!" Jim chimed in. "I think that's wonderful that your parents are so proud of you. They want to be a part of this happy day."

"Come on, Teresa. We don't have much time. The trolley will be comin'."

"But Joe, aren't we gonna *walk*, the *exercise,* you know! It's so *good* for you!" She snickered.

Joseph reached over, grabbing her by the hand. "Come on, you big tease!"

"Bye everybody!" Teresa said, turning as she and Joe went out the door.

"Can I take you out for some dinner, Bridget?" Jim asked after they left.

"Well, I don't know, Jim. Aren't you tired at all? From the train and everything?" Before he could answer, she continued, "Where's your suitcase?"

"Oh, I stopped and dropped it off at the Statler. I can unpack later on tonight. But aren't you hungry, Bridget?"

"You know, Jim, why don't we just relax right here. I can throw some sandwiches together and I have some fruit. Just take it easy, you know?"

"Bridget, you're an angel! That would really be great! It has been a long day—the train ride and all. Thank you so much. You're so considerate."

"Oh, you're welcome, Jim."

"But only if you promise me we can go out tomorrow, what do you say?"

"Okay. Sounds good to me. You relax while I get us something to eat."

"Best egg salad sandwich I ever had!" Jim remarked, holding his cup up for a refill on the coffee.

"Well, I can't really compete with the Statler's roast beef!" she said, laughing.

"You know, Bridget, I made it a point to go see Molly and Scotty when I was in New York."

"You did? Oh, Jim! Tell me."

"Well, first of all, they were so happy to hear that I saw *you* and wanted to know everything."

"A-w-w-w. Such sweethearts!"

"They are the best, aren't they? Well, anyway, they're still living on the *MOLLY-O* and old Scotty there still plays those bagpipes of his. In fact, he's become quite well known in the area."

"How's that?"

"Well, every evening at sunset the people around can hear him playing. And he has actually been listed on the tour guide of the *River Queen* as a point of interest—'The Tugboat Piper.' The ship passes by their tugboat just around the time Scotty plays. In fact, it's become common practice for the captain to slow the boat down as they approach the area the tug is in, and you can see all the passengers lined up at the railing of the deck to listen to Scotty's serenade!"

"That is *so* nice! And Molly. What about Molly? Is she okay? I love that woman!"

"Well, naturally she can't move the big ships around with her tug any more, but she still takes it for an occasional pleasure trip around the river. She's doing really well for her age—just a little problem with her knees. She uses a cane to walk. That's about it. Most of the time was spent with my talking about *you*! They want me to bring you to New York to see them." He hesitated. "Well, we'll talk about that later, okay?"

"Oh, yes, of course."

"Oh, one more thing. They did tell me that Joseph was married about twelve years back—*and* he has four sons!"

"Really? *Four*? Small Fry has *four sons*?"

"Yes, Bridget—four. And Bridget, he named the first boy Tom!"

Bridget's eyes filled with tears. Jim walked around to the other side of the table, knelt down on one knee, and held her, her tears warm on his cheek. "I'm sorry, honey. I'm so sorry," he whispered in her ear.

After a few moments, Bridget collected herself. "It's just ... well, it's just ... so beautiful! How beautiful! I'm sure Tom must see this beauty from Heaven—Joseph's boy, named for him." She thought for a moment of a time way past. "Jim, do you know there was a time when Tom and I thought Small Fry was a little thief? He stole some bread, and he was actually taking it to Nellie and the baby who were living in an abandoned building." She started crying again.

Jim felt helpless. He took her by the hand and led her over to the sofa. "Just rest awhile."

A few moments later, after composing herself, Bridget asked Jim if Molly had said anything about Captain Skully.

"Uh ... well, I was kinda hoping you wouldn't ask that, Bridget. I'm sorry—he passed away some years back."

Bridget indicated that she suspected that, but it brought a great sadness to her heart. "He was such a good man, Jim."

"He sure was—the best!" He poured her another cup of coffee, chatted for a few more minutes and then mentioned he wanted to stay longer but really had to get back to the hotel. He had a conference to attend at eight the following morning. "Now Bridget, you just get a good night's rest, and I hope we can go out a little tomorrow after work. I think it would do you good." He decided not to mention that she had promised to see him then. "Would it be okay if I come by for you at six? If you're feeling better?"

Bridget appreciated his kindness. "Yes, Jim. I'd like that. Thank you."

They decided to go to the early show and have dinner afterward. "Better we can relax over our meal and not be rushed," Jim offered, as the cab pulled up in front of 12 Broadway. "Two, please," he said at the ticket window of the Olympic Theatre. "This is supposed to be a very good show, Bridget—'The Thief of Bagdad.'"

"Yes, Teresa mentioned to me that some of her friends at Western Union were talking about how great Douglas Fairbanks is." Jim ushered her into a seat halfway down the left aisle. "I haven't been to a movie in *forever*!" she whispered as the lights went down.

Afterward, Jim suggested Giuseppe's. "They have the best spaghetti sauce in town, Bridget. All homemade, of course! Do you like Italian food?"

"Oh, I love it! Doesn't everybody? Besides, I'm starved—spaghetti sounds perfect."

Two heaping dishes of steaming red sauce covering the pasta were placed before them, topped with two of Giuseppe's famous meatballs. "Oh, my gosh! This looks wonderful, Jim!" She began to twirl the spaghetti against the large spoon provided.

"How about some parmesan cheese, Bridget?"

"Oh, yes, of course, please. And some of that garlic bread would be nice." He reached over, sprinkling the cheese on her meal. "Didn't you absolutely love that film, Jim?"

"I always enjoy swashbuckling movies—lots of action!"

"Typical man!" Bridget chuckled. "I personally thought the best part was the romance between the thief and the princess!"

"Typical woman!" They both laughed.

The waiter brought two long stemmed goblets of sparkling red wine. "Compliments of the house, Mr. Flynn. Giuseppe says, 'Welcome back.'"

Jim turned to the owner standing behind the bar and nodded as he lifted his glass to him. "He's an old dear friend, Bridget. I usually stop here on my visits."

"How nice of him," she responded, smiling over at Giuseppe.

The evening couldn't have been more perfect, as they continued reviewing the film and discussing plans for their futures. Jim seemed a little guarded as he spoke. "Oh, waiter," he signaled, "two of the same."

"Oh, I don't think I should drink another, Jim. I'm not used to it."

"But we're celebrating, honey."

Bridget felt a little uncomfortable being called honey. But just smiling, she accepted the next glass of wine the waiter poured. "Well, exactly what are we celebrating? I didn't even know we were!"

"I'm going to be running the whole New York enterprise, Bridget! It's a big promotion."

"Oh, Jim! How wonderful! Congratulations! I'm so proud of you!" She lifted her glass, holding it up to make a toast. "Here's to you! I wish you all the best." She drank the wine, forgetting she had said one was enough. It seemed to go down very smoothly, and she indicated she'd like still another.

"You wish me all the best? Do you, honey?"

There's that word again.

"You know, Bridget, this is a wonderful opportunity for me—but it's bittersweet."

"I don't understand."

"Well, you see, being top banana in New York means I don't have to travel anymore." She looked puzzled. "I'll actually be in charge of all operations in the state, and it will be a permanent thing. Someone else will be taking over in Michigan and here in Buffalo."

"You mean ..."

"I won't be coming back again on business." He looked so serious.

"Oh, I see." She felt badly inside. Is it what he just said, or is it the wine? "Well, gee, Jim, I ... I'll miss you."

"Well, you don't have to, Bridget."

"What?"

"Bridget, I want you to come back with me. To New York."

"Oh, well thanks, Jim. That's nice. I'd enjoy that— seeing everybody again. But maybe down the road a little. I mean, right now isn't a good time with Teresa home and ..."

"Not to visit, Bridget." He reached across the table, taking both her hands in his and held them very tightly. "I want you to come back with me, as my *wife*."

For a moment, she couldn't speak, wondering if she heard right. Oh, I knew I shouldn't have had all that wine. "What did you say, Jim?" she asked innocently.

"You heard me right, Bridget. Please ... please come back with me. I can't begin to tell you how wonderful it's been being with you. All these years of loneliness just seem to disappear when I'm with you. We get along so well. Don't you think so?" Before she had a chance to respond, he continued, "I'm sure this must seem so fast to you but ... well, I know we could find happiness together."

For a minute, she felt like she was in a vacuum. There was only silence in her mind, and she couldn't seem to comprehend it all. This was Mr. Jim Flynn sitting here with her. It couldn't be Mr. Jim Flynn asking me to marry him. She lifted her mind to Heaven, as though to implore assistance from the Mother of God. "Jim, I ... I..."

Seeing that Bridget seemed uncomfortable, Jim realized this was not a good time or place to continue. He looked over and hailed the waiter.

"Yes, sir?"

"Check please—and a cab."

"There's a cabbie in front right now, sir. I think he's waiting for a fare. I'll check it out for you right away." In the few moments of silence until he returned, Jim simply held Bridget's hand.

"Here you are sir," as the waiter handed Jim the check. "And the cabbie's waiting for you outside."

"Come on, Bridget." He took her hand and helped her with her wrap. "Keep the change."

"Yes, sir. Thank you, sir."

"1574 Delaware, Cabbie, please." Neither one spoke on the short ride back. Bridget didn't know *what* to say, and Jim thought it best to drop the subject of marriage for now. Arriving back, he indicated to the driver to hold the cab for him.

"Do you want to come in, Jim?"

"Only for a moment."

They sat on the sofa. Jim once more reached over to take Bridget's hand. "I have to leave early in the morning. Please don't think me forward, Bridget, but I meant everything I said. Give yourself a little time, but please promise me you'll think about it."

"Oh, I will, Jim. I promise. I will."

He reached over, caressing her face. "I'll call you."

"But I have no phone, remember?"

"Write me, Bridget ... *please*!"

She stood in the doorway watching as he climbed into the back of the cab. I wonder if I'll ever see him again. She waved back at him as the cab pulled away and broke into tears. I'm so tired. Too much wine. Why is it that men seem to come and go into my life so quickly—like fireflies that light up for an instant, then disappear. She slumped back down on the sofa, laid her head back, and just wanted to sleep.

Teresa and Joe continued to date, his father always welcoming her with a big hug. His mother, however, seemed a little more reserved, giving Teresa the feeling that she was almost protective of her son. "It is wonderful that Joseph has been accepted on the police force now. It'll give him some time to get his life in order—maybe put a little aside for future years."

Chautauqua Lake became a wonderful place to get away. Teresa and Bridget had visited there once and loved everything about it.

The landscape was dotted with beautiful vineyards lining both sides of the sparkling waters, row after row exploding with purple grapes as far as the eye could see—and only a couple hours from Buffalo!

"Elope? Elope, Joseph?" Teresa didn't know whether to laugh or to cry, finally just throwing her arms around him and holding him.

Joseph explained that Ted had agreed to let him borrow his car for the weekend. This was a well-planned "escape." The young couple would make excuses to their parents that they would be going away with friends. Teresa felt a little guilty, as though she might be deceiving her mother. That morning Ted picked up Joseph, and his parents thought nothing of it, waving happily as they pulled away. "That'll do Joe good, getting away for the weekend," his mother remarked, not suspecting that someone other than Ted would be going.

Dropping Ted back at his house before meeting up with Teresa, Joe thanked him profusely. "Oh, you're welcome, you sly dog!"

Teresa met Joseph at the train station as previously agreed. They planned to find a priest to marry them in Chautauqua; however, after going to the only Catholic church in town, they were unsuccessful and disappointed that the priest would not marry them because he did not know them and advised them to return to their own parishes to arrange for the nuptials. Joseph decided to try the church in nearby Mayville, but again was rejected for the same reason. Teresa was getting a little disheartened. "I don't think we'll ever find a priest who will marry us, Joseph. I guess we'll just have to wait."

They drove along in silence, Joe not really knowing where he was heading or what to do next. Suddenly, he pulled the car over to the side of the road. With a big smile on his face, he took Teresa's hand. "I've got it! I've got it, honey!" She looked puzzled. He went on, "I know just the priest who will marry us—Father Joe Burke. He's the pastor at the New Cathedral down on Delaware Avenue in Buffalo. He used to come over for dinner once in a while when I was a kid, and my parents are good friends of his."

"Oh my gosh, Joe! Why didn't you think of that before? I mean ... gee, we went all the way to Chautauqua for nothing?"

"Oh, I'm sorry, honey. I guess I was too impetuous! Didn't think we'd have any problems—just go down and come back married! That's all I could think of. After all, I never got married before!"

"Well, I should hope not!"

"Tell you what—I'll drive you back to Buffalo ... for a kiss!"

"Well, I don't know about *that*!"

"Then I'll just take one anyway!" He leaned over and tried to kiss her.

She quickly turned her head. "Nope. No kiss."

"What? No kiss for your almost-to-be husband?"

"Just kidding." She laughed and puckered up her lips. He decided to take full advantage of this, holding her tightly and wanting the intimacy of the kiss to last forever.

After what seemed much too long to her, she gently pushed him away. "We're not married *yet*, Joseph! Besides don't you want to get back to Buffalo before the year is out?"

"Teresa, you're too much! No wonder I love you!" He started the car.

The carillon rang out its announcement of the 6 p.m. hour—the time for the Angelus prayer, as Joe and Teresa approached the white marble cathedral with its 260-foot-high towers. Entering, they knelt at the front altar rail to pray. Muffled talk could be heard coming from the sacristy. Joseph rose and approached the cleaning lady who was busy arranging flowers before a statue of the Blessed Mother. "Excuse me, Ma'am, is Father Burke here?"

"Sh-h-h."

"Oh, I'm sorry. I didn't realize ..." He lowered his voice.

"Father's in the Sacristy working on his sermon for Mass tomorrow. I'll tell him you're here."

"Thank you." He started to tell her his name, but she left too rapidly.

"Hello. I'm Father Burke. What can I help you with?" He hesitated momentarily. "You look so familiar."

"I'm Joseph—Joseph Mang, Father."

"Oh, of course! Joseph! How good to see you! How are your folks?"

"Oh, they're good, Father. But Father, I really need to talk with you for a minute."

"Yes, certainly."

"Just one second. I have to go over and get my fiance'," pointing to Teresa, still kneeling at the altar rail.

"Father, this is Teresa Sexton. Teresa, this is Father Burke."

"Happy to know you, my dear. Now, what can I do for you two?"

"Well, we want to get married, Father," Joseph said.

"Oh, how wonderful! How about the two of you meeting in my office next week and we'll begin to make the arrangements?"

"Umm, well, you don't understand, Father," Joseph said. "It's like ... well, we want to get married *now*."

"Oh, I see. Well, Joseph, first of all, you must obtain a marriage license," the priest advised.

"Oh, don't worry about that, Father. I took care of that weeks ago!" He reached into his pocket and pulled out the license, handing it to the priest.

"Well, fine. First step accomplished!" Father Burke said. "Now the next thing ..."

Before he could finish, Joseph interrupted. "So when can you marry us, Father? I thought since you've known my family and I for so many years, there wouldn't be any problem."

"Well, that's true, Joseph. But what about Teresa? And how long have you known one another? And your parents? What about them?"

"Oh, we've been seeing one another for months and months actually, Father." He thought he'd best not say about four or five months, afraid the priest might indicate it was not long enough to decide to marry.

"I see."

"And, Father ... umm ... well, Teresa's father has been gone for all her life and her mother really doesn't have the funds to give her a wedding. And my folks don't have much, as you know. So ..."

The priest looked at Teresa. "Are you a baptized Catholic, my dear?"

"Oh, yes, Father. I never miss Mass on Sunday. And I'm actually a member of 'The Child of Mary Society'."

"Well, that's wonderful! Now, Teresa, I need to ask you ..."

"Yes, Father?"

"Would you be entering into this marriage of your own free will?"

"Oh, yes, Father! I love Joseph very much!"

"Well, I could make an exception and marry you now, but, you see, there must be two witnesses."

The cleaning lady couldn't help but overhear the whole conversation and offered to be a witness. "The janitor is over in the rectory, Father. I'm sure he would agree to be the other one."

Seeing the smiles on Joseph and Teresa's faces, Father Burke assented and left to get the janitor. The cleaning lady took a rose and some Baby's Breath from the bouquet she had placed before the Virgin and handed it to Teresa. "The bride must have a bouquet, of course," she said.

Teresa's eyes teared up at the woman's kindness and she hugged her and asked her name. "Annie's my name, honey. Well, it's actually Anne, after Saint Anne you see, but everybody calls me Annie."

"That fits you, Annie," Teresa responded, borrowing Joseph's handkerchief.

"Here we are!" the priest announced. "This is George, our janitor."

Joseph reached over, shook the man's hand, and introduced himself. "Thank you so much for being here for us, George."

"Oh, happy to do it, Mr. Joseph."

Father Burke motioned to George to bring a kneeler to the base of the altar. "Now let us come before God's Holy Altar," he said, indicating to Joseph and Teresa to kneel there. He instructed them that a Catholic marriage is a holy sacrament wherein a man and a woman vow before God that they will love and be faithful to one another for the rest of their lives. He then folded his hands and prayed,

"Oh God, who in creating the human race willed that man and wife should be one ... join, we pray, in a bond of inseparable love, these your servants who are to be united in the covenant of Marriage, so that, as You make their love fruitful, they may become, by Your grace, witnesses to charity itself. Through our Lord Jesus Christ, Your Son who lives and reigns with You in the unity of the Holy Spirit, one God, forever and ever."

The four responded, "Amen."

Father then asked the bride and groom individually if they have come of their own free will to give themselves to the other in marriage. He then asked if they would honor and love one another as husband and wife for the rest of their lives and if they would accept children from God lovingly and bring them up according to the law of Christ and His Church. "Now please join your right hands. Joseph, repeat after me..."

"I, Joseph, take you, Teresa, for my lawful wife, to have and to hold, from this day forward, for better, for worse, for richer, for poorer, in sickness and health, until death do us part."

Teresa repeated her vow then to Joseph, after which the priest blessed them. "May the Lord in His goodness strengthen your consent and fill you both with His blessings. What God has joined together, let no man put asunder."

These words of beauty brought tears once again to Teresa's eyes, as she couldn't help but think of her mother and father having once stated these vows to each other. Maybe it was good that her mother was not there, she thought. It may have made her heart ache too much.

"The rings?" the priest asked.

Joseph was not only prepared with one to give his bride; he also brought another that she could give to him. He placed it in her hand before they both handed theirs to the priest who blessed them and returned them to the couple.

"With this ring, I thee wed."

"With this ring, I thee wed."

"I now pronounce you man and wife." Joseph kissed Teresa. The priest and both witnesses hugged them, wishing

them all Heaven's blessings.

They left the Cathedral with high spirits, although no honeymoon had been planned due to their work commitment, nor had any arrangements been made for lodging due to their impulsive decision to elope that weekend. "I just got a good idea, honey. Why don't we drive up to Niagara Falls—it's not far—and we can stay overnight and most of the day tomorrow."

"Oh, Joseph, that's a good idea. Let's do that!"

"It's still early, and we can be there before dark."

The Clifton Hotel had two rooms available. It was a bit more than Joseph felt he could afford; however, he was relieved that they were able to obtain a place to spend the night. After checking in, they found a small diner close by.

"I think I will have the meat loaf, husband." She smiled over at him, thinking this was their first meal as *married people.*

Joe smiled back. "Good choice, wife!"

"Do you feel different, Joe? I mean, since we are married now?" She held up her hand, admiring her wedding band.

"Well, kinda," he responded, feeling a little nervous but not wanting to let on to his new bride.

Two glasses of water were set before them. "Two meat loaf dinners, please."

"Comin' right up!" The waiter's white apron seemed to be stained with every color of the rainbow, mustard and ketchup stains the two major colors of yellow and red. Teresa couldn't help thinking she was glad she wasn't the one who had to wash it.

The newlyweds didn't seem to mind that the mashed potatoes were cold and the green beans seemed undercooked. "Isn't this delicious meat loaf, Joe?" Teresa offered.

"Uh, well ... yeah, it's pretty good!"

"Coffee?" the waiter asked.

"Want coffee, honey?"

"if *you* do, Joe."

"Maybe we'll skip it. We're kinda in a hurry," Joe said.

The waiter had a big grin on his face. "Newlyweds, eh?"

"Well, yes, we are," Teresa responded, blushing.

"Wish ya lots of happiness, folks. Come back again."

Chapter 20

The End of the Line

"I absolutely insist on it!" Joseph's mother stated emphatically after recovering from the news of the marriage. "We have plenty of room here, and it will give you an opportunity to start saving a little, Joseph."

Teresa, being quite concerned at her new mother-in-law's obvious agitation at hearing of their elopement, decided to offer another possibility. "Oh, my mother mentioned that we were welcome to stay with *her*." She immediately crossed her fingers behind her back.

"Well, that's nice. But Joseph must stay here, Teresa. His job requires he live in Kenmore, you know."

"Oh, yes. I guess I forgot." Having nowhere else to turn and no funds to speak of, this seemed to be the newlyweds one and only recourse. Teresa decided she would do what she could to help with the housework and cooking. However, by the time she returned home from work in the evening, her mother-in-law had the evening meal prepared and the housework done. Teresa offered to do the laundry on the weekends; but as it turned out, Saturdays were the only time she had to spend with *her* mother, and Mrs. Mang wouldn't hear of work being done on the Lord's day. This was the day for church and family dinners.

Bridget had been quite surprised when she had heard the news of the marriage; however, she was happy for Teresa and thought highly of Joseph. After years of living with her daughter, however, she couldn't help but feel somewhat abandoned and shades of loneliness set in. She welcomed the weekends when she could spend time with Teresa and they could catch up on things. "How are things going, honey? Are you happy over there? I miss you terribly!"

Teresa wished she could do more for her mother who she felt had done so much for her all her life. She knew Bridget had put a little away in savings so she'd have rent money when the *Canadiana* stopped running for the season. "Now I want you to let me know if you need anything, Mom. I can help a little with the rent if you need it." She stopped suddenly, as though deep in thought. "Mom, did you ever hear any more from Jim?"

"Yes, honey, I did—last week. A letter came, talking about his new promotion and ..."

"And is he coming? Is he coming back, Mom?"

"Well, his work here in Buffalo has actually been assigned to someone else, Teresa."

"Oh." Teresa looked disappointed. "But, Mom, I think he really was hoping to see you again."

"I know that, honey. But he wanted me to come to New York with him."

"Oh, that's great!"

"I couldn't do that, Teresa. He wanted to get married, you see."

"Oh, that's even greater!"

"Teresa ..." Bridget reached over and took her daughter's hand. "Honey, I could never marry again. No one could ever replace your father."

"But Mom, you could learn to love someone else, couldn't you? In time?"

"Teresa, I already wrote him back."

"And you said 'No'?"

"Well, actually I said that I cared very much about him and that he was a wonderful man. But ..."

Teresa took her mother in her arms and held her tightly. "It's okay, Mom. It's okay." Bridget cried. "Sh-h-h. I understand, Mom—really I do."

That year Teresa and Joseph saved every penny they could, after giving room and board money to Joe's parents. They wished they could have more privacy, but it was a necessity to stay there for a time. Their thrifty habits brought them much hope for the future, however, as they sat and figured their finances every payday. Their social life revolved around St. Paul's parish and an occasional movie, as Joseph was given free passes to the Kenmore Theatre from his police job from time to time. Often, they would try to retire early after dinner, so as to have some time alone together. "It's only nine o'clock! You can't be that tired already!" his mother would say. "Why don't you sit and chat a while with your father and I."

"Oh, now, they've been working all day," Joe's dad would reply, understanding his son's needs. "Let them rest, Mother. They have to be up early again for work tomorrow."

By Spring, their hard-earned savings were enough to put a down payment on a newly constructed home on Lincoln Boulevard. The green and white wooden dwelling had a wonderful front porch where many would enjoy a cold drink in coming summers. "Oh, Joseph! I can't believe it! Our own home! Just *ours*! Can you believe it, Joe?" Teresa remarked as they stood admiring their house which was nearing completion. "We'll even have a yard! Oh, I can't wait 'til we can move in! How much longer do you think it will take, Joe?"

"They should be done with the inside ... oh, I guess about another week or two, honey!"

Every day, after dinner, the two walked the block from the farmhouse to Lincoln to survey their dream. "I don't think anybody could be happier than us, Joe! Isn't it wonderful? Oh, my gosh! Our own home!"

"Yes, honey—wonderful."

Not long after they moved in, Bridget and Teresa were having tea in the dining room. "Mom, Joe and I talked it over and we want you to come and live with us."

"Oh, no!" Bridget responded. "I couldn't do that."

"Listen, Mom. You had a hard time raising me and trying to provide in that old First Ward when Dad ... Oh, I'm sorry, Mom ..."

"That's okay, honey."

Teresa got up and walked over to her mother, taking her by the hand and leading her to the rear window. "Now Joe and I have it all figured out. Look, Mom, look at that backyard!"

"What about it?"

"Your garden, Mom! You can plant as much as you want. And if you stay here, you won't have any more money worries! Great idea, huh?"

"Oh, honey, I don't know ..."

"Besides, I'll need help with the baby!"

"*What*?" Bridget's eyes began to tear up. "Teresa! A baby? Oh, my gosh! How wonderful!" She hugged her daughter, then stood back to survey the girl's tummy. "Well, I don't see anything, honey. When is this baby supposed to come?"

"They think about December, Mom."

"Oh, what a Christmas gift!"

"Then you'll come? You'll stay with us?"

"Well, of course—if you need me. Of course."

"Oh, that's great. I'm so glad, Mom!"

For the first time in many, many years, Bridget had a wonderful secure feeling in her heart. Her whole life had been a fight for survival, from her beginnings in Ireland as an orphan to the struggle in her youth upon arriving in America, and then the tragedy of Tom's disappearance. The scars on that heart were many, Tom's loss being the deepest wound.

Teresa had her first child and retired from Western Union. Bridget was a great help in caring for little Mary who was born on Christmas Eve. Joseph was now the only bread winner for this little family, becoming quite well known in the village as he patrolled the streets. Teresa was extremely proud of her handsome young husband who soon was dubbed "Officer Joe" by the villagers and often followed by a few children as he patrolled the streets.

"Is that a real gun, Officer Joe?"

"Did ya catch any crooks today?"

"Are there bad guys locked up in yer jail?"

Joe enjoyed the children, hoping he could set a good example for them. The highlight of his day, however, was coming home to his family which soon grew, as little Joseph Jr., soon to be known as "Buddy," made his appearance into the world. Bridget couldn't have been happier, now that she was reunited with her daughter as well as enjoying the companionship of her two grandchildren. Her days were filled with helping Teresa with the housework, cooking, and caring for the children. She was a hearty woman, used to hard work. Happily, she perused seed catalogs in the Spring, choosing many vegetables for her garden and flowers along the sides of the yard.

"Ga-ma," little Mary would say, "get this one!" as she pointed to the colored pictures of corn and carrots and tomatoes. Bridget drew a diagram to show Mary where each of her choices would be planted. The child took great delight in doing things with her "Ga-ma." And "Ga-ma" was filled with joy, relishing the pleasure of sharing life with her and little Buddy. It became commonplace, however, for the new grandmother to feel many tugs on her housedress throughout the day when her attention was momentarily taken from the little girl to attend to the baby.

The 1920's were a time of great wealth and excess for many. But as they drew to a close, the Great Stock Market Crash of 1929 spiraled the nation into a depression which lasted well into the 1930's. Billions of dollars were lost, and thousands of investors were wiped out. Many lost their homes and jobs, and some who had previously enjoyed riches were reduced to poverty. It was not uncommon to see some standing on corners warming their hands over bonfires in metal barrels—others trying to sell apples. "Oh, my gosh! Joseph, what's going to happen to us? What's going to happen to our home? Will they take it away?"

"No, no. Don't worry. My job is secure. Besides, they recently announced a new program called the FHA. That will guarantee our mortgage. Our payments will just continue as they were."

Life was good for this little family in that small friendly village. Most residents were on a first name basis with each other and the local merchants. The next several years brought three new additions to the family—Kathleen, Barbara, and Donald. Although this made things a little crowded, the family was tight-knit, their lives revolving around their parish life at St. Paul's on Delaware Avenue where the children attended school.

Toward the end of the '30's, reports of war filled the newscasts. A little man with a small black mustache was elected Chancellor of Germany and, shortly after, began to gobble up Europe, beginning with an invasion of nearby Austria. His name was Adolph Hitler. Poland came next, followed by France and the bombing and destruction of their Maginot Line, a defensive fortification built before World War II to protect their eastern border from German invaders. Soon the Nazi terror was released upon Holland, Belgium, and Luxembourg, followed by the Blitz of Britain.

One cold Sunday afternoon, the Mang family was just finishing their afternoon dinner. In a heartbeat—everything changed. Joseph left the table to turn on his Philco radio in the living room. "Sh-h-h," he exclaimed. "Listen! It's President Roosevelt speaking!" He turned up the volume.

> *"Pearl Harbor has just been bombed by the Empire Of Japan. We are at War. This is a day that will Live in Infamy."*

It wasn't long before changes began appearing in every neighborhood—scrap drives, food and gasoline rationing, blackouts and air raid drills, and victory gardens on land donated by the government. And the landscape became permeated with women in slacks, red bandanas tied around their heads—"Rosie the Riveter" was born.

Bridget decided that she would make her own little contribution to the war effort. One morning, she came downstairs dressed in this manner.

"Mother! What in the world?" Teresa exclaimed. "Why are you dressed that way?"

"Grama! You look funny!" Mary laughed.

"I'm going to work at Bell Aircraft building airplanes," Bridget stated with a proud voice.

"But Mom, don't you think *younger* folks should be doing that?"

"We all have to chip in for the war effort, honey, and this is the best way I know how. Now help me tie this back here," she instructed, holding the two ends of a bandana at the base of her neck.

"I can't picture you as a factory worker, Mom."

"I know, dear, but don't you worry. I may be older than most, but ..." She paused, then raised her fist and shook it. "But this is my way of giving Hitler a punch in the nose!" She picked up her lunch pail, kissed the children goodbye, and left, joining a group of women working at Bell Aircraft on Elmwood Avenue, manufacturing Bell Airacobra aircraft and machine gun mounts.

Bond drives were started across the country, and American youth were drafted, many sent overseas. Those veterans who lived through the horrors of World War I were highly unnerved to see what was happening again. But the young and brave men called to duty now were unafraid and determined to take the fight to the enemy—and that they did! It was better that they weren't fully aware of the terrible cost about to descend on the world. They fought in malaria-infested jungles, frozen tundra, sweltering deserts, in the air, and under the sea. Normandy! Guadalcanal! Bataan! Iwo Jima! Saipan! The toll would be astronomical— freedom would come at a terrible cost. There were a number of men anxious to fight for their country but were found to be unfit for duty due to age or ill health—they were classified as 4-F.

The draft imposed itself on 78 Lincoln Blvd. as Buddy was called by Uncle Sam just two weeks after his eighteenth birthday. This caused a great deal of distress in Teresa's heart, though she did her best to hide her feelings. Her son always said he could "read her like an open book," however.

"I'll be fine, Mom. Now don't you worry." Buddy hugged Teresa tightly, as a whistle was heard in the distance, announcing the approach of the train that would carry her son and hundreds of others from Buffalo, New York off to war. Mr. Spitzer was seen standing on his ladder shortly after adding Buddy's name to the billboard on Delaware Avenue, listing the servicemen from Kenmore. At other times— sadder times—a gold star was painted next to the name of one of their fallen.

Teresa decided she would take a small step of her own for the war effort, renting Buddy's room to two young brothers coming from Ticonderoga to work in the defense plants in Buffalo. As time went by, these two would also receive draft notices, after which Teresa continued to take in others for the same purpose. Although boarders, they eventually became like family members, sending pictures back to 78

Lincoln from their basic training days. All of these ended up in a permanent place on top of the player piano in the living room. By war's end, that old piano top was filled with pictures of soldiers, sailors, airmen, Marines, Coast Guard and See-Bees—some who returned home—some who never did.

Joseph became an air raid warden, now patrolling the streets at night as well as day and making sure all lights were turned off in the homes during air raid drills. This caused much consternation in the hearts of the children, as they understood the reason for the blackouts; and they worried they might be bombed, although Teresa had instructed them it was only "practice," while she herself constantly worried about Buddy who had been sent to Okinawa.

Many nights, people would attend church to pray for their loved ones overseas. Some nights one could barely squeeze into the church, some having to participate from the entrance hall. Neighborhood homes were opened to all for evening rosaries. Even gruff old Roy Gannon, who ran illegal booze over the Peace Bridge from Canada during Prohibition, would come next door to the Mang home, drop to his knees and pray the rosary. Afterward, the men gathered together in the living room discussing their viewpoints of the movements of the troops and the progress of the war as the women set out sandwiches on the dining room table. Roy was always ready to share his stories of his World War I service. "War is a terrible thing," he would say. "We lived in filthy trenches with rats running all around. And if you popped your head up, it would get shot off!" He'd roll up his pant legs. "Ya see these scars? Mustard gas! Krauts used it on us." Shaking his head, he would add, "Saw many die from that damn..." He stopped suddenly, glancing over at Bridget. "Oh, I'm sorry—I mean *darn* gas! Well, maybe they were the lucky ones. You shoulda seen my sergeant! He had his guts hangin' right outa his stomach from a grenade that hit right near us. The poor guy lasted an hour or two like that—in agony."

"Sandwiches are ready," Bridget called from the dining room, hoping for a break from the war talk. The men, however, continued their discussion as they ate, speaking of the movie newsreels from the previous weekend, which added to the viewers understanding of the horror and stark reality of the fight their country had been forced to endure.

Bridget's life had become a beehive of activity, with her factory work in the daytime and the family life in the evening. Mary, being the oldest, had become a great help to Teresa, trying to assist her in household chores since Bridget had begun her job. She adored her grandmother, and saw to it that she rested when returning from work. "Grama, you sit down—I insist!" she would scold her sweetly. "You must be exhausted!"

"I'm not the least bit tired, my dear. What can I do to help with dinner, Teresa?"

"Nothing. Absolutely nothing, Mom. Please, sit down. You heard your granddaughter!"

"Oh, you girls! How you baby me!" They all laughed.

"You deserve babying, Mom. Lie down there on the couch now and rest awhile. I'm almost through getting dinner. Mary, go get a pillow for Grama's head!" Bridget loved living with her daughter and the family. The children all doted on her—and she on them.

The next couple years continued to show a great increase in strength through unity as the country stood powerfully behind the fight for freedom. Several gold stars had been added to the billboard by Mr. Spitzer and placed in the front windows of the homes of those who had lost their loved ones—and the neighborhood mourned their fallen.

Bridget's busy life left little time for thinking of other things. One Sunday morning, however, she decided to rise early before anyone else was up. She dressed quietly, left a note for the family, and took a bus down to the First Ward to attend Mass at St. Bridget's. She took a seat in the front row before the side altar where Our Lady's statue stood, staying after Mass for a while to pray. Realizing she was seated in the exact spot where she and Tom sat that Christmas Eve so long ago, tears welled up in her eyes; and she put her hand on her belly, as did Tom that night when the child inside was moving. She felt a hand on her right shoulder. "Oh, hello Father."

"Are you alright,?"

"Oh, yes ... yes, I'm alright, thank you."

"I'm sorry, I don't recognize you. Are you new to the parish?" He smiled. "I'm Father Leon."

"How do you do, Father. So nice to meet you. I'm Bridget Sexton. Actually, I'm not a parishioner here—I used to be some time ago—when Father Lanigan was pastor. I go to St. Paul's in Kenmore now." Bridget had a thought. "How long have you been here, Father? Did you ever hear about the strike back in '99?"

"Oh, certainly. People still talk about it today."

"My husband went missing in that strike, Father ..."

"Oh, I'm so sorry. What happened?"

"Did you ever hear anyone, by any chance, speaking of a man named Tom Sexton?"

"Well, no I haven't—sorry. Was that your husband?"

"This is him, Father." She quickly pulled a picture from her purse, holding it up to show him.

He shook his head. "I'm so sorry, my dear." His sad facial expression showed his empathetic nature.

Bridget rose from the pew. "Well, I guess I'd better get going, Father."

"Well, let me give you a blessing before you leave, my dear." He made the Sign of the Cross" on her forehead, saying a short prayer over her.

She walked the few blocks to 282 Alabama Street. It looked deserted. There were tall weeds growing up in the front and two of the windows were broken. Going up the front steps, she peered inside. Apparently, no one had lived there for some time. It was dirty—empty—cobwebs everywhere. It hurt her heart to see it. *Their* home—hers and Tom's. Their first Christmas. The night she told him she was pregnant. The scrawny Christmas tree. It all came flooding back, as though the interior of the house was a movie showing one scene after another from her past. She stood there and cried, remembering those happy times with Tom. My Tom ... my Tom ...

She was suddenly jolted from her memories when a loud voice called from the sidewalk, "Hey, lady! You okay?"

She turned to see a somewhat disheveled older man carrying a small brown paper bag. "Oh ... oh yes, thank you. I'm okay."

"I don't think it's a good idea for ya ta be peerin' in them windows there, lady."

"I used to live here. A long time ago. My husband was a scooper."

"Oh, yeah? Me too. What was his name?" as he lifted the paper bag to his lips.

"Sexton—Tom Sexton." An excitement built up inside her as she inquired, "Did you maybe know him, Mister?"

"Sexton? Umm. Name sounds a little familiar." He lifted the brim of his cap, scratching his head. "Nope, can't say that I did."

"Are you *sure*?"

"Sure'n as the Old Sod is green, lady." He turned and walked away, taking another swig from his "hidden" bottle.

The towering elevators of the grain mills loomed tall across the canal, the small guard house at the closed gate. Tom passed through there every morning. Could the guard on duty have heard of him? Too long ago. Too long ago. It wouldn't hurt anything to ask though.

But the wind suddenly picked up and large flakes of wet snow started to fall. She wondered if the family might be getting worried and decided she'd better head back. The bus stop was only two blocks from there, but it seemed as though the temperature had dropped ten degrees as she walked. She took a seat in the back of the bus, glancing out the rear window until the elevators were no longer in sight. Somehow she understood she would never return to the First Ward again as the bus made its way back to Kenmore.

"Watch your step! Watch your step, lady!" Bridget turned slightly to acknowledge the driver's warning, losing her balance on the slippery steps and crashing down on the pavement below. The pain in her left hip was so excruciating, she could barely catch her breath to call for help. Within a moment, however, the driver was at her side, along with a few passersby. "Can you move, lady?"

"O-o-o-o," she moaned, "I don't think so."

"We have to move you. You can't lay here in the street." The snow was coming down heavier now and a man came over, took off his coat, and covered her.

"I don't think you can move her," he advised. "She seems to be in terrible pain."

"It's my hip," Bridget said, trying to hold back the tears. "... my hip."

"Just leave her right where she is," the man said. "Better not try to move her. That hip could be broken. I'll call an ambulance," he said as he headed across the street to the phonebooth in Kay's Drugstore.

Some of the passengers were observing the scene through the bus windows, while a few got off and knelt around her in the snow, forming a barrier to shield her from the bitter wind.

The sirens of the approaching ambulance could be heard screaming down Delaware Avenue within a short time. It seemed like forever to Bridget, however, as she lay on the pavement praying silently, glancing upward at those concerned looking faces over her and in the bus windows. She knew Teresa and the family must be terribly concerned as well, wondering why she hadn't come home yet.

"Where do you hurt, lady?" the ambulance attendant asked, seeing the apparent pain in her face. She pointed to her left hip.

"She fell from the bus steps," the driver advised.

"Bring the stretcher!" the attendant called to his partner.

"Go easy now—real easy," he said, rolling Bridget slightly over onto her right side and sliding the stretcher beneath her. She groaned. "Okay, now just pull her over onto it a little bit. There ya go. So far, so good. You okay, lady?" Bridget shook her head. "Okay, now you take the other end and let's lift her into the ambulance."

"Whose coat is this?" his partner asked the crowd, handing it out to the man who came forward, then covering Bridget with a blanket.

"Thank you. Here's her purse," the man stated. "Hope you'll be okay, lady," he said to her before they closed the ambulance door and pulled away.

"Where are we going?" Bridget asked.

"Downtown—Millard Fillmore Hospital, lady."

"I'm worried about my family. They won't know why I haven't come home for so long—since this morning."

"Don't worry. We'll notify them from the hospital." He held her arm out.

“What’s that?” Bridget asked.

“Just a little something for pain.”

She became drowsy before they arrived at the hospital, almost unaware of her surroundings. “*Put your hand to the plow, Bridget dear ... Put your hand to ...* The last thing she remembered was the blurry figure of a man in a white coat opening the door of the ambulance.

“Mom! Mom!” Teresa softly nudged her mother’s shoulder. “Can you hear me, Mom?” Bridget reached her hand out to her daughter but didn’t open her eyes. “You took a nasty fall, they said, Mom. How are you feeling?”

Bridget, still under the influence of the morphine, answered in a weak voice, “Not too bad. Not too bad, Teresa.”

“You broke your hip, Mom,” but you’re going to be fine. You’ll just have to stay here for a little bit.”

“I shouldn’t have gone—shouldn’t have gone down there. I’m sorry, Teresa. I don’t know why I went down there.”

“Sh-h-h. It’s okay, Mom,” as she held her mother’s hand and leaned over to kiss her cheek. “Just rest.” Bridget started crying. “What’s wrong, Mom? Are you in pain?”

“No, it’s just ...”

“What?”

“I won’t be able to go Christmas shopping, and I’ve got my whole list made out! And the kids won’t ...”

“Now, now. We don’t care about *any* of that. We’re just thankful you’re okay. Besides, the doctors expect you’ll be able to come home by Christmas!”

“They *do*?”

“Yes. Isn’t that wonderful? Now, please Mom, just rest, okay? Go on, close your eyes. I’ll be right here. I’m staying with you tonight.”

“No, no, Teresa. You go home and get a good night’s sleep. You need your rest.”

“Mom ...”

"Teresa, I insist! Please honey—do it for me."

"Well, alright. But I'll be back first thing in the morning." She leaned over and hugged her. "Try to sleep, Mom."

"Well, how's the patient?" Dr. Stedem asked, the morning sun streaming in the window.

"Oh, Dr. Stedem, I'm so glad to see you," Bridget said to her good friend. "I guess I'm doing okay. I'm kinda drugged up enough so I can't feel too much pain."

"Yes, that's fine. You really took a nasty fall there, Bridget."

"And don't I know it, Doc?" She smiled. "I'll be alright though, won't I?"

"Well, looks like you're doing pretty good right now, my dear. But I want you to stay in the hospital for another week or ten days. You did quite a job on that left hip! But we can keep you comfortable—don't worry."

"Oh, thanks, Doctor. But I do have to get home by Christmas, you know. Teresa is planning on it." The door squeaked as it opened. "Oh, here she comes now."

"How are you today, Mom? Oh, hello, Doctor. Good to see you again. How's she doing?"

"Coming along, Teresa. These things can take a little time you know." He turned to Joseph, shaking his hand. "And how's Kenmore's Finest these days, Joseph?"

"Well, glad to say things are pretty calm, Doc. Just one thing—we did have quite a crime last week—right on Lincoln Boulevard."

"Oh, no! What happened?"

"Somebody stole the Christmas wreath right off Mrs. Flaherty's front door."

"Well, I hope they catch the criminal!" the doctor quipped. They all laughed. You'll have to excuse me now—gotta make my rounds."

"I'll walk you down the hall," Joseph said. "Need to use the men's room anyway."

The rest of the morning was spent listening to Bridget expounding on her day visiting the First Ward. "I started out to go to Mass at St. Bridget's, but I decided to go over to 282." Her eyes began to tear. Teresa squeezed her hand. "It's all overgrown with weeds—it's been abandoned, Teresa. Imagine—abandoned! Our *home*."

"Now, Mom. You're supposed to be getting rest, remember?"

"And then, I was looking in the window and this man hollered at me."

"What? Hollered at you?"

"Well, I think he was drunk. Anyway, then I was gonna go over to the elevators, 'cause I know there's always a guard at the gate, but I was so cold. That's when I decided just to come back."

"Oh, Mom, that's okay. It's okay." Bridget moaned. "Are you alright, Mom?"

"Just a little pain."

"I'll get the nurse," Teresa offered.

The medication soon kicked in, and it wasn't long after that Bridget fell fast asleep. Joe and Teresa waited for a while at her bedside, before Joe indicated they'd better get back home so he wouldn't be late for his afternoon shift. "What did Doc Stedem say, Joe?" Teresa asked as they walked down the hall.

"Well ..."

"What did he *say*, Joe?"

"Honey ... well, the x-rays, I guess, were kinda bad."

"Yes?"

"Well, you see, there's really not much they can do at all, Teresa. I mean, except to help the pain. But these things just don't usually have ..."

"Joe—I need to know what he said."

"It's not good ... not good, honey. Sorry. I'm sorry."

Teresa broke down and cried. He held her. A nurse walked by and wanted to know if she could help. "Would you like to sit down?" she offered.

"I want to go home, Joe. Just take me home."

The following week was a bustle of activity at 78 Lincoln as the family made ready for Bridget's return as well as decorating for Christmas. They all looked forward to their best gift—Grama coming home—and wanted everything to be perfect. The tree was decorated in the corner of the living room and several gifts placed below it, most marked either "Mom" or "Grama." Since all the bedrooms were upstairs, they moved the dining room table from the center of the room to one side, and the back wall was cordoned off, a light blanket hung on a clothesline to allow Bridget some privacy in this makeshift bedroom.

"How do you like this, Mom?" Donnie asked. He and Mary held up a sign of large red lettering against a green background—"WELCOME HOME, GRAMA!"

"Oh, that's perfect! Very Christmas-y looking!"

"We're going to hang it out on the front porch. It's the first thing Gram will see!"

"Well, hurry!" Teresa advised. "She'll be coming any minute now."

The ambulance backed into the driveway, and the attendants lifted the stretcher up the front steps, carrying Bridget right into the dining room. "Good luck!" the driver said, as they turned to leave. Before Bridget could say a word, she was surrounded by the whole family, hugs and kisses abounding.

"Oh, I'm so glad to be home!" she said, tears forming in her eyes. "Oh! and look at that Christmas tree!"

"Here, let me make you comfortable, Mom," Teresa said, arranging the four pillows behind her so as to allow her to be in a somewhat sitting position. "That feel okay, Mom?"

"Oh, yes. Fine, Teresa."

"Are you hungry?"

"No."

"Want me to read to you, Grama?" Donnie asked.

"Well, actually I'm a little tired, honey."

"Why don't you just rest right now, Mom. You've been through a long ordeal at the hospital. Maybe you'd like to take a little nap?"

"Good idea," her mother answered, resting her head back on the pillows, as Teresa covered her and pulled the blanket across the clothesline.

Bridget slept right through until the following morning, Teresa having kept watch over her by sleeping on the sofa nearby. She was awakened by the sound of moaning and rushed to her mother's side.

"I'm okay, Teresa. I was just trying to turn a little. Maybe you could get me a glass of water—I need to take my pain pill."

"You really should eat a little something," Teresa said, handing her the glass and medication.

"Oh, I'm not at all hungry. Maybe I'll just sleep a little longer."

The next few days seemed to show a slight improvement, Bridget being doted upon by all. She began eating a little and asked for the blinds on the back window to be raised. "Oh, my! Look at that! You didn't tell me we had so much snow, Teresa! Oh, isn't it beautiful!" she exclaimed, looking upon the winter scene, the bushes and trees glistening—the wet snow having frozen during the night. "I love winter! It's so beautiful!"

"Most of that just fell last night, Mom. Guess I'd better get Donnie out there to shovel."

"Where's Joseph?"

"On the beat! He should be home in time for dinner. I hope you'll be able to eat a little something with us."

"Teresa, will you do me a favor?" Bridget asked, ignoring her remark.

"Of course. What?"

"Go upstairs—in my top dresser drawer I have some Christmas cards. Please bring them down. And also my little purse."

Bridget bemoaned the fact that she hadn't been able to go shopping for gifts but proceeded to address a Christmas card to each of the children. She then opened her purse and placed two dollars in each one. "At least this way, they'll be able to buy something they want," she said to Teresa.

"Oh, they'll love that, Mom! Always the right size and the right color!" Teresa laughed. "I'll put them under the tree for you."

It was decided that half the family would attend the first Mass on Christmas morning and the others would go at noon, so as to have someone always there for Bridget's needs. They had decided to bring her into the living room next to the Christmas tree—Teresa, Joseph, and Mary lifting her gently from the bed to the sofa, on which they had propped four pillows on one end. Teresa could tell she was in some discomfort, but seemed to manage better after her medication.

"So can we open our presents now?" Donnie asked.

"Patience, Donnie—patience!" his father instructed.

"Get all Grama's presents from under the tree and bring them over here on the coffee table," Teresa directed Barb and Kathleen.

"Here, Gram, open mine first!" Donnie said excitedly, handing her a package. "Want me to help you open it?" he asked, tearing the paper before his grandmother could answer.

"Oh, my! Oh, thank you, darling. Chocolates!" She reached her arms out to hug the boy. "How did you know I liked dark chocolate best?"

"Oh, is that *dark* chocolate, Gram?" he asked.

"Yes—it's my favorite!" she fibbed. "Here, have a piece!"

"Oh, no thanks, Grama. That's for you," he said, not mentioning that he didn't care for it and quickly handing her another gift.

The pink bed jacket and the books from the girls were perfect presents for someone bedridden. "We can read to you, Gram," Barb said, "anytime you feel like it."

"That would be wonderful! Thank you so much. What a thoughtful gift! I always wanted to read that."

"Which one?" Kathleen asked.

"'Story of a Soul,' honey."

"Oh, sure, Gram. Of course. I should have known that, since you named Mom after St. Therese'."

"Do you like 'Gone With the Wind,' too?" Barb asked. "... hope so,"

"Oh, I do—very much! I heard it's a wonderful book. Thank you so much. Now it's my turn," she stated, smiling. "Donnie, take those envelopes from under the tree and pass them out for me, would you?"

"Oh sure!" he replied, anxious to see what was in them. "Oh, boy! Thanks, Gram—just what I need!" They all laughed.

They finished exchanging all their gifts, and by the middle of the afternoon, the turkey took main stage in the center of the dining room table, Teresa having risen early that morning to stuff it and prepare all the trimmings along with Mary's help. "Oh, it smells wonderful, dear!" Bridget remarked.

"I'll make you up a plate, Mom. You just stay right where you are."

"Oh sure," she replied, laying her head back on the pillow and closing her eyes.

"You okay, Mom?"

"Yes, just a little tired, honey."

Teresa asked Joe to lead the family in a prayer before eating. She then proceeded to fill a plate for her mother, hoping she would eat well. She returned to the living room still holding it. "She fell asleep, Joe. I guess all the excitement was a little too much for her."

In the months following, the girls spent much time at Bridget's bedside, sharing the news from Buddy who wrote every week or two and reading the books they had bought. The family was growing concerned, as her appetite seemed to diminish more and more, even with Teresa's continued efforts to make her nourishing meals. She was sleeping more often, even during the daytime hours. When she was awake, she spoke more and more of things past, often about Tom. Teresa felt perhaps Bridget wanted the children to hear everything about that grandfather they never knew. Dr. Stedem stopped by every week or two to check on her. It was obvious to him that her condition was deteriorating, and he could not offer much hope to Teresa. "Just keep her comfortable, Teresa. You'll probably want to spend as much time with her as you can."

Teresa continued to cling to the hope that her mother would improve, keeping a positive attitude before the family no matter how she felt. "How are you feeling this morning, Mom?"

"Oh, fine! Pretty good."

"Hi, Gram!" Donnie would run to her bedside right after school. "How you doin'?"

"Oh, real good, honey. Give Gram a kiss, love," she would reply.

"Ready for Chapter 10, Grama?" Barb asked one afternoon.

"Okay, sure."

"You're not too tired, are you?"

"Oh, no, not at all. Go right ahead and read, Barb." But she soon was fast asleep.

As the weather began to warm up and spring approached, the girls brought her a seed catalog. "You just pick out anything you want, Gram, 'cause we're gonna plant that garden for you."

"Oh, no! You don't have to do that—too much work."

"We want to, Gram. Really we do. Come on, just pick out what you'd like to see growing back there. You can watch everything come up right from the window!"

Bridget did indeed watch that garden grow, taking much delight in it. She was grateful for all the goodness and kindness her family showed her. It had been an abnormally hot spring, and it gave the garden a head start. In addition, the neighborhood boys often gathered in the backyard, playing catch and batting baseballs in preparation for the summer games to be held at the Mang Park diamonds. Bridget was happy she could see all this from her little cot next to the window, and joy filled her heart as she watched her youngest grandson and his friends. They were often forced to accept Barb as another player when they were short a man— both sides secretly hoping she'd land on the *other* team.

This joy was soon multiplied a hundredfold, news blaring from all radios that the Nazis had surrendered. "It's called V-E day, Mom—'Victory in Europe.' That means that Nazi Germany has surrendered unconditionally."

"Oh, thank God the war is over!" Bridget exclaimed, overjoyed at the news.

"No, not exactly, Mom. That's just part of it. We're still fighting Japan."

"But what about Buddy? Is he coming home?"

"Not just yet, Mom—but soon. He'll be home soon. Japan has to surrender yet, too." Bridget looked sad. "Let's have a cold drink, shall we?" Teresa offered, deciding it might be better to change the subject.

By summer, Bridget's weight had dropped to a little below 100 pounds. Father Joe Waclawski had been assigned to Saint Paul's and stopped by to see Bridget as his duties allowed, bringing her Holy Communion. At one point, she told him she wished to make a good Confession, as she had been unable to get to Mass for so long. He placed his stole over his shoulders in preparation for the Sacrament. "Whenever you're ready, my dear."

She hesitated for a few minutes, her eyes closed. He placed his hand over hers and waited, praying silently. A few more moments passed before she opened her eyes. She glanced up at the priest, a confused look on her face. "I can't think of anything, Father."

The priest offered his assistance. "Bridget, are you sorry for all the sins of your past life—any sins against God or your fellow man?"

"Oh, *yes*, Father."

"Can you make a good Act of Contrition, Bridget?"

"Yes." She said the prayer. The priest gave her absolution, after which he decided to continue on with the Last Rites of the Church since her condition seemed so severe.

"Through this holy anointing may the Lord in his love and mercy help you with the grace of the Holy Spirit. May the Lord who frees you from sin save you and raise you up."

The next few days showed a little improvement in Bridget's condition, a great relief to the family. A letter had arrived from Buddy saying the company scuttlebutt during the past week or so was centered around the news that the United States was negotiating the surrender terms with Japan.

Then, finally, on a hot summer day in August, the great news came—Japan surrendered—IT WAS OVER! That quiet little village of Kenmore suddenly exploded with crowds of people cheering in the streets and hugging one another—many crying. Cars were beeping their horns and church bells began ringing. Itzy was handing out apples at his produce stand on Delaware Avenue, and John the butcher at Federal Market was giving all the children slices of boloney. Mr. Seifert came out of his shoe store, shaking hands profusely with Tony who had repaired many Kenmore residents' shoes in *his* shop next door.

"Oh, Joe! Oh, Joe! Oh, thank God!" Teresa began to cry. "It's over! It's *really* over now. Buddy will be coming home!"

"Oh, how wonderful!" Bridget's strained voice came from her little cot in the dining room. Her daughter bent over her and hugged her tightly and they cried together— tears of joy—tears of relief—tears of anticipation—their loved one returning safely home from the war. They had no notification of the exact day of his arrival, yet the certainty that he would be coming lifted Bridget's spirits and gave her the resolve to "hang on." Teresa, however, determined to make sure Buddy would see his grandmother before she died, notified the Army authorities who allowed the boy an early release.

"Grama! Oh, Grama!" Buddy embraced Bridget, kissing her on her forehead. He held her for a few moments, aware of the fact that she seemed so frail. "I love you, Gram." She cried.

"I love you, too, Buddy. I love you, too."

"None of that cryin' now, you hear?" He wiped her tears and fluffed her pillow under her head, as the rest of the family gathered around him, his sisters and brother taking turns hugging and kissing him.

"Boy! What a super neat uniform, Buddy!" Donnie exclaimed.

"Well, actually, I can't wait to take it off and get back into my civvies!"

"So what's that eagle on your sleeve?" the boy asked.

"That means the 101st Airborne Division, Donnie," his brother replied.

"Wow! I think that's what I wanna do when I grow up."

"So Mom, what's to eat? I'm famished!" Buddy remarked.

"It'll be ready shortly, honey. Why don't you go up and change awhile?"

"Okay, Mom. Donnie, get my duffle bag, will ya? I left it out on the front porch."

The meal that evening was a joyous time, the family being reunited after so long. But the joy was not to last much longer, as Bridget passed away during the night. Teresa buried her head in her mother's shoulder, sobbing quietly so as not to awaken the rest of the family upstairs. After a short time, she tried to compose herself and went to awaken Joe. He notified the priest and made all the arrangements.

The funeral Mass was celebrated by Father Joe who did a heartwarming eulogy afterwards.

> *"...Bridget's journey was hard, coming to a new land alone at such a young age. But she always strove on in hard times, taking any jobs she could to support herself and her daughter, whether it be babysitting, sewing, working on boats or cleaning at the Expo.*
>
> *"St. Paul might have said, 'She has fought the good fight, run the race, and kept the faith.' In the end, you might say her life was lived between two memories—her father and her husband Tom..."*

As he continued on with his remarks, there wasn't a dry eye in the church.

> *"She was always loyal to her family and to her God. And you never saw her without a rosary in her hand—or at least in her pocket. I imagine the Blessed Mother will be standing at those Heavenly Gates to welcome her and personally escort her to her Divine Son!"*

Entering the gates of Mount Olivet, the clouds seemed to separate and bright sun shone through the blue patch of sky opening before them. Teresa was comforted by Father's prayer at the gravesite.

> *"May God remember forever our dear Bridget who has gone to her eternal rest. May she be one with the One Who is Life Eternal. May the beauty of her life shine forevermore, and may our lives always bring honor to her memory.*
>
> *Amen.*

All joined hands and prayed the "Our Father." At the conclusion of the service, people began to leave; but Teresa and Joe stayed for a brief time, standing silently at the graveside.

"We can go now, Joe," Teresa said, wiping a tear from her eye. Joe put his arm around her waist and they walked slowly away. Before they caught up with the children, Teresa glanced back at her mother's grave. "Oh! Joe! Look!" The white dove flew low over the grave, then rose high in the sky toward the East.

Teresa smiled. "Rest in peace, Mom! At last ... at last you'll be together with your beloved Tom."

Bridget O'Halloran Sexton was the grandmother of author Donald Mang

Tom Sexton was never found.

Made in USA - Crawfordsville, IN
31908_9781085816168
03.14.2022 1216